The Sab

By

Steve Zinger

authorHOUSE

1663 LIBERTY DRIVE, SUITE 200
BLOOMINGTON, INDIANA 47403
(800) 839-8640
www.authorhouse.com

© 2004 Steve Zinger
All Rights Reserved.

No part of this book may be reproduced, stored in a retrieval system, or transmitted by any means without the written permission of the author.

First published by AuthorHouse 05/28/04

ISBN: 1-4184-0236-2 (e)
ISBN: 1-4184-0235-4 (sc)

Printed in the United States of America
Bloomington, Indiana

This book is printed on acid-free paper.

Acknowledgements

Originally I wanted to dedicate this book to nobody. The characters all have some sense of forlornness and desolation, and all have some sense of isolation. I had written a lot of myself into each character, and in a sense they are all fragments of who I am and who I wish to be. And, perhaps to a point, how I view myself. In writing this book, I brought a lot of positive outcomes to what I put in.

Having said that, I started to wonder: Did I actually write this all by myself? Literally, yes, of course. Figuratively…well, that's another matter all together. Any piece of writing, whether it be a novel, a note, or even a signature, should belong to the author as though it were his child. And that birth is a product of the interactions with those we love and hate, and the daily influence of the world at large. There is, in fact, an enormous influence from society, especially with the advent of mass global communication.

Therefore I have numerous people to thank, all of whom had some part in this wicked scheme of mine. First and foremost, James Jolley and Mike Robinson, two people who were always there, and always will be. No matter how much time passed both of you came back and it was like you'd never left. As well, the Jolley and Robinson family's for being like my own, and giving me places to go when I needed to hide. Denise LeBlanc, for her ongoing, and blatant encouragement and friendship, and Serge Alves for the wings and beer. Jodie Clements, for giving me a second home in New Orleans, and for the Mexican food. M, for lighting the spark of inspiration. From time to time I think of you and what you used to be, and wonder why you ever let your soul go. And finally, Rob Mirkovic, for your opinions, sharp eye for detail, and unending patience and assistance with the little things.

To Heather: I have not heard from you in a long time. I am here, waiting for you to once again come out of the shadows and light the world on fire…

**Steve Zinger,
Author of The Sab**

Book 1:

The Turning, The Burial

Part 1: Sunset

It lit. And it had not the fury one would think; it had not the inspiring stature that was associated with it. It was still nice to look at it though, and people always noticed it when they drove by.

He liked to stand atop it, arms folded, to relish the sour irony that it brought to his mind.

Utter meaninglessness.

It brought irony because of what others thought, because he knew that the representations these symbols supposedly depicted always became skewered with misrepresentations and misinterpretations. It was supposed to be a literal representation. A man with his head hanging down and his arms out, the martyred saviour, but it wasn't. Nothing was completely literal. And no one could factually determine the existence of history's most famous majician. Someone had died that day though. It was just a matter of the world spending the rest of its existence wondering whom.

But no one could know for sure.

Well, that's not really true. Someone could have known. Hell, there must have been some that have survived from that time, but if it happened during the *day*, then they probably didn't have first-hand knowledge of it.

But he wasn't up here to ponder the murder of age-old prophets. He stood up here because he heard *remnants* again. Things like this have been happening for a while now, and they had been getting worse.

It was still here. It felt stronger. It actually gave him one of those little mortal shivers that tickled the spine in the most disturbing way.

The worst part about it was that it wouldn't come to him this time. It didn't do that anymore. It positioned itself in the shadows of cities, in the woodlands where the snow and trees would hide it, and it would wait this time, wait for him to find it.

And he hoped it was only his egotism and self-centred nature that made him think this way.

It would fester and then consume mankind like a cancer.

He was sure he heard the *remnants* from behind him, where he couldn't see with his eyes because the mountain jutted up behind him. But he could *hear*. He closed his eyes and tried to bring himself *back*...

The sun was a hard and murky orange as it bobbed along the horizon, not quite sure if it should set, hoping that all the children would know to go in when he could no longer brighten their world.

But he had to go; he had a whole hemisphere that waited for him.

It was tough to leave sometimes, because he could see everything from where he was, like a God. And so, caring like a God should be, he left a trail of yellow light that looked like a drop of juice, or a tear perhaps, for the pretty little girl in the red dress.

She was wrapped up in the joy of bouncing an orange ball. She loved the orange ball and sometimes she would hold it up for her friend the sun to see. All the sun could do was spread shadows and wink good-bye.

The ball went *bounce, bounce*.

He would try to leave a nite-light on for her.

It was easy to spot a victim from here. Look down with sharp eyes and see who happened to wander this way, past the park.

The park was empty, because it was night and it was cold. Winter in Montréal was always *biting* cold. Perhaps that's why he liked it here, why he chose to stay here, so close to a place that held such painful memories for him.

Memories! he laughed, and he didn't laugh much. It's all so made up, this game we play, and the only reality is the sliver called the present-gone. Gone. Gone. See? No use trying to catch it. And everything becomes fiction.

Or maybe it was because distance really meant nothing, that he could be a thousand kilometres away and he would still be haunted by *remnants*...

This trick of the mind, this fucking majic! Most people were blissfully ignorant of it. Others saw and disbelieved. And then there was the one-percent that actually gave into faith, the psychotic minority, the practitioners of the mysterious arts, the blood drinkers. Most certainly the tormented souls, and those unfortunate enough to be born with a poet's soul, like a Pisces, because they were tapped into the esoteric realm. Those were the ones who fell away from it all, who became isolated.

To be isolated is to be apart from the world, to be an imperfection of nature. Things fall away from the great cycle of nature sometimes, and they are not always accidents...

The pretty little girl in the red dress continued to bounce her orange ball, so absorbed in her solitary joy that she took no heed of the fingers of shadows that reached tantalizingly for her shoulders.

And no heed was paid to the cold, her coat flailing with her dress like a timed beat. No heed to the ground, to the ice that crackled and the snow that crunched, no heed to the laces of her boot that flailed with her coat and dress.

The ball went *bounce, bounce.*

She giggled playfully like little girls do, and paid no heed.

She chased the highest bounce of the ball-

-*Bounce, BOUNCE-*

-with the highest leap her little legs would allow. She grabbed the ball in mid-air with a triumphant HAH!, and crashed onto the icy ground.

No heed...

His kind was a *remnant*, tales told in celluloid and pulp, and under blankets with a flashlight. He was going to find a mortal who perhaps wouldn't go mad. He would haunt him to the very depths of his soul, and even if he went just a little bit mad, all he had to do was survive. Maybe one could survive. That's all it took with nature, just one and then an explosion.

Vampires had been dying for years, hundreds of years! Since before he'd become one himself. Then the Great Purge. The death of religion, of faith, the rise of science and logic, this is what had done them in. Logic eroded fears. But alas, it wasn't fear alone that trapped a victim. Ever hear of a serial murderer? Then how is someone supposed to kill each and every night? As communication became instantaneous, vampires began to starve. It became harder and harder to kill. Only the cleverest survived. And then a wave of drugs hit society and so many were easy prey and so many were made. And it was too tempting for a power mad witch. They were useless anyway, high on dope as mortals and drunk on blood as vampires. They weren't alive. They were shells, rotting away with each pleasure. That's why mortals die, stressing to catch the tiniest pleasure and it's the pleasure that rots their skin.

So he killed them all off. To let their blood run red in a river down the sewers, to maintain the strict secrecy of the creatures of the night. Mass murder of the already dead.

And now their number was less than that of the ones told in tales...

She wiped the back of her hand on her wet face to clean it of the dirt and blood. She felt the roughened ice beneath her. She looked up and saw her bright orange ball bobbing along-

-*bounce bounce-*

-content to be free of the constraints of grubby hands that could stain it with sticky chocolate.

The ice dulled the pain in her scraped knees to a throb. The wind would pick up soon and make her feel sorry that she didn't listen to her mother and put on her winter suit. She watched her ball-

-bounce, bounce-

It hit something and changed direction.

It could have ended a century ago. No; *he* could have ended it a century ago. But he thought it enough to flee when there was still a remnant of it left. There was enough left of it to survive, but he didn't care because they had killed someone dear to him, someone who was enthralled with what he was but wise enough to show him that he need not throw away everything he believed in.

Since that night he began to stop caring. Oh, it happened slowly. There was someone who had shown him his heart was not cold. But she died. She had to die. He wanted so desperately to save her but apathy gripped him about the neck like the Reaper and he didn't pull free of it until it was too late.

Everything was constantly crumbling. Even humanity was talking of the coming apocalypse. What bullshit, such self-centred arrogance to think that they would be important enough to kill *en masse*. Everything was constantly crumbling, and obviously it had to be in a state of constant repair. Such was the earth, ever turning, ever living, and ever dying. Apocalypse. Man is born and lives and dies as an individual, and thinks that way, in such linear terms. Thinking that it will all be gone when he is.

He spread his arms like a bat and leapt from the top of the mountain and the perch he dared to stand upon, the cross upon Mount Royal, and he flew down on his victim with exactly the fury one would think, fangs bared and malice in his eyes.

It was one of the few emotions he had left.

The girl wiped her knees on her dress, and shimmied up on the ice, paying more heed this time. Her palms and knees throbbed but the absence of her toy had overcome the pain. The cold winter wind bit as she looked for her toy, and she spied it (bright orange) resting under a park bench half hidden by some bushes.

The girl raced over to the bench (paying less heed), and snatched up her treasured toy (mine!) As she reached under the bench, a great shadow descended upon her and snatched her away-like a lost toy.

* * *

A vampire had plagued Heather Langden for about as long as she could remember. Sleeping at night was not the sweet bliss it was supposed to be. It was near torture to go up to her room and try to get a full night's sleep. Even when she did, it was not a restful sleep because of the expectancy of the nightly visitations. At first she would take them for nightmares because, upon waking, she could only remember bits and pieces of what happened the night before.

My God, I'm sixteen and I'm still pissing in my bed, she would think to herself. The dreams would take different forms; they grew with her, so to speak. They involved a mischievous friend who would come to her and take her out for a night of transgression. They started, near as she could remember, when she was about fourteen years old and, at first, she thought that her childhood imagination was trying for one last gasp at life.

The dreams weren't flat out *Boo!* in your face scary. There was a strange and eerie subtlety about them. This friend would come to her, sometimes frequently, sometimes not. She would control her. Sometimes she got Heather into serious trouble, other times she showed her something horrifying or obscene or uncanny. A lot of the times they indeed did just have fun. This girl was truly a friend to Heather, someone who could be counted on to look out for her if not always counted on to be there.

At first Heather did indeed think she was dreaming, that this was an imaginary friend. Being on the border of childhood and adulthood, she still felt at ease having a secret friend. As she grew older, she began to believe this friend was in fact real, but Heather had been so accustomed to keeping their relationship a secret and she had no way to prove the existence of her friend so nobody ever did find out about her, not even after Heather had died.

Heather looked out the windows of her house to watch the cars go by on *rue Ste-Catherine*. They lived on the corner of *rue Ste-Catherine* and Gladstone Ave. Except for rush hour, cars would constantly speed along the autobahn style streets of Montréal.

As Heather got older, the visits from this friend became more disturbing. She obviously was real and not a figment of her active childhood imagination since she was no longer a child and had never been diagnosed as schizophrenic.

The first night, she was sleeping lightly in her bed with the covers halfway down her body. Her window was open just slightly to allow the breeze in, the curtains moving almost imperceptibly into the room. She snuggled with her (stuffed) guardian, Bear, who was there to ward off wolves, zombies and the green glob of killer slime under the bed that was invisible during the day.

The window rapped open and shut a couple of times and it woke Heather with a start. She drew her blanket up close to her neck and clung to Bear ever tighter.

"Hello, Heather." There, sitting just on the edge of her windowsill, was a girl. She smiled coyly as she let her legs dangle from the ledge, childlike, as though she were keeping herself amused. Heather was frozen, except for a slight tremble. She was unable to breathe much less yell for help.

"Aren't you going to invite me in?" asked the girl. She was dressed from neck to ankle in a black body suit and on her feet were black socks-she wore no shoes; she also looked several years older than Heather was, at least sixteen, but possibly older, maybe as old as eighteen even.

Heather clung to Bear even tighter.

"I promise that I'm not here to hurt you. I just thought you could use a friend."

Heather was paralyzed. She could only stare at the stranger sitting at her windowsill and it took all her courage to utter a meek, feeble, *Who are you?* The girl smiled a little wider, a bit more toothier; almost, but not quite, a grin. Heather glanced at her nite-light on her bedside table and had thought of clicking it on but was still too afraid to do so. The moonlight was bright but coming from behind the girl it cast sinister shadows on her face despite her alluring smile. Heather gathered enough courage to reach out slowly and click on the light.

"Please don't," said the girl. "I don't want your parents to come in."

"How did you get up here?" enquired Heather.

"Oh...I can fly," answered the girl, like it was nothing special or out of the ordinary to say so.

Heather's eyes grew wider and some of her initial fear started to drip away with the onrush of questions that were flooding her mind. She thought about the possibilities.

"Bull," she answered. "Nobody can fly."

"But I can. Not all the time and never for very long, I'm not strong enough for that yet." As the girl spoke, Heather noticed that she was no longer actually sitting on the window ledge at all. She was sitting just a few inches above it, hovering.

"Cool," exclaimed Heather. "Wait till my friends find out that I know someone who can fly!"

"I'm sorry, honey, but you can't tell anyone that you know me. It's just the way it has to be if were going to be friends. Besides, no one is ever going to believe you anyway." That smile again, it coaxed.

"I guess you're right," said Heather, a trifle disappointed. She added, excitement growing: "This means were friends, though, right?"

"Of course it does. I'm new here and I don't have any friends. That's why I thought you could be my friend."

Ashamed of ever having been afraid, Heather relaxed her grip on Bear (who breathed a sigh of relief) and her blanket and shifted her weight to a more comfortable position.

"I guess it would be okay if you came in now." After all, she wasn't a green glob of killer slime.

"No, I've got to be going. But I promise I'll visit you again soon. And remember," said the girl with another of her coy and coaxing smiles, "this is our little secret."

Her teeth flashed under the moonlight. She popped one leg up on the base of the window and twisted as if to push off with a jump.

"Wait!" said Heather. "You still haven't told me who you are." Her fear almost completely gone, she said this with brashness. The girl barely peeked over her shoulder and said the name *Talissa*.

It was some nights before Talissa visited Heather again. In the meanwhile, she waited impatiently for her flying friend to reappear, all the time not knowing when to expect her or what to expect at all. Her mother, Susan, remarked on how withdrawn she was and was given the general reply: I'm just bored, or some variation of the phrase, the excuses that no one ever believed. In truth she was constantly distracted by the prolonged absence of her new friend, but she did not want to tell anyone out of fear of breaking her friend's confidence in her. She knew that if she did, that somehow Talissa would find out; surely someone who could fly could have other powers as well...eerie powers...

Heather stared out her window to look down *Ste-Catherine*. She wished she could be out there, wandering around, if only she could slip by her parents. She would love to see the people who lived while it was dark, the people who came alive at night. She knew that if she were to walk for ten or so minutes east on *de Maisonneuve*, she would find throngs of people that she could watch and walk beside, and see where they go and what they do when the clock had already struck midnight. She sighed and resigned herself to another night with her head against the pillow.

One night, after Heather had begun to give up faith in seeing Talissa, or even if she had seen her to begin with, there was a rap on the window. At first, her mind half-drugged by sleep, Heather ignored the sound, assuming it was part of a delusion. When it came a second time, and then a third and even a fourth, she blinked the grogginess from her mind and eyes and looked hopefully toward the window.

There was no one there, grinning like a delinquent child, sitting on the ledge like it was commonplace to do so.

Then, all of a sudden, *clonck!*, a large pebble hit the window. Immediately, Heather sprang up out of bed and darted towards the window, opening it swiftly as much to prevent its creaking as to confirm Talissa's presence outside. *Clonck!* Another pebble flew up and struck her forehead.

"Fuck!" cried Heather, touching her forehead. But she was okay. "What are you doing down there?" asked Heather in a shouted whisper.

"I can't fly tonight. I'm too weak. You'll have to come down here."

"Are you crazy? There's no way I can get down there without my parents hearing me."

"Sure there is. Scale the trellis down. I'll be here to catch you if you fall."

"No way! They're covered with thorny rose vines. I'd cut myself."

"Come on," persuaded Talissa, "how bad can it be? Besides, I had a really fun night planned for us."

Heather thought for a moment. She'd never been out past ten or eleven, and hardly ever awake after those times, so being out late was really enticing. Hardly a girl known for causing trouble, though, it wasn't a quick or easy decision, and when she finally made it, it was probably ten or fifteen minutes later with pushing and prodding coming from below the window every sixty seconds. Heather succumbed and put on a pair of jeans and a sweatshirt over her nightgown. To keep her feet warm, two pairs of thick socks, and, not finding a decent pair of shoes in her closet, she squeezed into a pair of thin canvass shoes. She stuck her head out the window and told Talissa she'd be right down.

She eased out of her window onto the thin ledge, her feet completely splayed. Nervously, she shuffled over the three feet that separated her from the trellis. Upon reaching it, she noticed that there was a thin stretch along the edge that the rose vines hadn't gotten a hold of and may be big enough to allow her to make her way down without having to deal with the thorny needles that jutted out randomly in all directions.

Heather looked around, along *Ste-Catherine*, and out over the night in general. Her fear was causing her to tremble slightly, as was the cold, which stung two floors up from the ground. A taxi sped by ignoring the red light, but otherwise the street was empty. Heather smiled a bit and her tremble began to subside.

She began to take hold of the first rung of the trellis and as she began to put her weight on it, it creaked with resentment at being disturbed. A shiver of fear crawled her spine from bottom to top and hovered around her neck, tingling. She placed her left foot several rungs lower and began to mount the makeshift ladder, her full weight now being transferred over. The rung under her foot snapped loudly-SNAP!!-and Heather half hung by her hand on the trellis and prayed that her foot wouldn't slip off the precariously thin ledge. She flailed a bit and got a good grip on the brick wall with her other hand and then, in one quick motion, she let go of the rung she was holding and reached for one in a more comfortable position. She then stifled a squeal because the rung she reached for was covered in the thorny rose vines she was trying to avoid in the first place. She got back on the ledge and opened and closed her hand in a fist to dull the throbbing. She glanced down at Talissa.

"It's okay," called Talissa. "It was just a weak piece of wood. Now get back on quickly and don't think about it. And above all, don't look down!"

Heather thought, *Don't look down, she says*.

Heather took the advice to heart and mounted the trellis again, quite fast this time, so neither she, nor the trellis, would have time to react to what was happening. She ignored the throbbing in her left hand from the pricking of the vines she received a moment ago, and made it down the rest of the way quite easily and with relatively few more cuts to her already tormented hand. When she had a few feet left she was already a confident and experienced climber (or descender) and she neatly dropped down and landed on her feet.

She straightened up and inhaled a gulp of fresh night air. The chill, which was stinging from higher up, became invigorating on the ground. It probably helped that the adrenaline in her system was kicking in. Finally she was on the other side of the window when it was dark; tonight she would see what went on when most people were supposed to be in bed. At this hour, Montréal was most definitely still awake.

For the first time she took a good look at Talissa in the half decent light that was coming from the street lamp nearby. She wasn't as tall as she seemed from across the room and her whole manner and attitude seemed to fool you into thinking she was majestically tall. Even now, looking at her from a few mere feet, and practically eye-to-eye, Heather felt as if she had to crane her neck backwards to look up at her when in reality she was only a few inches shorter. Her hair was definitely beautiful, long and curly and very dark, almost black, with very faint traces of gold flecked at the tips in some places, which could only be seen if you stared for a few seconds and somewhat closely. In fact, after a while they seemed to mesmerize and one got the illusion that they swayed on their own like they were actually glints of sunlight that had gotten trapped in a sea of liquid chocolate.

She was thin but by no means bony and very well proportioned, obviously a girl but with very little growing left to do. She seemed caught between being extremely sophisticated and quite childlike. Her skin was quite pale and it was really the only thing that stood out about her in the visual sense because everything else about her seemed so dark. Her eyes shifted between dark brown and absolute black, and seemed to absorb the light, as if they were devouring the scenery rather than just looking at it. If one wanted to examine her physical details one had to scrutinize and hope that you didn't get captivated by one particular feature; it was difficult to really see her as a whole and recreate each detail in one's mind's eye afterwards.

The initial attraction, what hooked one into all these details in the first place, was her warm smile. It could easily be described as alluring but there were so many other subtleties that emanated from it. Her teeth, barely noticeable, were a soft, pale, but clean white. If no one had dared to speak, Heather would have stood eternally in quiet awe, worshipping the statuette. There was something beyond appearance that effused from her, something quite intangible but ever present, that kept one's mind in just the slightest stupor so one could still formulate an argument but could never quite find the conclusion.

"Your hand," Talissa said softly.

Heather slowly remembered the dull throb of pain that had accompanied her down the trellis. She looked at her hand and saw that it was cut in several places in the palm and blood was slowly seeping from the scrapes that she'd accumulated on her descent.

"Damn," she said. "What am I gonna do about my hand?"

"Lick it off," suggested Talissa.

"That's disgusting! Besides, that won't stop the bleeding. I'd need a Band-Aid or something."

"It's not disgusting at all. I could even do it for you."

"Pardon me?" Heather, repelled by the proposal, had suddenly snapped out of her delirium.

"There's nothing sickening about it. Your lifeblood is the most powerful thing in the entire universe. It shouldn't be let go to waste." The way Talissa spoke was a little funny, a little unnatural.

Talissa gently took Heather's scarred hand in her own and lifted it reverently up for both of them to see. She inclined her head towards Heather's hand at the same time bringing the hand towards her. The blood gleamed in the shallow light. Talissa slowly and gently began to lap the blood up into her eager throat with her tongue. There was nothing obscene or unnatural about the way she cleaned the hand, as if she knew of religious traditions for what she was doing and was following them instinctively. Then, suddenly, Heather jerked her hand away with a giggle.

"That tickles," she exclaimed, like Elmo. "Do you enjoy this or something?"

"Blood is precious, Heather. Do not wash it away. It can heal you when you hurt." There was a distant look in Talissa's eyes, she was distracted by vague, yet perhaps hurtful memories. It seemed as though she was swirling the blood in her mouth with her tongue. After a short moment, though, she regained herself. "I'm sorry. I sometimes get carried away with my thoughts. I must be scaring you. You think I'm nuts."

"A little. But my hand, it's still cut."

"No problem." Again Talissa took Heather's hand in hers, and she gave it a slow, moist kiss that tingled like sweet iodine. Talissa's tongue spread the blood around like frosting on a cake, and it seemed so thick and alive. Heather looked at her palm, the muscles tightening involuntarily for a second, feeling strange, but the wounds were gone! Not even a scar!

"There, now we're sisters. Now, I promised my new friend a great night out and that's what you'll get. Come on." She took Heather by the arm and led her at a brisk pace to the end of the road, turned, and they made off under the canopy of darkness to the busy street corner not too far off, a place where two girls could find fun after midnight.

Talissa and Heather arrived on the edge of the downtown area. It was a vague border, houses becoming intermittent then non-existent as the bars and shops took over. The actions of tourists would constantly spill over into the more suburban areas, what with everything being so close in Montréal.

Heather's anxiousness increased when she and Talissa walked past a police car that was parked half-hidden on a side street, motor running and headlights off.

Talissa said, "Don't worry, they won't stop us," like she could read Heather's mind or something.

Police patrols had been increased after the lobbying of worried residents. After all, this was Westmount, the citadel of rich, Anglophone Québec, and it must be defended as so. In lower class Verdun, such action would not be so swift in its execution.

But the waiting police car and a twisted metal shell of a car parked at the curb, with it's blue paint blackened in some parts, served to remind Heather of the bombings.

"Talissa, let's go back, it isn't safe here."

"You're just scared because you've never been out this late. It's as safe as day."

As they passed the car it looked more like an abandoned wreck than something that had caught fire. But the pictures of the front page of the Gazette were burned into Heather's brain, the roof of a car torn open like some twisted surgeon had rushed an operation, the inside visibly blackened as though from a Dragon's kiss.

Heather was feeling a little relaxed-

"*You're with me, it's okay,*" Talissa said in her head, and it was so much more soothing that way, so coaxing.

-and, heart beating beneath her breast, she continued on.

The motor revved noisily as the police car sped away behind them, bored apparently, or perhaps other business called.

The sound reminded Heather of a motorcycle because of its loudness, and she wondered if she would catch sight of a notorious Night Stalker's biker, *sans* car bombs.

All the bombings have happened during the day.

"I know, but it's just something about the night that-" Heather stopped, looked at Talissa. "Did you say something?"

Talissa's suppressed smile broke into a wild laugh and she threw her head back as she shook.

All in all, the suburbs were quite safe, and downtown was also safe but nowhere is perfect. Heather's area, only minutes away from downtown, was rarely subject to the influence of the criminal element, notwithstanding former prime ministers and other politicians who lived in the area; but that subject in itself is a whole other volume. The frequency of police patrols varied according to the paranoia of the residents and a somewhat recent increase in kidnapping of children added fuel to the fire. This, coupled with the fact that she had worrisome parents, was a main reason why Heather had never seen much past eleven at night.

This night in particular, there was a group of guys and girls gathered at a local plaza, not five minutes from where Heather lived. Every once in a while their number would swell with someone who would come out from behind the plaza, having finished smoking or drinking something to warp the hours that remained ahead in the night.

And the police in Montréal, they were soaked in the decadence of the city, they would just tell them to fuck off and go home because they didn't want to fill out a report for something like that. It sounded lazy and arrogant when it was said with a French accent.

Not all of the people there were young, some were as old as thirty, and most of them were there as much by circumstance as by situation. Many of them were trying to get into the Night Stalker's. To substantiate their loyalty to the gang, these people would engage in petty crimes such as theft. Because the person who was trying to get initiated was usually inebriated, the victim of the crime may also get beaten or raped when things got beyond control. Fighting back usually spurred the attacker(s) on. But it was the bombings that occupied the police. Cars would suddenly explode. There was a small gang war going on, but the police couldn't figure out the motivation. Likely mere intimidation. Consolidating their hold on the drug trade. Montréal was nestled in the great St. Lawrence River, the first port of importance in Canada.

Montréal does have it's problems like any other city, but it is quite safe for residents and tourists alike; it is probably the least dangerous city after midnight, isolated incidents notwithstanding.

On this particular night, the group at the plaza was small, two guys and three girls, which meant someone was going home twice as lucky as someone else was. Talissa and Heather started towards them, at Talissa's behest, but the plaza rats had their backs to the street and therefore hadn't taken notice of them yet. Talissa walked slowly and confidently, followed by Heather who at least managed to walk quietly. Two of the rats took off for behind the plaza.

"What the hell are we doing here? Those people look pretty dangerous," whispered Heather.

"Just calm down, okay? I need a fix," she said, black eyes blazing deep within.

Another rat took off for behind the plaza, leaving one guy and one girl. Talissa continued to approach slowly, sexily and without fear. The remaining two took notice and glanced over.

"Pretty fuckin' brave," said the guy.

"Pardon me?" said Talissa. In control.

"Two young girls walkin' by themselves. Pretty fuckin' brave."

"No, what's brave is you coming with me back there." Talissa motioned to the back of the plaza, the side opposite to that of the one the other rats had gone behind.

"And stupid, too. Bitch, you just fuckin' asked for what was comin' to ya, know that?" The rat pulled a switchblade and sauntered over to Talissa. "And you, little girl," he said to Heather, "you're in luck. Shane over here likes fresh little girls like you."

Talissa and the rat disappeared behind the plaza, knife at her back, but it was like she was leading. Shane, her head half shaved making her look like a guy from one side, walked over to Heather and grabbed hold of her.

"Look at me you little tart." Heather's eyes were sealed shut by a glue of fear. Shane moved closer, her breath feather dusting Heather's left cheek. "I'm real gentle if ya co-operate, but be a shit and ya will get hurt. Bad." Shane's breath slowly cut through the air towards Heather's nostrils. It was vile and stank of hashish, vodka and spicy peppers. Heather didn't dare move and her eyes were still shut, her face trembling from timorousness and disgust. She felt Shane's wet tongue guide its way up from the top of her neck to just under her eye, slowly memorizing the exact texture of Heather's fresh, virgin skin. An eternity passed once, twice, and again a third time. Heather wasn't sure if she'd actually said it but she thought the words *Talissa, please*! had dripped out of her mouth but quite sure that if they did, no one could have heard them.

With a sudden jolt Heather was thrown to the ground as Shane was torn away from her. She lay there for only a second then glanced up, groggily, for she'd thumped her head when she hit the pavement and it throbbed, dulling her senses. What she saw, or thought she saw, was Talissa holding Shane by the neck, floating a few feet above the ground. Then Talissa slammed Shane into the wall of the plaza and her hand swiped claw-like across her face leaving an unrecognizable orb lined with glowing red streaks. Oh, did that blood ever glow! Talissa's clean hand then slammed Shane in the sidewalk and she dove on her, out of Heather's stupefied field of view. The only thing Heather saw before she lost consciousness was Talissa lifting her head for a moment and her teeth bared, now coated in red, her lips crimson as well, as she looked skyward as if in gratitude to some God. She then dropped her head down out of Heather's sight again and the sucking noises were the last thing Heather heard before the night pressed up against her eyes, blocking the world from view...

Heather woke up slowly, expecting to see the sun piercing the fog in front of her sleep filled eyes. In its stead she found only the darkness still there, as if it had become everlasting. She felt the wet grass under her fingers and realized that she was still outside, lying on it, her head against something soft. A hand touched her cheek, the same spot that Shane had violated, as if washing away the disgusting stain that had been left there, healing like blood, and she craned her head back to see who it was she was leaning on. It was Talissa. She felt a tremble manifest itself in the back of her neck and wash its way eagerly down her spine. She licked her lips and swallowed the cotton out of her throat. Her neck was stiff and she felt weak and hungry.

"So I wasn't dreaming," she managed, the thought of what had happened causing her head to ache. Talissa said nothing. Her face was almost expressionless, but for the faint trace of her ever-present warm smile, the smile that said everything was all right. It was nearly impossible to be angry at that smile.

"What the hell went on out there?" asked Heather. "You left me all alone with that despicable rapist girl. How can you claim to be my friend and do that? And then you with your hands and face covered in blood!" Heather's eyes filled with tears as she recalled how close she came to being part of that unspeakable horror. Talissa looked on with pity as tears rolled down Heather's soft cheeks, her innocence falling on the grass with them.

"I'm sorry, sweetie, I wasn't thinking clearly in the least. I got caught up in my fun."

"Fun?! That's your idea of fun? Taking on a bunch of lunatic gang-bangers? What would have happened to me if those others had come back? I could have been killed." Her tears began to pour forth, leaving her speech incoherent. "I've heard what happens to people who run into them. I don't even know why I went with you."

Talissa clutched her closer as Heather continued her relentless sobbing. Her experience of the world around her up to this point had not been as cold and cruel as the one she'd just had. She'd heard stories of these kinds of things from her parents and the news, but she was always given the feeling by those around her that these things happened among those people and our people were always lucky enough to not have it happen to us. She clung to Talissa's arm tightly because she was the only one around who she could hold on to and also because there would be no on else who she could tell what had almost occurred that night. They would have to be told about Talissa and that was forbidden-their friendship was a secret. Why did she feel so attached to this girl whom she hardly knew? Why did she feel so close to her?

"God, why couldn't this really be a nightmare?" she whispered hoarsely. Her head was spinning and she felt as if she were floating and the air around her tingled with majic. Talissa's arms were wrapped around her waist and she felt her lips come near to her ear and place a soft kiss on her earlobe. She heard her whisper in her head, *It is a dream, sweetie, a very bad dream. Sleep peacefully tonight. Don't be haunted by silly nightmares, they cannot hurt you. Nothing will ever harm you when I am near. I promise.* Her words were like warm maple syrup, soothing her into calm. She actually was floating and she saw that she was now in her bedroom but she wasn't sure if she was lying in her bed or still hovering because she felt so light and placid. She put her head lightly on her pillow and her thoughts were of warm peaches and smooth cream as she fell back to sleep, her nightmares dwindling away as the darkness faded to be replaced by a gentle glow on the horizon, a glow that was the colour of the peaches in Heather's dream, the first vestige of a cold sun that finally decided to peak over the edge of the earth.

For the next several weeks, Heather tried to forget what happened to her on her nocturnal excursion. She immersed herself in her schoolwork, did the chores around the house without argument and occupied any remaining time with mind numbing pursuits such as solitaire. Her mother was pleased with her zeal in completing the household work, but she was worried because of how withdrawn Heather seemed to be, especially when she had time on her hands; it was as if someone had switched off the part of her brain that controlled her personality. It wasn't hard to notice when something was wrong with Heather because she was normally quite friendly, optimistic.

Her father, Albert, was too fatigued to take active notice-he came home from work, scarfed down something bovine, washed it down with a beer and sat in front of the television with a cigar and some scotch. He would only get involved with what went on around him if it concerned him directly or interrupted what he was doing. He wasn't at all uncaring towards his daughter, or his wife, he was always willing to give attention to his two favourite girls. But after a while his attention waned and would return to TV, or scotch, and if he wanted to be by himself a second cigar would drop a layer of filthy smoke between himself and the world that few dared penetrate, Prince Prospero sealed up in his den, immune to the troubles of the world around him.

Bedtime for Heather was a trial. She would go to her room only after forty-five minutes of prodding from her mother, and then she would look for excuses to put off the inevitable; she would brush her teeth two or three times, she would look extra hard for adolescent zits and such. Sometimes she would go back downstairs, lie on the couch in front of the TV, and fall asleep there, but her mother would eventually drag her flaccid body up the stairs and tuck her into bed.

After a few days of this routine, Heather began to be more comfortable with sleeping in her room. There would always be a nervousness, a tentativeness, that accompanied her entrance into the darkened room, but after she had changed and buried herself under her thick comforter, after she clutched onto poor Bear, she would relax and drift into dreamland. It also helped that she would wake up safe in the morning.

Heather didn't do much dreaming, but she would think of Talissa before she shut her eyes (although she tried not to; the thoughts swam in the back of her mind, threatening to surface like a storm), and those waking thoughts invaded her sleeping thoughts as the two states interfered, sorted themselves out, then went their separate ways. *This is stupid*, she would think to herself, *I was obviously dreaming so there is absolutely no reason to be afraid.* But it all seemed so real to Heather, the cuts on her hand, the gang-girl's slimy, wet tongue, the blood on Talissa's lips as she lifted her head away from the body beneath her. Why was she afraid? There was no way she could have gotten out of the house. Her hands were sore but they looked as though they'd never been cut. There. That was proof. Her flesh would have remembered the cuts, easily. No one could walk around and not notice lacerations on their hands that would need a few days to heal.

Still, she wasn't sure. But that was the essence of thick, violent dreams. They invaded your soul and made you doubt.

To ease her timidity, Heather decided to start leaving the light on in her room before it got dark. That way she could walk up the stairs and into a brightly lighted room. She had resolved not to be afraid of peccant girls who flew by windows in her dreams. And for three days straight, Heather went to bed with very little difficulty.

On the fourth day, she did something very different. Instead of sleeping face down, as she was accustomed, she slept face up. She was drifting off, thinking of her classes that she had to attend the next day, when she felt a refreshing breeze kiss her visage. She grinned and, already almost asleep, thought the breeze would nudge her over the threshold, when she heard a voice that rode the breeze to her ears like a feather.

"Wake up, honey, I have something for you." It was a dream turned real again. Talissa had materialized. Heather pushed herself up on her elbows and gaped at the girl who crouched at the foot of her bed, cat-like. "Don't scream my darling, you'll wake up mommy and daddy."

"How'd you get through my window, it was locked," trembled Heather.

"Some things just aren't a problem for me. Locks are one of them."

"How about security systems?"

"Clever girl. I'd still find a way though." Talissa flashed her warm and wicked smile, so enticing.

"So what is it that you have for me? You can leave it on the dresser and go," said Heather. This time she was staying safe under the blankets with Bear.

"I just wanted to apologize," said Talissa. Heather was a bit taken aback by this, but she listened without interrupting. "Some of my tastes are rather shocking or extravagant and I really shouldn't have pushed you to confront those people the way I did. I didn't realize how fragile you were. I'm sorry I frightened you. Friends?"

"Well, where have you been for the last week? You could've said you're sorry a lot sooner." Heather relaxed, sensing she was more in control of what would happen tonight.

"I just thought you wouldn't want to see me right away. I was giving you time to cool off."

"Thanks. Listen, I don't think I want to go out tonight. I'm afraid I won't be much of a good time for you anyway."

"That's okay," said Talissa. "Do you mind if I stay here with you for a few hours? I don't feel like being alone tonight."

"What if my parents walk in and see you? I'm not sure that's a good idea."

"Hey, I kept you out for the whole night without them finding out. Trust me, they won't know the difference. I'll just snuggle next to you for a while till you fall asleep and then I'll split really quiet, like I came in. I can be your big sister for the night. We're still sisters, remember?"

Heather relented after a pause. "Fine, but be careful. I don't want any more trouble from you," she whispered. Talissa smiled and tucked her body close to Heather's, her arm draped over her chest and her hand grazing Heather's cheek and resting against her lips. Heather felt so warm and relaxed with Talissa pressed against her and she found herself drifting into a fugue again. She felt Talissa move slightly closer and it was as if this girl cocooned her, like she protected her and Talissa would let nothing harm her.

And nothing ever will, honey, remember that always, she heard Talissa say to her, the voice no longer traveling on the wind but right in her head now. All her thoughts of Talissa were good now. The doubt Heather had had of her character was washed away. Talissa was her best friend, she was her big sister. That night was veiled in the mist of the past, and the past couldn't harm you because it was over.

She felt comfortable with Talissa's arms wrapped around her, wholly safe. She smiled in her sleep as she felt Talissa's body near hers, as she felt every little nuance of movement it made, every subtlety. She was asleep and it was like she was still able to feel her surroundings as though she were awake, but much more acutely. Her sense of touch was more sensitive but the fugue still stayed over her mind.

She felt Talissa's hot breath near her cheek, the same one that Shane had desecrated, and she wanted to shudder but for some reason she didn't. She felt Talissa kiss her cheek and it wasn't anything like what happened to her before-there was no profanity about it. Talissa's hand slid down her side to her virgin sex and hover there, teasing. Heather felt herself being massaged slowly and gently, while warm, moist lips softly kissed her cheek. A slight coldness and longing touched her cheek as the lips departed but she felt them return to her neck, and she gave a sigh of relief. She then felt a prick at her neck, but before any pain could register, time seemed to warp into a gentle ocean wave around her.

This must be eternity, she thought. She felt moonlight bathe her soul and waves of the seas of time warm her and settle down to where they should be, bringing her back to reality. She shuddered as orgasm overtook her suddenly, quickly, and unexpectedly. *Remember,* said Talissa in her head, *just a dream.*

And when Heather awoke, she would have believed so, if not for the drop of blood spilled on her pillow and the soreness in her neck.

For the first time, Talissa didn't wait to visit Heather; she returned the very next night. She sat, her feet dangling out of the window, her childlike manner very apparent. She had a gleam in her eye, especially when she looked out into the night.

When Heather awoke, it wasn't with a start. She drifted back into consciousness as if a presence had drawn her back. She saw Talissa sitting at the window with her smile, glancing between her and the night outside. They sat there, Talissa smiling simply because it was a beautiful night, Heather confused as to what was reality. It was a gorgeous night though, with the crescent moon alabaster silver in the coal sky.

"Get dressed. Tonight were going out," said Talissa.

"There is no way I'm climbing through those vines again," answered Heather.

"Don't worry, I'll carry you down. It's just too nice out to waste it here in bed."

"Listen, T'lissa. I really don't want to run into any more thugs on the street-"

"Just sightseeing, I promise. I'm taking my friend out for a stroll under the crescent moon!"

Heather acquiesced, a little reluctantly. She put on sweat pants and a blue sweater, and she began to put on her shoes when there was a creak from the door. It was her mother.

"I thought I heard you talking to someone. Why are you getting dressed?" asked her mother, bleary from sleep.

Heather stood for a moment, knowing she was caught. How was she going to get out of this? And the girl sitting in her window, how was she to-

Heather turned towards the window and found it to be empty, still open, but with no girl sitting there, trying to coax her out with a warm grin. Heather felt her head spin.

"Are you okay, dear?" asked her mother.

"Um...I had a pain in my stomach and I couldn't sleep. I thought I'd go sit on the porch for some air."

Her mother thought for a second then said: "Well, don't be too long. And be careful. Three children have already been reported missing in this city and I don't want you to be the fourth." She closed the door quietly as she left.

"I'm not a child, you bitch," whispered Heather. Then she watched the feet pause at the door for a second before leaving.

Heather finished putting on her shoes and then went outside, though she used the front door this time. Talissa must've been a dream, there is no way she could've disappeared that fast when her mother came in.

When she got outside, the night air greeted her with a light slap on the face. It was chill, but fresh and invigorating. The moon cast a pale light, but set a wonderful mood, despite the interference of the street lamps. The streets were empty and quiet, no people whatsoever and no Talissa. She turned to go back inside.

20

"Hey!" came a whispered yell from behind. Heather turned and expected to see Talissa on the sidewalk, and she even did for a moment, but all of a sudden they were face to face. "You ready? Good, let's go."

They walked, this time avoiding the site of their last encounter, over to the downtown. The bars were still doing business and people still walked the streets in slowly dissipating numbers. Some glanced at Talissa and Heather but didn't seem to care at all that they looked young.

Talissa's skin seemed whiter than usual. It was hard to get a perfect, clear look at her face. It was always moving to look at something or other, and the dark hair that framed it seemed alive. It was like clusters of it would drift up across her visage to distract whoever happened to be looking from seeing the entire picture.

Heather was enthralled with the sights of downtown. She'd never been here at night, in person. It was wall-to-wall action, there was no time to catch your breath. Everywhere you looked there was something going on. There were billboards and signs that were dazzling with lights, there were people walking, people in cars, people sitting in restaurant windows and there were all kinds of people too. Men in sharp suits, women in the latest fashions, tourists dressed however they felt, people who dressed like they belonged on the street but were only dressing the part to live up to the latest trend. Most were dizzy with drink or life or both, and all were laughing and carrying on because it was good to be alive and having fun.

There was hair of all colours-cinnamon brown, copper, purple and green, and people just let it hang any way it wanted. The flashing lights from the signs created a glowing halo around the most interesting coifs.

Despite the fact that it was the middle of the week and after midnight, there were still enough people on the street to give the impression of a good crowd. Life lived in Montréal. Heather and Talissa walked on through the pulsing of the city, not saying a word, enjoying the life the city breathed into them. Talissa looked almost captivated by the city, like something was able to control her, which didn't seem possible.

They walked on for fifteen more minutes, talking, walking slowly so they wouldn't miss any important detail of the city that lived. Then, Talissa took a turn off *rue Ste-Catherine*, and Heather followed, not paying attention to their direction. They were going south along University, and in the alcoves there were homeless unfortunates lying around. The lights were less bright and still flashing, but the people around them didn't have the same glow of life.

The atmosphere had gotten *grungier* off the beaten path.

Heather noticed a woman standing on the corner of the street about thirty feet ahead, smoking a cigarette. She wore a red leather mini, and a tank top, was slim almost to the point of bony, and a little taller than normal. Her straight blond hair hung limply on her shoulders and back. Heather fixed her gaze on the woman. As she got closer she began to wonder why a pretty lady like that would decide to dress that way and stand on the street. Was this a prostitute? She had never seen one, or thought she ever would. A car approached the woman, who leaned on the window. A moment later she opened the door and got into the car. When the car passed Heather it hadn't picked up speed yet and she got a good look at the streetwalker.

She wasn't pretty at all, really, although she obviously once was. And she looked old, older than she did at a distance. The skin on her face seemed prematurely worn with time and her mouth looked sad and even a bit lonely. Her eyes, though, were a deep blue and they still retained their youth and vigour. Maybe underneath the trash that walked the streets at night there was a person trapped in a life that was torture to her?

How long would it be before my eyes grew old and tired, too? Heather wondered. Would her body die old and her soul young, or would life make sure it had her defeated before it left her forever? The car sped away and Heather hoped that the woman would survive the night, but she wasn't sure of it. Maybe it was a middle-class ideology to think that these people weren't happy.

They walked on a little more, Heather's sense of fear heightening at the sight of the surroundings.

"Talissa, this isn't a very safe part of town, there's no people around. Let's head back, I'm tired anyway," she said.

"Fine, we'll cut through an alley that's a little ways up the road. That will have us turned in the right direction," said Talissa. There were a few small, dead-end alleys along this road, so Heather wondered why they just didn't turn and go back. Then, as they passed one of the alleys, a raspy voice rose out of one of the depths.

"You fuckin' little mutt!" it said. It was a drunken bum, holding himself up against the wall with one hand and smacking a defenseless little pooch with his other. *Smack!* "You cause me nothin' but trouble. I's feed ya and ya whine and whine."

Smack!

Heather was disgusted by what she saw. "Look what he's doing to that poor little thing, Talissa!" The anger in Heather rose.

"Here," said Talissa. "Go ahead and stop him. You're strong, you can do it." She handed Heather a blade to defend herself with. Heather took it and looked at it as though it were a virus. She felt its dead weight in her hand.

Heather said, "I can't." She couldn't kill that guy no matter how mean he was being to that dog.

"Sure you can," smiled Talissa. "Look, take it just in case, okay?"

Take a peek, said a voice.

Heather nodded in acquiescence and approached the man, not sure why she suddenly changed her mind. She heard Talissa start to follow slowly behind her and it made her feel a little more comfortable, but not much.

Then, she challenged the guy.

"Leave him be," she said, with more authority then she thought she had in her.

The man spit on the ground and gave an iniquitous grin, which disappeared as soon as it was visible.

He said, "Fuck off," and the words sounded like a scratchy beard.

Heather held up the knife and the man only laughed in his sour voice. He started towards Heather, who continued to hold the knife in her trembling right hand. The man's hand had left the wall as he took step after rickety step towards Heather. She felt Talissa just behind her, whispering in her ear (or was it a voice in her head? She wasn't sure), *You have to kill him, do it quick, before he gets you. If he lives he'll just hurt more puppies. You don't want that, do you?*

The voice was like a hand pushing on her shoulder.

Heather bit her lip in fear and uncertainty. What else could she do? If she ran off that poor dog would get beaten even worse, but if she stayed she would get beaten too.

The bum moved closer, his odour becoming more apparent with each step. He smelt of booze and shit and sweat.

Heather wanted to turn her head and look at Talissa but she was stiff with fear. She raised her other hand to hold her right one steady. The bum's eyes were hollow black pits in his dirty face. He loomed over her.

It's either you and the dog or him, honey, said Talissa, again in Heather's head. She looked at the dog that shivered in a bed of newspaper, too scared to move or make a noise, like he knew what was going on. The bum was almost upon her and he reached out his filthy, creaky arms to take hold of Heather. The dog managed a feeble whimper.

Heather stabbed the man's gut. The knife went in clean to his stomach and he curled in pain, but managed to remain on his feet. Heather pulled the knife out and the man collapsed, gasping for air. Her anger was replaced at bewilderment at what she'd done. Talissa took over.

She told Heather to take the dog and go around the corner so that she could take care of the bum, who was not quite dead. Heather did as she was told. She went round the corner and waited for Talissa to come out. After a minute or so she began to hear the same terrible sucking noises that she heard the first time she was out with Talissa. She was too scared to peak around the corner. All she could think was *OmyGodOmyGodOmyGod! I'm a murderer!*

After another minute Talissa came out, said, "Hurry, let's get out of here!"

They returned to the suburbs and left the dog in a place where it would be found by someone and possibly taken in. A short walk was all that was required to get back to Heather's home.

"You were great tonight, sweetie," said Talissa. "I'm proud of the way you handled yourself."

"Thanks," answered Heather. "I just wish I didn't have to do what I did."

"Believe me, there are things worse than killing a dog beater. Trust me." Talissa flashed her cunning smile as always. It had rarely left her face. "You're a very good person, Heather, believe me. Your soul is truly pure."

Heather said, "Thanks," bemusedly, and they sat down under her bedroom window talking for a long while.

When Heather woke in the morning, she didn't remember ever going back to her room, much less leaving.

It would be several months before Heather saw Talissa again. She missed her terribly, because she always felt safe with Talissa around, despite the fact that Talissa often shocked her with her sexual escapades with total strangers, and the fact that Talissa would roam on in dangerous parts of the city to see who would challenge her. Heather felt safe because they were together. It was a strange duality in Heather, to feel safe in a dangerous situation because of who she was with.

Talissa would also teach Heather many things about life. She looked like she was in her late teens or early twenties, but spoke as though she was much more experienced. She would entertain Heather with numerous tales of people in far away places and from times long ago, and she told these stories as if she'd really been there.

She told her about Paris, and Rome and Berlin. She said Berlin was truly beautiful before it had been destroyed by war. Heather listened to all these stories intently, and wished she could travel to these places and see what they were like for herself.

Heather asked, "When were you in Berlin?"

"I must have gone there in '26 or '27," answered Talissa.

"Why?"

"That was the beginning of a beautiful time in history. I could feel it."

"You mean the Nazis?" Heather was intrigued. "What do you mean beautiful, there was nothing beautiful about that."

"Oh, I'm not talking about something as petty as racism. I could feel the chaos building to a climax. The chaos keeps me alive, I can thrive off it. And there was some brilliant political bullying going on at the time, kind of like there is here.

"There was an electricity of fear in the air, and I had the time of my life. Until the bombs dropped."

"But I thought you liked chaos," said Heather.

"I do, but up here," she said, tapping her temple with a clawed forefinger. "I hated when they destroyed all my beautiful buildings. Such Old World architecture will never be repeated."

Old World architecture-like in Montréal.

"And the bastards started stealing my lives. People think killing is chaos, but killing is the end of chaos, really. You can't have chaos when everyone is dead. (Then there would be no one to call it chaos.) If you ever want to see me angry, it is when someone commits an atrocity like that. I prefer to pick my victims off one-by-one. To let my children thrive and my tree spread as though it were a thorny vine."

This opened a new door of questions for Heather.

But she blinked and it was morning.

She'd completely forgotten her homework for that day, and it showed in an embarrassing attempt at calculus up on the chalkboard. Her teacher asked her to stay after class, asked her why her study habits were so erratic. After a few downcast glances and aloof shrugs, the teacher dismissed her.

She said, "Fucking bitch," louder than she meant on her way out the door and hoped she wasn't suspended the next morning.

Heather walked down the hall, thinking things like: "She's just picking on me because I'm Anglo, maybe I should tell her I'm one quarter French and she'll lay off."

That's how teachers were sometimes. Grades slip a bit because you're living life, and they treat you like you're shit.

Heather sulked for a few steps, felt a tug on her sleeve and turned to see Sarah, who had waited for her.

Sarah said, "What did Madame Dumas want?"

"You mean Madame Dumb-Ass. She wanted to know why I didn't do my homework. 'Erratic study habits,' she said, in that prickly voice of hers. When I had that 'A' on a test three weeks ago, she couldn't stop smiling at me like I was her prized pupil."

"She's probably just upset because she thinks you fuck more men than she does. You know how these old hags are when the looks start to go, they get jealous of anything that can steal the men from under their nose."

That seems more your style than mine, thought Heather.

Sarah said, "I was out with Henri last night," and Heather thought, *Here we go.*

"We went by your house to see if you could sneak out, but we couldn't wake you."

"I'm really not the type to do something like that," said Heather with a furtive glance.

"Not that it mattered. We went downtown, hit a few bars. I don't even know why they have a drinking age here, nobody gives a shit. It's almost like they encourage it."

"Are you complaining?"

"You've tried booze, haven't you? And I don't mean a sip of beer on your dad's knee."

"My parents don't let me drink. My dad's an alcoholic, remember?"

Sarah lowered her head, looked at Heather from beneath her eyebrows.

"Sorry," she said.

"S'okay," said Heather. "Anyways, get it over with."

"What?" asked Sarah.

"What you and your bad-boy Henri did afterwards. He does have his own place, doesn't he?"

Sarah nodded a yes with a big smile.

"How the hell does he afford it?" They entered the cafeteria and sat down with their bag lunches.

"Welfare. And he works under the table at some bar."

"Your mom must shit when you go out with him."

"My mom doesn't know," snapped Sarah proudly. "Anyways, we go back to his place, the room is spinning like one of those carnival rides. He pops a couple of beers, but that's like foreplay, y'know, because he wastes no time in pinning me down on the couch. He pulls up my shirt, kinda rough, but still gentle and caring, like he doesn't want to hurt me. I won't bore you with the details, but he gave me a fine bath with his tongue where it counted most, if you know what I mean."

"So you didn't..."

"No. I'll string him along for a bit, see if he'll stick around for at least a while."

"I didn't expect to hear that from you," said Heather.

"Hey, what's that supposed to mean?" Sarah gave her a shove from across the table. "Anyways, it was pretty good, didn't bring the earth crashing down around me or anything. It was a little better than what we talked about last week. Was that what you were doing last night?"

Heather took in a deep breath. "No, if you must know, that wasn't what I was doing last night."

"C'mon," prodded Sarah. "It's me. You know I can keep my mouth shut about the important stuff. It's been a whole month and I haven't told a soul about your crush on Patrick. Is that who you think about when you do it?"

Heather blushed a bit, tried to think of something to change the subject, but was at a loss.

"I haven't really done that more than a few times."

"You should. It's good practice. One day, maybe, I'll spend the night and we'll do it at the same time, see who's better at it."

"Oh, Lord, you have a sick mind," said Heather. "You know how that stuff disturbs me."

"Gonna have nightmares, Heather? Aaaawww!"

"Probably. If I can even get to sleep."

Sarah said, "You have had bags under your eyes lately. Maybe you should skip the rest of the day?"

"Nah, I'll tough it out. I'll just sleep well tonight. I've got class, I'll call you later," Heather said as she walked away. "That is, if you're home," she added with a coy smile as she looked over her shoulder.

The warmth and crispness of the air indicated that winter was almost over, and Heather decided to take advantage of the weather and walk home. It took her half an hour, but she'd hoped the exercise would also serve to keep her awake so she could catch up on her homework.

She thought about what Sarah had said about nightmares, and it brought a smile to her lips. Had she seen Talissa, her feet dangling at the window? It wasn't the first time Sarah had stopped by with a guy to get her to come out. But Heather never did more than chat for a moment at the front door and turn down the invitation.

Geez, all my friends seem to want to sneak me out of the house, thought Heather. *Must be the warm weather lately.*

Susan said, "Leftover meatloaf for dinner tonight, I've got a meeting," as Heather walked in the door. It was early, not even five, but Heather got herself a plate and put some cold meatloaf and potatoes on it, popped it into the microwave to heat. In this house, leftovers meant you served yourself at your own convenience, and Heather felt that she would need the extra energy to remain awake.

After scarfing down dinner (ravenous appetite!), Heather went to her room to tackle the pile of homework that was bigger than Mount Royal. She figured it would take her a good two or three hours and that thought did nothing to enliven her.

She got through most of it, but after a couple hours, found her head and eyes heavy and falling towards the desktop.

She switched to her history book and lay face down on her bed, figuring she could at least skim the notes so she'd be familiar with them. She glanced to the darkened window, no Talissa sitting there like a playful child.

God, I'm putting too much faith in these fantasies, thought Heather, and turned her eyes to the book.

(Are they fantasies? Are they really, Heather?)

She put her hand to her thigh, left it there because she liked the warm feeling. Her concentration waned from the text to the warmness, and she found her hand creeping a little higher and a little to the left until she felt it touch her nether region.

She tried not to laugh when she thought of the conversation of earlier today, figured that it planted the thought in her head.

Hm, who to think of? thought Heather. Decisions, decisions.

Another glance to the dark window, nothing.

Maybe...No. She didn't know why the thought even crossed her mind.

Patrick, she thought. *He'll do just fine.*

It had been a good two months since the last time, and since she'd never really been interested in anyone, her fantasies would jump from singers, to movie stars, to the cute boy who sat next to her in math class. This time, though, she stuck mostly with Patrick, though she felt she would never have the nerve to do this with him, much less talk to him.

(Nothing in the darkened window.)

He had an average build, firm but yielding, which is why he appealed to Heather. He seemed gentle, yet strong enough to be protective. Heather was a bit shy, not overly assertive though she wanted to be.

Which is why this fantasy disturbed her.

She pictured him standing inside the door of her bedroom, it didn't matter how he got in, damnit! He was wearing loose pants and no shirt, his arms folded. He looked bigger than he actually was, his jaw more stern and square.

Heather wore pajamas that were smooth and made of silk, and she stuck her chest out, daring him to come forward.

No one spoke in her fantasies, she couldn't imagine herself or anyone else saying those clichéd phrases from soap operas or porns.

She wanted to rip her top open, but she couldn't imagine it. Instead she let her hand find its way to her breast, like a serpent. Her top creased with the firm caresses of her fingers, she put her finger in her mouth and sucked on it like a lollipop.

She saw his hardness through his pants, he walked over and exuded strength and power, and tore the top of her pajamas open so her breasts hung open in the air.

He pushed her down onto the bed, her hair covering her face as she vainly tried to resist.

She'd read something about rape-fantasies, but she never thought she would have one. Though she felt the excitement, she still couldn't see the logic in it. She didn't care.

He had his pants off, she liked to see them naked before she was. He tore off her pants, looked salivatingly at her blond pussy as he thrust her legs open, his thing throbbing and hard.

(Was that a shadow at the window?)

He forced himself into her, she imagined that it would hurt and that she would like it. She tried to imagine something both pleasurable and painful and she wondered if she could really spread her legs that wide.

His image became a blur, all she knew of him was the one important part, or maybe his strong arms when he picked her up and slammed her forward into the wall and pulled on her hair as he entered her again.

She almost imagined him entering her ass. Maybe that was both pleasure and pain?

Again he threw her down on the bed, forcing her to come as his weight pushed her face into the pillow. She wanted to scream, so loudly, so loudly that people would come running because something must be horribly wrong for someone to scream that way, but there was no one around to hear her imagined screams of completion.

When it was finished, her room was empty as it was before, but she never opened her eyes. She felt the sweat on her forehead run into her eyebrows, she left her fingers where they were, and she wondered if the history text was a crumpled mess.

The satisfaction and fatigue took her into sleep almost immediately.

Heather.

The whisper had to break through thick layers before she realized that someone had said something to her.

Her head still felt heavy, she couldn't focus her eyes, wasn't sure if they were even open.

Heather.

Drawing her up and out, the worst feeling to wake up and still feel tired. Maybe her mother back from her meeting, wanting to give her a kiss goodnight?

I didn't know you could be so racy, Heather!

Did she inadvertently leave her shirt open? Would her mother call her racy that way?

(Was that a shadow...?)

Open your eyes, honey.

Stop whispering in my...ear? thought Heather. *Stop whispering like that, so close to me.*

Stop whispering in my head! Get out of my head!

Heather picked her head up, the sleep washing slowly away from her eyes. She looked towards the window.

"Oh, it's..." she said. At first she merely thought Talissa was hovering there, like she usually did. But then she noticed that the curtains were wrapped around her as she floated, caressing her, that the pink of her nipples and the brown pubic hair of her vagina were the only things distinct.

The curtain began to slip away, revealing her feet, her legs, showing Heather the smooth and curvaceous midsection of a fully developed woman, the white silk slipping away over Talissa's face like a bride's veil.

"I didn't know this was all you wanted," said Talissa.

Heather's back felt cold and she shivered. She didn't like this.

"Go away. You're not real," she said.

"Oh, I know you stopped believing that I'm your dream long ago. You know I'm real." Talissa ran her hands over her hips and legs. "All you had to do was ask for it," and she held her shoulder lustily.

"I didn't ask for anything," said Heather. She felt like she was in water.

"Is it a bath you want, Heather?"

Talissa put her finger in her mouth, mocking Heather's fantasy, she slid the finger out from between her lips, wet and glistening. She took the finger and slid it between her other lips, quivering, saying, "Ask me for it," her voice breathy.

"I didn't ask for anything," repeated Heather.

"You want it," said Talissa, her fingers running up her body, her nails making ruby tracks along her tummy.

"I don't want anything."

"Just a taste...to whet your appetite." Talissa beckoned with a finger, *the finger*, the one that touched the wetness of her...

"I don't hunger for that."

"Oh, but you do. You do, honey. You just don't know it yet." A smile. "Come closer."

"No." But she sat up.

"Give me one little kiss."

No. But she inched forward.

(Don't do it.)

"Just one..."

On all fours-

Don't make me.

"...little kiss..."

Only a little nervous-

"...on my..."

So close you can almost taste-

"...lips..."

-salt.

It gushed, the salty liquid, as Heather knelt lip to lip with the surreal form that hung above her, her face splashed with streaming droplets of it, rivulets running down her face, her shoulders, her white sheets stained from it.

Just a taste, thought Heather. *It was this that you're supposed to taste? Does it really matter where it came from?*

She snapped herself upright, the wetness on her own sheets merely her own sweat, and it smelled bitter but reassuring to her now.

She thought she felt a cold draft, but the window was shut tight, though the curtains did waft to and fro a bit.

When Heather looked down at her top, she saw that it was unbuttoned. She blushed slightly as if someone may find out what she'd done, like she was being watched.

The pair of eyes she felt were her own, staring back at her from the mirror across the bed, and she looked up at herself as she did up her top.

What are you staring at? she thought to herself. *So I masturbate, there's nothing wrong with that.*

Or maybe it was the post-masturbatory dream that sparked the guilt? The fact that you were doing it more often lately than you admitted to your friend at school?

The dark corners of the room conspired to push Heather out, she didn't feel like she could get to sleep anyway. She felt hot despite the sweat.

Opening her door carefully, she slowly walked downstairs, hoping the floorboards wouldn't creak and wake up anyone in the house. (In Montréal, every house had wooden floors, and they all creaked.)

Walking to the family room, she didn't notice the light seeping through the crack in the doorway to her fathers study.

"Princess?" Her father's gruff voice quietly issued from the dim light. Heather pushed the door open.

"Sorry," she said. "I didn't know you were still up."

"It's okay. I could use the company." He butted out his cigar, crunching its thick head into the ashtray. "Come sit on daddy's lap," he said, slapping just above his knee.

"Oh, dad, I'm too old for that."

"I don't care if you're ready to retire, you're still my little girl. Sit!"

Heather sat on her father's lap a little awkwardly, put her arm around his shoulder. She only pretended she was too old.

"So why are you up so late tonight? Hm?"

"Bad dreams."

"Did you want to tell me about it?"

Oh, God, no. "Nah, it's over. What are you still doing up, dad?"

"It used to be daddy. Unless you're too old for that, too."

"Okay, *daddy*. Mom's still not home, is she." It wasn't a question, really.

Albert looked at the ice floating in his scotch. "No, she isn't home yet. Long meeting, eh?"

"It's after two in the morning. I don't see how it can't bother you."

He took in a deep breath, an uneasy breath. "As long as my little girl is here," he said, and he planted a hot, alcoholic kiss on her cheek. Took a sip of his scotch. "You'll always be my little Button-nose."

"You'll never let me live that down, will you?"

"You were so precious. It must have been two or three days-"

"I know what happened, you don't have to tell me."

"You would be playing on the family room floor, and you were so curious-"

"Flintstones, meet the Flintstones-mmph!" Heather sang to drown out the words, Albert covering her mouth so he could continue.

"You'd grab whatever you could reach. Your mother left the room for a moment, and when she came back, the door to the closet was open. Of course, she closed it without a thought. I thought you looked funny when I got home, but I was tired and it didn't hit me.

"The next day when I came home, your mother asked me if your nose looked swollen, so I took a closer look.

"I told your mother, 'Get some Kleenex, I think her nose is bleeding.' And your mother, paranoid as she is, she runs with handfuls of Kleenex, screaming. You kept burying your face, you wouldn't let us near, but we held you down finally. You were crying and screaming and you yelled, 'Don't touch my button!!' We nearly died laughing when we saw that you stuck a little red button into your nose so you wouldn't lose it! We pulled it out with tweezers and you were so upset when we wouldn't let you have your button back."

He took another sip of his scotch, refilled the empty glass with the bottle that was on the table.

Heather said, "You shouldn't let mom stay out so late." Her voice was melancholy, dejected from the late hour and her father's front.

He slurped at the scotch, it was strong as ever now because the water hadn't melted into it. Heather patted his belly, he felt thinner. He used to be a bear of a man, the kind girls loved to squeeze.

"I'm in no position to tell your mother how to live her life now. No position for anything." He stared at the bottom of his glass.

"Is it because of your drinking?"

Silence.

"The doctor told you to stop, y'know."

"That was years ago. He told me to stop years ago."

"Still counts."

"No. It doesn't matter anymore."

"You can stop if you try. I'll help you. We'll all help you."

"I can't stop anymore. The doctor told me it's so bad that I can't stop anymore."

Night pushed rudely on the window. Despite the lamplight, you could feel the looming and foreboding, gruesome eyes and black-toothed grin staring in at the window.

"I won't be here much longer. I won't see you graduate, or marry-" he stopped. He needed another sip of scotch, but he could only stare at the glass that held his life, his life that was held in his hands, and he felt like the glass would drop. "If I drink, I die. If I stop, I die."

Heather just held on to his collar. This overwhelmingly disturbed her. It wasn't a surprise. But she couldn't cry. She felt like she should, but the tears wouldn't come.

Her father was crying a bit, she finally saw the man who sat in this room, like the president of some big company, about to go bankrupt. He was more than the voice on the phone behind a closed door. The time they spent together was always special, always enjoyable. But they never had much of it. Maybe he didn't want his daughter to see what he'd become?

"How long have you known?" said Heather, quietly, but it sounded so loud in the silence. The silence itself felt loud.

"A long time. Over a year." He squeezed her shoulder. "This was the most terrible thing I've ever done. I can't go one night without taking a drink. You don't know how terrible that is. I hope you never know how terrible that is."

They heard a car pull up in front of the house.

"Go, up to bed. Before your mother sees you're still up."

"I want to stay with you. A little while longer."

Albert nodded. He put out the light. Susan went quickly upstairs. It wasn't very long until Heather was able to fall asleep in her father's arms, but the hot tears that ran down her red cheeks left stains that would haunt her forever...

Heather said, "Sure, why not?" and they began to walk, despite the fact that it was almost the opposite direction of where he lived.

Two things dawned on her as they walked and talked. One, that Sarah had opened her fat, gossipy mouth, and two, that she really did like this guy.

Walking, she felt more like...oh say, a woman? More grown-up?

"I hear you've been getting in trouble with teachers," said Patrick.

"Just one, really. Who told you that anyway?"

"Sarah said you were kind of shaken up about it, that Dumb-ass yelled at you a bit."

She didn't.

"I'm feeling a lot better now," said Heather, and forced a bit of a smile without trying to *look* like she was forcing a bit of a smile.

God, I hope I don't look as stupid as I feel, she thought.

The time passed quickly as they found more teachers to argue about, more complaints about the amounts of homework and how it interfered with the strict and significant assessment of the new Metallica album, which required most of each and every weeknight.

Patrick said, "It is so cool to find a girl who doesn't listen to that awful dance crap," and Heather thought how wonderful it was that they shared an interest and decided to put off telling him that she occasionally listened to that awful dance crap.

When they had arrived in front of Heather's home, they both stopped and faced each other. Heather realized that they really hadn't made much eye contact.

"Well, this is where I live," she said with a gesture.

"Cute," Patrick smiled back.

Heather noticed her mother's car in the driveway, didn't bother to think anything of it.

"Did yooouuu, want to come in?" asked Heather, stretching the words in uncertainty with a raised eyebrow.

Patrick accepted, and they went in, took their shoes and coats off at the door. It was uncharacteristically mild for February in Montréal, an early signal that the end of the already short school year would soon come to an end.

"Mom?" Heather called, but no answer. Perhaps she'd just dropped the car off.

They heard a hushed tone from the kitchen and Heather said, "C'mon," to Patrick and they went into the room.

Heather's mother was on the phone, blotting tears away with Kleenex. Patrick felt a little awkward because something was obviously wrong and he didn't want to intrude.

"Mum, what is it?" asked Heather.

Susan wiped her tears, extended a hand to Patrick and introduced herself.

"I guess I should leave," he said. "It was nice meeting you, Mrs. Langden."

Heather walked him to the door. She was anxious, she had an inkling of what the problem may be but didn't let her thoughts stray that way.

"Call me later if you want, you have my number," said Patrick, and he touched her on her upper arm.

Heather said thanks and closed the door behind him, went back to the kitchen. She held her arm where he'd touched it.

It's tough to deal with emptiness, this nothing that we neither see, nor hear, nor touch, but *feel.*

And time, the rate at which emptiness is measured, that made up thing that makes that made up thing make us shiver, or cringe, or stoic.

Unusually balmy Montréal winter, like the bite of winter had lost to the fires of Hell, Heather standing in front of the lake, taking advantage of the warmth before it gets too damn **hot**!

"Heather."

Can I stop time? she thought. She took a puff of her cigarette, too numb to cough anymore, just suck down the toxic cocktail. Everyone must be left to their own (de)vices, by the by.

Everyone has their own regrets, everyone has regrets for others.

Though time regrets, nor forgives nothing, just marches to the beat of the distant drummer and chomp, **CHOMP!** consumes everything in its Goddamned path!

Except memories.

No, time has a damned good sense of **freak**ing ironical humour, and it leaves behind those unquenchable memories for us to savour, discard or dwell.

Toxic cock-

"Heather."

-tail. No.

No drinks, please. I abstain. Just a puff. Change the vice, everything's nice.

"Heather?"

*That voice, that damned voice! Get out of my-*Shaking, violent shaking.

"Heather, talk to me, please!"

Different voice.

Mumbled apology.

"You, um, spaced out, as they say," said Patrick, with a nonchalant wave of his hand.

"I'm cold. It's so cold out here."

He put his arms around her to keep up some warmth.

"You sure you feeling okay?" He touched her forehead. "It really isn't very cold out at all."

But it's cold in here, she thought. *But I can't tell you that, can I?*

Defend the void till the last.

"Take me home," she said.

They drove down the slopes of Mount Royal, away from *Lac aux Castors,* past the cemeteries (oh! what a painful reminder!), twisting down in a spiral.

Heather looked up at the cross, which had just lit at the onset of night.

Damned, lying bastards! she thought.

"I'm sorry," she said. "I guess I haven't been much fun lately."

"It's okay, really."

"No, it isn't-"

"Trust me, I understand."

It was, to say the least, bad timing that they'd met and begun to fall for each other, under these tragic circumstances. But, the drummer still beats, rat-a-tat-**tat**!, sometimes hitting the last note with extra forté.

Heather said, "Where are we going?"

"I thought you wanted to go home."

"Oh. No, I don't, really. Let's go out for hot chocolate. Anywhere, I don't care."

Downtown seemed as good a place as any.

They drove, mostly in silence, Heather still in a bit of a haze. Parked, got out and walked, the sidewalk a bit icy.

"When did it get so cold?" said Heather.

"It's winter. Be lucky it isn't minus twenty."

I could have sworn it was warm, thought Heather.

They walked along the sidewalk, heading for a restaurant that they'd noticed when they were looking for parking. Patrick had Heather's hand in his, but it didn't help because-

-Heather slipped and fell right on her ass, in spectacular fashion. The fact that she momentarily had her legs over her head and a decent hang time drew applause from passersby.

She looked up at Patrick, who'd already extended his hand to help her up, with a blank look on her face.

He was going to laugh, she could see it, the edges of his lips twisting in feeble resistance.

But it was Heather who started to giggle, she felt the void crack a little, like ice beneath a fallen ass. She took Patrick's hand and pulled herself up, wiping off her butt.

Her arms creeping around him, she said, "Get me out of here, my face must be red."

Patrick just laughed.

"You couldn't even catch me, Superman. It isn't enough to look great in the tights!"

They walked over to the restaurant, sat near the back where the hearth was.

When the waitress came to take their order, Heather said, "Two hot chocolates, extra whipped cream." She turned to Patrick. "It's on me."

He was happy to see her smiling, even if it would only last for the evening. Seemed breaking the ice may have broken the ice.

"Warm enough?" said Patrick.

"Yeah. It was so fucking cold out there."

"I thought you were warm before."

"Shit. Maybe I'm coming down with something. Anyways, I feel fine now. A night's sleep should help, too. Oooh, hot chocolate!"

The cups were so big they were practically bowls, whipped cream floating like icebergs, with cinnamon sprinkled over it. If there was a quick-and-easy route to heaven, the road must have been paved with chocolate.

They sipped at it, the smooth and silky liquid warming their insides like the fire warmed their cheeks.

Still, Heather felt the odd shiver scratch her spine.

"I'm so glad we came here," she said.

Go on, tell him you love him. I dare you.

"As long as you're having fun." (*Finally*, he thought.)

They chatted by the fire, enjoying the warmth of each other's company, ordered more of those delicious hot chocolates. It didn't seem long before the night had passed (time *is* funny), and they had to go.

"You look pale," said Heather, after Patrick had returned from the washroom.

"Too much hot chocolate, maybe. I hope I haven't caught anything."

On the drive home, Heather had to keep prodding him awake.

"What's with you? You can't even keep your head up," she said.

"Don't know. Feel really weak."

"Just stop at your house."

He did so, not thinking, just doing as he was told.

"You shouldn't walk..."

"I'll be fine," said Heather. "It's just ten minutes."

Heather took him up to his room, tucked him into bed. He looked like he was sweating, but felt cold, and he shivered.

Heather bent and kissed him on his forehead. Cold sweats. She kissed him on his lips and whispered, *I love you.*

She walked out, saying good-bye to his sister (who'd been kind enough to quietly let them in), and began to walk home in the chilly night.

Now that's more like it, she thought, as the wind bit to the bone. *This feels more like winter.*

She felt good, really good for the first time since-

Now, now, mustn't think like that, or of that, thinking is bad. Just let life lead you where it may, right?

(Why don't you follow me then?)

I'll think about it. Just leave me the hell alone for now.

It seemed like the powdery light of the moon caressed her shoulders:

Don't you love me, too, Heather?

Don't you want to be with me?

See what I see, know what I know?

Cast light upon shadows with an earthly glow?

Ooooh, that cold doesn't feel so good all of a sudden, does it?

Walk faster, have to get home.

(Don't you just love the night?)

Usually, yes.

But things lurk and creep at night. For some reason, God doesn't let us see the blacks and blues and purples, the three primary colours of darkness. Dogs can see and they howl. Cats can see them and they hiss.

(Hsssssssssssssssss, am I scaring you, Heather?)

Get out of my mind! Why won't you leave me alone?

Walk faster, what are you, stupid, a young girl walking alone at night? Move it, damnit! Your house is right there! Can't you see it? Run. RUN!

Twenty steps, if you run!

Through the door, slam it shut, up the stairs, under the blanket, nothing can harm you when you pull the covers over your head and curl up into a-

-little-

-orange-

-ball.

Steve Zinger

Look at the townhouses, all crushed together so cozy, the snow on the street ssslithering like a sssnake.

Bounce, bounce.

It came towards her in slow motion, from out of nothing, the dark gaping maw that was the end of the road.

Tick, tock.

It was the ringing of the phone that woke Heather, much more than the chill of the wintry morning.

Though the chill was a bit unnerving. She expected it to be warm, for some reason.

God, I don't feel like getting up, she thought. So young, everything to look forward to, and she wants to stay in bed. (A)pathetic.

Why did I even wake up?

Riiiing.

Oh, right. The phone. She picked it up, said, "Hullo?"

It was Patrick's sister, Patricia. I know, I know. Blame the parents.

"Heather? Where have you been?"

"Here. Why?"

"Patrick's in the hospital. *General de Montréal.* We've been trying to get a hold of you."

Awake all of a sudden. Heather got pen and paper and took down his room number, said, "I must have been sleeping. When did he get there?"

???

"What do you mean, three days ago?"

"The night you dropped him off. He woke up screaming, and..." she trailed off.

Heather's heart shook against her chest.

"Tell me," she said. "I want to know what happened."

Patricia took a breath. "He was screaming, there was blood all over the sheet, it was coming out of his mouth." She stopped for a moment, blew her nose. "They couldn't get near him. The paramedics, I mean. He was kicking and thrashing...Please. Just come to the hospital as soon as you can."

There was a pause, it sounded as though she wanted to ring off but wasn't sure quite how.

"Heather? Was he okay? Upset about anything?" Through the tears, speaking now.

Heather said, "He's been fine, very happy."

"They say it was poison, that he tried to kill himself. Oh, God, I can't imagine why! I'm sorry, I'm so sorry! I'll see you there." She hung up.

Tick, tock.

Three days. Any voices in your head, Heather?

Have I been asleep for three days? Think. She knew the mirror was across from her bed, but she didn't want to look, couldn't bear to look at herself.

Didn't feel like herself.

Have to get dressed, she thought. She felt a weight upon her, tried to shrug it off to think clearly. What happened in those three days? **Think clearly.**

Did I dream again? What happens to me when I dream?

Dreams have been trouble lately, haven't they?

Heather pulled off her nightclothes, began to look for something to wear. It felt like someone else was doing it for her.

Poison. My God, you know what it was, how could they say poison? What else could they say? That it was some disease, like anemia?

If that aseptic smell was soothing, one must have to be sick to appreciate it. It carried sterility upon the air, the feeling that the wards of people couldn't withstand any sort of impurity.

Or impropriety.

Everything must be white, pure. (And so much better to draw upon the walls with your finger in thick, luscious strokes of blood, to create a masterwork of madness, like Munch's 'The Scream.')

Heather felt the *thunk* of the elevator, she wiped her reddened cheeks so she would look more appropriate.

She checked with the nurse at the desk before she went into the room.

He looked chokingly, chalkingly white against the immaculate sheets, so hard to withhold the tears.

Heather put her fingers to his face, that face she knew was dead, her fingers being pulled closer and closer like a planet in a collapsing orbit. She didn't want to feel the fire of that face.

Why is it so hot this winter? Do you smell the pungent brimstone of Hell rising around you while Satan's trident pokes you like a-

"Daddy?" said Heather. The lifeless lids opened, there were holes where there should have been eyes that could look out over a-

There was blood on the sheets when they should have been clea-

He stank of booze when it should have been poi-

"Heather?"

"Heather?"

"Heather?"

"I...I...I..."

"It's okay, sweetie, it's okay." The hand that shook her shoulder gently now held on to it, like it was trying to keep her from falling.

"I guess I fell asleep." (Again.)

"You should go home. We'll call you if anything happens."

Who are you?

"Go. Take a cab." She gave Heather a purple ten. His mother. What was her name? Pamela? Petunia?

"Take a cab."

I'd rather walk.

(And you dare face me again?)

Go away. You're nothing. You're not my-

(Ah, ah, ah. Mustn't be so childish, now. You're a grown woman, you have responsibility.)

How, and when, did I get outside? thought Heather. *Oh, yes. Walking home. Can't be cooped up at night, must enjoy it.*

Why doesn't it feel so cold? It's winter, there's snow on the ground.

Heather bent and touched the snow. She felt acutely the cold, saw the crystal melt on the tip of her finger. It wasn't her finger she was looking at. It wasn't through her own eyes that she saw the world around her.

She picked up a pile of snow in both hands and pressed it to her face like an ice pack. She felt the melted flakes run rivulets down her cheeks, like her tears this...morn...

This morning?

Did I sleep the whole day? For the how manyith time?

No. It wasn't possible. Imp-possible.

The date. Have to find the date.

Her staccato steps were almost a run, like she was racing against the clock-

-tick, tock.

Through the dark streets-

-they always come out at night, don't they?-

-can you feel that hollow pit?can you feel the sweet sugar in it melting away?can you feel it getting bigger and all you want to look for is the time the date such a mortal thing to do can't move through this maze we call the mind unless someone draws you a friggin' map and labels 'x' time and 'y' space and tells you where to go and what to do and why you should do it and how it should be done and it's all really just bullshit because no one told you there was a 'z.'

(Lose any friends lately, Heather?)

What are you doing here?

(Check the clock, Heather. I dare you. I double dare you. That's the game, isn't it? You like it when they die, don't you?)

No.

(They shackle you, don't they? No matter how much you love them, they shackle you.)

No.

(Truth, now. We're on truth.)

....

(Well?)
I...No! Get-out-of-my-head!
More snow in the face.
Heather looked up at the billboard clock, the digitals flipping through various data:

9:57 p.m.
-22°C
Feb. 20/95

Three days. I've lost three days. I think.

Heather wanted to go home dearly. She started to feel the cold now. It was painful, stinging, like a honeybee. The pressure on her head was so great, but she tried to think through it, think about what happened to those lost few days.

It was obvious she didn't stay in bed, comatose. Her mother would have tried to wake her.

Violent spasms, the very earth beneath her feet shaking, and that heat, that terrible, terrible heat, Heather sinking to her knees like the Broken Man, whips upon his back, trying to shield herself from that fearsome fire.

He came towards her like some monster from a comic book, the flames engulfing him as he leapt from the car that exploded. He wore a leather biker jacket, and screams issued forth from his mouth, but Heather heard nothing. All she could see was the burning leather, and leather is *skin*, so all she could see was her own flesh burning in those flames. The man reached out to touch her, pleading for help, but Heather cringed at the mere thought of the fire, she jumped back like a frightened slave, backing away in a half run, but no matter how far she went, all she could see was the Night Stalker's pyre.

My house, she thought, *have to get to my house. Jump into the cold sheets of my own bed.* Monsters can't get you when you're under the covers in your own bed.

She made it as far as the front lawn before collapsing and burying herself in that cold soothing blanket called snow.

Please, God, tell me whose lips those are on my forehead.
(God doesn't exist. Don't you know that, Heather? I am God. My God.)
(MY GOD.)
Whose lips are those? They're so warm.

Water dripped down the side of Heather's face, running into her ears, down her little neck. When she moved, her pillow felt wet.

"Heather, sweetie?" said Susan. "Are you hungry?"

Heather tried to speak, but first had to moisten her throat. She was parched, positively.

"Whatever you want dear. Just eat."

"Mum?"

"Yes."

"What day is it, mum?" The words left her throat as though they were a spiked caterpillar sliding out of her.

"It's the twenty-first," answered Susan. "You've had a fever for nearly a week now. Been sleeping like a baby for days." Susan wiped Heather's forehead with the cold washcloth. "I spoke to Patrick's mother. She said you went to visit him. Which explains why I found you passed out on the front lawn when I came home last night."

"Thought I felt better."

"You will if you eat," said Susan. "What would you like?"

"Chocolate-chip cookies with chocolate milk."

"You and chocolate, my decadent daughter. You'll be fat before you're forty. Don't you think you ought to have juice?"

Heather said, "No. I want milk. Mom? Where's my picture?"

Susan glanced back over her shoulder without actually looking. "I put it in the drawer." Out she walked, quickly.

Heather looked at the empty doorway, the void of it.

She slid her legs over the edge of the bed, her feet touched the floor and simply felt like they hadn't in weeks. She got up and promptly fell on all fours.

"Okay, who took the damn muscles out of my legs?" she thought.

She picked herself up again, felt her heart pumping beneath her chest. Reached the dresser and pulled open her drawer, took out the picture, which was face down inside.

"Stay with me, daddy," she whispered, and she put the picture on the dresser in such a way so that only she could pick it out easily among the clutter. She lingered on it for a second, waiting for the teeth to rot and the smile to melt like seared cheese on a grill, the eyes to fall out and roll along the floor like marbles, but they never did. The picture remained whole.

Susan returned with a plate of five cookies and a glass of milk, as well as a glass of juice. She gave some aspirin to Heather and watched her swallow.

"I'm already late for work. You get some rest," said Susan. She brushed Heather's hair away from her face.

"Mom? Have I been asleep for the past few days?"

"Heavens, you've been burning up in here! Ranting and raving about this and that! I've got to go. We'll talk later."

The room was bright and empty, and Heather was left to nothing but her thoughts.

Patrick's dying, she thought. *I don't know why, but I can feel that he is. I'm going to lose him, too. But why does my heart feel so cold to it? I know if he goes, I'll feel it in my stomach, but why doesn't it seem as though I'll feel it in my heart?*

Heather turned on her side and curled up, pulled her blanket tight to her shoulder.

Talissa? Can you hear me? she thought, but these thoughts came from very deep within her mind.

Heather woke just after sunset, to the clatter of pans and dishes from downstairs.

"How are you feeling?"

She jerked her head to the window, saw Talissa sitting there, legs dangling off the windowsill.

Talissa said, "Gets dark quickly in winter, doesn't it? Quite all-of-a-sudden like, doesn't even bother to creep up on you. But I love it anyway."

"Where've you bin?" asked Heather.

"Oh, oot and aboot. Observing the rituals. I have another girlfriend!"

Heather said, "You're not my girlfriend," with one of her sidelong glances.

"What's the matter, Heather? Any good nightmares lately?" And she forced out an evil laugh.

"You're such a bitch, y'know? You're trash."

"Oh, c'mon," said Talissa, voice like nectar, and did you know she had her arm around Heather's shoulder now? "I'm just playing. I'm allowed to have fun, too, eh? Now admit it. You missed me, didn't you? Hm? Did wittle Heaver miss her Tawissa?"

"I don't even know why I invite you in."

"So," said Talissa, folding her hands upon her crossed legs, very lady-like. "I thought we might go to the Bio-Dome, they have some wonderful exhibits there, especially this tunnel of bats that I'm sure you'll love-"

"It's probably closed."

"Not a problem. I can sneak us in, we'll have the whole place to ourselves!"

Heather said, "I'm sick," and Talissa made a face and stood up in a bit of a huff, made a deep scratch on the back of her hand and put her lips to it as the blood seeped out, like it was a pacifier, licking the back of her hand like a cat licks it's paw.

"So we're just going to stay here all night?" She extended her hands upwards as she got down on one knee: "I need excitement, I need adventure, I need melodrama!" She folded her arms and put them on the edge of the bed, rested her chin on them. "Did you at least tape some afternoon soaps for me to watch? I always seem to miss them."

Footsteps on the stairs.

Talissa jumped up, said, "I almost forgot, I got something for you!" Went to the window and leapt the sill as if it were a horizontal bar, then dropped away.

"Heather, your dinner," said Susan as she walked into the room. "Stew, some fresh bread, mashed potatoes, and *juice*. You'd better eat every drop of it. You look disoriented, my dear, what is it?"

"Nothing. Just get out."

Susan raised her eyebrows, delivered a sidelong glance that was only half as good as Heather's, but a good indication as to where Heather had gotten her improved version from.

"Two-timing little bitch," she said under her breath.

"Pardon?!" Heather froze.

"Gotcha!" Talissa stood arms folded against the wall, glistening white teeth visible in a broad smile. "You thought I was your mother. You look as fresh as a corpse!"

"Must you...be so-childish?"

"Oh, Little Miss Maturity. Lighten up, *mun petit* cherry."

"Hey, none of that frog shit in here!"

"My, someone's crusty when they have a sniffle. What's that?"

"My dinner," said Heather.

"Uch, how can you eat that crap?"

"Listen, just turn on the TV or something, okay?"

"How?"

Heather handed her the converter, which Talissa pointed at the TV. Heather grabbed the controller away, clicked on the set. "You flip through the channels with this button."

"Oh," said Talissa, with a slight giggle.

Footsteps on the stairs.

Before Heather could say, "Is that my mom?" there was a quick rap on the door and it swung open.

"Were you talking to someone, Heather?" Empty room, only the TV chatter as background making it seem like movie silence. "Jesus F. Christ, child, you shouldn't keep the window open in winter, especially with your fever." Susan moved to close the window.

Heather said, "I guess I had the TV on too loud," and she turned it down.

"Well, get some sleep. All done?" She wasn't. Susan took the tray, turned off the light as she slipped out of the room. She said, "Sweet dreams," with all the affection of a prison warden.

Heather woke to sweat and tears, felt her face flush hot pink as she heard the howling of a snowstorm outside.

It took very little effort to open the window up, to feel the wonderful cyclones of snow whip into the room like Furies. But she couldn't bring herself to do it. All she could do was cling to the pillow and cry as the memories of the lost few days came rushing back, as she felt her mind become her own again.

The wetness covered her face as she thought, "God, why do I have to feel this way? I can't handle it!"

Drip, drip, on her wet cheeks, tiny pinpricks she almost didn't notice because of her tears, but these were hotter and thicker, and when they ran down past her nose, she smelled them, salty and metallic.

Heather turned her neck towards the ceiling, tried to focus in the darkness. So hard to *see*, when you can't see.

Drip. *Ow, in my eye,* drip, drip.

Where is that coming from? Heather looked down at her sheets, she could see the blood staining the yellow flannel like permanent marker. She put her finger to one of the spots, felt the tip of it moisten when she touched it. She looked at her finger, smelled the liquid, the throbbing, pulsating liquid that seemed so alive, and on the very tip of her finger! Another drop exploded on the tip of her finger, a bit splashed on her cheek. She sniffed it again. She was still crying.

Oh, Patrick.

She turned back up to the ceiling, started to reach her hand upwards, upwards. No way you can see now, through all those tears. Unless you know what to look for.

Heather pulled back her hand, wiped her watery eyes. She began to reach upwards again, through that blackness.

It wasn't darkness. You could still see in darkness. Darkness was *natural*.

When Heather's hand penetrated the layer of oil that hung from her ceiling, she felt its warm and slick touch, like a lizard's tongue.

This was by no means oneiric, of that she was now certain, and nothing scared her more.

It engulfed her now, this blackness, and Heather no longer felt firmness beneath her. With no focal point, she could not find any equilibrium. She couldn't tell whether she was helter or skelter.

It was as fearsome as it seemed to someone so ordinary looking up from her bed in a dark room. When you were in it, it was coaxing and friendly, like a man in a fine black suit. But you could tell that when he turned around, he twisted the edges of his long moustache and laughed sinisterly to himself.

Once you were in, there was no way out.

The ceiling, thought Heather. *Keep going the same way, up, and hit the ceiling.* Unless someone decided to turn this thing around. If this was death, it would lose its charm very quickly.

Is this Patrick's death, or...?

Heather thudded into the ceiling all-of-a-sudden, it felt as though the blackness had pushed her like a bullying big brother. Thinking too hard. Those night creatures don't like when you begin to get the gist of it.

On the edge of the oil and realism, Heather made a last grasp into the blackness. She could see it was only the size of a few people, tried not to look down at the bed hovering beneath her. She reached in, not really knowing what she was looking for, hopefully her boyfriend, though she felt a lump in her breast at the thought of how hopeless she knew that was. She smacked something, the blackness began to dissipate into a coal-like mist, and Heather fell roughly on the edge of her bed, nearly collapsed to the floor.

She peered up, eyes still trying to focus, saw Talissa hovering there, curled in a fetal position, just waking.

"Talissa!" whispered Heather. It was after two in the morning. Talissa uncurled and stretched, the coal mists enshrouding her, so dark it was like she disappeared again.

Heather felt a hand on her shoulder, she turned, startled.

"I didn't wake you, did I?" said Talissa.

"Don't sneak up on me like that!"

"How did I sneak up on you? You were looking at me the whole time."

Heather waited a moment for her heart to slow its beating. She didn't realize it, but she'd never stopped crying. She only didn't *feel* the emotion, she couldn't empathize with herself.

Talissa said, "You know, don't you? You remember."

Heather nodded, only barely. Talissa held her close, whispered apologies in her ear, and Heather felt a bit of the emotion that she knew she was expressing, but it was like it was seen in a movie, or that it was all from someone else's distant past.

"I'm sorry," said Talissa. "These things don't always work out right. The world is probably the most cruel creature of them all."

And some of us just play by its rules.

"Did you want your present now?"

Heather kept trying to dry her tears, she took a deep breath and felt some sudden but disturbing relief. Quick fix, her mind seemed washed of the bitter memories, but that itch tickled at her subconscious, trying to get back in.

Talissa went to the windowsill. The snowstorm had subsided, quite along the lines with Heather's mood. She opened the window a bit, breathed deeply of the stingingly cold but soothing air, and turned her back to the window, one hand behind her, hiding the gift.

She moved towards Heather with a smile and proffered what looked like a mere rose, but when the faint nite-light hit it, Heather saw it was more.

"Oh, *wow*," said Heather, her hands up near her lips. It was, indeed, a rose, but it was some sort of crystal, and it was blue, such a deep and resonating blue, that

Heather wasn't sure if she'd ever seen that shade before, nor ever would again. Calling it merely blue was almost derogatory. "It's absolutely gorgeous!"

"You can take it, you know."

"Ooo, I'm afraid to, I know I'll break it," said Heather, but she was so enticed that she gently took the rose.

"Breathe on it," said Talissa. Heather made an 'O' with her lips and let a gentle breeze touch the delicate petals. The blue shimmered, it made Heather's breath visible on the surface of the petals in the most violently striking shades of indigo and crimson. It was as though the shimmering colours were speaking to her.

Talissa kissed Heather on the forehead and whispered, "Happy Saint Valentine's Day."

Part 2: The Haunting

It has been said that endless hours of darkness have been known to cause madness in the most capable of men. Something so trivial as sunlight is what keeps people from losing their balance. It had been almost eight years since I had any prolonged exposure to sunlight. Not that I didn't have the opportunity. But working the night shift left me drained and tired by the time the sun rose. At first I tried to block it out. I'd pull the covers over my head and keep them there no matter how hot it got. Later, years later, I would just let the warm waves wash over my body. I guess I had a love/hate relationship with the sun for years. It may sound a bit funny. But I was seeing a psychiatrist about it for six months.

I would wake up just in time to see the sun set. I would lay my head on the pillow just as it rose. There was something special about a sunrise. Maybe because no one saw them too often. That's why I would make sure the last thing I saw before I slept was the sunrise. And it reminded me that I was still a part of the world. That's very important, to remember...to remember you're part of the world.

I felt enough like an outsider living at night. I saw my wife in the evenings before I went to work. There were still people on the street, though their numbers would soon die. There were my co-workers at the M.U.C.P.S., but I didn't talk to too many of them anymore. At least not seriously, like friends. Most of them wouldn't take me seriously anymore.

And so I always felt one step outside of the real world. Like everything was happening and I was only allowed to watch. And it would always happen, and then I'd go home. My wife would give me some tea, a little brandy if I wasn't on call the next night. She tried. She really tried. And I hoped that she could still look at me and respect me, if not believe me. She always did comfort me and I assumed that that meant she truly did love me. True love is seen as often as a sunrise, and appreciated even less. If it wasn't for love, I honestly believe this world would stop. And it took me quite a while to figure that one out.

That might sound lofty coming from me. After all, my life is a mundane mountain of paper work, shuffling files from cabinet to cabinet. Once, maybe twice a week I would walk the beat up and down *rue Ste-Catherine*. It was like therapy. Not that there was that much excitement, but it was a nice change. Gave me time to think, which I do a lot of. I think my boss took pity on me. Other than that, my nights were quite routinized, done very much by rote. I would come in, sign the log, change into uniform. I used to leave my gun on the corner of my desk, but that led to too many jokes. Now I left it in the drawer.

We had a decent bunch of guys working here, despite of what they thought of me. One of my duties was cataloguing the evidence that came in. For my own benefit, to relieve some boredom when things got slow, I would double check. Sometimes things went missing. You didn't have to be a detective to figure out who it usually was. But us cops stuck together. As long as the system kept moving, the other cheek would be turned. I can't say I agreed with it. But I was the outsider among an organization of outsiders. You learned about us against them when you were a rookie. It may seem stereotypical, but that's just the way things are. People stop talking when you're in the room.

C'est la vie, as we say here. I'd made my choices and I'd lived with them.

Wednesday would seem like an uneventful evening for most people. And usually it is. But this is Montréal. There's always something to do here. People could still be seen out on the streets in the middle of the week, walking, talking, gathering in small bars set beneath sidewalk level, or others a few steps above. And as I made my way down the famous *rue Ste-Catherine*, I was grateful for the urban creatures roaming the wilds. Gave me something to look at. Not that I would stare at anyone in particular. But the movement made the already vivid scenery come alive. Like some thing that had to be fed with the very soul of its inhabitants. *rue Ste-Catherine* would be Montréal's main artery, assuming a city could die.

I stopped for a moment and put my hands in my pockets. I tried to imagine how it would look totally empty. No cars, no people, not even a beggar. It was difficult to do, but eventually I pictured it. All the people had disappeared. There was no noise save for the hum of the electric lights, the whistling of the wind through the alleys and the rustling of newspaper that blew across the street. It was unreal. The closest analogy I can make is to that of a zombie. This thing could be alive. The electricity flowed like blood, the wind was its breath. It was as though there was an essence to the city that would awaken when it was filled with people. Until then, it would hibernate beneath the streets like a black bear. The people and cars returned.

And I kept walking. I always felt as though I were just killing time. Waiting for life to be done with me.

I stopped for a minute to clear my mind, to look at the stars winking from heaven. If only I was a star, then I would be able to see everything from a much easier point of view. The cars sped by on the avenue with a whoosh, and groups of people idled by enjoying the evening. The scenery around me faded into the background of my senses and the blue-black sky dominated me, overwhelming, hovering high above.

I thought it was strange that we look for answers up there, in a void where nothing lives, while the battle for life is being waged all around us. It shows us how empty our minds really are.

Looking at the sky made me a little dizzy and light-headed so I began to walk again, this time more slowly so I could enjoy the night. The people around me were distracting, but I didn't mind. Actually, I liked it.

I'd made my way to *rue Crescent*, and I walked up the crowded street a little ways. There were a few police vans hanging as crowd control, clearing out the kids who were off of school. They always flocked here, from everywhere. Dressing up like they were all grown-up, renting limousines, drinking and laughing. I waved and gave a half smile to some of the boys on duty. A couple nodded. One waved and smiled politely. A few pretended they were busy. I turned back to *rue Ste-Catherine*.

As I neared the corner, the noise of the crowd rose behind me. I stopped and turned. A fight had broken out between two young men who'd drank a little too much. It was broken up as soon as it was started, the belligerents detained in the back of the vans. The crowd dispersed as though nothing happened. Cool and efficient, what with riots being a tradition in Montréal. I backed off slowly, knowing I wasn't needed, but wanting to keep an eye on the situation to make sure it was under control. Shit, mobs of people, it could be a very scary thing.

As I turned back around to *Ste-Catherine*, I collided head-on with a girl, knocking her to the ground. She looked up at me, bewildered, the heels of her palms holding her up, her arms shaking. She did not look well, to say the least. I apologized and helped her up. She seemed to quiver as though she were cold. She muttered a feeble thank you and brushed herself off.

I hate to say it, but I couldn't take my eyes off of her. She was half my age and it was lucky that she walked away quickly, before someone thought something improper in the way I stared at her. She was...very pretty for her age, despite her ill pallor. But it wasn't her beauty that transfixed my stare. There was a certain look about her face, a certain deep darkness to those blue eyes of hers. I want to tell you that I couldn't place where I'd seen those features before. But it would be more accurate to say that I had pushed my memories of those trying events into the back of my mind. Not so deep as the subconscious. Neatly in a corner in the back, where I could feel them pushing and squirming to get out, to match the memory with the reality that was walking away from me.

I put my hand to my top lip and it shook as I thought. In that moment, I committed a sin. I lied to myself. I denied myself the very facts that were held in my mind. I denied myself the reality of what I just saw. And I denied myself tears. Tears of relief. Of a great burden being lifted from the back of my skull. I literally, physically felt an increase of pressure in the back of my head. Like I said, our minds are empty. But it felt like mine was filling up fast.

Despite the fact that I had lied to myself about it all, I shoved my hands in my pockets and started after the girl. After all, I was just walking my beat, right? I'd lost sight of her in my fugue, but I didn't rush my pace. I walked as though I were merely continuing my patrol. I don't even know what made me think I would ever find her, that she had taken a straight path.

I'd begun to lose hope of finding her at *rue St. Marc*. If I hadn't stopped to glance around I might have missed her. She'd turned onto *St. Marc* and had collapsed next to a bush. It looked as though she'd tried to hide herself. Perhaps she'd pulled herself off the main street. But her blond hair was like a candle in the night, albeit a dim one. The filth of the sidewalk seemed to cling to parts of her hair.

I looked around the street. It was pretty empty. Only a bum lying on a piece of cardboard across the street, shouting to himself. The roar as a Night Stalker's sped by on his motorcycle, eyeing me from behind smoked glasses.

I walked over to the blond girl, intent on helping her up. I figured she'd collapsed from too much drink or something.

"Madame," I said as I was standing over her. I didn't look at her face yet. Perhaps I was scared...no, apprehensive is more appropriate. I was apprehensive about looking at her face. All I saw was a mass of scraggly blond hair and a hunched shoulder. She was making slurping noises. I leaned over her further. "Madame," I said again.

My heart jumped in my chest. It horrified me to see that her face was lying next to a pool of blood, her tongue making circles and slowly lapping it up. The blood looked stagnant, tinged with blue under the orange streetlight.

I moved, a little tentatively, to shake her shoulder. Her head snapped around, her arm snatched mine, and she fixed me with a stare that, for one brief second, was hungry and feral. The strength of her grip astonished me. And that second passed, and her grip became weak and her arm quivered. Her gaze became that of a confused girl. I didn't wait for her to figure out the situation. I didn't need to hear her excuses. I didn't want to hear explanations.

"Come on, kid, let's get you up." I felt as though talking would alleviate the awkwardness of the situation. It didn't, but I kept speaking anyway. "That's it, sit up." I didn't bother asking if she was okay. That much was obvious. I tried to maintain the confidence that I'd been given in training. But I'd forgotten proper procedure. I was required to put on latex gloves when dealing with any kind of spill of bodily fluids.

I pulled out some tissue from my pocket and said, "Let's get you cleaned up." I proceeded to wipe her left cheek of the blood she'd lain in. She was like a toddler who'd spilled her apple juice and didn't know anything was wrong. The heel of her palm held her up and her arm quivered like before, like when I'd knocked her over.

I got some fresh tissue and this time she took them and cleaned herself off. She coughed into the tissue.

"God, this is embarrassing," she said, forcing a laugh, trying to make a joke of it.

"I've seen much worse. Don't worry, you're okay." I kept my manner professional. She seemed to be regaining her lucidity. She hadn't really looked at me yet. "What's your name?"

Now she looked at me, but still not right at me eyes. I gave a little smile and said, "I'm not going to arrest you."

She looked down at the sidewalk and said, "Heather. Heather Langden."

"I'm Constable St. Croix. Do you live near here?" I asked. She nodded, wiping the last bits of the drippy mess from the corner of her lips. "I'm at the end of my shift, Heather. If you want, I could make sure you get home okay." Just doing my duty. Heather pushed herself up off the ground.

She took a gulp of air and said, "I think that would be a good idea."

Luckily, she didn't live too far, just a few blocks down *Ste-Catherine*.

"Too much to drink tonight, eh?"

"Yes, that's it." She walked the entire time with her arms folded, never looking my way. Always looking at the street, like she was watching for something.

"You sure you're alright?" She snapped out of her reverie. We'd reached her house.

"Yeah, I'll be okay. Thanks. Thanks a lot."

I pulled out my pad and started to scribble.

"I think you should get yourself to a doctor. What happened back there wasn't pretty." I tore off the page and handed it to her. "Here's my extension at the station. It's always a good idea to have a cop as a friend." She gave a little smile as she took the paper and put it in her pocket. She thanked me again and walked up to her door. She sounded weak. I walked away, and committed her address to memory instead of noting it down. After all, a policeman's notebook is public property.

Still slightly sweaty from my hot shower after work, I walked up to my townhouse just as the sun was breaking the dawn. I slid the key slowly into the lock, letting out a slow sigh of exasperation. I noticed someone had left a little orange ball on my porch step. I rolled it under the ball of my foot a few times, then flicked it up onto my toe and gave it a good kick into the street.

I wasn't supposed to hit the beat again the next night, but someone had called in sick and my paper work was small. My boss would cover any incoming paper work, and I would get another night on the street. And actually, I didn't mind it at all. I had resigned myself to several more nights of deskwork, but I really did want to get back to the street. I had a feeling I would run into Heather again. I hoped I would for some reason.

I walked up and down *rue Ste-Catherine*, watching the street slowly empty. The night was cool and the cold kept my senses acute. I stopped into a café for a cup of hot coffee to warm my insides. It was bullshit, I'd never gotten a free cup of coffee in my life. I only spent a couple of minutes in the café before taking my coffee outside. I walked slowly as I drank.

Obviously, not much happened on these beats. It was merely a patrol to make the police available to the public. If I were to patrol the park on Mount Royal, I would be expected to greet everyone.

And of course, I didn't run into Heather that night. I decided to walk home, but I didn't go directly home. I went to the station, showered, changed into my civvies and decided to wander a bit. Strange, that I would want to wander after walking a beat, but off-duty was a different world. My home life was a different world. I didn't want to go home to my wife. I didn't want to jump between the realities. I was sick of it. Reality was a slap in the face. I thought I could perhaps escape it…at least until the sun came up and reminded me of the clock.

It was easy to forget yourself in Montréal. Whether through its vitality, the warm inhabited feeling of the streets or its dark, Gothic beauty, you could really enjoy losing yourself here. It was late and the vitality had shimmered. The streets hugged me gently because I was the only soul to grace the sidewalks. Stone churches loomed over me between the flashing neon signs that constantly espoused carnal pleasures to those who graced the remarkable *rue Ste-Catherine*.

And that's exactly what I did. I let myself get lost on the darkened streets of Montréal. I let those gentle hands that hugged me quietly prod me along some predetermined path that I had no way of knowing except to merely follow where it would lead. And she led me away from *Ste-Catherine*, onto darker streets, between the homes and buildings that were usually so lovingly crushed together. Onto streets that lacked the energy of downtown, onto streets that were dead in the night.

A shiver ran down my spine, causing me to stop and stiffen. I glanced back over my shoulder, a little fearfully. I had lost my direction. The street behind me was empty. I continued walking, more briskly, but still stiff from the feeling I got. Every minute I would look back over my shoulder only to see the dead street behind me. Going home seemed like a better idea now, rather than roaming the streets. I just had a feeling that gave me shivers. Like someone was watching over me.

I stopped for a sec, turned, looked back again, and sighed relief that I was just being childish and stupid. No one was there.

Suddenly, a hand reached out from a pile of garbage and grabbed my ankle. The hand looked weak and bony like it had been dead for a month but I felt strength in its grip. I shook my leg but the hold was too strong. I thrashed but I couldn't get free and I bent to use my own hands to pry off the dead one.

To the touch it was ice and slime. If I had to touch this thing much longer then I would throw up. I brought my fist crashing down on the dead/live hand and it let go. I got up quickly and without trying to think about what happened I turned around and began to run.

It lasted a step and a half. I had smashed into something that felt like it was made of brick and it made me fall back to the ground again, within arms reach of the corpse.

Slowly, I looked up at what I'd run into. It turned out that I had no need of looking behind me at all, because I wasn't running away from anything, I was actually running towards it. What I saw gave me another one of those spine shivers. It was a man on the surface, but something emanated from him that said he was much more than a man. He was immensely tall, about six foot seven, and built like the brick that he felt like. His shoulders were broad if one was given to understatement, for he looked, in a word, powerful. His figure cut a trenchant outline against the backdrop of night, and he seemed to control the shadows that swirled around him, especially those about his face. And his face, what you could see of it, was expressionless except for the faint malevolent grin that just touched his lips. Shadows danced upon his eyes to shroud them. He had long, dark brown hair, almost black, which was just past his shoulders, and it framed his face enough to make him look unpropitious. On the left side of his hair was a thin braid ending with a small group of beads that looked like they were ritualistic.

And his skin! It looked alternately leathery and pale. It was kind of a glowing darkness. The man before me was unmistakably an alabaster Indian. He looked like a physical impossibility. How did this man get around without being noticed in an instant?

It was as though I were looking at a close up shot in a movie. All I saw was his face in a frame of midnight bold against the black sky. I sat there on the ground looking up and all I could do was shake my head slowly from side to side, like I wasn't sure if I could even do that. Like someone in a movie, badly overacting.

"N-no...no..." I stuttered. I think I tried to push myself backwards, away from my fears manifest themselves. I say I think because the more I pushed myself away, the closer to him I seemed to get. His form loomed over me and his figure bled into the very darkness of night. My vision was overwhelmed with his image, his skin bright in my eyes until the light overwhelmed me, becoming a flash that exploded slowly, so slow that I could see the streaks of light traveling towards my eyes.

My God, I think he actually touched me.

It took a strong heave to lift my head off the pillow. It felt like I'd slept for a week, and I was surprised to see the sun shining bright when I woke.

"Breakfast, sleepy head?" It was my wife. She always sounded sweet. Sometimes I don't think I deserved that.

"No thanks. Mebbe later." My throat felt heavy and sore, maybe a bit of nausea. I sat on the edge of the bed, my hand rubbing my stubbly chin, staring off in thought. Julia stopped what she was doing and looked at me, smiled. I didn't look right at her, but I could see that smile. It was only on the outside. It was only for me, not for herself. She abruptly left the room.

As for myself, I was trying to figure out the blank slate of memory that sat in my mind. The night before seemed empty. I remember walking and walking...The night before that I remember...

My mind just wouldn't work. I couldn't make it do what I wanted it too. I hated that. I got up and went to the bathroom to splash water on my face, to wake myself. I decided I was hungry and went downstairs to eat. The plaster of the wall at the staircase had been cracked.

"Your breakfast is ready, sit." She put a glass of juice in front of me and I downed it in one shot, poured another and drank that quickly too. I poured a third and saved it for later.

A moment later a feast was laid in front of me. Eggs, scrambled, with cheese dripping through the bits of salami, the spices tempting and aromatic. Potatoes fried with onion, spiced with pepper and a hint of garlic. Some small pancakes and baby sausages soaking in a pool of Québec maple syrup. I looked at the steaming plate and felt as though food should repulse me now, but I was too hungry and it was too good. I took a forkful of egg and could feel it filling me as I swallowed. Julia sat across from me and folded her arms across the table.

"Do you want to talk?" she said.

"You're not having any?"

"I asked you something."

I cut a piece of pancake and let the syrup drip off before putting it into my mouth. I couldn't help closing my eyes for a second at the fluffiness of the taste. "This is absolutely delicious. You don't want?"

"I ate while I cooked." She sat there, arms folded, just watching me eat. She was waiting for an answer to her question. I somehow knew it had something to do with last night, but I didn't want to find out what she wanted to know. Her smile had faded a bit. I started to eat slower.

"You must've been pretty drunk last night." My fork stopped halfway to my mouth and I looked up at her from under my eyebrows.

"I don't drink," I said. I hadn't had more than one drink at a time in over two years.

"There's a hole in the wall that says you did." So that's how it got there. "What happened?"

"When?"

"Last night. I thought you were working."

"I was."

"You came home in rough shape. Do you remember?"

The truth is that I didn't remember. So I told the truth. "No. I don't remember." I think I said it loud enough for her to hear.

She looked at me as I picked away at my food. I didn't have to look up to know what expression was on her face. It had hours of conversation on it. And the worst part is that none of it needed to be said. We'd argued over it more times than I care to remember. And it was all summed up in that one sad, sagacious look. Her face itself was soft, but her eyes were deep.

She must've been sick of watching me pick at my food because she lifted the edge of my plate and gave me a moment to protest her taking it away. I just let my fork down gently, and she threw out the remains of my breakfast. This wasn't the kind of silence I wanted to endure.

"We should go somewhere. We haven't gone anywhere in a while." I didn't answer for a minute. The last place I wanted to be was trapped with her somewhere and forced to talk.

"Where did you want to go?" I asked.

"I don't know, but let's *do* something." That seemed reasonable to me. It would give me the luxury of taking my mind off what I was trying not to think about.

We went to the Bio-Dome. I couldn't enjoy the beauty of the place. I saw it all around me, but it was as though I was in a haze. I was outside of what was happening to me. It was as though an outside force was controlling me. We went into a re-creation of a tropical paradise. And it was like I read the humidity off a meter rather than felt the wet thickness of the air. I looked relaxed on the outside. But on the inside I wasn't enjoying being here. Killing time. I wasn't enjoying being with my wife.

She suggested coffee as we took the bus to the metro. I agreed, though I would really have preferred we go home so we could go our separate ways. I indulged her, though, because I'd be up all night. I sat. I had a cup of coffee, though I hated coffee. I made conversation, though I hated conversation. My mouth smiled at her. I tried to look at her, but I couldn't maintain eye contact. I looked at my coffee, watching the steam coming out. I glanced to the outside window...

I couldn't believe it. I saw him across the street, in a recess of shadow. But I could see his eyes looking at me. It was hard for me not to look. I kept glancing over. I thought Julia wouldn't notice. I kept my professional calm. But she was, after all, my wife. And she knew me for nearly a decade.

"Why do you keep looking outside?" she asked.

"Just looking outside," I said. She looked at me severely. She tried not to look severe but she did. Of course, I'd ruined her day.

She let her fork clang loudly on the plate, so people would look. She got up quick and left. I dropped more than enough money on the table before going after her. I had to go after her. I really didn't want to. I wanted to let her go. Let the last vestiges of my marriage slip away, with the rest of my life. But I had to go after her because she was my wife and I was still alive and still going through the motions.

I didn't have time to look at the figure in the shadow. But I knew that there was someone watching over me. I guess I'd always known...

Julia, when I finally caught up to her that is, was walking stiff backed and swiftly, her sunglasses covering her eyes. I had to dodge people to catch up to her and for a minute I thought I would lose her, that she knew I was gaining and she was trying not to make it obvious that she was running away from me. I got near her and grabbed her arm, turning her around. Tears were dripping from under her shades. God, I didn't want to do this now.

Before I could say anything trite, she said, "Is there any point?"

I stopped and looked her straight in the eye. For the first time in a long time, I looked her straight in the eye and she had sunglasses on. I took them off, carefully, so I could really look her in the eye. My God, she had beautiful eyes. She was beautiful when she cried. It was a shame how beautiful she was when she cried. And I never wanted to make her cry.

"Is there any point to what?" It was a stupid question. We'd been married long enough that we could finish the other's sentences, that meanings were taken as much from tone and expression and the words were implicit. But I was only human after all, I needed the clumsiness of communication. I needed her to actually say it to validate the facts.

"Us. You and me. I don't know you anymore. I can see you're inside there but you won't come out." She turned her head away and wiped her tears with two fingers. Years ago, I would have turned her head back to make her look at me. Years ago.

I left her in bed. I pulled the covers up over her shoulders and watched her tears drip onto the pillow. She would cry herself to sleep. I went downstairs quietly.

In the dining room, I knelt down in front of the cabinet. I opened the low doors and pulled out the Southern Comfort. There was dust on the bottle. I held it in my hands, feeling the weight of it. Rolling it around and watching the liquid splash against the sides of the bottle. I could smell it through the glass. I thought the coppery colour was stunning. It glowed in what little light there was.

"Always willing to share a drink with a friend." I jumped at the voice. I dropped the bottle on the floor and was I lucky it didn't break. I picked it up by the neck and ran at him, aiming for his head, my other arm ready to force him to the wall.

He caught my arms like they weren't moving. His hands were ice around my wrists and it was as though my arms had been caught in the mold of a statue. He was immobile and immovable. His eyes glowed red and flowed like mist into the darkened room. He didn't smile and I couldn't even imagine him doing so. Even though he threw me against the wall so hard that I blacked out, his image was burnt into my eyes as darkness overcame me.

The bubbles of colour would whoosh and fizz and pop as though they thought they were fireworks, except that they seemed to have a mind of their own. They would zoom fast as though they were going to hit the end and explode.

They would travel up, up, up, and hold high above, quivering in the imagined space of the mind. Then, deciding that the drama had built to a suitable tension, they would detonate and their fragments would travel in all directions imaginable, each morsel a different colour and texture from its mother.

Juicy bits of orange splashed on the floor, and granular gold collided with syrupy brown.

In the centre of it all though, was one wee, insignificant little black dot. It was a speck, really, a piece of dust that had managed to escape the broom unnoticed, and it had fixated itself in the exact centre of imagined existence. Shoo it away and it remained. It was immovable, so strong despite the fact that it was almost unseen.

It became bolder and grew, looming larger and larger.

The colours stopped jumping and playing and whooshing. All the movement slowed to a dull vibration that was accompanied by a faint hum, perhaps of prayer. All colours settled beneath the level of the dot so as not to offend it by looking down upon it.

It didn't burst like the other bubbles, it seeped like choking smoke, mixing with the other colours and assimilating them.

I thought I saw his red eyes coming at me, but it wasn't his eyes; it was dripping, off his chin, everything drawn in black except for the dripping chin...

"Graham...?" I was being shaken awake. "Come on, wake up." Julia put the bottle upright and pulled my face out of the pool of alcohol. She slung my arm around her shoulder and hauled me up to bed. I noticed it was morning. I could taste the Southern Comfort on my lips. I hated the taste of alcohol during the day.

Julia was about to lay me out for the day when I got the feeling. I covered my mouth, but I didn't have enough sense to go to the bathroom. Julia had to push me in there. I had my eyes closed most of the time, so I only felt what was happening. The muscles in my throat tightening and denying me air, my stomach being kicked with every thrust. The soothing spray of liquid pouring out of my mouth. I had my eyes closed most of the time so I hardly noticed when I'd finally gone to sleep.

I went back on the beat two nights later. After sifting through mounds of paper work, I was glad to be on the street instead of staring at black and white pages that blurred after hours of sifting through them, boring like reading always was. I walked up *rue Ste-Catherine* and down *boul. De Maisonneuve*, traveling that circuitous route for hours. It was past three a.m. when I noticed that the streets were nearly empty of people. I kept walking my beat.

I approached the intersection at *rue Université*. I'd done this beat for years, I wasn't stupid. I wasn't fooled by the gargoyle perched on the railing of the steps to the church. I walked closer, maintaining my pace, along with my professional calm. He sat on his perch, arms resting on his knees, hands in a downwards-pointing steeple, eyes riveted forward like he was actually stone. Like he didn't know I was walking towards him. I was about twenty feet from him when he swiveled his head to look at me.

"You've had a...*hell* of a decade," he said. I almost laughed! God knows why but I almost did! Of course I kept that inside me. He looked human enough now. Not the monster I'd previously imagined. His skin was an amalgamation of light grey, a pale moonlit blue and chalky, powdery white. He wore a black button down shirt, black trousers and a long black trench coat, his gargoyle 'wings.'

There were so many things I wanted to tell him. Like why had he put me through that kind of hell? Why had he shown himself again after so many years? Why was he following me?

But he jumped off his perch on the rail. If my professional calm was a bodily function, it was now a fart in the wind. I jumped back. I guess I'd had my hand on my gun, because I'd drawn it incredibly quickly. I fired three shots and the explosion of the gun was a bright flash in my eyes...

I was a few blocks away, *rue Mansfield*, I think. I hunched over, hands on knees, to catch my breath. I heard the car speeding towards me, stood up and wiped the sweat off my brow. I made as though I had been walking and they skidded to a stop when they saw me.

"*Bonjour*. We had a report of shots fired."

"From back there?"

"*Oui*."

"I just came from there. The street was empty, and I've heard nothing." The man's partner was writing everything down. By the way he was looking at me, it seemed like he was giving a description of my condition. My sweaty brow, my heavy breathing. Then again, I may have been a little self-centred and paranoid because of what happened. "I'll stick around here in case I see anyone."

"*Merci*." They sped off. I stuck around the street for a bit, checked in with headquarters to tell them my position. I was an idiot for thinking that...thing would show his face again. Half an hour had passed. I radioed central that everything was clear, that I'd be moving on. My shift would be over soon anyway. And that meant the sun would be up, and I could go home and sleep.

The ringing of the telephone woke me. I wet my throat before picking it up. I answered like I was at work.

"Sen Cwa."

"Hey, you up for dinner? Or breakfast, rather." I rubbed my face. Shit, I really needed a shave.

"I've got to go to work."

"You've got *hours*." I thought for a minute.

"Yeah, sure, what the hell. Usual?"

"Of course."

I dressed and avoided Julia as I left. I met Jerome at the *Cote St. Luc* Barbeque- the usual-on *rue Ste-Catherine*, near the old Forum. He was already there with a table when I arrived. He got up and he took my hand, put a hand on my shoulder for a moment. His hug. We sat and ordered right away.

"I'm gonna grab a beer. *You* want one?" He leaned into his you. Thank God he always grinned, otherwise I'd have thought this was an intervention.

"You're as subtle as a rectal exam, y'know?"

"Ya got people who care about you, bud. You can't run away from that."

We were interrupted by the arrival of our food.

Jerome said, "Julia called me. She's really worried about you. She thought you were getting better, but now she said you're seeing things again."

I stared straight by him and said, "I'm not seeing things." The words came out flat. We finished the rest of our meal discussing other topics, but the first had lowered the mood of the table. In truth, it lowered my mood, and I think Jerome picked up on that. It was rare that there was tension between us, even a little.

We stood outside for a moment to say our good-byes. He put his hand on my shoulder.

"Listen, you fuckin' talk, you got that? Don't go closin' off. Don't sink like before." He held up his forefinger, pointing at me like a parent. Then he smiled and we went in opposite directions.

I felt a lot better afterwards. Maybe because Jerome was more blatant about the issue than most. Still, I could tell he was trying to spare me the pain of the past.

At work I sifted through all the forms, requisitions, etc., and filed them away quickly as I could. My mind seemed clearer than usual. My vision didn't blur from the hours of staring at paper work. I was lucid for the first time in years.

I knew he was watching me the whole time. So I walked. I went looking for a vampire! I walked for about twenty minutes, then I thought, *This is stupid*. How would I just walk and find him? I thought about going back to the place where I saw him the other night. But why would he be there? Then I figured, *You don't look for a vampire, they look for you*.

"You're getting the hang of this, Mr. St. Croix." Fuck did I ever jump when I heard that. I spun and I was up against the wall, my body bent, taut, wary.

"Jesus Christ," I said. Or whispered, or mouthed. Who could really remember, with their mind racing and heart drumming the way mine was? He (it?) tilted his head back and laughed. His movement was so unnatural, yet it wasn't mechanical, it was still smooth. His hand was in a loose fist as though he held the neck of a wine bottle. And his laugh became soundless as though it choked on dust.

"They always say, 'Jesus Christ!'" he said. "Did you know all Christians are vampires? Drinking the blood of their Christ." He looked at me, his grey eyes glowing just a bit red. "We could do this in a church, if you want." I wasn't sure if he was making a joke, but I said okay.

He swept me away, and I'd like to tell you we flew to the church, but I'm not sure. It was so fast and I was shaking like a kitten, my skin was cold and wet with sweat. The wind rushed by my face and I had to squint my eyes. And the door to the church whose steps I'd seen him on slammed shut behind us. Thank God when we landed I wasn't standing next to him. Pardon my French, but I would have shit my pants if I were standing close to him.

"What the hell do you want from me?" That was it. That's all I came up with. After all these years. He pursed his lips and slightly raised an eyebrow. Such a human gesture! But it suited him. It breathed arrogance. And he was very arrogant. If I didn't maintain my professional calm, I would've called him a fucking Indian bastard. But it wasn't me to be like that. Oh, and I was still scared shitless.

"I think you know, Mr. St. Croix. You can piece it together." I walked over to a pew and slumped down.

"That girl..."

"*Very* good!" He was sitting behind me. I hadn't even sensed his movement.

"She looked like you..." God this was so hard for me. "She was becoming one of you..."

"For someone who's not even half a century old, you're not so dumb after all." I glanced back, very slightly, trying not to move my head. Trying not to let him *see* me looking. He was leaning back, one arm on the back of the pew, his left leg crossed on his right. This was *nothing* to him.

"Why me?" It was a question, but one without any intonation at all.

"Because I like you, Mr. St. Croix." He didn't catch my meaning. But then he realized, said, "Oh, you're still not upset about that? It was only, what, five years ago? I can't remember, the years seem to *blur*."

I was near tears, but I wouldn't let them out. I didn't want to give him the satisfaction.

"What? Oh, Jesu-See, now you've got me saying it! Get off it. Tears in the house of God!" His voice boomed inhumanly up the spires of the church. "God is about *love*, Mr. St. Croix." He flicked his tongue out at me and continued to shout.

I clamped my hands over my ears. The noise was deafening.

"Stop!" I yelled. "Stop it!"

He sat and folded his hands in his lap. "Yes?" Innocent little boy!

"Why me. You cost me years." I think he softened up a bit. Only a bit.

"Ah. That was an accident. When you saw me those many moons ago, I got things a little...mixed up. Happens."

"What. What mixed up." He was so cold, analytical about it.

"It's a remnant. They're a bit unpredictable sometimes-"

"What's a remnant?" I cut in. He seemed to show the slightest bit of frustration, like a teacher having to repeat herself.

"See, you're stuck *here*, now, and I saw you run into that girl, but I got to you a little earlier than I should've. It's really complicated, a conceptual thing." He looked down at his bare wrist. "Hm, look at the time, I've got to run. Listen, tomorrow, take what's coming to you, no matter what. I wouldn't want to ruin the surprise, but you'll know what it is when it happens. Can I offer you a ride home? Too bad." He got up and walked to the door, stopped in the open doorway and turned. "And remember Mr. St. Croix. I'll find *you*."

Needless to say, my anticipation at work was high the next night. I spent a few hours quickly filing everything away. The whole thing was a blur, then my commander, Francois Belanger, came out of his office.

"Graham, I need to see you in my office for a minute." It was still a shock to me. But this must have been what that...whatever it was he was talking about. I went into the office and sat down. The blinds behind me were drawn. But you could tell that people were glancing at the window, trying to look in.

He started with, "I know you put up with a lot in the last few years," and I really didn't like the sound of it. He continued.

"We stuck you with a lot, but I had to do it to keep you on. You know we like to think of our force as progressive, but politics will never go away, unfortunately."

"Especially in Montréal," I joked. He cracked a quick smile.

"Yes, yes. But I think it is way past time I returned some of your responsibility to you. You understand I meant to get to this sooner, but-"

"Very busy, I know, I know."

"Yes. And I have to say I had doubts, I have discussed this with many people, your counselor, for instance. Now, you know of the serial kidnappings lately?"

I nodded. Who didn't? It was big news, it was devastating the community.

"We're going to start a task force to deal with the matter. I want you on it. I hope you don't feel like were throwing you back into it, but like I said, I think you are growing stagnant. You're a good officer, Graham. I like to keep things around here moving."

I heard his words, but his tone was more: You *were* a good officer. He handed me a file folder, thick.

"Here are profiles of the victims, whether they've been found or not, etc. Take your time going over it. I don't want you to miss any details. Needless to say, even the smallest piece of information can lead to solving this." He stopped for a second, in thought. "I hate to get melodramatic, but this is on the verge of gripping the community in terror. Something like this...terrible, terrible..."

"You know what the press is like here, Graham. Were trying to keep this thing as quiet as possible. We don't want mass hysteria. Makes us look...unorganized."

"I may get to see daylight then," I quipped. Francois laughed a bit.

"No, they wanted you because you liked the night shift. Of course, you will be briefed on this when you join the task force. I just wanted to let you know what you were walking into. The information you need is on the top page of your folder. You join the force tomorrow." He stood and extended his hand, which I took. Before he let go he said: "This is a great opportunity for you, Graham. Use it wisely." Well, thank you Obie One Kenobi.

I thanked him, took the folder and left. I'm not sure, but I don't think he ever said congratulations.

I had trouble sleeping that day and I ended up waking early, which was noon for me. I was reeling, I had something to *do* at work now. I was a *cop* again. In my head, doors were opening. I could seriously pursue detective work with this experience under my belt. It had always been a passion of mine. Maybe forensics? Nah, I wasn't the scientific type.

I set to the folder, ready to start scrutinizing the case profiles. Of course, in my excitement-perhaps a poor choice of words, I was not excited about the prospect of assaults on children-I'd neglected to realize that I had to be transferred to the Specialized Investigations division. The transfer papers were the first things I encountered. Various sheets I had to fill out, taking me nearly an hour, but it went by quick.

I was moving, in effect, from Neighbourhood Station Twenty, the *Ville-Marie Sud-ouest*, nearly one hundred employees, to Specialized Investigations. What that meant was that I left a station-though I would work there as a contact as pertaining to this case-to an arm of the force that was three tiers below the director. I would report to the task force supervisor. Above him would be two assistant directors, one for general investigations, the other for specialized ones. And then the director of the Montréal Urban Community Police Services.

As well, we would have contact with people from subdivisions dealing with gangs, homicides, morality and sex assaults, which I figured we would have the most contact with. And, of course, forensics, but their role wouldn't come into major play until we'd put together a lot of evidence and had to catalogue and cross-reference it for arrests and prosecution. Forensics would be our claw, the killing blow in court.

So I had splashed into the big time, I guess you could say. I sat back and looked at the transfer form, finished.

And the thought came into my head. This was a pretty big leap for someone in my position. That is, someone who was coming from my situation. Working, really, in a token position that would be more suited to a clerk. I took a big leap over a lot of people. And that was bound to piss someone off.

As for my own view, I began to try to make sense of it. Hell, I wasn't complaining, but I had a nagging suspicion about the whole thing. It seemed too good to be true. What could possibly compel my commander to give me a promotion like this? Me, the cop who needed a psychiatrist. The cop who saw a demon. But after all my years of torture, or rather, enduring while others scowled and disbelieved, I didn't want to ruin this with my paranoia. I would take this as a way to improve myself, my life.

I heard the click of the door, Julia coming home early. I was in the dining room, and as I didn't want her to get a look at the file, I ducked upstairs quickly and hid it in my half of the closet till I could find a better place. I had developed a mistrust towards her after our recent outing. Actually, that just pushed the mistrust over the edge. It had to, of course, be developing over the recent years. And it didn't help that she worked as a reporter for the Gazette. My paranoia, full tilt.

We had a fine dinner, I answered questions about my day with non-committal answers such as 'same ole shit,' and then I got into a suit. I examined myself in the mirror, smoothed my lapels, straightened my tie. I walked downstairs and put on my shiny leather shoes.

"Where are you going?" Julia asked. I usually changed into my uniform at work.

"Work," I said haughtily.

"But why the suit?" she pressed. I looked at her from under my brow.

"Belanger called a meeting tonight. I thought I'd dress for it." I went back to my laces.

"Oh. Well, tell him I said hi."

"Sure."

Shit. My dossier. I left it upstairs. And I wanted to get it out of the house without her seeing it. I thought for a sec, then decided on my trench coat. I could hide the dossier underneath, easy. So I went upstairs to get my forgotten keys and then bounded out with a, 'Bye!' leaving Julia and her puckered lips behind the door.

I thought about how stupid this was as I walked to the metro. I would have to tell her about my promotion. Soon. I hated sneaking. Ha! A cop who hated sneaking! It sounded a little contradictory, but this was my wife. It was different with her. Or should have been, anyway. I mean, we shared our lives, why should I feel that I had to hide something from her? This was good news, anyway. I should have run to her with it. I settled on telling her that I'd gotten an assignment for a while, but I wouldn't give with the details. I'd grab a briefcase and hide my files in there. This wasn't much of a marriage anymore.

Walking down the street, I noticed a few glances my way. There was something about a suit that made a man something more! My suit was cheaply charming. I also had on a my trench coat, slung over one arm, and my dossier under my other. From the clothes and the looks, I felt...important, perhaps respected. I walked with my back straighter.

I noticed a friend of mine, Monsieur Picard, he owned a bakery café. I would stop there on my beat to grab a snack, enjoy the smell of sweet yeast rising. He was big and boisterous, looked like a baker.

A man said, *"Pardon, monsieur, quelle heure est ile?"*

I answered him, *"Sept, monsieur."* He nodded a thanks and leapt into a jog down the street.

"Ah, monsieur St. Croix-" he always pronounced my name exquisitely, rolling the r, "-you look marvelous tonight!" He took me by the shoulders, gave me a little shake, smoothed the material of my suit down. "You come in, sit, for a coffee, come!"

I raised my hand to him, said, "Oh, I wish I could, but I'm on my way to work. Hence, the suit."

"No more uniform for you?"

"Maybe not for a while, sorry. Someone else will be handling it."

"Ah!" he said. "So you have moved higher! You come back later, for a drink!" He spoke with his hands, he stuck his belly out. I liked him.

"I'll make it by soon, definitely!"

The flames burst up behind me, shooting up. Everyone ducked away from the force of the blast, me included.

Even my professional calm wouldn't let me stand stoic in the face of a blast. I pushed my trench coat into Mr. Picard's chest, pushing him two steps back.

"Call the police!" I yelled to him. I hung onto the dossier. It was stuck to my hand. I ran to the source of the blast. The flames licked up at the air, arms of orange and red swept the asphalt, alive. God, I hoped no one was in that car. I had the image of a man on fire staggering through the street; horrific, horrific.

Sirens in the distance, thank God.

"Back off!! Back off!!" I yelled, alternately in French and English, holding up my badge. Many people, close to the car when it went up, had fallen on the ground. Some had to be moved away from the flames. Some men-brave, oh they were brave; this was true bravery, putting their hands near fire to save a life-started to lift limp bodies away. I nodded at them, said, "Good, good, careful."

I ran to a girl with curly hair, she was lying on the ground still. Her mother ran over, purse hanging from her wrist, her coat dragging, she ran with tears dripping off her face, screaming. I had to hold her back, I had to, someone helped me I think, the woman's arms flailing at the edge of my sight, reaching for her daughter. I put my mouth to the girl's, pushed on her chest. Breathe...breathe...The dossier under my knee now. It was less than ten seconds before she started to breathe again. Ten seconds of an eternity. Everything froze around me, the great arms of the flames, the mother's hands. No noise, until the coughing and choking. She must have gulped smoke or something. I didn't know.

I was pulled away by paramedics, firemen. The dossier was stuck to my hand again, somehow. I backed away from the scene. I watched.

Some firemen patted my shoulder with heavy gloves. I walked over to Gauthier, he had the radio in his hand.

"Hey, I've really got to run. Catch up with me later on this?"

"Sure. I already called you in. You'll be at twenty?"

"No. I'll meet you there though, say about three hours." He nodded and answered the squawk on the radio. I turned and resumed my walk to work. I looked back over my shoulder when I heard a sharp whistle. Gauthier winked at me and gave me the thumbs up, mouthed *good job*.

Picard was neatly folding up my coat, he slung it over my arm for me. He smiled at me and stuck out his belly. He said, "You don't forget to come back for your drink." I think that was the first time his voice was quiet.

When I got to work, Korson-the vampire, he hadn't actually told me his name, but somewhere along the way he *told* me-was sitting on the rail of the front steps...wearing the same suit I was.

"You look stunning!" he said. "There's something about a man in a suit-mwah!" He blew the air a kiss. Then he was serious again. "Come on. Perk up. You were in a good mood. You're a hero now. Get in there and knock 'em dead." He gave me a shove towards the door-hard! Fuck, he had strength. I looked back and he stood there like a rigid father, he urged me forward with a wave of his hand. He looked almost disinterested. I walked through the doors.

I walked into the room, just in time. Though I had a perfectly good excuse for my tardiness. The head of the task force was Pierre Lacroix. I'd heard of him. Tough bastard, but fair. I recognized some of the people in here, but we'd have time to meet as we worked. Lacroix had settled us down, Hill Street Blues style, and he began to talk. He went over objectives, procedures, an overview of everything we'd be working on. He spent nearly ten minutes drilling into our heads the need for secrecy, as much as possible, about case specifics. Of course, the kidnapping and murder of a child would be big news, but he didn't want any specifics leaked. That could lead to cranks and copycat killers, and solving the actual murder would be hard enough. Not that anyone in the room didn't know this, but Lacroix was a stickler for details, a perfectionist.

All in all, the meeting was nearly two hours of making sure everyone was on the same page, going over generalizations and such. There were quick hello's and handshakes, and everyone dispersed to their respective stations, set to meet again later. I went back to twenty.

It was in my mind that the guy who'd stopped and asked me for the time earlier had a part on planting the car bomb. I wanted to get his description down, I'd been flashing the image in my head for three hours now. Of course, it was standard procedure to get descriptions immediately, as they are more accurate fresh. But I could always back up the time on the form if need be. And it was purely circumstantial that he was involved at all, but I'd hand over the description to Gauthier with that explanation-just in case. Police paranoia and all.

I was going through the suspect forms when someone told me that Gauthier had arrived and was waiting at my desk. I picked up my things and went over to meet him.

"Allo, *Monsieur St. Croix*," said a woman.

"*Bonjour*. Could I help you?"

"Yes. I had some things I wanted to go over with you."

"I was told someone was here to see me. Could you give me a minute, madame...?"

She extended her hand. "Isabelle Gauthier." I shook her hand, a little confused.

"Oh, you're the Gauthier that-"

"Yes."

"Sorry. I was expecting Gauthier to be a man." I gave a laugh, she barely smiled, but sweetly. "Uh, let me just leave these forms for him, with a note." I took a couple of minutes filling out the forms, left a note and put everything in an envelope. She sat there watching me, holding her briefcase in her lap. I stood up and said, "We could take a conference room. Less noise." She nodded and said *oui*.

I shut the door behind me, extended my hand to a seat, offered coffee and such. She declined, politely.

"Now, I said. What can I help you with?"

"We met a few hours ago? At the meeting?" I thought for a sec. Then slapped my head.

"Oh, right! I'm really sorry, it's been a hectic day-"

"So I heard. You were next to the Night Stalker's bomb earlier."

"Yes, happened to be there. Lucky."

"For that girl," she said. "She lived. I checked." I thought to myself, *Wow, I did something good*. I was introspective about it. I don't know why, but I didn't smile, I kept my small reaction to myself. I felt good, really good, but a subdued wow? That was all I could manage? Isabelle looked at me blankly, obviously expecting some sort of smile out of me. She was attractive, her eyes dark, warm.

"Mr. St. Croix?"

"Graham."

"Graham, then. I'm running a bit behind myself. I'll just leave with you these photos to go over and I may meet you tomorrow?" She pulled out an envelope and handed it to me.

"Sure. Eleven, here then."

"*Oui.*" She walked out of the room, clutching her file to her chest. She waved and gave me a smile as she closed the door.

I finished up my shift shortly and left, moving quickly down the stone steps.

"It's intoxicating, isn't it?"

I turned my head, looked behind me as I kept walking.

"Korson," I said. "What do you want?" I took a slight tone with him.

Suddenly! In front of me! "Don't you ever..." He had me by the collar, showing his strength. God, I couldn't even move his hand off me, it was like steel. "Answer me."

"I-I don't know-"

"Yes you do." His eyes had reddened and his fangs hung, ivory tusks from blood coloured gums. "I want to know how you felt." He relaxed his grip on me, only a bit.

"You want to know...what it's like to hold a life?" He hissed yes as his answer. "It's...powerful." He put me down. I wondered why a creature such as this would want to know what me-a mere mortal-thought on such matters. Would he not be more experienced?

He pushed me to the ground and said, "Remember that." When I looked up he was gone.

I yelled at the sky, "You're fucked! Fucked in the head!" But then I got up and walked away quickly. I knew the looks of the people who passed me by all too well.

He looked at the four pictures. Only for a few minutes, though. It was hard to stomach them. It took one a while to become desensitized to them. Or did he want to be desensitized? The pictures were all different, but of the same theme. They might as well have been the same pictures. It didn't matter.

He flipped through them stoically, trying not to let the images register, to stamp permanent impressions in his head that would be the last thing he saw before he drifted into sleep and the first fearsome image to greet his waking mind.

He flipped through them quickly at first, one-two-three-four, again and again. He had to stop after a while, because it began to look like flip book animation, the figures moving in a dance of the dead, broken, jilted motions and limbs flailing around like hands of the clock. It was as though everything around stopped and darkened because this kind of evil existed. He could feel his heart drumming in his chest. He could hear it, too. Or was that...? Was that real drums?

So he had to slow down, to go through them more methodically. Methodical examination was a dreaded phrase he didn't want to consider, but it was his duty to study society's crimes in an effort to prevent them. It was his duty. Duty to be in such a thankless position.

He looked at the first one and his heart actually thumped slower rather than faster. The neck of a little girl smiled at him with a gaping wound and he pictured the murderer holding the girl up with an arm around her back, her head bouncing back and forth like a jack in the box. The background fuzzed into grey smoke. He drank some Southern Comfort so his head would fuzz.

Steve Zinger

There were other pictures of the girl, and he cross-referenced them in his files by code number. (Oh no! Never by name, one didn't want them to become real, to have their ghost visit you in tears every night; to have them ask you where everyone is in the darkness.) The other photos should have been easier to take, they were just close-ups of wounds. But her face kept flashing before his eyes, like a strobe.

The police photographer had taken a close-up of her nipple. There were little teeth marks around it, red dots like measles. To him it looked like the murderer had sat there with a needle, poking holes in the young, powdery skin of the child (nameless...)

He saw the child sitting in front of the mirror in a...clown costume? The mirror had big frosted light bulbs all around the frame, and the child looked at herself with an ear splitting smile. A mother's hands tended to the details of the costume. Primping and preening the frills, pinching the girl's cheeks affectionately. He couldn't see the mother's face in the mirror. In fact, he couldn't see the room at all. Just the mirror, the lights and the child; the mother's hands holding facepaint. The girl nearly bounced out of her seat as the mother started putting the white make-up on her face. Thick, sticky streaks of icing sugar stuck to the girl's cheeks, her forehead. The mother carefully filled all the pinkness of her daughter's cheeks with white.

She began to use colours now, lining the eyes. She drew smooth blue lines that drooped sadly down from the edges of the girl's eyes. She made the girl's lips purple, the make-up pulling her expression downwards. The girl shook her head vigourously, she didn't like it. She wiped it off, her eyes and lips normal again. The mother touched up the white paint, and she began again. This time she showed her daughter the colours before applying them. There was some hesitation, then she consented.

The girl closed her eyes, and the mother painted them with gold glitter. The girl smiled again, gleefully. Her tongue stuck out from beneath her top teeth. The mother's hands put red lines at the edges of the girl's eyes, lines that were dense, bold. The girl looked up and nodded at her mother. More lines were made, red paint being drawn at the girl's brow, making it look furrowed. Some black was added around the bridge of her nose and at the base of her eyes for contrast. It made her look almost...menacing...She looked up at her mother and scrunched her nose at her, cutely. The menacing eyes held their expression over the girl's real ones.

The mother began applying paint to the girl's lips. She painted the lips orange and used black sparingly around the mouth as contrast. She made some lines perpendicular to the lines of the girls natural lips to show dimples. She drew some other lines that made the lips look withdrawn. But this time she couldn't make the expression sad because the colours were too strong and the paint and the girl's smile wouldn't let her. The mother finished the face by putting a big, bright red rubber nose on the girl, touching it with a finger after it was in place.

The girl was alone and she looked at the mirror and her smile was about to explode in joy at the way she looked. She pulled her knees up to her chest and hugged them, she threw her head back and laughed and giggled at the sky!

The stitch at her neck slid gently opened and her head bounced like a jack in the box...

Graham looked at the next picture.

Hectic. The pressures of processing it all, trying to stay calm, focussed, detached, analytical. Trying to remember *who I am*. Trying to be what people expect me to be, and forget about what they think I am. Trying not to say, "fuck the real world," or at least trying not to express it in my actions. Because it keeps going on viciously, mindlessly, no matter what.

But most of all, trying not to feel guilty about coming here. Trendy spot. *Boul. St. Laurent et Prince Arthur*. Cobbled roads closed off to traffic, restaurants and cafés littering the storefronts. Not so guilty about coming *here*, per se, but about who I was meeting here.

"Graham!"

With her too much outside work? Working too much? What was I doing here, nothing was going to happen here. Nothing would get accomplished here. Life, important to accomplish things in life, not get bogged down by it all. Easy to lose yourself. And the body...

"Graham!"

Stuttered, "Oh, sorry. Mind wandered. I guess."

She smiled, but I didn't return it. Couldn't, really, tried but couldn't. Took in her appearance, *detached* remember, but I did notice she was much more casual, faded pink sweatshirt, well-worn blue jeans. I guess she wore heals all the time cause damnit, she seemed so much shorter now. That and it was more relaxed outside of a work setting. Her smile faded, like a winter sunset.

"Are you okay?" I liked her accent, with the French lilt, though I could tell she tried to hide it when she spoke English.

"Yeah, yeah. To many people here. Let's siddown."

Greek restaurant, good place, *saganaki* (flaming cheese) preceded by glasses of red wine. The waiter said *'opa'* a little too quietly but quite friendly all the same.

"You don't like big crowds, lots of people. You're distrustful."

"Not true," I shot back, perhaps a little too forcefully. "Defensive, maybe. Sometimes I love the crowds. Just forgetting and getting lost in them." I felt weird tonight. Like I wasn't inside my body, like I had forced myself to respond with too much forced emotion to Isabelle's casual observation.

"Sometimes that isn't good. Better to deal with the situations as they arise instead of running to hide. But I know the feeling. Like caving in."

We were on the patio, quite unseasonably warm. The pleasant breeze, sweet and relaxing like the taste of the wine, much too romantic out here. Much.

"You sure you okay?"

I laughed, said, "You gonna ask me that all night?" *Trying* not to sound defensive, more like playful, force a smile maybe. But the body...

"But you won't answer. It's what happened, wasn't it."

Slight pause. "I'm not supposed to care about it. To stay professionally focussed is to leave emotions out of it."

"Then you're not living in the real world," said Isabelle. I mean, who the hell was she to talk? I had never seen her laugh, and barely a smile. Maybe that's why I felt I could trust her, because she never laughed, and the echo of laughter was the Devil's signature, written in blood still wet.

"Did we come here to talk about work?" Bit of venom in the voice this time. Well. Perfect. That shut her up.

"I, um...I thought I was talking more about you, Graham." The worst part about it was that now I felt guilty about being harsh. Wearing my heart on my sleeve and such, having to adapt to others emotions, constantly worrying about hurting others feelings. Finally getting selfish and standing up for myself and I feel sorry about it. I'm amazed that I'm still a cop. Such a soft heart beating within my chest!

"Hey, I'm sorry, I really shouldn't-"

"It's okay." Quick response, and more food came. I wished our waiter would stop smiling like that. Slaughtered lamb on my plate. Oh, that body...

"I guess it has hit me a little hard, the last few days. You just try to brush it aside sometimes."

"We're partners outside work, too, Graham. You need to relax. You need to allow yourself some-" she searched for the word, "-*companion*." Stumbling over the word and meaning with her accent. "You don't go out much after work?"

"No, not really."

"Well, I'm here to help too, to get through it. You know, if you don't feel you can discuss it with someone on the outside."

"Which were not supposed to." Further isolation?

"Smoke?" She'd finished eating.

"Hell. Why not."

Stated question: "You don't smoke normally."

I lit up, the orange flame pulsing rhythmically with each breath I took. I said, "I used to drink quite a bit, I'm sure you know. I would have one from time to time if I got really hammered. Just so I wouldn't remember the addiction the next day. Quit years ago, though."

"You don't drink anymore?"

I looked away, gave a laugh. I noticed her looking at me with one of those 'I'm glad to see you smile' looks. But it would later haunt me that I neglected to notice that, during the course of our conversation, the light had faded away as the sun had set.

I began to stare at the smoke, remembering many years ago sitting at my grandfather's table, watching the grey wisps float through the air. Trying to break them up with my fingers, thinking it was fun. How was it that he died? Too much smoke? His lungs slowly filled, choked unmercifully to his painful end, till all that was left was a grainy memory in my head, slowly fading like a sunset.

"Graham?"

"Yes? Oh! Sorry. No. Don't drink anymore."

She smiled a little. *Never* did that at work, not even a cursory one, not even out of politeness. Put her elbow on the table and leaned her head on her hand, looked at the smoke with me. That bo-

"You're thinking about it."

-dy.

The smoke mesmerized us both, and I moved my hand slowly as if in time to a softly played piano.

"Yeah. I guess I am."

Several more murders in the past few days, bodies mangled...well, not beyond belief, but very intricate, intimate mutilations. And some symbols inscribed in blood on the skins of the victims. Not necessarily on the body, on the skins; the skin torn away like scrap paper, like someone turned their back on the shock-filled, innocence-bled eyes of the poor little child to scratch out a morbid note.

Isabelle said, "It looked like a child had drawn them."

"Hm?"

"The stars. It looked like a child had drawn them." The symbols were of a moon, and a cross with pentacles on the end of each thick line. But at times it looked like the handiwork of a child.

"I just wonder if it means anything at all," I said.

"An amalgamation, perhaps. Pagan rituals with the epic splendour of Christianity."

"I always thought religions preached love."

"They do. But were dealing with a murderer here." Something more, Isabelle. But I don't think I could even tell myself that. And the moon is the night and I know all too well about who that could be. "Something bothers you?"

"It's the zeal. I've seen the love religion can inspire, but I've also seen the hatred. It's..." I broke off.

"You don't have any belief in religion?" asked Isabelle. "Isn't there even something in this world that makes you question your perception?"

"I wasn't raised religious, but I remember one thing from the teachings: Mary Magdalene kneeling at the tomb of Christ, in tears, begging forgiveness for her sins, only to find that he'd risen from his grave...

"And she was a hooker, and her salvation lay somewhere beyond death." Isabelle looked at me, a little slyly. "You don't even believe in magic, do you."

"No."

"Nothing mystical ever crossed your path?"

"Stop it. Okay? Stop." Now it was her who'd gotten to me. I bet she hadn't seen half the shit that I'd seen. And she was pushing it. I didn't want to be that person, I didn't want to deal with things from that angle, the opposite one of everyone else.

In a small alcove between two of the restaurants across the cobbled way, a dim pair of white eyes stared at me. The harder I looked to make out the form, to try and distinguish, the less I saw. Complete shadow, but for the eyes. The street was well lighted, but the alcove seemed enshrouded in darkness, as though no light were present. Smoke like...out of the body...

"What's so special about them," I said. "Children I mean."

Isabelle ran her fingers along the bridge of her nose, thinking. I tried to scrutinize the creature of the alcove. Gone. Nothing there. Just the wisps of shadow flowing and twisting like they usually did.

"I don't know," said Isabelle. "Perhaps...perhaps a connection between the purity of their souls and the power of enchantment."

"I can't take that to Belanger," I said, sternly. "I have to go to him with something concrete, something tangible." I emphasized my point by banging the knife-edge of one hand in the other.

"Graham, you saw him!" she cried, almost loud enough for the people around to hear. "Are you so atheistic that you deny the very evidence before your eyes?"

She knew, she knew, and she saw it in my eyes. I couldn't get rid of it, I couldn't shed my insides of it and it was reflected in my eyes.

"I didn't see anything," I said, quietly refuting her implications. In the back of my head I felt her dancing towards the conclusions I didn't want her to go towards, the answers I didn't want her to pull out of me. Perhaps I was scared that someone would believe me? Perhaps I was scared what that would validate?

"Graham," she said, taking hold of my arm. "You saw it. Coming out of him." Oh, right. The body. "That was unreal what we saw. That wasn't natural, or of this world. There is something beyond life and death here, and we have to find some way to expose it. I know you can do it." Still implying? She still had her hand on my arm, and I didn't like the way it felt. Or maybe, liked it too much.

"I can't get over what his eyes looked like."

Black. Empty. Forever deep. Like the shadow that came out of him. Flowing out of the dead body of the boy, his tormented, torn body, out of the orifices. And no one but Isabelle or myself had noticed. Nobody else could <u>see</u>. Except for the little girl in the crowd, who pointed. But in a moment someone had passed in front of her. And in a moment, she was gone as though she hadn't been there. That sheer innocence that must be broken by those who've had the world cave in upon their mind.

I started to shiver. I noticed it was dark. I looked around me, trying to find that strange pair of eyes in the shadow. I began to notice the people around me, and some of them I didn't like the look of. The haunting familiarity of their pale white images.

And who is majic for if not for the children? And where do the evil steal their majic if not *from* the children?

It wasn't so much the darkness of the night that I felt caving in upon me, as the oppressive colours of the crowd, as though mad, tittering clowns were swarming me. There were too many people here. I felt vulnerable, became jittery. Isabelle didn't notice, she kept holding my arm, and I felt thankful for that now as it provided me with at least one way of keeping myself *grounded*; of feeling as though I had an anchor in this world as things began to happen around me. She could, after all, *see* to a certain point. She saw what I saw coming out of that dead child's body.

I tried to get up. I had to get out of here. I think I got up, but I still felt Isabelle's hand holding my arm. I was having one of those *feelings*, like an anxiety attack, jittering, shaking, unexplainable nervousness, I *had* to leave, I was getting up, I knew it, I felt my legs moving, going away, or that's what I *wanted*. I could *swear* I was moving away. Out of here, but her hand was still touching my arm, I felt it. I think I pulled away from her. I didn't care, I would explain to her later, I just had to leave.

Three women appeared out of the myriad colours of the crowd, surrounding me before I could react. Pale white cheeks and ruby red lips with little fangs just denting into the skin. One pushed me back down into my seat, holding me down by the shoulders as she stood behind me. I think I still felt Isabelle's hand touching me. And then, casually, as though out of a pale grey mist, walked a gentleman, debonair with his cane that he swung from his wrist, and stood before me. And he gave me a smile that I somehow knew was much more deadly than Korson's...

Sometimes one can stare at something for hours and hours and still not notice every detail. He sat and studied the second picture, this one of a boy. His leg had been rotated on the socket, the ligaments snapped and bones ground to powder; his skin stretched until it was creased and wrinkled and torn. He could see the boy's face clearly in this picture, but he found one of only the face, the lacerations looking white on ebony skin. The boy's eyes were wide with shock, black pits so hollow and devoid of any understanding. And all he could see was the eye. And it became bigger all of a sudden. Bigger. Until it engulfed his vision, until he could imagine nothing nor see anything but that deep endless sadness and the horror of the candle being blown out in one swift, torturous whiff. Sweet red lips in an 'O' kissing air on the orange flame. Grey skin stretching into a smile.

"Good-bye, little darling. Sweet dreams for all eternity!"

That eye just staring so large from the photograph...OH! Did it just...blink? Could he still see what was happening? Is that why he was so afraid? No. It was because of what had happened to him. He died watching his own murder, and he watched it over and over and over...

And he stared over and over and over. Watching faceless hands twist his leg around and seeing the boy scream but not hearing it, no, not in a picture.

Sometimes one could sit for hours and stare and not notice how black the eyes were and how unnatural they looked. And how black the black skin was and how unreal it was, black on black like ink set deep into his dark skin with a needle...

*   *   *

Julia St. Croix also had a pang of guilt run through her spine, like a long, cold needle. It was while Graham was off at work, most convenient, and she went out to do extra research for some upcoming articles. And, most conveniently, at night, when the creatures who roamed smelled the succinct scent of opportunity. Julia had, by the look on her face, of her manner, obviously left her home to escape the quiet, cold solitude, the silence and the emptiness. She sat at the table, seemingly distracted as she looked around, her chin lightly resting on the heel of her hand, lights flashing and the music blaring. She obviously didn't belong here, her look was too quaint. It didn't take a mind reader to realize she was seeking some sort of escape.

And it was a vampire that smelled opportunity. One of the Sab. He often came to places like these, for escape as well. And he spotted the pretty blond lady sitting by herself at a table, spotted her through the myriad of bodies writhing in artistic ways on the dance floor.

Marie said, "Come, Paul, let's leave here, I tire of this place."

"Yes, Paul, come, we can find some flesh elsewhere, perhaps somewhere more intimate than this noisy barn," said Clarisse. Paul remained silent, his stare fixed upon Julia.

"What's with him?" asked Antoinette.

"Oh my!" exclaimed Marie, as Paul continued his fixed, stony stare. "He's in love again!"

The girls began to chatter and playfully shove at Paul's shoulders, poking fun at him by sticking their tongues out. Marie, the most vocal of the group, was closest to Paul, and he grabbed hold of her wrist, his claws digging deep enough to draw blood from the purply veins beneath her powdery skin. He finally pulled his stare off Julia and turned to Marie, said, "Leave me," though it was to all of them. His eyes were gleaming white orbs, on the verge of vampiric anger. The giggling girls cackling subsided, and the smiles faded from their faces. They slowly rose from the table, trying to look as though uncaring towards the rebuff of a man.

"In love again," said Clarisse, exasperated.

"Always seeking it out," echoed Antoinette, "but forever an arms length away from it." Saying it as though it were his curse to bear for eternity. And the three women left to find their own fun for the night.

Paul turned his attentions back to the lonely lady, and took another big drag of the air. He certainly smelled many things from her, most glaringly apparent the absence and longing of her heart. And most deliciously, the smell of his nemesis-the vampire Korson. Though the scent wasn't particularly strong. He took a glance at the vulnerable mind of the young woman. Oh ho! So this was the wife of the mortal Korson had been running with lately!

The broth of opportunity was too good for Paul to pass up. Perhaps he could see how close Korson was to this mortal. Those sick rumours were true-Korson with a mortal; Korson with a friend. Though Paul, thinking of previous murders many moons passed, was loath to tread this territory with anything but the utmost discretion and guile, for he didn't want to ignite Korson's wrath after a century of surprisingly dormant tempers. Perhaps, though, just maybe, she could be a sacrifice to the Queen Talissa? She would like that, something close to Korson, when she finally decided to bring the veil crashing down on a fated Hallowe'en.

He maneuvered his way over to the table, very nearly getting jostled on the dance floor (God be praised! He didn't come into contact with a mortal), and sat with the woman after whispering something sweet in her ear. Over the next few nights he would come to her with twisted faces, under the guise of many names, as he kept her under his majical swoon. She would never truly know he was Paul, a vampire of the Sab, and that all she really was was one more soul to be consumed among the masses.

Most certainly he didn't want to get too close to the mortal Korson was cavorting with lately, but he could certainly add some torment through the wife. He knew of the strings of love, and especially those of love lost, and he knew how one delicate tug in just the right way could cause searing pain.

The music slowed to a relaxing throb, and he took her out to dance. Not in the middle of the floor, though, never, as he didn't want any undue attention directed at him tonight. Normally he might stand in the middle and be quite flamboyant, wanting the eyes of all the girls upon him. And she, she was never supposed to be here in the first place.

They were practically in a corner, hidden away in shadow among the shadowy lights of the place, and he said, "Lean your head back, my innocent little flower," and she did. They always fell for that one, especially under the swoon. And then he kissed her full on the lips, though he hated kissing, and he had to resist the urge to taste her blood. Until she was full sway under the swoon.

"Meet me tomorrow?" he whispered to her.

"Kiss me again," was all she could say, but it was yes enough. She hadn't been kissed with any sort of depth or passion in over a year, and the pleasure she felt now was almost hurtful. It surprised her when the man was gone, and she was left swaying to the music on her own with puckered lips, but as he watched her from the shadows he was certain she would seek him out the next night-and that soon she would be his.

The third one was of a girl again. Most of them were girls, young, pre-pubescent, the flower of womanhood rended apart in bloody rips and tears. This one was thrown face first into the ground. Her jaw shattered to pieces at the impact of her fall. Tiny teeth tinkling out of her mouth like crystal shards. Her nasal cavity thrust upward, enough that she should have died then. But some miracle kept her alive.

The killer used some sort of weapon to slice open the skin sheathed over her back. "It-" the mortician paused while he spoke, his throat constricting "-was some kind of animal. A claw."

It, well, could have been a serrated blade, true, but the mortician decided to stick with his hypothesis about an animal's claw. Uncertainty crept through his voice. But he wrote down what he thought anyway.

"But if I didn't know better," he continued, "it was like someone was trying to pull off the skin in one piece. As though they wanted to make a Halloween costume out of it. Or something." He was clearly disturbed. "Never seen anything like it. Never...ever...seen anything like it." He put a cloth over his mouth as though he smelled something rotten, and walked away hastily.

My head had been turned completely to the right, and the clawed fingers gripping into my skin pulled it back as far as it could go, so as to painfully expose my neck. To say the least, I felt vulnerable. The vampire's hands numbered the same as my own, but I felt as though a thousand demon's hands reaching up from Hell had strapped me down. Isabelle, of course, remained ignorant, still chattering on about the murders.

"Amazing, isn't it," said the vampire who'd called himself Paul. "She sits there spouting off tripe about belief and esotericism, and here we stand, right before her very eyes-and she cannot see!" Paul moved closer to me, and I was helpless to whatever he wanted to do.

Though he certainly carried a sense of morbidity about him-it was quite apparent in his eyes, in the way his glance was sly and askance-and the vampires around him began to dance. The shadows around me continued their advance, and Clarisse and Antoinette were enjoying a prance. Needless to say, there was of escape no chance.

"So sad I am to tell you of this," the vampire Paul said, he teased with a kiss. His hot breath on my neck, so close I could piss. He leaned in close and said, "What's this? The soul of a child, that smell I can't miss."

"Fuck off," I told him and spit in his face, his century old soul feeling the sting of disgrace. With the fire in his eyes, the dancers picked up their pace, swinging their arms all covered in lace.

Isabelle kept talking of children and majic, the murders of them, which were all oh so tragic.

Marie and Paul and Antoinette and Clarisse, they wanted my body, my blood, Oh Christ! piece by piece.

This tale would come to an end much too soon, if the vampire Korson hadn't flown in from the moon.

"You shithead, you fucker, you cunt-sucking whore!" screamed the vampire Korson, come to settle the score. He hacked and he slashed and kicked and he tore, and as darkness descended, the world around me-no more!

He held Paul up by the neck like he was a puppet. Bullshit-to me he now looked like a Muppet.

He now spoke in French, shaking, nervous like a hermit. God-damnit I knew it, that frog he was Kermit.

Korson held his claw o'er his head, ready to land the killing blow; but for some strange reason, he just let him go.

I thanked God for my saviour, my White Knight of the Gore. Then to me he looked towards and his fangs he did bear, giving me an earnest and quite frightful scare. But wait, what was this, all caught up in the lore? Watch out from behind! Attack from a whore!

He twisted and turned and threw Marie off, spitting blood in her face making her look oh so Goth.

She landed on Clarisse and Antoinette and Paul, and they then took a tumble, not one but all.

"We'll be back, mark my words," said the vampire Paul, looking way up at Korson because he was tall.

"Your talk is so mighty," is what Korson said, looking at him as though he were dead.

"Next time I'm around I shall give you a call."

"It would be my pleasure, Paul, to see you fall."

And with that the vampires of the Sab did flee, though the only ones who could see were Korson and me.

The next thing I remember was going to sleep, and there were tears in my eyes as I made to weep. For from what I have seen the Sab was so keen, on stealing my blood and skinning me clean. But the scariest thing I think would have been, if this were to have happened on:

Hallowe'en!

*   *   *

I'd decided to go visit that strange, pretty girl I'd seen on the street, Heather. I'd been so busy with work, and I spent a *lot* of extra time with Isabelle, too. Working, technically, but really just talking a lot about stuff because I felt she understood.

I have to confess, though, that I did feel a little sorry for Isabelle. She lived alone and never really mentioned anyone-friend or otherwise-so I guess I kind of imagined her as lonely. But alone and lonely are two different things.

It was Saturday and I usually reserved that for Julia. Though it usually amounted to staying home and watching a movie or some other quiet activity. Or making small talk, that dreaded animal that eats precious moments. I was terrible to watch a movie with anyway, I always insisted on some 'B' action flick as opposed to those sweet romantic comedies.

But Julia was gone when I rose from my coffin of a bed, and as I showered the previous day away I realized I hadn't seen her in three days. In fact it was apparent that *neither* of us was paying much attention to the marriage.

I'd found Heather's home at Gladstone and *rue Ste-Catherine* with little difficulty. It looked nothing like I'd remembered it. The night can play tricks on you, it seems.

I knocked on the door, straightened my jacket, and put my hands in my pockets as I waited for an answer.

"Allo, yes?" It was a woman.

"*Bonjour*, I'm looking for Heather Langden?" I asked.

"You are...?"

"Oh, sorry," I extended my hand. "Graham St. Croix." Then I showed her my badge. "M.U.C.P.S."

"Come in for a minute, Mr. St. Croix, please." I stepped in. "Would you like coffee? Tea?"

"Tea, please."

She introduced herself as Susan, Heather's mother, as she prepared the tea. She brought a tray with the tea bags and teapot to the den.

"I'm afraid I have some disheartening news, Mr. St. Croix."

"Graham, please."

"It seems...Heather has passed on," she said with wet eyes. I was speechless and couldn't manage to think of anything to say. Susan looked at me as she topped up her cup.

"Oh, shit, shit, shit." She hadn't been paying attention and overflowed the china teacup.

"It's okay, I got it." I blotted the spill with napkins.

"Thank you. It's been very stressful around here. I guess you would realize that though." I nodded in agreement. "Was she in any trouble?"

"Oh, no, no. I saw her on *rue Ste-Catherine* late one night. She didn't look too well at all. I walked her home. I was just checking up on her."

Susan had poured herself more tea, carefully this time. "Her father passed on a few months ago. She took it quite hard. She was quite sick for a while, she was delusional. She wandered out of the house quite a bit. I don't know if she realized she was doing it."

"That's terrible. Just terrible." I really didn't know what to say, this was something I wasn't too good at dealing with. Death.

"Oh, can I show you her room?"

"Madame, I don't think that's really-"

"It will be just a minute, come." She was smiling a bit. Perhaps it took her pain away to be among Heather's belongings. Perhaps Susan felt as if she was still alive by talking about her and touching her daughter's treasures.

Heather's room wasn't especially surprising in the decorations. In fact, through my brief image of the girl, it was what I expected to see. There were white drapes hanging from the window frame, asking to flow in the wind. There was a thick comforter on the bed, maroon with shapes in blue and red scattered over as design. There were stuffed animals-cats, puppies and a brown bear that was flimsy in the neck from being squeezed so tight.

There was a picture of Heather, her arms around the shoulders of a bear of a man, her smile bright as her hair. The man had a stubbly face, and despite the fact that he too wore a smile, he looked like he normally didn't.

"Her father?" Susan nodded. "It looks good in black and white. You don't notice it really." She took the picture from me and touched her fingers to the glass. She held it close as she looked up at nothing.

"Oh, I'm sorry for being like this!" I told her not to apologize.

The dresser was cluttered and it caught my attention by the boldness of it. I could have easily missed it as it was almost hidden behind something. A rose so crystal and blue. But I touched it and it didn't feel like glass. I slipped it into my pocket before Heather's mother could turn around.

"It's such a lovely picture," she said.

Smoothly I responded, "Well, I shouldn't be keeping you any longer. Besides, I have some other business to attend to anyway." My heart was thumping, too fast. I felt as though I would break a sweat. Susan showed me out. She told me the funeral was tomorrow, that I was welcome to attend. She wrote down the address and I promised to show up.

I got into my car and sat for a second. I said, "Fuck, fuck, fuck!" and slammed my hand on the steering wheel each time. I shouldn't have done that, taking something from someone else's house. It didn't make any difference that the girl was dead. What if her mother noticed it gone? I drove off, quite upset with myself.

I finally got home, and went directly to bed. Heather's funeral was tomorrow and I didn't want to show up yawning and bleary eyed. I went to sleep, almost waking Julia as I readied for bed.

I had another strange dream. The little girl with the jack in the box head was in the middle of a one-ring circus stage. There was a big ball, like the one elephants balanced on, and it was sweet and bloody orange. The little girl was dressed up in her clown suit and she was trying to balance herself on a plank on top of the ball. She kept falling off, but she kept trying. Each fall made her more determined, her head lolling on her neck rhythmically to the undulations of the board. She finally triumphed as she held her balance, her head bouncing slower and slower on her neck as the ball stopped rolling beneath the board. She held her arms up in the air in jubilation, as though there was an audience applauding beyond the spotlight.

The only noise that broke this soundless fantasy was a sharp *crack*! The board splintered beneath the girl's feet and she fell into the ball up to her knees. She looked down in utter disappointment, and too late she realized...she was sinking into the ball! But she didn't struggle. She wasn't afraid, she was almost...happy. She looked a little contented-at sinking into...what looked like...her grave. A child's grave, made so she could rest happily after her torturous death.

The singular sound of tactless, arrogant applause broached from the shadows as Korson stepped into the middle of the ring. The broken plank was healed again, but had fallen next to the ball. Korson picked it up and looked it once over. He then placed it on the ball-with a grace I would not have thought possible from one as abrasive as he-and he slowly released it from his grasp, and backed away just as slowly. The plank remained perfectly balanced.

Korson turned his evil, fanged face to my mind's eye and went, "Blah!" I awoke with a start, his uncanny laughter fading into the distance, the image of his face burned away by the light of the sun and his laughter drowned out by the buzzing of my alarm.

Part 3: I am the Devil!

One evening, after Heather had been up all the previous night, she found it extremely difficult to get out of bed. She understandably felt quite tired and seriously considered trying to get a good night's sleep for a change. But something had Talissa more excited than usual, and she kept insisting that Heather accompany her in her celebrations.

And who was she to turn down a good time?

They were getting into bars and dancing the night away, so it was quite enjoyable for a girl Heather's age (she was now sixteen), who had been dreaming of clubbing it for a few years now.

And Talissa had begun to look at Heather differently now, too. She had this gleam in her eye. It made her shudder to be looked at like this. She put it out of her mind, just happy to be with her friend, out in the beautiful night, enjoying what Montréal had to offer.

They walked along the streets looking at the buildings and the people, like they always did, and sometimes they tried to guess what that person did or what they were like. Heather, who was a little bit shy at the outset with people she'd just met, would watch in wonderment as Talissa would ease up next to the meanest, crustiest looking hombre and manage to draw his face into a smile. Heather loved watching her use this art she had. It was a cultivated practice, came with years of experience. The ability to slip in and out of a social setting was one thing. Talissa created these settings out of thin air, ambling up next to a lone person and seconds later looking like an old friend. It looked like a damned instinct, she was so good at it, as though she had some psychic power. If she wanted to make a living as a prostitute, she had the perfect skill for it.

"I only wish I could be so casual with people, the way you are," Heather would say to her.

"Sweetie, in time you'll be even better than I am. You, my dear, have a charm that cannot be taught-innocence. You'd be amazed at how powerful that can be. You just have to open up more."

Heather would always talk to Talissa about the world. She loved Talissa's stories of places far away and long ago. They would sit on the patio of a rooftop restaurant, Heather drunk on alcohol, Talissa drunk on blood, and watch the sky turning above them. Heather would be staring at the purple-black sky listening to Talissa, and once in a while would be jolted into looking at her by something she said; something so vivid about the past.

"You've an excellent memory," Heather would tell her, "it sounds like you were there."

"And what makes you think that I wasn't?" Talissa would ask her.

"Well, that would make you so old you'd be farting dust!" Heather would laugh. Then they would smile at each other and go back to looking at the empty sky.

It was always Talissa who would shock Heather with something that she said, or did. Some of the things Talissa did were to be taken as the product of a sick mind. She seemed to have a good heart but could only accomplish something with violence. Like the time when she had Heather save the puppy, afterwards she came out of that alley with her lips dripping and bloody, her fingers dripping with strawberry juice, and she said something that Heather couldn't quite understand but her voice was so demonic because it was throaty and deep. When Talissa licked the blood that clung to her lips, she closed her eyes and looked upwards, she was in a state of utter orgasm like Munch's Madonna.

Put these two together and they were somewhat of a yin-yang, Heather the black swirl and Talissa the white. But there is a dab of white on black and black on white, so don't think for one minute that you know which colour is really beneath.

And then one day, it was Heather who made Talissa tear her eyes off the sky and look at her.

"My mom's out for the night," said Heather.

"I know," answered Talissa, "we didn't have to sneak you out, remember?"

"So...I was thinking maybe we could stay out all night and wait for the sun to come up."

This was when Talissa, for the first time since Heather had known her, seemed at a loss for words. Seconds passed and those turned into minutes, and all the while Heather tried to suppress a grin that was triumphant, boasting. She had gained an upper hand, they both knew it, and Heather respectfully let the next move go to Talissa rather than push any farther-at least for now.

"I have business to take care of and I have to get going before the time the sun would rise."

"Hey, I risked my neck many nights by sneaking out with you. What is so important that you can't enjoy one little sunrise with your best friend? Hm?"

Try to get out of this one, Talissa.

"Well, see...I kind of keep weird hours, I despise the heat, so I get things done when it's dark." She tried not to stammer much as she thrust out her excuses. Heather was good at exposing liars.

"Oh," said Heather, "I see. That's believable, really, even though it is winter. We'll just have to make it sunset then."

Talissa rubbed her temples in exasperation. One would think that someone who lived for centuries would get his or her excuses in order, but no, fooling around seems to be a priority. And it was well past the time that Talissa could use her vampiric powers, because Heather had known too much already. It just goes to show you-give someone an eternity and they squander it, if it is at all possible to squander forever.

"Listen," said Heather. "I am pretty damn positive that when you came out of that alley you were unclean. I do have a somewhat religious upbringing and I'm not sure if I even want to say what you are-by saying so it's kind of like actually acknowledging that you are real and really what I think you are-and that scares me so much because it means that you've befriended me for a reason."

"And will you resist me? I, who has centuries to wear you down. I, who has a power over you that you can hardly dream of."

Those strawberry juice lips, that sweet and divine nectar.

Heather sat there under the canopy of night, thinking of all that had happened to her. The 'poison' that had claimed Patrick, the things she'd done while roaming the intoxicating night-she'd actually slid a knife into a man and it felt more than good; it was exhilarating. There was an unseen connection between murder and immortality.

The thought of having centuries to do with what you pleased rather than following the same rank and desolate establishment that lorded over working class life. To be young and strong forever. To have power and authority over people.

"No," she said, "I want eternity. I want to live forever, and I'll pay the price. I want to be tall and strong and free, and alive, while everything around me crumbles to dust with age. I've thought about it for a while. I was mad at you because of what you did to Patrick. But I realized that it would have happened anyway. It happened with my father. Death came to claim him before his time and I have no control over him unless I become one of his agents.

"Nothing matters to me anymore. Life has lost it's...it's luster, and I don't really know why. My food doesn't taste the same; each day feels like another pointless step towards the inevitable. Maybe because I know it's going to end? I want to be able to tell hundred year old stories like you do. The end seems so near, yet I'm still so young. I can't bear to die. I can't stand the thought of time flowing like a racing river while I rot in a tinderbox."

A salty tear crawled down her warm, red cheek. "Make me what you are!" she pleaded in a hoarse whisper.

"You can't even say what I am! All this over-dramatization! All this agony! How mortal! And you can't even say the word!"

Heather whispered, "You're a vampire..."

"Scream it," dared Talissa.

"I'm not going to scream it in the middle of a fucking café."

"What do you have to lose? I'm putting myself at risk here."

"Yeah, it's only my dignity on the line."

"You're such a little wallflower!" laughed Talissa. "I love it! Priceless!"

The waiter came over to see if they needed to order anything else. He knelt, arms on the table, flirtatious, "Ladies, how would you like to try a fabulous drink?"

Heather said, "I wouldn't mind, but my friend here has discriminating tastes."

The waiter smiled at Talissa and said, "A connoisseur, eh?"

"You might say that," said Talissa.

"We'll show you a trick," said Heather. "Put your arm on the table. No, wrist up." And Heather put her hand on his to hold him down. "Now tap the vein three times. Make a wish." The waiter closed his eyes for a moment. "Done?" He nodded. "Now look at my friend here. She's a vampire!"

The waiter glanced between the two awaiting a punch line.

"And what's the point?" he asked.

"Try not to scream when you die," said Heather, tightening her grip on his arm and stuffing a napkin into his mouth before he could react. Of course, Heather didn't have the strength to hold him down on her own, and Talissa gave her ample aid by clamping her jaws around his wrist after bearing her fangs maliciously. It would be logical to assume that some of the other diners at the café would have taken notice of the murder scene. Some were too self-absorbed, too ignorant of their surroundings, to take notice. And Talissa was a skilled huntress, she clamped one hand firmly around the neck of the waiter, piercing his windpipe. Such might and strength! He could barely thrash, he couldn't manage a scream as little rivers of blood flowed out from the wounds made by Talissa's nails. She sucked his arm so hard it nearly shriveled, and when she was done-in under sixty seconds, mind you-she adroitly hid the body beneath the table so her feet would have something to play with.

"That was a little unexpected," she said, swaying from the dizziness of having drunk litres of blood in a mere moment. The redness was rushing to her face.

"I like to be creative. I couldn't just scream out you're a vampire!"

"Creativity is the only thing that fills this empty, endless world."

"You sound fucking drunk, for God's sake!"

Talissa just put forth her wide-mouthed grin, a little laugh.

"I drew a picture of you once, when I was younger. I still have it, I think. I could never draw too well but for some reason, this one came out beautiful. I'd keep it near whenever you were gone for a long time, to make me feel better." The backdrop of the café became a syrup of figures that coalesced into a mass of shape and colour. It stuck to the corner of Heather's eye but never once dared to interfere with her concentration.

"Does that picture mean something to you? You talk of it as if it does." Talissa looked at Heather's face, ripe and keen under the moonlight. Not a pang of guilt touched her withered, dying conscience that she would let the finger of evil touch such a sweetly beautiful face. "Would you keep that picture safe from decay?"

"I'm not sure. I guess I would, but with you here it ceases to be important," she answered, uncertainty punctuating her response.

"And if I were to leave forever? Then would it majically gain importance where once it had no meaning whatsoever?"

Heather looked at the sky full of empty. It was clear, which made it apparent that nothing was hidden there that would provide any insight for her. She ground out her cigarette with her toe and looked back across the table, ready to resume the conversation.

"Is art important? Does it have meaning but what we give it? Of course art has meaning. It means different things to different people, but it has meaning because society gives it meaning. And that meaning is rated by commerce. The more commerce a piece of art can gather, the better it is. The businessman uses the artist as much as he can, careful not to go *too* far, because he knows that his well being is rooted in the work of the artist. If he were to anger the artist beyond his breaking point, he would lose his source of income. And that scares him more than he could ever scare the artist.

"But still he steps on him. The best artists are those who can gain fame by shunning mass appeal. But they are caught in a loop-if they're really good, people will like them. How do they maintain their integrity?"

"Is art always about maintaining your integrity?"

"It isn't about popularity! It's a deep personal expression from within. It has nothing to do with getting people to like you, it's about the sheer honesty of the soul."

Talissa laughed, said, "Honesty of the soul? Does it always have to be so profound? Does everything have to have meaning? A why? What about functionless art? You've got some interesting people running around doing some cool shit, and it might not even mean a thing."

"You of all people have no cause to criticize functionless art. If it weren't for functionless art, there would be no vampire literature."

"So? What do I care if people write myths about me? Whether they're right or wrong, things they're clueless about! Things they don't know shit about, have no possibility of experiencing. How can you write about what you haven't experienced?"

"Because it validates you," said Heather. "Look around you! You're not a part of all this! You're a dream, T'lissa. You're a dream for people with lost souls. Sometimes you can cross over into their reality and steal a little piece of existence. Then you sink back to the shadows. You exist, but you aren't alive. It's sheer majic that keeps your eyes open. Dying is a part of life and you haven't lived till you've died.

"It doesn't matter if they've experienced it. They've thought about it. They've lived it in their minds, and the mind doesn't know the difference between reality and fiction."

Talissa was astounded at such insight, such vision, from a mere mortal. She sat gazing at Heather's beautiful visage. Her light blond hair made a perfect frame for her face, which had a pleasing roundness to it, her cheeks full and tinted red. Her eyes were a deep, dark, delicate blue that was reminiscent of ocean water on a beautiful afternoon. To watch them was to be mesmerized by their waves that lapped in her irises. Her smile had a vivaciousness that was positively infectious, a narcotic for the eyes. "Are you sure you want to go through with this?"

"Yes," answered Heather, letting the word snake out of her mouth. Eternity awaited her.

"Then stay, and watch the sun come up." And with that, Talissa got up and moved to Heather. She ran her fingers through the strands of gold that were Heather's hair and she smiled. Then she disappeared, like a spirit, like she'd never been, and left Heather to watch the sun come up, and she hoped that she would appreciate it. If she ever saw it again, it would burn.

Heather slept most of the next day away. The greatest luxury of being on March break was that you could sleep till two in the afternoon if you wanted to, so she took the opportunity. She woke to the heat of the sun on her back, making her slick with sweat. She rolled over and the light blazed into her eyes, white hot.

"It won't be so hard never seeing the sun again," she decided to herself.

She got out of bed, didn't bother to put on her robe since no one was home, and went downstairs to get something to eat. Opening the fridge, she saw what emptiness and desolation really were. There was not a thing to eat, at least not something you'd want when you first got up. She resigned herself to juice and cookies, and began to read the newspaper. The front-page headline showed another kidnapping, with no clues as to who could have committed it or where the child was taken. A nightlong search turned up nothing, and further investigations were likely to do the same.

Another Night Stalker's bombing as well. What *was* this city coming to?

The morning sun didn't hit the kitchen, being at the back of the house. Heather decided to sit in the bay window of the den, which was at the front of the house, so she could have some light and warmth. She picked up her food, grabbed a few more cookies and refilled her glass, and headed for the den, planting herself in a plush recliner, which was positioned so she could see out the window. She drew the curtains open just a little.

She nibbled away on her food and she slowly got the feeling of not being alone. She looked back into the house and the doors to her father's den caught her stare and fixed it for a substantial moment. Was he watching her or did the dead just die? That room had hardly been touched since Albert Langden died, and whenever someone walked in there, a layer of dust could be seen to have accumulated on his books and side table. She brushed off the presence in the room. It was a *remnant*, nothing more. Her father was no more than bones, and a room that some people had seen him sit in.

She went back to her paper and would glance up every once in a while to see the people and cars that were passing by. It was about ten or fifteen minutes before she realized that one of the neighbours had been staring at her curled up in her chair, and she then remembered she had nothing on but her underwear. It was Vincent, the boy from down the street, and he was leaning on the fence and trying quite hard not to suppress a grin. He was probably about twelve or thirteen now, Heather wasn't sure. Her cheeks rouged a bit, and she was at a loss, not sure if she should pull back the curtain or tell the guy to get away or both. One thing was for certain, it made her feel like an exhibitionist, this young boy watching her. They stared at each other for a full minute, neither one sure what to do exactly. Heather's spine tingled from the fact that someone had taken notice of her among the curtains, and even more so from the fact that it was someone who was just learning the meaning of the word puberty.

She was about to lift her hand up when she saw him do so, and he tilted it back and forth in the air a few times as if to say so-so, with a smirk breaking through his face. Heather laughed at him, the crudely urbane thirteen-year-old. He had also taken about five steps forward. She motioned with her finger that he should continue to come forward, and she got up to open the door for him, still wondering if she should bother with a robe.

She opened the door to him, and about his calm, collected exterior, which he had exuded all along, a twinge of trembling and excitement was evident.

"Vincent, right?" asked Heather. He had dark straight hair, which immediately began to drive Heather feral. Her hand did all it could to stop itself from getting lost in its luxuriance.

"Uh, yeah. Your name's Heather, isn't it?" he asked, his voice resisting the urge to crack, his heart beating at an inhuman pace. Heather smiled and nodded slightly to tell him he was right. She felt glad that he remembered who she was, and wondered how long he had been trying to steal a glance at her in the window when he passed by. Lord knows she hadn't given his presence a thought since she met him, which was probably five years ago now. She looked him up and down, noticing that he was kind of skinny, but his body looked on the verge of breaking out, growing. He had indeed come a long way from a skimpy seven.

Heather strolled away from the door, turning her back on Vincent without a comment, and she heard the door close behind her.

"Should I take my shoes off?" he asked her. Heather nodded, again with a smile and said sure. Vincent removed his shoes and walked a little further into the house to catch up with Heather, who had wandered back to her chair in the den, her knees against her chest. She told him to sit on the couch and he obediently obeyed.

"You're not embarrassed?" he asked her.

"Do you think I have a reason to be?" Heather said to him, with no reproach. He looked her up and down slowly, thoughtfully, his eyes stopping longingly between her thighs. Then he answered, "No, you shouldn't be embarrassed at all. It's just that most girls wouldn't be showing off like this."

Heather ran her fingers through her blond hair, the sun tinting it strawberry, enjoying how velvety soft it was today. She hooked her finger in her lower lip and fixed her stare on Vincent's eyes. He was going to be fought over by many a girl some day that was for certain.

"You're lucky. Today, I'm pretending it's my last day on earth and I've decided to enjoy it however the hell I feel like." She got up out of the recliner, away from the beam of heat that was coming in through the window and stretched languidly in the middle of the room, her arms out high in the air, her breasts pressing full against their restraints to break free. She then bent down and massaged her calf for a moment and walked over to where Vincent was sitting. She touched the side of his face and her fingers found his hair, which sent a shiver throughout her body, both of excitement and nervousness.

"Follow," she said to him, trying to make her voice sound like silk. Again he obediently obeyed. Heather led the way up to her room.

She sat him down on her bed, taking off his shirt, every once in a while glancing at his puppy dog eyes that looked up at her with innocence. Sometimes he looked like a man and sometimes he still looked like a boy the way he did now, and that pushed Heather forward, making her heart thump fiercely in her chest. She ran her hands over his chest, over his nipples, feeling the hardness of them. She knew his hands were cold from being nervous, and Vincent stiffened a little at first but then relaxed, pliant to her touch. His skin was hot and Heather closed her eyes to concentrate fully on its texture, which was smooth and silky, as if he'd barely been touched by the harshness of the world and it had left him still feeling baby soft. It made Heather shudder with pleasure to touch him. She could feel the hairs just breaking through on his chest, and they, too, were soft. She knelt to kiss his nipple and as her mouth passed his ear she whispered his name, *Vincent*, softly, her breath landing hotly on his lobe. And his hand found the small of her back and touched it gently, like he was afraid he might break her flesh if he were to do anything wrong. His hand was chill and trembling a bit, but after a moment his fingertips settled more firmly on her back and his palm followed slowly. He began to lean back onto the bed, partly because he was pulling her down, partly because Heather urged him back. He liked it when she urged him. They rolled over a bit so they were each on their side, Heather's hand under his face, her other hand on his shoulder. He reached down and struggled with his zipper, awkwardly sliding out of his pants, not wanting to break the position they were in. When he finished, Heather drew him closer to her, and she felt his hardness against her belly button. She shivered with animal excitement. He looked away from her eyes to her breasts and Heather smiled coyly. She pulled the straps of her bra off her shoulders to tease him a bit, but his hands seemed to have other thoughts. He pulled at the straps eagerly, but she stopped him and turned so her back was to him, telling him it would be easier if he would just unhook her. Bright boy, it only took him a minute to figure it out. Heather pulled her bra off slowly, one shoulder at a time, again to tease him, then turned over with her back to the ceiling before facing his hungry eyes again. He put his hand gently to her full, well-shaped breasts and massaged them slowly. He reached lower with his other hand and snuck his way beneath her underwear to feel the silk that was hidden there. Heather helped him by taking off her panties for him and he made his way deeper, searching for her inside. His hands fondled the orifice and probed deeper a little harshly, until his fingers felt the slick membrane that enticed from within, and he began to massage every inch of it. Heather's hips began to move with the rhythm of his fingers, a slow methodical beat that matched both Heather's and Vincent's pounding hearts. She grasped tight to him as she shuddered with pleasure and he pulled his hand away from her fire.

    She sighed and moved lower, kissing his chest and stomach, and teasing at the flecks of hairs that led a trail to beneath his waist. He was completely ready for her and she claimed him with her mouth, all at once. He throbbed and threatened inside of her as her tongue worked its way up and down, around in circles. She expected him to be quick, but she kept him inside her anyway, the danger of his explosion exciting her. Vincent's hand clenched at her hair and she released him, putting his sex between her breasts and smothering him with her soft, supple bosom. His thrusts became agitated and quick, and he couldn't control himself anymore as he released his passion over her. They lay there, exhausted and exhilarated.

    Heather got up and went to the bathroom to get a towel to clean herself off with, and she brought it back to her room, mostly to tease Vincent with her nakedness. He lay there and looked at her with puppy dog eyes and she felt a touch of guilt at seeing him look so innocent when he was no longer. Guilt, or excitement? No question, her guilt turned into excitement and drove her towards him, even now after being satisfied. She went downstairs, naked, not caring if someone else saw her in the window.

    Right now, I'd fuck them all, she said to herself. *By tomorrow, I'll be dead anyway.* She spotted her plate of cookies and brought them upstairs for Vincent and herself to eat. He had probably worked up as much of an appetite as she, and when she went back to her room she could tell by the way he was slumped that she was right. He had pulled the blankets up to his waist to diminish his self-consciousness.

    Without being asked, he took one of the cookies off the plate and ate it in two quick bites. After a while longer, Heather told him that he would have to leave, as she had some things to get done. When he asked if he could come back tomorrow she told him, "Sure," knowing full well that she would be found dead by the next day.

    Night blanketed Montréal, darkening its streets, the moon and street lamps competing to see who could cast the more ghoulish shadows. The city, especially *rue Ste-Catherine,* only catnapped very early in the morning. It was to *Ste-Catherine* that Heather decided to walk. She had waited till night had fallen, a slow tantalizing wait that was delayed by that intermediate called evening. She watched the yolk of the sun break on the surface of the horizon and turn to orange and then a deep grapefruit, and finally to bloody crimson before its light turned completely to syrup and flowed in a rivulet to shine on the other side of the world.

    She dressed in snug but warm clothing, her pants black and her top orange like the ball of the sun. She ate her last meal, savouring the sweet liquor of hot, syrupy chocolate bursting out of fluffy pancakes with each bite she took; the moist, smooth richness of cheesecake buried in strawberry jam and the sweet soft bite of the cocoa graham crust making her mouth numb with sugar.

    And she looked at her mother, who seemed, in the year and four months since the loss of Albert to have merely accepted that she was to live her remaining years alone, with no one to share her life with. Her happiness had died with her husband. She still had some of her looks left, and the suitors to prove it, but she was content to let them pass her by. It seems guilt had been born when Albert had died.

    Heather didn't agonize over how her mother would react to losing yet another member of her family. She was going to leave her utterly alone, and it bothered her that it didn't bother her. But she thought of how her mother disrespected her father and it left a taste in her mouth quite the opposite from flapjacks and cheesecake.

    Heather walked out of her house and turned east on to *rue Ste-Catherine*, the wind warm and soothing at her lobes. Night kisses. She could smell change in the air, she knew that tonight would be a night of opportunity. The question was how to find Talissa to initiate the change.

    Ah, transaction. When dealing with Devils and doctors, one made a transaction, a deal.

    Where did one go to seek out immortality? The answer was somewhere, out in the openness of nature, lurking about in the deep richness of the city. She could smell the electricity that buzzed out of downtown, the life. The one that awaited her, perhaps? Tonight was the beginning of her second life, the one that would never end.

Heather stopped for a moment, to inhale a breath, to remember what it was like to feel mortal. She closed her eyes and let herself bathe in the smells, the sound, the kiss of the warm wind.

How would this feel the next evening, when I'm an immortal? she asked herself. The thought struck her fully for the first time: an *immortal. I will never die. I will never be sick, or grow old, or anything so mundane and trivial as that. Leave that for the rest of God-forsaken humanity.*

She continued on, more slowly this time, having eternity ahead of her to do with what she wished, and it was only a short while before the buzzing electricity of downtown Montréal enveloped her. She had become certain that Talissa would come find her tonight, seek her out, to bestow the gift. Unless maybe...maybe she was watching. Heather gazed languidly towards the darkened sky, seeking out the puffy, smoky white clouds that hung there. Was Talissa's presence holding them there? Was she in there, a part of the sky, able to look down upon civilization, demiurgical in her power? Heather slowed her pace a little again, letting the gaze she felt from above, whether it was real or imagined, peer down upon her. She wondered how long Talissa had lived. She wondered how she'd managed to survive the years, viewing the changes of the world with animal eyes, watching friends and loved ones die while she moved forward with each turn of the earth, staying one brief step ahead of time and decay. She wondered what fuelled her desire to keep going.

Heather felt some strange *press* on her mind and shoulders.

Heather had walked along *rue Ste-Catherine*, looking at all the familiar sights, seeing for the first time how they contrasted one another. At the corner of rue Bishop was a Catholic Church, one of many in Montréal and not far was another one, also along *rue Ste-Catherine*. They sandwiched bars and nightclubs and places where women did exotic and sexual things for drunk, sweaty men who gave them money, and sometimes gifts. If you were to stand on the right street corner, then sin and salvation could be at your fingertips.

What was it to be a vampire? Sinful or redeeming? For God's sake, to drink the very blood of His children and to live in probity of Him and see His schemes to fruition, can there be any benediction more worthy of His glory?

If, perhaps, one day you happen to meet a man of Italian and French descent, a Mr. Vachon, first name Sal, you should be kind to him. He *could* do you a favour. But then again, transactions...

Anyway, it was a convenient arrangement for someone who had a guilty conscience. She (Heather) continued past the church and closer to the flashing lights that proclaimed their sin a doorstep away from the almighty saviour, and shortly she reached the corner of *Ste-Catherine* and rue University. She stopped and turned a slow, lazy circle where she stood, surveying the area, trying to compare it to a mental picture of how it looked bathed in the golden light of the sun. Her mind was not acute enough to do it justice, but her eyes peered at the crossroads she'd reached. She felt a tug, two actually, and she knew that the direction she chose was both literal and symbolic. She could continue on her preordained path, and lead the life that was fated to virtually every living soul on the planet. Or she could turn, down rue University, and find her new direction. She looked down the road and felt a tug. She saw haze, a distortion in the warm air that swirled down the street. She felt power. The choices she had to make were exciting, enticing. She crossed the street, taking a few steps in her original direction, teasing at the power she felt from down University. By the time she reached the opposite curb, the tug gripped and seized at her, pulling her by her skin to come towards it, to taste of its secrets. There was a strange urgency in its clutch, something eerie, something that awakened a slight disturbance in Heather, which she refuted as the overworking of her fear, her nervousness, her overactive imagination. Maybe her life was a figment of her imagination, too? She stood another moment on the corner furthest from the potency, the puissance that she felt tugging at her soul. She lingered to tease it, showing it that she was strong enough to throw immortality into the river if it suited her whim.

Then she crossed. She made her way across the street, towards the presence that emanated for her sole audience. The people in the street, those who crossed her field of vision, whose voices reached her ears, whose perfumes stung her smell, they were oblivious. Except for one, who slowed his pace, his wife on his arm, speaking in an eloquent French tongue while he, he turned his attention to the spot for the briefest moment. He felt or saw a disturbance, and maybe he would have stopped, maybe if he were alone, without the momentum of his darling's feet to keep his in motion, he could possibly have stopped.

Or not. He brushed aside the oddity as a bubble in his brain, one that was small and insignificant, that went **POP**! And he continued, turning his gaze and thoughts to make his darling his focus once more. This man was merely ignorant. In that respect he was more fortunate than most. It meant that he had abilities, that his mind was open to possibilities. He just chose to dismiss them. The rest of the lot was quite oblivious. Heather stopped for a second and watched him disappear down *rue Ste-Catherine*.

Almost, she thought. *You could have known everything*. And what would happen if he did?

Then Heather turned. She crossed over, back to the west side of the street and walked listlessly down toward the presence, the one that now actively beckoned to her. She made no exhibition of eagerness, nothing to say that she was overjoyed to be presented this gift. She still teased it, as it in turn teased her, letting only the barest essence of its existence be felt. It was now an absence. Heather's heart began to race a bit at the absence, she thought it may have misunderstood her playfulness and left, thinking the gift of eternal life too grave for one so juvenile. She took a few quickened, clumsy steps and let her agitation show on her face, her confidence draining away somewhat.

"Please," she whispered, her voice pleading for the presence to return. Her eyes showed the signs of regret at having mocked immortality with her childish games. She shed a tear in penance for her foolishness, and felt, as if in acceptance of her apology, an unnatural wind come to wash the lone tear away. The absence left.

Heather continued forward, slowly, respectfully, until she felt herself awash in the presence. She looked about her and noticed that her journey had taken her to where she encountered the puppy-beater. Her first kill. She remembered what it was like to stab the man, to drain him of his life, and it made her feel like she had been ready for a long time, ready to assume the role of executioner now that she realized she'd been judge and jury once before. She moved into the alcove where she had lain the shit to waste, her heart thump-thumping under her breast. She closed her eyes and waited for the gift to be bestowed.

She felt a hot breath at her neck, Talissa's breath, and she opened her eyes just a sliver to glance back at the beauty that would bring her life through death; that promised the ultimate happiness through the ultimate ending. She felt strong hands take hold of her arms and felt the press of Talissa's body against her back.

"Do you still choose what I offer?" asked Talissa, her minute fangs sharply grazing Heather's ear. "Will you wallow for eternity in attrition?"

"No. I want your gift. But don't make me beg for it. I have paid already. I have endured what you've shown me, I've kept your secrets. My soul has strength. I know I can be with you forever."

"I want to be with you forever, too," answered Talissa. "And you have learned some eccentric and unusual lessons. You've learned life and death, sorrow and ecstasy. You learned how real your dreams can be. But there is one more lesson, the one that will signal the end of your mortality, your life."

"I will endure it," said Heather, a shiver passing over her entire body, her throat coarse. She felt Talissa's grip on her arm, and now her face, and she felt vulnerable, timorous.

"You don't even know what it is! You don't know what it is to die! You don't even know what it is to *live!*"

"You've loved me and wanted me as your companion. What you offer is going to hurt. To know pain is to live. To inflict pain is to be a God."

"My little tigress. Even when threatened with death your beautifully strong spirit engages me to no end. You know me too well. And it hurts me to have to do this but it is necessary. Your final step *is* pain. I have grown to love you, first from a distance, then near. But for you to join me forever I must cause you-"

"Do it quick," said Heather through clenched eyes. "I can take the hurt if it means forever." She felt every muscle in her body constricting from the thought of agonizing pain. Talissa's breath scratched at her throat, a precursor to the venomous bite that would bring her into another world. "Don't antagonize me anymore. Finish what you started years ago. I can't bear the sun anymore."

With that, Talissa's lips moistened a spot on Heather's neck, as if tenderizing it like steak, making it soft for her to be able to tear a hole in the flesh. Heather felt Talissa's eye teeth pricking, teasing at the skin of her neck, and finally felt them break the surface and enter into her veins, Talissa's tongue slowly lapping away, her lips clamped over the surgical wound so as not to spill a drop. Heather felt the gush leaving her neck, and she did her best not to make a sound, quelling a scream that still managed to find its way beyond her lips, only to die as a disappointing moan. Her legs began to weaken as the bite got deeper, and the pain she felt showered down to her arms and back and stomach, and then became a hazy numbness as a fugue encompassed her. She felt Talissa's iron grip on her face and around her waist, holding her tight as if she might float away if there was nothing to keep her moored to the earth.

Heather saw a dot of inky blackness hanging in the air above her, what she at first took to be spots of delirium floating in her eyes. And Heather couldn't quite be sure, because of the weakness, the loss of blood, but she thought she heard a belligerent laugh issue forth from the blackness.

Heather felt herself falling all of a sudden-her head tilted back and her legs lifted, her arms spread out to provide her with some semblance of balance. She still felt feather light while she fell, like someone had turned the world upside down and inside out so as to confuse her. She could still have been floating for all she knew, or simply spinning. The paradox brought her some giddiness. She realized she had been falling when her head thudded on the pavement, but such a long fall it seemed! She opened her eyes to look out of the alcove, out to the street that had very few people on it. If she had had any desire to call for help, there would be little chance of an answer anyway. Besides, she doubted if anyone could have spotted them in the shadows, the ones that had come to life to hide from view what passersby were forbidden to see. She looked up to see Talissa on her knees next to her, her head bent so as to draw the attention of Heather's eyes. She felt entirely soporific, felt as though she would slip away at any moment.

"Come," said Talissa. "Find the strength within yourself to take back the life that I've stolen from you." She held her wrist out over Heather's lifeless head. Heather uttered, barely audibly, that she hadn't the strength to lift her head up, that she didn't know what to do.

"Take back your life. Take the way I took it."

"I...can't," Heather answered her, her voice making audible the weakness in her body.

"Then you will die."

Heather felt a choking in her throat, as though Talissa's power had held death's grip at bay and now her words had called him forth.

(Or was it the Shadow, entering her mouth and choking her like some wretch in a rag who lived as black smoke?)

Heather gathered her meager strength, and tried to pull herself upward to the wrist that held life. It took her several attempts to get just halfway there, and a few more to finally clamp her jaw on to Talissa's arm. She bit her teeth down. Nothing. "I can't," she said to Talissa. She felt her life draining.

"Use your eye teeth," Talissa told her. She did, biting as hard as she could, with as much strength as was allotted to her. She tried over and over to break Talissa's alabaster skin, and nearly gave up hope when a single drop of blood touched her lower lip. It gave her the bit of desire she needed to continue with this perverse deed. She dug her teeth deeper and made a sloppy, crooked tear in the flesh, and blood began to flow languidly over her lips, into her throat, down her chin. She lapped at it, hungry for blood, felt the power that was carried in the salty warmth. And there was a strange familiarity to the taste.

She felt herself renewed, felt her body grow strong, while an ecstasy washed over her like never before. She felt her body turn preternatural with every passing moment. Until Talissa pulled her wrist away.

"I'm not finished," said Heather. "I need more."

"Not from me you won't," stated Talissa firmly. "You're on your own, to satisfy your own needs now." Talissa walked out of the alcove and down the street, and Heather was so stunned at the fact that she was left to her own devices that it took her a moment to follow.

"Wait!" she said. "You can't just leave me here by myself. I have no idea what to do." But it was too late. Talissa had disappeared, like she'd never been down this street tonight. Heather touched at the wound at her neck-it had begun to heal and would be completely so before dawn. She wiped the rivulets of blood that were on her chin and drank them up, a shudder of relief tingling her spine as she swallowed.

But anger overcame her swiftly, and she turned and screamed up at the sky, "You bitch! I fucking hate you!!" Then it subsided as quickly as it came.

She looked around at the street, at her hands, her new vampire skin. She felt her eyeteeth with her finger-they were small but razor sharp. Her hair was still a beautiful gold, but it felt silkier than it did before. It had a sheen, as did her skin, which looked paler. She could see her veins thumping at various points of her body, like they had desires of their own now.

Looking around, she saw the world with a glow that it never had before. Whenever she shifted her gaze to something in particular, it would jump out at her, alive. She had the sight of a cat, or fox. Lights were brighter and shadows no longer hid things from her. She could pierce the very darkness with her vision!

She walked back to *rue Ste-Catherine*, turning west towards her home. Her head was constantly craned upwards and around, looking at everything her range of vision would allow. It seemed as though objects were slightly convexed and blurry at the limit of her field of vision. The incredible focus was clearly in the centre region. It gave her a view that was suited to hunting a target, forcing her to fix her gaze upon her prey to keep it in clarity. She wondered if Talissa saw this way. She'd have to remember to ask the bitch when she managed to catch up with her.

The blur was slight, and was at the farthest reaches of her field of vision, and it seemed an extremely minor inconvenience. Especially when she took into account her other senses, which had heightened considerably. It made her feel incorporeal. She could put her senses to use for survival, for hunting. Before they were mere accessories, tools that could be done without if necessary. Now, though, they were highly honed weapons.

Her ears picked up sounds that were from around corners, or a far distance off; no one would be sneaking up on her soon. Her sense of smell was equally adroit. It noticed every nuance of a scent, every ebb in the wind-she could sniff out her prey. She inhaled deeply of the world, of the new smells she could acquire by breathing in. Some were so intensely familiar, and so intense, that it made her dizzy. Others, though, were completely alien, as though there were another world that was denied by lack of scent. She concentrated on these foreign scents for a moment. A strange desire welled up in her abdomen. She realized that this desire would increase when someone passed close to her, that the smell would get quite strong, and she recognized it as the potent scent of blood. It was like smelling the noxious fumes of boiling acid. Her desire for it waxed, indignantly. There was a perversity that erupted in her, and she tried to quell the desire and diminish her disdain, but it fought its way to the surface of her instinct- it became an utter priority. She felt the need to drink like one felt the need to relieve a forbidden, secret urge. She pushed it down, grappling with its indomitable will, telling it later, not where the throngs of tourists congregate. The struggle within her nearly brought her to tears and vomit.

The wind shifted, bringing a distraction. She smelled blood again, but blood with a taint. And she had a desire to find it, yes, but she did not have an overwhelming hunger to consume it. Heather allowed herself to forget her desire while her senses were distracted. It seemed that her senses, now preternaturally strong, were not hers to control, at least not without some practice. She began to move on, making her way towards her home in Westmount where there wouldn't be so many people to overwhelm and overload her. She concentrated on the tainted scent. What was it? Was it someone with a disease? Was it animal's blood?

Another vampire!

The thought crossed her mind with a flash of insight-she hadn't even thought of finding another vampire, obsessed as she was with Talissa. If there was one, and she just became one, it was guaranteed that there must be others. She picked up her pace considerably, not realizing that in her excitement she was becoming a blur to those who saw her whisk by. A brisk walk to her looked like a sprint to mortal eyes.

She reached the border of Westmount, at *rue Ste-Catherine* and Atwater. Another few minutes walk and she would be in the middle of the richest region in

Montréal. And with all the money in the world they couldn't by what she had in her possession-true power and eternal life.

It made her think. She thought about the energy she felt now, and then thought about the years, the centuries, that lay ahead of her. There was so much ahead of her that the horizon was hidden by sheer distance. How much could her power grow? She prayed that she was not the weakest vampire ever because it would be an obstinate cancer on the world for there to be someone who was stronger. What would stop such a creature from unleashing itself on humanity? Who could stop it if it did?

Heather looked around at what she saw on this street corner. The air of dilapidation could be smelt. Just waiting for a statute of limitation to expire so it could settle itself in. The corner was just the slightest bit unclean and it was like something important used to be here but left because the majic had died. It was shameful that no one had seen fit to preserve the electricity that used to be here. It felt as cold and heartless as a museum; and no one went to museums anymore.

Heather drew in some breath, a slow drag on the wind. She could barely smell the Taint anymore. The wind had shifted a bit and she was no longer down wind from it. Maybe it had caught her scent too, whatever it was. And now she could barely make it out, like it had purposely hidden itself from her.

Or perhaps not. It sounded unlikely that one could hide one's scent, but anything was possible, as she'd seen.

Heather continued on into Westmount, towards the mansions that stood stately on the sloping terrain. She felt the desire gurgle in her belly, but since the streets were empty, the smell of blood locked behind brick and mortar, she was able to force it to subside. At least for a bit. She knew she'd have to find her first victim soon. It was like a sexual hunger that couldn't be masturbated away. This was an instinct that had to be fulfilled. It was so different than just being hungry for food. People skipped meals all the time. It became apparent that vampires *had* to be satiated.

The tall trees and darkened sky conspired to overwhelm Heather. It was a drastic change from the lights and flash of downtown Montréal, although it was only moments away. The streets were quiet, dim, with the dignified mansions looming overtop, looking down upon passersby with the watchful eye of a King surveying his subjects. Why had she come here? She first thought she would look upon her house, perhaps for the last time. But she'd avoided the street altogether.

Maybe a wander in familiar streets? Perhaps. There was very little to find here in the way of prey, since most had gone to bed. The throngs were downtown. But, alas, Heather preferred it empty. Allowed one to have time to think. Someone was bound to walk by, and until then she would gape at the vista ahead, around her. She would only think of the kill when there was prey to stalk. Only a few hours into immortality and already a huntress's callousness.

A few streets away, Heather's attention turned to a woman in a window. She was middle-aged, but still attractive, her face barely touched by age and wrinkles. She sat in front of the television, watching a show, but every once in a while would do something curious. She would get up, walk over to the stairs, put her hand on the rail as if to go up, then turn away, go to the kitchen (which Heather could barely see-her acute sense of hearing made up for that completely), get a glass of water, fill it, pour it out without taking a sip, and sit back down in the den, scrunch herself in the leather recliner and rock back and forth. She would do something like this every few minutes or so.

Sometimes she'd pick up the phone and then hang it up in mid-dial. She looked agitated, more so with every passing moment. She also looked sick to her stomach. Heather wondered what could have her so tortured and tormented. A muffled yelp from the upstairs carried her answer. Heather peered upwards, scanned for a window with some activity behind it. She caught movement in one of them but couldn't make it out from her low vantage point. She looked at the old oak that stood metres away. It would allow her perfect view if she were to climb it. She placed her hands on the bark, hesitantly.

I've never climbed a tree in my life, she thought to herself. Another muffled shriek from the window forced her into making an attempt. She amazed herself. After a few clumsily set footings, Heather climbed the old oak like a pro. She found her agility had increased, along with her strength. Her hands gripped the bark with ease and her feet gave powerful pushes to move her upwards. She found a suitably strong branch and sat in its crook, her knees against her chest, and looked directly into the window.

She saw a girl, the daughter, in her nightgown, and a man, the father and husband, wearing the remains of a suit, his tie partially undone, his pants wrinkled. His hand held the daughter's arm tight, while the other undid the buttons of her nightgown. Whenever the girl would struggle the father would increase his grip tenfold. When she uttered, "Daddy, don't," he silenced her with a look, or a smack like he was beating a puppy.

She looked barely thirteen. When the father had gotten frustrated, alcohol making him left-handed, he tore the nightgown so the girl's pubescent breast fell out, his fingers fondling her virginal nipple. Downstairs, the mother continued her distracted routine.

Heather's face flushed red and hot, and she descended the oak so fast she may as well have jumped down from where she sat. She walked over to the house, standing under the window, ready to burst through in malice. Scaling the brick would be no problem. But something stopped her. She knew that hurting the father, scaring him, would only be a temporary deterrent. Eventually he would slip back to his old ways, and back into his daughter. The girl let out another cry and her mother responded to the stimuli with another distracted routine. How the hell did Talissa get into a locked house? Heather decided to let her anger simmer a bit. Maybe calm was required.

Rationality and calm. She would go to the front door, ring the bell, and confront the mother. Maybe the woman just needed to realize that someone might have noticed what was going on and she'd get off her cowardly ass and call the police. That's what she would do. Heather marched up to the front door, and rang the bell. It was only a moment before the mother answered, her face stained with signs of sorrow.

"*Oui*, can I help you?" the lady asked in broken English. "You look pale, my dear, is something wrong?"

"I heard a scream, from upstairs. I thought something may be wrong," answered Heather.

"No, my dear, you are mistaken. I heard nothing and have been awake all evening." A cry, muffled and desperate, came again. The woman at the door stood frozen, petrified.

"Madame, your daughter is being abused." Heather tried to state this as flatly as she could, but her voice choked on the last words. "Do something," she urged.

"Please," insisted the woman, "go away. If you interfere she will get hurt. He'll beat her after you've gone."

"Call the police, Madame!"

"The police can't be here all the time. I don't want my daughter taken from me." Tears streaked the woman's cheeks, her face now looking much older than it had moments ago. Trauma had made her look older than she really was when she clearly should have looked younger. But the pleading look on the woman's face couldn't soften or dissuade Heather. She pushed past, almost misjudging her newfound strength, and made for the stairs.

"If you won't do anything, Madame, I will." She climbed the stairs fast, the woman in teary pursuit, begging her alternately in French and English not to interfere, that it would only make things worse. Heather ignored her pleas, intent on injuring the bastard at the top of the stairs. The daughter's anguish had increased in volume, and Heather burst into the room.

The daughter was bent over the bed, her face pushed into a pillow so she could barely breathe. The father's pants were around his ankles, he was inside his own daughter and not even the tears that soaked the pillow, or the screams that died in the down, had given him any pause. He continued to take what he obviously would not be granted by any other woman other than by force. And even at that, he had to pick a thirteen-year-old girl.

His face showed astonished bewilderment at having been caught in the act. It was shifting into anger, anger at the stranger in his house, anger at his wife standing behind her, bleeding tears of sickness and revulsion, anger because someone had the fucking gall to walk in on him! Who dares disturb the master of this house? Who dares question the actions of the man who earned hundreds of thousands of dollars to provide for his family? Well, if they didn't like it they could goddamn leave! And he would have said so to Heather, this strange young bitch who had no place being here, except it was Heather who had gotten mad first. For the first time in her short immortal life she bared her fangs, keen and cusped. Her face contorted, her soft, ocean blue eyes blazed boiling and black and charred while a faint, almost suppressed guttural snarl escaped her lips, which had retracted to form a voluptuous frame for her fatal fangs. Her blond hair framed her face in a way that made her look devilishly angelic. She advanced upon the bastard, and he backed away in fear, afraid of the unknown that came towards him. Heather felt the desire rise in her, till it reached a crescendo, and it burst. There was no stopping her now. She grabbed hold of the man firmly, the way he held his little girl and said to him, "Is this what you enjoy? Do you still like it rough?"

He choked on useless words and thrashed pointlessly. Nothing could save him now. He was no longer fat and powerful, just fat. Heather wrenched his head back, cracking a bone in his neck. She bit, cleaner than she had before but still a ragged, disorderly tear in the man's flesh. She drank of him while the mother held her daughter, both of them crying at what had happened and what was happening. Heather let the steaming, salty blood rush to the back of her throat and into her. She felt the man's soul leave his body, felt the maliciousness with which he treated others go with it. Serenity remained in its place, a quiet rapture between her and the sustenance that imbibed her, saturated her to the capillaries. It made her feel more in control of her capacity.

The man went limp in her arms. She dropped him to the floor and he made a thud. She was glad that he was dead, disgusted that he had been allowed to live in such luxury. Someone should have stepped on him a long time ago, crushed him like a cockroach.

Heather felt the warmth circulate her, lapping over her and going right to her toes and fingertips. She looked at the mother who clutched the girl in her arms, whispering tearful apologies to her daughter. The girl thankfully resembled the mother more than the father, which comforted Heather for some unknown reason. The girl was beyond tears, beyond feeling, her eyes devoid and vacuous. The only sign of animation from her was a short, shallow breath and an occasional fluttering blink.

"Will she be okay, Madame?" asked Heather, as softly as she could so as not to startle the pair, what with blood splattered over her chin. The mother looked at her, speechless, and looked at her dead husband, then back at Heather with abhorrence. Heather moved closer, slowly, to comfort the mother, to tell her that everything would be okay. The woman pulled back, yelled at Heather to stay away, leave them alone, despite Heather's assurances. The woman trembled in fear of Heather, the *vampire* Heather, and suddenly it struck her: *I'm a monster*, thought Heather. She looked at her art on the floor. She'd certainly been efficacious. But wasn't that what she wanted when she saw the father sodomizing his own daughter? The revulsion she felt must be human, mortal. Didn't she leave that part of herself behind hours ago? The daughter lay against her mother, catatonic.

"This is your fault, Madame," said Heather. "You should have stopped him."

Then she walked out of the room without a backward glance, though she was tempted to look at the diorama she'd created. Maybe she was a good artist, though her tools were repulsive, and her brush deadly. She wasn't sure. All she wanted to do was get out of the house before the mother had the time to realize that she should scream. All this was sloppy, not worthy of a good haunting. Next time she would have to be more careful. It was stupid to let the woman and the girl watch while she drank. She should have taken the man somewhere remote. Too late now, anyway.

"Oh, shit, I got blood on my shirt," said Heather, grimacing at the stain. She smiled and gave a short laugh as the absurdity of the situation struck her, clashing with the reality all around. She lifted her arms up and bounded down the street singing, "I am the DE-vil, I am the DE-vil," sounding like a schoolyard child who'd just won a game of tag. She strangely felt more complete without Talissa around, like there were more possibilities for her.

Heather walked up to *boul. de Maisonneuve*, trying to put out of her mind the incident that just occurred. She walked distracted, without any sense of direction, taking no notice of who came near to her. She ended up sitting on a curb at the corner of *de Maisonneuve* and Metcalfe, not far from her home. She thought about what had happened, why that man did what he did to his daughter. It was mammonism, pure and simple. That was what had skewered that man's morals. What he couldn't buy, he took.

Heather looked up at the sky, which had looked a little lighter. Whereas downtown she saw action and excitement, here everything was quiet. Here, at night, everything settled to a molasses pace. Everyone had gone to bed, or stayed in their homes. But the undercurrent of this wealthy community, when the lights had gone out and there were no men in suits and women in dresses to act as solicitor, to show passersby that they live in perfect comfort and contentment, was a lurking melancholy. It oozed beneath the surface, hidden by palatial mansions and behind expensive smiles and painted faces. But it didn't make it better. The wealth only served to act as a shield for the corruption that could easily be seen in less fortunate communities. It wasn't really about money, though. It was about power, of which money was a means to an end. And, now that she felt true power, it sickened Heather Langden more than anything.

Heather found her way back to her house. The faintest bit of light that was visible to her brightened only the tiniest bit, but it made her aware of a problem- where was she to sleep? Where would she go every night when the sun came up, whose rays were surely deadly? It was obvious that she couldn't live at home and not make any appearances during the daylight hours. She had died for real, now she had to figure out some way to fake her own death in the real world. She wondered how long she'd be able to put off leading a normal life till she came up with something. Maybe draw the shades real tight and fake a fever?

Being only hours old, not counting her mortal life, Heather had a sort of instinct in her, one that gave her an intrinsic fear of sunlight. It was much like a bad allergy, when someone knew that if they ate peanuts they would die, so they avoided them like the plague. The instinct was within Heather but it lay somewhat dormant, only because there was nothing that would have triggered that fear yet. She'd never, of course, been exposed to sunlight when it could do her harm.

As she walked towards her house, though, she felt flushed and warm. Sun up, the deadly dawn, was fast approaching, less than an hour away. She felt the warmth, and it felt like her head would catch fire. It *burned*.

"If you can't stand the heat, get out of Hell's Kitchen."

Heather spun around, startled at the voice when she thought no one to be near. She was relieved when she saw Talissa standing a few metres away. Somehow, it didn't surprise her that she appeared at an alarmingly appropriate moment.

"What?" Heather queried.

"Calm down. It's just a saying. I've always kind of liked it. Don't you?"

"It's lovely. Now where the fuck have you been all night?!" Heather's face, now chalky from death, became flushed.

"Temper, temper. You may be a vampire but don't forget that you're still a lady." Talissa smiled coyly at her. "I left you alone because it's the best way for you to learn. You did well for your first night."

"You were watching me?" said Heather, astonished.

"For most of the night. The exciting parts, anyway. Now we don't have time for chit-chat, we have to fake your death. Come, up to your room." She hustled Heather along, who had become a little speechless. She wondered how Talissa could be so insensitive to things like death. She herself had some apprehension about killing herself for the public record. It was one thing to die and be reborn, but to actually die, officially, now that frightened her. She thought of her mother, alone and in tears.

Heather began to climb into her window via the trellis, a late night ritual. She was no more than a quarter of the way when Talissa grabbed her about the waist, and climbed with such swiftness and confidence, especially considering the fact that she only had one free hand to use. She scurried up the side of the house like a lizard, or a rat. They both entered the window and Heather readied herself for bed. She lay down in her bed, got herself comfortable, and looked at Talissa. She saw a dim brightness from her skin, one that had looked different than when she saw with dull, mortal eyes. There was more beauty to be had with vampire vision. Would it dull after an eternity?

"How am I to die?" asked Heather. She said it more calmly than she thought she would. A melancholy had set upon her mood. Despite the brightening sky she felt a gloominess. Talissa just smiled at her, softly, gently, somewhat reassuringly. She bent over her head and placed a kiss on Heather's smooth, pale skin. She kissed Heather's cheek. Heather felt her body weaken, go cold and flaccid. Talissa gave her a vampire's kiss to her neck, like the one she had received shortly after dusk. Only this one had drained Heather of the vampiric power. She felt only a glimmer of life in her body. A faint ember that barely glowed. She felt a sharp prick on her arm. And she heard Talissa whisper something in her ear. An apology? She wasn't sure. With the last bit of strength, she fluttered her lids open, saw Talissa gazing back at her from in front of the window, her brown eyes puppy dog sad, and turning reluctantly to leave. As the sun began to break the horizon, Heather felt the sting of its pain searing her flesh, and she lost what little consciousness she had left in her.

Part 4: Last Rites

That morning, I changed into beige dress pants, a white button down shirt with blue pinstripes and a conservative tie. I then made my way to the funeral of Heather Langden, hoping the heat wouldn't make me too sweaty. It was to be held at the *Cimetière Mount Royal*, in the middle of the pentacle that shaped the Montréal murders. I noticed, of course, the obvious coincidence.

I'd called a trusted acquaintance of mine at the morgue, asked him if he knew of the circumstances surrounding the death of Heather Langden.

"Well, the official report," he began, *"lists the cause of death as* Meningococcal meningitis. *The tests showed signs of the bacteria on her spinal cord and brain. There was some evidence that she may have also had* Menningococcal septicaemia. *But none of the tests for that were conclusive."* He explained that the same bacteria as meningitis caused septicaemia, but that the two are not necessarily present concurrently in the host.

"Septicaemia is a form of blood poisoning," he said. *"Her mother had called the family GP and told her of the symptoms of heavy fever, vomiting, delusions. Changes in mental state. She began sleeping long hours mostly during the day. She couldn't stand bright lights of any kind. The GP tells the lady to drag her in here immediately, but by the time she can get the girl to the hospital she's DOA."*

He lit up a cigarette. I guess there was no one to complain but the dead bodies.

"But, shit, Graham, if that girl wasn't missing litres of blood. I couldn't find one concrete explanation."

"So you didn't report it?"

"I left it out. For God's sake, the girl is dead. Let her rest. There's no need to have me tear her body apart. If someone asks, she vomited it into the toilet before she was carted off to Emergency. Sometimes it's better to keep you mouth shut about these things. YOU of all people should know that." Of course. Well, that evened us up for the favour.

"I admire your morals, Logan, really I do. But do you know that there's a murderer out there? Are you going to take the risk of burying the evidence?"

"Graham, she died of Meningococcal *meningitis with the possibility of* septicaemia. *I have the plate counts and five other tests to prove it."* He took a deep drag on his smoke, squinted his eyes a bit. *"I know it's not glorious, but at least everyone can move on as quickly as possible."*

Too long in a morgue. Death meant nothing, another body on the pile. But I knew Heather Langden was more than that.

Heather. Langden. Her name tumbled through my head. She was a victim of a vampire's fatal bite.

I entered the church as quietly as possible and murmured to the usher that I was a friend of the family, and he urged me quietly to a seat at the back.

The church was sparsely populated, most of the people mourners. I noticed Heather's mother tearfully seated at the front, flanked by aunts and uncles who handed her tissues and patted her hand.

The service was short, yet eloquent, after which time each person was allowed to approach the coffin to have a private moment with the late Heather Langden. I waited until almost everyone had had his or her chance at viewing before I took my turn.

I just sat and stared at the coffin, trying to picture the girl inside. I stared numbly, trying to think of the emotions that all these people who'd been close to the girl were feeling, trying to feel the empathy of the situation. It just made me feel cold and tired.

I was roused by a scream, and Heather writhed and blood dripped from her mouth and fingers and the coffin shook and the mourners just cried like nothing was happening but the scream was so feral and deafening and the girl was a demon rising-

I snapped my head and looked around. The last of the mourners went to the coffin one by one, the church silent but for sniffles against tissue.

When I got near to the coffin, what I saw made my heart weep. Lying in the coffin was a girl who was astonishingly beautiful. She looked as though she were merely sleeping, waiting to be awoken by a knight's kiss. Her hair was a radiant, deep gold which made her look like an angel. Her skin was pale, white, and when the sun brightened up the church enough it made her hair light up like a soft flame and her skin glow aureately. I looked at her youth, her beauty, and thought how unfair it was that she had to die so young, with so much life to look forward to.

The service made its way to the cemetery, the cars chugging and struggling to climb the mountain while maintaining a pace that was appropriate for a funeral procession. After a few more brief words by the minister, they began to lower Heather's casket into the ground. All were silent, except for the distant sounds of children in the *Parc Mont-Royal*, the odd car that passed by, and nature, to whom this was merely part of the cycle. Give and take. The grind of the gears that lowered the coffin scratched at my spine, like chalk on a board.

Finally, Susan broke into tears to cover her tears. She'd been crying all along, but these tears were the deep ones. Seeing her daughter being lowered, a pile of earth waiting to be thrown on top of her with the horrid sound of the shovel scooping into the mound of dirt. The tears were because of the finality of the situation, and when it came time for her to throw in a ceremonial handful of earth, she nearly followed it into the grave. She was escorted to her car by her cousin, her face soaking wet. As they passed by me, I tried not to look at her, to look away, but couldn't help myself.

As people began to filter out, as the custodians of the cemetery began to fill in the grave so the only thing making it discernable from the rest of the world was a stone marker, I thought of the tragedy that had ended this girl's life so young. The book was closed on the life of Heather Langden, the final chapter scripted in disease and dirt.

Book 2:

The Orange and the Purple

Part 1: The Majician

The plane gave a sharp drop, which awoke Jerome from his slumber. He returned his seat to an upright position, then took a look out the window to watch the approach. The skyline of Toronto always interested him with its geometries. The buildings, running low for most of it, then broken by the needle of the CN tower that stuck up in the middle of the air. The clusters of glass high-rises where big business took place. He took the candy offered him by the stewardess, and sucked on it so his ears wouldn't pop. He always enjoyed the bump when the plane touched down.

He waited until most of the passengers cleared out before he did so, not being in any hurry. Then he grabbed his carry-on from the overhead and headed for the luggage pick-up, which, thankfully, didn't take too long. He then made his way out to find himself a cab, but got a nice little surprise instead.

"Hi, Clyde," said Jerome. "Nice to see you."

Clyde smiled his slightly slovenly grin. It always looked like he was chewing on something.

"Hey, Jerome." Clyde spoke in a sluggish and laggard way, because he was somewhat dull, and had been from birth. But with patience and kindness, one would fond out that he was an amicable person, the type that was nice to everyone and just wanted to be friends with you. "I thought you'd...need a ride."

"Clyde, my man, you are too good a person. I told you I'd find my own way to the city."

"Sorry Jerome." Clyde hung his head forlornly and scratched his pot-belly.

"Hey, perk up, buddy. I'm kind of in the mood for company anyway." Clyde's smile brightened immediately. "You know..." said Jerome thoughtfully, "I was thinking that I'd maybe open up a deli down here soon. Maybe you'd like to work for me if I do?"

"I'd love...to, Jerome. But I do like working at the school, too."

"I thought some of the kids made fun of you there."

"Only a few...but the principal doesn't let them, if he catches them. Most the rest are nice...real nice to me."

They got into Clyde's beat up old car, a clunker with some of the most charming rust spots you've ever seen, and headed east on the 401 to Clyde's home in North York, which was just north of the city of Toronto. Clyde's apartment, actually, was just a few minutes walking from the Toronto border, which was at Eglinton. Clyde's house was north of that, just off of Bathurst St.

When they arrived at his apartment, which was a basement of a small, lovely old house, Jerome got settled in, after which they both sat down to a midnight snack of leftover Chinese food. Both of them fell asleep half way through an old movie that was playing on the television.

The next day, Jerome woke up to find Clyde gone. Clyde worked as a custodian in a school. He would probably be home by mid-afternoon. Jerome made himself breakfast, showered, changed into shorts and a T-shirt, and began to go about his business, calling friends and business associates. Later in the day he took the bus to the eastern side, looking for potential locations for a new deli. Half-hearted comments had a way of growing into big projects with Jerome.

When Jerome returned to Clyde's apartment, he found Clyde there.

"Hey...there, Jerome," said Clyde, his sloppy, lovable grin etch-a-sketched on his face. "Did you go to...the carnival today?" Clyde was in one of his boisterous and eager moods. Clyde was usually in a boisterous and eager mood. Sometimes he would calm down or get tired and then he would just be eager.

"Nah," said Jerome, "I thought you'd want to come along, keep me company or something."

"That was thought...ful of you Jerome. You're a friend!" Clyde's smile was brimming at the thought of going to Carnival.

"First, though, we eat. I went to the grocery store and picked up something to make for dinner. Your favorite: tapioca pudding and bloody steak."

"And...?" Clyde's eyes were wide and drooling with anticipation. "And?"

Jerome smiled a grin that was full of slyness and chuckles, his hand digging in a grocery bag.

"Chives. I could never forget the chives." Clyde loved chives, and was known to munch on them for the sheer of joy of it. Jerome tossed him a stalk to nibble on, which he did contentedly.

They ate well, and sat around talking after dinner, letting their meal settle. Jerome munched on a small cigar. Clyde was the only person in the world who didn't mind this habit of his. They watched the evening news, sometimes discussing the what they saw, sometimes turning the conversation to inane chatter.

Clyde was entertainment enough, sometimes. Certainly more witty and informative than the news.

After both had rested, they changed into something warmer for the coming night, and made their way to Carnival by bus. In Toronto, carnivals popped up everywhere once the summer started. They were the classic traveling circus show, setting up in parking lots of malls for two weeks then moving on. There were probably ten or so that could be found every summer, and the one that took place every year at the corner of Victoria Park & Eglinton was the biggest and the best. It had everything anyone could want in a carnival. Rides, both mechanical and animal, side shows, events, psychics, homemade baked goods. The bus ride was about half an hour from Clyde's place, which Jerome was unused to because in Montréal, everything was about ten minutes from everything else, people wanting to live life rather than drive to it.

They stepped off the bus, and from the street corner could feel the electricity tingling and licking at their senses. There was a certain mysticism about carnivals for Jerome, and Clyde too. They both got caught up in the atmosphere, the smell, the noise. They crossed the street and went over to the ticket wicket at the front to buy some rides tickets. They went on a few-the Ferris Wheel and the Vortex amused Clyde to no end-and then decided to do some wandering, maybe sample the delicious smell coming from the bake section. Jerome made more than one stop at the beer tent.

"Hear ye, hear ye!" blared a man with a megaphone and top hat, and the crowd quieted somewhat. "Once again we would like to thank each and every one of you for joining us on the opening day of the sixty-fifth annual Queen's Fair carnival." A slight congratulatory applause, to which the crier smiled congenially and held up his hand to say he wasn't finished. "In honour of our long and esteemed yearly celebration, and as thanks for your very loyal patronage over the generations, we would be pleased to offer every child under twelve free cotton candy before ten o'clock, after which we would ask the parents to put them in their beds, where they belong." Slight chuckles. The man then placed the megaphone on the podium that was beside him, and from his sleeve pulled a long red and green handkerchief. He showed both sides of it to the audience, proving it was ordinary in all respects. He then lightly tossed it above his head and allowed it to feather down onto his hand, which was positioned palm up, his fingers and thumb meeting in a point. He snapped the fingers of his other hand and, in a swift, blinding motion yanked the kerchief from his hand to reveal a bright, pink fluff of cotton candy, which he presented to a boy in the front row who was so grateful that he took his finger out of his nose and grinned a toothy grin.

"Ah ah," said the man. "Pink is for ladies." And he withdrew the saccharine gift. The boy's smile faded and his eyes became moist with disbelief and disappointment. The man placed his fingers at the base of the cardboard stand that held the cotton candy, with the candy part pointing towards his body. He took the red-green kerchief and let it settle over the candy and his arm. With his other hand he pulled quickly on the cardboard holder, the kerchief fluttering a moment before deciding to touch ground.

"Blue," he said to the boy, who accepted the proffered sweetness with a new found grin and snotty fingers. The crowd gave polite applause for the man, mingled with a few sighs of satisfaction at his kindness. The man stroked his white mustache, satisfied with his handiwork.

"Things like that give me a warm fuzzy," smiled Clyde. "I'm in the mood for cotton candy," he said, slathering. Jerome rolled his eyes in friendly exasperation and went to get Clyde a stick. They wandered the Carnival some more, took a few more rides, saw a magic show (by the man with the megaphone), and afterwards stopped to talk to the Majician, who was quite an amiable and genteel old fellow. He happened to also run the Carnival. He amused them with a few tricks, took out a deck of cards to play a friendly game of poker (Jerome was astonished, he'd never lost to someone with five aces in his hand; Clyde didn't catch on until he saw the trick for a second time), and they even learned a trick or two, albeit simple ones. It was getting late, and Clyde had to work tomorrow, while Jerome wanted to meet some friends downtown to sample some of the nightlife and catch up on old times. They promised the Majician that they would be back the next day at the very latest, especially since they still had a couple of rides tickets. He smiled and tipped his top hat, retreating into the darkness of his tent.

Jerome took the bus home with Clyde to make sure he got there okay before heading south to Queen St. and some late night enjoyment. Jerome met three of his friends when he got down there. They grabbed a late night snack at a bar and grill before heading over to a club to dance the night away.

The next day, Jerome woke with a haze over to his head, one that bordered on a hangover. His temple throbbed. He went to the kitchen to get some breakfast, and upon checking the time, decided to call it lunch instead. Potato, patato. Clyde would be home in a couple of hours and until then he would relax with soaps and talk shows and aspirin to clear his head.

Clyde came home at three-thirty, a little later than usual. He was all excited about going back to Carnival tonight, and wanted to go early so they could have plenty of time to see everything twice.

"Can we meet...the Majician, Jerome?" he asked with no little enthusiasm.

"If we see him we'll meet him. Now, let's work on dinner cause I'm famished."

Clyde's fridge had just enough food for a few days, partly because he was so fickle and partly because he didn't have the foresight to plan any farther ahead than that. After looking through the fridge, freezer and cupboards and taking a thorough verbal inventory, they both agreed on ordering in. Exactly what they would order was another question entirely, but after seven suggestions (run through two or three times each) and a coin flip (which turned into best two out of three, then best three out of five, before Jerome finally acquiesced), they settled on chicken wings, a double order at that. Shortly after dinner they went outside and walked off their meal for a bit before catching the bus to Carnival. It was still light out, which bothered Jerome a bit. He much preferred the atmosphere after dark, but he was patient and willing to bide his time. Besides, he wasn't going to nit-pick, it was just that beer tasted better after dark. The more Carnival the better. That's the main reason he came to Toronto, anyway.

When they got there, they were both shocked. The place was teeming with police and paramedics. They had cordoned off a large area near the Ferris Wheel and were questioning quite a few people who were now witnesses to something. Jerome and Clyde moved as close as they could to the action and stood watching with morbid curiosity for a long while. Their patience was rewarded, albeit woefully, when they saw the body of a boy who looked to be in his early teens lying face first on the asphalt. Clyde hung his head in mourning, his eyes moistening with regret at having witnessed such a sad display. He loved teenagers, or little grown-ups as he called them, and hated to see them a victim to the sick mess that growing up had become these days. He noticed a boy sitting in the back of a police car and made a connection. He felt both anger and shame that someone so young could have dreamt of this scenario and committed it. Jerome just stared stoically at the scene, taking in every detail. He wondered what the world was coming to. A hand on his shoulder woke him from his excogitation. He turned to see the Majician, his top hat pushed back on his head like a baseball cap, his white gloved hands locked at the fingers, thumbs twiddling respectfully, distractedly and slowly. He looked forlorn, restrained. Neither said anything for a minute, allowing the scene before them to speak on its own behalf.

"Such...tragedy," said the Majician. Jerome noticed, for the first time, that he had a slight Slavic accent, which added to his mystique. "Never in my life has one of my festival begotten such an event as this. It is shameful."

Jerome looked at him, tried to look down, to think of something to say. "Well, it isn't your fault. Don't blame yourself." The words tripped on the way out over his lips. A police radio made annoying Rice Krispie Sounds. It seemed strange to see in one direction a murderer and victim, in another a Carnival which looked like a slice of the fifties come alive, preserved for pleasure, and in between the Majician with his gloves, his mustache and goatee and knee length satin cape, black on the outside, red on the other, seeming Victorian. He looked like the conduit through which these two eras could mingle, he stood out yet no one noticed him, like he was invisible, or didn't exist.

He smiled a wry, dry smile and turned away from the scene, the red flashing lights illuminating him rhythmically, and took a step.

"I put an aura round this place," he said, now looking slightly skyward. He spoke in slow, melodramatic tones. "Sometimes though..." he paused with a sigh. "Sometimes human nature can override it if the emotions are powerful enough." There was a longing in his dark eyes. "Enough. Come. I will entertain you myself. There is no need to let everyone be saddened."

The three of them walked over to the Majician's tent, where he pulled out a deck of cards, and they all sat at a table.

"What did you mean, there was an aura around here?" asked Jerome. The Majician grinned again, almost chuckled. Jerome waited patiently for him to answer. Clyde munched on some chives.

"The majic you see me perform on stage is parlor." He placed the Jack of Clubs between his palms, and, pulling them apart in a flash, showed the card to be gone. He turned over the deck of cards in front of him to reveal the bottom card. It was, of course, the same Jack. Jerome's eyes looked on in wonder. Clyde smiled warmly and scratched his ample belly. "I do parlor to make a living, entertaining the masses. But sometimes even majic has its limitations on the subconscious mind."

"So this aura makes people want to spend money," said Jerome.

"No, no. I would never use majic to cheat someone out of a dollar. I do not play Three Card Monte on the street. This aura keeps people from thinking bad thoughts, from feeling sad. But all it really does is make the atmosphere more festive. If people choose not to spend money here my spell will not sway them. At that, it is a weak spell anyway."

"So it's parlor majic."

"Again, no." The Majician's mood seemed to be brightening a little, having taken his mind off the tragic events of before. "It's a conjuration. You can't learn a trick like that out of a children's majic book. The parlor majic can be duplicated with some practice, quickness of the hands. If I were to ask you to pick a card, and tell you that I could find it after you've returned it to the deck, you would trust that I could do so?" Jerome nodded and chose a card from the proffered deck. He memorized it and returned it to the deck, after which the Majician found it. "But see," the Majician said, turning the deck upside down. "I have flipped the bottom card, so the deck looks upright no matter which way I hold it. When you returned the card I need only search for the one that was returned upside down. A simple trick that can amuse someone till his eye knows to look for my turning the deck." Jerome took the deck in his hands, fondling it absently.

"So you started learning parlor majic, then you moved up to white majic?"

The Majician laughed a short, breathy laugh. "You misunderstand. Black and White aren't kinds of majic! They are merely metaphors that are used to distinguish. Majic is merely majic. It is the Majician who makes it black or white. It is the Majician who chooses to suck the energy of those around him to perform the conjurations. Alas, in recent years, people have lost their faith. The few practitioners of majic left have mostly turned, lulled by thoughts of grandeur and power. Others have given up, becoming believers of science." Again the Majician looked forlorn, like he'd seen another die.

"Then you're dying. You're endanger of becoming extinct," said Jerome.

"Like the dinosaurs," added Clyde. He made the room seem happier for a second.

"There will always be someone."

Jerome was confused. "But if the few left are evil, then-"

"Where there is evil there is good, and vice versa," interrupted the Majician. "It can be seen everywhere. For years my Carnival has been the sight of joviality and cheer. But today a stain has been placed upon it. Nothing is completely good, nor completely evil. All is a part of the cycle. Some would say that evil does not exist, that some people do harm but are not evil."

"Well," said Jerome, with triumph in his eyes, "what about a nuclear missile. Where's the good in that?"

"Why, it is neither good nor evil! It is the one who uses the technology that makes it wicked."

"But is it possible to put that technology to good use? What good can come from something that is built to destroy?" Jerome knew he had him there.

"You are right. The missile itself cannot be put to good use. But the nuclear capabilities can."

Somehow Jerome's victory seemed a bit hollow because of the Majicians geniality. He didn't expect him to admit he was wrong, but it showed he had class, a distinguished air about him.

"What other spells can you do?" Jerome's curiosity turned back to the majic.

"Well, I'm quite good at auras. I can conjure them, sense them. Your friend here, for example, has a warm pinkish aura. It means he is extremely and purely kind. And honest."

"That's Clyde. So you can see these without any majic phrases?"

"True majic is the training of the subconscious mind, whereas parlor majic is the training of the quickness of the hands. Majic is a belief."

Jerome thought for a moment, while the Majician dealt a hand of Blackjack out to the three of them. "How would you go about picking a successor? Would he have to be psychic, then?"

"It would help. But it can be learned by the one with a strong aura too." Jerome pulled out at cigarette, and the Majician made his hand into a fist with the thumb inside. He then flicked out his thumb, upon which a blue-orange flame flickered. Jerome lit his cigarette off of it, amused and delighted. The Majician blew out the flame, charismatically. He smiled at the wisps of smoke that hung in the air. "I find fire simply beautiful, cleansing even." He paused. "That, for instance, was the power of the mind over oxygen."

"Ah," said Jerome. "Now you sound like a scientist."

"Oh, my friend. So naive, so naive. I never said science and majic were at odds! They are both part of this world, albeit they encompass different realms of it.

But they do tend to overlap, sometimes greatly. It is today's society that has chosen to believe solely in science, while abandoning majic."

"But why? Both could be put to good use, couldn't they? I'm sure that what medical science can't cure, majic may be able to help out with. I've heard of faith healers and people who turn to voodoo to cure diseases because drugs don't, and they end up alive because of it."

"People lost their faith because of Charlatans and the truth. Even as recently as the early nineteen-hundreds, there were people who sold miracle cures from traveling wagons. They were bottles of alcohol, nothing more. These people were out to make a fast buck, and that created a distrust between the common folk and majicians. That and the fact that the general public didn't have ready access to majic. But people have easy access to science. One need only to read a book and comprehend. They see the proof of science in ink. Majic can be read from the Book of Shadows of the Majician, and from old, old books for spells, but comprehension is not so complete without training the mind. The Majician must build his laboratory in the brain, and that takes time and practice and patience. It is not something that can be learned by rote. It is much more than a skill. It isn't a truth, it isn't empirical. Science is fact. Majic is an art."

The three of them played cards and talked, Jerome and the Majician debating and bantering back and forth, Clyde eagerly listening to what was said, just happy to be a part of the group. The Majician had decided to retire for the night and gave them each a ticket for a ride on the Ferris Wheel before saying goodnight.

"And you, my friend," he said to Jerome, "I suggest you visit our gypsy." He motioned in the direction of a tent on his right. "I believe you would find her intriguing."

Clyde and Jerome did some more wandering, rode the Ferris Wheel and some other rides, grabbed a sausage before heading over to the beer tent to relax. Clyde, who rarely drank more than one had a few with Jerome, who rarely stopped at one. It was a sort of tradition for Clyde, *a few beers with my buddy Jerome*, he would say.

Now, both of them reasonably imbibed, they decided to walk out among the open air again, to absorb some aura.

"Jerome..." said Clyde, "did you believe what the Magician was telling us?"

Jerome smiled at Clyde's child-like innocence. "He seemed very sincere, that's for sure. I'm sure he believed every word he spoke. Whether it was all true or not, I don't know."

"But what...about his flaming thumb?" asked Clyde.

"Shit," said Jerome. "You got me there. But then again, people have come up with incredible majic tricks, and it comes only with practice. It's their job to deceive you, so they spend lots of time thinking up ways to do it."

"It isn't too hard to deceive me, Jerome!" They both laughed. Clyde was great at laughing at himself, although few made fun of him. He tended to do plenty of that himself.

"Y'know, Clyde...if I didn't know better, I'd have to say that you have low self-esteem. But knowing you as well as I do, I can honestly say that you make those jokes about yourself because you're confident in the person that you are." Clyde just grinned and blushed a bit.

It was getting later into the night, so the air had cooled a bit, though the humidity of summer still hovered threateningly, waiting for the next day to unleash its dry wrath. The crowds had thinned somewhat, and in a couple of hours the only people left would be clean up staff and the performers. Jerome and Clyde walked a little ways, thinking of maybe going home, when Jerome noticed the Gypsy's tent. He decided to go in, the Majician having piqued his curiosity. Clyde agreed, as long as the would go home after. Clyde was not a late night person.

They approached the tent, not sure if they should walk in or not. All was dark inside, until a small flicker of candle light caught their attention.

"Jerome, I don't feel so good in my stomach. I'm going to find a bathroom."

"Shouldn't have had that last one. Meet me here after?" Clyde agreed, and left to search for facilities. Jerome turned his attention back to the candle light from inside, its illumination offering no insight into the interior of the tent. Jerome decided to just go in, nothing to be gained by standing at an empty doorway.

As he entered, he began to see bits and pieces of the furnishings, which was good, since he didn't want to bump into anything. He noticed the tables and stands to the edge of the tent, which seemed bigger than it looked from the outside, and the exotic bottles that were on them. One in particular contained a light green liquid that seemed to glow dully. "This must be the black majic tent," muttered Jerome under his breath.

"You wish to challenge the Gypsy, do you?" said a voice, which was grating and thickly Slavic. The candle flared a little brighter, allowing Jerome some vision to see who startled him.

"Shit! Don't do that! Uh, I was just sort of saying, y'know? A kind of joke."

The old lady who was sitting behind the table harrumphed. She was dressed in typical gypsy fashion, a shawl wrapped around her stout, bent frame. A scarf was wrapped around her head, and a gold necklace tick-tocked back and forth from her neck.

"You should have more respect for the powers that are around you. You young people mock what you do not know, coming in here and asking for your palm readings. I should open a telephone service if I wish to do that. Seventy-five cents a minute. What do you think?" The Gypsy scowled, more so than what was her usual.

"I didn't mean to mock you. The Majician sent me here."

"For what?" The Gypsy's voice was even more grating than before. Jerome had not won any trust.

"He said I'd...like you."

The Gypsy's scowl turned to a snarl. "Sit down, then. I'll read your palm." She spat the order, like it disgusted her to have to put with a visitor.

"What else do you do? I mean, if you don't like palm reading, you could do something else. The Majician said something about auras."

The Gypsy, almost intrigued, picked up the candle by its brass holder and, wax dripping on the table, held it close to Jerome so that he felt its heat on his cheek. "Oh, my," said the Gypsy; she almost began to sound kind. "You do have an aura about you. The Majician was right."

"So, what kind of aura do I have?" Jerome felt a little more comfortable and began to show some eagerness. The old Gypsy lady studied him with an earnest look on her face before answering.

"First, you pay," she said gruffly. She slammed down a jar full of folded old five dollar bills in front of Jerome. He pulled out a crisp, purple ten, folded it neatly, and thoughtfully placed it into the coffer. The lady nodded approvingly and withdrew the jar, this time politely, having been satisfied with the generosity.

"You are in balance, spiritually. Your life is as you would have it, but...on the horizon there is a disturbance. It ebbs and flows in your aura, sometimes growing large and disruptive, other times receding to utter blackness. The choices you make decide the magnitude of the disturbance."

"So something bad is going to happen in the future?" asked Jerome, almost nonchalantly.

"No, not necessarily bad, you could become rich and it will lead to problems with a spouse, so something like that. Or you could die." Was she joking?

"But what is it that's going to happen?"

"You don't listen, maybe you need a hearing aid, not a Gypsy! The choices you make determine your future. They are not written in stone, not the way you think. There are certain things that are fated to cross your path, but should you recognize them for what they are, if they are good or bad, then you can choose to walk away, we will have no problems." Her tone was casual now. Her accent and her rolling R's made her seem endearing, once you got past her sandpaper exterior. "You are disappointed, I can see. You were expecting a detailed account?"

"Um, no. But I was expecting something more...concrete." The Gypsy gave him a look as if he had spit on her best china.

"Why didn't you say so?" She banged her palm on the table and pushed her chair away noisily as she got up. "A charm is what you want." She stepped over to a table laden with jewels and trinkets, the shadows scurrying away like a field mice as she brought the candle closer. The jewels sparkled with radiant luminescence.

"Wow. They're all very beautiful. Which one do you recommend?" The idea of bringing home a souvenir was rapidly growing on Jerome.

"You are to pick the one that calls to you. I can only tell you of its properties. Remember-life is of choices." The melodrama of her voice went beyond Jerome's hearing-he was too busy picking out a charm. He scanned the table. Rings, bracelets, necklaces, earrings, they were all so extravagant. Some he found too feminine; most too dazzling to wear on a daily basis. His eyes oscillated from one end of the table to the other, his mind following the same pattern. Each choice was instantly replaced by one better, which in turn was replaced by a better one still. Too big, too small, too fat, too thin. Each trinket had a flaw that made him look for one better. The Gypsy's toe tapped rhythmically to his right. His eyes rested a moment on a ceramic gray jar that sat at the back of the table. It was dull and somber, especially among the jewels, but what caught his attention the most was the jewel at its base. It wasn't set in anything but it was beautiful, its golden-brown hue shining dimly among the sparking of the others. It nearly hid itself behind the jar; Jerome picked it up. The glow seemed to brighten, only slightly. The jewel was about three inches in length, and was round, with many small faces to give it that shape, and from it protruded a sharp point, which seemed out of character with the look of the gem. It was an inch or so thick.

"I can let you have that for one hundred dollar," said the Gypsy. Her voice was quiet, but it seemed piercing since the noise of the Carnival had died down.

"A hundred? I don't think so, that's more than I want to spend." He put the jewel down, though he left it in plain view. The dim glow seemed to fade, though he wasn't sure.

The Gypsy harumphed again before speaking, more to command attention than to clear her throat.

"Maybe you really do want it? Maybe you higgle with me?" And she grinned like a hag.

"I'll give you twenty-five bucks. It's a dime-store trinket. A toy."

"An insult!!" the Gypsy bellowed. She calmed down almost immediately. "All my jewels have a spell on them, for one purpose or another. This jewel that you ogle in particular is very old, as well. It is you who receive the bargain. Eighty-five!" Again she smacked her hand on the table.

Jerome thought for a moment. He picked up the jewel and examined it again. It ebbed in his hand. Maybe a gift for Graham's wife? He could have it filigreed and hung from a chain.

"Fifty, tops."

The Gypsy wore a grim smile that was flanked by shadows as she brought the candle close to her face. Her eyes sunk into dark, black wells as she said, "The next price I give you, you will accept." Jerome thought for a second then nodded slowly. "Sixty-five."

Jerome paused for a moment. He thought he heard Clyde calling him from outside, but it still sounded far away, a different world altogether. The Gypsy's face began to twist with anger, until he reached for his billfold. He pulled out the necessary amount and handed it over to the Gypsy's coffer. She smile a twisted, old smile and picked up the jewel, handing it to him.

"This jewel," she said, "may serve you quite well in time, if you put your faith in it. It has access to the soul of the bearer, among other powers."

"It's going to be a gift anyway." Jerome fingered the point on the gem. It was needle sharp, though it didn't look it. "Don't matter to me."

The Gypsy gave a smile, muffled a laugh. Jerome was sure he heard Clyde calling, so he turned to leave, thanking the Gypsy for her time. He glanced over his shoulder, but the candle had been put out and the room seemed an empty space, but for the muted murmurs that touched his ears, making him chill. He stepped out into the night, the night that seemed blazing and bright as midday after the deepness of the tent. Clyde was ambling towards him, his face white and pale, but he wore a broad smile-he obviously felt much better after throwing up for the past half hour in the bathroom. Jerome felt like he was in a different world altogether; none of it seemed real. He brushed off the feeling with a shudder and a shake and put on his trademark good cheer. He and Clyde walked to the bus stop, Clyde to go home and sleep off the rest of the booze, Jerome to meet three friends downtown and drink some more.

Part 2: The Little Brother of War

I sat down with my volume of *The History of Witchcraft and Black Majic*, by Andreas Lurik and began to read through it cursorily to start. I wanted to get a feel for the topics I was going to study. Of note was the warning with the introduction that under no circumstances should the rituals be taken lightly. A guardian, or observer should be present when attempting the more complex rites, and those with little experience with ceremonial majic should not attempt the advanced rites. The observer would interfere only if bodily harm were to come to one of the participants.

The book itself looked quite unimpressive to me: black cover with the title printed in decayed yellow, as though scrawled into the page. And I figured the narration would be morbid and Lovecraftian, but it read almost like a cookbook.

I have to admit I was a little disappointed. The spells were…well, poetry. And not very good poetry at that. Simple phrases calling to Gods, Goddesses, asking for things to be done. Simple rituals, nothing grandiose. Nothing harmful! This was light-hearted, esoteric hippie shit as far as I could see. But the point was for me to look farther than I could see.

There were some things in this book that rang with a clear familiarity to me. Historically, witchcraft, paganism, call it what you will-when it came to religion, wasn't it all majic?-had been amalgamated by the church in order to facilitate conversions. In the introduction to the book, I'd read a little poem-*spell*-that I had no idea was from witchcraft. The author had used it as a simple example to teach the structure of spell-casting. To me it was merely a childhood rhyme:

Rain, rain, go away,
come again another day.
All the children want to play,
happy, pretty sunny day.

It illustrated a request, a reason for the request, and it allowed the rain to return later so as not to cause a draught. Simple. I found it ironic that it mentioned children though. Was there a connection between children and majic? Or was this a coincidence, or just my own mind working away?

So this was majic, and I was trying to put it together with what I knew. The reality of Korson, the murders I'd hoped it would help me solve. Faith and belief. The possibility of the unseen.

Julia wasn't home, I hadn't seen her at all today, but after an hour or so of perusing through the text (and, I might add, getting drawn into it somewhat), I decided to try one of the spells. I gathered together the available supplies and went down to the basement.

I used some candles for light, the flames burning the motes of dust from the air. Using the wax from a white candle, I drew out the pentacle on the floor in a counter-clockwise direction. I placed candles at all points of the star. Lurik said to use black candles but all I had were white. I left them unlit until I performed the incantation on invocation.

Truthfully I thought I would feel a little silly, perhaps childish. This was Hallowe'en stuff. Was I naive to think that witchcraft had died with the onset of Christianity? That medieval flames claimed all the last witches in the world? And I chastised myself for my narrow minded view of humanity. That because I couldn't see something that I thought it wasn't there.

But what was it I set out to invoke? My passion, my obsession; the face of a murderer.

Your honour, if you would allow me to draw my pentacle in the middle of the courtroom, the face of the wavering sprit you see clearly matches that of the accused!

I thrust the book down at the floor, dust clouds bursting out from under it. This was stupid. I looked down at the book, the pages crumpled as it lay face down and open. What did I really expect? Was I doing this for my own benefit? I picked it up again. I had to believe. I had to see for myself.

To open the circle I had to light each candle in a counter-clockwise direction after reciting a chant line by line:

By the God and Goddess under the moon (I lit the first candle),
whilst thou bring they love unto me?
Through knowledge divine I wish to see (the third cannel lit. I felt lighter),
come through the veil, up through the earth,
unto my circle where power flows forth.

I lit the fifth and final candle. The circle was opened. I opened myself up to the power. I left my disbelief outside the circle. I didn't force myself to believe, rather I allowed myself to see, like the poem/spell said.

In truth I felt isolated. The flames of the candles cut a hole in the darkness, the smoke drifting up in rivers above my head. I looked closely at the smoke; I wanted to see if it was alive, but it wasn't. It was ordinary smoke.

I felt isolated, but I didn't feel alone. I continued to read through the text of Lurik's book:

There is a veil between words. Between that of deities and man. It exists as much in the mind as in any literal representation in nature. Man's lack of knowledge of the divine, his inability to see, is what hides this veil. To discover the veil, both figurative and true, man must abandon his secular, scientific world for that of the esoteric. Man mustn't throw all his faith unto science; for there are those that can't be explained in technical terms. For nature was created before science was invented by man to explain that which he wished to understand of the world. But science is growing beyond necessity to fill man's hunger.

The mind itself is vast as the universe; largely ignored and unused, as well. To understand the concept of the veil is to understand the duality, the link, between the natural world and the mind and physical representation of the spirit. That stepping across the veil was akin to stepping into the unused portion of the mind.

It made me think: What was in that unused portion of the mind? But I had trouble transposing the metaphor to fit the universe. I couldn't see the connection. After all, did we not exist on earth?

The majician must strive to break the bonds of man's selfish morality, to again become one with nature, a part of her. The explosion of the population of man is due to the lack of love man has displayed throughout history: for himself, for the earth, and for the cycle. Through patriarchal philosophies, man sees this explosion as his triumph over the planet, while in reality it will be his downfall.

One with nature, a part of *her*. Witchcraft was matriarchal, polytheistic. Isabelle had explained that it was a nature based religion, rooted in philosophies that were opposed to harming others around you in addition to yourself. That spells could backfire if not careful.

Though I could see the rites and practices of Lurik's book as being beneficial to a practitioner, whether as literal majic or metaphor for the soul, I was a little questioning of his lectures in between. It seemed to have the slight intonation of a diatribe against secularism and monotheistic religions. I reread the paragraphs again, and decided that he hadn't really put down any other beliefs. He went on, in fact, to say that he was in no way trying to evangelize as that would go against the philosophy of the majician, that this world was to be sought after. And that practitioners should try to learn about the other paths of faith and take from them beliefs that would strengthen their souls as opposed to condemning other beliefs.

Upon thinking and rereading several times, I found myself nodding agreement. The religions I was most familiar with-the Big Three-were all fundamentally sound as a system of morality. I began scanning the pages quite quickly. I checked the index. It was a fairly thick book, one that required somewhat extensive study, but I couldn't find one mention of Satan. Of Hell and heaven. Despite the self-serving tone, there was nothing that said anything about evil. In fact the closest I found were phrases that denounced the belief of evil and demons. Perhaps that was where the patriarchal religions faltered: in their acclamation of the existence of the Devil. I found it ironic that Christianity would evangelize its followers by appealing to the dark side of their souls, while at the same time forcing them to deny that dark side.

And the self-serving tone of the narration, perhaps that was just my own ignorance? My own preconception of language? When shouldn't man be a little selfish? As long as one didn't force their beliefs on, or harm, others...

I decided to try a summoning incantation ritual. I took the book and left the circle-how much thicker the darkness seemed from inside of it!-and went up to the kitchen to gather supplies. Most of the ingredients, witchcraft being an earth-based belief, were herbs and natural products. I gathered together several ingredients, but upon reviewing the introduction to the spell, I found that the spell was a general one. As the belief system was founded in one's self, so too were the incantations. I could adapt the spell to suit my needs, and if I put my heart into it and believed then it would-should-suit my purpose.

I wanted to summon a specific spirit-by spirit I referred to those in the esoteric world-and as I was swimming uncharted territory here I would stick to what I felt to be concrete. To represent the blood I gathered roses (it had occurred to me to use my own blood, but as I had no observer and hadn't totally breached sanity yet...), to represent claws I clipped the dog's toenails, and all I needed was something to represent death. I decided on tracings of the photographs of the dead children. My hand shook as I redrew some the grizzlier details of the twisted figures.

(As an aside, I did find blood rituals towards the end of the text, and, obviously, the use of knives as a part of the ceremony.)

I sealed myself in the circle again, and on a piece of paper began to compose a chant. I wanted it to be specific to the summoning of a vampire. To call directly to Korson himself. Time lost its sense in the confines of the circle. I think it was an hour or so before I finally came up with a chant I was satisfied with.

The sun no more as night has fallen,
the creature who lurks in the shadow roams.
Haunting the streets he exists outside time,
tearing of flesh to drink his subsistence.
Come to my circle come into my power,
tell me your story, I beckon you speak.

I know. I know. I fucking suck at poetry. But life isn't about being good at things, it's about doing things. I was being a good cop.

In a censer I burnt the photographs, and sprinkled the nail clippings in accordance with my chant. I put a rose petal under my tongue to symbolize the consumption of blood. I hoped I'd covered everything I had to. I believed it was essentially my faith in the majic I was practicing that would lead to its success. The strange feeling in the circle seemed no different, albeit it did thicken somewhat. But no change in the air as I waited for the results of my majic. I watched the thick shadows and the smoke from the candles swirling around me.

"O, were it that those shadows not such a frigid reminder of the howling of wolves!"

I jumped, nearly swallowing the rose petal.

"Fuck, don't do that!"

"I love watching you freeze, you're like this." Korson stretched his face into mortal shock.

"Heather is dead." He shrugged. "You don't care?"

"Death doesn't mean much to me."

"It does to me."

"It shouldn't."

"Why?"

Korson shrugged, said, "I suppose you'll find that out for yourself eventually."

"Does death make an asshole out of everybody or just you?"

Korson's foot kicked over a candle.

"Oops!" he said. "I broke your circle. That's a bad, bad omen!" He put his fingers to his mouth like a clumsy pantomime. "Do you like movies, Mr. St. Croix?" I nodded yes. "I love movies. That's what's kept me alive, all these years! Things were very boring until you mortals invented movies."

"How did you get in here?"

"While you were busy..." he gestured to the circle and the door, "with your hocus-pocus mumbo-jumbo, you forgot to lock your front door."

I got up and closed the book, said, "You might as well come upstairs." I led him up out of the basement. I put my hand on the knob to open the door but stopped when I heard voices from the main floor. My finger went to my lips to keep Korson hushed.

Two voices...man and woman...my wife's...after midnight...and I wasn't due home for hours...I pushed Korson back down the stairs.

He said, "You look like death," but I didn't laugh. Profanities filled my head, steaming rage. Why didn't I confront her? Didn't I care? Did my anger stem from the disrespect rather than the love we were supposed to have? I was up against the door again, my eyes wet with anger, fists in a banging motion on the door. I was stuck here with a dead bastard.

Korson whispered to me, "Stay here. I'll get rid of them," and he slipped quietly onto the main floor before I could protest. I pressed my ear the to the door but heard nothing more than muffled voices, for twenty minutes nearly. The front door slammed closed and the basement door slid slowly open under its own power as the picturesque image of my living room, curtains crimson wet, the walls splashed with blood dripping down to the black pool covering the floor-flashing-flashing.

"You've got to relax, Mr. St. Croix, you'll make yourself crazy thinking about those things." He gestured towards the living room. "It's your house. I shouldn't have to ask you to have a seat." His tone was less abrasive, still a bastard, but less abrasive.

"How did you get them to leave?"

"Would you want to stay in the same room as me?"

It wasn't real, my hands, my house, the clock ticking away its seconds over the fireplace. Someone else was feeling my throat choke. Korson poured me some Southern Comfort over ice and slammed the glass down in front of me.

"Drink." He said it austerely.

"I don't want any. My throat hurts."

"Drink," he repeated. "It'll make you feel better, trust me." But he wasn't *bon mot*. And I couldn't really argue with him, so I didn't sip, I gulped half of it down and then the other half, then he poured me another glass. "You're taking this well."

I shrugged. Maybe I didn't care anymore? Maybe it hadn't sunk in yet. What else could I do but drink?

"Is Korson your real name?" He pursed his lips and shook his head. Neither of us said anything, me because I was shaken and drinking. Korson was never one to say anything, he kept his cards close. It was frustrating to be teased by him but reassuring. If he had told me everything he knew, I would have to consider him my enemy. Enemies are closer than friends, closer than lovers. No man has ever felt such passion as that he felt for his nemesis.

"Do you believe all that you were doing in the basement?" He seemed more sincere now. Perhaps he had some emotion. Perhaps he felt he had to scare me to live up to my expectations. Or maybe he wanted to see my strength? Who was to say that he let his prey feel fear? It would be all the more furtive to be sweet and charming to your prey.

"It isn't very pretty, usually, when we kill." He could hear me thinking. "They usually void themselves. Or go mad when they see us."

"I don't feel strong."

"Why should you?"

"Because I almost went mad. But didn't."

He pointed to his watch and said, "I still have time." I laughed out loud, he wore a watch! He lived forever and wore a watch.

The phone rang.

"Hello? Yeah-shit." Isabelle. "Fuck. On my way." I hung up. "I gotta go, more children were found." Korson nodded, followed me out the door.

Don't be afraid...I'll be close... But I was in too much of a rush to care.

I met Isabelle at station twenty. She briefed me on the past night. Five murders, all quite close to the points on the star of the pentacle. I was willing to bet that they occurred in a counter-clockwise fashion.

"How were they discovered so quickly?"

"One phone call. Just before dawn."

"Trace?"

"Nah, cellular." She played the tape for me. The voice was dead, almost crying, almost simple, hollow with a scorned lovers resentment.

They're all dead...(a choke, a tear)...you're all so blind...soon there will be nothing any of you can do...

Where are you?

I'm everywhere, I can see everything.

Where are the bodies?

Université de Montreal...(long pause)...Parc Jeanne Mance...Oratoire St. Joseph... She only gave up three, the rest were found through manpower searches.

Soon the Sab will rise again...(did she say: I'm on to you St. Croix...?)...Humanity is mine...

The rest was very garbled due to the connection, and then the line was cut with an electrical zap in the air.

I wanted to tell Isabelle about Korson, that she was right about it being ritual murder. But how could I tell her that vampires exist? Who was to say that Korson wouldn't kill me if I gave up his secret? And I didn't want to be the madman again.

"I already said I would believe you, Graham."

"Yeah, well, that's humanity's nature, to be neurotic, insane, lethargic, stupid. Besides, how can I trust my own senses, after-" Stop it, take me back. "I mean, was anything I ever saw real, did anything really happen-" Stop, "-to me cause after a while it sure as fuck don't feel li-"

"Do you believe in evil, Graham?" I just looked at her, expressionless. How could I answer such a question? Of course there was evil. How could a police officer ever have faith in man? "I don't. I believe that there are people who do terrible things, but I don't believe in evil," she said. We sat in the conference room, the buzz and brightness of fluorescent lights in our ears, reminding us that nothing was ever silent. "I'm sorry. The voice on that tape...not what she said, but something was very disturbing. The tone of it, the inflection."

I made a copy of the tape, to study it.

"I better not play this over too much. I may go insane."

"You're not insane. You're the most sane person I know. Some of the others, it's just a job to them. And you can tell that they're numb to what's going on."

I underestimated how much Isabelle was affected by this work. I poured some coffee for her and when she picked the mug up her hand shook and she dropped it, she spilled some on her hand and jumped from the heat. She began to wipe up the spill with some napkins before it spread to the files. She was visibly shaken, and shaking.

I said quietly, "You okay?" She pushed her chair back and stood, her hand to her forehead.

"I've been having such terrible dreams." I found that hard to believe, it looked as though she hadn't gotten much sleep.

"It's hard to have a thick skin about these things. You don't need it, fear isn't a weakness." But she was a woman, she was bound to be sensitive to these things. "Maybe you do believe in evil, maybe you would if you saw a demon." I sent her home, told her to eat and sleep. I would call her before our shift tomorrow. She hugged me, kissed my cheek. And whispered in my ear, *I believe you.*

Did she say: *I'm on to you, St.Croix...?*

Perhaps it was the endless hours of darkness, but Korson always seemed to me to be a man teetering on the brink. It wasn't the gleam of insanity in his eye as he listened to the tape that made me think he was maniacal, it was the gleam of intelligence-supreme, vast, unsullied by morality. But as many times as we played it, the message to me was no longer there.

I begged the question that I had held back when I was with Isabelle: What is the Sab?

And for the first time since he'd shown me his face, after years of trying to keep my sanity from breaking like an egg into the vastness of my mind, he looked at me like a man who knew too much.

He asked me, "If your death was staring you in your face, would you accept it as your destiny or would you fight like hell to keep your life?" It took me a minute to answer. Years ago, young and brash, I would certainly have said fight like hell. But I had lived barely half my life and already there were more and more times that I was ready to just accept cold fate and sleep. I'm not talking about insanity, about keeping your head in this world. Just because you're dead to the world doesn't mean you're dead.

"I think I would find a way to live. I'm not going to be trite and say life is precious, but, well...Some of us have claws too. And I was never insane. You bastard." He laughed, silent, mirthless, tilting his head back. Like he was acting. "We're players to you, this is a stage."

"Not at first. It gets that way after a while. You notice the patterns." He steepled his hands. "Things have to play themselves out. Everything follows the cycle." I had to get out of my house. I didn't want to run into my wife.

"You know where I'd feel safest now? On the mountain." Though that was irrational, it was in the center of the circle of power. But the scenes of the murder were to me the points of power.

It was strange driving in my car with a vampire.

"I come here a lot myself," said Korson. But we never got to the lookout. We stopped at the *cemetery* to visit Heather's grave. And Korson said, "By the fucking Shadow." He was astonished and I followed his gaze. Heather's grave, some bastard had dug it up. I was naive for a moment, she was murdered, and it was her murderer who had dug her up. The hole ragged, dug by hands that cherished the earth, and the coffin splintered open by hands that knew figuratively and literally power. Such raw power!

Korson fell by the hole, and if one such as he showed no emotion at the murder of innocent children, then what was it that he showed feeling now? He made a fist and the barest audible whisper, *'again,'* issued from his grey lips. I put my arms on his shoulders, I felt no revulsion or apprehension now, just my heart beating at the imminent danger of being caught in such a compromising position. Not, perhaps, with the splintered open grave, but with a demon. I led him across the road to *Lac aux Castors*. He was distressed, and I had no idea what to say to him.

"Did you ever realize," he said, "what kind of power ideas carry? Is it enough when so many believe in a myth? Does the myth have to be real, or does it become real?"

"Honestly...I haven't been able to figure out what's real since I saw you." He snorted a laugh. I don't know if he was laughing at my wit or at my lightness to the situation. I summoned my professional calm. "Are you the cause of these murders? Are you putting me through all this just to *mock* me?" Was there any point in questioning an obvious murderer?

He pulled out a dagger, silver blade glinting fiercely in the moonlight.

"I need your blood, Graham." There was too much kindness in his voice, too much familiarity. I hoped his tone wasn't reaching past the bounds of friendship. But I showed no fear, I stood still under the night, in the darkened park. How many children had died like this? Though my heart was beating like a drum in my chest. And a creature such as Korson would smell the fear from my mind no matter how much I outwardly disguised it. Or the vicious pumping of my blood through my arteries.

He took the knife by the dagger, and gave it to me by the handle: "I need your blood. Then I can tell you how, over a century ago, I could have stopped all this."

* * *

To the south, across the Great St. Lawrence River, a tribe of Blackfoot Indian settled near Tupper Lake in the Adirondack Mountains. A young boy, on the verge of manhood, who knew of love only for his lacrosse stick, for the earth beneath his feet for which he was grateful for the gifts that provided life, had his destiny decided for him.

The elders of the tribe, though proud of his skill at the hunt, at his oneness with the earth that allowed him to track prey, also were a little bit fearful. At his loneliness; at his pleasure while decapitating the corpse of the evening kill; of the gleam in his coal black eyes of something that spoke of dark shadows beyond their knowledge, perhaps touching the divine.

Perhaps out of sympathy to the young Blackfoot, one of the nah tova, the medicine man of the tribe, acted as guardian to the boy who would later call himself Korson. The nah tova knew too, himself, what it was to a boy to be fatherless, directionless in the cycle of the village. The nah tova was the strongest and most divine of the tribe, of the region fact, and it was also out of a little bit of selfishness that he regarded the young Korson with extra care. For he could see deeper into the boy's eyes than any of the other elders.

The nah tova, the Shaman, would always watch Korson at the lacrosse games. The children would play three, four times a week, before their dinner called at the setting of the sun. It was not uncommon for the elders to watch the dance, as the game told the story of their place in life. It was not uncommon for Korson to draw blood early in the game. But he also excelled at the skills of the game, mostly as a goal scorer because he was not adroit at passing to others; though he was not the least bit selfish, but the game told the story of his isolation from the society of the tribe.

His behavior was looked at as somewhat a source of embarrassment, more so when the tribe was visited by an outsider. They would wonder, *Who was this boy who was not beside his elders?*

A messenger for a nearby Cherokee tribe arrived one day and studied the boy Korson, he'd noticed him before but not as clearly as he did now, and he studied him in detail. Korson looked back at him, his face blank but his coal eyes deep. But his eyes did not scare this man, he was leathery and his arms brawny, bulged with muscles. A warrior, and a master with the stick.

Peace reigned between the tribes; it had been quiet for many, many years. Though the race of Indians was not warlike in general, as accorded by the historians in Hollywood, they did engage in the art of war to defend themselves.

The village was tense at the presence of the Cherokee messenger. His massive frame accorded their respect, so that they issued only furtive glances and gave him a wide path for his bulk. As Korson gave no hint of the massive size he was to reach when fully grown, he was but a speck in the Cherokee's shadow.

The Cherokee tribe were the barbarians of the north-eastern Amerindians. The brawny, muscled messenger was typical of one of their kind, arrogant and guileless in his display of ego. Cherokee Lacrosse-the little brother of war-was military training more than it was sport and metaphor. The games would consist of hundreds, even thousands, of participants per team, the whole tribe or village would engage in the game, and, as goals were expectedly few and far between, only the luckiest players getting sight of the ball, the object was to injure your opponent with your stick. The massacre could last up to three days.

So despite many years of peace between tribes, the Cherokee messenger was in essence issuing a challenge to war, to lacrosse. The Blackfoot game was more civilized, it consisted of only a dozen or so players per team, but the game was still quite vicious compared to its modern day form. But the Blackfoot would not back down from the challenge. They would be hard pressed to gather resources to match the massive attack of the Cherokee, but to disregard the challenge was cowardice. Women would fight, children too, if necessary, but to disregard the challenge of the Cherokee would mean the disrespect of other tribes.

The messenger noticed the eyes of the boy, and he himself had something of the same look in his eyes, though diluted. Korson met his stare, the only one who would do so other than the village chief. It was the Cherokee who broke the stare, but not out of defeat. The chief had come out to meet him, he commanded enough respect, or rather the tension in the village had called the chief out. The Cherokee had issued the challenge of war lacrosse, the chief accepting. As he left the village he looked at the young Korson as though he were already bruised, beaten; perhaps even dead.

The other villagers had busied themselves with other tasks to occupy their minds, the preparing of the evening meal, the skins of the corpses of animals hung to be made into clothing later. The chief met with the elders and wise of the village to pick the players; in essence, to pick who would be sent certain to return with chopped bones and torn skin.

Korson had wandered away from the village with inks. He decorated his lacrosse stick with red and black ink and during long games the ink would sweat onto his skin. He would rub his reddened hands on his cheeks and brow, he wore no war paint other than what was sweated off. His war paint was a story of the game he was playing, the patterns chosen by nature, the Gods. He was searching for feathers to tie to the stick as decoration; birds were powerful.

But he was not chosen to play. The wise ones, the elders, they thought him too roguish, that he would be cut down early and be of no aid to his teammates. It was known that bad choices led to accidental death. The game was meant to strengthen the weaknesses of the tribe, not decimate the numbers. As it was the Blackfoot tribe would have to draw upon reserves from other villagers to bolster the lineup. Korson was calm, he still searched for feathers in solitude as though he would play. He still prepared his war stick meticulously with inks.

The forest darkened quicker than the open land. He met the eyes of a wolf who had *his eyes*, and he was frozen to his spot and stared. The wolf looked at him, almost like the Cherokee did.

"There is such depth in his gaze, you fear him. Why not take him to the game? If he does well you will be better and if he loses you will be free of him. That is what you want."

"Nah tova, with all due respect I will not send him to his death. He is harmless as he his."

"He is a shell of what he should be."

The nah tova, the Shaman who believed in the one who would grow to be Korson, he knew of destiny. He knew that man must take the hardest road and death was the land's way of taking unto itself the weaker of men who could not transcend death. He saw, though almost blind, he saw and knew that Korson's destiny was assured, but would be shaped by that fateful death on the lacrosse field.

"He is a lone wolf." The Shaman laughed at this. The chief bowed his head in respect to the powerful nah tova. In some ways the nah tova was like Korson; above the chief, beyond the fringes of the society of the village. Perhaps beyond the cycle. And this power, though respected, was also distrusted when personified. Anything outside the circle was unknown.

The nah tova, the Shaman, the medicine man of the tribe, he was a witch; a healer, a doctor. Witch meant wise one. But some became distrustful of people with knowledge, they appeared to have powers that those of lower intelligence couldn't comprehend, they thought that perhaps there was some sort of dealing with evil spirits. Though it was more lack of understanding on the part of outsiders that these views prospered.

"Wolves travel in packs," said the Shaman. He was fearsome, logical, but gentle to Korson, sympathetic. The Shaman left the chief, he was not one to debate intellect, to dispute points of view on facts.

Korson held the gaze of the wolf-the lone wolf!-and stared into the depth of his own eyes. True fear is looking into one's self. Some see how shallow they are, others are astounded by the vastness of their own mind, knowing they will never dip into that so precious of gifts that the Gods and Goddesses of the world have bestowed on their most favourite of animals. Even as he was on the verge of manhood, his heart was cold to those depths. He was used to isolation and loneliness and being with himself. Looking at himself was nothing new.

He returned to the village and took his meal. He didn't even look at the chief. He sat with the Shaman, his nah tova, and he told him of the lone wolf at the verge of sunset. It was known that majic was more powerful at points of change, day to night, fall to winter, and to see an aberration of nature was something of interest. The Shaman could tell by the young man's voice that he was affected in some way by what he saw, but he sensed no fear. He kept his counsel.

The chief was a little wary of the Shaman, of the man's knowledge. He looked at Korson, pointed to him with a lacrosse stick. The signal that he would accompany the villagers to the game. It was a great honour to be picked, to do battle for your people. Korson made no acknowledgment, he left his stick sitting by his thigh.

He dreamt of the wolf, thick grey fur and deep grey eyes that glinted red under the moonlight. The deep fangs of the wolf left him unable to return to sleep. He woke and the Shaman was standing over him. He turned and left, his hands out to guide him as he'd not brought his walking stick. Korson rose and followed him, but immediately lost sight of him. He moved fast for one almost blind.

The dream of the wolf left him unable to return to sleep. He sat on the ground and meditated. He was unused to being awake so late in the night. In his meditations he found a sense of things he couldn't find under the sun.

Why would the wolf leave its pack to come to him? Both in reality and his dream? It was his animal, but he wouldn't tell it to others, not even his nah tova. After all, he had no real friends and who should know about him that didn't care? The Shaman had most certainly saw his dream as he stood over the sleeping Korson. Behind his back, the others taunted him as the lone wolf. Perhaps not out of cruelty. Perhaps.

Sitting stiff-backed under open darkness, he looked as though he were sleeping. He went somewhere else, but wouldn't remember what it was he saw...

The Blackfoot tribe was the first to arrive at the lacrosse field; they held sticks in hand and waited for the Cherokees. Were the Cherokee watching them, thinking them fools for standing open to ambush? The Cherokee were brutal, not clever. They were expected, they wouldn't be so underhanded as to sneak up on an enemy.

A cloud of dust was seen on the horizon. The Cherokee were arriving, their most fearsome warriors and leaders driving horses to kick up clouds of dust to make their arrival dramatic. Perhaps unnecessarily the Blackfoot set up nets. There were nearly four hundred Blackfoot and the Cherokee had more than enough to match that number. They could drag the game out for days using their reinforcements, their bench.

Korson remained back, he didn't show his inner force as a leader, and the chief held him out of the game for a while. He debated putting him in as a goaltender. Normally only the bravest took up being the guardian of the net, but it was a figurehead position in this game. In three days competition there would be perhaps four goals per side if they were lucky.

The Blackfoot, they were fine hunters, but were not nearly as brutal as the Cherokee. Brave, honourable fighters, but the Cherokee were their Goliaths. The nah tova of the Blackfoot were busy early, because of arrogance; arrogance of the Cherokee's game plan, arrogance of the persistent Blackfoot who simply refused to quit until injury forced a nah tova to call him off the field against his will. Often one of the children far too young to play lacrosse would get a taste of the stick while dragging their injured warrior off the playing field. They saw pride and honour in his glassy, far away eyes.

Korson remained impassive while his Blackfoot were on the verge of slaughter. It was out of quiet respect for the tribe's chief that he remained so, but the chief thought him a coward, more of an outsider than ever. He was somewhat tall, wiry, not yet grown to full fearsome bulk, but the mind grows before the body, and he was beginning to carry an arrogance about him. One of the elders touched his shoulder. He was in the game finally. The chief would not be bothered with acknowledging the young wolf, as though the command were not his.

Only the Shaman laughed at Korson's arrogance as he stepped quickly on to the field, stepping on the face of a fallen Cherokee. The chief was impassive, but you could read distaste in his eyes at the disrespect shown by Korson. This was a game, after all. There were lines. The chief was thankful that the fallen Cherokee was alive. It would do no good to disrespect the dead.

Korson had kept his eye on the ball all the while and chased after it through sticks and hacks and kicking legs. His dogged pursuit was rewarded with only a few minor scrapes and bruises. Despite the fact that he quickly and efficiently cut down the sizable Cherokee who'd owned the ball, the chief was beginning to think him cowardly of being hit. But it was exactly the opposite, for Korson now had the ball and he was the most marked of men in a field full of marked men.

To the astonishment of all present, except the Shaman, Korson held onto the ball for over an hour. Through pure skill, dogged determination and sheer force of will he stormed the Cherokee defenses and scored the opening goal of the game, so all important in this type of competition. Though technically, credited with two goals for both injuring the opposing goaltender and stuffing him into the net after the goal had been scored.

But he would never regain the ball. Vengeance was on his mind. The game had taken over and, though an outsider, introverted, not truly one of the society of the tribe, he belonged through birth, through blood. The strength of blood was stronger than anything and now he was stepping in the very blood of the Blackfoot, feeling it on his bare feet as it soaked into the wetted grass.

It was not uncommon for some to lose their life in such a game, but they were honoured for their bravery despite their obvious weakness. For, if they couldn't survive lacrosse, how were they to survive actual combat? The little brother of war chose its warriors cunningly.

But Korson, with Cherokee viciousness, began purposely cutting their number. Intent to injure was one thing, adrenaline would flow after all, but there was murderous rage in his eyes. The wolf's eyes turned red; deep, dark, soaking red like that of the Blackfoot blood on grass. The veins in his arms and neck became grey ropes on his body as he used his stick to crush the facial bones of any Cherokee within reach. Cherokee flesh was torn like cloth by his stick. Korson had put thirty on the verge of the other world by the time night had fallen.

He'd become a murderer on the lacrosse field that day. He was out of his gourd. From far away the field looked as though it were stampeded by a herd of buffalo. Thick clouds of sand and dust mingled with a storm of blood, the ground had become soaked with Blackfoot blood. Not since the days of war had so much Blackfoot blood been lost. The disrespect that Korson had shown-his skill and ferociousness as a warrior-had roused the utter brutality of the Cherokee. The lacrosse ball was soaked with blood, it was no longer white.

Korson cracked the skull of a Cherokee, he put stick to the side of the Cherokee's head and watched it disappear like the flesh was mud. He wasn't himself anymore, he was pure animal, his actions all instinct. He was outside of himself. He had his war paint on, his face was red and black.

The brawny Cherokee had been watching Korson, out of the edge of his sight. He chopped through Blackfoot, his superhuman size no match for any of them. Korson stopped, he heard a sinister, deep laugh, a laugh of derision, of arrogance. Through the dirt and dust, through splashes of blood, the big Cherokee cut an imposing figure as he slashed through Blackfoot like brittle branches. He was sketched in the blacks and browns of the shadow and dirt; the artist used no colour, no red to accent anything. Though his bulges and biceps needed no emphasis.

He stood over Korson, making him look like a speck. The wind was stopped dead by his thick dirty hair. It was as though he would crush Korson with the size of his chest. Korson looked into familiar eyes.

"Ahpacee," said the Cherokee. He spoke Blackfoot, as though he plucked the word from Korson's mind. "Caquay Ahpacee." Korson swung the shaft of his stick, to cut across the face of the Cherokee. The big Cherokee, he was so fast, he caught the lacrosse stick with his hand on the side that the blow was coming from, looking at the stick severely. He turned his gaze to Korson, he smiled so evil, teeth sharp and white. He twisted the lacrosse stick, tore tendons in Korson's arm.

He shoved him backwards, and he fell to the ground like a boy. He was no longer a murderer under this one's shadow. By all rights the Cherokee was toying with him. He should be dead now.

"Caquay Ahpacee," the Cherokee said. He smiled and laughed the words out. He folded his muscled arms, stood there as though the war that rained around him was soothing and of no consequence. Korson looked into the eyes of the wolf. The sketchy blackness of the figure, the huge Cherokee, it was as though there were mists coming off of him. They surrounded Korson and the Cherokee, as though separating them from the little brother of war around them. The lacrosse players had become grey ghosts battling each other. Korson and the Cherokee were on another plane.

Korson would not be cowed by the size and arrogance of this large Native. Though Korson himself was not yet big, his fight was. Who was this man that so arrogantly renamed him Caquay Ahpacee? The name he was teased with as a child. Korson could hear the children whispering derisively ahpacee, the wolf. They looked at him as the lone wolf and the symbol of the animal carried no respect with it. It was an honour to have a spirit animal, and any animal was part of the Great Circle. But the belief in the Great Circle of time is what had alienated the young, lonely Blackfoot who was chided with the name Ahpacee.

Though the wolf was a great animal, and deep inside him, in a place not yet found, never found by children, was a pride in being a wolf.

The father of Ahpacee, of Korson, was a warrior in the times of war. He fiercely fought every battle, denying none the bloodlust in his eyes. But no warrior is truly fearless, and those that seem so are all the more shattered when fear finally fires an arrow into their heel. His son, distant, withdrawn, did not carry the vindictive and powerful air of a fighter. As much as for an example to his son as for his own pride, Ahpacee's father drew blood on behalf of the Blackfoot. He knew how powerful blood was, that his blood flowed strong in his son's veins. And the stigma of disgrace scarred the lineage of the family.

Though Korson had become a ruthless killer on the lacrosse field, he had known murder since his first breath in this world. He had torn his way out of the womb, and the fortitude of his mother had been too weak to withstand his early exit from her body. His body dripping in the blood of his family, in the water of life, the baby Korson looked upon the lifeless eyes of his mother. He had blood in his veins and on his skin, he had grown into a human in the water of the womb. But he was denied the sweet nurturing of mother's milk. His mother's eyes were reflected in his immediately as he set gaze upon them. The wise ones, the nah tova, of course sensed the imprint of death that had reflected itself in the baby's eyes.

The father was forced to nurture the child. He received little help from the village women. None wanted to look into their symbolic death, the one in Korson's eyes, the death of the mother. The child would have been abandoned when the father went to war, if not for the Shaman.

The Shaman gently rocked the child back and forth. The villagers were furiously packing away belongings, folding up tents and mounting horses. War had raged dangerously close to the Blackfoot settlement. The Blackfoot were nomadic to the area surrounding the Great Lake of Ontario. They were accustomed to moving around, whether because the Gods and Goddesss beat the land with the fist of nature, or the land itself grew tired of them and no longer was fertile, and sometimes due to battles with other settlers. It was such a terrible era, the normally pacifistic Natives turned against each other; strange settlers raping the land.

The Shaman chanted a lullaby to the young baby in his arms, as the child watched his father slaughter the tribes enemies nearby. Perhaps because he couldn't see his own death imminent, the father of Ahpacee had been cowed. As he slaughtered his last prey, he turned, his jaw dropping open in awe, in utter terror, his legs losing their purpose, and he dropped to his knees. The Shaman, already with nearly no vision left, rose abruptly to his feet, his chanting cut short. The young baby had his eyes riveted on the only person in the world that he recognized. But none could see what the father saw. Only the knife in his hand rise above his head and plunge into his own heart. His dead body fell forward and he smashed his face on the battlefield, the dagger in his chest plunged deeper and tearing a track along his lungs.

The eyes of the child had reflected a second death, a disgraceful death. The Shaman, placid at the carnage that raged before him, oh so close, sat back down in his seat. And chanted. Black mists had crept over the dead body. No one found out, nor had anyone seen, what had happened to Korson's father. But it did nothing to save the baby from being in bad graces with the Blackfoot tribe. They had assumed the father had fled the war in terror. Though no one could explain what terror would have overcome a skillful warrior.

And, death in his infant eyes, Korson knew what had happened to his father, the way he knew what happened to his mother. It was burned into his soul. Both his father and his mother were no longer part of the cycle. His eyes knew death.

Korson looked at the same eyes, looked into the visions of his very life. The black shadows had surrounded him and the brawny Cherokee. He had risen to his feet-sprung, into attack position, but not tense, never tense, the spirit of the wolf ingrained into him. The battle raged around them, but it didn't dare its way into their circle. And every warrior on the lacrosse field was already dead to Korson. Dead because the Blackfoot chief was forced to call the game. The losses of the Cherokee were numerous, but nothing compared to the spilled blood of Blackfoot. On the ground was their dignity, their pride. Blood was blood. The Great Cycle would renew it. To die with honour for your people was a coveted deed.

Desperately, Korson leapt back into the little brother of war. Into the deadly mists that he'd seen his own father engulfed in. Fear was not to be considered, only the pride of the tribe. Only the momentum of the game mattered, it had turned from a brutal test of manhood to absolute adrenalized slaughter. The players had left themselves, war cries filled the air, drowning out the utter dreary death moans of the fallen warriors. And into the shadows Korson leapt, boldly; and it spit him back into the Circle with the brawny, inhuman Cherokee.

"Caquay Ahpacee," he laughed, his voice guttural, the laugh from deep in his belly and only in Korson's head. Who was this beast, this thing who was too large to be real, that so arrogantly renamed him? Who knew the name the tribe had given him? He called him the night wolf, but the intonation, the quality of the words were different. Korson leapt into the fray again; again he was thrust back into the Cherokees presence.

Was it fate that forced Korson to do battle with this beast? To abandon his people as his father appeared to? Who was he but not even a man in the face of this abomination? His hands tensed around the shaft of his lacrosse stick. The red and black inks were just a little but slippery, it gave the stick a loose feel, made it a relaxing weapon rather than a mere firm piece of wood. But now it felt as though it were a twig in the face of the Cherokee.

Korson, his blood hot, bubbling, took the stick in both hands, he laid a vicious, powerful cross-check to the face of the Cherokee. The Cherokee stood there impassive, a small smirk on his face, his arms still crossed. The lacrosse stick was in two pieces, one in each of Korson's hands. In that moment, in that slight hesitation of astonishment, Korson was a dead man. But for the fact that the Cherokee didn't land the killing blow in so obvious a predicament to any warrior worth a feather. How could someone, no matter their size or temperament, stand stoic in the face of a blow to the bridge of their nose? Such an inhuman reaction! He even smiled at Korson's bravura.

Korson pulled out his dagger, he'd hidden it so he could keep it with him on the lacrosse field. He stabbed overhand at the Cherokee's heart. The blade couldn't penetrate deep into the skin, as though the sinews and tissues tied together into steel cables. But it did break into his skin, and there was almost no blood.

The players around him were grey, disintegrating dusty corpses half-heartedly dragging their feet along the bloodied, trampled field. This smoke, this black mist, it was the shadow of death. Everyone was dead in the smoke; but for the Cherokee and Korson, who stood in he circle of reality.

Korson's feet were soaked in Native blood, he felt the ground squish every time he shifted his weight. But the circle of reality they were in was a vessel of death. The spilled blood of lacrosse warriors diffused through the shadow ring. Though Korson couldn't leap out of the ring, pure spilt blood would soak its way in. It covered his ankles, rising slowly...slowly but noticeably, thick, crimson, opaque, steam rising up to Korson's nose, the cooling of warriors blood that once boiled hot with confrontation. His death imminent, under drowning by the blood of his own and his enemies, the presence of the Cherokee boldly outlined against the black shadows, the warriors crumbling around him to dust, to be soaked up by their own blood, fear never entered Korson's mind. But reality wavered, flickered like tiny ripples of tide as the blood filled the chamber.

He fought the instinctiveness of struggling, he had nowhere to go. He was guarded by the Cherokee as well, if escape was at all possible. He fixed back on the eyes of the Cherokee, the wolf. The same wolf he'd seen in the forest? The eyes were absolutely unwavering, not a flicker evident. Like the body, not a flicker of muscle movement, but for the point of breaking the surface tension of the blood pool. As though the Cherokee warrior himself were melting into the very pool of blood.

Korson was too young to achieve any balance of thought, any true spirituality that comes through experience and coherency of thought. But briefly, briefly he lifted his chin in defiance of his own death. He propped himself up on his feet, silently fighting fate. Then realized in a flash of insight that whatever fate there was, whatever God or Goddess decided this for him, whatever trenchant force that allowed the Cherokee to bring this otherworldly smoke to the earth and rain havoc upon a pogrom, it was foolish to fight fate. Who was he to angrily refuse death? To step out of the cycle? Yet every time someone died he saw fear in their eyes. From the day he was born; he saw fear in his mother's eyes, perhaps anger at this weak young baby who sprung bloody from her legs, who had the force of will to kill her in the first few minutes of his life so <u>he</u> could enter the world. Saw the rage of a warrior melt into cowardice as his father died in front of him on the battlefield, in the last of the Great Tribal wars, melt against some unknown force...now so obviously the same force as this, the Cherokee.

 He would not fight his fate. But he would be damned if he was defeated! And laughter filled the air, (perhaps only in the vessel though. Who knew what went on outside of it?) distant laughter, quiet and teasing and fading off on the wind that it came in on. Throaty...a woman's perhaps? That of a Goddess?

 Korson put his palms together in front of his chest and sank slowly down to meet the rising blood in the vessel of shadow, the instrument of death. Perhaps even death itself. Who was to say how death came to greet the earth's inhabitants? In the form of a smiling beast of a Cherokee, on a field where fate was met as stick clashed with stick in a game that tested, to the utmost, most brutal and harsh of human limitations of pain and suffering.

 The blood seeped over the crevices in his cracked and broken and scabbed lips, filling his sores and clinging to the tissue in his mouth. His first taste of blood, blood that wasn't his own. Though his soul was already soiled with patricide and matricide. He was forced to swallow the blood, it crept into his body through his nostrils, through the ocular cavities in his skull. He sputtered as it began to fill his lungs.

 But he could still see! Though the blood looked opaque he could see as it surrounded his senses, as though there was another reality within the liquid of life, as though it was sentient in its own way, its own right. And who was to say it wasn't sentient? It carried the unbreakable code of life, of death, of power, lineage, it could turn man against man by differentiating the colour of their skin! And whose heart didn't race just a little at the sight of their own blood oozing through a break in their wrist?

 The Cherokee actually <u>was</u> melting into the crimson pool! Was it possible that everyone's fate had a loophole? Korson, his flash of insight sparking some wisdom in his youth, didn't hesitate to debate this good fortune, he just dove to the exit. He stretched through the shadow vessel, the smoke holding him back as though they were living, rubbery cables, as though they didn't want to let him go. (Sticky hands of fate!) And perhaps his perseverance had angered whatever God/Goddess it was. Perhaps it impressed the higher powers. He was thrust out of the shadow like a rocket, trailing bits of smoke and blood and soaked mud and grass. He landed rudely and hard on the now empty lacrosse field, coughing up the swallowed blood, emptying his lungs of the precious liquid, striving to fill his body with another valuable commodity, oxygen. He kissed the ground reverently, a little humbly, grateful to be feeling the cold reality of the wet earth, apologetically for bruising the grass with his abrupt arrival.

He was alive; the cost his perception of reality, his precious lacrosse stick that he carved from his own hands. The war paint was washed from his skin.

Big circles filled his mind: fate, the loophole, the very earth; the stars and sun, the migratory path of his people. Eggs, even his testicles.

"Caquay Ahpacee." The words carried the same tone as the Cherokee used..

"Nah tova, what happened to the world?" Korson hadn't learned to speak in the harsh modern tones he used with Graham St. Croix. He was barely over a decade in age, nothing close to a century yet. Did the Shaman witness his struggle?

"You have followed your father. You are thought of as a disgrace to your people, for your murderous ways, for deserting game in fear afterwards."

He spit blood from his mouth, said, "I don't care. Who needs them? They never loved me!"

The Shaman, the nah tova, who is the wise one, he never got angry. What was the use of anger, such unbridled, uncontrollable emotion? But the solid look in his eyes, unwavering and stern, said that if anger was his option he would exercise it now.

"Do not ever deny that you are Blackfoot! You have been drenched in their blood, you are of them and they of you. They have never loved you. You were outside of them, apart from their world. But they cared for you, made you what they are. They fear me, too, they think I am so much more than they. I am the witch of the witches. But do I hate them? I give, I never ask but what I need."

"But I can never return to them."

The nah tova shook his head. He tilted as though listening.

"They deny your name, the same as they denied your father's name." Even the Shaman, entrenched in the ways of Blackfoot, would not speak the name of Caquay Ahpacee's father. Even saying 'your father,' a reference to the disgraced warrior, could be tantamount to scorn. He tilted his head again, listening. "They are preparing to leave so you cannot return."

"Are you there now?" The nah tova nodded his head. "So my belongings are no longer my own then." In the space of hours Korson had to become a man, truly solitary; he had to wrestle with a higher force for his death, he had lost his precious lacrosse stick, lost his people. Though, to the Shaman's word he was not to deny his heritage. He would crumble to dust a Blackfoot.

"I will return to where they are leaving then." Korson had decided he would return to the forest and mountain region, to where he saw the wolf.

Only a broken lacrosse stick and footsteps reddened with the blood of his people left in his wake, Korson, Caquay Ahpacee so named in Blackfoot by the

Cherokee, began the journey to where he last held a bond to the real world, to the circle. The wheel was turning, and the coming season was winter, the time of the God. Chilled winds brittled bones in Korson's fingers, the chill crushingly numb in his appendages and crawling lizard-like into his thighs, his arms, his chest. He felt bigger, stronger, the test of fate and the little brother of war thrusting him to a state of resilience. The stars were eyes watching him as he shivered back home, the last place his nomadic people had settled.

The chill had bit his ears and his thoughts, he hugged himself and, without consciously realizing it, overshot the lake where his people had not lingered long so as to shun his presence. It was only when the sun came up and he collapsed at the base of Whiteface Mountain that he came to his senses as to his location. Though his inattentiveness actually benefited him in the sense that the constant motion of his body had kept him awake and safe from lapsing into a coma from exposure. He curled up against the comfort of a large rock and under the lukewarm sun.

He hated being awoken and at first thought it was the early chill brought about by the cover of the Adirondack mountains. Though he'd slept enough and his senses became somewhat aware of what was going on around him. But as his awareness rose with the setting sun, he fixed stares with a lupine lolling it's spittle drenched tongue at him. According to Native legends, when one chose a spirit animal as a familiar, that animal, whenever encountered, would be a protector. The wolf had obviously followed Caquay Ahpacee, as it could be no accident that they both appeared in the same place. It had the unmistakable glassy grey eyes that glinted red when struck by the light.

Korson shook the sleep from his eyes, and rose, bones cracking painfully at their joints. The wolf jerked its head and paw, scuffing the ground. Was this the Cherokee? Had he become a servant to Korson? Korson approached the wolf slowly but confidently, not a trace of fear. This was, after all, his spirit animal. It had accompanied him on his journey, he'd spent the night with it. Why would he need to fear harm from it? He was taught to commune with the natural world, with the soil. And things that Christianity feared and preached as evil were not necessarily so to a Blackfoot. The Christian Devil, the Christian God, that linear thinking, had no place in a world of circles.

He put his hand to the head of the dog, stroked the ears and between the eyes. He crouched down next to it and looked at the marvelous orbs. But saw nothing but a beautiful creation, a phenomenon of nature akin to water falling like a crystal spray from a great height. No depth of perception, no utter realization. Just simple beauty.

And purple, black and blue descended over the mountains, bathing the majestic vista of Whiteface Mountain in darkness. Korson had no idea if the Shaman's spirit could find him, ever perhaps. No matter how strong the nah tova was perceived to be. But the wolf next to him was comforting, his sprit animal.

Blood had caked to Korson's teeth and he tasted the flakes of it, tasted disgrace, bitter separation from a bitter relationship. But why did he feel the disgrace that was thrust upon him? It was, after all, misplaced. Though the reality of it was that all the Blackfoot had abandoned him, denied his existence. And he'd been taught a lesson in reality, the dissipation of the Cherokee proof that his eyes may not perceive what is really occurring.

The Blackfoot held the belief of cristacoom sah, the evil sprit, as part of their heritage. One of the myths, though a small and seldom told story, was of the caquay ahpacee, the night wolf, that which the Cherokee had renamed Korson. Korson knew nothing of the tale of the caquay ahpacee, the vampire, but had gathered from the connotation of the words issued from the Cherokee that he was being referred to as a cristacoom sah, perhaps even by one of their own. Was it the unwilling matricide that planted the seed in Korson to be set upon the left path by the fates? Would he see the wrath of the Gods and Goddess's if he chose to spit on his path? The world is a puzzle, the pieces large and intricately cut, such fine corners and details so human yet so impossibly replicated by the very beings that are the very pieces themselves.

The trick is not intelligence. It is understanding, the way some instinctively understand lacrosse, or love, or art. And some instinct buried in Korson, sparked at birth by the accidental murder of his womb, knew what his namesake legend, the caquay ahpacee, meant. But still he didn't have full realization nor any remote understanding, nor did he seek it. That would raise a new series of questions: Why would the Gods want to confound us? Why would they pluck a mere mortal out of the great cycle of the very earth? Wouldn't that mean that their puzzle would never be complete?

Now he merely sought food, and found only some berries to tide him over. He would conserve his strength until he came across better sustenance. The coming winter would not be friendly. He wouldn't have the stores of his people. By denying him, they essentially condemned him to death. Someone-perhaps a Goddess with a throaty laugh-tittered because his fate was indeed death.

The berries were okay for him, but his pet may start slobbering at the sight of him if he didn't feed the beast. He was tired but had lost time, and so he walked with the wolf at his side. And it was obvious that these two, from different planes of the same world, had found friendship with each other, both lone wolves. Though perhaps the wolf was not even of the earth...

Indeed Korson's life, his very soul, had reached a dark season, and he headed north despite the coming winter. It was an option to enter a town. But he laughed when he thought that. It was insane to lead such a life! Not to live off the land! The cold felt good, made him feel alive, and he was bright and his legs energetic despite the later hour. He trotted with the wolf beside him. Amazingly, he had no idea where he was, despite his knowledge of the area. It was telling how attached he really was to the tribe of the Blackfoot. Despite always being the outsider, the loner, there was certainly a connection he hadn't fathomed in his formative years, though he was taught of the teachings of the cycle, that everyone had their place in this life.

And with the coming of morning he found himself growing weary, and he slept. As the sun hotly intruded into the night, he found himself getting heavy and tired, the heat sapping his strength. His arm was a pillow, and his pet, his namesake spirit animal, was his blanket, the rhythmic breathing and steamy innards wrapped in fur such a relaxing dream, such a warm carpeting across his prone body. And once in a while the wolf would shift, and he felt as though he lost a part of himself as the cold sun was nothing compared to his wolf.

It was as though it were a mirror, the seasons, the changing of day. Night was winter and the dusk and dawn were spring and autumn and the Goddess ruled the night, the God the day.

In the early evening he woke wolfless, his stomach rumbling of hunger. He saw the wolf a short distance away near the trees, his eyes fierce and reddened, the foreboding black smoke spewing from his wet nostrils as though they came from a steam engine. He approached his spirit animal and it was calm, smiling a bit as it looked up at him. It lolled out it's tongue and panted. A normal wolf. Just a normal wolf. Korson had taken to calling him meetah, which was Blackfoot for dog, as he already had the name of the creature as his own. Though animals were extremely respected and worshipped among Natives, the Blackfoot didn't keep many pets. They were worshipped as gifts from the Gods to be used, never wasted, always revered.

Why was it that mortals looked to animals for their inspirations? A so-called lesser being? Korson didn't yet comprehend his connection to the wolf. It was a connection born of instinct, of a desire to be part of nature. To learn and expose one's own piece of the puzzle. The Gods had obviously shattered a mortal mind and from its fragments sprung every living being that was not man. But in the mind of each man one animal gained a hold, dominated his soul and his path and his being. Thus the other animals receded to the shadows, mere aspects of a larger personality.

He woke dry, the sun bright but cold. Even the cold couldn't invigorate him now. His energy was low, he hadn't eaten since before the lacrosse game two days ago, but for the berries. He found water and drank it, it alleviated his hunger, but only for a short time. He was reluctant to kill, and had neither weapons nor any means of carrying the leftover remains. And he hadn't seen much; his time occupied the obsession of travel and the burden of sleep.

Meetah, the dog-wolf, was again gone when Korson awoke. He crouched at the pond and slowly drank the water, though it was gritty and black. Again the dog appeared some distance away. And with something in his mouth. He'd killed a squirrel and had brought it back for Korson. He dropped the animal to the ground when Korson had approached him. Though the meat was raw and the blood was cold, Korson was grateful for the nourishment.

It got dark quickly as they were surrounded by trees most of the time. It was deceptive, as when they got to a clearing there was still plenty of light, but the trees managed to filter it out with shadows. He knew his fight with fate was not over. It never was. But was he condemned to die in the forest, alone? Again that throaty laugh, a giggle. Everything blurred into a swirl, the last few dots of light making bright yellow streaks between green-black leaves and thick brushstrokes of brown bark. Struck, awestruck, by the mesmerizing removal of reality, the dank misconception of his perception. Alone he was, his face in the cold dirt of the forest floor. He spit out the dirt, his tongue tasting earthworms and squirrel. He'd struck the ground hard and his cheek was scraped from the pebbles in the earth, and they seeped tiny pricks of blood.

"Don't lose too much of it." The voice spoke to him in his own language though no words were spoken. Korson had jumped, threw himself onto his back, propped up by his arms. Before him the speaker, a dark haired girl, she giggled. That throaty laugh. "Don't be afraid! Please?" But she didn't look mortal to him, and her skin was fair. Her eyes like those of the wolf, the Cherokee. Were they all one and the same? Was this a Goddess? And meetah, the wolf, was gone, too.

His hands shook out of fear. He knew true fear, deep and passionate fear. Though he put a mask over it. His warpaint, it was still on, his mask. He had never known such fear as this, the only fear he did know was the rush of adrenaline from the heat of a lacrosse game. He'd never known true war, only its little brother. He was never taught fear of the Gods, that the Gods were vengeful. But he did hold the belief of the cristacoom sah, the evil spirit. And there was a very thin veil of difference between the two.

"Please don't go away." Her voice was musical, soft and pleading. It was difficult to deny such sweetness. "I'm lonely too." Though her visage was beautiful, but also foreboding, the very thought of such beauty being associated with death.

In a rare moment of speech, Korson said, "I have to go."

"Where are you going?" He didn't answer, just looked at her with fading awe, his features becoming unreadable, even to her. "You don't know, do you? Well, maybe I could come with you. I know you want a companion!" Was this meetah? He wasn't bold enough to ask, he didn't want to offend what was obviously a Goddess, or at least a spirit. And he didn't want to give away his hand. Perhaps she expected him to have knowledge? Why else would she reveal herself? So this is what the elders saw when they smoked too much peyote.

He got up and began to walk, neglected to brush himself down. She burst out of the shadows to join him at his side, much like the meetah wolf did. She was naked, as though just born of the very earth; dirt matted the shine of her hair, her toes were wrapped in thick wet earth and her skin was fair beneath the black-brown soil clinging to her. Korson merely stopped and looked at her. She was small, but she carried herself as though she were taller. He pulled off his top and covered her with it.

Korson looked a little emaciated, the full day of battle and days without food having taxed him. But food was a more mundane reality now. His hunger lay in other places.

"How can you go anywhere if you don't know where you're going?" Korson stopped and looked at her.

"I'm going that way," he said, and he pointed north. It was the most likely route his people would have taken. They would reverse their tracks before continuing on a new one to confuse him. And he had to find the Shaman again. There were only so many days one could survive on one's soul. They walked quietly together, one a just born sprite, immortal and alive, the other a warrior on the verge of manhood. She skipped beside him, full of mirth and happiness, a contrast to his young angst and brood.

"What's your name?" He disliked communicating with her, she hardly moved her lips when she spoke and when she did the words were gibberish.

He answered, reluctantly, "Caquay Ahpacee," the first time he'd ever referred to himself as that. She had to think for a minute, as though her memory was failing. And then her name hit her brightly.

"Hm. Ummmm...Talissa!" Then they didn't speak much. Her way of speaking was eerie and disturbing to Korson. But Talissa was vivacious, prodding, bursts of energy as a new-born kitten has. "How come you're going somewhere when you don't know where you're going? How come you don't smile? Why don't you talk? Do you want your shirt back?" Korson ignored her presence, he focused on his path, on the journey. But Talissa persisted. "How come we look different? Why is my skin lighter? How come some trees are green and some are red? Why are those two animals fighting like that?"

"Quiet." Talissa abruptly silenced herself, and her mirth was doused by the wetness in her eyes. She was sensitive, empathic, and picked up more meaning from Korson's tone than he meant to convey. But Korson hadn't bothered to look at her, and she cried silently for a few minutes.

Then she touched his shoulder, said quietly, "I'm sorry." He didn't answer her, but she wouldn't be deterred, she tugged his shoulder, not enough to actually stop him but enough to prod him into stopping and she hugged him, put her head on his chest. "I'm sorry. Do you forgive me?"

He was quiet, and her eyes conveyed the tension she felt, so he nodded his forgiveness. She immediately broke back into her kittenish effervescence. She bounced back into the walk, her first step taking her high in the air. Korson walked stoically, Talissa bouncing beside him like a sprite, a pipe-smokin' leprechaun. He was wary of her, quiet, but less afraid. She seemed a cristacoom of some sort, but less like the Goddess he first took her for, and his upbringing didn't allow for vengeful deities to a great degree.

And he did, secretly, privately, enjoy the companionship, though he kept an eye open for meetah. It was pointless to search for the wolf, though he hoped that somehow they would cross paths. The wolf could track his scent, and perhaps she was looking for more food for him. Or rather, tired of his company and returned to the pack, where she belonged.

The chill of the night, and Korson now shirtless, began to dig into Korson's bones, his shoulders and nipples. It seemed to affect Talissa not a bit. And neither did she tire, her step continued to be bouncy and her back was erect. Though Korson, more from stubborn pride, outwardly remained as though he could walk on endlessly.

Talissa had shown herself to be emotional, her moods a rainbow on a pendulum. It seemed as though in the space of one instant to another, that her strength was sapped. Her steps made tracks in the damp dirt of the forest floor. Korson remained rigid, he didn't fall in for her suggestive idiosyncrasies. He continued to walk.

Talissa said, "Can we stop? I'm so tired." Her voice had assumed a contradictory maturity, quite in contrast to her childish mannerisms earlier. And the unwavering Korson didn't align himself easily with enigmatic personalities. Talissa's heart thumped like a rabbit's foot, she grabbed Korson's arm and chest in her hands, her nails tore his reddish-brown flesh and made train tracks that slightly bled, acutely throbbing in the cold. "Stop! I can't go on. I can't...move..." She slid to the ground and pulled his skin as she fell to her knees, choking, grabbing her throat, spitting the foul taste out of her mouth. She dug her nails into the mud, squishing tiny bugs in her palms.

"I travel by night. The days are hot for walking." There was still night left and Korson wanted to continue walking. He cared nothing for her ills. Ills were common, people were sick some days, others not, and why should illness be a reason to desist in daily routines? The sun still swung the earth around, why waste time over discomfort?

"Please. I can't. I swear I would if I could, but something is pressing on my insides." She reached her hand out, and she reached out her empathy, she tried to elicit his sympathy. She wasn't mortal, but she was still a woman, and her attractiveness held the danger that all beauty held. That love could steer men down improper roads and swerve them from the rigid logic they usually adhered to. "Please..." Korson acceded. He was hard hearted but not heartless. And perhaps because he himself was abandoned, he wouldn't abandon her. This, despite the fact that no friendship had yet been forged.

Talissa trembled, shook nauseously on the earthen floor. Korson looked down on her, took silent pity on her, as she was most certainly immobilized by her illness. She lost control of her limbs, as though her bones were gelatin, and a stench rose as she unwillingly voided her body of waste, her thighs looking as though spilt over with steaming coffee. She choked and coughed again, and remained still and silent afterwards, her seizure seemingly over. Korson bent over and picked her up, somewhat carefully so as not to upset her stomach. She put her arms around his neck, he felt her grip, flaccid and weak. Her entire body fluttered with a spasmodic tremble, almost imperceptible. Korson carried her to some water and made her drink form his cupped hands. She drank slowly, then eagerly, the water soothing her quite noticeably.

Korson gathered some wood and struck up a fire for warmth. The lack of motion made him more aware of the cold. He wasn't sure how much darkness was left, it felt endless now. And they had nothing but one set of clothing between the two of them, the open air, fire and the stars above.

While Korson searched for some berries, Talissa sat before the fire, recuperating. She looked at the dancing flames, the colour of the body deep and tangerine, the heart blue like a sapphire. She would glance towards the wiry, tall silhouette of Korson, perhaps a little afraid he would leave her alone. But she was vulnerable of mind now, the physical state of one's being reflected upon the mind. She didn't have clarity of thought and was obviously unaware that Korson was most certainly not dishonourable. Korson returned and sat down not too close to her, allowing for a buffer zone. He had two handfuls of berries and held one out to Talissa, but she refused it. He thought her foolish. They had nothing to carry water or food with, why should she not eat a little while the opportunity occurred?

"My stomach hurts too much," she said, as though answering the expression on his face. Or his thoughts. Korson popped berries into this mouth, slowly and one by one, though his appetite was ravenous. Gluttony would only serve to destroy his resolve for the upcoming days, though it would quell his hunger for the moment. And Talissa trembled in front of the fire. The only noise was the crackling of burning wood and the occasional flutter of wings. Both of the figures were insignificant under the vastness of the blackened sky. While the image brought further shudders from Talissa, the vastness like a weight, Korson remained relaxed. He would devour insects to keep the last spark of life left in him going. Talissa, in her current physical state, looked as though she would make a bed of the earth once again.

The separateness, the space between them made Talissa feel more alone. As though Korson weren't even there, and she had to keep looking at him to remind herself of his presence.

"Caquay?" she ventured. He merely raised an eyebrow at her. "Can you say my name?" The question puzzled him, and he looked at her, his face still blank but obviously wondering at what she was asking. "It's just that you've never said my name. I want to hear you say it." Korson popped a few more berries.

"Talissa." He put no emotion into it, stated it. The word was rough, his tongue being used to Blackfoot. This name was very smooth and musical, it required skill to truly say it properly. But she appreciated the gesture and she smiled. Her pain was less now. Or that she had endured it long enough to be numb to it. The cold was numbing and they could see their breath on the air.

"Why do we look different?" she asked, then rephrased it: "What are you?"

"I'm Blackfoot."

"Oh." She drew in the dirt for a second. "I don't know what I am. Or where I'm from. I can't remember anything."

"You are a cristacoom sah."

"What is that?"

"An evil spirit." She looked at him with a curious expression. Why had he called her evil? She didn't do anything bad, or wrong. Perhaps he was just bitter at having to stop walking to wherever it was he wanted to walk to.

"All I remember is a great waterfall, I think." Korson kept his counsel, he neglected to mention that when she'd ambushed him in the forest she'd hovered mere inches off the ground. And that when she'd stepped from the shadows her visage had reduced from the gleaming, unconforming ghoulishness to a more palatable, less foreboding view. As though something enigmatic in her had snapped as she crossed the veil. That to exist on this earth one had to cut one's wings. "It hurts to remember sometimes." Korson nodded with her, was empathetic with her statement. "You have memories that hurt?"

He nodded again. Talissa asked him what it was that had hurt him.

"My people think I am a disgrace. They will not set eyes upon me." He summarized the tale for her, leaving out the full details of the Cherokee and only referring to him in the most abstruse manner.

She had slyly moved closer to him, and he amazingly didn't realize it until she was close enough to put her arm around him.

"We need each other." It seemed so true, so right, as he felt her chilly heat, the inner warmth fighting against the outer cold. On a journey to nowhere, under the open sky, they'd found each other. And perhaps later, when Talissa's mind was free of enteric pain, when the lucidity that revealed itself in sparks was hers again, she would realize why Korson journeyed aimlessly like he did. If not for serendipity she would be alone with her vomit and feces-caked thighs and the burden of this reality would consume her.

Her wish was granted when a shudder of pain overtook her intestines and she found herself leaning in Korson's lap, his arms around her. Though she trembled and even the force of his grip-the only sympathy that she could gather from him-couldn't stop her shaking. She shook herself to sleep, the last thing she could recall being the slow and silky fall to the earth in his arms, like that of water falling from high up into a lake and not even causing a ripple.

There was tremendous heat and discomfort in her slumber, and the only thing that kept her grounded to the world she was in was Korson's touch. The heat made her slick with sweat and every opening in her body was hot and sticky and uncomfortable. Though the sun was in a cold autumn phase, it felt like Indian summer. And she would not wake until she felt the coming of moon and Korson was trapped beneath her, feeling her wet weight upon him. It was strange and new, the bond possible between man and woman unbeknownst to him.

Korson woke to find the burden on his chest relieved, Talissa having risen and now attempting to light the fire anew. All that was left of it was ash. The blanket of night had again begun to roll itself over them. She couldn't strike up the flame the way Korson had. He took the rocks from her hands and began to work on lighting the teepee'd wood, when suddenly it burst into flame on its own. He looked at Talissa. She wore a little grin that marked her guilty of this little mischief.

"You want to walk again, don't you?" she asked. He nodded to her. Korson gathered another handful of berries as nourishment before they set out again. He looked so undernourished his ribs were visible from under his skin. He had an obsession to keep walking, as though his literal path would become metaphysical. His hunger had become an entity unto its own, so voraciously powerful it was distributed to the very limbs of his body. Yet, somehow, perhaps out of some twisted, nonsensical desire born of the very hunger itself, he managed to strive ahead despite the expected weaknesses. Three days he had subsisted by slowly popping berries into his mouth. He'd been spared the initial stages of hunger due to his involvement in the little brother of war, and the pangs had stabilized over the past few days of travel. But, like walking in to the calm eye of a storm, one had to overcome enormous odds to come out again. The breaking point was upon him.

The fire was doused with handfuls of water, and they drank before they continued in case they didn't happen upon another source of water to camp by. Korson's mind thought again of murder, as they would need supplies for the coming winter, and soon. It was already difficult enough to find animals as food and would be more so in the cold months. Plus one dead carcass was worth more than its weight in food; it was worth the tools that could be carved of its bones, the clothing that could be made of its skins and the steamy warmth of the freshly cut belly. A deer or a buffalo would be a blessing from the Gods right now.

Again they set out north. Korson's soul chasing the winter it was reaching, chasing the path of the God. Talissa, energetic and vivacious, brightly bounded along beside him. Her energy seemed boundless, until perhaps the Witching Hour, when her enthusiasm began a noticeable decline. And again, like the previous night, pain overtook her bowels and they had to stop, still with plenty of darkness left, too.

Talissa hugged her midsection as she sat in front of the fire. Despite the heat she shivered a little. Korson was next to her, still disciplining his hunger by slowly popping berries into his mouth.

"You miss them don't you?" she said. He raised an eyebrow. "The Blackfeet." And he laughed. He actually laughed! The sky boomed his guffaw back to him.

"We're just called Black*foot*," he said. A berry burst in his mouth.

"So do you miss 'em?" He had to think a moment.

"Yes. I do. I didn't realize that I had my place there." The fire crackled rudely and spit sparks at their feet. The wind had died to a dull kiss, though the cold was ever-present.

"You used to dream of running away. You thought they never loved you and you wanted to leave, just run off and roam the woods by yourself. You're living your dream." Such a succinct and upsetting insight into his character! She had pulled this from deep in his mind. This disturbed him, not because she saw into his soul, but because Talissa had offended him with her interpretation of his thoughts. That he would live a dream! The implication that the world in his mind was better than the reality that was provided by the Gods! This was not a Goddess, one who uttered such blasphemous statements. Though maybe he was angered because he *was* living out his dream. And the reality of it was an utter disappointment compared with the imagining. "It's okay to dream."

"Dreams are like shadows. Fleeting unreality's that run from the light of truth."

"Are you going back to them?" He said no. "Why don't you just go back to them?"

"Because I'm a disgrace in their eyes. Therefore *I am* a disgrace." It didn't make sense to Talissa. He was unhappy in his dream yet stubbornly refused to return to his reality.

"At least you have dreams. I can barely remember how I got here."

"Maybe your pain is the key to your mind."

"I don't understand."

"Do you know the cause of your pain? The mind sends messages to the body. Any physical manifestation of pain is due to some anguish unresolved in your mind." What is the cause of earthly anguish? Intelligence? Or rather, a consciousness of being. Knowing you are alive and being able to contemplate the meaning of existence. More likely though, emotions. More likely-

"Love. I think I was in love." And love is the sweetest of nectar to suckle, until it turns sour and yellow. One has to be strong. It is a test of character, of the passion of your convictions. "You've never been in love, have you Caquay Ahpacee?" Did she see some weakness in him? Perhaps his bitter severance from the womb? Would it not make sense that a baby who viciously and maliciously tore his way into the world would naturally be looked upon with disdain by sensitive women?

"You should eat. You haven't eaten in days." Still she rejected the offer of food. Snips of nauseous, empty hunger and thumping, throbbing dizziness of the head were affecting even Korson, a young man budding quickly into sturdy conviction and stubbornness of character, on an almost constant basis. Talissa had moved next to him, she took his arm and put it around her, to feel warmth, to feel attachment to the world. She needed his affection every night, every time the illness overtook her. It satisfied her pain, to have him touching her. In such vast emptiness, broken only by trees holding their shriveled, gnarled branches over them, two abandoned people sat so utterly alone in front of a fire. And nature didn't look so spectacular as it did foreboding. As the sheer emptiness of the land was quiet anger at having been trampled on for centuries by thankless mortals who lived striving to mark their existence and died like everyone else: as dust and nitrogen and food for soil.

Talissa turned Korson's chin towards her with her fingers. She pressed her lips up against his, cautiously at first, only the bare-branched trees and blinking stars a witness to their adolescent awkwardness. Though nature is wise and knows how to overtake the passions of two lost souls, and their kiss quickly and naturally became deep and intimate, *en francais*. With a warrior's buried instinct brought to light, with the gentleness of the slight wind in the air, Korson lowered Talissa to the ground slowly. She let out slight moan as his weight pressed atop her. The wind picked up, this time with some warmth, as though a blanket for them. Korson began to make love to her under the night.

"Ow, careful. It hurts. Slowly." And he felt the sticky, cold friction of her, the deadness of her love. But she wouldn't let him stop. He felt pain too, and neither would he stop himself. The thrill of love was enough to overmatch the hurt. And his inexperience left him ignorant of the abnormality of her physical means of love. It took most of the remaining night to find completion, and when the climax of their tale took effect, their skin tore from the burst of frenzy and they mingled blood from their lacerated genitals. In each other's arms, the last of the shakes leaving them still, they slept another day, not in the least bothered by the inconsequential heat of the sun.

Korson woke second, Talissa having again shed the pangs of her illness, to find her sitting on a large rock, staring at the most spectacular sunset. He walked over to her and she put a finger up as if to silence him, as if he needed silencing. There was a fascinating spectrum painted across the sky, and the chill fall air shellacked it, making the tones shiny and permanent. Between the brown-black swaying branches of the trees was a fading, sparkling gold, like someone had melted the most precious of jewelry instead of using mere paint. And with such precision blended the tone into a bold, bloody orange, as though the medium was the juice of the fruit itself, but much more purified and striking. The orange faded into a red, vapid yet quietly powerful. And that quiet power became the dark, overpowering black of the night, spreading across the sky. Talissa stared for over an hour, entranced by the sight, enamored by the pureness of colour. The fading presence unbearably sad. The absence of colour, the black, carrying something far greater, far more powerful, hidden inside it, something unimaginable. Korson tried to match her will, to stare at the disappearing sky a long as she did. But his eyes would eventually hurt, so he resigned himself to occasional glances at beauty and collecting berries and watching Talissa watch nature. Only when the colour had bled and melted into the horizon would she remove herself from the rock and begin their travels anew.

The look of the wolf had returned to her eyes. Korson remembered meetah, his wolf-dog, and indeed had some emotion for the creature, as well as for the Shaman. Though the void of companionship could be filled, there was something hollow about the replacement. As though intangible pieces of us were left behind as gifts for the intangible pieces we took from others. Neither memory was as fulfilling as when the two came together.

They had walked for several weeks, and with less time needed for Talissa to recover from the fatigue of illness with each passing night after their first tryst. Though lovemaking was painful, Korson found that constant sex filled Talissa with piss and vinegar, and she was less affected by her illness and she could travel longer. She felt the same pain as he, and curiously Korson, still determined to melt miles beneath his feet, had developed a limp and now had to plumb the depths of his stamina to keep up with Talissa. Lovemaking can awaken untold desire, passion beyond that of the fleshly variety. The most astounding creations of man, the brutalist atrocities, have been because of love; and each and every creator is born of woman, of the mother, who is bred to love and create.

They'd reached the raging white froth of the great *rivière St-Laurent*. To cross it would be an impossibility without a bridge. It was calm in parts but neither had confidence in their swimming abilities. Korson knew of the great river, and it afforded them two possibilities: one, to have a constant guide and water supply, as they could simply follow the north-eastern lilt of the river; two, they had enough clear water to bathe in, rather than the muddied waters they'd had to drink from. Talissa, who amazingly had no appetite, in fact looked as energetic as ever. She'd even seemed to be losing the eerie pallor that she'd displayed when she'd first frightened Korson. The clear waters of the *St-Laurent* served to invigorate her more, as she shamelessly stripped off her borrowed shirt and immersed herself in the polar waters. She splashed the water on her face, the droplets that fell from her hand glinting crystalline in the dying sunlight. Her small appetite was in no way associated with her thirst as she drank handful after handful of water.

Korson, sore from night after night of coitus, stripped and dipped himself into the calm recess of water, his throbbing purple member eternally grateful for the soothing wet chill of the water that crept beneath the scabs of clotted blood. Rising out of the river, both with long and luxuriant dark hair dripping water, their bodies glistening as though oiled, they stepped onto the shore and, the earth's muddy fingers squishing between their toes, celebrated the shivering coldness of the night with an embrace. Icicles nearly formed from the tips of their extremities as they had nothing to dry themselves with, though they tried with kisses. So as to prevent their joints from freezing they began to walk by the riverside and carried their garments with them until they were dry enough to put them back on.

Across the great river they saw faintly (in fact, it was Talissa who spotted it) the fires of the town of Cornwall. Neither of them knew, nor had any way of knowing, that they were crossing the border from America to the Canadian province of Québec. In fact, Korson had very little concept of political structure, in the sense of divisions and borders. Political concept to him was of the democratic hierarchy of a tribe.

Talissa had become openly contented, while Korson was quietly so. The openness, the emptiness of nature was a misconception. It was the trauma of change for Korson, for Talissa the uncertainty of an amnesiac, that had caused them worry. As well as the pangs of Korson's hunger lending credence to delusions of Talissa, his interest in love peaked by physical manifestations of lust, crying in her sleep and constantly vomiting a burning red liquid; though come the next evening he always awoke to find her resumed to her sprightly nature. The emptiness of nature was merely a reflection of the uncertainties of their minds, of their lack of a common goal. But who needed a goal? To apply a goal to an activity was to imply some desire to search for a meaning to existence. And the only desire awakened in them was the intangible, intoxicating desire that arose from their fucking.

They both maintained an aura about them, though it glowed dully now due to the lack of nourishment, the chill air, the fatigue of constant footsteps on uneven ground. Korson saved bursts of strength to pounce on squirrels and chipmunks for some meat, and when his acumen temporarily abandoned him, Talissa was surprisingly more than able to dart away in a blur and snatch up the creature. And always more efficiently than Korson, as though something in her was attuned to the earth.

They'd been traveling for nearly three weeks, and finally encountered an encampment of people. They couldn't immediately approach the encampment as they'd only discovered it in the waning hours of the night. Korson ushered Talissa to a distance from the camp that would ensure their safety, where they could themselves set up a fire without fear of being discovered and get some much needed sleep. They slept in each other arms, though Talissa gave the weary and scabbed Korson a reprieve from the nightly fucking that made her step with a spring.

Korson dreamt strongly, and he loved to dream, he hoped that the Shaman would visit him in his dreams. He held Talissa tightly and saw his eyes open wide, a bit suddenly, as though sleep snapped out of his body like it had been exorcised. He lifted his head up and over Talissa's shoulder, her skin was grey-white and dull, powdery, the smoothness contrasted against her dark and wavy hair. She was so beautiful, perfect and statuesque, shoulders rising almost imperceptibly with each breath, and though she looked beautiful to him, she would have looked sacrilegious to a Christian, almost dead. She let out a small moan with an exhalation of breath, and her lips, very grey, parted slightly to let out the sound. And the grey grew bright, runny carmine, blood spilling over her lips and smothering her chin, pouring out as though a waterfall. He thrust her away, she rolled listlessly in the fallen and now stained leaves, the blood turning dark and disappearing against the thick brown of the forested floor. Again he would look at himself holding his passion, and again she would lose her blood through her mouth. Atrocity! He held her and pushed her away several times, his dream black and grey and white until the splash of red was painted in, as though a mislaid pigment had slyly stolen its way to the canvass to create a masterpiece.

Talissa hung from a low-hanging, gnarled branch of a wise tree, swinging as though the wind was pushing her along rather than her withered muscles. Her skin-shirt barely touched her thighs, and a shadow met an inverted triangle where her legs met. Korson tended to the camp and prepared for departure-that is, he doused the fire that Talissa had lit while he still slept. Talissa, swinging and grinning mischievously, hopped down from the tree branch and they made their way to the clearing of campers they'd spotted the night before.

And, dismayed, came upon an empty clearing. Clearly there had been someone there, as indicated by the dead embers of a fire, the disturbances in the ground. This hadn't been some sylvan oasis, some false hope. (Had it? The throes of hunger caused more violent convulsions of reality in souls stronger than Korson's.)

Talissa said, dismayed, "They've gone. They've left us." Korson bent to the ground and examined the wagon tracks. There seemed to be a bit of a rush to their departure, there were several dropped items-among them, thankfully, a canteen to put some water in, though now they were traveling near the river and were in less need of it. They picked up some other items, and though they had no sack to carry them with would trade them for blankets and clothes later. They followed the direction of the tracks.

Korson had, from time-to-time in his travels, the feeling that eyes were upon him. And if he'd happened to push back the drape of a nearby shrub he would have come upon a pair of cold blue eyes that stared back at him from the pallor of death, from atop a skewed pile of bodies.

The only indication that they had switched nations had come from the fact that, when they finally caught up to the fleeing travelers, was that they were of French descent. The travelers had veered off the road in such a way so as to confuse any pursuers, turning left and backtracking, then straight and circling then off right in a zigzag pattern, as much as the trees would allow. Korson, well trained, was able to decipher the markings and pick out the true path.

Talissa followed Korson's lead as branches crunched in the night, cracking the silence. They saw the blinking of a fire between the old tree branches and moved to the clearing. But, upon entering it, found the camp abandoned, the fire untended and wagon left unguarded.

A man hidden to his left snatched Korson, he was grabbed around the throat and the cold metal of a blade pressed to the flesh of his neck, breaking into the skin near his jugular. Talissa had leapt to the right, the open side, with incredible reflexes, one step ahead of the moment. The branches that cracked beneath their feet had alerted the encampment to their presence. Though obviously they'd expected only one, or perhaps were lax from fear. Talissa had herself snatched one of the travelers who'd emerged from the trees, her hands becoming claws, the bones of her hands seemingly rising out of the taut skin. Her eyes blazed red and her lips became deathly, purplish-grey and formed a pouty yet angry oblong shape, teeth glowing, especially her fangs, oh so visible now. Korson's fear contained a duality: the knife at his neck and the monstrosity of his lover.

The captors uttered threats in French-threats obviously from the tone. Korson could not understand, of course, but Talissa spoke with almost perfect inflection, the words plucked from the minds of the ambushers. Though the men were uncultured they were logical, and one pointed to Korson, to the fact that he hadn't turned into the Gothic woodland creature Talissa had. She looked as though formal intelligence and consciousness had abandoned her in favor of a lower sentience, like that found in animals such as tigers, and with all the grace and ferocity. A strange situation had unfolded, made stranger still by the stalemate of the failed ambush and the stillness of the forest around them. The settlers had realized enough that a one-for-one trade-that is, Korson's life for their own captured man-would tilt the balance out of their favor. That the only thing holding Talissa back from an all out massacre was the fact that Korson was alive in their hands. If his body fell dead, her hand would drop. Korson, though all evidence before him would suggest otherwise, was capable of disengaging himself from his captor under his own strength, but his obstacle was an unfounded fear that Talissa herself would lower her guard once he'd done so and would in turn lose her life. That and the fact that he couldn't think quickly enough in this tense situation to make anything out of the change in her state. He was a warrior and his training instinctively took over despite his lack of experience in true battle; his concentration would not be swayed by realties, as was proven by his successful encounter with the Cherokee.

The line in a hostage situation was a strand, so delicate. For the bargaining chip, the very threat of the pleas, was tentatively balanced upon the survival of the hostage, and one's plea must be both vicious and sincere because the scale would crumble if the weight of the hostage were suddenly removed from the pan. To stretch the stalemate, to facilitate their escape, the French captors had reigned the horses and, the branches of trees scraping at the sides, moved their wagon through the narrow path leading away from the clearing. Korson allowed himself to be dragged away, the knife at his throat an excuse. An excuse to flee from his twisted love, and where could he be more safe than in the hands of terrorists? If he were to escape, who was to say she wouldn't chase him?

He was loaded into the wagon, his hands bound and a knife wielding Frenchman sat by his side. They must have heard the rumbling in his stomach because (Gods be thanked!) they gave him some food. It had been so long and he felt nauseous after a few minutes of eating, and couldn't eat his fill even. Which was beneficial as he would have vomited it up anyway, his shrunken stomach weak from undernourishment. But the food, as was the goal of his captors by giving it to him, calmed him, like candy to a screaming child being led to slaughter... He tried to peek out the back of the wagon but couldn't spy Talissa's form. And how could it be possible that they would abandon their captured comrade?

They had been discovered twice though, and were cutting their losses for escape. They'd already faced this demon at their earlier camp. They strategized hastily in French, Korson trying to listen to their tone to see if they had any inclination of killing him. Finally he spoke up, he raised his bound hands and tried to signify the rising sun, he grabbed his stomach feigning illness as he tried to communicate the fact that their pursuer fell nightly to a strange sickness before the dawn. But the French had misunderstood his attempts, they thought the young Blackfoot warrior was himself ill and they, out of fear, prejudice and underestimation of Talissa, threw him from the wagon so that he landed off the path and thudded his spine, and bumped his head against a fat tree. Shrugging off the pain he began to rub the rope on the tree until it frayed enough so he could break it with his own power. He thrashed and fell convulsively when the report of a shotgun frightened him to the ground in fear of his own safety. Several more shots were fired, and silence reigned king after the terrifying neigh of the horses was suddenly cut short.

Korson cautiously and quietly crept back to the edge of the path, moving forward so as to follow the continued route of the wagon. He found it stopped, the barricade in their way Talissa and her captive. One of the horses had fallen dead, blood pouring out of its exploded neck, parts of the wagon ripped from the falling of the animal attached to it. The Frenchmen wielded shotguns and knives, and Talissa had entered a wild rage because of Korson's absence. She plunged her hands into her captive's chest, ribs being splintered apart, plunging in to the wrist, and she pulled, a horrible cracking sound as the bones broke, the ribs opening to reveal the beating heart of the man, who would have screamed in scathing agony had his lungs not been torn to deprive him of air. Talissa, ever cruel, didn't completely murder him. She dropped him, his heart slightly thumping, showing he still had life, awareness, as he lay on the dirty ground of the forest all inside out.

One of the Frenchmen had enough sense left in him to overcome his frozen limbs, and he leveled the barrel of his shotgun at Talissa, but misfired and hit her shoulder, an explosion of fire and flesh. Talissa stood in the line of fire, completely uncomprehending of the concept of firearms until she'd been taught the lesson first-hand. Perhaps she'd had enough quickness and adrenaline to move her heart out of the line of the shell? The thrust had caught her off-guard and it threw her back, but she recovered, and with great vengeance turned upon her enemies. While Korson watched, rooted to the spot like a tree, morbidly fascinated with the slaughter, the graceful dance of the warrior far outnumbered yet so passionately devoted to victory. Talissa twisted heads half circle, plunged hand into heart and tore flesh with teeth, fangs razor sharp and so unnatural, yet so stunning as a weapon.

As the men lay dead around her, as she lapped up the blood from her lips and teeth and hands, she turned to look directly at Korson, though he'd begun to back away without a sound. Actually, to one so obviously preternatural as Talissa, the fear that made Korson's heart pound away at his chest, like the native oghtum, the drum, wooden stick on stretched leather, was audible to her sensitive ears. Her rage softened when she saw her love still alive and coveting her privately from behind the leaves. But her hunger remained strong. And Korson, who procrastinated leaving, was not completely stupid and kicked up leaves as he dashed away through the woods. Again he could feel those eyes upon him and wondered to the extent at which he underestimated Talissa's majical powers.

Korson discovered an amazing dexterity in him as he dodged branches and roots that thrust up from the forest ground. He listened for pursuit, and it sounded to him as though pursuit came from the air, rather than a ground attack. He wouldn't look back though. Not that he didn't dare, but he didn't want to sacrifice speed or risk tripping over a rock for a fleeting glance. He burst through a thick copse, almost thrilled at the thought of freedom that would be afforded by the cover provided by the thickening of trees. He slid as he burst out onto a gravel road, actually stopped for a second as the openness startled him. There was a field that would afford no cover, and he was too late to leap back into the forest if he so decided, and it would have been stupid to do so because he'd have leapt back into the arms of his now monstrous beloved.

It was only beauty that he saw emerging through the curtain of green and red and yellow leaves, beauty flawed only by sharp teeth and reddened lips, chin dripping with someone's juice.

She said the words intoned exactly like the Cherokee: Caquay Ahpacee. Korson stood there tense, knees bent and body held so rigid by his muscles that he nearly shook. He didn't know if she was naming him or just saying his name.

"Please don't be afraid of me. Please don't run away. You must have known what I was." And that was partly true. He'd had some inkling. After all, he wasn't stupid, he was raised in a culture drenched in myth and the belief of gods. Of higher powers. "I woke up." Perhaps she felt owed him an explanation, a repayment for his companionship. "I slept for a thousand years. I remember a love. It's hard to reach back over the darkness. To remember. But I didn't really awaken until now."

In the quiet darkness, the open air, Korson asked, "How old *are* you?" And with a rare moment of inflection in his tone.

"I'm as old as time." The answer struck Korson with awe, that someone was as old as that. That someone could fathom the concept of time to its beginning. But he mistook her meaning, she spoke in scriptural terms, in biblical meanings. For her time began when Christ was born. "It's been so long since I've tasted another man's soul. Come and kiss me." Korson shook his head no. It was like being trapped with the Cherokee again. He would not succumb to fear. "Don't deny yourself. You've seen my power. Imagine for yourself how good that power would feel. It's only a matter of time before I spread my wings over the earth. It's been over a thousand years and now it's only a matter of time."

"You speak in my head. I never liked you speaking in my head."

"Do you distrust me because of it?" Her tongue had not yet mastered the art of languages, and Korson's was based not on the Latin she knew, therefore she couldn't pick it up as easily as she would French. "Just have faith in me. Faith is so important." She was close to him now. He put out his hand to push her away by the shoulder. She was cristacoom sah, an evil spirit. She grabbed his hand, kissed it gently. It had the blood of her wound on it. She kissed every finger, every bloodied finger of his hand, and her grip was more than human, stronger than his, and each time she kissed him his fingers were dangerously close to her fangs and no matter how hard he tried he couldn't break the grip. There was no savage effrontery to this capture. He'd been netted in a spider's web, the strands delicate and soft; translucent, therefore visible if one looked closely and tread carefully. "You'll want it after you have it. You'll understand."

He struggled against her advances. There was no malice in her eyes, not the way there was when she'd murdered the travelers. She was bestowing this out of love. One was struggling, the other caressing. She pushed his head back and the very muscles of his neck flexed in resistance. But the taste was in him, they'd already mingled blood through their lovemaking. Such a treacherous fuck it was! Her bite upon his neck would complete their bond. It was a feral experience, her strength forced him to surrender to it and his muscles relaxed, became numb to the pain, tingly. He heard her growl, deep from her diaphragm, and her tongue rumbled against his wounded throat. It gently lapped up the blood dripping out of his bitten wound. The growl made his spinal cord vibrate, more so when it was joined by another growl, low and guttural. Talissa shook and suddenly disappeared.

Korson snapped from his delusion. Talissa lay on the ground. Now her neck too was gashed and bloody. The other growl, it had leapt from the trees. The wolf-dog, meetah, was crouched into attack position, the grey-white fur of the wolf bristled and tense. The fangs less lovely than Talissa's, but no less a relief for Korson to behold, dripping Talissa's blood and bits of her flesh clinging to the yellowed teeth. The wolf had been following Korson ever since Talissa had awoken in the forest. Meetah held a long, low growl at the base of her throat and released it slowly, guarding the space between Korson and Talissa. Perhaps animals, with the barest spark of sentience, with their senses more attuned to the earth and without the ignorance and egotism that man has bestowed upon himself, could understand what kind of creature Talissa was. Innocence can easily be found in animals and children.

Talissa, thinking herself faster, better than the wolf, made a move towards Korson. She didn't understand the connection, the Shamanistic properties, of the spirit animal. Korson was himself the wolf and under protection of his spirit animal as long as he was part of the great cycle. Meetah understood, through some hidden instinct, that her companion was about to be robbed from the cycle. (Though with mingled blood he was already doomed...)

Korson struggled to break the link, both with Talissa and the wolf. He had been robbed of blood, and already had the vampire's blood within him. It was only a matter of time before he would be too hungry to resist his first kill. But for now he would summon strength (and he had to go oh so deep, his reserves tapped to the limits already) to leap back into the forest. As painful as it was. His last sight was of meetah, the wolf, leaping upon his lover and fangs meeting flesh, claws meeting fur. The wolf itself had broken the bond, given her life at a vain last gasp at letting her companion escape to reality. She fought so valiantly, brilliantly. Knowing she was doomed to lose, she didn't fight to win, but rather to tie. To merely prolong the battle long enough for Korson to be able to put safe distance between them. Korson knew the exact moment when his spirit animal died, but, lamentably, couldn't hear that she died not with a yelp, but a vicious growl, an honourable death, worthy of a warrior. The effect was two-fold: the immediate reprieve provided by the dog was extremely beneficial in the short-term, but the further reaching effects were far more disastrous. The spirit animal was the last link, now severed, for Korson to the great cycle. He was no longer a part of the tribe of Blackfoot, though no one could steal his Blackfoot blood so long as it ran free in his veins. He had apparently been abandoned by the Shaman as well. And the spirit animal, the link to the earth, and therefore to the very cycle itself, had been severed through loyalty to save him. But, unbeknownst to the animal, Korson already had one foot outside the cycle...

He hadn't actually been fully turned towards vampirism, he'd been able to stave off the illness-his era being on the rising cusp of science diseases are looked upon with awe and misunderstanding. His body, ready to spring into powerful manhood, was woefully deprived of blood, and he had a gnawing thirst rise in him whenever someone came near. His willpower, coupled with the botched initiation to the Undead-he'd had the blood inside him before the bite on his neck, a reversal of the ritual-allowed him a small reprieve.

He resisted the first kill for days, braved the sunlight despite a wild growing aversion to it, and stole his way further north, finding temporary work with a man who smuggled furs and skins up the St. Lawrence. Korson would inspect the furs, cut and sew them, chew skins till they were pliable, all skills he had some knowledge of because of his Blackfoot background. There were many, in fact, who were of Indian heritage working for Adams. He was strict, his eye everywhere in his business, but wasn't a slave-driver. He knew all too well that greed could make his operation, already illegal, crumble. Some of the other native workers could communicate with Korson to a small degree, and they began to teach him English. Adams had given him some clothing to wear.

Adams had access to boats, of course, and Korson planned to find a way to stow away on a boat as passage to Montréal. But after less than a weeks work, Korson looked so ill and withdrawn that Adams released him rather than risk contamination of the rest of his workers. As a gesture of good will, he took Korson across the river to Montréal.

It had been the first city Korson had ever been in, and it attracted him because it was across the water, out of Talissa's element, and there was a large mountain breaking the middle of it. Korson climbed the mountain and collapsed at the top of it in a forested area. Here he could be out of the city while surrounded by it for protection.

He dreamt of the Shaman, his nah tova, and dreamt of a place where he was. He was no longer with the Blackfoot, he'd fallen more ill and blind than before. The nah tova awoke suddenly, grasping at the air, grasping at Korson's mind's eye, as though he sensed him. He fell back to his sheets moments later, convinced that a raccoon was scratching at the door. Or maybe that his head was not well. As real as it seemed, Korson could not communicate with his beloved mentor. He woke suddenly, to the chirping of crickets and the thick, sightless dark of a forest. His heart grumbled with hunger as he lifted himself off the ground and descended the mountain.

Korson was starving, drained almost totally of blood, and he woozily made his way towards the Old City. He even marched right into an isolated house, and he seemed as though he were drugged up. He burst open the door of the house, his hunger giving him the last boost it could possibly give. A married couple was sitting down to dinner, the man rising in protest at this intruder. Emaciated as he was, Korson still proved a menacing figure: he had great height, his features skeletal, his skin tanned slightly and long black hair that looked solid and unnatural. The woman froze in her chair. The man issued a profane challenge, but Korson could smell his fear. He moved closer. The man snatched a shotgun and fired a shot almost point blank distance and hit Korson in the right side of his chest. Being bloodless he bled not, and the bullet passed clean through taking a one-inch diameter chunk of his body with it, the exiting bullet exploding out Korson's back and spraying bits of flesh on the door behind him. Korson fell backwards to the ground and thudded his head on the wooden floor.

The Sab

The man looked to his wife, shaking and hysterical at the dinner table, her hands up to her mouth. Her eyes were wet but for the most part any reaction beyond shaking was denied to her. The man sighed and lowered his weapon. And his wife gave a reaction: she pointed. Korson had risen, hungrier and angrier than ever, gaping hole in his chest giving clear view of the log door that was behind him, bits of flesh dancing in the wound. Majic had kept him alive. Lack of blood meant life couldn't spill out of him. Overcome and succumbing, Korson flew at his first victim.

Though he was only half vampire, his hunger more than compensated for his lack of fangs. He bit right down on the man's neck, and the jugular sprayed a fountain of blood over Korson's lips, his throat, and when he choked, his face and hair.

The woman recovered enough to scream, and Korson, more lucid, drew his knife and cleanly slit her stem to sternum. Peeling open her belly, he pierced vital organs, the beating of the heart waning as he peeked under the ribcage and stabbed through the muscle. The husband, unable to move or speak but still able to see, registered his comprehension with a look of bright, wide-eyed horror. Korson let the woman's blood drain into her intestinal cavity while he went back to finish drinking of the man.

He lapped up the man's blood, off the floor, out of his spurting appendage. Such sweet liquor as he'd ever tasted! Succulent bovine juice! And intoxicating, but in such a way as to make one more lucid rather than drunk. God's alcohol, divine nectar. And who was to say blood itself wasn't a God, the DNA its mind? Can man decipher the mystery of DNA? Any more than he can the mystery of miracles? He was feeling more powerful, finally, after the trials in the forest, rejuvenated.

His first victim had to be conquered, through viciousness, thirst. His second, she lay on the floor, stomach splayed open and full of blood. To dip his hands and bathe his wounds. Reality didn't register as he looked at the gaping hole in his chest. How could he live and have this hole in is body? The blood healed his lacerations, but would it heal something such as this? Or would he be doomed to walk the earth forever with a hole through him? He dipped his hands into the blood filled intestinal cavity, cleaning his wounds and drinking of his second kill.

The rib bone made a sticky pulling sound as Korson tore it off from the meat. He pulled flesh and tissues from the body of the woman, stuffing his wound so as to close it. He was no medicine man, but it was worth at try. After each morsel of flesh was placed into his body, he anointed it with the woman's blood.

Two things interrupted him. First he vomited, pure red blood spraying out of him, as though he were a sacrilegious demon. He had to lap up the blood, regurgitated, tinting bluish. He vomited again, drank again, and vomited again, the blood bluer every time. The bodies were nearly drained of blood, and he decided to drink of them rather than the regurgitated blood he'd spit up several times. (He squeezed every drop he could, as though wringing a rag of flesh.) He hated his body.

Rejecting the very life, the nourishment. He'd steeled his stomach, he felt sickly, but tingly, as though he were calming.

A child screamed and he raised his bloodied head. She screamed louder. He stood, to full and fearsome height, his gaping chest exposed now. She screamed even louder. She saw her murdered parents and screamed louder still. And louder still when Korson moved closer to her. But it was not fear in her voice, her eyes. It was understanding. And perhaps that is the greatest fear. Korson crouched in front of the child. He put his fingers to his lips and said, "Ssh." He felt majic in him. He was weak but felt it nonetheless. He kissed his fingers and touched the girl's forehead, said, in Blackfoot, "Dream...just dream and forget." The girl's eyes drifted back to slumber and she stood, swaying as though to a gentle breeze. Korson returned to tending his chest. Though the wound would heal, it would take nearly two years, and it was always visible as a scar that looked as though the skin was metal melted under heat.

With the blood of two bodies inside him (he'd eventually lapped up the blue regurgitated blood, after several more trials), Korson headed to the cobblestone roads of Old Montréal. He was immediately out of place because his attire didn't match that of the stiff-collared, late nineteenth century style. Not wanting to draw attention to himself, he broke into a shop through the back way and managed to outfit himself in garments...a few sizes too small. He had to be creative-high boots to cover the short pant legs, extra frilly cuffs combined with hands clasped behind his back-in order to mask the ill-fitted attire. And he did the honourable thing by relieving the drawer of all the profits. He stashed his other clothes in the alley behind the shop, keeping his knife though.

For weeks he lived on the blood of the destitute, the forgotten souls who hovered and wandered aimlessly. And on theft.

A loner by nature, Korson had to find some niche in this culture. He learned many things, the language, the manners of the time, the very streets of the city. And commerce. He was only aware of trade, and money meant nothing to him. His third night, he boldly picked up a young woman's purse and began to relieve her of her cash. She started screaming and her escort began to beat Korson. The brawl spilled into an alleyway and Korson, up to this point stunned, rose to full height. He picked the man up by the shoulders and slammed him into the wall, thrusting his chin up and sinking his fangs into him. The woman of course followed, screaming, and he drained her as well. When he began to collect the coins and bills, he looked at them in his hand. They were filthy. And he realized they had value to these people. To him they were nothing. As much as he despised them, he had to learn the theory behind money.

He found an accountant, a timid, bespectacled man, and burst into the office just after sunset. Fully intimidated him. The man nearly choked on his own fear. Then Korson calmed him, said he wanted information. The man explained money to him. Investments. Korson put a large sum on the table.

"Increase it," he said. He gave the man twice his required payment, in return for utmost secrecy. It had only been weeks, but he knew what he was and that his majic would cause fear in people. The accountant set him up in a house, which was most discomforting to Korson at first. He slept in darkness in the basement, using a coffin, the most convenient means to keep the sun out. He now had money, a home, possessions. Blood every night. The many thoughts he heard were his company. He made friends every night and killed them. And with each kill his frame filled out, becoming muscled and brawny.

And one night he heard his name. Caquay Ahpacee. The name no one knew, the name he'd abandoned. In his head, or did someone say it? He walked swiftly around the streets, searching frantically. Pushing mortals aside like rags. Find it. Find the voice. The source, track it. Running in circles, back and forth, zigzag.

"Guess who I've found, my night wolf." A game. Find me. "I have your only friend in the whole world." Running now. Bombarded by images, so confusing, and then darkness. Death. And from his hands, destruction, his throat tearing the night with a scream.

* * *

It's quite a feat to resurrect the dead. It takes skill, determination, knowledge of the dark ways. And obsession. The one thing madmen and lovers have in common is obsession. When Talissa had first risen, her thousand-year sleep hadn't quelled the pain in her heart she felt from the destruction of her love, St. Valentine. Korson's subsequent snubbing of her dark and bloody desires had pushed her further across the thin ledge of obsession between love and madness. She followed the tall Blackfoot warrior as he discovered his new existence in Montréal. She knew she couldn't approach him-he was strong, and the blood made him stronger, while his heart was cold, made colder by death. And what she stole from him was so precious, the fact that she'd taken his love under the stars and made him cristacoom sah, the evil spirit. She'd pulled him out of the precious cycle so treasured by his people and could feel the heat of his hate when he looked into her eyes-hate mingled with fear, fear of what she was that led to a bitter self-loathing in his heart.

So she followed him. That was all she could do for now, knowing that though she may be physically weaker than he, her majic was still more cunning than his and she could sneak around behind his back without him knowing it. She was, after all, still a woman.

Her nights consisted of rising, feeding, than finding Korson as he frequented his usual haunts-mostly bars, brothels, and back-room casinos. He loved to play games of chance, to test karma and see how he could manipulate it with the new found majic twinkling in his eyes. If the night droned on and she hadn't run in to him, Talissa would begin to get a little anxious, clenching her claws until her palms bled. But Korson was young and as yet not adept at hiding what he was, especially to another vampire. There were occasions, though infrequent, when a mortal would pick him out for what he was, usually one who'd just lost a game of poker, or perhaps pool, and Korson would have to...creatively...figure a way out of the situation. (He was an unconvincing liar and was often forced to release the souls of many people who could no longer be coerced into ignorance by his charm.)

It became a little redundant, watching him from the shadow, despite the fact that her obsession and desire for love, and for his attentions, hadn't waned in the least. She did miss out on an existence of her own, sleeping in the earth, stealing clothes when hers became too worn to wear any longer. Talissa discovered two things: one, Korson's secret, and two, that she could manipulate men. It took a little doing, with her being filthy and weather-beaten, but eventually she'd amassed a small fortune acquired because men had desires.

She could feed, earn herself some blood money in the process, then finish her night by climbing Mount Royal and watching Korson as he looked down upon the city from the Cross at its peak. It wasn't a particularly large or impressive piece of nature, but it afforded a great view of the cityscape of Montréal and was quite relaxing, especially at night. Roads were paved to take one most of the way up, to walk the parks, or the lookout, or the cemetery, but to get to the cross one had to do some actual climbing and though it wasn't the most treacherous of terrains it was by no means easy either. Talissa would usually wait among the graves of the cemetery until she saw Korson's unmistakable form walking under the secluded piece of earth, or nestled in the branch of a tree. On more than one occasion, Korson looked over his shoulder behind him when Talissa's foot had cracked a branch or accidentally kicked a small rock. Once he was so sure he heard something he even retraced his steps, but Talissa was quick enough to evade him, despite his prowess as a hunter.

Talissa couldn't have done what she was now attempting to do-that is, destroy humanity and tap into a vast well of majical power-but for the fact that she'd harbored an irrepressibly large capacity for desire. She was a mimic. True to vampirism, she stole ideas, majic, power, even love. In love she was destined to always be the fraud, not the conjurer. If she had the drive of a man, she likely would have taken the earth by now, had she not destroyed her soul in the process. She was not a true conqueror, though as a woman she had a power of her own.

For weeks she watched Korson from behind, the only thing really visible his back, and she thought he was meditating. When the wind died and no longer carried the murmurs of Montréal to her sensitive ears, she could hear him quietly chanting prayers in his native Blackfoot tongue. Though they weren't prayers in the Christian sense of the word. More like talking, but with a musicality in his voice that implied more meaning that just mere words. Was he speaking to the souls of his victims as they floated around in the night air? Was there some deity that Talissa couldn't see or some dear friend long dead?

She noticed that he sometimes did something with his hands. After some weeks of watching, her curiosity was piqued and she found a position at enough of an angle to him that she could see his hands, the profile of his face. She was in greater risk of being spotted, but that excited her all the further. And what she saw in his hands made the darkness in her heart erupt.

Talissa had slept most of the last one thousand years in the earth, and in that time had forgotten much, including herself. She'd had glimpses of the Shadow since her awakening, but, like many mortals who catch glimpses of the occult, had brushed it off as a trick of the dark. This, despite the very majic in her blood! But majic was something that couldn't be seen to be believed, it had to be *felt*. So for many nights Talissa watched as Korson wove the shadow with his fingers. It wasn't anything specific he did-he merely played cat's cradle with a dark piece of energy-but she was mesmerized by the fact that he actually *held* it in his hands. No, not his hands even, his *fingers*, the very tips of which could transmit the energy of one's soul to the body of another. And Korson sat there, atop a lighted cross on a mountain, chanting to the souls of his dead victims, and playing with this powerful piece of majic as though he were an engrossed, prodigious child.

It was then that she dreamed of going to him. Walking slowly towards the cross and floating up to him, putting her hand on his shoulder. He would turn, looking up from his work, and his face, as usual, would be expressionless, but only for a moment. Then it would stretch into a smile, and even though he tried to make it a warm and inviting smile it would still look harsh and hard just because that was the way his face was-cold.

She would say, "I love you," and he would go back to his weaving, and she'd put her arm around him and hold him tight as he wove, so she could feel the power of the thing he held in his fingers as it flowed through their souls and inhale it as bits of it managed to escape the weave and waft up to her nose. They would sit there under the stars, like they used to nearly fifty years ago, looking out upon Montréal's cityscape, at the tiny lights of red and white and orange and they would be one. Talissa would lose herself in her dreams until the cruelness of reality slapped her cheek and she realized that Korson was no longer there. She would climb the cross and cry and cry because she knew her dreams would always die when she opened her eyes, and she'd cry until the first rays of the morning sunburned away her tears and forced her to quickly scamper to the ground and hide herself in the earth. Whenever this happened it reminded her of her thousand year sleep, of true death, and a part of her felt a hatred for Korson for making her feel this way. Even in dreams he never said, "I love you."

But still she was obsessed with him, and when she finished her pursuit of earthly wealth and passion and blood, she would go the cemetery and wait until she saw his figure stealing its way up the road. She snuggled up to a gravestone and tried to snatch bits of shadow for herself, tried to remember how to do it. Many times she merely grasped at the mundane kind caused by lack of light, but eventually she was able to tap into the same well of power Korson had discovered. Though her fingers didn't have the intricacies his did, she tried her skill at weaving, at controlling the power in her palms. So engrossing and enthralling was the task-and who isn't excited by the prospect of power?-that many nights she nearly missed Korson's dead, dark form walking up the road. She still watched him, but more for his skill now. Perhaps her love for him had died in a burst of hate? She wanted him just to have him now. Not out of love, just to control him and weave his words the way he wove the shadow.

Talissa would lean next to the same gravestone every night, as it afforded her the best view of the road while keeping her hidden. John Hartley Watkins had become a good friend of hers over the many, many weeks that she knelt by his marker, and she caught fleeting glimpses of his life as she waited for Korson to come, usually when she got bored and let her mind wander. His stone read that he had died of disease at the age of forty-seven, and on the rare occasion that Talissa found roses by the grave she wondered who may have left them. In life he had been an artist, poor and starving.

From time to time she felt the earth beneath her move. She'd usually just drank, two, three, four victims blood, and naturally assumed it was just from the wooziness of her inebriation. The strange scrape was just her brain sloshing back and forth in the sweet juice of the men she'd seduced.

Talissa sat and wove the shadow, and finally felt as though she had some skill in it, after watching Korson for many weeks. She was so lost in the workings of her fingers and despite the fact that the drunkenness of the blood was wearing off, she ignored the ebb of the ground beneath her folded legs. Her hands had dipped downwards for a moment, and in that instant a dead hand broke through the soft, wet grass and tried to grasp hold of her wrist. It wasn't a particularly quick movement, but Talissa was so surprised that she froze a mere moment. Obviously, she cared not that a dead hand was trying to touch her, herself being dead.

"My queen," said a voice from behind her. Talissa turned, almost a jump, and though she was slightly startled she had enough sense to stuff the dead hand of John Hartley Watkins back into the ground. She remained on the ground and looked up to see Paul Lancombe, a young vampire whom she'd turned to the dark way for vain and selfish reasons-he was handsome, though quite neutrally so, almost to the point of androgyny, and she was lonely. He had a reasonable amount of wealth and was a gentleman, so she figured him quite capable in her mind to be of assistance to the growing seeds of desire that hungered for power within her.

"Paul," said Talissa, nonplussed. "What are you doing here." To be the hunter is to be hunted.

"I'm impatient, my queen," said Paul. Though he'd taken the initiative in this matter, he was totally subservient to Talissa's will and beauty. "You've made many promises, and I long in my heart to see them fulfilled."

"You're a vampire six months, Paul. Curb you impatience immediately or you'll never survive eternity."

"But my queen," he said, going down on one knee and taking her hand in his-she'd stolen his love as well as his blood. "I sit in the shadows and steal the blood of one or two a night. I want to boldly enter a room and have all eyes gaze upon me in fear. I want women to walk up to me and open their veins willingly to my throat."

"We all want that, Paul. None of us wants to sit and hide in the shadows like some monster or outcast. But be patient. It will take some time. That much we have plenty of, while mortals must endure death after death and the precious few who have hints of our secrets have them constantly die with each generation." She noticed Korson's figure stealing it's way towards the foliage and she used her power to rivet Paul's attention on her eyes. Jealousy could incite the deepest of betrayals... "You're bored, Paul. Go find yourself a woman or two, to occupy yourself when I'm not around." As a gentleman, he was shocked by this suggestion, though it would eventually entice him to create several who would forever satisfy him and alleviate his longing for his mistress. "And Paul," said Talissa, rising and taking several steps over to the retreating disciple, then gripping him tightly about the neck so his toes could barely touch the ground, a bluish tinge of dead blood staining Talissa's fingertips.

"Don't ever follow me again."

Talissa had felt that Paul had stained her secret, the ritual of her observing Korson in his meditations, but she didn't exact revenge on him, even though it could have been construed as a sign of weakness. That, and the fact that he may have had hints of her obsession, and he could have seen that as weakness on her part as well. As much as she wanted to punish him, merely out of sadistic tendencies, she told herself it was petty and was able to curb her desire. Though petty revenge usually was a strong enough argument in most cases, Paul was blindly loyal and had been of good service.

"Paul, that man over there handing out money to the poor. Kill him," Talissa would say.

"Yes, my queen." And he would wait in shadow until the man was alone and then strike with a malicious and devilish slash of his claws, making sure the Good Samaritan had the fear of God in his eyes as a demon destroyed him despite his deeds. He would drink enough to weaken the victim to delirium, to the point where the words life and death had no meaning, and then drag the carcass on the ground-though he did have the strength to carry the body in his arms, it was more degrading to drag it, and it amused his queen further-to the waiting Talissa, and she would lift the man by his chin and suck the rest of his blood out of his body. Sometimes she was a little sloppy and would spill a little on her dress as she reached the bottom of the well, and would always have some covering her chin and lips.

She would wipe the blood off her chin with the back of her hand and say, "Thank you, Paul." She always said his name a lot, and would reach out with majic in her voice whenever she did. It solidified her hold on him. Paul, Paul, Paul, and each time she said his name it reminded him of the love he felt. Then she would kiss his lips with hers, her lips still bloody, and he would think it the most wonderful gift because he would get another taste of blood mingled with a taste of his love, Talissa.

So it was that Talissa was reluctant to obsess over Korson in secret for the next few nights, nor would she keep company with her servant. She made several more over the course of those nights, merely out of boredom, but they weren't a danger to her because she made sure they were of weak majic in their blood. But most of them were men and they were hungry for power and desired battle, and would fight all too willingly to their second death if need be. The only problem was keeping them restrained and hoping their chains wouldn't break. She did have to destroy one or two, but that was of no significance to her. She left Paul occupied with the task of watching over her new young minions.

Talissa returned to Mount Royal but this time her curiosity was more focused on the artist, John Hartley Watkins. As with every night she went to his gravestone, but could not see any sign of the man's corpse. She dug a little ways into the hole his hand had come up through, but saw no signs of any flesh trying to worm its way up through the earth. Korson was already perched on the cross, mired in his weaving, and Talissa thought how pointless it was that he sat there, merely playing games with majic so powerful as the energy she felt from the shadow.

(Korson, if he'd been privy to those thoughts, would have soberly remarked that purpose and skill were separate entities, and that the acquisition of this skill with majic was not done out of any grand purpose such as Talissa was mapping out in her mind, but with the intention of bettering himself.)

Talissa again wove the shadow in her fingers and kept her conjuring close to the ground. Hours passed, but to her fingers it felt like nights, and still she saw nothing of the hand of John Watkins. To have such power coursing through one's veins-despite the fact that it was merely a sliver of the what the shadow was-would eventually lead to a drain on one's system. Talissa released her hold on the shadow and slumped up against the grave, her fatigue the only thing staving off her disappointment. She rose to her feet after a moment's rest and stole her way back to the main road, first just walking then a little more swiftly, and finally breaking into a soft run. She didn't, after all, want to be seen by Korson, and it was almost dawn. She'd been lax and hadn't paid attention to whether Korson had already gone, or if he'd even showed up.

She returned several more nights in a row and it was always the same-shadow fatigue and no corpse. Raising the dead was more tiring than she'd first anticipated, but obsession, madness and desire were far stronger in her mind and wear and tear on her body was a small price to pay. It's the little things that make eternity so sweet, attention to detail. True lunacy was being able to see entire grand schemes in one's mind's eye one moment, and minute, specific details that would lead the plan to fruition the very next.

Talissa again wove the shadow with her fingers close to the ground, but, sick of her many failed efforts of the previous evenings, this time tried to weave the shadow into the fabric of the earth. She wove it into a sort of netting, thinking perhaps that poor old dead John just needed something to grab on to to pull himself up out of the earth. She wove an intricate and beautifully patterned netting into the wet earth, and began to draw it upwards, as a puppeteer would pull on strings to manipulate a puppet. She watched intently. Nothing happened. She pulled further, and further yet. Nothing happened. Then slammed down her hand so her palm hit the ground, crushing the shadow into the earth. She was sick and frustrated with the intricacies of majic. It had lost its enticement to the brutal simplicity afforded to her by her kamikaze band of eager young vamps who were all to willing to tear a bloody swath in humanity. She thought of them now, their necks tense as she had them chained up on the leash of her threats of brutal destruction if they disobeyed her. All she had to do was call across the night to Paul and tell him to let them loose.

Then something brushed her hand.

That's when the glimmer of corruption became a permanent gleam in her eye.

That's when her skills as a puppeteer began to truly take a spotlight in her scheming mind.

She drew up the threads of the shadow, slowly, gently, her fingers making c's and s's in the air. The hand began to break through the dirt, grasping at the remembered freedom of clear air. There was a moment of confusion and it stopped it's ascent, as though it was sure it should remain in the earth, dead. But Talissa coaxed it, as one would coax a kitten learning to climb down stairs.

"That's it. Come on," she said, her voice soft and musical and light. Her lips wore a big, triumphant, fanged smile. She began to see the arm up to the elbow, and she stood, waiting for the rest of it to appear. She felt the sheer energy of the shadow coursing through her, a rising feeling as though she were lifting herself as well as the corpse. Her control of the majic was by no means absolute, and she could not give the corpse enough strength to lift itself out of the ground, nor did she possess the power to make it rise by her will. The hand became frantic and began to thrust upwards over and over in an attempt to escape.

"Fucking Hell," she said, giving the moon a frustrated look. "Do I have to do everything myself?"

She took hold of the hand, calming it in a moment and then tugging it upwards. It took a momentous effort on her part, as she not only had to lift the body but the large mound that covered it.

The earth split open like the crack of a wound, and out of it fell the body of John Hartley Watkins. For a corpse he was young, still with his skin though it was in the first stages of decomposition. It looked as though it would melt off his body if the sun were to rise at that moment, and it had a grey-green hue to it, sickly and morose. Dirt clung to his body, and his clothes were rags.

He fell to the ground, tired from the effort of returning to life. Talissa still had the web of shadow attached to her fingers, and after allowing him a moment's respite, lifted him up using her majic. He was quite like a child, as her hold of the shadow was tenuous and she couldn't infuse him with enough life to satisfy his basic needs. She spent the remainder of the night teaching him how to walk, how to manipulate objects with his fingers.

His eyes were enthralled with what he saw. Talissa thought it was because it was like he was seeing everything for the first time, but then she noticed a deep, dark sadness in him. As he was a young corpse, he still had some recognition of his previous life, albeit on a shallow and cloudy level, and he remembered his art. It hurt him that his fingers didn't work, that his talent was not immediately resurrected with him.

"I think, John, my new friend," she said, running a finger under his chin, "that you may not be the warrior I had been seeking." But she liked him nonetheless. He was, after all, an artist, an aristocrat of sorts, though he lived and died in poverty. Talissa liked him as a child would a puppy.

And as an artist, it was easy for him to fall in love. He was, much like a majician, a creator, and even in death his mind could look at Talissa and form things his fingers could no longer. And she was the liar, the ghost, her truth hidden in shadow.

He would follow her as she followed Korson, and she liked the innocent attention he provided. And she didn't have to care for him much, nor would he become bitter, like Paul would, if she didn't reciprocate the attention. There were times Talissa would merely forget about him and he would be forced to fend for himself, battling the bitter rays of the sun, for the sun would disintegrate the dead, make the majic in his veins boil over and explode. He spent most of his time haunting the mountain-that is, that's where Talissa left him and he hadn't the intelligence to seek out anything in the world on his own-and it was with a mere glimpse into his mistress's mind and careless irony of Talissa's karma that he did what he did.

He'd seemed to become constantly weak and ill, and it was after nearly a week that Talissa had realized that she'd neglected to do something-feed him. For man could not live upon majic alone. She gave him a few drops of her blood to see if he liked it. He lapped it up a bit, and it gave him strength for a few hours. She then had Paul bring him a victim containing only a few mouthfuls of blood (for she didn't want to instill any great hungers or desires within his soulless body.) She ordered Paul to leave and then had a wound opened in the throat of the victim, and she squeezed the body until the wound was blood soaked. She brought John over to the body then put his dead, cracked lips to the blood. And she laughed.

"John, you vicious little monster you," she giggled at him. He was meek, yet even he was a murderer at heart.

"Have we an army then?"

"Paul. What did I say about spying on me."

"Don't do it."

"Correct." Talissa got up and went over to him. "Don't tell me you're jealous of John, are you? Look at him, lying there on the floor. He can't possibly compare to you, my dear."

"Then let's make more of them and be done with it! The shadows begin to bore me..."

"You're only a year old, Paul. Patience, patience," she ran her finger along his cheek. "Go play with your friends. Think of different ways to murder, and drink your fill. Look at him. We can't very well send that out into the world, it wouldn't inspire fear. It will take time, and that we have plenty of. Now, I think he's eaten enough. Go take him back up the mountain. We can't leave something like that in the house. I'll tend to him later."

Reluctantly, Paul acquiesced, and he got the collar and chain and strapped the corpse of John Hartley Watkins into it. Not that it was necessary, he just liked it that way, to pull him like a dog. He gave a good yank to pull the man to his feet.

"Careful, Paul. Corpses are fragile, you know. I wouldn't want you to sever the head or anything like that."

"Yes, my queen," said Paul, with a bit of a sneer.

He walked John up the mountain and then undid the collar when he got to the gate of the cemetery. He pulled the corpse close to him and said, "You'd damn well better learn fast," then thrust it through the gates with such a push that he flipped head over heels before landing upon the ground. He looked back at the vampire with a confused and almost fearful look, but Paul had already turned his back to him and was walking away.

And this was the first night Talissa had neglected to tend to him. On other nights, when she was lax or lazy, she would have Paul put the corpse back in his grave. But tonight he was left to himself and the only thing he knew was his loneliness and the fear of the coming day. He wandered the graveyard, and for nearly an hour had nothing to do but sniff the air.

Korson, as on many nights, was walking to his secret place upon the cross, and John saw him and began to follow, not knowing what the figure was. Perhaps more food. But he was a corpse, and his motor skills not as intricate as that of a living mortal, nor, needless to say, a vampire's, and couldn't catch up to Korson. He did, though, catch a scent on the air and it was that of Talissa's. On many of her tearful nights she'd lain in the ground at the base of the cross and dug a hole for herself, a place where she kept the earth soft so she could rest if need be. Her scent was all over it. And thinking he could search her out in the depths of the earth, he dug.

At first he unknowingly mimicked his mistress, digging into the hole and, seeing the rays of the sun, burying himself there to sleep. For nearly a week he was neglected, and for nearly a week he dug from dusk till dawn, searching. The initial hole was small, and no one would have taken much notice of it, if anyone had bothered to venture to their own area. Which no one did.

Needless to say, Talissa eventually came looking for John, and she did find him, shortly before dawn. It was too late to return to descend the mountain and find her usual shelter, so she was forced to remain in the chasm with the corpse. Unnecessarily, she hid her disgust at having to share a bed with a man long dead. It surpassed even her sense of morbidity. But he worked diligently for weeks and the chasm he'd created was quite vast, though the walls crude. And when the sun set the next evening and the majic in their veins rose in power, Talissa had distinct difficulty in getting her zombie slave to leave the chasm. She led him to the opening in the ground but he suddenly became resistant, like a child at the school doors for the first time. After a few more attempts, Talissa's temper became short.

"I command you," she said, her tone firm, her dark eyes hard. Her words almost moved the corpse, but then he stopped again. And she saw the chasm had some hold on him, perhaps her scent. She could see that softness was required. "What is it, John? What's here? You haven't become a *reclusive* artist have you?" She looked into his eyes, and into what little was left of his mind and saw-

-the merest glimpse of the greatness of the artist he once was. It nearly made her cry.

"Oh, John," she said. "So that's it. I suppose everything needs its purpose, even monsters. Okay, you can stay. Build me a shrine." She turned him back into the chasm, and if he were capable of smiling he would have. He spent many months digging and tunneling a chamber for his queen, and at the head of it, far from the light of day, he carved an intricate throne in the wall. Many abstract symbols and designs adorned the dirt walls, one of which looked suspiciously like the name of the dead artist who'd carved out this den for his vampire queen.

Paul, of course, hated it. Talissa loved it. It was a place beneath the earth, symbolic of Hell, where she could pontificate, judge, rule, and whatever else it is that royalty does.

"Perhaps a real throne, instead of that dirt mound you're sitting on?" suggested Paul.

"Nonsense. This is perfectly suitable. I'll just drape a rag over it so I won't get dirty." Talissa glanced up at the dirt ceiling. "Perhaps you should go play with your friends up there rather than leaving them waiting while you sulk."

And so it was that Talissa had both raised the dead and found herself a hellish little lair, quite close to where Korson tried his skill with the shadow, away from humanity. He was her love and her hate and she kept him very close, and he never did catch on because she hid her scent from him by coming and going with remnants, or waiting till she was downwind. They were vampires after all, but not truly Gods, and not all-powerful or all seeing.

In the coming years Korson found the nah tova, his Shaman, on a reserve outside Montréal, and made most of his residence there, where he could more easily immerse himself in nature. Talissa, keeping close to him, had found his other little secret, a weakness, a friendship with a mortal. She once more asked Korson to join the Sab. And Paul had all too much pleasure in killing something dear to Korson's heart. If not for Talissa's protection, Paul would have been soon dead himself, but he was able to hold a smug smile up to Korson's blank and pallid face. The remaining years also saw more experimentation with zombies, much improved over the first of the resurrections, John Hartley Watkins, which Paul would forever deem a failure. One by one dispensable warriors were amassed from the ranks of the recently dead to help spell the growing legion of brash, young, vindictive vampires like Paul, who made the Sabaoth, the Host, the Army, that would, as prophesied by vampire lore, destroy mankind...

Korson gave a smile, coupled with a slight laugh. He went into the kitchen, got himself a wooden chair, and brought it over to the window to sit in. His long legs stretched out as he leaned back, continuing to look out the window. I was actually impressed with him. He wasn't flawless. He had depth of character. He made mistakes and tried to learn from them. And he was an honourable killer. He wasn't indiscriminate; he murdered those worthy of death. I would never make it as a vampire. I'd be haunted by each soul. I'd cry every time I killed someone. I've never had to shoot someone as a police officer. I'd given beatings, and they usually felt good. But there was always the wall. I could put a man in the hospital without thinking twice but I could never kill a man.

After sitting under the eerie silence of the night, the twinkling stars, he'd quietly insisted we continue the tale within the walls of my house. Muttering something about separating himself from nature.

"She fucked with me," said Korson. "I'm not sure if she found him at the time, but she sat there fucking with me because I'd abandoned her. But I refocused myself. I knew the Blackfoot had migrated north and I had to set about to find the Shaman before she did. I called to him, but nothing. It's not so simple, this trick of the mind. Over great distances it all becomes jumbled and the Shaman would have his defenses against black majic up.

"It was years," he said. "Each winter I would give up hope, knowing that they'd migrated south. The summers, the short nights, were spent scouring the outskirts of Montréal. I searched completely alone, rarely drinking, while the winters were blood filled nights. I trusted no one. Yet I dared not wander too far because of the sun. Many times I risked my existence at dawn because of my searches. The only hope I clung to in my bitter loneliness was the fact that there were tauntings of his death. Talissa would threaten that she'd found him, that she was tearing his limbs apart, but I knew she would leave me proof of such. To me, no body meant he was alive. It may have been specious thinking, but I was left with no choice. I had the rest of his life to find him.

"He taught me many things, about the changes in our culture, about what it meant to be a man. He put his faith in me, let me have his life in my hands. I could have killed him at any time I wished. I didn't, obviously. I wouldn't. He clung to life until he was a papery husk of flesh, seemingly living long enough to fulfill a bitter destiny. I think he was about one hundred and twenty years old when he finally did die.

"He reminded me of the ways of my people, he told me to practice them no matter what I had become. It had been fifty years since I became a vampire. I would have been this man's age had I lived out the course of my life. And I had done so little to prove my worth to my birthright as an Indian. The Shaman told me, though, that I *am* one of God's creatures. I am no worse than the white man who has caused the buffalo to be endangered. In fact I'm better. Though I must kill so I may live, I follow the customs of my people. I waste nothing of my victim. Every last drop of blood is taken into me. Their deaths are as quick and as painless as I can possibly make them. I pray for their souls to find peace, to return to the earth as a creature that will not have the misfortune to cross my path twice. I bury them deep in the earth so they will become part of her."

I interrupted: "What happened to the Shaman? Did he die in peace?"

Korson continued to look out the window. Was that a tear in his eye, a tear tinged red with blood?

"No. His death was sudden and tragic. It is why I have never befriended a mortal. He was discovered to have knowledge of vampires. Somehow, maybe someone saw him with me, though I will never be sure. And it was a vampire who took his life a mere two years after I had found him again, stuck on a reservation outside Montréal."

I spoke softly this time. "The one we're looking for now?"

"Yes, it is she. She didn't do it directly, she ordered someone to do it, but the blame must lie with her either way. The man was kind and gentle. A healer. He was of no threat to anyone, mortal or vampire."

"Is it true that a new born vampire is under the control of its maker? You did say that she had someone kill the Shaman for you."

Korson's tear streaked face broke into a grin. Two lifetimes certainly let him learn how to deal with his emotions.

"A vampire is born knowing all that he knew as a human. He need only learn to be a vampire. But this vampire we seek is powerful, no doubt. She is old, older than even I can imagine. I don't think anyone really knows how long she has lived, even herself. Hell, you know how women are with their age. She has developed strong telepathic powers, and is able to coerce both the human and the inhuman to her will. She makes them fall in love with her. And this vampire had, at the time I speak of, nine under her consolidated control. She spent years recruiting vagrant vampires, turning humans to her way. She would court a mortal for months, make them believe that they needed her and she would turn them with droplets of her venomous blood. She made sure to keep them weak and obtuse, which further strengthened the link between her and her consort. And if someone were brave enough to turn their back on her she would burn them, or have them murdered. It was all about love. She was obsessed with love.

"The worst is the burning. I remember once when I let my hand stray accidentally to a candle flame. It was just for a second, but my hand burst into flame like a soaked wick. My little finger and the back of my hand were scarred soot for the next three years. Fire is the absolute enemy of the vampire. It is said: You can close your eyes to the sun, but fire will eat you alive. It means that the vampire, with time and stamina, will be able to resist the sun for short periods. I myself have been able to stand the light of dawn, if only for a moment. It is the young ones who usually cower from the sun, out of fear."

"And the stake through he heart? Is there any truth to that?"

"It is possible to kill a vampire by dismembering their body. But it is difficult. Tough skin." Korson paused for another moment, looking out the window contemplatively, trying to recall the thread of his story. "This vampire had assembled, by that time, nine, like I said. And these nine were powerful, quite powerful, but they were weak enough to remain under her control. She'd duped them into believing so. She'd quell any resistance with her power, which was always to be greater than theirs. But resistance was rare. They all loved and adored her. *My Sabaoth*, she called them. That name struck fear among the vampires who dwelt in Québec, south to Ontario and even into the northern U.S. You'd be amazed how many vampires roam the rural areas of your nation. Most tend to avoid the cities for long periods of time. But this group of vampires, this Sabaoth, they were feared and reviled. They brought death and suffrage to many. They wiped out small towns. And they didn't even care who knew of them. Their presence became known to some humans, even, in tales...

"And one day, the Shaman told me he foresaw their coming. Well, by this time I had become somewhat of a protector for the reserve that the Shaman lived on. And I would let no harm come to the Shaman himself. I knew the ways of the Sabaoth, and that they would come one by one as they infiltrated the village. They would terrorize the inhabitants. One by one they would reveal themselves. And as people gathered their strength to defend their residence, more would appear. *Look, there's one behind you*, someone would scream. *And to the left, is that another walking out of the fog?* By the second night, the Sabaoth would be completed. And their leader, this she-devil, would come and kill the leader of the village, or its mayor, whomever it may be. They turned it into a fucking religious ceremony. The fog would descend nightly upon the village, so thick no one could see their way around. They danced and chanted like pagans around a man who was bound in the center of town. Some strong enough to brave the fog would watch, and retch at the sight of the murder, a useless, needless sacrifice, the puzzle of the flesh undone.

"I had watched these people thrive under my secret surveillance. I felt kinship with them. Their successes I took as my own. I could not let this happen to the people of my village.

"I woke early one evening. I took up sharpened sticks and hid them at the outskirts of the village. I prepared sticks soaked in alcohol that I would use to light into flames and burn the vile, raging blood of these jackals. And the center of the village would be their pyre, for all to see.

"First, though, I should tell you something. Talissa's taunting subsided after a while. She became hungry for power and I, as you can see before you, have that commodity. She began creating the Sabaoth. And she had asked me to be its second member, to which I of course refused. She told me: "Power comes in three's. We could be powerful together. Just the three of us." It was tempting, but I declined anyway.

I interrupted, said, "You say three. I don't think it's a stretch of the imagination that Heather Langden is that third?" Korson nodded, agreeing. But that raised new questions. Why was there such a gap in time between Korson and Heather? And Talissa as well?

"I knew that power would come to me with training and effort. And this vampire pestered and tried to haunt me-children's frights, like the monster in the closet. Stupid things really. But I was still young and foolish, thought I was so strong. Thought nothing could defeat the great Indian warrior turned demon. And when she found someone to join her, I killed the first member of her Sabaoth. And I gave no care to the retribution that I was sure would come. I was, after all, already dead. I was nonchalant and arrogant as I walked the night, in the reserve, in the forest around it, when I went into town to feed. But I knew, I felt those crimson vampire eyes staring at me from behind a bush, from atop a house. I felt the warmth of their anger in my subconscious. I was frigid with tension at the revenge I knew was to be meted out. But it never came. Not a night later, not a week later, neither month nor year. I walked like a confident, smug stud but I had one ear pricked over my shoulder to make sure no one ran at me with a sharpened stick and blazing flame." Korson touched the back of his hand to his lip, his cheek. He could still feel the burn throbbing there. Sometimes he could not be indifferent to it.

"So this vampire carried a vendetta against you for years. And she built her group until she thought you would not be able to challenge her," I said. Korson nodded in agreement.

"She may have been weak or frightened of me. Maybe I had been more powerful than I thought. I'm not really sure. I do know that I have always been physically strong for a vampire, this I noticed about five years after my unbirth. I noticed that my strength of mind and heart had grown as cold as vampires who were already a half a century old. My strength now, after one hundred years of vampirism is as good as one who is three hundred years old. But remember, my experience is the exception to the rule. I think I was lucky."

"You judge your strength by the coldness of your heart?" I asked.

"There are many ways to judge the power of a vampire. I found myself rising to see the sun dip below the horizon. Most vampires are lucky to witness anything remotely like that until they are at least a century old. Imagine spending one hundred years in the dark. It would cause anyone to become morbid, to follow the dark ways. Evil thrives at night. Almost every culture associates sin with the night. Man's symbolism is a powerful tool. Sometimes I wonder if it is a result of instinct or if it is a learned ideal..."

He continued:

"A few nights later the fog rolled in. It was thick and syrupy, most of all unnatural. It clung to the cabins, to the trees. Dogs and cats growled at the scent in the air, its fumes stupefying the villagers. But my head was clear. I was wise to the tricks of the mind. The Shaman had honed my mental strength to a fine metal point. I waited. And listened. The wind was weak, but I caught a scent on it as it changed direction. And I moved towards it. They would begin an attack from a small side road, one that was seldom used, and I made my way there. A lone vampire was walking, her hair a blaze of red curl, her skin gleaming white, and her eyes green as emeralds. She walked at a brisk and dire pace, holding her dress with her hands so as not to muddy it.

"'Ho there,'" she called to me. 'Some assistance, sir!' Her face was troubled and urgent, but her eyes gleamed with a deep vampire hunger that only another vampire could have detected. She stumbled in haste and steadied herself by catching on to my shoulders. I supported her with my left hand. 'Are you in trouble, my lady?' I asked her. She nodded, thanking the Lord that she was able to find me so soon. She staggered over to a tree a few feet away and leaned on it, calling for me to support her as she had no strength left. I did as she asked. She said that her wagon had lost its wheel not far down the road. She would be very appreciative and would repay in kind, now if I so desired. She lifted up her skirt a little to present her offer, and her lips moved to my cheek. I felt the tips of her fangs protruding beyond her mouth, grazing my skin. A small hiss escaped her throat. It was followed by a sharp scream which I muffled with my free hand. In my other was a sharpened stick that I used to impale her with. She hung from the tree, her feet inches above the ground, dangling. Blood seeped and soaked the folds of her clothing. In her mouth I stuffed handfuls of leaves and grass to keep her from calling for help. I hammered in the stick further.

She would live, but she was helpless to the others in her coven. She choked and gurgled on the leaves.

"The next attack would come from the main road, I suspected. I went across the village and waited there. This time there were two vampires, a male and a female. The male walked slightly ahead as they approached the village, as though he were husband and leader. I hid behind a copse of bushes to their left, unwilling to take on two vampires at once. The man approached a villager, one who was assigned to watching the main road at night. They spoke for a moment, probably the same wagon wheel story the other one had fed to me. He waved to the wife, spoke a few words to her, and ushered her on into the village. The man stayed behind a moment, and I chose to follow the woman before she infiltrated the village. I hurried on ahead of her, out of her sight, and came out in front of her, by a cabin near the center of town. She noticed me and began to walk toward me.

"'Sir!' she called. 'Our wagon is broken and we were told we could find lodgings for the night.' She hurried towards me, impatience and hunger in her eyes. I continued to lean nonchalantly on the corner of the cabin. 'Would you happen to know where I could stay for the night?' Her fangs were already egressing. She was impatient and young, but had some power. A shame she didn't have the sense for it. 'You are most welcome to stay here, my lady,' I said to her. She came towards me as if to hug me in gratitude, a thank you forming on her fanged lips. She got close enough to smell my blood, and she sensed something was not right. But it was too late. I grabbed her about the neck and pulled her round the corner, throwing her down on a sharpened stake that I had placed in the ground, the point coming through her stomach, the wood of the tree red. She was in shock. She looked at the stick protruding from her abdomen and her mouth gaped open, her dark eyes trying to register if this was really happening or if she was having a nightmare. She tried to speak or scream, which I don't know. I took another stick and thrust it down her throat, pinning her neck to the ground.

I made a convulsive expression, which Korson noticed and smiled at, but said nothing.

"I made my way back to the front of the village with a weapon. Everything was going as I'd hoped up until then. But I caught the scent of others near. I had to act fast. Some villagers were coming out of their homes to see what the scream was about. Someone was talking loudly, saying that no one was at the main road keeping watch. I moved quickly and shortly found the male vampire and the guard in a deadly kiss away from the light of the village gates. The scent of death permeated my nostrils, emanating from the man. The vampire had drained him beyond hope. I took up my machete and sliced the bastard's head off. His victim fell back, a small cut in his neck from my knife next to the fang marks that the vampire had left. The vampires hands trembled, not sure if they should live or die. I dismembered the rest of him and put his body in a sack, and made my way to the red-headed vampire that hung from the tree. She still hung there, her body struggling somewhat on the stake. It was time to finish her suffering. I placed the sack with the remains of the male under her feet and I lit both of them afire. Neither would rise again. The flames cut through the fog, making a beacon in the night.

"The warning had been sounded for mortals and vampires alike. The villagers came rushing out of their cabins. I heard the women scream and the men curse when the dark eyed vampire had been found beside the cabin. If she had the will to live she would spend a decade with a hole in her throat. But no one would go near enough to set her free, and she gurgled on in pain, *help me, help me,* a stick in her mouth stifling her voice.

"But there were six more vampires unaccounted for, plus their leader. I could smell them, the scent of living death that they carried with them. And I heard the screams of women as they began to take the villagers, torturing and draining them. The pyre I had erected did nothing to dissuade them. It didn't even seem like a dent in the armor. I did what I could to help, but it wasn't much. I had reacted too slow in disposing of the first of their number to arrive. Now the Sabaoth had struck in full force. And they had grown since last I had heard of them.

"Fifty-six male and sixty women vampires terrorizing a village of five hundred or so. They used tricks of speed and wit to make their number seem greater than it really was. I heard shouts that there were as many as two or three hundred of them. I think I managed to get over two hundred to leave the village until it was safe to come back. The rest fought through most of the night and perished. I spun with delirium at the destruction. One hundred and sixteen against three hundred. I was sick to my stomach.

"Then I realized, the Shaman. I had to save him if I could save no other. I went to his cabin-it was made out of clay, like some Indians used to do-but he was gone. I scanned the room. His pipe was going, a few things were out of order, but it seemed as though no struggle had taken place. He had left of his own accord, sensing the commotion. I left his hut and decided to make myself scarce. The village was lost. I had few personal belongings, all hidden, and none that couldn't be replaced, so I headed for the side road, hoping the glimpse of the red-headed vampire would leave me with some semblance of satisfaction. As I began walking, I heard shouts from the center of the village-they were erecting the pyre and about to begin the sacrifices. My heart was thick and heavy with sorrow as I took step by aching step away from a place that I felt I'd adopted. A place that had been the only one to call home in fifty years. I thought of the few villagers that I had met, the fact that they took no distrust of the seldom seen stranger who lived a few miles out in the woods. I think, for the first time in fifty years as a vampire, that I actually cried. A tear tinged red rolled down my cheek in a hot river of emotion.

"But my reverie was disturbed by the increasingly loud shouts from the village square. And then I heard a voice bellow with vampiric power: 'There is among you one who is as strong and powerful as we. But he refuses to become a part of the Sabaoth. He envisions himself above and beyond us but in truth, he is just another murderous devil like the rest of us, doomed to walk in the shadow of God, with the earthly powers of an angel, but the heart and soul and appetite of the one who is cast from heaven forever!' This, of course, stopped me where I stood. I gave my attention to the speaker and my feet began to carry me toward the center of the village. He went on: 'To help in making your decision swift, let it be known that we have here a friend of yours.' The Shaman!

"I began to move quickly, faster than a mortal could. I grabbed a branch and wrapped the end of it in a soaked cloth and lit it afire. Then I walked into the village square. The Sabaoth had numbered over a hundred members, who guarded the hundred or so villagers who remained. They were set up in a circle and if one were brave enough to stray or attempt any escape, a vampire's claw would slash them at the jugular. It was a quickly learned lesson. In the middle of the circle was a wooden pole in the ground, a makeshift pyre, to which was trapped the Shaman. He looked neither grim nor forlorn. He was just *there*.

"And I had been foolish to think that Talissa had only nine cohorts under her command. She was amassing legions.

"I moved slowly towards him as the circle broke to allow me passage. I held my torch as high as I could but I felt its heaviness straining my forearm. My steps were somber and leaden as I moved as close as I dared. The male vampire, the speaker who called to me, grinned a malicious, fangy smirk. Paul. A supplicant if I ever saw one. His lips were deep red, and moist. All of them were like that. The village dripped from the corners of their mouths.

"'So,' he said, his voice arrogant and slightly adenoidal. 'You have the bravery to show yourself.' I didn't answer him for a moment. I let my sight wander, memorizing each and every undead face that held the crowd captive. I saw nothing of their Queen.

"'Let him go. Let them all go. Your war is with me.' He laughed, his manicured little devil's laugh.

"'O, but we owe you retribution!' He flung his short salt and pepper hair with a jerk of his head. 'Tonight alone you have reduced our number by three. And there was one other, one earlier, that you had the gall to challenge. We owe you retribution!'

"'Then fight with me!' I told him. 'Let these innocents go and have it out with me. If you so much as harm him you'll start a war.' Again his practiced laugh.

"'A war, you say?' He turned to the female who stood by the pyre with him. 'He means to start a war!' He looked back to me, his eyes filled with gloating delight. 'What will it be? You against sixty? Or maybe we will be sporting and half our number for you.'

"'That won't be necessary,' I said. 'I can half your number on my own.' This, of course, brought raucous laughter from the rest of the clan.

"'And what of your precious Shaman? Can you save your friend from death, too?' He took a long talon-like index finger and drew a scar down the left side of the Shaman's cheek. His eyes welled with pain, but he would not scream. He stood as stoic as ever. The blood trickled down his face, still hot with life. 'It is unwise to lead the life you lead and make friends,' he told me. 'Now, you will watch him die.'

"I couldn't take it. The only person who ever let me feel as though I had self-worth in this foetid afterlife, the only person that was a friend in fifty years, and he was about to die. I couldn't let it happen. As a mortal, he was nearly a hundred and twenty years old, and frankly, that impressed the hell out of me. I began to move forward to do something. The vampires of the Sabaoth were shocked into action. Some ran to stop me. Others, I saw, were readying themselves to kill the Shaman before I could get to him.

"'Stop!!' bellowed a voice. It was the Shaman's of course, but for just a moment I thought it perhaps a savior. Everyone froze. His voice carried in it a preternatural tone. He sounded almost God-like. To look at him though, was to see otherwise. He was bloody and broken. He looked at me as he spoke, his eyes still dancing as his body was dying. His voice now sounded withered, but was still audible. 'I am an old man, now. I am not worth dying over. Leave and fight these demons another day, on your own terms. Their only strength over you is their number. Each by themselves is not even half your strength in mind or in body.' He sighed, a sigh which turned into a cough. 'I won't see you die!' I said to him. He smiled at me. 'Like I said, I am an old man. I have served the Gods for all of my life. I have no need for this shell that houses my soul, anyway. Do not worry about me. They are only setting me free.' I looked at him, tears filling my eyes. I knew what he said was right. Even if I chose to stay and fight now, even if I could beat all one-hundred of them, there would be no way I could save him. What distressed me the most was that he didn't seem the least bit disturbed by his imminent death. He seemed so calm though his demise would be so violent. But he was right. I could beat these brat vampires one by one, or even in a group of two or three. Thirty would overwhelm me by sheer force of numbers. I had to leave. But I had to make sure the Shaman died quick, without much torture, if that was possible. The vampire at the pyre, I think, sensed that my blood was boiling, that I was at my breaking point, and would not tolerate more mischief, not with regards to this execution, though I had resigned myself to its occurrence. The Shaman smiled at me again, warmly. He uttered something in a native tongue, an older one that gave me trouble in figuring out the words. I believe he said: I will be watching over you. Then he turned to the vampire at the pyre. He nodded and maybe he said, 'Do it.' He was doused in alcohol and sent up in flames, to the heavens, I'd like to believe. Or maybe he became part of the earth. I know he would have liked that. But that was the last that I, or anyone saw of the Shaman. And when his body had become a charred silhouette, that is when I turned and calmly walked out of the village for the last time. None of them tried to stop me.

"They were *afraid*. So I came back here. To Montréal. To lose myself. There is something compelling about Montréal. And of course you know the saying: Don't ever give up on Montréal."

"What about their leader? She didn't arrive to take her revenge?" I asked.

"No. She was watching, I know it, but she never made her presence known. I'm sure she stayed in the shadows when she saw that her plans weren't going as smoothly as they usually do. The Sabaoth was known for overcoming an entire village in less than an hour. They were a dominating force. And I believe she is trying to create another."

"What happened to the old Sabaoth?" I said. Korson laughed a bitter, dry laugh. He looked at me with an old anger in his eyes. Then he spoke.

"I killed almost every one of them. Some in groups. Most alone. And I made sure each time, before the fire caught their blood and burst it into flames, that they knew who did it. It took me little over a year. A few cowards scattered. Their Queen, she wouldn't run. But she hid in the shadows. I'm positive that she is trying to put together a new Sabaoth. I just wonder whey she waited so long."

"She was waiting for Heather," I said. "But how would she have known about Heather?" But Korson was lost in his story, like an old man reminiscing.

"Oh, she had her little groups. But they were small, weak, never numbering more than three at a time. Yes, they often numbered three unless one was lost for some reason or another. But never was there a Sabaoth so powerful as that one. And Talissa has been very busy of late. That is what has me so worried. This girl, Heather, the one who died. Her soul is very strong. She could make a powerful vampire, if trained right. Her skill would rival an old one's in a very short time. It didn't make sense for her to be killed by a bite."

I thought for a moment. *What could we do?* I said to myself. *Dig up her grave?*

"Tomorrow," I said, "I'm going to see if I can speak to Heather's mother. Maybe she knows something that she's not letting on to." Korson nodded in agreement, looking a little more satisfied but still troubled.

He then left. I held my throbbing wrist, finally allowed to attend to the wound now the tale was told. The knife felt sharper than I thought it would, the blade made of the bone of some long dead animal, cold and sleek. I felt woozy and was a little worried that I may bleed myself to sleep, that maybe Korson meant to charge me my life for his tale. He'd taken my blood ceremonially, drawing on my forehead a circle and pentacle, and I felt the blood drip into my eyes and down my nose. But I now knew something that no other mortal did–the history of a vampire.

Part 3: Things to do When You're a Vampire in Montreal

It was cold again. The only way to tell if it was night or day. The days were so sweltering and oppressive. Or was it summer and winter? It was impossible to say which. The nights, or what were the cooler periods anyway, were a short reprieve from the heat, welcome, but short.

Yes, it was night and day. They passed too quickly to be seasons, though they might as well have been.

Some bugs had already begun to crawl over her skin. They were all so cold and soothing. Their twiggly little feet tickled her cheeks as they crawled over her face, occasionally stopping to nibble away at her flesh.

The heat parched her mouth, made her thirst for any drop of liquid to touch her lips. If there would have been room to shake and thrash, she would have. Sometimes she did, only to have tiny cold pieces of earth crumble onto her arms and legs.

How can something be cold with this heat? she thought.

Then, one day, she became scared. More afraid from what was happening than from the fact that she'd retained her faculties while trapped emotionless in this cocoon. She felt the air grow cold again, stale, but sill cold. And then she heard a harsh, scraping sound. At first, she was thankful to hear something, because it meant she was alive. A loud noise like this was real, not the result of dreams.

I am alive, she stated to herself, *I am alive*, she said out loud, to make sure she could still speak. Her voice was hoarse and it felt like a long, sharp needle was scraping her throat. She put her hands in front of her, as far as she could, touching the top. The sound came quicker and louder, stronger, until she heard a thump. No-felt it. She felt a thump against the top. It startled her, making her cringe, or at least try to. The scraping sound went round her several times, quickly. She tried to push the top again, but she realized that she had no strength, never had, in her limbs or her neck. Every movement she had in this dream had been imagined.

She felt the liquid drip on her mouth, moistening her parched lips. She felt it flow down her throat of its own accord, and she tried to swallow though she couldn't, but it made her feel better to try. After a moment of soothing refreshment from the rusty *water*, she tried to open her eyes. She saw only squares and circles and funny shapes which she couldn't put a name to, and they came in hazy, foggy pastel colours. They moved closer and farther, across her vision, till she realized she had never opened her eyes at all, but had sensed a light that was shining above her closed lids. The water still flowed down her throat, and she began to feel weakness, which was good, because it occurred to her that before she felt almost nothing at all. To be alive is to be weak and suffering, to know you exist is to be able to feel pain and sorrow.

She'd forgotten how to drink and choked on the liquid, her body convulsing and doubling over, her first real movement in a long time. She put her hand to her lips, and then both hands to her face and nearly cried because she could move, she could feel the sleekness of her own flesh, and smell the open night air. She found herself rubbing her eyes to open them, her hands dirty from the water that gave her the ability to move now.

She looked up to see the bright face of the moon smiling down upon her. Someone had left the nite-lite on for her, was watching over her.

She lowered her head a bit, trying to focus on the figure kneeling next to her. Her head spun with dizziness, delirium, and she adjusted her eyes to the untrained vision she had savored before becoming comatose. The statue that sat next to her was enshrouded and dark, but she knew who it was. Looking up she realized that the night would be bright but for the fact that she was surrounded by earthy hills. No, not hills. Mounds of dirt.

It was a grave she was in, her very own.

Her hands rested on the satin comfort of the lining of the coffin. Talissa stroked her hair so gently and imperceptibly that she didn't even realize that it was comforting her, it was the only thing that stopped her from screaming in the absence of sense. Her hand stroked the satin, the smoothness of it making her shiver. It was white, pure and virginal, except for a moist, red stain that her hand had passed over in its fondlings.

Heather tried to stand, her legs quivering with infirmity and decrepitude, but she struggled against them, ignoring the paradox of pain and unfeeling that her nerves registered to her.

"Rest a moment, honey." The voice, though quiet, rang in her ears high-pitched and immense. She felt her head throb, her body stiff with atrophy, as she began her debouchement to the air that was truly fresh, not the air of some pit for a carcass and worms. A slight though unwanted nudge from behind put her over the threshold and she fell prone on the soft, dewy grass, her senses overwhelmed by the tantalizing touch of Mother Nature caressing her with the arms of a gentle, warm breeze. She breathed long, heavy breaths but when she put her hand to her heart, the drum didn't beat. She sensed rather than saw Talissa, again kneeling at her side. "You should feel like yourself in a few minutes."

Heather listened to the throb in her head, focusing on its rhythmic beat rather than listen to the silence of her heart. She tried to speak but her voice was throaty and garbled, and it took her a moment to clear it.

"How long?" she managed. "How long did you keep down there?" Her hands went absently to her throat to rub it.

"That's not important now-"

"How-**fucking**-long!!!" screamed Heather, her voice catching the attention of squirrels, and corpses not yet deep in sleep. Talissa looked at her forlornly.

"Two weeks, about," she said bemusedly.

Heather was agape, anger seething as her blood boiled and raged in her veins.

"Two weeks," she repeated, validating the statement. "Two fucking weeks?! In a wormhole! How the hell could you do that? You said you loved me. You told me you bestowed a gift on me, you said nothing about covering me in dirt for days on end."

"I had to do it. I had to make sure there was no tie to your former life."

"That's fucking trash! You could have had me out the next night or two. I never agreed with *this*." She kicked at the dirt pile.

"Now, don't be mad. Come on. We've the whole night ahead of us. Let's enjoy it."

Heather spat dirt, both from her mouth and from her mind. She had to clear her head, think about what had happened, decide what to do.

"I'm not spending the night with you, like some Whore of Satan."

"Please, Heather-"

"Shut up and listen for once. I don't know why you sought me out in the first place, and I don't know why you wanted to make me a vampire. But I do know that you've been very little help ever since. You threw me to the werewolves that first night, and then you buried me like a corpse for two weeks. Do you know that I felt everything? I felt the sun beat down upon me like a rain of fire. I couldn't move or think. I was stuck in a fugue the whole time. My stomach twisted and turned and the stale air clogged my nose and throat. It was like someone held a mask over my face and deprived me of sight or thought. Is that how you treat someone you love?" Heather didn't wait for an answer. She barely glanced at Talissa's cheerless face. She just got up, the feeling in her legs coming back slowly, and began to walk away.

"Wait," called Talissa, "where are you going?" She got up and followed her, and when she caught up and was about to put a hand on Heather's shaking shoulder, Heather turned round, quicker than one would think possible on account of her weakened state. Talissa stopped abruptly, shocked still by the fire in Heather's ocean blue eyes.

"Where are we?" asked Heather, her voice now strong and terse. Talissa stared at her a moment before answering, her face expressionless, sadness trying to break through the corners of her lips.

"*Cimetière Mont-Royal*," said Talissa, her voice cracking and betraying her.

"Thank you," answered Heather, with sarcasm and rolled eyes. She stood there, seething, directing the energy of her anger at Talissa, tears welling in Talissa's eyes because she knew that she was going to lose Heather to emotion, at least for a while. Heather's upper lip started into a slight snarl and she said, "Don't bother following me. Don't even think of it." Her body was in a clenched stance, her muscles flexing in their newfound freedom. Heather raised a hand-no, a claw-the tissues in her hand so taut and stressed so the veins on the back of it were clearly visible, making it look like it belonged on a wild animal, and took her nails, which were long and protruding and brought her hand in a swift, preternatural motion across Talissa's cheek. Blood seeped from the three ragged wounds, but Talissa stood stoic as though it was a breeze that had grazed her face. Heather turned and walked away, not even glancing back.

* * *

I had just spoken to Susan Langden. The woman was alone, distraught, but obliging and she spoke freely, as freely as her tears would let her. Her home now consisted of two memorials-one for her husband, one for her daughter, both prematurely deceased. She seemed lost to the world; she had her friends, who were as supportive as possible, but they had their own lives to lead. Her life, the one she had painstakingly etched from marble, was being chiseled on its display, into a disfigured and tortured creature. The stability and beauty of it were being made unclean, and she was the last piece of the statue that stood teetering on a bad leg.

She spoke fondly of her husband, said he was jovial and kind-hearted though somewhat reclusive. Everyone has their way, though, and she accepted his, leaving him space knowing that he'd find a moment to throw her a smile behind his veil of cigar smoke. He died a victim of his excesses, his drinking.

And she loved her daughter dearly. She was an outgoing version of what her father was. She brimmed with confidence and excitement and curiosity. It was so shocking when she came home from work one day and found her sleeping still, and more so when she tried for twenty minutes to wake her. After that, she decided to take her pulse, though the decision was more unconscious than an active one. When she couldn't find any thumping of a heart, she called for an ambulance, screaming in hysterics. She was full of tears and nausea for the entire night, after Heather was pronounced dead on arrival at the hospital. An elderly aunt, one of the few relatives who was still around, had stayed as much as possible to comfort her but it was of little use. Her life had become senseless and barren. Susan entered counseling nearly a week past Heather's death. And that in itself was not enough. Few people can find their self-worth in bite-sized weekly sessions, and Susan had lost more than her self-worth. She'd lost her daughter and her husband, really the only two people who had a strong presence in her life. (A note from Korson: Susan's lover dismissed her when he became her sole emotional base, the only the basis for their relationship having been jack-hammer fucking. Graham St. Croix was, of course, unaware of her infidelity.)

I thought about the poor woman. She was a pathetic wreck, a shell. But there was nothing anyone could do. She would spend the rest of her years trudging against a bad current, trying to figure out what had happened, what she'd done to deserve this karma. And then she would end in a wild, maniacal state, cared for by nurses who would wonder why this old lady's sanity sat on a chair across the room from her, giggling and laughing like a pitiless child.

* * *

Heather had spent the night in an abandoned shack near the foot of the runway of Dorval airport. She closed herself in as best as she could, covering the ragged, dirty window with newspaper and masking tape. She climbed into a stolen sleeping bag and pulled it over her head to block out the light of the sun. It was the best she could do for now, and other more suitable arrangements would have to be made for tomorrow. If there was a tomorrow; she was not oblivious to the risk she was putting her life at. It served its purpose though, as she found out when her eyes fluttered open for a moment at midday and she was still enshrouded in mostly darkness. It wasn't the light that stung, though it was painful in its brilliance. It was the searing heat which caused her both to wake and to desire the fugue of sleep. She would sweat and turn throughout the day. She had to find a way to overcome the simoom.

Curiously, she discovered that by sleeping directly in the path of the window was more effective than trying to hide in the shadows.

When night fell, it was a blessing. She had woken from her slumber, which was at times satisfying. And went out of the shack just as a plane was taking off, its engines roaring overhead. She found it curious that the noise hadn't woken her since her senses were animalistically keen now. As she thought about it, except for the heat waking her, she remembered nothing at all of her sleep. No dreams, no feeling of having lost twelve hours of her now endless life, nothing. Maybe sleep was death for a vampire? If that seemed to be the case, then sleeping in shacks at the foot of a major airport may not be the bet idea if she wanted to remain undead. Then again, who would look for her here?

She began walking towards the airport, and slipped into the crowd unnoticed, though she was nervous that people would be pointing and whispering about the girl with the bright blond hair of an angel and the skin of a corpse. Not a soul took notice of her. Heather checked what passed for her belongings. In her wallet she had her identification, useless now except in an unofficial capacity, and over a hundred dollars that she'd had the foresight to leave in there. With the money she decided to hail a cab to take her to the city, and she told the driver to drop her at the corner of Queen Mary and *boul. Decarie*, where she would walk and decide on what to do next. This was, incidentally, north of downtown and her beloved *rue Ste-Catherine*, about a ten minute drive down the Decarie.

(Note: An interesting point about Autoroute Decarie: It was built below ground level, a highway, and the off-ramps rose up and merged with *boul. Decarie*, two one way routes running parallel to the highway on either side. Every so often there was a bridge over top of the autoroute to allow for turns. In the mid-seventies, heavy rains backed up the sewage system and flooded the deeper parts of the autoroute, trapping numerous cars and drowning several people, further evidence that nature still has great sway in man's domain.)

She stepped out of the cab, said *merci* to the driver. She started to walk south on Decarie, her thoughts lost in the night. The two weeks she had lost filled her with a sense of emptiness, of having missed out on something. She stopped, scolding herself for being stupid, because she had till the end of time now. What did two weeks matter, not only in the grand scheme of things, but in *her* grand scheme? Why was she angered at having been comatose for that time? It was about control. Control over her body, her actions, what she did with herself. It wasn't plain and simple, but it had a lot to do with that, with the fact that she was being handled in such a disrespectful fashion. She didn't even have the courtesy of being told what to do. She was forced into that awful situation, cheated of happiness.

Heather had walked at a brisk but comfortable pace and in a short time she reached Monkland Ave. and *Girouard*, and smiled. She saw the open-air cafes and restaurants and it was just what she wanted-to sit and watch, rather than walk and search. She would let the world walk down the runway for her joy, as she looked on in appraisal. She felt as though the Earth were a crystal ball, and that she held it in the palm of her hand, caressing and fondling it, lolling at it through eyes that were keen and fresh, newborn's eyes.

She sat down on the patio of a café, against the railing that separated her court from the peasants who were to parade in front of her. The waitress asked her what she would like and she answered, *Vin blanc, si vous plais*.

The waitress brought the wine, with a napkin and some breadsticks, and told her to enjoy. She would, most definitely. Heather brought the wine to her nose. It was sweet and fragrant. The smell was intoxicating, she closed her eyes to appreciate if fully. She almost giggled aloud as the bubbles tickled her nose, which then startled her into opening her eyes.

Champagne? She hadn't ordered that. Ah, well. It was a pleasant surprise, anyway. She could almost hear the bubbles popping as they reached the air. She took a minuscule sip, letting the bubbly reach high tide in her mouth before swallowing. It was almost tasteless, and she coughed and choked on it several times before composing herself. She looked around, hoping no one took notice of her fit. She didn't feel like being noticed right now. She looked back down at the glass, sitting isolated on the table. It still gave forth its fragrance, the bubbles still popped cheerfully for her pleasure, but it held in its golden tinge a stain. She couldn't appreciate it in a way she did before. She couldn't drink it down.

She tried again, rising the glass slowly to her lips. She took a tiny sip again, and swallowed, ready for the convulsion. She didn't sputter like the last sip, but her throat was choked with nausea and sickness, which spread down to her stomach, a vile, puking feeling welling up in her.

"No champagne, I guess," she whispered to herself. "Probably no food of any other kind either." A throb started in her head, a familiar one. It would seem likely that all consumables were to be enjoyed under glass, to be smelled and touched and seen but not tasted.

"Cigarette?" queried a voice from beside her ear. She looked up casually to see a handsome man, slightly older, proffering a cigarette to her from a silver case. Slightly corny, but charming. Heather shrugged indifferently and took the tobacco. The man went to light it for her but before he could she extended her open hand to the direction of the seat across the table from her, to which he accepted her invitation and sat down. Then he was permitted to light her cigarette. She smiled at him warmly, and he gave her back a practiced but sincere half smile.

"What day is it today?" asked Heather. The man smiled more broadly.

"Wednesday. Too much champagne for you lately?"

"Not enough, actually. I don't think I can drink too much to tell you the truth." Heather smiled at him, just so he would return one of his own. He had a bright, friendly smile, though it was rough from the years. But that made it alluring, the fact that he seemed to be wild, uninhibited-initiated.

"Forgive me. I had forgotten to introduce myself."

"No. Don't. Monsieur will be just fine." The man almost laughed.

"A girl that likes the mysterious. I like it." Yes, monsieur suited him just fine because of his age, his demeanor, his accent, which was only hinted at from the bottom of his voice. "Are you Francophone?"

"Partly. My mother is three-quarters French, while my father was all stubborn Anglophone pig."

With *savoir-faire* he said, "I'm sorry."

"Don't be, that's what made him charming."

"No, I mean about your father. You said *was*. I take that to mean he is no longer with us."

"I am a little impressed. You're perceptive, Monsieur." He took a sip of his wine, of which the effects he was already feeling. Heather, using the pause, put her glass to her lips but drank nothing. She could smell his blood, the rush of it through his arteries, every pump and thump of his heart. It made her own heart fill with a sexual anticipation, a crude and basic desire to have him. It was amusing that she would judge him by his looks, that they would attract her to him, when all what counted was his blood, the same blood that flowed freely through every vein in the street. Blood is blood.

"You seem to lose yourself in thought, my dear," said the man. His voice was also sexy and intoxicating, the hint of the accent teasing to the ear.

"I was just wondering about why I chose to stop at this place of all places. Why it happened that I met you, if it was fate or accident."

"This place, it is beautiful, *non*? You chose to sit here because the view is prettier than over there, next door, or even across the street. This vantage lets you look down the gradual decline of the boulevard. It is like being on a hill so imperceptible that some people don't even realize that there is one. But you have a sharp eye, and you chose the top."

"This whole city is built on a mountain. Yet do we choose where we are to live according to that?"

"The rich live closer to the top, *non*?"

"True. But is that an accident?"

"Maybe. Perhaps. But it is also their dogma. To be the best. To be higher. To have more, to have better. The poorest sections of town are away from Mount Royal, are they not? But whether that was chosen or not, whether the decision was subconscious or a calculated act of will, that cannot be known. I myself would think that the rich, based on the history of Canada, would want to live near the shore of the *rivière St. Laurent*. It would make for easy escape. Actually, I would think they would want to do it now too. Politicians are always vilified, but especially so in Québec."

"And where do you live, my handsome Prince?" The man gave her a toothy, embarrassed grin and he put his head in the palm of his hand to hide his face.

"I live close to the mountain, but not so close that I don't have to go to work every day." He paused a second, just to look at Heather's cherubic beauty. "As for why I met you, I simply saw you from the bar the minute you walked up the steps and sat down on the patio. A beautiful girl shouldn't sit alone."

"What if I was waiting for someone?"

"You weren't. I'm perceptive, remember?"

"Right. But what would people say to see a girl like me with a man of your age? You wouldn't mind the whispering?"

"They would be whispering of your beauty, and of me they would be jealous. Even the ladies." He stopped again to look at her, without having to concentrate on speaking or thinking what to say. Just to look and bask in this beauty whose golden, shining hair framed her face like a painting of a princess in a castle, her hair caressing her shoulders lightly. Her eyes were oceans of tropical blue sea that danced back and forth on her sweet face, their light providing the glow of a blue flame with which to sit by and look at and absorb, simply appreciate.

"Monsieur, you're old enough to be my father. Though I might add you would have to have had me young. What would your wife think?"

"Oh, I'm not married, if that's causing you worry."

"But you were."

"Now you're the perceptive one."

"It has nothing to do with perception. You're a well-spoken, older man, though not aged by any means. You still could pass for late twenties, and people would be shocked if you told them you were in your forties. You have a confidence in speaking to women, so we are not a mystery to you. You have experience, and it shows. You can't hide that. Besides, I can read your mind!"

The handsome stranger laughed a full, masculine laugh. "And what am I thinking now, my dear?"

"That you want me."

The man looked at Heather impassively. Then he smiled his flirty, practiced smile. "And would you have me?" he said, with an air of some confidence.

"Maybe," said Heather, "if you promise to be a gentleman."

"Why wouldn't I be? We will only go so far as you want."

"Good. I think I can trust you, but you never know these days. You hear of so many brutal rapes. But I feel that I have been seduced by an honest man."

The man grinned at her as he said: "I think it is actually you who has seduced me!"

They talked a moment longer and then paid the cheque to the waitress, the man leaving a generous gratuity, and left the cafe to walk arm in arm down the boulevard. The man lived only fifteen minutes from where they sat. The air was refreshing, smelling like spring though fall was nearby.

"You won't tell me your name?" asked the man, without coercion. Heather shook her head politely no. "Then you will always be a mystery to me, as I will be to you."

They reached his home, a townhouse in which he occupied the top floor. They went up the darkened, creaky steps and inside. The place was nicely furnished, and he had a good eye for coordinating the colours and good taste in useless trinkets to fit over the fireplace. The walls were somewhat bare, except for a large picture over the fireplace of a snow covered log cabin in the lake at sunset. Heather stared the beautiful purples and pinks that melded gently into each other, embracing rather than combating each other. The artist-it didn't occur to her to look who had painted it, and it didn't matter-had captured the sinking sun with such poignancy and clarity that it almost made Heather weep. It reminded her of the fact that she hadn't seen the light of day in almost a month. What was it she said? *I don't care if I never see the sun again.* Maybe she did miss it. But everything had its price, bartering was what made the world itself turn. The world bartered with the sun and the moon for the right to cast night or day. She bartered with a demon for the right to live forever.

And won.

And won!

She hadn't given up much, though her life would seem a lot to some. But she'd gained so much. Unbridled freedom. Her senses had a passion in them that no mortal could ever hope or dream of.

Everything has its cost.

The man, the sweet man, took her though the house, offering her a drink, which she turned down. He led her into the bedroom, or rather she let him lead her, and there was no presumptuousness to it at all. Heather excused herself for a moment and went to the bathroom, closing the door behind her, seeing the man loosening his clothing.

He is old enough to have fathered me, she thought. *But I must learn to transcend age now, I'm beyond such things.* She turned on the tap, splashing cool water on her face. She thought it would revive her, make her feel more awake, and it was startlingly invigorating. The hunger, that hunger had been welling up in her for a long while, but now, with the man naked in the next room, with his salty flesh exposed for the taking, she couldn't control it anymore. She knew what she would have to do, she knew that she must satiate her dead veins with the life of others. She dried off her face, her wet face, and went back to the bedroom.

The man was prepared, his shirt untucked, unbuttoned, and he sat up against a pillow on his bed. He looked inviting to her, his warm face friendly, his casual, uninhibited demeanor, his relaxed posture. His hot, throbbing blood that flowed audibly just below the surface of his tanned skin.

Thump, thump.

And Heather could see why he was so smooth when he talked to women, it was to cover his inadequacies, to conquer so as to boost his ego. He had a pathetic phallus. He used words to mesmerize and hypnotize.

Heather wouldn't be rushed, or overanxious. She would prolong her orgasm until the right moment. She walked over to the bed slowly, letting her hips sway a little for him. And she bent down over him, pulling back his shirt to let his hirsute chest breathe. She bent her head low, with the emotion of an experienced adulteress, and she teased and tickled his phallus, licking it with her cold, dead tongue. It was not very long for him to complete his longing, as it must have been a long while since it saw use. And with his need satisfied, with his body relaxed and drugged with debauchery, she bit her small, sharp eye teeth into this throbbing sex, and he moaned from stupor and dull pain, not realizing it was pain because of the ecstasy and inebriation that had clung to him.

Heather drained him a second time, moving up to his belly and biting, his arm and biting, his mouth, and there she bit too. He was shocked into stillness by what she did to him, by the lack of energy he felt. If he had the strength left to scream he would have done so. But when Heather had finished her feast of feeding and frenzy, when she pulled away and surveyed the disaster she had made of this being, this life she had found so precious she had to have it for her own, she was drawn to his eyes, his dark and empty chips of coal that once told the world what a wonderful man this was. And in that emptiness was a speck of pain, of an odium at what he had been victim to.

Heather took a piece of paper and pen. She searched the house for a sample of his writing and set about to copy it. She wasn't sure why she did this (maybe her heart was still soft?) and it took some time and care to do it right, and with tact. Maybe he deserved better. Maybe he just deserved something, rather than the legacy of being killed by a nameless murderer. She made his note as eloquent as possible, trying not to sacrifice believability in the process, and she took care of any evidence that would reveal her presence there. She left the suicide note on the night table next to the bed. It was, of course, unsigned. Everything has its cost.

The walk from where she was to her old neighborhood took a while, a good half hour, but it was something that Heather felt drawn to. She wasn't quite sure what pulled her, as no ties, other than maybe her mother, were left over from her old life. But it had been nearly a month since she'd seen her old place, or any of the city for that matter, and a little bit of nostalgia needn't prove harmful. She had no engagements otherwise, so the time was plentiful.

She walked in a haze of thought, not paying much attention to the night that had so enraptured her earlier. She had seen only death and torture as a vampire. Was there a link between the evil in her blood and the evil in the air? Did her mere presence augment the two age-old forces, tilting the balance in favour of darkness? The irony was that she herself hadn't brought about as much of the death she thought she would in two nights as a vampire. Her thirst seemed satiated by her will and one life per night. Of course, she had only been a vampire for two and a half nights now. Things could change, and probably would. If Heather had any naiveté as a mortal, it was rapidly vanishing.

She was snapped to attention from her reverie by a familiar scent in the crisp night air. The Taint. It was present only for a moment, then gone. And it wasn't so strong as to give away any valuable information, like its direction. It just gently wafted in on a low breeze. And it both captivated and nauseated Heather at the same time, which flummoxed her as much as trying to figure out its source. With the scent gone, she put it out of her mind and continued over to *rue Ste-Catherine* and Gladstone.

When she reached her old neighborhood, she was at first reluctant to approach the vicinity of her house for fear that her neighbors may recognize her. But it was after midnight and the streets were quite empty, and she scolded herself for being irrational, (she was a vampire for God's sake, a Goddess of the night! People should submit to <u>her</u>), and she walked towards her house with the intention of walking by it slowly, just for a look, and not to stop.

But something caught her attention. A smell maybe, a sound. She could just see her mother, not really see her but she pictured her there, walking around, turning off lights, putting lunch in the fridge, telling her to go upstairs to bed already. But now she had no one to tell, no laundry to fold but her own, no husband to share her dinners and problems with. She was utterly alone. Heather listened more closely, (or perhaps she walked closer to the house?), and she thought she could hear her mother talking in her sleep in the upstairs bedroom. She thought she heard her mother calling to her to come and snuggle up next to her like she did as a baby, and sometimes as a child. It was nonsense to be hearing voices with such keen hearing, but a part of her mortal self was still anchored in the real world, the living world, and she felt a mortal need to walk to the back of the house and stand under the window and listen as closely as possible and dismiss the voice as imagination. So that's exactly what she did. Fear was grounded in the unknown, and she was a representative of the unknown, therefore knowledge was her right. How else would she strike fear into the hearts of her victims if she were to come up against something else unknown? After all, two unknowns in the same room would just make for trouble.

Heather stood under her mother's darkened, silent window. Everything indicated that the room, the house, was dormant. She should just walk away. But if she could just feel the touch of the woman whose womb had bore her once more! To just let her know that she wasn't a random victim of death, that she'd chosen a different life from the norm. A secret life.

So romantic. So touching. And still she thought her mother a bitch.

C'mon, Heather, you'll never make it as a vampire if you don't toughen yourself up, she scolded herself.

Before Heather could stop herself, she was climbing the brick with animalistic skill, climbing like she had for those many years when she was haunted by Talissa. She clumsily and loudly opened the window, rending the metal latch out of shape, but her mother remained asleep, though aware of a presence in the room. Her eyes fluttered and her hands searched the air around her for something. Her eyes opened a bit, shuttered still by the grogginess of sleep.

"Heather?" she whispered. Heather moved closer, like a wraith, the moonlight shining through her white silk blouse making her look ethereal. Her languid locomotion across the room made her seem as though she was carried by a soft, scented breeze and had no need of legs. Her slender waist and smooth sides gleamed from under her shirt, with the light behind her. "Heather?" her mother whispered again. "My baby? Is that you?"

Heather reached the bed where her mother half slept. She stood as an angel of God, her blond hair a halo of perfection, her face cherubic, yet her eyes glimmered with a fierce maturity that belied her youthful visage. Her body swelled and curved like that of a woman's. And if one looked very close, you could see the tiny points of eye teeth that hid themselves, disguised themselves, to make her look mortal still.

"I thought you were dead, darling." A tear tinged the weathered cheek of her mother's face. "I can't live without you. I can't live alone." Heather realized how selfish, how self-serving she'd been in leaving her mother with nothing, nobody. She should of at least thought of a way to take her with her. But it was too late.

"I'm here mother. I'm okay."

"Then you've come back to me! You'll stay?" Her voice cracked.

"You're dreaming, mother. I'm not really here."

"But you look so real! I can feel the sheets beneath me, I can feel the air from the window." She reached to touch Heather's face with her fingertips, but Heather remained out of reach. "It's so cold."

"I just came to tell you that I was okay. I just wanted you to go on living."

Susan cried a little harder. "I can't. Stay with me. You don't understand how much it hurts to be alone."

"I'm not real, mother. Open your eyes. Look at me. *Look*." It was a command. "See my skin, how pale and white it is, like chalk. Look at the veins on the back of my hand, how withered and purple they look under the chalk. My nails are claws on the ends of fingers that look like branches from a wizened old oak. I'm a ghost. That's all. I'm just visiting. I just came from my grave. I'm dead as a doornail."

Susan examined Heather through watery, old eyes, but she couldn't tear her sight form her daughter's face. "Look at your face, though. It's still beautiful. Let me touch it, please? You look like a beautiful woman, like you did before. I can see through your blouse that you're a woman."

"It's an illusion, mother. I'm only looking pretty for you. Touch my skin, go ahead." Heather bent near, extending her hand for her mother to touch. "See how cold it is?" Susan reached for her daughter's cheek instead, and Heather didn't pull away. The skin was smooth and icy and unnatural.

The tears from her mother's eyes began to dry a bit. "See," she said, "I knew you were real. I knew you'd come back to me."

Heather became forlorn. "I can't stay, mother, I just came to tell you that I'm okay. I won't be here tomorrow." The tears resumed their torrent from Susan's eyes. She took Heather by the arms and tried to pull her close, but she hadn't the strength.

"Why do you do this to me? Why do you leave me so alone? Please, can't you just stay with me the night? Can't you lie next to me like when you were a little girl?"

Heather moved onto the bed, one knee at time, and curled up next to her mother who held her closely and tightly.

"Please," said Susan, "please come visit me again. I don't care if you're a dream or not. Please visit me again..." Heather turned and it was now she who cradled her mother. She could hear her heart thumping and gushing. Susan became a babe in her arms, curled and crying. Heather rocked her back and forth, back and forth, trying to comfort the woman who had become a shell, a waif of a person. They lay there together for a while, daughter cradling mother like a distraught child, whispering assurances into her hot ears, kissing her wet, hot cheek with her cold lips. And Heather found that her eyes had tears in them as well, for the life she had left behind, broken and torn, for the woman who had to endure its tatters. For the fact that she couldn't function because of grief for a lost family, and would continue so until the day she died. She began to cry because of what she was about to do, relieve pain with pain. She tried to ignore the hunger in her, it wasn't because of the hunger that she was going to do it. It was out of pity and love. It was out of remorse and regret and guilt. It wasn't out of hunger, anything but hunger. But it was also out of anger for the way her mother disrespected her father. Murder was such a complex puzzle to piece together. Pain was life. And too much pain was death.

Her small, sharp teeth dented the flesh of her mother's neck, and she wasn't sure whose heart raced more, or if she had a heart, because sometimes she could hear a thumping and sometimes everything was quiet. Her mother thought she was being affectionate and she nuzzled closer and bore her neck more. Heather's teeth slid slowly and smoothly into the flesh, breaking the veins that contained the sweet elixir of everlasting life. Her mother moaned of pain and drowsiness as she began to feel weak because of her loss. Heather moaned with her at the sensation of the suckling, the paradox of eroticism and nurturing making her shiver with a dark delight. In moments, she felt the beat of her mother's heart grow slow and faint, and she felt her fangs withdraw from the wounds and she felt mostly relieved that her mother would suffer no longer, that her mind was at ease before her death because the last thing she'd seen was her daughter's angelic visage. She was relieved that she didn't have to continue to endure the experience of killing her own mother. To live with it was to put it out of one's mind. To experience it was to endure the experience of killing her own mother. To experience it was to endure the pain that she had caused the womb that gave her life. She was shaken at the what she had done but she couldn't let her mother continue to live under those circumstances, with her mind in such a horrid state, shredded grey tatters.

Heather got up and walked away from the scene of her matricide, and when she got to the door, pushing it open to allow her passage, she looked back into the dark and quiet room. The last knot had been cut.

In the hallway, with the door to her mother's room closed, and with it the last door to her mortal life, Heather surveyed the darkened hallway of her house. The scent of the place was as she remembered it, though stronger and more aromatic. It looked alive with her vampire vision, even though the lights were off and it should have looked drab and dull. She walked slowly down the hall, past the guest room/computer room where they would store their extra blankets and work on school projects. She went into the hall bathroom, the one that belonged to her, to see the place where she fussed and crimped herself to perfection each morning before school. Nothing had been moved really, though it seemed sparse of supplies such as soap and toilet paper.

Then Heather caught her movement in the mirror. She turned to look at herself. She'd never gotten a clear look at her reflection since becoming a vampire. Now, here, in her own house, the place she shouldn't have come back to, she had all the time in the world to thoroughly examine herself. Her face was wan and surreal in the dimness of the moonlight. It was a shadow of a reflection that stared back at her. It was a shadow of humanity, the other side of its coin. The part of humans that were denied to the, shunned by religious dogma:

Thou shalt not kill.

Thou shalt not covet thy neighbour's blood.

Thou shalt not steal his soul.

Was it the vampires fault the it would kill just to remain alive? Any more than the fault of the dog who kills by his own instinct and sleeps for it? Heather fixed her eyes to the ones in her reflection.

She clicked on the light. What she saw gave her a shock.

Her eyes were even more brilliant than they'd been in her life. They shone with a deep opal-like blue, and they had a cavernous depth. Around her eyes, the lids and just below were dark, as though a permanent eyeliner had been applied to make them stand out, like on an Egyptian Princess. Her skin was pale and chalky and white, but it had a sheen to it, probably for the warmth of the blood, and it looked aery. In the shadow of the darkened room, she thought she looked like an angel, or a virgin in a church. In the harsh brutality of the artificial bulb, she looked like a minion form Hell. Her eyes made her look inviting and whorelike. She bore her teeth to the mirror and gave a terse, challenging growl. A part of her hated what she'd become. A piece of her simply loved it, adored it. It invoked the duality in her.

She went into her room, which had been left more or less the same as she'd left it, except for the bed which was stripped of its sheets, the covered mirror. She drew back the curtains to let the glorious moonlight in. She was developing an affinity for it, for things that were of the dark. Heather loved its pale purple light.

Walking over to her closet, she opened the door to look at herself in the full-length mirror that hung on the other side. She stood back from it a few feet, and the darkness gave her no trouble in distinguishing her features. The see-through white blouse she wore was definitely effective, and not as revealing as one would think. The shadows teased all over her in sensuous ways. Now wonder Monsieur had been so taken aback by her, so much that he didn't care if he was old enough to be her father. She saw the slender curve of her waist disappear into her snug black leggings. She held her arms out to see more. The swell of her breasts was just barely outlined by the light that shone from behind her.

She saw herself purply-red. Thank God she wasn't hungry or she'd just see herself red!

Her hips curved smoothly and subtly became her legs. She turned to the side to see the shape of them. They were luscious, healthy, perfect to be touched and caressed and felt. She looked at her ass and it was perfect and round. She turned her back to the mirror and pulled off her shirt, and looked back over her shoulder to the smooth curvature of her supple back. And she turned and moved a little closer to the mirror, her finger imperceptibly touching her cold, hard nipple, then the rest of her breast. It felt real, but cool to the touch, but still, it felt human, looked human. She pulled off her leggings and shoes and stood naked and dead before the mirror.

What about down there? she thought to herself. *Would that still work?* She sat on the bed, the mattress scratchy without any sheet on it, and opened her legs up slowly to see the dead thing between them. She touched it with her index finger. Whereas it used to be a little warmer than the rest of her body, now it was a little colder. It was also numb to the touch, without the expected sensation arising from it, and it was dry, not moist. She entered herself slowly, so as not to hurt herself. It was a mere umbra of the feelings that were once inspired from there. It was an ornament, like on a nun, there, but unusable because of promises to a higher power. She belonged to a different lineage now, one that progressed in another fashion. She felt a sadness at losing what she did-the taste and pleasure of food, the pleasure of her own body.

But there were other pleasures to be had. Suckling blood was her food now, she nourished like a tiger who'd been separated from it's mother-fierce and without compassion. Her senses were something that awed and astonished her with every new sight or sound or smell that she received. She would make herself determined to find more pleasures in the afterlife. There must be even more than what she'd seen and felt in the three days she'd spent as a vampire.

The clock read five after five. The sun would be up soon. She decided to stay here, in her house for a few nights, until people became suspicious of her mother's whereabouts. For a few nights, she would have a mental reprieve from being a vampire. She could pretend to be Heather Langden, and she could come and go from her house as if she was still alive. She walked down to the basement with some old, familiar blankets that she'd found and she sealed herself in for the day.

When she woke, it was sudden and abrupt, and she'd had no realization that any long period of time had passed. It felt like she closed her eyes, went numb for a moment, then awoke fresh. Thinking back on it though, there was the feeling that something had happened to her. At some point, when the sun was too bright and hot, she had the memory of a feeling of uncomfortableness, but it felt as though it were someone else's memory, or it was like something she'd watched from a distance but wasn't quite sure what she saw.

She also found herself directly under the window, rather than hidden away in the corner.

All in all she'd closed off the basement window quite well and it was small anyway. She'd covered herself with thick blankets since the warmth of it didn't seem to bother her the way the sun's heat did. In fact, the warmer an object was, the more enticing it felt. It was like she fed off warmth because she had none of her own.

Heather climbed out of the pile of blankets that she'd buried herself under, and went upstairs to her room to dress in fresh clothes. The house was dark and she'd sooner leave it that way. And it would help if anyone happened to peak into a window that they wouldn't see someone roaming around, especially someone who wasn't supposed to be there.

She went downstairs and had to struggle with the urge to make breakfast. Upon searching her feelings she found that she really had no desire for food, but the habit was so engrained in her routine that it was hard not to think in those terms. With time, she figured, she'd adopt the new feelings and habits as her own.

She did notice, however, that she did hunger for blood, that it was keen and fresh on her tongue, that a drop would alleviate the longing that manifested itself there. She wanted the hunger to swell and ebb in her. She wanted to feel desire. Gluttony was not something she wanted to be a part of, sitting in the gutter, blood covering her chin and nose and teeth, some street rat that devoured whatever came into reach. She felt the skin of her face, the coldness of it, how lifeless it was compared to how it felt after last night's two course feast. How many would it be tonight? Two again? Three? When was the desire satiated?

She decided to go outside, to walk around a bit and enjoy the fragrance of the August evening. She looked at the clear night, the stars winking their admiration at her icy beauty. She looked at the light and wondered at how old it was. She wondered if she would see any stars die, just snuff out because they had exhausted themselves. She wondered if a vampire could exhaust itself. There were so many unanswered questions she had. So many things she didn't know about. There had to be more than waking up from death and drinking so you could wake up from death again. What if she were to stop drinking? Would she then die? What was out there that could harm her now that she was immortal? Did she have a field of protection around her, that drove off infection and pain and suffering? She thought about Talissa's scratched face, the last time she'd seen her. It was obvious that it was possible to harm another vampire. She relished the idea that the scratches would still be there if-no, when-she ever saw her again.

A thought came into her head, one that was timid, just a little, a bit cocky and amiable, and it asked or wondered 'why she scratch.' Before Heather answered it, she realized that the thought was overly simple, quiet childish, very incoherent and most certainly not her own.

"Meow," a little voice said to her from just behind her, only a few feet away. It was a tiny kitten, his fur gray, alternating between light and dark, and his underside and paws and chin were white. "Meow," he said again. He approached Heather, unable to sense any danger, and sniffed the air that came from her, perhaps hesitant to come closer.

"Hey, you!" Heather said to him. She could gather no further thoughts from him. The thought she had before was most definitely from this little three pound kitten, but now his mind was blank, at least to her. She reached her hand to pet him, and he instinctively cowered down and away from her, but then he sniffed and reached up a paw, and gestured for Heather to bring her hand closer. He sniffed her fingertips again and he licked them in affection, then he rubbed his entire body against the back of her hand the way cats do.

"You're a brave little fellow ain'tcha," said Heather. Like it or not she had made a friend. Her first friend she'd made since her decision. "I could really use a friend right now, y'know? I'm glad you're not afraid of me. I have a feeling that I'm going to be scaring a lot of people for a very long time."

Heather tried to actively transmit this thought to her kitten friend, to see if maybe she could communicate with him. It seemed to open a pathway of some sort because she received from him a jumble of warm, friendly feelings, the same childlike ones that she'd felt earlier. She also received more nudges and rubs, with extra vigour. When she tried to transmit her name she received only confusion. Communication was apparently limited to simple, basic emotions and needs.

The kitten curled up against her thigh and purred.

"And where did you come from?" Heather realized that it was needless to speak her thoughts out loud, but it made her feel more comfortable. She was disturbed, however, by the kitten's response. He'd been in an unwanted litter, and he had a strong, fresh image of one of his littermates who was smacked and thrown across the room, though only the barest conception of the humility and pain of the torture. He himself narrowly escaped a broken bone. Being a creature of instinct, he had run at the first opportunity of an open door. He ran for freedom, out of fear, because he was lucky enough for his tiny brain to be blessed with an intuition that he was better off trying to chase down birds and mice on the street. Lucky for him it wasn't winter or he'd have had trouble trying to keep warm. And it was especially lucky for him that these memories of abuse would fade because they were infrequent and his animal brain thought in linear patterns. If the abuse had been more frequent it would have made him timid to any socialization whatsoever. But he'd found Heather, through the hand of fate, sweet succulent serendipity, and he felt rightly safe. These thoughts that Heather had gleaned from him nearly made her weep at the fact that someone would needlessly hurt a defenseless creature.

She stroked his fluffy fur.

"You need a name, little one," she said to him. She realized that any words that she tried to transmit to him would be met with confusion, so she looked at him and tried to figure out what he reminded her of. "Clouds," she said, "you look like clouds. Would you like the name Cumulous?" She gave him an image of big, puffy grey and white clouds and the kitten increased his purring, relaxed by the image. "Cumulous it is, my friend."

She picked him up and he hung from her hand, upset to be removed from his comfortable, curled position next to her leg. She brought him into the house, putting a box of dirt out for his litter, and finding some cheese and sliced chicken, put it in a bowl for him to nibble on, while she went out to buy him food.

On her way back from the store, she smelled the Taint again. Determined not to be beaten by it once more, she rushed home, threw the food in a bowl, and in another milk, and rushed out of the house to chase down whatever it was that gave this pale pungency its source. She hoped it was the smell of another vampire, she knew it had to be. Above all, she hoped it was a vampire that she hadn't met before. She wanted to know if there were vampires running rampant across Montréal, across the country, the world. How did they hide? Where did they live? She ran down *de Maisonneuve*, east, towards downtown, where the smell came from. She ran and ran, pushing past people, making women drop their purses and men yell bitch *en francais.* But the turning of the wind did her in. She'd lost it.

She turned down Chomedey and then went east on *Ste-Catherine*, hoping that her direction would carry her back into the path of the Taint. It had to be another vampire, she was sure of it. She tried to sniff her own skin, to see if the same smell emanated from her, but she caught nothing. And on she walked.

She came to *boul. St. Laurent*, a small district of streets that were paved with red cobblestones that were faded with time and use, and where throngs of people walked on the street itself, which was closed off to traffic. It was an area where people would gather to relax, some dressed in fashionable causal clothing, others in a standard t-shirt and jeans, and they would loiter in the numerous restaurants and cafés that lined the curb, sitting on the patio if it were a gentle and warm night. It was entertainment enough to sit and chat with friends over a drink, have a bite to eat, watch the crowd ebb and flow in front of you. To watch the stars come up and the streetlights come on.

Heather had wandered a bit out of despair, a bit out of boredom, and found herself in the middle of the crowd. It may have been fate, or karma, or an accident that she hadn't turned around sooner, but she caught a faint hint of the Taint on the air. She turned slowly, looking to her left, then behind her, then to what was her right, and back the way she stood before. She didn't want to scare it off this time. Every other time she'd chased after it and it teased her and when she turned the corner it had disappeared only to tap her on the shoulder and run once again. This time she would wait and see and look out of the corner of her eye for it. She knew it was another vampire. It must be.

But did the other vampires smell her? Did she give off the same Taint? Did they purposely avoid her like a disease? She began to walk forward, slowly, her head looking at the cobblestones before her, and every once in a while she would tilt her head to the side and look into the restaurants and cafés.

Over there, on the patio of that Greek place, was that one? The man seemed to glance at her and laugh, as though her were taunting her, then he'd go back to talking to the person at the other end of the table. But was he really taunting and just pretending to talk? Did he just happen to look like he had laughed at her? His skin was so pink he couldn't be an immortal.

"It's your ego, Heather," she thought to herself. "Talissa just wanted to make me feel important. I'm just another vampire. Get it through your head. There is no conspiracy against you."

Why was it so difficult to spot someone with fangs and white skin? How did they hide their obsidian eyes? Heather remembered the stranger she'd taken the night before. She remembered that it was only moments after she'd sat down at the café that the man had approached her. She had a preternatural charm, something that emanated from within her unnatural psyche, a telepathic power of sorts that would attract prey. Was this how vampires hid? By dampening the emissions that made people become enamored with them?

But she was all alone. That was the fact. Her world had shrunk and become skin tight and the only company was herself and you know what happens when that happens people go crazy just trying to live with their own thoughts that's why we like fucking but after drinking blood the other one's dead and you're left holding a rag but they're both messy and everyone who's dead is really dead and it was an accident that Heather had risen but wasn't that life big fucking accident and it was all so pointless but it didn't have to be boring the future's the page and everything's fiction so how about let's write and see where life goes and let's have a drink because it's all about blood and the madness the madness the madness-

"Shit," thought Heather. "Fucking woozy. I won't make it through eternity at this rate. Deep breath. There. Drink. Find a drink."

She continued on, turning her gaze up towards a patio on a balcony. A woman with thick, gorgeous black hair, wavy and part of it put up, she looked down and met Heather's eyes and held her gaze for a moment. She had a look on her face that was almost blank but for the trace of animosity that seeped across it. This woman did nothing to disguise the look. Then she smiled a polite and diabolical smile. Her sculpted cheeks shined under the lamplight. Then she turned her attention away, back to the man seated across from her.

Everywhere Heather looked she saw people gaze at her with an expression similar to that of the woman. And each one seemed both intentional and accidental. Each person could be put into the category of vampire or human. The world was not made up of vampires. That was a logical impossibility. Yet all these people gave her these looks, all these people and it couldn't be by mistake. Some of them had to be a vampire or know of vampires. But which? Why couldn't she pick out who was who? What was the trick to it? And why did the Taint tease her? The smell permeated the very air, but it was neither strong nor weak, it certainly ceased to give any sense of direction the way it had before. Heather turned back the way she came, she made her way down to *rue Ste-Catherine* again, and she wanted to go home, at least get away from this confusion. She was beginning to feel as though she regretted leaving Talissa because she was the only other immortal that she knew of. The others didn't seem to want to show their faces to her. That much was apparent. She knew they were there, she could sense it. But for some reason they chose to remain in the shadows.

And those shadows, they seemed themselves alive now! Whereas before they were merely places the light couldn't go.

She left the district and its crowds and restaurants and shy, sly vampires that seemed abundant but invisible. She would have to find a way to communicate with them, but on her own terms. She wouldn't be toyed with, not the way she was toyed with when she bought into immortal life. But now she felt a hunger, *the* hunger, well up in her, strong all of a sudden as though it waited for her to turn her attentions towards it. It seemed to be a being in itself, within her, writhing and trapped and struggling for blood.

Was this what it would be like to have a penis? she thought. It threw a tantrum in her throat.

She walked along, sending off her signal, consciously, trying to attract a victim. A teenage boy, one who tried to look a lot older than he really was offered her drugs. It was too easy. She took him into an alleyway, his friends grinning knowingly, smiling at his dumb luck.

She took him into the darkened alleyway and she took him.

Walking west on *rue Ste-Catherine*, Heather felt an urgency to find others of her kind, others besides Talissa. Enough of wandering, of wondering, of brooding about her preternatural body. She needed information, she needed a guide. She needed someone to tell her about her powers-and she knew she had powers, she'd already communicated with an animal-and she needed someone to show her the proper way to use these powers, and how to interact with mainstream society.

It was so hard for Heather to admit that, after years of despising her high-school teachers, but maybe all she needed was a teacher who knew the meaning of the word relevance?

Being alone, though, gave Heather no opportunity for mimicry. She couldn't cunningly learn by watching others out of the corner of her eye.

But most of all she felt vulnerable. Vulnerable to the vampires who she knew had her surrounded at *boul. St. Laurent.*

The Vampires of *boul. St. Laurent.* It sounded eloquent, eerie, gothic. Unnatural creatures dressed in fancy dresses and silk suits, pretending to drink and eat, pretending to be human, socializing with them. A great farce it was, to be human when you're not. Heather herself felt much more comfortable keeping to the shadows and luring prey to her. She had a compunction about broadly displaying herself in public. Something felt wrong about moving too close to the world of mortals. To be so close, to interact so you couldn't tell human and vampire apart seemed perverse, and a little bit too cruel, though Heather felt flashes of cruelty course through her body when the desire to kill came upon her.

But she couldn't tell vampire from human. That was the point, wasn't it? She herself didn't feel comfortable in fooling an entire crowd of people. She had too many physical aberrations on her; her tiny fang points, which could be seen if she opened her mouth too often; her pale skin, which made her look corpse-like; her nails seemed to grow almost claw-like, sharp. No, she would fool one or two even, but not crowds and crowds of people.

She walked quite a ways, was twenty more minutes from home and feeling satisfied that she'd fed enough. She'd reached *rue Crescent*, a place littered with bars and clubs where tourists and residents of Montréal alike gathered. There were also several big name fast food restaurants that remained open all night because it wasn't worth the effort of closing for only a few hours.

Uch, I've never smelled such rancid meat, thought Heather as she passed McDonald's.

She glanced in the window of one, memories, some blurry from drink, of times with friends when they'd just come from a bar and sat eating the greasy food and laughing over nothing in particular, or the loser who sat in the corner.

She was about move on, when a lock of scraggly dark hair caught her attention. She stopped and looked, trying to seem like she wasn't staring, which was difficult since few people window shopped at Burger King. She focused her vision on the back of the head, the familiarity of it coming in clearly.

"Sarah," she whispered to herself. She stood, looked behind her, down the street, at the sky to see if the sun was visible on the brink of the horizon. It had been almost two months since she'd seen her, one of her closest friends. But with her increased responsibilities at home, with the loss of her father and her boyfriend, Heather didn't feel much like getting together with friends and she'd lost touch with a lot of them, at least on a regular basis. But Sarah she still spoke to a few times and on weekends they still went out whenever.

Heather looked at the young man sitting across the table from her. He seemed agitated, he was saying something, using his hands a lot, and he struggled to keep his voice down. Then the girl turned her head to her left. Her cheeks were tear-stained and pink, her eyes glassy from sadness. It was Sarah. Heather then recognized the young man as a boyfriend that she may have recalled meeting. Henri?

Sarah got up from her seat and went upstairs to the washroom. The boy pulled his eyes away from her in exasperation as she passed him and put his hands on his thighs, leaned back in his seat. A moment later Sarah returned, looking no better than before and picked up her purse to leave. The boy reached for her to stop her but she eluded him and she put on her jacket and walked away. He made no effort to follow. He sat there aggravated.

As soon as Sarah had exited, Heather leapt to her side and took her by the arm, turning her off the main road. Sarah tired to pull free but she wasn't strong enough and she kept saying, *What the hell do think you're doing?* and other such phrases. Heather felt a few eyes turning to her and she loathed the attention.

She felt undeniably strong so close to a mortal.

"Hush," she told her friend. When they were far enough from the main road and the throngs of people, Heather said to her: "Listen to my voice. Familiar?"

Sarah managed to turn her gaze a bit, to take a look at this mugger or whatever that had pulled her aside. She was still tear-streaked and ragged, but the feelings of desertion had been pushed to the side momentarily in favor of confusion, anger and a little fear at being robbed. But the face she saw, the voice finally registering in her memory, these left her with confusion, and disbelief and shock and so on. She stood mouth agape and looking down the street and back at the face and away again, not expecting it to be there when she looked back to it. A thousand scenarios ran through her mind and dismissed themselves as ludicrous, only to be replaced by a thousand more. She managed to mutter half the word 'how' before becoming silent again.

Heather just stood there, holding her up by the arms, smiling warmly, ready to burst out laughing at the severity of the situation.

"Don't you miss me, Sarah? Don't I look just divine?"

"Oh, this isn't happening," she said. "I'm hallucinating. My mother was right, sex is bad for you."

"No, Sarah, look, it's really me. It's Heather."

"But how is that possible? I buried you a month ago." The possibilities continued to turn over in Sarah's mind. "I put dirt on your grave."

Heather said, "Listen-" then stopped. What was she to say? I'm a drinker of human blood now? Like in the movies? *That's* how I escaped the grave. There was no way Sarah would believe that. She'd think someone was trying to play a cruel hoax on her. She'd try to tear the mask and wig and see who was really underneath.

"Your skin, it's so red, and chalky." Heather put her fingers to her face. It must be the blood she just drank. It must make her pale skin redden, like when you put your finger over a bright light. "Your hair's shimmering." Sarah went to finger Heather's radiant blond locks. "It feels like velvet, or kitten fur."

Oh, no! Sarah was becoming enamored with her. Two minutes ago she was about to faint with shock, but in her excitement Heather must have not realized that she was sending out her pheromone that seemed to hold people rapt! Sarah looked at her and touched her like a star-crossed lover. In her weakened and saddened state she must be very vulnerable.

"Listen, Sarah, it was great seeing you again but I should be going, you probably want to be alone after what just happened."

"Don't go!! Please?" Sarah took gentle hold of Heather's arm. Heather moved her hand off and began to walk away. Sarah followed, longingly.

Heather turned abruptly, took Sarah by both arms and shook her, trying to turn off the fount that enraptured.

"Sarah, look I've got to go. I'm not real, I'm dead. Remember? You buried me!" Shit, she didn't want to say this. "You're dreaming me." It seemed that she only existed in her own mind, and in the dreams of others. She began to walk away again, her mature, manicured walk, the walk that drove men crazy.

Sarah followed.

"I'm not dreaming you, you're real, I know it. I just felt your hair." All the pain and tears had left her voice. She caught up to Heather, put her hand on her shoulder. Heather spun and wrenched her arm back and away, took her by the back of the neck with her other hand, her mouth open and surgical fangs bared to the wind.

"I'm your nightmare! That's what happens when you don't let sleeping dreams lie!" She thrust her intimately close and bit her teeth into the yielding skin of her neck. The fountain had turned the other way, had entered the realm of the physical and the liquid, spurting forth down the vampire's throat and gushing throughout her body with an ecstasy like no other. Sarah shuddered and shook in Heather's hold, too weak to struggle by the time she realized what was going on. She slid slowly down to the ground as the hold was released, only a glimmer of life still ticking within her.

Heather looked down at the tangled form that was once her friend. Her head throbbed with the coursing of fresh blood, with the morality of what she'd done. She had no idea why. It felt so good, it was so hard to resist, but she hadn't even felt the urge well up in her this time. It seized her by the hair and she'd taken he first person in arms reach.

A friend. She'd killed a friend. Heather had never felt so alone as now.

Part 4: Catholic Quebec

The next evening Korson fed early, on a whore who tried to solicit him. He made it look like a suicide. Always believable, she didn't have much to live for anyway. It was still early, not yet midnight, and he hoped to catch the girl at her home. It was there that he went, and waited across the street.

For hours he stood, still as an animal waiting for it's prey to peek from a hole, and for hours he saw nothing. He crossed over to the house and snatched a look into the windows. Everything was dark and quiet. He went back to the front porch, looked into the sitting window in front. Nothing. No scent, no movement, no glimmer of life. He shivered. So close. His fingertips were within reach of grasping the mystery, the shape of the piece of the puzzle that eluded him. He had this sickly feeling creeping over him. It told him to quit. To give up and leave. Québec wasn't worth it anymore. In the entire century or so that he'd spent here, not only were the events around him unsettled, the people in conflict with their own identity, but he hadn't yet found the peace he was looking for.

He could go out to the sea, the east coast, Nova Scotia. It was gentle and quiet there. The waves crashing against the shore the only conflict to think about. He wished he was through with it. He thought he was, those many years ago. But the strife seemed to continue, it would consume itself and rekindle out of its own ashes. No matter how long or how hard it was to beat it down, it would rise up again with a flame as bright as before. And each time it would carry more danger with it. He slumped himself down in a patio chair, which creaked under his giant frame. And a terse little motion caught his eye.

There, at the end of the front walk, stood the angelic, blond little vampire. Her right foot set a little behind her left, her knee bent at the ready. To turn or to fight, he wasn't sure which. She held a tensed hand at her side, showing she was able to defend herself if necessary. Her deep blond hair glowed warmly in the moonlight, and her eyes were the romantic droplets of water they always were.

Korson fixed upon her eyes. The rest of her looked somewhat battle-scarred. Her skin was chalky red and vampiric, her hair glowed bewitchingly, and her hand seemed clawlkike at the fingertips. But her eyes, they were mixed. They had the alluring vampiric glow to them, the one that emanated both from the sight of them and from the coaxing of the power of the mind, but there was still that tinge. That small part of them that showed she was still young. They weren't hollow. An old vampire, his eyes were hollow, and cold, and empty. His eyes showed the callousness of a murderer's essence. Hers though, hers had that tinge of remembrance. Remembrance of humanity, of innocence.

They also radiated fear. A stifling, choking fear. Her hands shook, and her shoulders, as well. She was frozen in the stare of the aged vampire on her doorstep.

Korson rose slowly. The other vampire tensed. He took a tentative step forward. She hopped two steps back. Clearly on edge, jittery and nervous. Korson raised his hands, palms out, in front of him. He could hear her heart beating, wildly, in her chest. She was a beautiful young girl. But that beauty now masked a vicious danger for anything living, himself included. To intrude on the territory of another vampire was treacherous ground indeed. A creature that always felt hunted, watching for the one mortal in a hundred thousand that knew, that could burn you out and destroy you. It was almost instinct to be distrustful and skeptical of another who was intruding. They stood watching each other for many long moments, one afraid to move for fear of frightening the other, the other unwilling to move for fear of her own self.

Finally she took a step forward. Korson kept his hands high, in front of him, remaining as still as he possibly could. She moved closer and closer, until she finally stood at half the distance, and stopped. She discreetly sniffed the air, inhaling large breaths through her sculpted nose. After several times she looked more confused than scared, dizzy. But the memory of where she was came back quickly on the cold night air of mid-summer. She tensed back again, crouching a little, her legs ready for a lunge. Korson remained at his absolute stillest, despite the screaming of his mind to grab this one about the neck and hold her, not to let her get away again, not to chance it. She moved forward, slowly, slowly, and she was within arm's reach. He was going crazy with inactivity, he felt and fought the impulse in his appendages to move into action, he sweated just in the attempt. Heather reached out her hand slowly and touched his face, to see if he was real.

In the ultimate risk, their lives were in each other's hands.

You have her trust, he thought, *she will curl against your wing if you can just resist the violent urge within*. Tears welled up in Heather's blue and innocent eyes. Korson laid his hands slowly and gently on her shoulders. She clutched him and put her head into his chest, and the tears flowed from her like rainwater from the eaves.

"I was so lonely," she whispered. And she shook in his arms.

Inside Heather's house, in the front sitting room. Korson positioned himself in a recliner next to the widow, Heather lay on her side on the couch, more relaxed. She had Cumulous next to her and she stroked his back as he meowed intermittently.

"Was that you? The one I saw last night." Heather looked at Korson, in awe. He put his hand to his chin. "Watching me."

"No. There is no honour in spying."

"Oh." Heather waited.

"Do you always act so impulsively?" asked Korson, with no attempt to stigmatize. He elaborated: "I have found some of your kills. Sloppy. Not worthy of someone capable of the nuances seen in your beauty. The police are out there a lot lately. I had to cover your tracks."

"Oh. Sorry," she answered. The words sounded pale against the memory of what she did. She was beginning to feel comfortable around him. Or maybe it was curiousness, and the diminishing void of loneliness. She knew that she wasn't alone in the world beneath the world. She had questions burning in her about the social structure that kept itself hidden. Korson spoke, suddenly it seemed, for he looked statuesque watching Heather watch him.

"So you've never been taught or guided in vampiric ways?" Heather nodded in agreement. "You have a strong natural drive in you, completely uninhibited." Was that a smile from him?

"I really don't know what happens to me. It seems that the urge wells up in me all of a sudden. It just overtakes me without my realizing it."

"Do you also know," said Korson, crossing his legs and putting his hands on his knee, "that a mortal was here last night?" Heather shook her head no, a little nervous at the answer, a little scared. "He just came to check on your mother. He spoke with her once or twice about you. He was concerned for her welfare, she seemed lonely and withdrawn. Is she here, by the way?"

Heather put her palm to her mouth and bit at it. She began to see through teary, watery eyes. Korson was patient with her, he waited for her to give her answer as she wished, and she finally uttered, no, her mother was not here.

"What happened to her?" asked Korson.

Heather began to relate the story, how she came to her mother as a dream, that she just wanted to see if she was okay. Through half sobs and a choked throat she was comforting her, that she was about to leave when the urge just splashed her, the scent of live, pumping blood was too much to take. That she took the life of her own mother. And she justified it by making herself believer it was euthanasia, that her mother's life was too broken for her to go on living it, and the fact that Heather had visited her gave her a false ray of hope that would have made her condition worsen when she woke up in the morning.

"And what's done is done," she cried, "and I'm learning that the hard way."

Korson waited in silence, for her to stop crying, to regain some composure. It took nearly an hour, Heather being so swept up in the emotion, the sharpness of her senses making every needle of pain that much more acute. Every detail of her own mother lying dead in her own room.

"I'm sorry," said Heather. Her cheeks were still wet and her eyes purplish and sore. Her chest heaved as it took in air. "I'm sorry."

Korson said, "You have nothing to be sorry about."

"Yes I do. I've been such a terrible witch and now I can't stop crying over it."

"You have no idea what you've become."

Heather shook her head no. The pastel of sadness still grazed her consciousness...

"A vampire is more than a blood sucking demon from the depths of Hell. You once were a creature of habit. You were trained how to eat, how to defecate, how to speak and walk. But now you are that creature transformed into a creature of instinct. An instinct is something you can't restrain, but you can regulate it. It is your instinct to kill for your sustenance, and instinct to be suspicious of others because you know they will fear you and want to destroy you. Your instincts don't have to govern you, you don't have to be a slave to them."

"I'm not sure if I understand you."

Korson shifted in his seat, leaned forward. "You can train yourself to reel them in. Have you ever known hunger, real hunger, like that of the starving children of this world?" Heather said no she hadn't.

"It is common practice to restrict a vampire's feeding for the first few nights of his existence."

"The first night I was a vampire, I was thrust into the world hungry."

"Mmm." Korson was thoughtful. "It's ingrained in you, this urge? The first night, were you overwhelmed by the search for blood."

"The first night, I had no idea what to do. But I saw something that made me angry, that's when the urge seemed to overtake me."

"True," said Korson, "anger and sadness are extreme emotions. You can forget yourself in either. This is why the urge overtakes you. Because you forget yourself."

Cumulous meowed in Heather's lap, quieting down once she began to pet him.

"Can I die?" asked Heather. "Am I really going to live forever?"

Korson smiled at her naivete. "You can be killed, yes, but otherwise you will live for as long as the universe survives."

"Pretty awesome thought," said Heather. "I don't think it's really sunk in yet."

"It probably won't," said Korson. "Not for a while at least."

"But how do I learn? How do I know that I'm doing the right thing?"

Korson laughed at what she said, his expression returning to the morose quickly after. "You have in you a raw power that matches your cherubic beauty. You are pure," Heather shook her head no, "whether you think so or not. You are the vampiric picture of innocence. Is the black bear a sinner because he kills a man? No. He kills out of fear. If he thinks the man is dead he will leave. But the man who kills the bear for his paw and bladder, for money, his is the sinner. He is the evil one. You kill for food or fear. You haven't sinned. Not like some I've seen." His face went forlornly dim.

"You have to show me!" cried Heather. "I need to see others, other vampires. I'm sick of being the brooding, wandering waif. All I've done is wander and kill. I've seen nothing that was promised to me, no grand revelations of the world. Immortality seems to be eluding me, showing me only boredom. I want to see more, I want to see what there really is," she pleaded.

"Heather, you are young and foolish. And I hate to say it, but naive, because you shouldn't be. You have the skills, the intelligence. But you have to open your mind. You are no longer a teenage human who can giggle and grin her way through life. You are a vampire. A hunter! A creature that is callous by nature. And the grand scheme you speak of may be right under your very nose."

Heather was perplexed and said, "What the hell are you talking about?"

"You don't see it? In my face, in my eyes? Although I have embraced my native ways, the ways of the Indian, I used to be a more vicious and ruthless killer than yourself. I tore at my victim's throats and left them breathing and gasping, clutching at the air, wondering, *'Why? Why me?'* They died in absolute agony. There were few that survived, and those that did did only because I allowed it. I watched as they went crazy, insane. Their closed minds couldn't grasp the fact that a creature such as I existed outside the imagination. Remember, at the time I was born machines and science were sweeping the earth. The age was becoming stale and antiseptic. Religion was losing its foothold. And it was the perfect time for a vampire to be born. No one would believe, not like they used to. People lost their superstitions, they stopped listening for the *remnants*. We would kill as savagely as we wished, and everyone would put the blame on bears or wolves. It was the great vampire joke to tear the flesh from a person's bones and then howl loud and long at the sky while the man screamed in pain.

"As I said, I let some live, and they were overcome with psychosis. No one would listen to them, and I would watch, from a distance, as they tore their own hair out. One even bled himself every night, despite the best efforts of his restraints. The doctors wouldn't allow anything in his room, nothing sharp or anything like that, so he eventually bit his own flesh and tore it so he would bleed on the floor so the 'demon' wouldn't devour him. That night I went into his room, his restrained and helpless body shivering in the heat. Shivering in *heat!* And he trembled, his skin was icy. I looked down at him. Imagine it. A creature, whose hands could resemble claws at times, nearly seven feet tall, eyes shimmering when there was no light to shimmer by. I must have looked like a God. I know I felt like one. The power over another's life. Isn't that what makes a God? And I just stood there with a tiny grin on my face, and I outstretched my hands to him, like I would accept his suffrage unto myself and release him from his pain. I must have reminded him of a dark Jesus, one who allows others to suffer rather than taking the pain into himself. He shook even more and opened his mouth to scream but all that came out was a dry rasp. All he could do was give himself to me. And it was then that I bent down to the floor, one knee at a time. Then I placed each hand on the floor, again slowly and one at a time, so I knelt over the pool of blood that he had torn from himself. And I casually moved my head to the floor, to the steaming, hot blood-it was still flowing out of him, by the way-and I dipped my tongue into it and I splashed it into my mouth with the ease and tranquillity of a deer at a calm lake. I knelt there and licked up half the blood, taking my time as though it were a feast of fat king, a king who looked down a long table filled with food and was in absolutely no hurry.

"And finally I stood up, again the God that towered over this broken disciple. I still smiled. And I said to him, 'Thank you for your sacrifice. I will leave you with your life.' I left. And it was only moments later that I heard his scream tear the night in two. I think that they killed him, out of shear mercy for his soul. The priests of the village were baffled. Come to think of it, they were happy to see him go. This was, after all, a thickly Catholic Québec. There was no function for a blasphemer who saw demons. They dismissed him as a creature forgotten by God."

Heather was speechless. She couldn't even think of the pale murders of her own compared to this.

"Ironically, it was a human who drew me back from the evil, the excesses. It was a mortal who conquered his fear of me, who trusted me with his life, and showed me that the way of the Indian can be meshed with the way of the vampire. I was a good man in life, very virtuous. I'd like to think that if I ever do die, that if I have a soul, it will be redeemed." Korson sat plaintive, as did Heather. The air was thick with the brooding she so wanted to forget, to dismiss.

"Can we meet? Again I mean."

"Of course," answered Korson. Heather smiled, and for just a moment, she looked more like an angel than a dark angel. "Come to me, Heather. But you must become mine, I warn you. You know of the fount, the rapture."

Heather nodded. "Thank you," she said, very much. And then her eyes went wide with recollection. "The others, you have to show me the others!"

Korson looked a little perplexed. "What others do you talk of?" he asked.

"The others! Can't you smell it?" Heather sniffed at the air, in this direction and that. "I want to meet them!"

"Heather," said Korson. "Young one. There are no others. I don't know what you are talking about."

"I can even smell it a bit now. It comes and goes, but I can almost always smell it if I don't think about it. Don't you smell it, too?" Heather pleaded.

Korson shook his head no, slowly. "Heather," he said soothing, gently, "I've hardly seen another vampire for over thirty years. The numbers left are less than that which you could count on your hands. I think you are just sensing the one who created you."

"No!" she screamed. "It is the scent of others! And I can smell the difference in it. Can't you smell it? It's so strong sometimes."

"I think we are about the last of our breed, in this part of the world anyway. Not that I've left Québec, or Canada, that much, but whenever I do I very, rarely, see another. I think vampires are becoming overwhelmed with a self-loathing, and they commit suicide without making another. Since the Great Purge, it has always been dangerous to make another. We are dying, slowly, a slow immortal death."

"I am absolutely sure of this." Heather was adamant. "I have smelt this over and over, and whenever I chase after it hides from me. But I know it's there. I can smell it around the corner. Why can't you smell it?" Heather slumped back in her chair, tired and frustrated.

"You are positive about this?" asked Korson. Heather looked him a yes. "You have a strong instinct, that is true. Untrained, but strong. Tomorrow, come stay with me. I have a cabin, hidden, outside Montréal. I'll draw a map, but burn it when you are finished with it. Or eat it, I don't care. And make sure you aren't followed!" Korson's intensity, sudden as it was, shocked her. "Bring only what you need. It's probably best that you leave here soon anyway. What is it?"

Heather held up her kitten. "Cumulous. I can't leave him here. He'll starve."

"You care for this...cat?" He looked a little repelled.

"I can't leave him here. Will you take him tonight? Please?"

"I suppose," said Korson, taking hold of the tiny creature, wondering why someone would put their faith in such a timid and insignificant kind of animal. But maybe it was good that she could still care. "What does he eat?"

"Raw meat."

That figures, he thought.

Finding Korson's cabin house proved to be more difficult than it sounded. It was hard to picture distance and length of time from words on a piece of paper, no matter how many times he'd said that this road would go on for many miles and such.

But all the same, she was both excited and thrilled, and the only thing to be accomplished was the reality of it. To have finally come into contact with another of her kind, to find out those many secrets. Ah, but she set herself up for disappointment.

Again. What if there were no secrets? What if there was only unlife? To hell with it, anyway. She wanted to know. And she would.

But first, to leave her home a second time. This was proving trying. She knew that she shouldn't be here in the first place, and that someone would come calling after her poor mother, especially when they found where she'd put her. But to leave for a second time, it was tough. And this time she was the icy demon vampire Heather, this time she clung for different reasons. She felt that this wasn't the safest place for her.

But then, isn't the most dangerous place the safest? She knew the geography of the area like the lines of her body. But was it really the safest? Talissa, after all, knew where it was. And the fact that she'd seen neither drip nor drop of her was paradoxically the best and worst sign she could possibly have. It was best to leave, for certain. She had to disappear.

But for different reasons, other circumstances! She should never have come back here, the troubled, necromancing angel, haunting her old house. She had the entire world to practice her dark arts and she chose her closed little environment to return to, the thing she wanted to get away from. Oh, but to control time and life as she did. She felt the strength coursing through her veins whenever she took a life into herself, whenever a man went soft in her arms.

It was troublesome for her to take women now, she seemed to shy from them. Perhaps it was because of her friend? Her mother? Homophobia from her past life? Who knows if a little Freudian slip of the tongue might change her mind in a few hundred years, eh? She might get sick of the mindfuck that went along with every man.

But back to leaving home for the second time. The first time around she wanted to be free, free of the constraints of life, of time, of rules, those petty things that teenagers are prone to, when they believe the world ends at the tips of their fingers.

And she had conquered those restrictions, she did cross the boundary to another world, one shrouded in, well, she really wasn't sure yet having only experienced two vampires in her company. This time, though, it was familiarity, the territorial. She had cat-like instincts and she marked down her territory along pre-existing patterns, but mark it she did. After all, there appeared to be no other vampires willing to invade this area. Perhaps they feared her (unlikely), or maybe they were watching her from a distance and debating with their preternatural minds about whether they should destroy her enlivened remains (a possibility), but the bottom line was that they stayed away. For Heather to come back a second time, though, was like a heroin addict shooting up all over again for an entirely new set of reasons. If he starts again, based on his old reasons, he can quit easily because he has had that experience before. Though to invent a new set of circumstances was to also have to live through a new experience of cessation.

She began looking around the house, gathering small items together. She placed some of her mother's more cherished belongings together on her bed, her wedding ring, her favourite book, a dress she liked. It was a small and unfitting tribute but it was all she could do, and it alleviated her feelings.

Unresolved finality. That was what she felt, something ending when it shouldn't, when there was more to be done. She hated long good-byes, and this was the longest. It started years ago.

Heather walked slowly to her room to finish her packing. It sounded too human, too out of place.

I'm a vampire and I'm packing and moving to 666 Brimstone Ave. Nah, didn't work. Maybe a vocabulary lesson was in order. Shift your thinking is what Korson would say. Bloody morbid bastard.

She liked him actually, is what she was thinking as she picked through her belongings. Seemed...wise. Or something. He did know something, she would get it out of him sooner or later. And she thought that he liked her too, though it was difficult to conceive of it. He was constantly in shadow (those damned living shadows!), expressionless. Even his smile seemed forced. No, practiced. Like he was supposed to do it. Tall fucker, too, must've been a blot back in the 1800's. Would fit in okay these days, what with people being taller.

She ruffled through her clothes and changed into her leggings and white lacy top. She liked the tight, dark clothes these days, and the white lace gave her a touch of the Goth. Fitting.

But soon she stopped her distracted shuffling and her attention took to her surroundings. It all started here. Right in this very room, that very bed in fact when she slept with the Devil Talissa. The road to Hell was a long, twisty branch. She wasn't surprised that many people fell off along the way. She could remember that first day when Talissa was sitting like a jubilant cherub on her balcony, *floating*, above the window, just barely. Maybe there *was* a monster under the bed. Maybe it had come out. It was all so simple when she was a child.

Heather couldn't help but laugh, a small one. How in God's name would it be possible to recall the past when she was a thousand years old? Oh, what a powerful preternatural brain she would develop by then!

She continued to think of the events that led up to her unbirth as a vampire. If you were undead then you *must* have been unborn which then meant you were unalive or maybe caught somewhere in between. The thoughts flashed quick as lightning through her sharp mind, the thoughts of all the seemingly random events of her mysterious friend, and she tried to organize them into chronological order. Focus the blur. Next she remembered her mother coming into the room and her thinking she'd been caught, but she was alone. And Talissa standing at the bottom of the window, where she had dropped to. And her, Heather thinking she'd imagined it, but being called to the window, walking to it, like she did now, retracing her steps, and seeing Talissa at the bottom telling her to come down the trellis, standing there like a ghost who wasn't even there—

—But she was. Down there, like that other night, was she calling to her? Did she feel a tug? Heather froze, panic slammed the window shut and locked it, Talissa down there looking up, *she's come back for me!* Her mother of darkness, her blood sister. Heather backed away from the window, waiting for it to smash into tiny, glittering fragments, like little electric sparks, expelled outward around Talissa's sprung form, her dark, thick hair spread across the frame blocking the shimmering moonlight making the window an umbra. She backed away, but her walking was slow and syrupy from fear, she couldn't tear her glowing blue eyes from the window though she knew she should, should turn and run—

She slammed into something behind her, though she didn't feel like she was going fast enough to hit anything, and she turned and there she was, Talissa, the thing that looked so beautiful, like a statue, until you touched it and then you were in trouble.

Leaving for real this time? Go ahead and run, my Sab will find you anyway!

Heather let out a scream, it wasn't possible, she shouldn't have been in the backyard, she couldn't have been in the house, it was crazy, and all Heather could think to do was double over and scream. She was one of them now, whoever they were, and she shouldn't be afraid. Action, she needed to do something now. The window, the only way in was the only way out. It would be her that darkened its frame, not Talissa and it would be her that would crash through it like a blackened phoenix.

Blond, she thought, *I'm blond and I'll look more like an angel, I hope.*

She turned and took a few fast steps and leapt through the window, surprisingly majestically for someone who was supposed to be trembling with fear like a little waif vampire. And she landed softly and smoothly in a crouch while the electric glass tinkled to the ground around her, her holy circle. From which she leapt from her crouch and began to run with speed and fury and determination.

She ran to *de Maisonneuve*, thinking to lose herself in the nearby downtown. She could do it, run that way, without stopping, probably without breathing heavy at all, who knew? But something stopped her from making the turn east. The lights, flickering and flashing, the hordes of people, something stopped her. Prevented. She was prevented. Maybe other vampires were lost in there, too? Maybe friends of Talissa? She had met Korson by accident after all. She clearly didn't want to run into anyone else by accident. So she turned west after heading to *Ste-Catherine*. And all the time she was looking over her shoulder, waiting to see if the Devil had followed her.

And it came into her head that she'd lost something, something she had to get back, dearly. She lost territory, true, but also a piece of herself.

A piece of me is human. I'm not letting it go because I don't have to, it's a part of who I am. But she felt as though there was a battle of some sort going on. That if she didn't stand up to the Queen Mother that something else would be lost.

And that is really what Talissa was, and seemed to be. The Queen Mother with all the precious knowledge and power and it wouldn't surprise her one bit if she was the first ever vampire. She lacked the goodness of evil that was apparent in Korson. Too early to contrast, though, she had to meet others.

Her marathon had taken her to a cobblestone tunnel near the end of *Ste-Catherine*, just a south turn. Quite rustic. And it was in the arms of this tunnel that she found respite from her chase. She could see who approached from either direction and nothing would come down from above.

Fuck, if I could only fly already, she thought. She hunched over, her hands on her knees, her breasts showing through her white top because of the bloody sweat. She breathed somewhat heavily. Some things never change. At least she felt herself recovering faster than a mortal.

The ringing of a train sounded and Heather felt its rattle acutely in her tired bones. Tracks ran over top of this tunnel. The clattering sounded louder and louder with each moment, the earth beginning to shake with the weight and speed of the vehicle. Metal clanged on metal, and all that was needed was the chug, like from the old steam engines.

Heather looked up from catching her breath and she noticed, strangely, that each individual cobble was vibrating and shaking as though it were alive, independent of the wall. And as the sound of the train (the real one, not the steam engine she pictured in her head), as the sound came closer and became more deafening, she noticed that the cobblestones were indeed trembling in their mortar. And the closer the train got, the more they would tremble, the closer they would come to her. The tunnel was a haven for some reason. Maybe the stones had something to do with it. The stones were carved out of the bones of dead men of the cloth and they knew that she, Heather, was really not the evil creature that she really was. In her heart she was of pure soul and she deserved safeguard from her pursuers. Though God himself probably didn't agree. It seemed that way to her lately.

But as much as she tried to channel the energy of her mind to see reality (whatever the fuck that was), she saw only the rattling, trembling cobbles coming closer and closer with the ever increasing thunder of the train. And between the stones a light appeared. It must be her personal judgment day. It was God and the bones of priests who were after her now, she needn't worry herself with a petty Queen of the Vampires. God has decided to look down upon her and judge her actions because she was too much of a whimpering teenage coward to do so. She couldn't accept her fate as a vampire and she didn't even have the moxie to leave the tunnel and deal with the judgment of her peers. So God decided it was time to take it upon himself.

And try as she might, the walls still closed in upon her and, though her eyes were shut tight, the light still penetrated the thin lids, they went through her hands when she covered them over her eyes. And the light grew brighter, too. It must have been her imagination, but the walls began to push her from behind. It was too much for her, the walls touching her. She felt violated. By God, yet. How dare He. The tears welled up in her eyes, but she wouldn't let them flow. She wasn't a child anymore. She was a supernatural being who was being assaulted on all senses by a God. But she didn't truly believe in God. If he didn't exist he wasn't there. The assault increased. Bad move, saying God didn't exist. He could hear you, after all. The thundering in her ears was deafening, the touch of the wall at her back was slimy and disgusting, the light in her eyes harsh and blinding and not at all the peaceful light of heaven that the Good Book talked about. All that was left was the Taint to clog her breath. But it didn't come. The roar of the train loosed a scream from her mouth but she held back the tears, she would not shed another. The thunder was right over top of her now, so deafening, so painful, so utterly unbearable. The light so blinding in her eyes that all she saw was a sheet of bright white. It was so unbearable, indescribable. It was so close she could feel the rattle, feel the heat of the light, and it was the hand of God come to take her back.

And the light ceased, suddenly. It was the headlights of a car that was passing through the tunnel, the crescendo of the train dying down into the distance. Heather let herself relax, she leaned up against the cobblestone wall of the tunnel. Her chest still heaved and she stank of a cold, stale sweat.

Thank God it wasn't God, she thought.

Part 5: The Great Feast of Samhain

Curled up and trembling in a cold and dank forest, a large copse, really, Heather shivered from the bite of the wind. She had no real idea of how long it had been and how she'd made her way here, but thanks to fate, intuition, and anxiety, she had the delirious sense to collapse in a place where Korson would find her as he searched his way to the main road. He scooped the trembling little vampire up in his arms and carried her the rest of the way to his cottage house.

He settled her into a glass box, a sort of casket if you will, and covered her with blankets to keep her warm, closing the lid to seal out the sun.

When he awoke he found Heather standing by the window and looking out at the imperceptible glow of light that kissed the horizon good-bye.

"If you're cold you can wrap yourself in a blanket," he said to her, noticing her shiver.

She continued to look out the window. "No. Thanks anyway."

"You know you're not doing any good with these self-inflicted punishments."

Heather took her gaze from the window and sat down in a chair, covering herself in a blanket. "Happier now?"

"Much," answered Korson. He could see that Heather's mood had changed from when they first met. A few days ago she was eager for his knowledge and tutelage. Now she seemed content for four walls and a cadaver. And self-loathing. She seemed perhaps a little embarrassed at what happened last night.

"We all have trouble with coping, you know. There are times when even the best of us has to lose ourselves."

Heather shot him a look of contempt. "Don't you understand?" she said, hoarsely. "I went completely insane out there. I would have burned in the sun if you didn't happen to come by."

"I didn't," Korson said deprecatingly, "happen by. I was looking for you."

Steve Zinger

"Whatever. My point is, I'm going to do some serious harm to someone for no reason at all. Killing because I had to live, that I could take. But to just kill someone because I can't control my faculties, no. I won't let it happen."

"So you're never going to leave this house? That's being very unrealistic." Neither said another word for a while. But Heather was thinking that what he said was true. She was afraid of herself more than anything. She had these new powers, skills, actually, that were really beyond her. When they finally spoke again they talked about that. About why she was more powerful than most other newborn vampires. And it was agreed that she would have to exercise her mentality, control the part of her mind that seemed to be at the root of her instability. If only she could block out that noise.

"What noise?" asked Korson. He was like an intrigued doctor studying a patient with all kinds of exotic problems. By now Heather had her hands over her ears and was gritting her teeth. "What is it you hear?"

"It's like buzzing, a whirring." Heather trembled again. "It's so…simple, narrow-minded."

Well, Korson of course heard no buzz but he began to think on something about which Heather had said and about the way she acted with her kitten.

Cumulous, get down here and stay out of that, she would say sometimes, but he'd be nowhere near. He concentrated on her and called her attention.

"Heather…" and threw her a thought of fire and hot silver. Heather hit the floor in pain and agony, such utter agony to see a vampire and it's acute senses so in tune to the sensations of the limbs. One often thinks of vampires as creatures who are cold and callous of the heart but their senses are animalistically sharp and very fine so as to aid them in the dark of night. Not that they needed much help, their eyesight so perfect that the sun would blind them. Such is the accident that is nature. To see Heather on the floor in this state would have been agony to the witness.

Korson was on her immediately and giving her all kinds of images of cold, dark lakes and strawberry ice-cream. But the moment he touched her she only screamed louder. It took him what seemed forever, but was really twenty minutes, to ease her scream by forcing her to concentrate on his image of blackness. It was the most trying mental exercise one could imagine, projecting a dark and noiseless void from one mind to another. He kept it up as best he could, seeing as every time he slipped away from the image, Heather looked on the point of vomiting and would become a pale white (paler than even vampire chalk white.)

"You're a river for thoughts," said Korson. "You have no control over a power that most take centuries to develop. And all the energy in the world around us passes through your mind. It must be strong in this area. Did you believe in the power of mind as a mortal?"

"No," Heather managed.

"Even worse. If you have believed than at least your mind would be willing to handle it."

"I think I've made a believer out of myself." Her voice was hoarse with fatigue.

"Come," beckoned Korson, "and keep your mind's eye focused on me." They walked out, into the palely lit night among the trees and foliage of the surrounding area. Korson's cabin house was remotely set in a remote area and seemed essentially to be in the middle of nowhere though it really wasn't. And it wasn't all that far from the city of Montréal either. But it had the aura of being nowhere.

"Where is it we're going," asked Heather. It seemed to her that she had to crane her neck upwards more than ever to peek at the upper portion of Korson's lofty frame, something she didn't feel like doing right now. She was tentative but more controlled now.

"Just to a lake." They walked on for a few moments and came to a glass topped body of water with the moon reflected in it, like one of those paintings you see in someone's basement. "Now tell me, what do you think the buzzing was."

"You had to bring me here to ask me that?"

"Don't question me. Remember that I died over a century before you were even born. Now, what was it?"

Heather hugged herself and trembled at the thought, though Korson's black mental blanket was of some comfort. "I don't know."

"Don't be afraid to tell me what you think it was. I'm not going to laugh at you."

"I don't know, really." She couldn't help but stare at the ground, wet and mucky.

"Heather..."

"It was bats, okay?! I think it was a horde of screaming, hungry bats!"

Korson had a little smile playing on his lips as he looked at Heather.

He said, "Does that scare you, that you can hear these things?"

"It's like someone's in my head, and I have no control over what I see or what they see. I'll be walking by someone on the street, and I'll see this awful image of them being beaten by an abusive boyfriend or something like that. I wonder if they can see into my head, if they would even realize it if they had. That's where all the nightmares come from. Vampires walking beside you on the street. Yes, it scares me! Scares me a lot."

"Imagine that someone knew of our actions now, by means of reading thoughts like a book. Do you think that person would be scared? Don't you think he would be thinking to himself, 'Is this girl nuts? Does she not know how to think, or what fear really is?'"

"But that person watching wouldn't know what I meant until he stopped to think for a moment, to apply my circumstances to a personal situation. If that person felt for me, he would do that, he would sit with a book with the rain beating on the window at midnight, look up into the blackness and say: 'What if that happened to me...' His emotions would move with mine."

"Do you think you could call one over? A bat, I mean."

Heather shot him a look of reproach. "I don't think I'd want to do that. They didn't sound to friendly."

Korson laughed. "Forget the myths you've heard of them. They're really harmless. And they keep the bugs away, too. Now, call one over. Just one. You'll have to open yourself for a moment and then focus your energy. Use simple thoughts. I'll be right here if you need me."

Heather swallowed the clammy night air and went for it. She nearly tripped over the first hurdle, opening her mind completely, but closing and focusing was not problem. She was almost scared into it by the din that assaulted her at the start. The focus was random and the first creature she picked out was timid, simple, not at all willing to talk to the voices in it's head. She searched, almost too quickly, hopping from bat to bat, finally slowing her pace till she found on that was able to communicate with her, albeit on a very simple level.

She found herself focusing on the moon, its fullness and pale brightness comforting, its stately, unwavering authority soothing. And she almost scared the shit out herself. The iridescent sphere of the moon was broken by a shoal of bats, cutting across the visage of the moon like an arrow, their wings whipping the wind out of its silence.

"One, Heather, focus on one."

It was tough to narrow her mind down to just one. She realized that the creatures were on a much lower level than herself, and that she'd been communicating with dozens of them. She concentrated herself into one tiny beam of thought and actually broke a sweat doing it. The black cloud of bats dispersed across the face of the smiling blue moon and took their shadows with them.

All but one. This one came to Heather, landing on her shoulder. Jittery little thing, really. Would feel the need to get up every two or three minutes to whip around the clearing, across the lake, into the forest, land on her shoulder for a moment and repeat the procedure. It was only when Heather realized that bats like to hang upside down that she extended her arm and the creature settled down on the edge her hand. It made her giggle with delight, something she hadn't done in quite a while.

Korson said, "Remember to keep your focus." And she did. "You have a wonderful gift, communicating with animals. It is something that my own people have prided themselves on. Being in communion with nature. Though you yourself are more in tune with it than anyone."

Heather distracted herself from her preoccupation with the bat to listen to Korson. "Can other vampires do what I can?" she asked him.

"Not that I've ever heard. Bear in mind that I've not seen my own kind much in fifty years."

"Why is that?"

Korson paused thoughtfully for a moment. "I can't condone the evil with which they align themselves." There. He'd said it. He had ego, he was better than the rest of the soiled lot. Heather let the bat go. "You, though, you have been given an immense amount of power. To communicate with nature through one's mind is unheard of." He took her arm and brought her over to the lake. "Put your hand in here," he told her.

She did so and said, "It's freezing."

"Your senses are much too acute for your own good. Try to dull the sensation. Make it feel acceptable."

Heather closed her eyes and tried the focusing trick again. It was the only way she knew how. Slowly but surely the water began to feel warmer, more like she thought it should.

It was like she felt a knowledge flowing through it.

She opened her eyes and grinned up at Korson with her accomplishment. He looked down at her with only a little lack of astonishment.

"What?" she queried. He pointed to the lake, where her hand was immersed in the water. She looked down and realized why her hand didn't feel as cold. It was because the water had moved away from it, swirling around it in a miniature whirlpool. "What the fuck am I doing?" Heather looked up at Korson again with longing and bewilderment in her blue eyes.

"You can move things with your mind," he said.

"Pardon?"

"You're doing it," he answered. "Mind over matter. Never in my life have I beheld such power from a vampire. Never have I <u>seen</u> a vampire so strong that it's mind can move the very earth."

Heather pulled her hand away from the water, though the little whirl remained.

What if I could do the whole lake? she thought.

"No," said Korson. "Do you not think that would not arouse suspicion? The very waters of the lake spinning against their will? You must guard this power. Your life could be in danger if others discovered it."

They walked back to Korson's cottage, Heather pleading to him to let her try more, to go into the city, anything. It was useless. He finally locked her in a wooden box to shut her up.

"Korson, I'm starving!" she screamed from its confines. He could only tell her once that she needed to learn hunger to control her urges, that her gluttonous ways had to end. After a while her screams and pleas became too disheartening to answer to and he just sat atop the box until she slept.

The next night, Korson with a deck of cards playing, appropriately, solitaire. The lid of the wooden box burst open and Heather lept out of it, her eyes afire. They stared at each other for a long, angry moment.

"Hungry, yet?"

Heather all but spit at his feet, her look said it all. She left the room, and came back shortly in a different set of clothes, her top a velvet red, her pants tight and black. Another sharp look at Korson was all she gave before she exited the house with a firm shutting of the door that rattled the panes. Korson continued with his cards.

A scream interrupted his train of thought. He got up casually, his lofty frame filling in the space between the floor and ceiling. He walked out of the cottage and it was only too short a way down the road that he caught Heather in an embrace with a woman, who was limp and almost dead. The woman then fell to the ground and she was certainly dead. Heather looked at Korson with blood coating her lips like make-up, and she licked every last viscous drop of the stuff slowly and languidly off of her lips with her tongue, as if to say, *Gluttonous enough for you?*

Korson walked causally over to her, glanced down at the body, and took Heather by the collar in both hands. He picked her up high, damn high, and smashed her into the wall of the woman's cottage with a surprising amount of force, at least to Heather. It was a wonder that her frame wasn't imprinted upon the wall.

"Don't ever disobey me like that again," he said. Not that he had to say anything. Heather got the picture that though she probably had the strongest vampire mind in history, Korson had the strongest vampire arms out of all the people present. It was perhaps the reason that she couldn't suppress a little laughter, the fact that she was back to being a teenager who had to sneak around under the nose of the watchful parent. She was one for nostalgia, having missed her former life as much as the loved her present state. It was nice to have a little psychological trip down Freudian lane, helped keep her from tearing into two. But why did it seem like he was trapping her…?

Over the course of time, important in any vampiric existence, the world developed like a photograph. Heather grew, quite rapidly I might add, and the figurative rosy warmth replaced her pallor. Concurrently, the leaves drained their envious green in favor of them any hues of fall; reds, yellows, oranges and that one distinctive mixture that speaks Indian Summer whether it happens to be or not. Which it wasn't.

The air, other than the odd day or two, gave with its biting chill in the form of a gutsy wind. Certain trees had completely shed their leaves and stood naked in defiance of the chill. But it was the perfect segue into fall and, more specifically, Heather's favorite month: October.

With October comes all the aforementioned events; the leaves, the cold, perhaps the odd tickle of a snowflake on the tip of your nose. And, of course, **Hallowe'en**. And it was, most deliciously, Heather's first as a vampire.

Ah, a vampire on Hallowe'en. Fat pumpkins and white sheets and orange and black swirled cakes for the kids. But Hallowe'en is for the monsters, not the children, and don't you dare let anyone tell you the contrary.

First off, though, the intervening month or so between mid August and the end of October. Heather was feeling the fingerprint of Korson's thumb upon her head a little too tightly. She appreciated his help, his guidance, but they were really an isolated twosome. Heather still had the heart of a young and vibrant woman who really hadn't gotten it as much as she'd liked and had the unquenchable urge to roam. Not to mention the most important lesson that Korson insisted on repeatedly imparting to his adopted daughter and quick study:

"You are now a creature of instinct, not the creature of nurture and habit you once were. It is in your nature to consume blood and in your nature to hunt, though those instincts are under your power to control."

Admittedly, Korson can be quite stuffy and, well, okay, anal. Only just, maybe. Can't blame him for living and dying in the 1800's. Live and let...

Though he had the sense of duty and honour one finds from the main character in those God-awful karate moves. He was a good match for Heather, they could bounce their personalities off one another. A little conflicting, a little disagreeable, but opposites attract. It did tend to get tense, what with Korson exerting his fatherly tendencies on her a little too much. With Korson it was all about purpose, deep and utter meaning.

He was quiet reluctant to let Heather loose on Montréal, and the trips for their nightly sustenance to the similar outlying countrified areas grated on Heather after, oh, a night. She loved the dazzle of Montréal. Korson, on the other hand, liked his privacy. Like most vampires, he savored his anonymity, both with mortals and vampires alike. And he was still unsure of Heather's restraint.

It got her fairly riled when he would lock her in a wooden box for all or most of a night and, though no repeats of the first incident occurred, the tendons in her chalky neck would tighten noticeably. Silence would often ensue as well. Whether it was through fatigue, or increased patience, a strengthening of the psychological muscles perhaps, Heather eventually stopped her puerile cries to 'Let me out right fucking now!'

She longed for the safety of her glass casket, but could endure the pain of sleeping in the wooden box, though it felt like trial by fire. And Korson, though Heather didn't know it, was imposing starvation upon her the way he imposed it on himself when he first became of the dark ways.

After mere weeks of the periodical jailings, she would lie quiet and still in the box, hands at her sides, and wait for Korson to remove the lid he was perched on.

The length of time decreased remarkably with her increasingly good behavior. And to prove her self-control further still, Heather took to the habit of walking silently and stoically out of the cottage, scaling the side with her claw-like nails and adept and shapely legs, and perch on the roof cross-legged, willingly denying herself satiation of the blood-lust. Though her pose was meditative and contemplative, she looked not at the navy night sky but at her nether regions, as if she were seeing inside of herself a vastness far greater than that of the earth's canopy. It was clearly not an empty vastness for it sometimes occupied her for hours before she ventured from her lioness's perch to, quite surprisingly, hunt her prey with a calmness and restraint that was astonishing. She would be so neat with her surgical bites that one was hard pressed to determine the whereabouts of the customary little holes that one would find on a victim of a vampire.

Korson, introvert that he was, was quite impressed with Heather's progress, witnessing for his very own eyes what was probably the most powerful vampire he'd ever seen, at least at such a young age. He rarely said so to her, of course. It may have been in his best interest to apply a little bit of encouragement because, though Heather visibly clicked along at a remarkable rate, the strain of the exercises that Korson was applying were taking their toll on her mentally. It wasn't until he was attacked by a large group of bats, with Heather perched on the roof with a Devilish grin belying her youthful and angelic visage, that he realize this. Needless to say, her next session in the box was quite a long one.

Korson, not one to be unreasonable, did offer the encouragement that was forthcoming and they bit and made up, or whatever it is that vampires do.

Korson would watch Heather from a distance usually, sometimes close-up, but not often, and he was from time to time shocked by the cruelty with which she would kill. He himself once a ruthless killer, this was no small act, indeed. It was not so much the act of killing where her cruelty lay but the hunt itself. Heather had the habit of leaving her prey in a state of mental, and sometimes physical hysterics. Like the woman who she led into the woods on a thrilling chase on what happened to be a Friday the 13th in September. The young woman, home from college for the weekend, stumbled and tripped as fast as she could through the trees and growth while Heather used her preternatural speed to have her perform a vice-versa pattern. The horrible part was the removal of appendages that accompanies some of the directional changes…The woman in tears and clutching frightfully at her missing right hand while trying to outrun an unnatural monster that was once Heather Langden. Just an awfully misbehaved girl sometimes!

Korson watched but neither reacted nor discussed these incidents. He was more concerned with Heather's control of her instincts on a more basic level. Her removal and exile from big city life was probably manifesting itself in these overly cruel gestures. It was also known that younger vampires are more blatantly nasty until they become more desensitized to the whole thing, if that ever really happens.

Over the course of the next six months or so, Heather saw little of the city. It was Korson's fatherly disposition that kept her from her travels to the high life. Occasionally, she would rise early, and sneak off. Or so she thought. Korson was a master hunter in his life as a Native Indian, and it carried over quite well to the dark side. It was more often than not that Heather would be caught dead (ha, ha, yeah, it's a pun, now get over it) in her tracks at *boul. St. Laurent* and Prince Arthur. Other times, though she thought she'd gotten away with the act, Korson merely watched over her. He was never *really* mad, though sometimes it was hard to tell if he was being mocking or not. It was more of a general concern, and though Heather fancied his affections she could never quite figure the source of his caring and overprotectiveness.

But back to Hallowe'en, a heartwarming tie-up to the aforementioned events. Heather had her moods, as we've seen, and they were psychologically in line, though a bit extreme, for a young vampire. She learned quite quickly in a short time about hiding her extra power, not that it mattered much. In the time leading up to Hallowe'en and the six months afterward as well, she saw and sensed absolutely nothing of any other hematiphagic life form.

And Hallowe'en absolutely took her by the throat. The first night of October on, she was gripped by an excitement that swelled and ebbed until it burst on that fateful night, when all the spirits are freed on the earth.

Heather carved a pumpkin. It was to be her costume for trick-or-tricking. She carved out the eyes with care and inspiration, and gave ol' Jack pointy eyebrows and a triangle nose that pointed downwards. The mouth, she loved. Her little joke for the kiddies. It was a big, half-mooned smile, broken in the middle by two pointy fangs. She loved the smell of pumpkins and that was made all the more thrilling with her vampiric sense. It excited her like nothing she'd known, except, of course, that rush of syrupy blood down her throat.

She wore all black, and the clothes hugged tightly to her skin. She then found a classic cape while rummaging through Korson's belongings. It, too, was, of course, black. She painted her nails orange to match the pumpkin, and tied her hair back. And ol' Jack was placed on her shoulders.

"You're going out like that?" inquired Korson, who looked up from his Dickens. Heather turned to face him and said nothing, but Jack smiled back. "Just remember your curfew, dear," he said, and went back to his reading. Heather put her fists on her hips, a little nonplused at his passiveness. As long as the children were frightened, it didn't much matter anyway, and she left the cottage and began walking to the clusters of homes that were not too far away.

Heather reached the main road in a short time, and it wasn't too long before the first houses began to creep up and thicken in their numbers. It was not long dark and one could see little white sheets roaming with half-filled garbage bags, goblins with green faces and pointy ears, and superheroes like Batman. Some teenagers were out and carrying cartons of eggs.

Heather garnered some attention by making brief yet visible appearances at the edge of a copse of trees, leaning up against houses with her arms crossed, that sort of horror film foreshadowing evident in her actions. She certainly succeeded in drumming up some rumour and talk among parents and kids alike, and sent the few brave enough to follow her into a back yard running soft-seated back to their parents.

Eventually she snuck up to a house and put her chin on the porch. The numbers of children started to filter down by this point and all that was left were adults in drag and on their way to costume parties, or teenagers out to scare each other, their girlfriends and whatever children happened to be left unattended. Three of these decided to start the customary game of smashing pumpkins, and got around to the patiently waiting Jack perched on the porch.

"It's stuck," said the first boy in French. His accomplices answered him with remarks about just how much testosterone he was really carrying and each tried to pull the Jack up in turn.

"Shit, it really is stuck down," said the second.

"Out of the way. Let a man try." This boy moved in and with all his might pulled as hard as he could. And God did he ever move the wrong way! Heather clutched him and dragged him into the bush so fast it look as though he'd been eaten by the grinning pumpkin, though it, too, had disappeared. The two other boys were stunned still for a moment. It finally occurred to them to follow, search or whatever. They leapt down over the railing and, seeing nothing in the bush, walked around the corner of the house in time to see the legs of their companion dragging out of sight into the backyard. They followed hungrily, frightened yet wary of the fact that this could be a practical joke.

Turning the corner into the backyard, they saw their friend lying adjacent to the other side of the house, his entire body visible except for his head and neck. Resuming an upright stance (people tend to crouch when they are anticipating a fright; the shorter you become, the less likely you are to be scared), they looked knowingly at each other, and gave with a customary jab to the ribs that they were now on top of things. They walked up to the fallen body of their friend.

"Oh my Lord," said one. He put his hand to his mouth and held his friend back from the scene vigorously.

"What, what is it, let me see," said the other, though it took much brute force to get through. This is what he saw:

The body of his friend, sans it's skull. And a rat, jammed into the newly created orifice that was once sealed, its feet and tail wriggling and writhing, struggling for air, a muted squeal echoing from the decapitated shell. Both young men were now on the verge of throwing-up, and were practically in each other's arms out of sheer fear. They both ran to the fence of the backyard, which would deposit them on the road that led to their respective homes. The fence was covered with thick and thorny brambles throughout most of the links and only one of them could struggle over to the other side at a time. The boy who had witnessed the body first seemed to be the fastest in getting to the fence and had first turn at climbing. He scampered over with some grace, though shivers of fear and cold ran through him. He dropped down the other side feeling the sting of the landing in his feet. He looked up at the top of the fence, which seemed mountainous in height right now, and heard or saw nothing of his friend. Could it have been the joke was on him all along? Was he duped into whimpering and running like a frightened child? The short eternity passed when he saw the fence rattle and a hand grasp the piece of wood across the top.

"You were looking back at him, don't. Let's just get out of here."

His friend was not as adept at climbing, or not in any condition to be doing any, but he managed to pull himself up with a moderate struggle. He peeked over the fence-top, his friend at the bottom with an urging look on his face, a hand out to help him down. He froze, his mouth agape as his friend, who stood there in bewilderment, whisper-yelling, "Come on, get down here!" and turned to go-

And stopped to see the Jack that was on the porch staring back at him with it's maniacal grin, with it's pumpkin-meat fangs hanging deliciously in the carved mouth.

The next day, three boys were neither seen nor heard.

Completely satiated, Heather slumped on a porch front. She put her elbows on her knees and rested Jack's chin on her fists. She'd had her fun. Alone, albeit, but fun nonetheless. But as the night dies, the mortals sleep and things get very quiet. Somber. Only crickets chirp and stars twinkle. The porch light, if anyone had cared to watch, (perhaps Korson? Perhaps someone else?), spotlighted Heather in a macabre Hallowe'en scene.

Boredom set in, just a little, as Heather's energy was low from all the activity. She was self-absorbed in her fatigue and didn't notice the veil. How thin it was. This was the night of the dead after all. And majic filled the air and Heather, so in tune with majic, didn't even feel the surge of power that flowed through her. If only she could have spent one night in another vampire's body, she would never again take for granted the dark ways. She would realize how powerful she was.

"Trick or treat."

It was in Heather's nature, though, to struggle for the top. Even if no struggle was required, she would create one. She needed a sense of achievement.

"Trick or treat." The little girl held out her bag.

"Sorry, no candy here," said Heather. The little girl was dressed up in a clown suit. Clown's were scary. Oh, they were okay during the day. They made their living at circuses, they tried to make you laugh. They let kids beat the hell out of them and throw pies at them. But once night came, then everything changed. Clowns became mean. Murderous. On Hallowe'en, you could bet your life that a clown committed a murder as revenge for all the crap he took during the year.

Heather realized the time, said, "Aren't you out a little late, little girl?"

The little girl put her hand to her mouth and giggled.

"Sssh!" she said. "I won't tell if you won't! Don't you like to sneak out?"

Heather laughed, said, "Yes, I've done my share of sneaking out!"

"Gets you in trouble, doesn't it?" asked the little girl. She sounded a little more mature now. Heather, sick of the echo in Jack's head, pulled the pumpkin off and let her hair out with a shake.

"I guess it does get you in trouble. "

"You don't have any candy for me do you?"

"Nope. Sorry." The little girl hung her clown head a little bit, looked slightly forlorn.

She asked, "Why do your wear a mask?"

"It's Hallowe'en," answered Heather.

"No, I didn't ask why *I* wear a mask, I asked why *you* wear a mask."

"To scare little kids!!! Grrrrrrr!!!" The little girl squealed in delight. Heather playfully shook her by the shoulders.

"You don't need to wear mask if you're already a vampire," said the little girl. Heather stopped.

"You're just spouting childish nonsense." But Heather wondered if this little girl could see her for what she really was. If it was possible that mortals knew. That the world wasn't ignorant.

"Silly, it's Hallowe'en! All the vampires come out on Hallowe'en!" The little girl skipped off and shouted, holding her arms high in the air. Heather began to follow her. "You just have to know where to look for them!"

There were a few cemeteries near Korson's cabin, located on the outskirts of Beaconsfield. There was a tiny church and a small cemetery adjacent to it, and the little girl skipped her way through the wrought iron gates. She began putting a candy on each of the graves.

"Why are you giving away your candy?" asked Heather. The little girl didn't answer. Just kept placing a candy at the base of each of the gravestones. Heather bent down and picked one of the sweets up. The girl ran over to her and squealed in terror, like a rat:

"Nonononononono!! You can't take them away! Leave them there!" Heather picked up the little girl. Tears stained her cheeks and made her orange and black and white make-up run.

"Hallowe'en is supposed to be fun. Don't cry. Please? For me?" Heather brushed the girl's wig to keep the hairs out of her face. She was Raggedy Ann, so sad and limbs floppy. The little girl wiped her tears away and smudged her make-up. "Why are you leaving candy for dead people?"

"Sometimes the dead come back. Sometimes they're angry." Bass drum thunder ripped the sky, and electricity crackled and lit the clouds afire. Living smoke crept between the graves, utterly black and deadly. The little girl hopped out of Heather's arms. "I have to go. Please leave the candy. It might make them happy. It might help them sleep."

She ran away and it was as if the smoke reared up around her and consumed her as she rounded a gravestone. Heather followed and rounded the gravestone, but, as expected, the girl was gone.

The search for the missing boys luckily avoided the cottage, though how long that would remain the status only time would tell. And the punishment that Heather figured was forthcoming never landed. Why, she could never really figure out. Maybe Korson liked the strange things she did?

But the stuffiness of the cottage was affecting Heather. She needed Montréal, and she needed its night. And sneaking away was becoming tiresome. It was especially disheartening to be cooped up in a forest when winter was beginning to blanket the city. As beautiful as the countryside is in the winter, Montréal glitters all the more brightly when covered in icing sugar. And Heather was dying to see it.

Korson, on the other, was reluctant to let her leave too early in the night, and reluctant to let her wander city streets too frequently. Though she could never find out why. It was finally cold and January before her temper boiled away the memory of the box top suffocating her. Perhaps if she hadn't been buried unborn she wouldn't harbour this fear of staying too long in a casket?

Choke on it, she would probably tell you.

"What is it you are protecting me from?" was a common phrase that Heather would utter, and eventually spit forth. And she was feeling confident enough in her nocturnal gifts that her ego had grown back to the point where the universe ended at her fingertips and the limit of her range of vision, which, by the way, was gagging on the lack of nourishment it was receiving lately. Which is why she ran away from Korson. At least for a while. He would allow her back in whenever their moods didn't contradict one another, but he always had to screw her thumb. It was grating on Heather, each and every moment. Bats were meant to fly, after all.

Heather's powers increased remarkably, not to the point that she couldn't be beaten, but she did possess a power of mind that was astonishing. Her telekinesis was her bicep, though her physical strength naturally increased with her turning. And her symbiosis with nature increased as well, to the point where she had more animal friends than any other species. And that was probably what prompted the question:

"Why haven't I seen any other vampires?"

That was the one Korson dreaded. And through major stalling and vacuum silences he only served to arouse Heather's interest and curiosity. She'd been desperate to find the underworld, as she called it, the place where the vampires went after dark.

And after weeks of trying to squeeze it out of Korson, she broke. His arguments against it were such as the fact that vampires are very suspicious, wary creatures who would rather kill you first. None was willing to take a chance on letting a young one foolishly start a power struggle with the older ones, with whom an uneasy truce was usually in play. See, the old ones were filled with ego and power and everything else that comes with living one, two or three centuries. And young ones were known to latch onto older ones, and this would be the start of vampire battles. Nothing big, but it could escalate. If, for instance, there was an old vampire, well-respected and worshipped because of her power and age, she could garner a lot of sympathy if another old one, perhaps as powerful though maybe not as respected, were to try to rid the world of her. The first thing the antagonist would try would be to send a young and susceptible vampire, probably one she'd made herself, to gain access to the hidden lair of the other. And vampires, always wary of this, would kill any young one who got too close too soon. And though Heather was powerful, she was till a young one. And stubborn, too, because this point would not sink into her, though Korson tried repeatedly.

"That's fucking trash you're giving me, Korson," she would say. "I've read all that schlock horror fiction some loser hack writer came up with because he couldn't find a girlfriend. Me, no thank you. I would much rather go with what is around me in reality. Don't give me that old ones/young ones shit."

What she couldn't accept was the fact that Korson was different, and her too, for that matter, but we'll get to that later. Korson was all the things that a vampire was, but in a much different way. He was also very much those things that a Native is. He was much the loner, much the one to stay away from the pettiness and vanity of most vampires, so if there were other vampires around then they would very likely not link up with Korson. But most were governed by vanity, power and their animalistic instincts for blood and territory, and though these things weren't evident on the surface they were indeed present.

What was also present was Heather's confidence and power, and they were abundant. Still not as sharp as they could be, but they were strong. So it was that the Vampire Heather, the one with the regrets, the ferocity, the emotions, and the extraordinary qualities became a vampire hunter. She left Korson, on fairly good terms this time (though from their final conversation it was hardly evident), and set out back to Montréal, to the city she loved.

It was actually Korson who set her up with a place to live, paying the giddily grinning landlord a year's worth rent by candlelight. He gave the excuses as to why neither of them would be seen by day (they both worked long hours), and explicit instructions that the house was to be left alone at these times anyway. It was reinforced with another bundle of bills.

Heather now had her place to live, north-east of downtown Montréal, and a few bank accounts under false names, of which she was to set up more. She also had the number of a good investment agent (Korson's, in fact), and he was to help her produce an income through interest and investment.

She also had Korson's blessing to return to him whenever she wanted, or if she was in danger, which he suspected wouldn't be long. But a disclaimer came along with that blessing. If she was to ever draw another vampire to his whereabouts, then the danger would come from him.

* * *

They stood over him, the three of them, after they'd stolen into his home like ghastly thieves in the night. Looking down upon him and smiling that all-knowing smile, waiting for him to awaken. The mere fact of their presence eventually enough to arouse his suspicion, as his dreams would turn slowly to darkness and liquid and unbearable heat. For the three of them were vampires of the Sab, evil in all of their emanations, but more importantly the three of them were women.

The fourth, he didn't concern himself with the same petty thoughts that crossed the minds of the women. He was here merely on a mission, searching. He'd been in a foul, unrepentant mood of late, and the only thing he concerned himself with now was searching. He had no blood-soaked thoughts of late, and he was paying some sort of penitence. And now he searched, for his queen, much like he constantly sought out love.

"Hush, Paul," said Marie, as he loudly sifted through drawers and cupboards.

"We want him to wake on his own," said Clarisse. The three vampires began to lean over him, like midwives tending to a fresh babe, their fingers dancing slowly in the air above his body, as though sprinkling him with their majic.

Paul continued to sift through the belongings, he now had his hand in the proverbial junk drawer in the kitchen.

"This is pointless," he muttered, just loud enough for the others to hear as they made playful little noises, sweet baby noises. "Infernal, blasted, psychotic witch."

"Paul," said Antoinette quietly, as she went over to him. "Hush. You'll get yourself in trouble. You know she *hears*." She draped an arm around his shoulder and began to give him soothing kisses and licks to his cheek and ear.

"Be off of me you woman," he said, and shoved her away. She gave him a lingering, scornful look, and then returned to her consorts. Paul took a deep breath and sighed. He looked at the three of them, standing over the husky corpse of a sleeping man.

He thought, "You're sleeping through every man's dream, you unknowingly lucky bastard. A blond, a brunette, and a redhead."

He remembered when he'd turned Marie to the dark way, oh so many moons ago. He constantly wondered if it was he who'd trapped her, or her him, with her luxuriant black hair and opulent blue eyes; her long, enticing legs. It was quite likely she'd seduced him as much as he'd tried to be the predator, and years later he realized that of course, she was good at it, as it was her profession at the time.

"Oh, he's waking!" gasped Clarisse. Antoinette leaned close to his cheek, so he could feel her rank and metallic breath on his skin, and she whispered sweet cradlesongs in his ear to keep him soothed. Marie stood at the foot of the bed, her clawed hands held hungrily over him, her face beginning to grow an eager, crazed grin.

"Wake up little Clyde," said Antoinette. His eyes slowly opened, and he lay there, his body still, his head lolling slightly. The look on his face was glazed over, partly from sleep, partly from bewilderment, but mostly drunk from the spell the women had cast upon him.

"We've come for you!" It was tall Marie, and now the grin on her face broke into one all-out maniacal.

"N-no. N-no," was all Clyde could say. He tried to move but he felt as though his limbs were lead. He could barely turn his head from side to side, and Antoinette put her hands beneath his chin and on his cheek to steady him as she gave him the licks and kisses Paul declined. "D-dont."

Paul watched with a detached, distracted interest. Still thinking about the women. Clarisse, with her shocking red hair and green eyes, once a schoolteacher; Antoinette, the blond, smaller than the rest, her hair thick and wavy, her eyes mahogany brown. He looked at Clyde's drugged up head trying to lift itself off the bed, and he moved away and into the shadows. Why break the mood of their little fandango? Let them have their fun.

He continued his search. He realized his time was running short, as the women would end their game shortly. And once done, they would certainly want to be off, and they would whine and become *such* a disturbance when they did.

Paul took a sniff of the scents here. For certain one who was close to the mortal of Korson had been here. And the Queen wanted her jewel.

"Little witch," reiterated Paul. "Having me chase after meaningless trinkets and legends of lore." He hardly thought he would find the fabled Tiger's Eye in the most mundane of all places. But Talissa had become adamant, and Paul knew all too well of her compulsion for obsession. So he continued to scrounge, like a rat, and he really didn't know what he was looking for, but Talissa had told him to see it would be to know it.

"You'll feel it in your dead, brittle bones, Paul," she said. "It's a jewel that can show you the reflection of your soul, and looks as though it had burned carved of dried and dirty blood."

A scream from the bed was muffled. Paul glanced over. Clyde had begun to thrash, his body thumping up and down on the bed as though he were in seizure, his fat belly bouncing like a heavy sack. The smoke of the shadow had begun to envelope them, small towers of black smoke rising from the ground as if from Hell.

"Marie," said Paul, quietly, yet oh so forcefully. Marie turned, the grinning mania on her face fading, as though she were a schoolgirl caught smoking and knew she was in trouble. "Not the shadow. Not here."

"P-please...l-let me g-go," pleaded Clyde, who could only stutter out his words. Antoinette continued to work her tongue along his neck and cheeks, putting heavy pressure on his thick-skinned neck.

"I want to see it," cooed Marie, her body swaying side to side like a cobra. Clarisse leaned over Clyde's body, pulling up his shirt to reveal his ample belly, sliding his pants down to show Marie her treasure. She ran her hands on his thighs, around it, hanging her tongue out of her head which hung over his drooping piece of clay, salivating over it. "Do you think anyone's ever touched it?" she mused delightfully.

"It smells fresh to me," said Clarisse. "And if you're not quick I may steal the first bite!"

"I b-beg you, d-don't, p-please d-don't," cried Clyde, his eyes becoming swelled and red and hot with tears. Even Antoinette's affections couldn't soothe him further. Over and over he kept saying, "I h-have a s-soul. I have a s-soul."

The three women laughed, like Devils in High Court, their faces mockingly, glaringly white, a reflection of death. Marie bit down and sucked out from his appendage the blood of the soul that he held so precious, the fact that his life held a spark of meaning to him despite the fact that the Gods afflicted his mind from birth. The other two followed, Clarisse biting into his belly and Antoinette clamping down on his neck. He shook as though the pain alone would kill him, and all the while he hopelessly comforted himself with his words: "I have a s-soul."

Paul said, "It's not here," as he walked over to the scene of the macabre. He looked down at the three on the bed and said, "You women sicken even me. Let's go. Leave the retard already. I've thoroughly lost my taste for Toronto."

They continued to feed a while longer, and Paul put up with the slight insubordination only because he knew it would be a long ride back to Montréal, and the last thing he wanted was for these three to be hungry. Let them fill their stomachs and wallow in blissful sloth all the way home.

Done with their meal they rose up, lips drenched in ruby red richness, and the three of them looked to the sky and sighed in ecstasy and delirium as the warm blood filled their cold, dead veins.

Clyde was left quivering on the bed, clutching the bloody tragedy between his legs and rocking back and forth as his sanity slowly slipped away, his voice echoing, "I have a s-soul...I have a s-soul..."

But there was no one around to hear.

It was with a foul taste in the mouth, much like that of unwashed genitalia, that Heather left Korson. She did love him dearly, despite the fact that he was a disciplinarian. It was, really, the discipline she liked, because she couldn't discipline herself. Korson was straight up, he was an honourable murderer. But this honour was pulled in two directions, and he committed, what was in his mind, the ultimate sin- he lied. He had told Heather that she was the most powerful vampire he'd ever seen. Now that Heather, who was beginning to taste of her potential, was leaving, Korson could hold his tongue no longer. She would be alone again, and subject to assaults on all fronts.

"There is one who has achieved great power," he said. Running through all the little trite explanations, trying to soften the blow.

Heather said, "I'm not stupid, Korson. And my social ladder as a vampire is somewhat limited."

"I never wanted to let anything hurt you. That's why I brought you here." It became obvious to Heather that Korson afforded some protection to her. That he was not without some great power within him. Perhaps he just held back on it a little. The greater power is restraint. And Heather looked feeble in her attempt to restrain her look of disgust.

"You couldn't just tell me you knew who Talissa was?" Heather didn't give him a chance to speak. "How are we going to survive if you keep secrets from me? I thought you were a friend." She began to walk away from him.

"Heather, please-"

"How do you know her? Where is she?"

"I have no idea where she is. As for how I know her: she is the one who tainted my blood blue."

Heather stopped still where she was. Something deep within her made her more solitary than Korson. And therefore, more suspicious. Was Korson jealous of her power? Was he merely using Heather to lure Talissa to him?

"I still have to go." She kept her suspicions to herself, thinking logically that they were unfounded. But she wouldn't forget them.

"Heather, this is very important to me. I never wanted you to doubt me. I never wanted to lose your trust."

"You have a funny way of achieving that." As she got her things together, Korson hovered around her. Openly worried, showing some emotion. And Heather wondered if he was worried about her or about his own agenda. The tension that developed didn't allow for open communication.

Heather was finally ready to leave. Ready to all but storm out actually. Though she wasn't completely angry, there was some forlornness apparent in her. Korson grabbed her by the shoulder to stop her. To make her say a proper good-bye, even if it was forced. Heather, though, was a sincere person and they hugged-they were, after all, brother and sister-and they left with a different kind of bond than they started with.

As Heather walked down the path to the main road, sparse belongings in tow, Korson asked himself, "Why did I not inherit the same power as she?"

Part 6: Catherine

They saw each other infrequently, and she missed him. Though it was her choice to be alone, it was not her choice to be lonely, and her search of the others ended in miserable dead ends. It was at these times that she would fall back into his arms no matter how callous they may seem. But mostly she was alone. The months, all the more seemingly useless now, whittled away and were mere wood shavings on the floor of the front porch. The hints and teases of others were now nothing more than the manipulations of her senses, of which she now had a more firm control, and therefore was less susceptible to them. But still, the odd one would catch her eye.

Mostly, though, she was alone. As the ground warmed and the water melted away the sugared tops of the buildings and the fudge slush of the streets, she resigned herself to the fact, more and more each day, that there was no purpose to it at all. She had forsaken Talissa, and to an extent Korson too, and she was left with herself. Not that it was at all a displeasure to gaze upon her forever cherubic visage with its mother-of-pearl skin that glinted orange and purple like the sunrise she missed so deeply; of her ocean blue eyes that were so deep and dark they reminded her of the centuries she had before her; or her razor-sharp nails and teeth which showed what she really was. But there had to be a point, a structure, a society. There had to be more than three. How long had it been? About a year or so? Summer became fall became winter and now spring was going to bring her back to summer, where it all started.

At least she'd grown so much! She felt like a baby before she was unborn, caught in that cloudy brine of change from child to adult, though she probably shouldn't have taken that left fork. What was it that was wrong with her life? Was it so trivial that she'd forgotten? Did she just want to be a vampire because she was obsessed with that luscious occult world that was subterranean to the world that each and every average fuck left themselves to? The confusion of juggling all those new responsibilities, the longing to hang on to freedom and childhood. The pull had won for freedom, for the forbidden.

Though in all this time she'd seen neither God nor the hidden world and she herself played the part of the Devil so really there was nothing more to know. Perhaps there were only three vampires. Perhaps the world didn't need Devils anymore.

Heather picked up her flute, which she'd been teaching herself in her ample spare time, and played a lilting melody. The Pied Piper she sometimes fancied herself, leading the sheep to slaughter. Or was it the children? She couldn't bear to take a child, though God-knowing she tried. Something stopped her, months ago when the child actually recognized her, and days after the whole family celebrated their last Christmas together, and the child his one year birthday even, so in a way it was good that the parents weren't around for that extra spoonful of grief. And that paranoid bastard Korson wouldn't even look her in the eye and admit that he'd been following her and he was the one who did it.

Was it the flute that was the Devil's instrument? Didn't make a difference, today it was the electric guitar. Or drums! She would learn the drums next, and bring her next victim to her very home and find and excuse to sneak off and she'd play a beat on the bass and snare: thrum-ta-ta-tum-ta-ta-ta-ta-ta-ta-tum-THRUM! And she'd use her preternatural hearing to match the bass to the beating of the person's heart and use her coercion to make them think it was still there when she walked into the room in her negligee with her alabaster skin glinting kaleidoscope colours so faint that the mortal would be mesmerized by that alone, and her breasts of course because they were so lovely; and her eyes would be red with hunger and her fangs would be just visible and making little dents in her lower lip and Cumulous would be curled up in the corner and wishing he could laugh because that's just how he would kill a bird if he could.

Heather put down her flute and decided it was time to go out, and feed, and maybe search a little more for the vampires she so longed to find. She walked, she almost always walked to the downtown because the metro had such a glare and she felt so visible underneath it.

She changed her mind and decided to take the metro after all because she might as well save some time and be visible. Maybe a vampire would find her instead of her finding it. She walked up to the man in the glass booth, whose gaze had fixed upon her as soon she'd descended the stairs into his view. He didn't take his eyes off of her even as she was right up to the glass and dropping her ticket in, not even to look at her hand, which, had he been paying attention, may have made him think, or even jump, because the nails were just a little unnaturally razor-like. Heather sensed his gawk even as she walked away and just to be a tease she flung her hair over her shoulder in that sexy come-and-get-it way that some girls do. It was *so* hard to turn it off sometimes!

The metro was a joy, the jilting, speeding bullet ripping through the tunnel like a giant sandworm. A group of young men kept glancing over Heather's way, but she really wasn't in the mood just yet, so she threw up a veil and switched seats on them. She almost laughed out loud when she noticed people staring at them staring at an empty seat. Boys that age are usually turned by something empty anyway. One of the guys actually went over to say something to her and that's when she decided to tap him on the shoulder as she left the train. Needless to say, they were bewildered and had a reason to drink that night.

Muddling men's minds required precession timing and that caused Heather to get off a stop early, which wasn't too bad at all. It also didn't speak too well of men's minds, at least that group of them. And up she went to the glitter and throb of downtown Montréal, which always made her smile. She was countless times glad that her house was so close. It was a good night for bars in Montréal, which isn't saying too much because it's usually a good *day* for bars, which is when everyone is supposed to be working. Night was just that much better. Add to the fact that the downtown population swelled in size by an extra sixteen thousand because of the hockey game, which also meant that most of the ghosts were in attendance there, and she was probably the only miraculous being who was actually walking the streets tonight. As long as the crowd thronged around her, she didn't much mind.

She still wasn't in the mood to drink, so she found a quaint little café that she'd never been in before and sat down with a red wine. She wondered when the thirst would hit her, and it was at this time that she was beginning to appreciate Korson's forceful tutoring of her nightly hungers. It used to be that she would run out and grab the first morsel that happened by and drain to the point of death. Now, though, she was more selective, and she would try to prolong the drink and even steal a kiss without the victim realizing it. Though it was less orgasmic than it used to be, it was more satisfying in the long-term. She could feed off less in a night than she used to and the less bodies there were about the better for all.

And it was quite a while before she noticed the girl that was looking at her. It wasn't the fact that the girl wasn't directly looking at her (she was being viewed through the mirror behind the bar), but the fact that she'd not seen the girl sit down. She was very accustomed to the fact that her senses would alert her to all of the movements in a place this size. She couldn't have been drifting that much, could she?

And of course, the first thought that popped into her head was, *Is this person a vampire?* She thought it was best to control herself and mask her thought, so she did so. Just think in a calm and orderly fashion and let each thought slip slowly through her. Let nothing go.

Let nothing go, let nothing go. It was difficult to think when that was the only thought that was sifting through your head. She looked at the girl-no, woman-she had the eyes of a woman. She looked at her through the mirror for some reason, thinking maybe she existed in there. Maybe she was a messenger of God? But if she was in the mirror, wouldn't that make her a messenger of the Devil? Would that mean the messenger of God would be sitting at the table that she hadn't bothered to look at? She didn't look because she didn't want to lose the image, though she couldn't see the woman's face behind the glass held before it. The woman smiled slightly at her. Mockingly, perhaps? Daring her to look at the real image? Heather figured that with her preternatural speed she could manage the task. A quick glance-

-And the woman was gone. An empty table. Back to the mirror and nothing was seen either.

Shit, thought Heather. *Now I'm back to imagining things.* She had to wonder if this was another vampire, but moreso, why was she being avoided? Could someone leave the room without her sensing it, coming and going as they pleased?

But no one had left the room. The Cheshire grin in the opposite side of the mirror confirmed that. And when Heather noticed, she knew that she'd been played. That this was a vampire and that she was being tested to see how strong she was. She couldn't read anything from the woman's mind, it was screwed shut. She had the choice of trying to match this lady physically, or she could use her mental powers which she knew to be superior. Or she could turtle and pretend that she was a weak little waif.

Then she remembered the mirror. And without taking her gaze away from it, she scanned the crowd in the mirror. The woman's face was still hidden behind the wineglass, but Heather wasn't interested in that anymore. She was interested in the rest of the people in the pub. None of them were looking at the woman directly.

Dreams, thought Heather. *People think their dreams have come true when they look at me.* Or nightmares, but that was a different argument. And this lady was putting up the barriers between worlds. If a psychic mortal were to walk in the pub, they'd *really* have to be on their toes to catch the emanations from this one. All Heather could feel was an absence. And, still with her eyes on the mirror (Heather decided to bend the rules end over end rather than flat out break them), Heather decided to pinch the pub awake, as well as keep her head out of the shell.

She turned slowly to the image of the woman in the mirror and gave a glance at her glass-which then abruptly shattered on the table. Every head in the bar turned to look at the woman-there was no defense against this many eyes upon her and she was caught off guard so she didn't flee the scene in time-and the bartender was over in a moment to clean up the mess, fending off the apologies of the woman. He even brought her another drink. And when the fuss drizzled, the woman looked up to see Heather staring at her with raised eyebrows, one elbow propped up on the bar, and only the wispy smoke drifting between them.

Heather was quite enamored with her, the way she looked, the way she moved, the utter grace that reminded her of a machine come alive. She cold have scratched the tip of her nose and made it look artistic. Her hair was dead straight and shiny black and at times it looked as though a sheen of white would pass through it.

Did Korson hold back these enticing waves of Gothic beauty? The woman, with the embarrassing moment passed, gave a minute smile to Heather. Her skin was dark and smooth, as though it had been coated in olive oil. But it also had a leathery, tough quality about it, like if one were to cut it she would just shrug and sew it back together. And her eyes were deep and dark, but if one focused and looked deep enough, one saw that they were actually, quite amazingly, purple. At first, Heather thought that they were just picking up the colour from her lipstick, which was a colour that was close to that of her eyes. But no matter what light hit them, or which way the woman looked, her eyes remained the same deep, purple that first caught Heather's attention.

But she wouldn't outwardly show it, the fact that this woman had her enthralled. And who wouldn't be, after seeing only two other of their own species in a year? Heather's heart burned to go over, to purr out her questions at this woman's knee and have them answered lovingly and completely. But something stopped her from walking over. She felt awkward at the thought. Was it because she was so used to being alone? She wanted to just appear there, the way the woman had switched places in the mirror. That would make it so simple. But, she'd come to learn, life, in any form, isn't straightforward. One has to do the clumsy, time-consuming things like walk up to people while they study our approach. One has to be ready for the jolt of rejection.

So Heather arched her curvaceous back, slid off the slick leather stool, and found herself in front of the table, face to face with the vampire who had the purple lips and violet eyes.

Maybe it was time to stop hiding? Something terrible must be happening, more so because it hadn't happened already. It should have been over and done with by now. But when things have to be perfect, that's when one tends to drag them out, making sure every detail is just so. And more so when the years lay ahead of you.

But could it be starting all over again, over a century after it was quelled? Why the wait? What was it that made this time different, after so many failures? Perhaps the failures weren't actually attempts. What if Talissa was searching? Refining her technique? What if Korson was her fated nemesis and she was looking to expose his flaws?

The ultimate in procrastination. Korson should have wiped out the problem when it presented itself years ago. But that was just the point. The root of the problem never did present herself those many years ago, she hid behind a Sab that was doomed to fail. And she was the germ. And she still existed. Spreading her disease.

Not doomed, though. Due. She must have known he was around, she must have known that he'd oppose her, and no one is so stupid to allow a host of vampires to run riot over a place they'd come to call home.

But what could really be accomplished with that mislaid plan? There were no *thrones*. There was really no purpose except power. *Control*.

It seemed like a meaningless, vain pursuit. It mirrored life, a meaningless pursuit in itself.

He wasn't exactly sure why he even got up every mor-

Night, he got up at night now. And it had been a while since he'd stayed awake in the morning, watching the sun blink a cheerful English hello.

It had also been a while since he'd gone into Montréal. Being cooped up here in this cottage area must be getting to him by now. Room to roam! Nature was quite fulfilling but the bustle of Montréal was unmatched. City full of personality.

He decided to take the car, the unassuming grey sedan that hadn't been started in years. He hoped it would start, it would make him feel human again, like he was part of all those people who raced down the pavement day and night.

After several tries, the car started. Now he had to remember how to drive it.

When you learn to rely so much on your senses, you learn to love the feel of the ground beneath your feet. You learn to love crossing distances that would make a human being gasp and vomit at the mere thought. You loved using your strength. The exhilaration of releasing the stored potential. As opposed to largely lethargic humanity, stifled by society because they weren't allowed creative freedom.

Which made driving a moot option. But it was fun, like go-karting and its like they'd never seen a car before when they got in one of those.

He made his way to the highway, opening his window to feel the wind, at least give him that much. He took the 13 to the 40, the Trans-Canada, and from there hopped on to the *Decarie* which took him into the heart of Montréal. It had been months.

Which reminded him of Heather, and in turn of purpose, more specifically, hers. Was she to be the vampire princess, holding court at the foot of her creator? Was humanity doomed to feel the wicked press of power from the fingertips of the vampire Talissa?

Nonsense. She didn't even know her creator. Her purpose was to wake up every night and play her games of cat-and-mouse, scaring her victims with her photo-negative image of the fallen angel gone rotten.

Though the only problem was, her photonegative wasn't black and white, it was a colour negative. She still had her heart. She cared for that little puff-ball Cumulous like she'd borne him herself. So she had a taste for the macabre? So what? It was in her nature, now.

Speaking of nature, it called, meaning he was hungry. He'd have to find something soon.

He passed certain areas, wondering if there were others who were still living there.

And then he slammed down on the brakes (they held!), and abruptly turned the car into one of the side streets.

Enough wondering, he said to himself. *It's time I stopped in to old acquaintances.* The socialization should do him some good. You'd be stagnant too, if you spent years at a stretch basically alone.

He stopped the car with a bit of a squeal. He looked at the house, it seemed forlorn and dark, like it tried to be separate from the houses around it. Like it knew a vampire lived in there. Or used to.

He walked up to the door, and double-rang the bell, waited a second, then rang again. A bit of a code, so you would know that it was one of your own at the door.

Korson remembered when he used to live in the city, and when someone rang his doorbell. He recalled the time that it was a vampire, but he just rang the bell, no secret code ring, and he was so hungry he'd whipped open the door nearly pulling it off the hinges and had torn the throat of the foolish youngster before either of them had realized what was happening. Paranoid bunch, vampires. Hunger made them worse.

He heard footsteps and the handle jiggled and turned, the door creaking open, like it knew it should make a suspenseful noise like they always seem to do in the movies.

"Yes, can I help you?" An older woman, not a monster. Forget you're hungry, your heart screaming for the blood it doesn't have. "Yes?"

Forget the blood, go hungry, don't deserve food. Or drink. Don't deserve drink.

"Uh...sorry, wrong house, I believe." Feeling like he's going to fall over.

"Are you okay, *monsieur*?"

Fine, just show me your neck.

"*Monsieur*? Do you need a drink-"

Yes.

"-of water? Are you all right? You look pale."

Dizzy and delirious because my veins are empty. No. Not my veins. My heart. And blood has nothing to do with this one.

"Madam...I haven't been all right in...years."

She looked at him as though he were breaking down. But he wasn't, he was building up. Something dormant gains rust, yes, but it also harbours its energy. He had enough now.

"I'm sorry," said Korson, "to have disturbed you. It seems my friend has moved on."

And he walked back to his car.

Trying not to let the nervousness cause her voice to crack, Heather said, "Hi."

She was face to face with the violet vampiress, only the third she'd met in nearly a year as a siren. She had no trouble luring men and women to her maw, but she hoped that now she'd found the break in the curtain to the underground. But she could only open with a banal 'Hi.'

The vampiress was idly twirling the ice in her refreshed cognac, a little smile playing gleefully upon her lips. She raised her head slowly and looked up at Heather. Despite the oddity of her make-up, it suited her, so well in fact, that she seemed to blend with the surroundings rather than stand out.

And she glowed naturally of violet, as well as it being her colour of preference in clothing and make-up. And she was beautiful. This was Heather's second thought, after the purple had so enamored her.

She had full, round cheeks, like juicy plums, and eyes that were dark, with a hint of amethyst when the light struck them. Her hair was long, straight and dark, very luxuriant, the kind of hair that made you want to stroke.

But what Heather liked the most was the smile, the fact that it was meant for her. Which she took as an invitation to sit down. The vampiress stopped twirling the ice in the glass and sucked off the wetness from her finger, dried her digit on a napkin. Her cheeks looked flushed and hot, like the way Heather felt right now. Flustered, but excited.

"Bold of you, taking the glass out of my hand. It's been a while since anyone's caught me with a swift movement like that."

Heather remembered Korson saying that vampires weren't exactly known for telepathy. Maybe better to keep her attributes to herself.

"Just lucky, I guess." It felt good, to talk. Made her feel as though she belonged to the wet blue orb.

"You young ones usually are," said the vampiress, uncontemptuously. She was still smiling.

"How can you tell how old I am."

"You get a feel for these things."

"Mm. Are...you from Montréal?"

"Near here, yes." Reluctant to divulge anything too quick. And Heather was running out of small talk. The vampiress clinked the ice in the glass. It seemed stupid to ask how she did the trick in the mirror, since she was supposed to have the speed to do it too. And all she really wanted to do was touch those hot cheeks and silky hair.

"You must be the new one."

"New? Well, just how new do you mean?"

"Couple months."

Heather thought about telling the truth, decided to keep playing along instead. "Yeah, couple months."

"And who bled you?"

"Is that more important than, say, my name?" Meow!

This wasn't going so well as it seemed it would. What did she expect? Creatures of instinct, not habit. Fighting for space, territory, throats. She was handling this like she was still a mortal.

"I'm Heather. You can tell me your name if you have the courage to."

"Sorry. I'm Catherine." She stretched backwards in her chair, her purple sweater holding back her breasts. Something else that Heather decided she liked. "Vampires usually take a lot longer to approach each other. I had a feeling you were trying to attack me."

"Do I look that vicious?"

"No. But beauty is the most dangerous thing of all." It appeared Heather wasn't the only one who felt a magnetism. "And young vampires tend to attack the old ones to prove themselves."

"Out to prove themselves? Sounds like the new bully in the school yard syndrome."

"Youth and power are a bad mix." Heather felt the comment was more specific than general.

"It's weird, really, that vampires get stronger as they age."

"And what makes you think that? You haven't been there yet."

"Well, that's what I've been told."

Catherine laughed, her voice like rich maple syrup on a chilly day. "Ah, a protegé. And who might your mentor be?"

"I'm not at liberty to say. A promise, nothing personal."

"Smart girl. You're tough to crack. I like that. Most new ones spill words like drinks."

"I just spill drinks, right?"

"Right," said Catherine, and smiled.

"Anyways, I have to ask. Is there any way you can trust me? I mean besides my letting you read my mind, like you've been trying to for half an hour now."

If Catherine's cheeks weren't already flushed, she would have blushed. Caught peeking, she was.

"It's just that," continued Heather, "I really haven't had much of a friend for a while. I thought you looked like a good one."

It seemed the bar got quiet, though no one took any notice of them now. Catherine let her attention wander around the place before she settled her eyes back on Heather, warmly smiling again. A good sign, the fact that she made the extra effort to smile when she looked at her.

"What about your mentor? You don't speak to him at all?"

"Mentor. It sounds so stuffy. I think of him more as a brother. We speak from time to time, but we parted ways for...strange reasons. I mostly needed to be on my own."

"A lone huntress. I like it."

251

And me too, I hope, thought Heather. She'd never thought she'd find such attraction in another woman, but many things changed since she'd uncovered her sexuality.

"Yes, I like you, too," said Catherine.

Little slip, should keep your guard up more rigidly. Though it was hard when you were developing an instinctive trust for someone. Maybe vampires needed a partner to put a drain on the mind? Blood from the mortals and soul from your breed. How much psychic residue did you pick up when you sank your teeth into someone else's throat? How did you manipulate that residue so it didn't eat at your cold heart for centuries? A simple cerebellum to cry on?

"Do you think we could meet again, Catherine?"

Catherine stretched her lilac lips into yet another smile and said, "My friends call me Cat. And, yes, I'd like very much to meet you again. And thank you."

"For what?"

"Thinking I'm beautiful."

A little embarrassed, Heather said, "I'll meet you tomorrow, early, front of this place."

She walked out of the bar, looking back at Catherine twice before she left and started walking up *rue Ste-Catherine*, on her way home. She decided, because of the gorgeous night, still with plenty of darkness, and her warmth and good spirit, to walk home instead of taking the metro. It would take a while, but whoever it was who was following her didn't mind putting in the extra effort.

Driving across *rue Sherbrooke*, window open, his head cleared and he felt that curious feeling that you feel when you know you're hungry, you know you'd better eat, but you also know that you could go forever without food, or at least feel like you can. It was more than adrenaline, more than stamina. It was a lucidity of *mind*. A sense of purpose, perhaps. Purpose lost and found.

He decided to go to Heather. It was usually her that came to him, and he didn't want this relationship to dissolve into an unanswered knock on a front door.

And besides, he *liked* Heather. Who couldn't? He wouldn't readily admit it in the presence of anything breathing, but she had been as good for him as he for her, though he was a little hard on her at times. Brotherly love and all.

Sometimes he let his jealousy get the best of him, but she was a toughie, and, when he had regrets of his acidity towards her, it was apparent that she was still the headstrong lass who loved to haunt *rue Ste-Catherine*.

That was Heather, haunter of St-Catherine street, angel of the fête. How could he have ever denied her the nourishment of her soul? How could he deny her Montréal? He had been to other cities and he always came back to Montréal. He'd heard mortals talking and saying that one day they would go back to Montréal. Despite the conflicts, the constant arguing and political bullying.

He had to see her before he left and hoped to be able to keep her unsuspecting enough about where he was going.

He'd reached the other side of the downtown of Montréal, turning to where Heather hid her alter-ego, Heather St. Amore. Pulled up to the house and stopped, was about to get out of the car, even had a foot on the pavement but stopped suddenly, jaw open, when he saw-

"Oh, shit." It was impossible, nothing on the news, no word from her. Did that mean...?

He didn't want to think what that meant, he didn't want to think that he could have seen her once more before-

And all because he was absorbed in his own self-loathing, self-deprecating commiseration. How many friends must die before he realized that they were as precious as a drop of blood? How many centuries did someone need to wallow in defeat?

"You fucking cunt!!!" he yelled at the night, slamming his fist on the roof of the car and denting it noticeably. "I won! I'm not the one who was defeated! I'll tear your eyes out and squeeze them till they burst!"

He squeezed his fists tight and lowered his forehead to the dented metal of the car, feeling its cold touch on cold skin and whispered, "So why do you still haunt me? Why do you still linger, nipping at my soul?"

He felt a hot tear drip off his cheek, onto his fisted hand, and it was more than emotion that poured out of him. It was release. He had emotions, but stored them up somewhere, not in his heart, not in his head, but in his bowel and who knew what kinds of feces festered in the deep of a demon?

He sat back in his car and slammed the door closed. He didn't feel like driving anymore, but neither did he feel like sitting here, lest he look at *that*.

Korson brought a hand to his dampened cheek and wiped away the tears, but only literally. He felt the burning scar of the cleansing water and knew he'd feel it until the conflict within himself was resolved. Until the *conflict* was resolved. Period.

And he hoped to whatever the hell Gods controlled the night that Heather was okay, because he couldn't forgive himself this time if-

Gods. He wasn't sure if he believed in them anymore, he wasn't sure if it was even proper for a vampire to believe, much less try to live by their doctrines. The sacred body of the victim, honoured for their blood. It was just food for the demons, that's all. Why bother? Why believe in a higher power, they controlled the shadows and everything that most humans only believed happened in fiction. Mortals themselves were so fucking egotistical as to consider themselves the higher power of the planet because they couldn't see the very products of their own imaginings come to life. The vain belief that they could even imagine a higher power! That it was within the grasp of their minds when the hardly made use of it all!

This is something I have to do, he thought, as he drove off. He used to be a killer. A long time ago. Now he just went through the motions. *No matter how difficult. The most rewarding road is the most impossible.*

It was time he saw another old friend, and well past time he found his roots. Again.

Oh, and by the way-the real Korson is back. And he's had one hundred years to get really...fucking...angry.

Heather struggled down *rue Ste-Catherine*, wiping tears from her face, clutching a sooted grey kitten in her arms. She rushed through the throngs of people unaware that they were there, bumping them out of the way and drawing attention to herself for only a dangerous moment.

She hoped she wasn't late to meet Catherine, having been understandably and unavoidably delayed. But the bottom line was, if Catherine got sick of waiting, she would leave and who knows how long it would be till their paths crossed again? Who knows if the fate that brought them together could ever be duplicated?

Cumulous meowed and coughed a choked, hair-balled cough. He would need water soon, food, too, probably. A million things were rushing through her head, she not knowing how she would accomplish any of them, and the kitten in her arms sending out trembling, fearful vibrations that were worse than if he were to scream and meow because these were his inner feelings she was listening to. He was scared.

As she approached the bar she'd been at last night, when everything was just perfect, it took her a moment to spot her but Catherine, she was there, thank God, and less noticeable because she was sitting down which hid her behind the people walking by who admired her.

Heather wanted to melt at the warm reception she would receive, as apparent from the smile that Catherine gave her immediately upon seeing her appear from a break in the crowd. That smile faded immediately when she saw Heather's condition.

Her clothes were ragged and torn, her hair and face blackened and splotchy, with tears trying in vain to wash away the dirt that muddied her beauty. The light bringer had fallen and fell into a pile of coal dust.

As Heather approached, Catherine had a quizzical look on her face, one that was suppressing worry in the hopes that it would be unfounded by jumping to conclusions. Heather arrived and put Cumulous on the table, where he crouched and trembled alertly, his fur all mussy. She herself sat down and looked as though she wanted to gush.

All Catherine could say was, "What the hell happened to you?"

Heather sucked in a ragged breath, a cleansing breath, but cleansing wasn't something she wanted to think about right now.

"I walked home last night," she said, "and I went to bed feeling good." She wiped a tear from her cheek and looked at it, but all she saw was black chalk.

"I don't know when it was, but all of a sudden I noticed how hot and constricting it was, lying in that box. After a while I had to get out, but when I opened my eyes, I saw through the glass that the flames were all around me. It felt like I was going to just..." She trailed off, too saddened by the thought of her house burning down, too worried about who did it and why.

Evaporate, thought Catherine, *it feels like you're going to burst into flames and just evaporate,* but she didn't feel the need to clarify that common fear they shared.

Heather sniffled and said, "The flames were blocking the door to the upstairs so I had to burst through them, and I grabbed Cumulous from under the couch and escaped through the window-"

"Mmm," nodded Catherine, sympathetically.

"-which was shattered inward."

Again Catherine nodded, knowing but trying not to think about what this meant. Heather stroked Cumulous behind the ear and he stretched out on his side, claiming the table top as his temporary territory.

"Can't you tell if you're being followed?" asked Catherine.

"Oh, don't jump on me and say that I could've prevented this! I have enough shit with the fact that I've got no home to live in now. It's not like I've got so much money that I could afford one, even if I could buy one before morning came."

Catherine looked down, twirling her drink with her finger, as she liked to.

"I didn't mean to say that you were lax, I just wanted to know if you could tell if you were being followed."

"Well, usually I can. But I've go more on my mind right now than my skills as a huntress. I've got to nowhere to stay."

"Where did you stay last night?"

"That reminds me," Heather said, putting her fingers to her forehead, "there's a dead family of three a few blocks from where I live. I tried not to let it happen, but they heard me break into their basement." She looked Catherine in the eye. "The mother wouldn't stop screaming."

Catherine looked down in thought, put off by the events.

"You can stay with me," she said, the thrill that would have been there gone because of the circumstances.

Don't sound too excited, thought Heather. "Thanks," she said dully.

A cone of silence descended around them, like these events were predetermined and pushed upon them. Not that they wouldn't have ended up spending inordinate amounts of time together, maybe even living together anyway, but on their own schedule, not fates.

"Your cat," said Catherine, "does he need a vet or something?"

"No, he's fine. Just a little scared. And hungry."

"You're sure he's okay? You don't want a doctor to check him out just in case?"

Heather gave a little smile. "He's all right, but he's starting to smell food. Any minute he'll bolt after a bird or a hamburger. I think I'm ready to go home now."

Catherine paid the cheque, tipped the waitress a twenty, and they made their way north, up Mount Royal, until they reached the other side of it, where Catherine lived.

Catherine had a lovely little townhouse, which at first looked crammed in between all the rest, but when you got inside, snuggled was a more appropriate term. Maybe it was because the living room was so comfortable, filled with a thousand throw pillows both big and small, which made you want to fall backwards on them and let the fabric mold to you and caress you. It might have looked strange that she didn't keep a couch, but right now it looked inviting.

Before they could collapse, a certain soot-covered kitty needed a bath. Heather and Catherine both held him down while Heather ran a wet cloth along his slinky little body. He looked as though he was undecided between being bewildered and being angry at having someone bathe him. The shame of a water bath, when he had a purrrfectly good sandpaper tongue!

That done, he leapt off the counter to the bowl of food they'd set out for him, and he ate and went to mark his territory in a plant.

Catherine and Heather went back to the living room, Catherine turning on the television and Heather flopping on the pillows, most of which were black or purple, a colour that Catherine showed a natural affinity for.

Catherine lit a large, free standing candelabra that had seven candles sitting in its arms. The light from it was bright enough, but soft and pleasant. She sat down in a plush black beanbag not too far away from Heather. Right now Heather wished the room was even smaller, so she could feel even more closed in. But the fact that the other rooms were only pools of darkness made her feel as though the world ended at the walls of this room, and she liked that.

Alfred Hitchcock's Vertigo was being shown on the late moved channel, the flickering old colours making everything feel just a bit more proper. Kim Novak's painted face a reciprocal of the realism of the story. And besides, Heather felt as though her life was flipped upside down, that she was falling and spinning.

But it was Catherine that Heather was more enamored with, her purple lips like a bruise that didn't know it was supposed to be ugly, her amethyst eyes like glowing crystals. Her olive oil skin looking soft and smooth and sensuous in the flickering glow of the candles.

"How old are you, Catherine?" Heather felt like a child asking that question, like it was unnecessary to know the answer, but Catherine smiled while holding her gaze.

"I was born in the year 1900. And I was killed in the year 1930. That makes me ninety-six, nice and simple math, thank the Devil."

"Do you really believe that we serve God or the Devil?"

"I just like people thinking that I do. It perpetuates the myth. And the more I'm a myth, the better I like it. I can belong to the world when I choose."

Heather flicked her sharpened nail, remembering that she wished she could belong to the world when she felt like it. Only she wanted to belong to the underworld, the mystical one that no one can see, the one that she couldn't find. Three vampires in about a year. Some society.

"You count your mortal life in your age. Why?"

"Why not?" Catherine countered. "I lived it, did I not? It's part of what makes me what I am."

Who made you what you are? wondered Heather.

"You feel guilty about what you are, don't you? The killing bothers you."

That brought a smile to Heather's face, her cheeks brightening as they plumped up and caught the candlelight.

"God, no, I love the killing. Not that I've never regretted any victim's deaths, but the killing is such a thrill it never ceases to hold fascination. It's more than food, it's-"

"Sex?"

"No, thanks, I'm a vampire. It's like liquor. No, it's more than liquor. It's liqueur. The sweetest, aromatic liqueur you've ever tasted, and to get drunk on it is to know a life. That's what's so special. You don't know every life. You know *a* life. One life, all to yourself, the most precious thing you can take from a person. Any crazy fuck can commit genocide, indiscriminately killing whoever crosses his path. But to choose one life and know it, from start to finish, for them to seize at the sight of your chalky pallor, your ivory fangs that mean oblivion begins hard and round and white and becomes red and wet and gushing before the darkness descends, that is the ultimate state of existence a being can achieve, and it's more than mere power. It's taking a piece of the earth, one at a time."

"If that's the ultimate state of existence, what about all the other creatures who can't achieve it? All those humans who are stuck in the rut of living and dying."

"Don't tell me there aren't humans who don't at least try to achieve it. The world is filled with psychopaths who rant and rave, stalking their prey before thy kill them. And what do the mortals do? They lock them up and *study* them. And sometimes they kill them, mercifully. Don't forget, we die before we even think of achieving a higher plane. We're elevated to a state that has the instinctive ability to achieve a Zen. It's like we've been given a spiritual appendage to our brains that manifests itself as the fears from our existence as humans. Look at us. We don't cease to look like mortals. And don't forget, we aren't the only creatures who live off blood. If humans can evolve from apes, why couldn't we have evolved?"

"But you are bothered by something, some part of your existence is disturbing to you, is it not?" asked Catherine, actually stating it more than querying it.

"It's the point of it all! It must be the Pisces in me. I always look for the deep and utter meaning."

"Nothing wrong with that," said Cat.

"But I mean that I try to find the parallels. It might seem stupid but I look to nature, to see how the world is connected. To see the pieces of the puzzle. And for me to think that we evolved is extremely difficult. I look at the few creatures in the world that live off blood and they're all insects. Mosquitoes. And the more I think about that, the more I think that we're an aberration, a bigger accident than humanity ever could be."

"What about bats, Heather?"

"Oh, shut the fuck up."

Catherine threw her head back and laughed, said, "You are so precious! Look at you, your face is red!"

"I guess I really haven't thought this through as much as I should have," said Heather, a little dejectedly.

"It isn't your intelligence. Your argument is logical, but you still need some experience. You're so young and there is so much inside of you that I can see you haven't even realized for yourself. It's in all of us, but sometimes we lose it. And some people can't get to it. But you, you just need to be patient and allow time for realization. Intelligence is valuable, but experience is absolutely irreplaceable. Your body has to experience what your mind already knows."

"I have trouble accepting that sometimes. I guess everyone hates an armchair quarterback, though."

"When I asked what bothered you about existence, I meant yours specifically. I love that about you, that you aren't self-centered and egotistical. But you sit there trying to figure out the grand scheme of things and how you fit into it. I want to know what bothers Heather, about your existence specifically. Instead of trying to figure the entire purpose, you should look more to *your* purpose. That's what I think is bothering you."

Though Heather would contemplate these things to herself, her lack of ego-centrism prevented her from discussing it openly with others. Her unselfishness focused her on the larger picture.

"I guess," Heather couldn't really put her finger on this one, couldn't spear it with that razor sharp nail. "I think it's the why. I know I was chosen for *something*, but I've no idea what, or even if I've been rejected. And I think that my house being burnt has something to do with my being rejected. I think that was a message that my time is up."

Not to mention that from time to time, she still heard voices in her head.

It was not even midnight, still enough time to make it there, set up, and ready himself for the serious stuff. He headed through the darkened streets of Montréal, taking in the view for one last time, until a flash of red caught his attention. Not good.

It would do no good to try and outrun them, probably even worse if he allowed himself to be pulled over, but that way was quicker. He turned into a side street, empty because of the late hour. Stopped the car and saw the man walking towards him in the rear view, noticing that he was alone, no partner in the car. But HQ would know where he is and why, might even know the information pertinent to his vehicle.

Which, the officer told him, was why he was being stopped. His plates were twenty years out of date, and ownership and a license were requested.

Korson reached into the glove box and pulled out a few cards, handed them to the officer.

The guy looked at them, saw they were outdated, and looked up at Korson with a skeptical look on his face.

"Is this a joke?" he said.

Korson had a sly little smile dancing on his lips, and he extended his hand reverentially, each finger gracefully following one another until the palm was open and waiting and grey, the nails glistening and small and sharp-and waiting.

The officer gave back the papers, a little confused, but thinking the proper documents were now forthcoming.

Korson opened the car door slowly, got out in thick movements that suggested he was made of something liquid rather than solid. Of something far more ethereal than a human.

The officer began to feel anxious, particularly when the strange, white man with the out-of-date car, with the papers he handed him that said he was twenty-six and the year was 1954, a guy who probably should be dead now; the officer began to feel anxious when this eerie, ghostly thing before him stood at full height and towered over him as though he were floating down from the dark sky and there was a special plane for him to walk on that was higher than the one that everyone else was relegated to.

After muttering *'step back into your car, sir,'* (and just why the fuck did he call him sir? This guy had the look in his eye that he was going to kill him), the pig pulled out his gun. (A far cry from the U.S., where, if you so inclined to pick your nose while being detained by a member of the highway patrol, a team of specially trained individuals with guns that put their penises to serious shame would have you surrounded before you could check for snot on your finger.)

The gun only broadened the smile that Korson had, a smirk, really. An intelligent, knowing smirk. A mean, salivating grin. He stepped forward as slowly as he had gotten out of the car, his body flowing on the light breeze.

Both his hands were out now, palms up and visible, grey, so that any movement of them could be seen clearly. He wasn't hiding a thing. He didn't have any weapons. But nothing was more deadly than those hands of his.

Except maybe his teeth.

And those were no longer hidden all too well either. Those lovely pinpricks began to dent his lower lip, his tongue flicking back and forth on the left fang until it had a small slice in it. It was all that much better when you had an open wound in your mouth, when the blood hit it and bypassed the gastro-intestinal tract and went directly into the bloodstream like it was being soaked up by a sponge. A hungry vampire bled in.

The officer fired his gun not once, not twice, but thrice. The first bullet caught a shoulder, the second a leg. The third was itself caught by a hand, one that had picked up the timing of the bullet leaving the gun. His phalanges cracked from the impact and in the skin a small tear that bled a little bit blue.

He held up the bullet between forefinger and thumb for the officer to see. The cop dropped the gun in complete and utter awe, fell partway to the ground wanting to run but caught between fear and duty.

The least he should have done was turtle and hide his face between his arms and the sanctity of the pavement, but he stared as Korson took the bullet and threw it-

-and embedded it in the socket which held the man's eye.

With the eye pushed back into his own skull, the man began to utter guttural, whimpering noises, noises that would build themselves into a scream. Those sounds became louder, more pronounced, when he closed his other eye. What he saw inside his own head must have scared him more than anything in the outside world, more than the vampire whom he had closed his sight from, because he never screamed at the vampire.

Korson looked down at the mess he'd made of the man, heard his useless, pleading screams. That really disgusted him, the pathetic coward quivering on the pavement, his face a monstrosity, a mockery of what it once was.

The man stopped screaming and began to shudder and sigh, on the verge of death. Maybe what scared him was the fact that he didn't see the light at the end of the tunnel? Only a mind that was ninety percent empty and throbbing blood vessels that pumped on, not knowing that something was wrong in the machine.

Korson picked the man up by the back of his head, looked at the mess. He took his long, bony grey index finger and slowly, teasingly slit the man's throat from right to left, like a lover playfully tickling the neck of his partner. Such a beautiful grin that now played upon the man's neck! Much like Heather's Jack that she wore on Hallowe'en!

He looked at the blood that hung like a raindrop from the tip of his finger and put it between his lips, swallowing it down gently.

"Uch," he said. "I'm not hungry anymore."

Still a little wary of each other, what with instinct ruling the roost, Catherine and Heather slept at opposite ends of the house, Heather in the basement, Catherine upstairs. Really a petty thing to do, but vampires can be petty sometimes.

The snow had by now dried up, and March had gone out like a slaughtered lamb. Spring was budding, the breeze carrying the scents of daffodils and fresh laundry hung out to dry on the air.

And the days got longer. It must have been an accident of nature (or maybe not), or just everyday perception, but the length of the night increases with the decline of the season. More time for the demons to roam, they say, and it's true.

Which is why Heather so loved the winter, with its acute nip of cold that suited a creature whose blood had run that way, whose heart would harden with icicles after centuries of watching the world fold and unfold its petals.

That's what drew Heather to Catherine the most. Her colour. The fact that, after almost a century, she didn't run pale white the way that stoical bastard Korson did.

And maybe that's what drew her to Korson, her revulsion of what he'd let himself become, though she still counted him among her friends, what precious few of them there were.

Drawing herself together, she pushed open the lid of the box, smiled when she saw the grey little sphinx perched on the lower half of it that she'd never bothered to open. A little guardian, a sentinel. He knew where his food came from.

And up the stairs she went, companion in tow, and she fed him something crunchy and something raw, then washed her face in frigid water. It felt like it took off a layer of dust that accumulated through the night. She didn't know why the water felt so good, didn't care.

Seating herself on the amazingly large accumulation of purple and black throw pillows, Heather looked out the window at the thin glow around Mount Royal, the glow that blocked out the dying rays of the sun, a glow so faint no mortal eyes would have detected it with ease. She remembered how she used to cringe at the heat the sun would bring, and was thankful that it was now only a fading warmth that she felt. Maybe the fire had desensitized her to the burning ultraviolet?

Whatever, it was a nice segue into the cool night which she so loved, and convenient as well, because she didn't have the protection of her glass box and she didn't seem to need it anymore.

Footfalls on the stairs alerted her to the presence of another ultraviolet, that glow much more beautiful, yet probably just as deadly. It acutally was a bit of a glow she saw in the rising shadow, perhaps the light amplified the effect?

"Up late, are we?"

Catherine smiled at Heather with her acute mother-of-pearl teeth. She said, "I hate the sun. I always wait until it's completely gone."

Heather went back to looking out he window, noticing the emptiness in her heart. Catherine sat down next to Heather and brushed away some of the spun gold that was her hair, pushed it away from her thick, full cheek and said, "You're hungry already little one."

Heather felt a sharp nail tease the side of her face, her spine tingling at the touch.

"Oooh," she said. "Look at that." She pointed at the full, low-hung moon, which was a shade of dusty pastel red. "It looks like a melon."

"Sure," said Catherine, still playing with Heather's hair. "More like a dollop of blood, I'm sure, is what you're thinking."

"Yeah, yeah, guilty," confessed Heather. "But wouldn't it be wonderful to sink your teeth into that, and let the juice run down your chin?"

I'd like to sink my teeth into something, that's for sure, my full-breasted beauty, thought Catherine.

Heather laughed bit of a giggle.

"What," said Catherine.

"Nooothing," Heather cooed.

Had Heather heard that? Evil mind-reader!

"Go ahead, you can say it," prodded Cat.

"All right." Heather ran her tongue over her upper lip. "What do you see when you look at me?" She stated it more than queried it.

"What do I see? Can you be more pacific?"

"Okay," said Heather, "well, when I look at you, I see purple. I was wondering if you see me as a colour."

"Oh, of course," said Catherine, "that's easy. You're golden, like those golden Santas they sell every X-mas."

"My eyes?" Heather purred.

"They still blue," said Catherine, raising her hand tentatively towards Heather's lashes, "but they have an opulence that is very reminiscent of gold."

Heather felt a cold flush over her cheeks, an emptiness in her heart that was her hunger. She took Catherine's hand in hers, pulling it down to the pillows, and then quickly and playfully kissed her on the forehead, still with her alluring giggle.

"Enough play for you, baby. Coming out?"

"Nah. Not in the mood. I'll just stay here and stare out the window or something."

Catherine squeezed Heather's cheeks and said, "Since you've been such a good little ghoul, I'll bring you home something sweet."

"Fangs a lot! Yer a pal!"

Yum, thought Heather, and she watched Catherine's hips tick-tock as she walked out the door.

It really wasn't that long until Catherine returned, and with her was a young girl, Monique, about thirteen, fourteen but struggling to look older. A few shots of brandy and some fine chocolates was all it took to relax Monique and she'd accommodated by subtly undoing the top button of her blouse.

"My, such a mature young woman you are," said Catherine, "to be in such a position. You wouldn't prefer to be seducing some young boy your own age?"

"People don't seduce anymore," said Monique, quite matter-of-factly. *Thought the world ended at her fingertips, would tonight, too, if I may let you in on something not-so-secret!*

"Besides," continued the tart-in-training, "I've had boys before, some as old as seventeen, if you believe me."

"Mm, it's been a while since I've had seventeen year old. Male or female," said Catherine.

"That's probably on account of the fact that you look forty." Monique's mouth was a river, flowing fast with no rocks. "I mean, don't get me wrong, you're a very beautiful woman, but if I were you I'd save the grief and stick with stockbrokers and doctors and other such older gentlemen, no shame in that."

Oh, Lord, Catherine, thought Heather, *if you don't put her out of her misery then I will.*

"So," said Catherine, taking Monique's fragile hand, "you have been with boys. My, such an experienced young woman. Have you tired of them already? Boys, I mean."

"Oh, somewhat, I like to try different things, y'know, meet different kinds of people and have different kinds of fun."

Ah, that's how you keep your friends, by removing your shirt, thought Heather. Coincidentally, another button had mysteriously come undone.

"Dear, dear, no need to be coy," tutted Catherine. "You're among *friends*, people who *want* you. Heather, you've been such a pooh, why don't you help our precious little guest feel more comfortable. That's it."

Heather slinked over on all fours, cat-like and sexy (read: sleazy.) She looked as though she was going to crawl up Monique's slim and undeveloped little body. Her hands rode up Monique's boyish chest, over the partial bumps that would soon be breasts, and rested on her shoulders, holding them firmly and slightly massaging them. She (Heather), bent closer, and closer, until she could smell the baby powder freshness of Monique's skin, scolding herself only a little at the fact that she let it reminder of diapers and felt no revulsion. Heather let her nose lightly graze the cheek of the fresh little girl and her wet, slithery tongue drew a line in the blush that powdered her face.

Withdrawing a bit, Heather's dexterous fingers found tiny buttons on a black blouse and undid them, both her and Catherine salivating at the little breast in the lace brassiere.

"Now," said Catherine, breaking a lovely silence, "tell me, dear, why is it you're tired of boys. Is it because they aren't yet large enough to fill you up?"

"Oh, no," said Monique, like she was having a conversation over coffee. "It's not the penis itself that I'm dissatisfied with, per se. It's really the fact that most boys under twenty-five really haven't figured out what to do with it, from this point of view anyway. Now, that's all fine and good for them, but if they're going to ride this vessel, y'know, you better keep the captain of the ship happy. It's not like I'm not willing to do my part, either, so I figure a little feminine expertise is what I really need."

Which is what Heather had begun to give her nether-regions.

"Well, if you don't mind, I wouldn't mind parting with some of my own knowledge, if you'll let me have just a little taste?" said Catherine, hanging her forefinger from the corner of her mouth.

"Oh, sure, age and experience, it's always worth a shot. Hey, what you're doing with your tongue, that's great, keep it up. Ow!"

Heather had bitten her quick and hard. "Ssh. Let's not ruin this moment with words."

By this time, Catherine had joined in, fondling a now naked little breast, playfully toying with Monique's short burgundy bob. Lips and spittle teased a nipple, more a teat really, but Monique, poor little bitch, had begun to grow weak, her vagina slowly bleeding into Heather's waiting throat and lapping tongue, the nerves rubbed raw from a vampire's hunger. The little girl fell numb and tired and was going bloodless.

And, shockingly, the more delirious she got, the chattier she became.

It was all Heather could do, when she raised her bloodied lips and reddened teeth, to roll her baby blues before she twisted Monique's neck to shut her up.

Catherine looked up from a bloody breast, sucked some blood off her finger between her full lips and said, "What the hell are you doing? I was having fun! Besides, maybe I wanted to save her for tomorrow, too." Her tone had lost the condescending, sultry tones that lulled little Monique into her arms.

"You would have put up with that until tomorrow?" said Heather with a raised eyebrow.

"Point well taken. She's empty, almost. What should we do with her?"

"Ach, let's just leave her here for a bit, enjoy the irony of it. She almost looks shocked. Would you have thought that possible?" She turned to Monique, whose eyes were a little widened in some surprise, and put her index finger on Monique's nose, spoke in toddler tones: "Do we know the ways of the world Monique? No we don't, no we don't! Are we dead and cold? Yes, we are, yes we are!"

Catherine smiled a wide grin, licked some more blood off the breast and Heather laughed her most practiced maniacal laugh-MUAHAHAHAHAHAHA HAHAHAHAHA!!!

These two definitely had a rapport.

Later, the body stuffed into garbage bags and hidden in cold storage in the basement, Heather had curled up in Catherine's arms, listening to the dulcet tones of her voice singing a song that was older than time.

Though the honey-dripping moon had vacated to some other part of the sky, the view of the night was still as beautiful as if it had been carved in diamond and blackened with charcoal strokes.

Both Heather and Catherine were warm with blood, and they felt each other's heat against their cheeks.

"That was good fun, though, wasn't it?" said Heather.

Catherine said, "Mmm," stroked Heather's thick, soft hair, her fingers making train tracks as they pushed their way through the strands of dead cells.

Heather got up, went to the sink and splashed water on her face. "I don't know why, but sometimes I get the urge to do this over and over."

"We all do." Catherine got up and went to the kitchen, came back with a glass filled with water. "Drink," she said.

"What? No way, I'll throw up."

Catherine snuggled back into position. "What makes you say that?"

"Well, I've tried drinking wine, eating things, bloody things like rare steak, and all I want to do is vomit."

"Tsk, tsk, raised very poorly, you were."

"I've found myself quite happy subsisting on blood, thank you. It's not like I've resigned myself to it, I do enjoy it."

Catherine took a sip of the water, exhaled a sigh of satisfaction a it cooled her, her violet glow fading just a little. "Go ahead, take a sip."

Heather took the proffered glass, looked down into it like it was a crystal ball. "I just don't get what I've been missing. I thought we gave up being human, that all we needed was blood and fun and making the night come alive. I thought that was what set us apart."

"We never really gave up anything, little one. Our priorities just shifted a bit. You had the misfortune to be mistaught and abandoned by two callous individuals."

Heather winced a bit at the derogatory reference to Korson, because he did have a part in making her the sleek huntress she now was, and she loved herself that way.

"But we're still after the same three things, the blood, the milk and the water, that drives the humans on. Our desires differ from the mortals, we have different priorities. We're their improvement."

Heather craned her head to look up at Catherine. "Our priority is obviously the blood. But what's the water? The milk?"

"The water, my dearest," said Catherine, "is what makes up the blood. It's blood in its purest form, really, unborn blood, if you will. They should really be more strict in science class these days. Now drink, take a sip and see what the water does."

Heather sipped slowly at first, unsure, then drank it down like a whore drinks cheap wine.

"Wow," she said. "It's like thin, thin blood. We could live off it if we had to, couldn't we?"

"Yes, we can, but it's much better when you use it to dilute the blood already in you. You probably won't even be hungry tomorrow if you drink a few glasses." Catherine took a sip herself and continued:

"Humans, or mortals, as you like to call them, can live off of water. Their priority is reversed from ours."

"That's trash," said Heather. "I've never heard of humans living off of blood."

"What about cannibals?" said Catherine. "And don't forget, many religions used to hold sacrifices. Pagans had blood rituals. Christians too. Who's to say that we're not still human, living another reality?"

"How can we be living another reality? I see the way I used to live. I'm different now. I'm not human."

"So what's real Heather? If you're a secret to the world then how is it that people know of us through myths?"

Heather thought for a moment, said, "Because there is truth to the myths?"

"Exactly. But who hid them. Where is the code?"

"But we don't write anything down."

"The secrets must be somewhere, Heather. Where have you looked?"

"I've been all over the city. I can't find anything."

"Think," said Catherine. "This is what you wanted, isn't it? The secrets behind the darkest parts of man's soul."

"Tell me, then."

"*No,*" heard Heather, in her head, and the intimacy of the way it was conveyed carried the pain in a way that would make mere words melt like frost on a blade of grass.

"You *won't* tell me? Don't you even care for me?"

I would tell you if I-

"Say it to me!! Don't try to blind me with your wet thoughts. I want to hear it in your voice that you don't care for me!"

Catherine put her arm on Heather's shoulder, said, "I have loved you dearly from the moment that I set eyes upon you. But a very long time ago, I swore an oath. Not knowing, I agreed-"

Heather held back tears, or rather, she had none left, perhaps, but she did cling to Catherine. Who else could she cling to? But if there were a hundred suitors with a thousand promises, she would still have clung to Catherine.

"Why is it that none want me? Why does everyone want to keep me in the dark?"

"I want to help you any way I can, but I swore an oath-"

"Fuck your oath!!! Whose blood did you sign that oath with? Isn't it me who counts now?" The sea of Heather's eyes boiled with resentment and frustration, her arms tensed and her feet lifted off the ground several inches.

Catherine said, "Heather, calm down. *Come* down. You have to believe me when I say that I care for you immensely. But all I can tell you is that you have to follow faith."

"Can you at least walk with me if I need you?"

"There are demons lurking underneath the fabric of everything. And sometimes those demons come out to play, or haunt. But whether or not you are one of those people who can feel them, they are there. They do exist. It all depends on how we manifest them."

Catherine uncurled from Heather, stretched with an arched back, and walked towards the stairs. She was about to round the corner as she climbed them when Heather stopped her.

"Cat?"

They looked at each other for a moment.

"You can stay in the basement with me if you want."

Catherine smiled. "Maybe another time. Right now, I'd be more comfortable sleeping by myself."

Heather was a little disappointed, but understanding.

"Tomorrow," she asked, "do you think you could tell me about the milk?"

"Of course," smiled Catherine.

As she disappeared up the steps, all Heather could see was the fading violet glow that followed her friend.

Heather woke at the exact moment the sun dipped below the horizon line. Of course, by the time she made her way upstairs, the world had taken a bath in coal, rolling out the black carpet for her and her kind.

The night felt vivacious, zinging with electricity. Like it was ready for anything to happen. And that was contagious for Heather, she was ready herself.

Just a mood, though. But one made one's own fun, taking what one would from the lemon.

She waited for Catherine to wake, lazy old bag, but it wasn't long, and she told her she was going out for a walk, needed to clear her head.

No use moping and sulking any longer. No use wasting eternity, it wouldn't be there forever.

Oh, yes, it would, but that wasn't the real point, was it? It wasn't eternity that you wasted, it was the *past*. That was still the challenge, even more so now.

You had the future, the present, but no one had the past. The past was sand in the breeze. Only writers and children could change the past.

Society was sand in the breeze. The creatures of the night got only bits and pieces of it. Vampire or no, if you live at night it was a whole other world.

After walking briskly for a few minutes, thinking on all of this, Heather slowed and found herself looking in a bay window, like the first night she became a vampire, looking at a family of three watching late night television on a Saturday. No, four, there was a baby sleeping upstairs in a crib.

Two girls, so much future.

Just like the night she was unborn. Except this father wasn't beating his children.

Sometimes the children bite back, don't they Talissa?

Heather snuggled up to a tree and crouched, the *voyeur* in her taking over. She massaged the backs of her arms with her hands, and her pony-tail flip-flopped in the mildly strong breeze, a loose strand of hair tickling the tip of her nose, her cheeks and chin.

Could she sit here forever?

She remembered what she talked about with Catherine last night, the words stuck with her.

You have to follow faith.

But Heather had no faith, no hope and worse, no belief.

Catherine had, like, ninety-five years on her, but it seemed as though the one who accepted her plight more readily was Heather. Maybe because she bought into it with more knowledge, more expectations than Catherine, that she was more disappointed with what she saw as a vampire than being branded and outcast. She was used to not being Miss Popularity. Not that she didn't have many friends at school or anything, but she wasn't one of those people who had others falling over her. That would have come when she had gotten older, when guys put less emphasis on putting out.

But that was over, no use to dwell. What was on her mind was more the fact that the woman she loved considered herself an outsider, and though she wouldn't admit it, she had regrets, she had lost or failed ambitions.

Much like Korson, and why was it that she kept coming across this forlorn, lonely feeling? She felt it acutely within herself as well.

Maybe the very answer was in the very problem? Perhaps her turning was the very incident from which these feelings sprung?

Maybe there was a way to get back?

At least for a while. Banish all thoughts of reversing the surgery, there are some things you just can't undo, like a tattoo.

Heather remembered how she used to read Batman comics, the only girl who did. Every other girl played with dolls, practiced make-up and holding high tea, she dreamed of a cape and pointy ears. That's what started her on this dreary, no-end-in-sight road, looking at things that were black.

But she was still fascinated with the idea of her own real-life comic book escapism. It was hardly a moment before she was done mulling over her thought when she found herself crawling in surprisingly comfortable cat-like position on all fours, crawling towards the house from her place on the front lawn.

Just a *click!* of the mind to open the door slowly, just enough space to slip in like a wraith-of-the-mist, her body lithe and thin, her golden aura dim as it kissed the shadow and clashed with the artificial glow of the God TV.

She'd been reluctant to use her mind powers all this time, reluctant and reminded when Catherine had tricked her in the mirror. All this time spent searching for the hidden world without and ignoring and smothering the limitless world within.

What could be deeper than the vastness of the brain?

Korson's training, telling her to hide her powers because they could do as much harm as help. She needed a reason, should have demanded some, but didn't care, was too caught up in the intoxication of blood and power. It was so easy to be drunk on blood, easier still on power.

But Catherine spoke to her as an equal, it was like she was trying to point her in some direction.

Heather loosened her mind of those intangible constraints, *I am a shadow, I am a shadow,* and she felt her body melt into the thick and viscous darkness.

She settled comfortably against the wall, the sound of the God and the odd comment from the supplicants giving her a feeling that she found soothing for some strange reason. What could be so relaxing about sitting with three unfamiliar people in a familiar but out-of-reach setting, listening to the inane but funny chatter of a gap-tooted ass on the super, really late show?

Ah, ours is not to reason why, just to do and die.

She was at the door frame that opened onto the room now, and she leaned a cheek and shoulder on the corner of the wall, put her hand up to the frame. The daughter was lying on her belly, holding her head up with her hands, the parents crushed together under a blanket in the middle of the couch, and their backs were directly in front of the door.

A little creak roused the man. Heather tensed as he turned his head. He whispered something to his wife, Heather relaxing as she saw that the creak only stirred from him a passive comment to his spouse. She wasn't sure if the creak was her or the house.

Steve Zinger

She listened as the TV babbled on, the little box that captivated so many and held their attentions for so long for a variety of reasons, and she began to relax and for while she nearly felt a part of the *tableau vivant*.

After a few moments, she found herself watching what was going on the screen, like she'd been invited over as company, and the guy in the tube said something pretty damned funny because Heather stopped a snort that tried to force its way out of her nose with her hand.

And, needless to say, she drew her attention of the mother and father, while the daughter only gave a cursory perusal of the door before going back to watching. The parents, though, both stared for a long and flummoxing minute at the darkened doorway, Heather frozen like a pantomime who'd forgotten her next scene.

I am shadow, I am shadow, she kept praying to herself over and over. She made herself believe it. She sucked in all the golden light that she could possibly bottle up inside her five-foot six or so frame.

The two fully grown mortals on the couch exchanged bewildered looks and shrugged it off.

Thank God that houses are known to creak, thought Heather, *but another slip like that and you surely will land yourself in trouble.* She had a strong feeling that, no matter how strongly she hid herself, if one of those people came looking for her-

Hell, if one of those people followed the sound of her snort and bumped into her, she would most certainly be found, majic or no. And why was she worried? Was she not the demon here? The Angel of Death?

Not that she'd have any trouble defending herself, but she wanted to leave this situation unsullied, she wanted to stay here as long as she could. She didn't want a repeat of the screaming mother in the basement the morning she was chased out of her house by licks of flame.

The closing theme of the show flickered by, accompanied by credits, and the girl hopped up and went to get herself a Coke, but settled on Canada Dry because she wasn't allowed to have the caffeine at this late hour, according to her mother. The girl settled back down and sipped at her fizzy drink.

As the clock ticked half past twelve, a movie came on TV and the man got up and announced that he wouldn't sit through it.

Heather looked for an out, and realized that the man would have to pass her to reach the stairs, that she had no time to dart to a room and stay shadow at the same time.

She willed herself twice as hard to be a shadow, pressed herself against the wall, and hoped as the man came around the sofa and towards the door that he had left all his fears of the dark with his childhood, that maybe that would help keep her hidden.

He passed by her, *so close,* that all he had to do to touch her would be to raise an elbow in a meaningless gesture.

And, two minutes later, the mother lost interest in the movie, her lids leadened with sleep. Her daughter told her to be careful going up the stairs, at which the mother smiled. She, too, passed Heather with tensity, without incident.

Heather relaxed, told herself that she's supposed to be the demon here. But for some reason she wasn't in the mood for haunting, she didn't want to cause a stir. Her victims told her she looked like an angel, and they all screamed when they saw her emerge from the shadows. She must be the ultimate paradox.

Or just a mirror of the world.

For the next few hours, buoyed by the thin but rich blood in her veins, she leaned against the wall, her face a marble carving that should have been visible, even in shadow. For the next few hours, she felt like she was the sister she had always wanted to be. She didn't feel like something bred to strike fear in the hearts of victims from whom she stole precious drops of blood.

But the scariest thing was when the little girl turned on her side, stretched, and rubbed her eyes, then looked directly at the doorway and said, "Oh, are you still here? I though you had to get home before the sun came up."

Hugging the branch of the oak, Heather perched like a carrion bird at the base of a limb of the tree that was in front of the house she'd just hastily retreated from.

Perplexed at how two people could walk *inches* away from her and not notice her standing in the hallway she could understand. It was her doing. She was shadow. But how the little girl could *see* her, when she was hidden in the dark, as shadow no less, that was what confounded her. And it had happened before, on that beautiful first Hallowe'en.

It was the children. The children still believed. That was why she hated stealing the children, they were too fucking easy. They were too goddamned innocent. But the worst of it all, they were never as afraid as any of the grown-ups.

What was there to be afraid of, when you held the belief that vampires did exist?

The fear came when you had lived two, three or four decades and all your illusions were shattered like glass, everything sprayed over the pavement with the glass shards piercing pieces of your shorn brain.

Little bitch. She had eyesight as clear as any vampire's!

But what did Heather run from? Herself? It was all she wanted to be a part of that little grouping, and more so in fact to be a big sister to the little girl. Maybe she ran because the reality of it was scarier than the theory. Maybe she had coagulated into the netherworld she claimed not to have found and by actually slipping back, just for a moment, she felt the change in the environment so acutely that it made her nerves run cold.

It wasn't as though she'd never spoken to a mortal since her turning, but the fact that she'd never spoken to one in an intimate setting without the alcoholic thirst for blood. She'd never spoken to one who had the knowledge, who was on an equal level.

She saw herself moving away from the house, carried on the wind, her mind still light and free.

Through her finger she could still feel the bark of the branch, but the clear breeze of the night engulfed her skin entirely, and when she thought she saw the whole city beneath her, the cross on the top of Mount Royal lit up to guide the way for wayward souls, she closed her eyes.

She listened to the thumping and the rush, to the tap-tap-tap, she smelled the salt and copper, and the wind rushed at her face, over her arms and between her thighs.

Heather opened her murderous maw and a throbbing and vibrant neck slammed up into the sharpened fangs, her arms flailed for the branch and found flesh, and the bittersweet taste of everlasting life cleansed her throat, hands gripping desperately at the backs of her arms and trying to escape. The body was of a young woman and she smelled a blood that was quite different from one she had known, she smelled a water and milk.

And, as Heather looked around, bewildered because the house was nowhere in sight, because the obnoxious pull of *rue Ste-Catherine* was within earshot, she realized that two people had died in her arms tonight, that to close one's eyes and succumb to the instinct of vampirism was to have a basic and feral need for blood.

Blood.

Blood that knew no race or creed or colour. Knew no age, and indiscriminately allowed incurable diseases into the veins of its host. Blood is life and death.

And all it really is, is water. And all the water was the same to her.

Despite tonight's accident, despite the fact that it was indirect, she still wouldn't take children.

She didn't know why, but at the same time, she felt no remorse, and left almost as quickly and discreetly as she arrived.

Talissa, on the other hand, would openly drink from babies, she adored them. She would cradle them, sing to them, play with them and make them laugh. Sometimes she would keep babies for a little while, then she would drink them down and discard them like trash.

And Heather was sure that the rash of kidnappings was because of the very mother of her darkened soul. And who else could it be really? The frequency of the abductions always, always increased when Talissa's presence was absent from Heather's side. The smell of the air indicated that events were coming to a head. That burnt yellow smell as though a tornado were imminent.

She'd seen Korson's papers one night, the ones he kept in his locked drawer. Whatever it was he was working on, he wouldn't tell, secretive bastard. And he rarely left her alone in the house, partly why she left.

Anyway, she ruffled through the file, and there were no notes, just clippings of newspapers and a piece of paper with several addresses on it. Thinking the addresses were of other vampires, and since she was planning to leave, she copied them down, but when she eventually sought out the places, they were nothing but dead ends, though the faint scent of vampires long gone did linger.

But what caught her attention were the newspaper clippings. They were all about missing children, and some of the children had been found dead, a vampire death, though the papers had all sorts of scientific explanations. But it was clear to a vampire that it was a vampire death, one of those instincts. But more so to Heather, there were a lot that had the mark of Talissa on them. The picture of the child that accompanied each one, that was a first hint, a big one. She liked beautiful little children. Maybe that was why Heather was averse to snatching the little darlings from their beds. There was such majic in children and Talissa was trying to steal it. But for what end?

But when she put the clippings together, the relevant ones anyway, the dates fell close to one another, within times that Heather hadn't seen Talissa, which were near eventful days like Christmas, or Valentines, or Hallowe'en. And all in the winter. The ones from the summer, she dismissed. There was some pattern, some regularity to the killings.

And the fact that one of the addresses was around the corner from her didn't come as a shock. It was probably that house that everyone knew stank of shit.

But the connection, other than a binge of blood lust, eluded her.

And she hadn't dared ask Korson, nor bothered to ask Catherine, but she would as soon as she walked home.

Finished her walk, actually. She chided herself openly that she did so much nightseeing, but she never had too many of the peaceful walks she planned to take. Always rocks on the path, but they made for an interesting drink.

North she went, on *ave. du Parc*, letting the cross of Mount Royal guide her way. She thought it would be a great joke to tear down that cross and drag it behind her, through the streets of Montréal, streets that espoused transgression as a way of life, saying, *I'm a creature of blood, and I know some of you are, too. Look at what your drunken ignorance allows to fester in the corners!*

She realized that she'd been buried there, for about two weeks. Just long enough to let her soul die. She remembered the heat and the thirst and the dark and the worms.

For some reason, she never went back there, she never went up the slopes of that mountain, and she found herself standing in front of the statue of the Saint that fronted the parkette at the foot of the mountain.

Why put it there? Why not put it at the top? Must be all down hill from here, eh?

A large drop of rain stung Heather just below her left eye, making her jump. She wiped it away with two fingers, but continued to look at the statue.

It was a strange rain that fell. Big gobs of spit, like the angels were spitting tonight instead of crying. Or was it God who did the spitting?

It must have been God because, because she always forgot, *I'm the angel here, the Angel of-*

Another fat raindrop fell, and struck the eye of the Saint, trickling down the carved and weathered cheek until it fell from the chin.

Heather took a step closer to the statue, to the mountain, and the rain fell quicker and harder, but these were big drops of water, meant to force her back, the womb of nature from which she was born rejecting her, forbidding her from the place that she was born again for the last time.

...keeping her away from...the mountain...

The water trying to cleanse the higher ground of something wretched and unclean, as though it were sick to death of strange creatures and tortured souls traversing the holy ground of Mount Royal.

Hell, she was un-everything, it seemed.

More drops fell, and she realized as they matted down her ponytail that they fell *harder,* not faster, never faster, just with more force and fury.

She loved fury, she lived fury. She wasn't afraid of fury, but something bigger.

And she looked at the eyes of the Saint, and she saw the drops hitting with the fury of God or nature-she didn't know which was stronger-and they, the drops, they kept hitting the same spots under the eyes so that the statue was crying.

Heather looked around, but she was the only one here, not even a car passed at this late an hour. No one to scream revelation, that a Saint would cry when looking out upon the world! Upon the city that was in psychological chaos.

Then she remembered what Talissa had said about chaos, how she'd thrived on it. There was definitely tension in Montréal. There was most certainly life. And conflicts would rise and fall in one form or another; it could be the French/English or the Natives; the cults, the Night Stalker's or *Les Canadiens.*

She looked at the eyes of the statue and was so *certain,* unmistakably positive that those drops were tears, because they started where tears would start, they dripped off the chin like tears would.

Had this happened before somewhere else? It had, in a church in Toronto, tears from a picture of the Virgin hanging on the wall. Did people laugh, did they dismiss it outright as a leaky roof, or a coincidence? Would those same people be so quick to discard such an occurrence if they could see it happening again, see it with their own eyes?

The raindrops were big and fat, but the tears that washed away the years of erosion from the cheeks of the statue were small streaks, like there was an invisible hand wiping them away.

Another step closer, mounting the stone steps past the watchful gaze of the stately lions, and the fury of nature thrummed the ground harder still.

Another step closer to the rusted green copper and she saw that the tears of the statue ran dark red, the eyes were crying blood, and they were crying blood for her.

Blood, milk, and water.

Was nature on her side? Was the water just nature's offering because it had no blood to give? For that matter, she started believing in instinct and nature so much, that she wasn't sure whether or not that nature and God were interchangeable or separate. And she was uncertain as to which one had the power. Or which one was real. And who was to say that is wasn't just some splash of the confusion of humanity, the many facets of faith colliding and splattering in a million different directions and landing in different parts of the world and in different eras and God popping up everywhere in every imaginable form? The isolation of people cutting them off from their brethren and causing everything from distrust to betrayal to war.

She remembered that she had some purpose, she realized that maybe she was the connection, that Korson was the one who was trying to quench the flow of information.

That part of the reason Talissa stayed away was because of Korson's mere presence.

He said how *uninhibited* he'd been once, how he killed with the delicious fury that Heather so loved of herself.

Talissa, Korson and Catherine. A triangle, and Heather was in the middle, and they were all looking in at her but she couldn't look out. But perhaps the children would keep her company? Maybe they could see with their innocent eyes?

She couldn't get anything out of Korson. His mouth was sealed she felt he was her *barrier*, or protection from it. She couldn't bring those children back to life.

But she could start at the top of the triangle, find the Queen Bee, whose sting ingested the sweet nectar of life.

As Heather walked away, back to Catherine, it still rained water, and the statue still bled tears.

And Heather realized what it meant to follow faith.

Catherine was asleep already, and the heat of the sun could be felt only by something that dreaded its scorch. Heather wished that she'd maybe had her glass box now. She drew the shades and turned on the ceiling fan, curled up around Catherine as she felt the burning warmth wash up around her as she went to visit death for several hours.

Ah. Welcome to-

Hell was the sound of constricting and convulsing muscles, a loud wretch from the bathroom. Heather woke. Catherine was no longer beside her.

Another sound of vomit brought Heather to her feet, drawing her to the bathroom with some anxiety.

She saw Catherine on her knees, hunched over the porcelain, her fingers looking bony, gripping the edges and trembling, crystal tears poised on the top of her cheekbones, waiting to fall.

Her whole body stiffened and she made that horrible sound again, something like blood but more mucousy white, like semen, gushing from her throat. She looked at Heather, with those eyes varnished with tears that uttered pain rather than sadness. She took a deep breath, a hope that it was over.

Still, she kept trembling and wouldn't let go of the bowl.

Heather went to the sink and filled a cup with water and said, "Here, drink a little."

Catherine sipped a bit of water. Cooling, soothing.

"How did this happen?" asked Heather.

Catherine's breath was raspy and she took a moment to answer. Her chest heaved in and out with some struggle.

"It happens every year. I guess I traded one cycle for another. I got taken, if youre wondering."

Loathing the after-life, she always had that sentiment, except when she was hungry. She took another little sip of water.

"Every year at about same time?"

"Yes," answered Catherine, "every year. At exactly the same time. Say: 'Happy Birthday, Catherine.'"

Another sip of water.

"Oh...you became a vampire today."

Catherine took another deep breath, said, "Don't worry, I don't think you'll inherit this pattern."

"You feeling okay, yet, Cat?" Heather stroked her neck, her soft dark hair, it was so straight and luxuriant and thick.

Another sip of water.

"Yeah, thanks, I think I'm O-Oh, God-"

That horrible choking noise, that awful spastic motion, her back arching with the muscles so tight that you could see the definitions of each vertebrae, hear them grinding against each other. Catherine had her head bent over to let it all out, it flowed clear and thin, the water coming back up.

"I think I'll go hungry tonight," said Catherine. The vomiting was so painful it brought about more tears on her smooth olive-oil skin. "I shouldn't have fucking drank last night."

Heather helped Catherine collect herself, dressed her as all she was wearing was an orange t-shirt that barely touched the tops of her thighs.

They went downstairs to the lovely array of pillows, Catherine taking a well-deserved flop. Heather got some water, assuming this would be her three squares tonight, as Cat hadn't stopped trembling. Maybe she had a vampire virus?

Heather snuggled next to Catherine, trying to stop her shaking by holding her tight, and it worked a bit. Strange, but she actually seemed cold, and, since vampires were cold-blooded (or no-blooded), they had no problems with feelings of frigidity. It was that dreadful sun, the heat that gave them fits and fevers and made their blood burst in explosive fury.

"So today's really your birthday?" asked Heather.

Catherine nodded to her, she was still fresh with pain. More accustomed to inflicting it, hm, my dear?

Heather turned over her thoughts, trying to recall what it was that she wanted to discuss with Catherine, something that had to do with a few nights ago. Birthday, birthday.

"I was wondering about something," said Heather, her voice tinged with a last drop of childhood innocence that refused to fall. "Do you resent becoming a vampire?" The question hung in the air, the last word echoing as though it wasn't real-vampire-ire-ire-ire.

"You've led too short a life Heather," said Catherine, raspberry voiced, "to understand that we don't really make choices in life, that the events choose us."

Heather said, "I know about karma," but Catherine shook her head.

"It's not a belief in karma. I never chose to be a vampire, and the vampire's never wanted me, either. That's why I throw-up on my birthday, each and every year. And the more blood I consume the day before, the worse it is. I should learn to deny myself, maybe, go hungry for two or three nights. Discipline like that would make me look like a virgin saint."

Heather continued to stroke Catherine's hair.

"The blood hates me tonight." But she spoke the words as though she'd lost a friend. "And it feels like every vampire in the world knows it and they're all wringing my neck and punching me in the stomach. Oh, Christ, I should be dead by now!"

It was a curious thing, disturbing, really, mourning the absence of one's death on the night of one's re-birth. The grandest of all missed appointments, when you missed your demise, because it was always penciled into fate's notebook.

Catherine was done with tears, her fount was dry.

"Do you throw-up because you're sad, or bitter?" asked Heather.

"When you were made into a vampire, were you given the choice? Did you follow the pull, but still receive the option of turning away?"

"Of course," said Heather, "I thought that that's how all vampires did it. The lure. A simple transaction, costing you very little, that sort of thing. That's what my vampire did. It never occurred to me that I had met my maker."

"There was a vampire who loved me dearly, he loved to watch me, perched on a window sill, while I slept, just watching my chest go up and down beneath the covers. Or he'd watch me have dinner with a friend. Because he felt like he was a part of my life. Which is just the reason he didn't want to end it. Maybe he would have, eventually, but for the time being, he just enjoyed watching me, for years he watched me."

Catherine scratched at her nose, continued:

"It all changed when the border moved in, down the hall from my room. He also liked to look at me, to, but looking wasn't nearly enough for him. He wanted to touch, but he wanted to be the only one to touch me.

"My father would leave town on business quite a bit, he was working on projects in Toronto. And the border was referred to by a trusted friend, so we didn't have many apprehensions about a stranger being in the house. He seemed nice enough, to be sure.

"But with my father gone from time to time, and my mother the timid person that she was, he easily crept to my room, and slipped through the black crack in the door, slipped into my bed and into me.

"God, his hand was suffocating over my mouth, I could barely breath with those fingers pulling my cheek and chin together.

"That was when I heard the tap on the widow, saw that figure standing on my sill, the silk curtains majically parting like the window was a stage and I was to admire him, with his hand gripping the frame in anger, those piercing red eyes melting the cold air between us.

"The border left me with the usual warnings, that no one would believe me, that I'd be making a mistake if I tried to tell anyone. All I could do was curl up against my pillow and cry, shaking like I was before, and let my lip bleed."

Heather looked around at all the pillows, picked one up and hugged it.

"A breeze hit my forehead to tell me I was still awake, to tell me that dreams don't feel like this, and a hand pushed away my sweaty hair to tell me that someone was in the room.

"I looked up at him through red and watery eyes, and he loomed over me like a ghost, I thought, because I was lying down.

"And he didn't try to hide the fact that he was a demon. Not like that bastard who lived down the hall, who walked among me and my family like a brother. No, he let the moonlight hit him full, his dark hair absorbing the light, his skin reflecting it with a pallid glow. He let me see his fangs protruding, making those interesting little dents in his lower lip, and he was dressed like a revenant of another age. Dressed like a gentleman.

"I couldn't care less if he killed me then and there. I hated myself. I felt the throbbing in my thighs and I hated myself and wanted to die.

"He looked at me with such a curious and malevolent glare, but I wasn't scared, not of him, anyway. All he did was bend close to me and whisper in my ear: 'The man dies, at your request.' He ran his finger across my reddened lip, took a drop of me down his throat.

"I lay there shaking and didn't answer. It wasn't in my nature to answer ghosts and spirits, and things out of Dickens. I squeezed my eyes, and he was gone, and the window was as it was, except for a flutter of the curtain.

"I dreaded going back to bed the next night, and the expected happened. When my father returned the next day, I couldn't bare to look him in the eye. But it wasn't long before he would leave again, and the dread returned to me, like it was my personal deity.

"Over the course of the week, I thought I noticed the vampire, lurking in the shadow, but when I turned my head, I saw nothing and no one.

"And then my father left again.

"I crawled into bed that night, praying for a miracle. I actually felt better knowing I had a guardian angel, even if he was a devil. But I didn't have the nerve to tell him to act.

"The door cracked open, and in he came. The gargoyle crouched in full view in my window, the air visible as it left his nostrils, the eyes glowing with brimstone. But the border didn't see him, his attentions were turned to me. Or, perhaps, my vampire didn't let himself be seen by anyone other than me. He just crouched there with his elbows on his knees and his hands steepled, the round moon behind his form.

"Lord, how many bruises I got that night. I was a ragged teddy bear, and he was a sick and lecherous boy, ready to pound my stuffing after his desires were satiated. And pound me he did, my eye swelling shut with bruises and blood, my arms and back covered in bruises, and something sick running down thigh.

"But my angel wouldn't let it happen. He was in the room suddenly, he took the man by the throat and held him up with one hand, the man's head hitting the ceiling, my angel standing inches above the floor because he was divine, he walked above the plane of mortal men.

"I would never have let him kill that man, though. I was no killer, I didn't have the stomach for it. My vampire looked at me and said, 'The man dies, at your request,' but the fire in his eyes told me he was going to kill him anyway.

"'Call him off, lady,' said that bastard who raped my soul. He had the nerve to ask for his life after what he had done to me, and all I could see was the fear in his eyes and I thought, 'If he were to die now, his face would be frozen like that. The last thing his mind would know would be the same fear that I felt tonight, that his life was over.'

"I struggled out of bed. I fell to the floor because my legs couldn't support me, but I crawled to the feet of my angel, looked up at my suffering hanging there by the thread that was his neck and his life and said, 'Let this man die, at my request,' and I said it with the callousness of dry skin.

"I kept my eyes on the two as best I could, watched as my vampire angel held the man by the hair and his back and thrust him onto his waiting maw.

"I heard a thump on the floor, a slump of clothes and dead weight, and then I felt cold but caring arms pick me up and put me back to into bed. I hung limp and broken in those arms and I can still remember what that felt like.

"'You would have been a sweet young woman, Catherine,' he said to me, in a voice I felt I could drown in. It felt like I was slipping away. He touched his cold, sharp fingers to my face, my shoulder, and I felt the bruises through *his* hands. I was covered in them.

"That's why she glows purple," thought Heather. "Her body can't forget the bruises."

It's ironic to think that in life a bruised and broken body loses its beauty, whereas the gift of death turns it into something beautiful, alluring. Sensuous, even.

"He wouldn't let me die," continued Catherine. "His eyes had gone from hot and red to cold and grey. He looked as though he was going to cry. I was supposed to die that night, and I still don't know if it would have been from the bruises."

"He didn't let me, of course. He bit into my neck with a reverence and gentleness that I never thought possible, and then he gave me back what he'd taken. You don't steal from those you love. When I awoke the next evening, I saw through those mystical animal eyes that vampires have, I felt stronger than I'd ever felt before. My body had healed and become beautiful again. And this time the beauty would be dangerous to those who would be attracted by it.

"And every year since that day, my body just can't handle the thought of what's happened."

Book 3:

St. Valentine's Inamorata

Part 1: The First Church of the Sab

Bound and determined to find the elusive Sab, Heather told Catherine she was going out for a few drinks downtown. Catherine was content to watch Cumulous fumble with a ball of orange yarn. It was only when she'd reached downtown that Heather thought she may likely not return. Though failure didn't cross her mind, it was a distinct possibility and a buried fear.

As the months wore on and winter graced the rooftops of Montréal with snow no more, Heather began to wonder at the whereabouts of the Sab, and more importantly, the whereabouts of its leader, Talissa. She wondered how it came to be that she was chosen as the love of an eternal's life.

And she was sick with herself of how she avoided confrontations. She was disgusted with her own timidity, at the fact that she was afraid of failure. She knew she could be so much more, but for the fact that she was satisfied with what she had. And fate knew nothing of time! She was now immortal, and fate would wait as long as she!

Not that she didn't believe in purpose, she just didn't believe in higher purpose. She didn't like the fact that Talissa lied to her about the afterlife, but she was content to be her own demon and live by her own terms that she wasn't disappointed with what she'd seen. She lived in the vastness of her own dreams and imagination and it could carry her through the millennia.

Though she was generally introverted and emotional, Heather knew she could play whatever role necessary to strive through the muck of the years and come out clean. Being a woman she could fuck her way out of anything.

She went to *boul. St. Laurent* and Prince Arthur and ordered a glass of water for herself and a plate of garlic bread for show. She waited for the vampires to come out, she knew that the few left loved it here because of all the people. That's why she avoided this place. She didn't want to face their taunting thoughts.

Heather hoped Korson would show up. Just by chance, that they would meet here and he would be by her side for just a little while. But it was unlikely that he would be in the city, unlikelier still that he would come to a place where others of his kind congregate. Korson was quite content being solitary.

Heather thought, 'The night is so beautiful,' as she saw the inky black shadow pass overhead. She wondered what it was, that mysterious cloud that appeared every so often. She wondered if it was like the Taint, if only she could smell it. She sniffed for the Taint and only caught the aroma of garlic.

She decided she would forego drinking tonight, unless something good happened upon her path. Drinking wasn't as much fun for her when she was alone, she'd found.

She scanned the crowd and still found none of her kind. Was it possible that they watched her and avoided her? She'd made no hostile overtones, why wouldn't they make themselves more visible? It was apparent to Heather that Korson and Catherine knew something of the Sab-and perhaps of herself, as well-because they seemingly had compunctions in meeting her face-to-face. Unless...they themselves were a part of the-

"No," she thought. "I can't start thinking that way about my friends." She seemed to be able to find doubt in anything she looked at since Talissa left her. Sometimes against her better intellectual judgment. But Heather was ruled more by her intuition, she had good gut feelings that stemmed from a subconscious expression of her knowledge. There were some things she just knew. And if Korson and Cat were traitors, she would only deal with the betrayals when they arose. And harshly. Assumptions, though, were unnecessary as they only led to unfounded fears.

Heather heard a little giggle. She scanned the crowd, she knew someone was aware of her presence. She saw a pretty little girl in a red dress smiling at her from across the walk.

"It's amazing," she thought, "what the children can see." She smiled back at the girl, trying to pretend she was human again. The girl made claws out of her hands and growled and laughed before disappearing into the crowd again. Heather spotted the girl looking back through a crowd of people and laughing. Then the crowd became too thick to see through the cracks. There was just no fooling some. Children were the real monsters.

Heather was thankful that she hadn't smelt the Taint in a while, and glad she didn't catch it's scent now. She thought the Taint might be the stench of the vampires of the Sab, but she wondered what it was that separated them from ordinary vampires.

A few of which she just spotted now. She tried to watch them without looking. She tried to be as elusive and nonexistent as the Sab she was chasing. In her year or so as a vampire, she had never approached one of her own kind. They had always approached her. Heather had no idea how to make herself known. It could be as simple as slowly approaching the table they had seated themselves at. But she wasn't sure if her radiance would give her away as soon as she stood up. For now, she thought it best to remain where she was, to retain her inconspicuosness.

But to sit here and do nothing? To watch and wonder why no one else noticed their terrible fangs and fearsome smiles as they sat there laughing? Were they laughing at her, at the world, at the expression on someone's face that they just killed?

To sit here and do nothing was to let everything continue to be the same. She got up, started walking towards them. Was that the giggle of the little girl she heard? Or was it her own imagination come to haunt her?

She left money on the table, more than enough. Then she moved slowly through the crowd. Heather looked at the inky blackness that hovered overhead.

"*I am shadow,*" she said. She felt herself darken, her beautiful aura dimming, her essence becoming part of a different world. She was at the table, now. They didn't even notice her. She remained in shadow and said, "Hi!" a look of insolence on her face.

The three vampires looked blankly at her. Maybe they were a little angry underneath. They were definitely caught off guard.

"If any of you move, I'll enshroud you in shadow." Heather remembered Korson saying how dangerous it was to play with shadows. "You three are the only ones who can see me." Maybe she could scare them a little. She pulled out the chair and sat down. "I just want to talk."

The man spoke: "What makes you think we have anything to say." His voice was flat.

"Because last time I was here, you all avoided me. You taunted me. But I know something you don't."

"Don't lie to us!" broke in one of the women.

"You can't trick us into telling you anything," said the other. "You're not so insidious as you think."

Heather said, "I'm not lying. There were others here that night. The Sab was here and none of you even knew."

"And how is it that you knew?" said the man. They all seemed to try to hide the touch of shock on their faces.

"Because I can smell them. I'm the only one who can. There's no stopping them this time. They could be all around you and you wouldn't even know it. I hear things too. I hear voices from vampires that you thought've turned their backs on you."

"If you know all this," said the man, "then what is it you need from us?" The two women had malice building in their eyes.

Heather thought for a moment. "I want you to tell me where to find the vampire Talissa. So I can kill her. So this madness will end. So the demons can be themselves again."

The woman said, "What makes you think you're of any importance?"

"Maybe you're just bitter because you've been left to eternity by yourself," said the other woman.

"I'm not bitter," said Heather. "I just want to resolve myself. My identity. I know that I have some significance because you've all avoided me. You're scared of me."

The vampires burst out in laughter, they slapped their hands on the table.

One of the women said, "Us? Scared of you? You're silly. Don't be silly!" And she wagged her finger at Heather.

"Quiet," said Heather, but none of them heard. "Be quiet," she said again. They laughed through her. She waited for them to calm down. It seemed that their laughter was like an infection, that once it was scratched the itch lingered and had to be scratched again. Maybe laughter was rare in the afterlife and they took every opportunity they could? Their laughter died suddenly and they looked back to Heather. The vampires thought perhaps she looked shameful.

One of the women vampires began to rise up out of her seat, into the air. The shadow had consumed the table, rose like smoke from a raging flame. They couldn't be seen. Nor could they escape. The man tried, he ran through the shadow and when he came out he was back where he started. The female vampire was lying prone, as though she were on an operating table. The only movements she could make were jittery little movements, shakes and such, but she couldn't break free of the hold that kept her afloat. Against her will her hands were spread and claws bared. Her top was ripped open and hung from her like torn curtains. Her clawed hands constricted and the nails dug into the flesh at the base of her neck, they dragged the dead skin down, tearing her breasts and her stomach open. She tried to hold a scream in her throat but it wouldn't come out anyway, it bled out the wounds at her neck. Her claws began tearing tracks between her legs, the blood dripped down on the table as though the woman was urinating uncontrollably. Heather never thought she would see another vampire cry.

The man said, "Enough! Stop it."

"I don't think you're truly scared of me," said Heather.

"Please. We'll tell you what you want to know. You have scarred her for an eternity."

The woman stopped eviscerating herself.

"Some scars run deeper than flesh," said Heather. She ensconced the woman in shadow. Maybe she could find solace in darkness. More likely she would only find further fears when she looked into the black of her mind. "Sit."

The man returned to his seat. He offered no information, he still waited for Heather to ask of him the knowledge, just like a vampire, sucking and waiting to be sucked.

"I want you to tell me the purpose of the Sab."

"They are a cult. They think our kind better than man, that we should be in the light. They want to make man subservient so they can rule."

"And what would the leader of the Sab want with me? Why would I be chosen as the object of affection?"

"I don't know."

Heather fixed her gaze on his hollow eyes. She looked so deep into him for a moment that he felt her stare burn like the noon sun. "You're lying. I can tell when someone's lying."

The man thought of his friend hovering in the shadow. "I...I cannot say. I would grieve for my friend if you murder her. But I cannot say."

"Why not?"

"I took a blood oath."

Heather looked up at the shadow with the girl in it. She thought for a second to make her scream, just to be mean, but decided against it.

The man said, "If I were to say anything, the others would know. I cannot break my oath."

Heather thought about Korson and Catherine. How they'd told her little or nothing. She knew that they'd taken the oath. That they were bound by blood to keep their silence, that even their love for her couldn't break the blood. The powerful blood magic.

"Then tell me without telling. Tell me a story. Tell me of vampire lore."

"You ask for my life."

"No. I ask for a bedtime story about vampires. It's been so long since someone's told me a bedtime story. I'm still a bit of a child, and the children know everything, right?"

The man sighed and put his grey hand to his forehead.

Heather asked, "How many took the oath?"

"Everyone," he answered. "It was after the Great Purge. There weren't too many left anyway."

"So tell me of vampire lore. If you break the oath then I can protect you in shadow." Unless, of course, that is where he was to be cast to Hell.

"It has been said, perhaps since the time of Christ, that one would come. And she would be female. But the legends have been so twisted, the purpose has been lost. Confused, but why or from where I do not know. Some say she is the savior. Some say a demon that will plunge us further into darkness. Some say she will let us live in the light again." Heather thought of her blond glow, like sunflowers.

"Our history is unrecorded. Vampires don't write anything down. If there is a vampire who has all the knowledge from the beginning of time, then that knowledge would die with the vampire. The risk of it falling into mortal hands is too great. The world already has enough demons without their power being augmented by unholy blood. I can say no more."

"Have you broken your oath?" asked Heather.

The man laughed, said, "I'm still here, aren't I? I haven't burst into flames, have I? If someone heard something, I may be sought after. But who knows?"

"I think I'm the one. The One Who was Foretold. But I'm not sure how to take that journey, or even if I want to."

"All I can offer you by way of advice is to look to yourself. If you are the Foretold as you believe, then the journey may be as much inside your mind as literal. Ask yourself why you think it is you."

"I don't know, I just think its me."

"There must be something within yourself that tells you this. But you are right. If you think you can make the journey, then you shouldn't put it off any longer. These things tend to become...haunting." The man stood, and the woman joined him by his side. Heather released the other woman from the shadow and she floated into the arms of her counterpart. "There is nowhere to run. Go where your feet take you and do not shun the darkness." He gestured to the shadow. "Darkness does not always equate evil. My name is Paul. If...when everything breaks, when light is upon the truth, I am at your service." He kissed his fingers and said another word, a bare whisper. *Did he just say...Goddess?* thought Heather.

"Will you make it out of here okay?"

"Yes," said the man. "I'll use a remnant to make her look as she was before. We'll be thought of as drunk fools. Good luck to you, for all our sakes."

The veil of shadow dispersed. The vampires left.

Notice of Heather was garnished from other vampires, and she in turn gave small acknowledgment to their existence. She left Prince Arthur without making contact with them. They were not of the Sab, they didn't challenge her and they were likely under the blood oath that left her utterly alone.

But she did take comfort in the fact that the oath left her isolated. No one would fuck her but herself. She could look on everyone as an enemy. And that's about as safe as life gets. Sometimes, because of your own limitations, you can't even trust yourself.

The difficult way of stemming the tide of the Sab would be to seek out each and every member and crush them one-by-one. She'd scented them numerous times and knew where they were likely to be. No guarantees, but it was a start. She wanted to see the Taint for what it was.

Easier still would be for her to find Talissa and go fang-to-fang with her once and for all; for her twisted cause, for her lies and for her betrayal. Heather could almost care less about what Talissa's loftier goals were. But she didn't have to fuck Heather off in the process, when all Heather did was care for her and be her companion. Chilled revenge was the sweetest dish. And the fire of quiet little Heather's vengeance would make Hell seem Arctic. She wasn't one to be crossed.

She would like to pull the Sab up by the roots. But she would have to stick with what she knew. She went to *rue Ste-Catherine*, where many of the events of her afterlife took place. She absolutely loved it here. She would not trade Montréal for the world. No one in their right mind would.

The voices in her head had been fairly quiet lately. And Heather had hardly tried to talk back to whomever it was that tried to haunt her. She thought of calling Talisssa this way, of maybe drawing her near. But she wanted to go in on her own terms. And she always wondered if there was one who would fight the Sab from within their own ranks. The thought went quietly from her head and to the places she had scented *Sabitants*.

And the Taint drifted in on the air. She was at *rue University* now. She went down the road to the darkened alley, slowly, following the Taint but not chasing it. After all, she was shadow and shadows never chased.

Heather looked up at the sky and saw the black ink spilling out of the clouds. She wondered if the shadow was angry at her because she was using it. She wondered why it was dangerous to play with the shadow.

The alley was familiar to her. There was a forlorn derelict sitting in the darkened recess of the street, he lay there as though he were thrown down like a child's forgotten toy. He wore a drab long coat that was brown, but it looked as though it were brown from the filth he lay in night after night. He wore a toque to keep away the chill of the night and he hid his face behind a raised collar.

Heather felt pity for him. She wanted to kill him. She wondered what death would bring to one who was no more than a log in the street. She wondered if he would be a God in the darkness, if he would thank her for letting his miserable existence end.

But the faint odor of the Taint drifted up to her, and it came from him. Had he been beaten and broken in life and as a vampire as well? Did the Sab make its own sit in filth as initiation to the rites of the evil empire?

Heather approached the broken vampire.

Look at me, she said in his head. The vampire looked up. His eyes were devoid of life. He saw Heather and he hid his face, he cowered against the wall. Heather was afraid he might flee, but he merely cowered. He told her to go away. And in his voice Heather heard why this alley was familiar. It was the sight of her first kill. She was crouching over the puppy-beater. Talissa had converted him into one of her own.

"I've seen such terrible things," he said. "She shows me such terrible things." He was shaking and he kept hiding his face. Heather could only see his lifeless eyes. She didn't want to kill him anymore. She wanted to let him live like this. He wasn't much of a warrior.

There were several half-dead bodies in the alcove behind him. They were hidden so people who walked by wouldn't think them anything but bums if they saw the strewn shapes. The puppy-beater pulled something out of his pocket and chewed on it. It looked like taffy, but it was really a piece of flesh from the thigh of a Chinaman.

Heather listened to his thoughts. He was selfish, cruel, pathetic. He had refused the Sab his soul and they tormented him with the brilliance of Hell, its fabulous images splashed red with hot blood and sadistic spikes of bone. He would be tormented forever but he still resigned himself to eating filthy taffy in a darkened alley. Heather asked where she should look for the Sab and he said that they were everywhere. His world was small. But still, they were coming out again. They would be everywhere.

She left him. He was an exception. The other members of the order would not be so meek. They would be fearsome! But she would remember his hollow eyes and their bloody glow. The pupils were slits like cat's eyes and they were an icteric yellow.

As Heather walked down *rue St. Catherine*, she noticed those eyes peeking from alleys and sidestreets. They seemed to sense that Heather was going to challenge them tonight. They sensed that she was going towards where she thought Talissa would be.

(Heather...)

And she realized for the first time that she could have wasted an eternity waiting for the Sab to find her. That they would have haunted her for so long, like they did to the puppy-beater. And prophets and Goddesses never had their destinies chase them. They always had to seek them out. And they always did. If she didn't seek out her destiny then perhaps another would take the grail. And perhaps no one would ever remember what Heather Langden went through because demons didn't write anything down. They let history turn to dust under the fist of time.

But if time consumed all, what did it do to someone immortal like Heather? Did they just walk into the shadow, forgotten? Was there something beyond vampirism and its lust for syrupy blood and drunken power? Did they live so long that they reached the end of time just to start all over again?

(Heather? What are you afraid of?)

The voices were in her head again. She thought it was Talissa talking to her, trying to haunt her. But when the voice was in her head it echoed in her skull and sounded so loud and like there were so many people trying to pull her. It scratched down her spine and made her ears ring and her eyes tear. No matter how hard she tried, it always made her scared. And she could feel the demons of the Sab gathering behind her. She wondered if the hid themselves in the shadow the way she did.

(It doesn't have to be difficult, Heather.)

Heather looked behind her and could pick off the demons in the crowd. She saw them closing in. She didn't want to fight a losing battle. She wanted to finish Talissa. She picked up her pace. The demons were closing in beside her now too. She started to run, she thought she'd run to where Talissa may be. She'd be finished if she couldn't find her. These monsters would overwhelm her. She hoped these demons weren't in her head. She could *never* escaped them if they were in her head.

She tore down *rue Ste-Catherine*, the flashing lights becoming streaks of colour, the laughter of the demons of the Sab sounding like a sadistic clown who scared children from behind balloons.

She ran until she reached *rue Bishop* and she stopped to look behind her, to see if they were following. It's been a while since she felt like she had to catch her breath and she wondered if it was from running or from fear.

A voice whispered, "Hey!" from the shadows. Heather turned her attention to the voice but couldn't find where it came from. She saw the specter of an old church loom up in front of her and it didn't make her feel any safer.

"Hey!" said the voice again. Heather found the speaker now. It was the little girl in the red dress. It looked as though it was the same one at Prince Arthur but something was different. She looked a little younger. The same but younger. The girl motioned for Heather to come away from the street, she said, "Come on," urgently but she still had her gigglish smile the whole time.

Heather moved closer. When she reached the girl she asked her, "You can see me?"

"Of course, stupid, I'm a kid!"

"You're not afraid of me?"

"No. I want to be a vampire when I grow up. I love vampires!"

Heather looked tentatively back to the sidewalk. She neither saw nor smelt the aroma of the Taint. She turned back and the girl laughed.

"You're pretty! I want to look like you when I grow up."

"Why are you trying to grow up so fast?"

The little girl's lower lip fattened as she pouted. She bent her head down and her eyes watered.

"The monster keeps coming to get me. I'm scared of the monster."

"Which monster?"

The girl shook her head. "I can't say. If I say his name he might come and get me again. It's part of the majic." She seemed sad, her smile had faded like the colours in a sun bleached drawing on the refrigerator door. Heather took pity on the poor child, she wanted to cheer her up.

"You know what monster I like?" The girl shook her head no. "The Cookie Monster!" said Heather as she tickled the girl's tummy.

"He's my favourite, too. Gookie, gookie, gookie!" The innocence of childhood was astounding to Heather. They could see all the monsters of the shadows yet still giggle despite that. All they needed for protection was a blanket and a nite-lite.

The girl stopped. "They're coming!"

"Who?"

"The monsters, silly. You'll be safe in here." She opened the side door of the church that was hidden in the darkness.

"What about you?" asked Heather.

"I'll be okay. My monster won't let me get hurt. I'll grow up to be as pretty as you...maybe." She ushered Heather in and let the door creak closed. Heather slipped inside, putting her faith not in the hands of the church but with the pretty little girl in the red dress.

The little girl went out to the street. The demons of the Sab caught her scent and they followed her as she led them away from Heather. She called on her monster, the shadow-demon Magog, and he came and snatched her away-like a lost toy.

Heather entered the church and was bathed in a soft honey brown glow from the candles. She realized she'd never been in a church for some reason. She had no fear of religion, but she did wonder in the black of her mind about God.

Gods, more specifically. She wondered if Gods roamed the earth. And she wondered if some of the voices that spoke in her head were the voices of earthly Gods telling her what to do. She wondered if the Gods took the blood oath. She wondered what the blood of a God would taste like.

Heather figured she was safe, that the Sab would have ritualistic doctrines that made them afraid of churches and sacred articles. Or maybe the little girl was her only hope. It was strange that she trusted the little girl of all people. Sometimes Heather felt as though she put too much faith in others, that she should look to her own strength for guidance. That she should have turned and stood up to the Sab by herself. But sometimes you have to put your faith in others and hope you weren't blind to their intentions. How could a child's intentions be anything but innocent? And sometimes you just got fucked.

The church smelled of citrus from the waxed floor, the wood was glazed to a shine that made it seem unreal. Heather ran her finger over the slick surface of a pew. She wondered if she should stay here till sunup or continue her search. The Sab could have devoured the girl and been waiting outside by now. She didn't really believe the girl had a monster who could save her. But then, she herself was a monster. And the girl could see her.

Heather stopped short when she heard ticking footsteps outside. The big wooden door at the front of the church opened, a little noisily in the dead night. The sounds of the street rushed in only for a moment. A young looking man entered and the door banged closed behind him, and silence took hold again, but for his steps on the floor.

He looked young, but his face was a bit wrinkled. His soul was tired. He could be young or old. He approached the pews to choose from one of the empty seats and smiled at Heather when he noticed her there.

She didn't want to be seen. She called the shadows to her, they rushed from the corners to her aid, the light blue-grey and the preternatural scream, the statues moving and the saints in tears. Heather opened her eyes. She thought she felt herself falling. She saw the man standing over her. He kept saying something to her but she wasn't listening, she looked around her for the shadow. Why wasn't the shadow around her?

The man asked if she was okay. Heather drew him close.

"Leave," she said in his ear. "There are demons in this church." The man pulled away and he looked into Heather's eyes. Heather thought he might have been able to see something in her eyes and she smiled her fanged smile. He knew but he was disbelieving despite the evidence before his eyes and it made Heather laugh. It was scarier when you come face-to-face with your demons and they laugh at you. The man dropped his liquor flask on the floor and walked quickly out of the church keeping one eye on the fallen demon. He would spend the rest of his life wondering if what he saw was because he was drunk or because it was real.

Heather got up and stretched the kinks out of her back. The church was empty again. The shadows back in their corners and the statues quiet and still. Her head felt dizzy from the sights in the shadow and the fall. Korson always told her it was dangerous to use the shadow. She'd been controlling it a lot lately. And nothing had happened to her till now. But to leave the church in secrecy meant to leave by the shadow. She had to call upon it once more. This time she would be ready.

They flitted out of the corner like a shoal of bats. She called them more slowly this time. This time they clung to her like the inky blackness in her bedroom. The shadows swirled in slowly like living clouds gathering to storm. Then everything changed. The light was pale grey again, and the statue at the altar let out a moan. The smell became thick and smoky. There were worshippers lying on the ground in supplication and all you could see were their backs and the black rags for clothes, puddles of tears at their knees.

The voices were here. Heather thought that the statue at the alter looked like Munch's Madonna in full orgasm. When the church was engulfed in shadow, when you were on the other side of the mirror, it was the Church of the Sab. That terrible secret netherworld was in the shadow. But Heather felt there was more.

"The shadow is alive," she said to herself. Heather thrust the shadow away. The church returned to normal, except...except...

The roiling black fog creeping under the pews, covering the floor. Heather had brought the shadow back with her. It was alive and creeping in from all sides like the Sab. And Heather was not of the Sab. She didn't know how to worship the shadow, to be subservient to it.

Sssssssssssssssssss!

She saw the shadow well up and gain form on the alter, the mists like an enormous cape. The figure looked like a man and he had his back to her.

Heather looked at the monstrosity before her and said, "My God."

No. It's Magog. But you are not the first to make that mistake. Magog idly stepped around the alter. He seemed to peruse the church, as though he wasn't used to seeing it in this light. **You've been a very naughty little vampire, Heather.**

"What are you?" asked Heather.

I'm a shadow-demon. And I know you've been told not to play with shadows.

Mists swirled and licks of them nipped at Heather's calves. She heard high-pitched giggling. The mites weren't far behind Magog in entering this world.

"I had to get out of here without being seen. I was going to surround myself in shadow."

Am I your supplicant?

Heather didn't grasp the importance in Magog's tone when he asked this question. "What do you mean?"

Do I serve you! He lashed a black, smoky hand in her direction.

Heather didn't jump when the demon directed his anger at her. She wanted to figure a quiet way out of this but could see none so she said, "Yes, I control darkness. I control the shadow." She thought Magog would laugh and castigate her with demonic ferocity but only silence hung in the air. Shadow roiled along the floor and the church was covered in it now. Worlds were colliding.

And why do you dare?

Heather didn't want to play cat-and-mouse with him. A creature like him was probably adept with his tongue and Heather didn't want to lose the advantage she felt she had.

"Show me your face, Magog."

Why would you want to see my face? You can't even look into the shadow without falling over!

"You're what I wanted to see all along. Now I've found the other world. I want to see your real face."

Would you dare to go into the shadow?

"Yes! I would dare!" Heather felt her heart beat for the first time in over a year.

Careful, said Magog. **You may not like what you see in there. You may not want the choices you have to make.**

"I'll see what I want to see. Isn't that the trick? Don't we all create our own realities?"

Perhaps...I may not be the only voice you hear. The licks of shadow began to coil around Heather's legs and arms. She felt something she never thought could happen: the mists of the shadow-demon Magog penetrating her to the very core and entering every orifice in her body. It seeped into her ears and she felt the mist twisting in the coils of flesh that brought sound to her mind; she squeezed her mouth shut and it still found space in the cracks between her lips to worm it's way in and fill her throat; it filled her nose and clogged it so tight she couldn't scent danger on the wind. Heather got a little scared when she thought of the inky blackness in her room and how she had trouble finding her way out. She wondered if she would find her way of the bowels of Magog. She got a little scared when she realized the inky blackness in her room may have been a piece of Magog himself.

The shadow sealed her eyes and the last thing she saw was the church of Christ transformed into the Church of the Sab. As she entered the world of demons and darkness, they now had access to the world of the living.

Part 2: Ghosts and Zombies

"I'm s-scared, Jerome."

The rudest, most intrusive-albeit petty-thing in the world was being woken up by the ringing of the telephone. So it was with no little annoyance that Jerome lifted the receiver while trying to gather some semblance of perception. Whatever words tried to come out of his mouth were barely audible, hoarse noises. Until he realized who it was.

"C'mon, Clyde, it's just a bad dream. Go back to sleep."

"N-no, I can't! E-everything's b-b-b-bl-" And Jerome knew that something was wrong because Clyde couldn't spit the word out.

"Black?"

"Yes."

"Your apartment isn't on fire, is it?!" yelled Jerome.

"N-no, not th-that k-kind of b-black, e-e-everything i-is-" Clyde's speech impediment had worsened so much so that each sentence was a trial to speak. "I'm s-scared, Jerome." It became all he could say.

Jerome said, "Clyde, listen. Do you want to come here for a bit?" Clyde agreed. Jerome checked the time. Shit. Almost four a.m. "I guess you might as well leave now if you want."

"N-no. T-tomorrow n-night."

"Okay. Just gimme a call."

Jerome went back to sleep. Clyde sat up against the wall, shaking, unable to move, sweat breaking out on his brow, watching the oily dark mass hover on the other side of his room across from his bed.

Shit, thought Jerome, *phone rings at four a.m. and I'm asleep...I'm getting old.* Jerome got up and took a shower, trying to wake himself. He'd been working long hours at the deli because someone had quit and it seemed to take its toll. He'd been out of touch with most everyone he knew, other than, of course, the friends who stopped by late at night to take him out to party. Picked up the phone and called Graham.

"So how's he been lately?" It was Julia, Graham's wife.

"Working. They've got him on something big down at the station. He's gone all night and then he's either asleep or goes out. I don't think we've said more than two words to each other in over a week."

"Yes, but how has he *been*?" Silent moment from the other end of the line.

"I don't think he's too well, to be honest. But if I even try to bring it up he shoots me this look..."

"Kinda like 'there's nothin wrong so shut up about it' look?"

"I wish. Worse than that. Almost like I've betrayed him."

"I think you may be reading too much into it. He's probably just stressed out." He hung up with a message for Graham to call him.

As he was getting ready, Jerome thought about his brother. He really didn't believe what he told Julia about Graham being stressed out. Just sort of said it to put her mind at ease. He could tell from the few recent conversations with his brother that something had changed. He had different look in his eyes and who wouldn't when you knew that not one soul in the entire world believed you? But it had been years since his breakdown and Jerome had to wonder why things suddenly changed. Wondered if he began to see demons again. They were close, but this was one thing that Graham didn't confide to his brother with.

Jerome had a full day ahead of him. He checked in at the deli and put a few hours in because it was busy. Thankfully there were enough people to cover for the rest of the evening and he had a well-deserved night off. Clyde was coming in so he kept checking his messages at home via cellular phone, he had to meet with suppliers because of a problem with a previous order and wanted to hook up with his brother at the police station.

There was some question as to his whereabouts. He hadn't made an appearance at work for two nights, he was hardly at home and his wife was worried because he seemed to be slipping back to his former psychosis. It was obvious to Jerome that something was wrong and he made a resolution to show a solid, grounded foundation when he came upon his brother. He was shrugging off work, his marriage, his family and it would do no good for him to be aimless in his path. He needed to be focused and if that meant Jerome had to constantly be around him then so be it. Anything to hold him to the ground.

The question did beg, though, at Jerome's mind: Should I just tell him I believe him? Had his brother been carrying this thing around with him for years and years until it finally dug a hole in his soul and it snapped him in two? Jerome's problem with that was that he didn't want his aid to be false; he wanted it to be deep and true. He wanted to bring Graham out of this in such a way that he wouldn't fall back. Which seemed to be what was happening. Psychiatry, it was, Jerome believed, that sat there weekly telling him what he wanted to hear so he was layered with a false sense of pride like sweet icing covering a tasteless piece of cake, that was the problem. If the hard truth was a punch in the gut then maybe that was what Graham needed to wake him up.

He tried Julia again, but nobody was home, so he left a message on the machine. Clyde was coming into Dorval pretty late and when Jerome stepped into his buddy Mario's Jetta, Mario could tell that Jerome wasnt his usual jovial, outgoing party-animal self.

"Hey, Jer, what's wit you?"

"Nothin's 'wit me,' what's your problem?"

"Hey, Saint C, chill, I just figured we'd have some fun."

Jerome said, "Yeah, it's just my bro, I'm kinda freaked abut him."

"He's a big boy, he can take care of himself. Take your mind off it tonight. Where you want to head?"

They drove around for a bit and decided on the *Casino de Montréal*. There were no one-armed bandits for Jerome, he liked to play the high roller. They hit the craps tables first and Jerome pulled in a three-hundred dollar profit. He met up with Mario at the poker tables and caught his pal in the middle of a showdown that lasted about a half hour. He had nearly a grand on the line, and he had to stare down a nerdy little fellow in a high-priced suit. A guy who you wouldn't think could bluff his way out of paying for a stick of gum, but as it turned out Mario lost because his resolve wasn't up to the task. The guy kept pushing the ante up and as it turned out the only thing he held was a really big wallet. There were really no cards of consequence in the guy's hand. He just had a lot of money that he was willing to lose. So Mario folded because the guy seemed so sure of his hand. Out nearly a grand and he was ready to call it a night. He wasn't used to losing.

Jerome was up, though, and he convinced Mario to stay a bit.

"I can't believe I let a shit like that bluff me," he said.

"Hey he had the cash to back up his words."

"Not the cards, though."

"That's why I play my own game, not his. He got all flashy with his cashy and you got bedazzled!" Jerome laughed and slapped Mario's shoulder.

They settled at the blackjack table and Jerome almost played a hand till he noticed the guy at the other end of the table.

"Mutherfucker...Hey! Graham!" he called and walked over to his brother. "What the hell you doin'?"

"Playing blackjack," answered Graham. He looked somewhat a wreck, unshaven and clothes a bit ragged and dirty. He rested his head on a hand as though he hadn't the strength to hold it up by his neck.

"No! I mean you haven't been home or at work in a few days. What the hell you doin' here?"

"Trying to win at cards."

The dealer said, "He isn't doing a very good job. He doubled down when I had an ace, and hit showing eighteen."

"Obviously the mark of a madman," said Jerome. He began to gather up his brother from the table.

"No! I know the cards! I can tell the next card. There's a way..."

They drew the attention of some of the security guards, and Mario stepped in to help Jerome drag Graham out before the burly security guards sniffed blood. He put up a struggle but he was too weak to be more than a nuisance as they tossed him into the back seat.

Graham said, "Fuck, I was going to win, you bastards!"

"Yeah, how much you in the hole for?"

"...almost three grand..."

"Sounds like a king to me," said Mario.

"Just drive. Let's get him home." Jerome pulled out his cell and called Graham's house, hoping Julia was there by now. He told her that he'd found Graham and was bringing him home.

The drive was short and they pulled into Graham's driveway as Julia came out to meet them. Graham seemed somewhat catatonic and shook slightly as the two men carried him up to his room.

"I think he's drunk as hell," said Mario. He then respectfully retreated to the car to wait for Jerome.

Julia said, "Seems your friend is right." Jerome just nodded. "I called him in sick to work. I'm not sure what to do now."

"Keep him here, obviously. I gotta run home and get my car to pick up a friend from Dorval." Julia hugged Jerome before he had a chance to move. He held her as she began to cry a little bit, from uncertainty, from worry.

"I just don't know what to do about him," she said as she sniffled. "It's been so many years and he's never really been the man I married. I can't, I just don't, it isn't fair that-"

Jerome shushed her. He felt the beginnings of a confession coming on and didn't want to hear it. He didn't want to have to compromise his allegiance to his brother because his sister-in-law saw fit to confide a personal secret to him. He just said, "Look, everything seems bad now. You're upset, it's dark out, no one's in a state to accomplish anything. Go relax, have some tea or hot chocolate, get some rest and let everything settle down so you can think. There's no rush. I'll be by tomorrow as early as I can and I can talk to him, too."

Julia thanked him and she kissed his dark and sweaty cheek. He went to the car, waved bye, the car speeding him away as she closed the door to the receding room. She stood in the entryway to her home, unsure of what she should do. She couldn't sleep, not with what had been happening to her marriage, not with her husband up there; not with this wicked chill penetrating, making her shake a little. She decided to take Jerome's advice, make some hot chocolate. He always had his wits about him, he never seemed rattled by anything.

She got a small pot out and put it on a low heat. She made hot chocolate the old fashioned way, heated the milk and used cocoa and sweetened with sugar. Her mother had always made it this way and it tasted so much more real that way, and now it was as much the memory of it as the actual drink that warmed her.

Julia set the timer and sat on the couch anticipating the chocolate drink, knowing that it was a taste that would at least relax her and help her sleep if not make her feel better all together. She felt a little guilty that she was indulging at this time. The only thing she could do, though, was listen to Jerome. She felt as though she would faint if she tried to follow her own mind.

Julia St. Croix, born Julia Burton, in *ville St. Laurent*, north shore Montréal, sat in her house and wondered why she deserved this. She'd been raised in a perfect lifestyle. Her childhood was filled with happiness, she never wanted for anything, and, when she was twenty-one, on the verge of graduating from *Université de Montréal*, she bumped into a law student named Graham St. Croix. Handsome, educated, funny, it seemed as though her life would continue on the same perfect course she'd been raised to believe was proper. Her family had never been subject to the many ills that plagued dysfunctional families-bitterness, anger, depression, violence.

She'd met Graham in the cafeteria line-up and after he'd said two words to her she was so nervous she'd spilt her drink all over her tray. They'd got to talking after the mess was cleaned up and soon would end up in a romance that was rather more appropriate but had enough excitement in it to sweep the young journalism student off her feet.

Julia had simple but pretty features, blond hair that was dead straight and a lively smile. She'd harboured a small fear that she wasn't good enough for Graham, but her mother pushed her into marriage, and, despite her inexperience with relationships, her naiveté about the world, everything felt right and she married him. Shunning the whirlwind pace of the news department, she freelanced her special interest articles with magazines until she landed a permanent position with the Montréal Gazette as an entertainment and lifestyle writer. The only skeleton in her closet was the time she recently went out with a fellow co-worker-one who'd had an obvious affection for her-to check out a new club on opening night in downtown Montréal. They'd gotten caught up in the atmosphere and drink, and he ended up kissing her on the dance floor, much to her shock. She'd never told Graham for fear he would overreact, and wondered if he may have known just by looking into her eyes.

The buzzer dinged and she went to the kitchen and poured some hot chocolate from the pot into a mug. Went back to the couch and sat there, feeling the warmth in her hands. Everything was quiet and she wasn't sure if she was glad for that. It felt like the events had frozen time. At least if it was daytime, noisy, the city active, cars whooshing by and honking, she wouldn't have felt so isolated. It used to be her husband would be the one to be by her side in a crisis. Not that she'd experienced many crises.

As she sipped at her drink a gentle murmur touched her ears. It actually relaxed her for a moment until she realized it was coming from upstairs. Sounded like...voices? She listened for a moment.

Voices. What else could it be? She put down her drink and slowly and quietly climbed the steps. It was dark and she only put the light on in the living room, so her ascent was on a darkened stairwell. But she could see enough from the light behind her to move in the shadow. It felt like forever to get to the top but when she did she put her ear to the door and listened for a moment. Voices...a conversation. Graham was speaking to himself. She thought it had happened once before, when her husband had been delusional and spoke of demons. She never mentioned it because she was unsure at the time, but this was confirmation of the previous facts, as well as an obvious symptom of his returning psychosis.

She thought for a moment. She was no psychiatrist. No good at dealing with this kind of stuff. Just leave it alone and tell his therapist when they saw her. Let him work through the night himself. Julia stopped again. This wasn't her husband behind that door. Whoever it was, the real Graham was somewhere in there, buried behind the heavy chest of that stranger, and she was deserting him. Being unsympathetic to his situation. Maybe that was the root of the problem? The fact that he carried this...thing all alone inside of him. There'd been a severing of the bond between them since that time and that was when he'd never been the same. Began to act all isolated and bitterly contemplative. In order for him to get better he would need someone and she had to be there.

Julia opened the door slowly and the first few steps she took into her bedroom were with her head down. She expected to see her husband lying on the bed and talking in his sleep, or sitting on the edge of it talking to himself, in a reserved state with a nervous demeanor about him. She didn't expect to see him standing on the bed, his shirt ripped off and strewn of the edge of the bed, his neck in similar tatters and blood all over his hands.

Julia put her hands to her mouth and yelled, "Oh my God!" She wanted to burst into tears but it was her husband standing there, crazed and insane and bloody by his own hand, yelling.

"Tell me you don't see him. He's standing right there! Fucking believe me now!"

She ran to the bathroom and got wet washcloths and gauze. Kept thinking, "Thank God he didn't go for his gun." He was surprisingly compliant when she pulled him down off his feet. Wiped at his wounds and was thankful they weren't deep. Just bled a lot. She gauzed up his neck. He was breathing okay and she held him, despite the blood on the white sheets, the sick feeling of his skin, she held him and he shook and she kept telling him everything would be okay and he seemed to calm down in her arms. She was right. He just needed to be held in familiar arms to remind him he was part of the world, but only barely...

Jerome was in Dorval Airport just in time to see Clyde walk out of the arrivals bay.

"Clyde, my bruh-tha, how's it goin'?"

"I'm...feeling better, Jerome." At least he had his speech back. He seemed haggard, slouching more than usual and scratching his pot-belly, making it jiggle. He'd hardly slept the night before.

"Let's get you back to my place, you must be tired."

"Th-thanks, Jerome..."

Jerome gathered up Clyde's luggage for him. Clyde seemed...slower than usual. They got into Jerome's car and made their way to his townhouse.

"Have you ever...read the bible, Jerome?"

Jerome looked over at Clyde a little funny. It was unlike Clyde to ponder things theological.

"Not really, man. What the hell was going on in T.O.?"

"I d-don't know, Jerome. I think...I think...it was covered..." Clyde couldn't speak.

"S'okay, man, take it easy," said Jerome. Clyde seemed to be okay until Jerome would ask him about why he freaked out, then he got all rattled and his speech impediment returned. So Jerome decided to leave well enough alone.

They got into Jerome's place and Jerome insisted Clyde take his bed while he would take the couch. Clyde was too tired to argue. Jerome warmed up some leftovers and brought them to Clyde but he wasn't hungry at all. He sat in front of the t.v. and ate by himself, which he was used to anyway. He called up Graham's house but didn't let it ring too long as it was late. "They must be sleeping peacefully," he figured.

*   *   *

It was with some trepidation that I went into work that day. It was obvious that Julia, out of concern for me, reported my situation. And it came as no shock when my boss told me I was suspended pending psychiatric evaluation. With pay. Thank God for socialists.

So now I had nothing to do. Except go home. Maybe I was done with it all. I could just pick up and leave and forget it all ever happened. Whatever. That was unrealistic. I don't think 'it' was done with me. A guy with Korson's temperament wasn't to be taken lightly.

I got home and Julia was waiting for me. I had several messages from Jerome, which were not unexpected. What was unexpected was the fact that Julia was trying to be really receptive to me. Asking me all sorts of questions, if I was okay, what had happened. Truth is, I couldn't remember anything happening last night after I'd left the casino. If not for the bloody scrapes at my neck there would be no proof of my breakdown. Which I didn't believe had happened. I felt fine, after all.

An internal therapist, Simon Dubois from the M.U.C.P.S., paid me a visit that day. For the most part Julia left us alone while he asked me questions, but I could tell she was eavesdropping. Usual line of questioning, and I really couldn't keep my mind on topic. But he was insistent that I don't deny something had happened the previous evening, as evidenced by my wounds. Julia brought some refreshments in-she insisted on providing for every visitor who dared set foot on our property. Even this anal bastard who thought he knew everything about the inner workings of my mind.

"I would like to have a word with your wife as well, Mr. St. Croix. You are welcome to stay of course, as we are keeping no secrets, no secrets. And it is your house!" He tittered at his little attempt at humour. Julia joined him.

I said, "I think I'll go make myself a cup of tea," and went into the kitchen while they started off exchanging pleasantries. I ran some hot water out of the tap and put it into the kettle.

"Look at them out there talking like they know about you." I jumped, startled completely, and I dropped the kettle and nearly scalded myself from the splash of hot water.

"Motherfucker, don't do that," I exclaimed in a whisper.

Julia said, "Graham? You okay?" I told her I was fine, the kettle just slipped and I would clean it up.

"What are you doing here, it isn't even night yet."

Korson pointed to the window and said, "Sundown. Close enough." He glanced towards the living room. "You listening to that shit?"

"...your husband is suffering from a mild depression that is manifesting itself in the forms of paranoid delusions. Imagine, if you would, a part of him closing itself off in a shell, hiding from the world. But the rest of him can't get along without the complete whole of his personality, and therefore this part of himself that has hidden itself away in his mind has to manifest itself in some form. Demons, monsters, what have you. They are all really representative of one's fears. Rather, his personal fears. The more intelligent the demon, the more complex the fear. The deeper rooted it is. It may seem strange to us, maniacal, but if we-along with your husband-can rationalize the fear, make it seem more reasonable, it may not seem so outlandish and it will eventually diminish, then disappear like-" and he couldn't resist suppressing a little grin at this, "-a rather bad zit..."

Korson, on the other hand, quite skeptical, had this look on his face like he'd eaten rotten sushi. He went over to the fridge and pulled out an egg, said, "This is your personality. It has encased itself in this shell as a means of protecting the Host. There must be a way to get it out..." He turned and reared back like a Major League pitcher and launched the egg at the back of Dubois' head, splattering yellow yoke all over his greasy yellow hair. Bow-tied little geek.

Of course Julia came rushing in from the living room, followed by the egged Dubois, and she promptly asked me what the hell I was doing.

"I swear I didn't do it." What else could I say? I love you? And Julia was ready to rip into me, I could tell by the look in her eyes. Korson, on the other hand, had disappeared. Dubois then intervened:

"Oooh! This is wonderful! He's confronting his nemesis! I see great progress for you Mr. St. Croix," he said as he wiped egg out of his hair. "I see this as a very positive sign!"

Julia was still eyeing me as Dubois said his cheery good-byes and made to leave. And then...God, this is the scariest thing I can think of...the *lecture*...(cue eerie music.)

"I can't believe you would do such a childish thing," she began. I filled in with yes, dear's and no, dear's at the appropriate intervals, and it was when I was nearly tuned out that I noticed Korson's imposing form filling the entranceway to the kitchen behind Julia, his hands against the door frame holding him up as though he were sick and tired of it all. I tried not to let it register on my face that I was looking beyond her, hoping she wouldn't turn around.

"Are you listening to me?"

"Yes, dear."

I swear this guy was going to make me insane. And, well, in the eyes of others it appears he already had.

"I can't believe all this," she said, her head thrust into the fridge rummaging around for food. "I'm going to bed." She closed the fridge door and I just about jumped to stop her from turning into the fearsome bulk of the vampire Korson. But he was gone. Silly me! Of course he was gone!

Julia said, "What is it?"

"Nothing. Goodnight, dear."

She gave me a little bit of a dirty look before she turned away and walked up the stairs. I followed a few steps, rested myself in the doorway where Korson had stood. Ignorant. Fucking ignorant. My own wife. And could I blame her for disbelieving? She could have at least sympathized, though. Isn't that why men take up with women? For sympathy? I didn't need it anyway. I could live alone from the rest of the world, or so I thought.

Korson said, "You need music in your life Mr. St.Croix," and again I jumped because he startled me.

"Jesus Christ!" What else could I say? The bastard was pissing me off, I never knew where he would be next. His face drooped in exasperation, and then he blew.

"Don't fucking say that! I don't want to hear anymore shit about Jesus Christ!" He didn't even move near me but it felt like he had me up against the wall. But I couldn't let him scare me, I had to shush him.

"Are you crazy?! Keep your voice down, my wife'll hear you."

""I thought she was ignorant."

Smart-ass.

"Insults will get you nowhere, Mr. St.Croix."

"Could you stop reading my mind, please?"

"Then stop mentioning Jesus Christ." He said it with forceful anger in his voice. Needless, that was what developed the ensuing silence between us. The one that felt as though it would never end.

"What have you got against Jesus Christ."

"It's a long, drawn out story," he said, flatly. "If you can figure out the weave of the fabric, then you can thread it together yourself."

"I think you hate that biblical shit as much as I do."

"Yeah, but don't discredit it. It's not all invalid."

"All the shit about last night. That was you wasn't it?"

Korson glanced to his left and shrugged a yes off his shoulder.

I said, "You love haunting and torturing me don't you?" Korson laughed. He leaned his head back, way back like a cat yawning, and laughed his usual mirthless laugh.

"I think it's a side-effect of my presence. Causes nightmares, y'know?" His mouth cracked into a smile. I looked at him and could tell he was enjoying the expression of bitter anger on my face.

"How long have you been drinking my blood? What, you got one taste and just had to have more?"

"Now you're just being neurotic, Mr. St. Croix."

"Tell me you aren't drinking my blood." He turned towards the door and started walking.

"I think you should be more concerned about the direction you're going to take." Before I could respond he was a blur, the door swinging open and closed as he left. And what could I really tell him? That, against all rationality, I would continue to hunt down a murderer?

"Hello..." Julia St.Croix answered the phone, her voice a little indifferent. She wasn't in much of a mood to speak to anyone in an unexpected manner such as this.

"Can I speak to Graham, please?" A woman. Few men called her husband, much less a woman, and this aroused suspicion in the madman's wife.

"May I ask who's speaking, please?" Digging.

"Isabelle Gauthier."

"From where are you calling?" Can't you hear the shovel going shuck shuck?

"I was his partner at work for the past few months on the serial kidnapping case. Can I speak to him please?"

"Oh, I'm sorry, he went out a little while ago. With his brother I think. I was just writing down that you called."

Isabelle said, "Please have him call me soon as he can. Thank you." Then hung up. Leaving the impression of callousness to the voice fading from Julia's memory, to be replaced by a dial tone.

Julia nearly slammed the phone down. She wanted to hurl it against the wall. *Partner?!* she thought. Why hadn't he mentioned anything about her? And the biggest case of the year, all the kidnappings, and he didn't even tell his own wife of the promotion? *Bastard...*she thought, gritting her teeth and clenching her fists. She wanted to hit something, anything, but she couldn't direct her anger anywhere. Just sat there letting the energy gather in the squeezed palms of her hands.

No, she thought. *I'm not going to bicker with him.* She was so ready to start a huge argument but that seemed like all they did lately. For certain she couldn't let this slight go. This was too much, but the rift between her and her husband was greater. It was time to stop the pettiness, the arguing. And she sat there, all alone, and as determined as she was to put this past her, she turned it over in her mind for several hours because it was something else to think about as she watched her marriage fall apart.

"I saw the Rocket tonight."

It took a second for what Jerome was telling me to register. I think I sort of zoned out while I was looking at him, but he did nothing to rouse me. Just kept looking at me, perhaps ready to be a little defensive.

I hadn't seen him in a while and after all the shit we decided to get together at *Côte St. Luc* Barbeque for our usual chicken dinner. We were talking and he just sort of sprung it on me. *La Rockette*. He was speaking of Maurice 'the Rocket' Richard, the fist player ever to score fifty goals in the N.H.L and a Montréal icon. And from the tone of his voice I knew that he hadn't encountered him physically. I never got around to responding to him.

"Since I picked you up that night at the casino, I've been doin' a lot of wonderin'. I saw you raving like a madman, tryin t'force your luck. Like you could control it. But it wasn't anything you said. Just seein' ya, man. I went to get Clyde at the airport, I saw you in my head. Went into the deli, saw you in my head. The last five years of you. You've never really been the same." He took a pull on his cigar. Filthy habit, but I wouldn't have it any other way from him. "So I been thinkin' about belief. The fact that not one person in the entire world believed you. And I wish I could say I'm sorry but I can't. Because there is no apology for what I did to you. I could've at least been that one person who stuck by you."

"If it helps..." I wasn't sure how I wanted to put this to him. "If it helps I never held any bitterness towards you." He nodded in acceptance, slowly chewing the nub of his cigar. "When did you see him?"

"Last night," Jerome said. "I was thinkin' about belief as I lay in my bed. Next thing I knew I was asleep. I wish I could tell you for sure if I'd woken up or not. But I lifted my head off the pillow and there he was. Powerful old fucker. Stood there smilin', his hair all silver and that look in his eyes, deep and red. Just grippin' you. I don't know how long I looked at him, but it wasn't too long before I realized he wasn't real. This deep, black mist-really subtle, so I didn't realize it at first-it came up and he seemed to get lost in it. Then everything was gone and I woke up to sunlight."

"His ghost," I said.

"But why didn't he say anything?"

"Maybe he couldn't," I stated. Jerome smoked his cigar thoughtfully. He looked a little disoriented, like a Toronto Maple Leafs defenceman without the puck.

"Why do y'say that?" he said.

"Maybe ghosts can't talk."

"Really. Have you seen any ghosts lately?"

I couldn't answer him right away. I sort of looked down and wondered if my brother knew me that well that he could read me. Then I had to laugh, but when I tried to look at him my gaze passed over his face and I was looking off to the side.

"Yeah. For the last few months, I've been seeing ghosts. This guy wearing thorns on his head and a loincloth keeps visiting me at night. Just before dawn, before I'm going to sleep. He stands at the door, looks at me. Smiles at me. I'm shitting my pants. He always says something to me, but there's no sound. And I can't quite make out what he's saying. For a while he gets insistent about it. Acts like he's yelling, his hands lashing out at me. After he realizes I can't understand he starts wandering around the room. Tries to open drawers but can't. This is too funny! He starts sticking his head into the drawers. Looks all over my room for something. Guy looks like a fucking martyred saint but I can't figure out what the hell he would want from my house."

"I believe you, man," said Jerome.

"You don't have to say it."

"Yes, I do," he insisted. "What are you gonna do now, man? You're off the force for a while. What are you gonna do?"

I took a deep breath. Rubbed my eye with my fingers for a second.

I said, "I'm gonna keep looking."

"For the murderer?"

"Yeah. I got demons in me, man. They're not gonna leave me alone. I gotta chase 'em down. This isn't about earning my paycheque anymore."

Jerome said, "Fuckin' shame. I always thought it's a fuckin' shame we had based our lives on money. Some people never do what they love. All over money. I gotta respect you for what you doin'. But how you gonna live once they cut off your pay?"

"I'll starve if I have to. But one things for certain: I'm going to expose this thing somehow."

"I gotta ask, Graham Cracker: Why are you looking for the murderer? Why aren't you looking for the connection to yourself? Haven't you wondered why it was you?"

"Yeah," I thought to myself. It did cross my mind, why Korson picked me. Why the ghosts were haunting me. I felt so arbitrary under his gaze. The ghosts visiting me at night seemed against all reason. But man's vanity had always disgusted me. I didn't want to be self-centered and arrogant to the gravity of the situation, to the fact that harmless children were being murdered in their sleep.

"I can't concern myself with that, Jerome. I don't think it matters why it's me. Or that it is me, at that. I've come to the belief that nothing really matters and things just keep going. Either way, we'll all be chewed up in the end."

Jerome became thoughtful for a moment. Chewed on his cigar and looked at me. Then he reached into his pocket and pulled out his cell phone and handed it to me.

I said, "Nah, I don't need it. Thanks."

"Hey. Keep it on you. Just in case. This thing, you disrespectin' your wife, that ain't cool, man. Keep the phone. The only people who have the number are you and Julia and one or two friends of mine. I just use it to call out for business. You disapppearin', that ain't right. We need you, we need to get in touch with you. You wanna be alone, fine, but we need to get in touch with you."

He left me, 'to hang wit Clyde,' and I felt a little different. A lot different, actually. I didn't realize what it was to have one person in the world believe you. Not so much believe me, really, as the fact that he accepted everything and I could confide in him. For God's sake, I couldn't even tell my own wife! The one who's supposed to be the other half to my soul. It was as though I were less isolated, as though my brain could shrug off the weight that made it sluggish and I could think again. Not just stand there as though I were watching someone else live out my life, completely indifferent and cold to everything going on around me.

I laughed! Oh shit, I laughed, loud enough that people looked at me strangely. (Not that I wasn't used to it by now.) I *wanted* to see my ghosts now. I couldn't care less that I was haunted anymore. Things had become a part of me and I had to accept them. And where was I going to go? I hadn't touched Lurik's book in a while. I'd flipped to the end and found inserts-and this was the curious thing-inserts that had been placed at the end of the book, pieces of essays. Even more curious was the fact the book wasn't actually published. No info on the inside jacket, just the name of the author and inscription stating: '1923-?' Did this mean he was still alive? It might be difficult finding him now that I was suspended. Something told me he wasn't in the phone book.

With all that, I headed over to McGill, the scene of one of the murders and the historical old library within the elderly walls of the university. The place was virtually empty as it was getting late in the evening. As the sun was beginning to set, the lighting was receding in dusty beams from the window, leaving only the tiny spots of illumination from the individual desk lamps. I dug up books-Lord, did I ever dig up books!-everything from the Holy Bible, to books on the occult to tomes on magic and paganism and even a dictionary of the saints. What was I hoping for it to tell me? That ghosts really don't talk? I kept skimming through things, scanning pages and indexes for topics until I tired of them or thought I'd hit a dead end, then moved on to the next book. It was hours and everything had darkened, except for the private desk lamps, and I was so absorbed that I forgot the deathly silence around me.

The interesting thing about all the biblical history that I was going over-and, mind you, there was so much that I was certain I would miss as much as I covered-was the interwoven threads that wound up each and every religion I looked at. Paganism and magic threaded their way into Judaism; we're all familiar with Moses coming down from the mountain and smashing the tablets because the tribes were worshipping false idols. Both Paganism and Judaism followed the lunar calendar, and magic still had a special section under Jewish rites. During the atheistic Roman era, when Christianity was on the rise, the evangelism of non-Christians involved plastering the Christian holidays over the Pagan celebrations. It led me to ponder two things; one, how much was lost in the misinterpretations of these interweavings? Two, were these religions rewritten to confuse us?

Korson said, "Man is in constant confusion about everything."

"For Christ's sake can you stop sneaking up on me like that? You're going to give me a fucking heart-attack."

"Christ's sake, Christ's sake, always Christ's sake...you...*mortals*-" he said the word with derision "-all of you, no matter what religion, it's always Christ's sake..." He threw his anger to the ground in a gesture. "Fuck," he spit.

"Why do you hate Jesus Christ?" I asked. Korson laughed, dry and bitter. A dead man's laugh.

"The most ironic thing about puzzles, Mr. St. Croix, is that the one piece that eludes you is the most perplexing of them all. Isn't it, though? You look at the information spread out in front of you. And you haven't even scratched the surface. You'll never find that one piece sitting here in a library."

"Why are you here, Korson?"

"Blood," he said soberly. "Always blood!" He stuck out his tongue in a playful and maniacal manner and it was deep red. Like it was the only part of him that was alive, the part that lapped up his precious blood.

"Y'know, you could be a big help if you would maybe tell me half the shit you know." Again he laughed at me. I hated his laugh.

"Why do you assume I know it all? Because I'm better than you? Because I'm a God to you? You're not taking risks, Mr. St. Croix. You're sifting through facts. And that will only get you so far. All this is beyond facts." He was emphatic.

"You're not much help, Korson. You may be a God, but you're not much help." He still laughed his evil, dead laugh at me and then spun in a blur and mingled with the shadows outside my private little desk light. I couldn't see him anymore and didn't hear any movement.

"Korson?"

I glanced over my shoulder at a lone student some distance away from me. He didn't break his concentration. Maybe he didn't hear me. But Korson was loud enough for him to hear. And I wondered if he even wondered. Or, like the rest of the world, thought me a madman.

"Korson?" I ventured again. His absence disturbed me more than his presence now. I prayed I was not interwoven with my ghosts. That could get dangerous. Not that the psychosis could run any deeper in my veins than it already did. And that dirty man on the street who spoke to himself, maybe I wouldn't look at him like he was crazy anymore.

I went back to my studying, despite Korson's utterings. Digging away, and it was barely an hour before I thought that my efforts were as futile as the vampire made them out to be.

"Korson?" He was long gone, and still I wondered if he just watched me from the shadows. Frankly, it was a great history lesson I gave myself that night. But I had no other avenues to venture as yet, still reeling from my suspension from the force. I continued on, determined, figuring there must be one person in the world who would have, whether deliberately or by chance, recorded some fact that would help my cause. There was, after all, one person in the world who believed me.

And now his phone was ringing. Figures. I have the damn thing for three hours and already the chain's choking me.

"Hello?" Static. Must be because I'm in the library, so I move my head around a little bit.

"Hello?"

"...I'm on to you, Mr. St. Croix..." Despite being suspended, I still had my professional calm.

"Who are you?" I demanded. I spun around. Whoever was calling must've been watching me, to at least know I had the cell phone and where I was.

The voice got raspy, demonic. Difficult to make out anything but an evil inflection from it.

"I...know what you're *up* to..." The words slow and drawn out. I slowly got up, trying not to scrape the chair, and began to walk.

"DO NOT MOVE AWAY FROM THE DESK!" I cringed, the voice crackling and booming through the receiver...(and...in my head?) I had to grab my ear for a second, it felt as though blood was seeping out of it. It took a second for the throb in my head to dwindle. I didn't want to switch ears lest I become more than half deaf in the immediate future. I put the phone back to my ear. "You are...closer than you think...Mr. St. Croix..." There. Proof that I was being watched. The thing on the other end spoke immediately when I returned the receiver to my ear, and could only have known I'd have done so if they were looking at me. The voice kept babbling on, demonically, incoherently, drunkenly. I kept looking around. It was so hard to see in the large darkened room. I looked towards the lone student. He had his head buried. Sleeping? I couldn't see one of his hands. I moved over there slowly, wary of the voice at the other end of the line. It kept on rambling, and it sunk into a language I couldn't comprehend. Pieces of English, French, Italian...Latin?

I moved closer to the guy at the desk. I was so close all I had to do was reach out and grab the son of a bitch. I pulled the phone away from my ear. There was some murmuring, and I tried to match it up with what was coming out of the receiver. I couldn't quite place it. Was he talking in his sleep? Was that a cell phone hidden in the crook of his neck? I had no choice. It was either stand there being neurotic or take action. I grabbed him by the arm and throttled him.

"What?! I-I-" Nothing. He didn't have a phone, nor any clue what was happening. He'd fallen asleep at his studies. I let go of his arm.

"Sorry, buddy," I said, as placatingly as I could. "My mistake." I backed away from the bewildered student in the white t-shirt, put the phone back to my ear. Lots of static still. But the voice was still there. Tittering.

"Maybe your brain is more wretched than I first thought, Mr. Sen Cwa." This was a game, obviously. I hadn't lost my nerve, nor my bladder, and I was being mocked to twist my mind away from my purpose. But could I go back to reading after all this? Could I just hang up?

I said, "If you don't identify yourself, I'll hang up."

"You...*know* me, Mr. St. Croix. You know me already..." I could feel the sinister smile from the other end of the line. But I wouldn't give the voice the satisfaction of hearing me give a name. I wouldn't be drawn into childish guessing games with monsters.

As much as it hurt, I pulled the phone away from my ear. True to my word, I slowly flipped the mouthpiece closed, ending the call.

Catherine said, "She's been missing a good week now." Korson just nodded, looking towards the ground in thought. They sat in a café at Prince Arthur and *boul. St. Laurent*, near the window, watching people pass.

"And the sky is black at night. Big fucking deal."

"Korson, for once can you please just tell me what is in your head?"

"What do you want me to say, Catherine? That I tried to stop it all from happening? That I tried to keep her with me against her will but she left anyway? It was her choice to leave. I was faced with a decision, and it was morally wrong for me to control her. I had to let her go."

"Wow. You're moral all of a sudden. That's wonderful. Yet you sit there, all arrogant, holier-than-thou, and you won't tell any of us who are left what it is exactly that's going on. We can all smell the air, Korson. It's like it was thirty years ago when everyone was being killed. And there are so few of us left that it just isn't fear that we're feeling, it's a matter of survival."

Korson looked at her blankly, betraying not a single note of emotion on his face.

"Can't do it, Catherine. You know Talissa listens."

"I've never thought I would hear myself say this, but you're a *coward*." Catherine put a heavy emphasis on her final word, and it was one of the few words in the world that could cause Korson to be driven to needless murder. Him, a coward? Ha! It was laughable!

"I'll pretend you didn't say that. But watch yourself."

"Go back and play with your mortal. You've become a *joke*, playing night after night with a mortal." They sat in silence for a few moments, angry with each other. Then Catherine said, "Why do you care so much for him?" Korson looked at her purple-black eyes and knew she was asking in all sincerity.

"Because if destruction is visited upon us, I want to be able to keep just one around."

"How sentimental. Not at all becoming of a hundred and fifty year old creature."

Korson said, "You don't think we need them?"

"No. We're immortal. I don't think we'll ever die."

"Then you're naive," he said. "We need them as much as they need us to haunt them." Catherine just looked at him, seemingly blankly at first, but it soon became apparent that she was masking her disgust at his mingling with a mortal.

"Have you drank his blood, Korson?"

"It's not all about blood, Catherine."

"Answer the question." Korson nodded a reluctant yes. Catherine looked at him accusingly.

"So I'm no better than you now, hm?" said Korson.

"How do you mean?"

"You, falling in love with Heather. That's why you suddenly care. What happened for the last thirty years, you were asleep? You're in love with her and don't deny it." She couldn't. She was absolutely in love with Heather, utterly smitten, and when Heather didn't return, Catherine knew the fire in the air was a harbinger of things to come. She couldn't help but shed some tears, not because she used to be female, but because of the feelings she felt.

"I feel like a puppet," she said. She was holding back her tears, cold from a century of death. Korson didn't use this opportunity to lash back for her previous comment regarding his sentimentality. "A fucking puppet. I wanted to protect her. I think I just ended up pushing her further into the shadow. Ironic, huh? All because I fell in love with her."

"I don't think you should blame yourself, Catherine. We're all just playing our parts."

"This doesn't sound like you, Korson. So defeatist. And still you won't tell what you know."

"That's because I don't know as much as everyone thinks. I'm in as much a fog as the rest of you. Just because I know Talissa people assume I know what she's up to."

"Oh," said Catherine, a trifle disappointed at the lacking details. "Then were all her fucking puppets."

Korson nodded, said, "Perhaps."

Their conversation was cut short because the shadow hissed into the air.

I had sat back down to my studies only to find my mind wandering. Wondering what a vampire would do with immortality. It must be like being a writer. Staring at the vast blank sheet of the future and having to make it all up. And what would I do? I hardly had a sense of urgency as it was, I'm sure if I had all of time ahead of me I would just shrivel up and forget it all. It would certainly be like death.

Now, though, I was content to sift through mountains of theologically based books in order to piece together the puzzle that was forming in my mind about the imminent war. I tried to track the dates and times of the murders in my mind (my files, of course, were confiscated) and, to some extent, they corresponded to holy days on the calendar. It had occurred to me that the holidays were rooted in majic and geared towards children. What was it Korson had said? Jesus was a great fucking majician?

It was the purple light that caught my attention. Brilliant in its own dimness, gleaming between a spectrum of white and black and always reverting to the metallic purple, as though it were a star. Held between the palms of my Jesus-ghost. He held the ball of energy and looked at it with hungry eyes. He glanced up at me once or twice and smiled. Then, carefully, as though he may lose the star-ball, he lifted his hand up and touched the thorn wreath upon his head. I was a little shocked. He bled. He became more enamored by the blood seeping out of his finger than with the star-ball. He stared at his hand and it began to shake, as though he were palsied. The energy ball lost its form, its luster. As the brightness bled out of it all that was left was a dark and sinister purple. It didn't so much as dissipate as melt and disappear into the shadows near the floor.

The ghost's hand stopped shaking after another moment. He smiled and showed me rotted teeth that matched the colour of his dirty brown hair. And said something...

"Sowen." He spoke! I heard something come from his mouth. Though it made no sense to me. And I was sure I heard an actual sound, not something in my head. Could I train him to live in this reality, rather than appear as something ethereal? As though he heard my thoughts, or perhaps because of the thoughtful expression on my face, he moved (he never seemed to walk) over to the table. Put his hand near a book. It took some summoning of effort, but he managed to move the book a few feet across the table before tiring. His image flickered a moment and I was afraid I might lose him. But he restored his image and, though he looked a little drained from his efforts, his form remained in this world.

How the hell did this ghost find me? I kept thinking and thinking...Was it Korson's presence? Unlikely. He'd first appeared to me five years ago and nothing since then had happened, till now. I flipped through Lurik's book quickly, searching for a piece of information.

(Now this was fucking research!)

I knew it! The majic circle in my basement. I never closed it. Could it be ghosts were finding their way to this world through that vessel? I didn't buy that theory. The circle was definitely part of it, but it wasn't as though I'd littered the world with ghosts and demons. Maybe it was Korson's presence that helped. Though, because Jerome had seen a ghost as well, I, whether it was arrogant or not, tended to think that the connection was myself. Could it possibly be...my belief? Perhaps Korson had more to do with it than I gave him credit for. Perhaps it was my belief in him that helped me catch glimpses to the ethereal plane.

"Can you speak again?" I asked. "Your name?" He opened his mouth to speak, but no sound came out. It was obvious it took a lot for him to do things on my level.

I sifted through the pile of books on the table. I pulled out the dictionary of the saints and began to flip. There were paintings of the saints printed near every picture. For fuck's sake, they all looked a little like Jesus. And the book was thick as hell, but I kept flipping page by page hoping I could make a match between the face of the ghost and one of the saints in the picture. It was a tenuous quest at best, I knew, the fact that these paintings could merely be artists interpretations done hundreds of years after the saint himself was deceased.

I'd been flipping between the page of the book and the wandering, flickering image of the ghosts when suddenly he caught my attention. He held his hand up to me, palm out, and with his other hand he pulled his baby finger and thumb together. It took a moment for me to figure his gesture out, but I deduced he was telling me three. Three what? I swear I went over every combination of everything I could think of. All I really had was 'sowen' and 'three.'

Jerome's phone rang again.

"Hello."

"*I'M GOING TO TEAR THE VERY FLESH FROM YOUR FACE!*"

"Whatever." I hung up. It was already three a.m. I only had a few more hours till the ghost would disappear. Till the sunlight dissipated the majic in the world to an ash flying in the wind. I could attempt to call the ghost through majic if I found that necessary, but it was already likely that he was somehow bound to me. Perhaps because it was I who opened the circle? Either way, I was confident he would keep appearing to me, as I'd seen him more than a few times already. As night dwindled to day, his image continued to flicker like a candle low on wax. His grip on this reality was losing its hold.

I had to try and touch him. If he cold move the book maybe some physical contact was possible. Though, when I saw him moving the book, I wasn't quite sure if he <u>actually</u> touched it to move it. My worry was that I had waited too long and his essence was too weak to accomplish what I wanted to try. I could've waited till the next evening, but...hell, I was impatient. I didn't want to take the risk of not seeing him again.

As I got up, the cell phone rang again. I answered it, frustrated.

"Yes, what."

Jerome said, "What's your problem?"

"Oh, sorry. S'you. Thought it was someone else."

"I was drivin' by your house and noticed you weren't home, so I decided to call."

I said, "Yes, I'm heading home very soon," quite patronizingly. "Guess I should get some sleep, I did want to do a few things tomorrow."

"Atta boy," said Jerome. We promised to meet later and then hung up.

Back to my ghost. The delay due to the call caused him to fade further. I put the nuisance phone down-hell, I can't lie, I turned it off-and stepped up to the saintly ghost. I was, to say the least, a little tentative. I thought of all the stupidities I'd seen in horror movies, like the guy who goes back to check for the monster. But the ghost seemed harmless enough, and I liked the prospect of hands-on research a lot more than the theoretical. I touched his surface with my index finger. A strange tingle. Mind you, I hadn't actually broken the essence of his form. I was testing the waters. So I tried again, this time pushing my finger beyond the barrier of the outer edge of the ghost's form. I felt something there. Nothing gooey, but there was something there. It didn't appear that the ghost had any sense of what I was doing to him, either. The problem was that I couldn't get a good sense of feeling with just my index finger. A little shudder passed over me. I'm not sure if it was nervousness at the experimentation or just a general feeling of unease at interacting with a ghost. I don't think it was dread. I'm pretty sure it wasn't dread.

I pushed my entire hand into the ghost's body. For a moment nothing happened. Then-it was as though my skin rotted in an instant, becoming a sickly blackened green in colour. My hand shook. I lost my sense of feeling in my hand, and I couldn't find the muscle to pull it out of the ghost. It felt as though something was being sucked out of my skin. As if the very energy was being sucked out and my hand was dying a death of its own. I could also see the bones peeking through the decaying and rotting flesh as it fell away from my hand.

I couldn't take any more. I grabbed my arm with my free hand and pulled. I fell away from the saint's image, quite easily, as though it was only in my own fear that I'd been trapped in his body. I sat on the floor, holding my shaking, traumatized hand. It looked normal enough, but for a sickly pallor and cold feel. The saint kept about his own business. Looking at the books as though trying to decipher something, or searching. Mimicking my search, perhaps?

It was close to four a.m. I hated to go, but I had to, and his image had faded further anyway. He'd be gone by sunup, surely. So I left reluctantly, hoping my ghost would follow me to the next night.

Love is a magical idea created by two people; one is the majician, the other, the liar. Perhaps, because I was at one point in love with my wife, I may have had some majician in me. It may explain why I was attracting demons lately. The only problem with that theory is that it makes my wife the liar. And because my marriage was deteriorating, it meant I'd lost control of my majic. I'd spent the last few weeks searching for that tenuous line in my mind, trying to cross it and become what I once was. But with all that had happened, I think my wife saw my tricks for what they were. She was just clinging to her lies as evidenced through the fact that she was still with me.

I had a pile of messages waiting for me; the few old acquaintances I'd kept in touch with, Jerome checking on me, one from Isabelle. I started returning my calls, and the message from Isabelle I left for last. It seemed ages since we last talked, but in reality it was only a week or so.

"Isabelle, it's Graham," I said when she picked up.

"Graham!" she exclaimed. She was usually very calm, very subdued, so to hear her voice excited was something uncommon. "How have you been?"

"I've been okay. Trying to keep busy."

"I heard all that happened. I wish you would've called me."

"Been a bit of an upheaval lately. Everything kind of went in a blur."

"Understood."

"You're off tonight, huh?"

"Yes. Maybe we could go out and catch up?"

I said, "I'm not really in the mood for large groups of people right now. I would like to talk, if you don't mind staying at your place." She agreed, and I left for her place after I took care of a few things.

I took the metro to Isabelle's apartment at the other end of downtown. I figured the walk from the station would do me some good. For some reason I was a little nervous about seeing her. I was always a little nervous about seeing people that I hadn't seen in a while. That, and I had no real reason to be seeing her as I was no longer working for the M.U.C.P.S. I got to her apartment door and I was about to turn away, just to leave without bothering. (I told myself I was being silly; sometimes I have to tell myself what to do instead of following my enigmatic instincts and buried fears.) I took a deep breath and knocked, and I really don't know why I was nervous.

When Isabelle answered the door, I wondered if she'd had other plans for the evening because she seemed a little bit dressed up.

"Graham, hi!" she said. "It is so good to see you. Come in." She gave a little tug on my arm to pull me inside. "I've been worried about you. You've got my messages?"

"Just one."

"Oh. I've left several. To tell the truth, your wife didn't seem to thrilled to hear me. You didn't tell her we were working together?" We sat on the couch.

"Honestly, I don't tell her much lately. Or anyone for that matter."

She lit up a smoke and said, "That's not good for you."

"What's that?"

"Keeping secrets. Keeping everything inside like that. It has to go somewhere."

I didn't respond, and she looked over at me through the veil of smoke escaping from her mouth. "You sure you're okay?"

"Yeah. I'm fine."

"It's okay to tell me. To talk."

I ran my fingers through my hair, said, "What do you want me to tell you? That I went mad? I'm sure you've read the reports. Probably more interesting than me telling it to you."

"I don't think you went mad, Graham."

Again I didn't say anything. Isabelle said, "I believe you saw what you saw and sometimes we all see things that confuse us and we lose it for a bit. But you're not mad."

I gave her a skeptical look. I was suspicious that she was just trying to get me to talk.

"Graham, I have no reason to doubt what you're telling me. If what we saw coming out of that dead child is a fraction of any indication of what were dealing with, I have no reason to doubt you. I believe you when you tell me what you saw, and I even believe what happened to you years ago."

"What happened years ago was a long time ago and is over and done with."

"Really? I don't believe so. I can tell by your face. It's still with you. You never told anyone and it's stayed with you all these years. Am I right?" I didn't answer. "This is strictly on a personal level. Out of my concern for you. I'm not reporting this to anyone." She got up and went to the kitchen, offered me some sort of alcohol, and I said yes, not caring what kind it was. She brought me a beer in a glass and then went back to the kitchen. Clinckging away. I think she was doing dishes or something. Once in a while she would say something to me, simple questions to which I could grunt a yes or no answer. I was faced with a choice right now; I'd closed myself off-I knew I was doing it and still I couldn't help myself-and the danger was if I continued to do this I would lose what tenuous connections I had left with this world. I would slip further and further away until I fell victim to Korson's deadly bite. Then I would be his. Then I could maybe lie to myself and blame it all on madness and misconception of reality as opposed to blaming it on myself. I could make the conscious choice to let Isabelle know what was going on in my head. Despite what she said, I still felt the risk of doing so. I still had a complete distrust in opening myself up to the hurt that could be caused by making myself vulnerable to people by letting them know what was going on inside of me.

Isabelle scared me, and I felt myself cooling off. Not only did she hold a belief in me, but she seemed able to look into me. To tell me that my demons were still with me after all these years and not be put off by my brusque comments and callous attitude. To not walk away or give up on me. Not even my wife could offer me that after nearly a decade of marriage. To top it off, she even said she would keep everything to herself, and I felt Jullia was reporting everything back to that fag bastard psychoanalyst Dubois.

"You sure you okay?" asked Isabelle as she topped up my glass.

"Yeah. I'm fine." I think I was starting to feel the alcohol for some reason. Is this what happens to alcoholics? The blackouts? It had been years since I'd drank-I mean *really* drank-and I had to wonder if I had, in my moments of turbidity, been subject to imbibing to the point where my perceptions had become skewed, to the point that I really wasn't sure what was going on anymore. I had no clear view of the world left. No set definitions, no dogma, no true friends...no faith, not even in what my own eyes told me. Frankly, I couldn't understand why Isabelle or Jerome would even bother pretending to believe me. I was truly content to be left to my own devices and deteriorate in my own little world. Which, of course, was impossible due to the hauntings from vampires and ghosts. And with all this fucking majic swirling around me lately, I wondered if I had enough strength in my soul to be able to handle it.

Isabelle said, "Graham," as she shook my shoulder. "I was speaking to you."

"Sorry, just thinking."

"Understandable. Must be a lot going on in that head of yours. Take your time, Graham. I'll just be in the washroom for a moment."

I sat by myself in the living room and wondered at my isolation. There were no sounds coming from the kitchen anymore and only intermittent noises from the bathroom. And in the silences I wondered if the isolation was in my own head, of my own doing. Like the madness, like the visitations from Korson. There I go again. *Doubting myself.* Not good, Graham, not good. But Korson was so *real*. The ghost was so real. I looked at my hand, the one that touched the ghost and thought-no, felt-that for one moment it may have been dead inside of him. That a part of me may have experienced death. Was that my proof? This intangible sensation in my fingertips?

Proof. Hell, what proof I wanted was another visit from Korson, figuring that he showed up nearly everytime I-

(-was that Isabelle calling me?)

That's what was bothering me! The fact that his appearances were so convenient! Could it be that, in actuality, I'd created his character out of my mind? That he was a manifestation of a side of my personality that was trying so desperately to speak out to me and show me something? But I had touched him, he had cut me, and there was no way I could have done that to myself. No possible way I was that crazy, that I was as crazy as the look in Julia's eyes told me. Not a look of fear as though I were maniacal, but as though there were something forlorn and pathetic reflected in her eyes. If this was all true, what was it that I was trying to tell myself? I couldn't think like that. If I was trying to tell myself something then it meant that nothing was happening. My brother came to me and put his faith in me and saw a ghost. That was real. The mysterious-

(Isabelle?)

-death of the Langden girl was real. The other murders of innocent children were real. I had to align myself with factual evidence in the real world, the bright and living world. I couldn't cling to such grandiose fantasies and fairy tales as midnight hauntings by ghosts and vampires and the crumbling walls of the castle that used to be my marriage. Of the fact that I'd failed as a majician and a lover. Perhaps in my struggle for truth and clarity my mind got muddied in the swarm of intangible ideas? That all these concepts I was trying to digest had begun to pull the sanity from my mind as though tearing off a limb from my body?

Concepts were intangible; facts were concrete. I had to focus my mind on the facts. All this delving (deviling?) into majic and scripture and the occult turned my mind toward something I could neither touch nor see nor feel. It was all-despite the reality of Korson-theory. I couldn't let my head swim in dreams when there was plenty of reality that needed tending to-marriages, murders and the reinstatement of my career. I knew what was real. I-

(-was that Isabelle calling my name from the bedroom?)

I stopped for one moment, to be sure. Let everything get silent except for the ticking of her grandfather clock. I thought I'd heard her call my name several times before, but why so quiet? I couldn't bring myself to just get up and walk down the hall because I felt it may be construed as improper. Then again, what I said about intangible concepts...

There was only so long I could sit and listen to tick-tocking before I really and truly went clinically insane. I heard the absolute barest whisper of my name from down the hall...*Graham*...as though a ghost were kissing the words into my ear with only the slightest of breath, and I had to get up and walk down the hall if only to refute whatever trick it was my mind was playing on me. I don't know why I didn't notice it before, but the walls in Isabelle's apartment were done up in a faint pink hue and I got the feeling that I should have thought it a bit tacky. I stood at the end of the hall surrounded by doors on three sides and the path to the living room seemingly long behind me. The door to my left was obviously a linen closet as it was a smaller door than the other two. The one ahead of me was slightly open and I saw the bathroom countertop adorned with toiletries peeking out. I gave a quiet tap on the door with my index and middle finger and wai-

(...my...name...?)

I pushed the door open a bit and saw nothing but an empty-pink-bathroom. So. Her bedroom. How fucking appropriate. Who knew what the brink of madness could drive me to? Even if something just barely suggestive happened I could not, on the basis that I was a sane man, defend my honour. And that was extremely important to me no matter how tenuous a thread my marriage hung by. Isabelle was such an attractive...

Shutupshutupshutupshutupshutupshutupshutup. Stupid. Isabelle was a great woman, fabulous co-worker, a strong person. I was giving in to my isolation and loneliness and looking for easy answers in the flesh.

(...my...)

If I'd just gone out more and kept in touch with old friends and socialized I would have at least some sort of outlet, somewhere to push all these extraneous, silly, nonsensical, neurotic thoughts instead of letting all the frustrations build up inside me until they needed to be burst forth in a gush from between my legs.

(...name?)

I gave a tap on the door and quietly called to Isabelle. There was only so long I could stupidly stand there debating the merits of my sanity in relation to the tapping of a door to signal my presence. I heard nothing. Not a peep. No one called my name. So I turned the handle and pushed the door open as quietly as I could. For some reason, I associated loud noises with impropriety. Silly, I guess. Human, I guess. The pink walls hushed their colours and faded into a thick, powdery grey-black as I entered the room. Isabelle was standing with her back to me, looking out the window and wearing a robe who's colour had been drained dead by the dark. I wasn't sure if I should say anything.

"The night's so beautiful," she said, holding her robe together at the neck, still facing the window.

"You okay? I've been out there for a while." She turned her head slightly to look over her shoulder. In the dark it was hard to tell if she gave me a warm smile or a sinister grin. The tricks of the shadow...

"My apologies. I came in to change and I lost myself looking out the window. The night's so beautiful, don't you think?"

"I've thought about that a lot. I haven't decided yet." She looked back over her shoulder again, her face hidden by fingers of shadow that crept over her shoulder, and I thought she whispered a laugh to herself.

"Are you going to tell me there's danger in such beauty?"

"Why would danger disguise itself?" I said. "I would think that crap would walk around as crap."

She turned toward me a little more. I felt a little claustrophobic as the darkness tightened the room around me.

"You should be a little more wary of the lies your eyes can tell you."

"I can only go by what I see, Isabelle."

She'd dropped one arm away from her robe. Turned towards me and I saw that, when she presented herself to me, she didn't have her robe tied at her waist and it hung on her body leaving a dark line of nakedness running from her neck to the floor.

"Isabelle...?"

She lifted her arms up a bit.

"I'm not so scary, am I? You think I'm beautiful, don't you?"

I nodded a slight yeah, but in truth I couldn't see anything but the bare colour of her robe and her silhouette in the darkness. The light of the stars in the window wasn't enough to see by and the streets of Montréal were too dark at this hour to shine any light in.

"You can't see me too well can you, Graham. Shall I turn on a light?"

"No!" I said firmly. "I should go. I'll come back some other time maybe."

"Then I am scary. Why are women so intimidating?" She turned around to face the window again, and it looked like her hands were on her hips and the robe was open and she bared her body for whoever happened to be passing beneath the window. "Is it because we control everything?" She walked over to the bed and lay down upon it, the robe barely covering her body. And I couldn't bring myself to maintain my resolve and just turn around and leave. I saw her lying there and she wasn't Isabelle anymore. For some reason, I don't know, she became just a warm body and she pushed her midsections upwards and her lips beckoned to me. She'd slipped her robe off now and she hugged her breast to her chin and it hid her face so all I could see of her was her femininity. It wasn't Isabelle and I couldn't figure out if it was some sort of conjuring on my part or her lies that had gotten her naked and faceless on the bed. I couldn't figure out if it would benefit me more to see if I could weave some majic through her lies and make her come or if I should be strict in my dogmatism and remain a dutiful and faithful man.

"Please, Graham," she quietly pleaded. I almost forgot she had a voice, or a mouth to speak with. Her midsection raised itself a little more in invitation. The scent of it was so intoxicating I couldn't stop myself from going towards her. She was really just lying there. Talking, prodding a little and I had to wonder if they were lies. "Sometimes I even take a taste of it myself. It isn't so bad, really." I was kneeling on the bed in front of her and I got a scent of something subtly vile and sharply metallic. There was a little bit of red dripping out from between her pink. But if I had done any conjuring, whether deliberately or subconsciously intentional, it had overtaken me and my forward motion was unstoppable. Whatever feelings of disgust that had risen in my throat and stomach were suppressed almost to the point of nothingness, and I could barely feel the weight of their remains. I extended my hands towards her and could feel a flow of energy through to my fingers, and was more so sure of that fact when the body in front of me responded further. I pressed my fingers gently to her and opened her up and wondered if a further gush of blood would spit out from her mouth. I stared for a moment at the mystery before me, at the complete darkness that faded into being from the pink opening. I opened her up further with my fingers and nearly lost my hold because of the slipperiness, and the slightly vile smell began to draw my mouth closer, as though the scent itself were fingers into my nose. My lips made only the barest contact to her flesh, and my tongue started to lick the syrup river that was dripping out of her as though I had to find her source no matter the discomfort to my body.

"Oh, Graham..." she whispered, lifting higher to meet me. I drank of her, I could feel drops of her blood hit the back of my throat as they were whipped in by my tongue. If I'd been a stronger majician perhaps I could have deciphered whether there was enlightenment or lies carried in that bitter juice. She moaned a little bit. I felt her hands pushing my head into her body, and it made me wonder for a moment where my hands were. I think they'd decided to wander upwards to replace where her hands had been. Her quiet little moans excited me, made my movements more enthusiastic. She was pushing so hard and high towards me that I felt as though we'd risen off the bed. Her hands began to tighten around my head, squeezing my ears to block out any noise. I was deprived of sound and sight and I couldn't get any read on her stage of completion. From her erratic motions I assumed my conjuring had reached the height of its power and was about ready for one final burst of energy before subsiding. Though I had no sense of the visual, not anything more than a few muffled noises in my ears, I tried to focus my perception on the tastes in my mouth, on the touch of her sweaty legs to my cheeks.

The grip of her legs became so tight I felt the pressure on my skull. Her movements stopped for a moment, her grip remaining tense, and I thought she'd finished, that she'd relinquish me from her hold. She seemed to relax and I began to pull away from her. But her legs, they'd reinforced the grip they had on me. I thought she was just being playful, a little viciously playful, and tried again. Her hold increased, I felt her legs crossing behind my neck to close the circle of her grip, and it was so tight around me now that I was practically forced to swallow the little blood droplets if I wanted to have any hope of taking air into my lungs. It was difficult to breathe and drink in the same breath. I started to thrash my hands. Fear was beginning to set in. I couldn't get a good grip on the body in front of me and I figured my only hope to be to find the edge of the bed, pull both of us off and hope the fall to the floor toppled us apart. I thrashed to my right and couldn't find anything, so I struggled the other way and-

-no-

-impossible-

-there was another body there.

Someone else was in the room with us, on the very bed. That was impossible. I couldn't have missed it when I walked in, when Isabelle had first lain on the bed. I guess the darkness had caused some madness in me. The shadows had played tricks on my eyes. The only explanation that remotely allowed me to keep my sanity was that Isabelle was so flexible she was able to contort herself in such a way so as to seem next to me at the same time as being in front of me. Some two-torso, six-legged demon. If I still didn't have my face buried in her pussy I would have expected to see flaming torches beside the bed and tribal masks hanging from the wall.

The next, um...this is hard for me to say. I think the next twenty-four hours were really sketchy. All I remember is thrashing at the body next to me, thrashing at Isabelle all entangled around me, her legs squeezing my neck so hard it felt as though half of it would be wrenched away from the whole, and I think my name was screamed several times. Serenity set in. My wrists felt as though they'd been bound, and my ankles as well, I think. But I don't think I could've moved if I wanted to. All I know for certain is that I was uncertain of everything. It felt as though the limitations of my flesh were slowly bleeding away into the air around me. I wasn't sure where my body was, and my soul was turning to gas. My mind was melting and each thought I tried to form melted with it, turning to liquid before I could decipher the substance of it. I might have opened my eyes from time to time, but all I was left with were the residuals of whatever fleeting memories I could snatch from those around me...

My dreams are of darkness...and clutching tightly to a blue rose made of blood...

Jerome arrived at the hospital just before evening was about to set on Montréal. He'd been, to say the least, agitated. It appeared, though he was trying to make a subtle and valiant attempt, that his brother Graham had relapsed into some sort of madness. That he was haunted and tortured of the mind. And it was going to destroy his body, as well.

He asked the nurse at the front desk where his brother was, and she directed him up a few floors. He found the room and saw a few people waiting outside. Julia, a woman, and a man. He touched Julia gently on the elbow and kissed her cheek, rubbed her shoulders to comfort her. The woman introduced herself.

"Isabelle Gauthier," she said. "I worked with Graham for some months." Then the man, bow-tied and hair greasy dirty blond, introduced himself.

"Simon Dubois." He was a psychologist with the M.U.C.P.S and had been assigned to Graham's case. Jerome shook his hand and hoped his psychological expertise was firmer than his handshake. Jerome pulled Julia a few steps away from the other to have some semblance of privacy for a family matter.

"What the hell's going on?" he said. He took Julia's hands in his. It looked as though she was tethered right now, her emotions held barely in check, and that she could fall off the line at any moment.

"I woke up this morning to his screaming," she said, talking to the floor. "He kept thrashing at something and when I tried to grab his arms and stop him, I noticed the blood. It was all over his mouth and his neck was torn and...I just couldn't get near him. I called the paramedics and I sat there watching him beat the hell out of himself."

"Who tore his neck," Jerome asked flatly.

"He did."

Jerome looked away, a little skeptical, thinking. Julia picked up on it, said, "They found skin under his fingernails."

"His skin?"

"They didn't do a DNA test or anything, but it wasn't mine and there was no one else there."

A doctor came out of Graham's room and Julia rushed over. The other three crowded around as well. A middle-aged Jew of a man, he introduced himself as Mendelbaum.

Julia said, "Doctor, how is he?"

The doctor glanced at his chart a second, then said, "He's stable. He's lost a lot of blood, but a transfusion isn't necessary just yet. He'll be out of it for a while, his heart rate was all over the place, but he's going to sleep it off. We'll keep him here for a few days, let him recover, then we can work from there. I've listed him as a danger to himself, so we'll give a complete psychological analysis before I'll give the go ahead to release him."

"Is he awake?"

"No. We've got him drugged up pretty good. He'll sleep at least the night, and when he wakes up he'll probably be very groggy for a while. Keeps the pain away. But somehow I don't think he'd be awake if he was sober. I have a feeling his scars go deeper than his skin."

"Can we see him?" asked Julia.

"Sure. One at a time, and keep it very brief. Please." They thanked the doctor and he shook their hands with a gentle and practiced handshake. Julia, being Graham's wife, was allowed to go in first. The room was a dim fluorescent blue, and they could see barely more than the silhouette of her figure as it sat next to the bed and her arms extended to the body lying there.

Dubois remained seated on the bench next to the door to the room, seemingly more interested in his fingernails than with the events at hand. Jerome held both his elbows and stood next to Isabelle, said, "What do you think?"

"About Graham? I like him. He's a good guy."

"I mean about what's happened. You think he did it to himself?"

"Why do you ask me? You would know him better."

"Yeah, but you're a cop and you are also his partner. And you're the only one who showed up who wasn't under any professional obligation. Says something."

Isabelle paused a moment, considering her answer carefully.

"There's something...stopping me from thinking he's crazy."

"You don't know what it is either, huh?" She shook her head no. And they were quiet a while and it was only broken when Julia opened the door and came back out again. She said he was asleep. White as a ghost. She left and would be back the next day to look in on him.

Isabelle said, "What are you going to do?"

"I'm gonna stay with him. As long as it takes."

"You should go home and get some sleep. Come back tomorrow." Jerome nodded, and Isabelle left after telling him goodbye. Jerome stood there in the white sterility of the hospital, a little apprehensive about entering the room. Nobody cared. His brother was just another bed there, and the nurses walked by with their heads down. He went into the cold blue room, disappearing into the darkness as the door closed off the light from behind him. Sat down in the chair next to the bed. Graham looked a bit like a corpse to him, lying there on the bed, a blue hue sickening over his pale whiteness. A nurse came in after an hour or so and told him he should leave but he refused.

"I see both of you are awake." It was Mendelbaum, the doctor. Scribbling in his chart. Jerome looked over at Graham. He was certainly awake. "He hasn't spoken, if that's what you're going to ask. I'm not going to sedate him unless it's necessary. But I think he's pretty mixed up. A psychiatrist will be in later today to evaluate him."

Jerome left the room with the doctor and thanked him, then got a drink of water for himself. Isabelle was walking in and they ran into each other in front of Graham's room.

"How is he doing?"

"I don't really know. He just woke up, and the doctor said he isn't speaking."

"Catatonic?"

"Naw. Not even close. I only looked at him for a second. But he looks completely aware to me."

They both looked in through the window in the door. Graham lay in the bed, his eyes surveying the surroundings of the room. His face was almost completely expressionless, but for the slightest trace of an unfavorable frown. He didn't lack any intellect in his eyes, though. It wasn't as though his mind had become a vacuum. They pushed open the door and slowly walked up to him.

Isabelle said, "Graham?" He looked up at her. Not speaking a word. But it looked as though a thousand thoughts passed across his eyes. "Can you speak to me, Graham?" Nothing.

Jerome said, "We'd better leave 'im. They said a psychiatrist was coming later."

It was so cold...worms slowly inched across my face and I wondered how long it would be before I could see beauty again...

"Do you think he's closed in on himself?"

"It looks like that's what's happened. A total severing from the world around him. He'd been pulling away for so long and it looks like he finally fell down a chasm. Like he was holding a rope and it broke." Jerome took a bite off his cigar. "I held my hand out. I thought he would take it."

Isabelle took a moment to reply, she was concentrating on making a left turn. "Was your effort sincere?"

"Of course it was. He's my brother."

"I remember early in my career on the police force, I was the first to arrive on the scene of a suicide situation. The guy was in an apartment, or hotel or something, a good ten stories up on the ledge. I thought myself a hero, and I went up and I was the only one there. No one would be on the scene for several minutes at least, and the staff was going crazy, so I decided to try and talk to him. Turn here? I stuck my head out to talk to him, calm hi, and once I started talking to him it seemed so easy. He was neurotic, I was smarter than him, I thought. Some medical staff arrived and I was even going to leave, but the guy didn't want me to. I backed them off and they didn't want to break a touchy situation so they stayed away. What it was though, was that I didn't care about this guy. I could care less if he jumped. And all I wanted to do was do my job well. I put as much sympathy into my voice as I thought possible. I thought myself so clever." She stopped and puffed on her cigarette. "Anyway just as I was about to get smug and pleased with myself, he looked me right in the eye-right through me-and he said I was just as false as the world he was trying to escape.

"And he jumped. Leapt high in the air and swan-dived face first into the pavement. What I'm saying is that no matter how psychotic someone seems, they can still see into you soul. Sometimes more so than any sane person could possibly attempt to."

"Thanks for the story. And the ride. Here's good." Jerome got out of the car and leaned in the window. He took out a pen and scrap of paper and scribbled his phone number on it. "Here. We better keep in touch, I'd say."

Jerome watched her drive away and then went up into his top floor townhouse apartment. As he opened the door he was relieved to find Clyde snoozing and snoring away on the couch, his belly hanging out of his shirt and chocolate smeared on his lips and fingers. It had been nearly twenty-four hours since Jerome had bothered to check in on his guest and he was feeling a little guilty about it. Obviously Clyde had found something to occupy himself-gluttony and sloth. Jerome shook him gently and tried to wake him.

"Clyde?" The only response was a wet snort from Clyde's nose. Jerome let him sleep and went into the kitchen to start on dinner. It had been a while since he ate a proper meal. He'd saved some steaks in the freezer for Clyde and set about to make them, as well as potatoes and corn to go with it. After he'd set everything to boiling and set the steaks aflame on the indoor bar-b-que, he went back over to Clyde and shoved his feet off the couch, sat down next to him.

"C'mon, buddy, up and at 'em." Clyde just lay there contorted. "Jeez, I wish I had your worries," said Jerome. He watched a movie on t.v. for a few moments before going to check on the steaks. Being in the restaurant business, he was always concerned with presentation and was putting together the plates with the dripping red meat and fluffy mashed potatoes when he heard some rustling behind him. He glanced over his shoulder and saw Clyde standing at the entrance to the kitchen.

"Up and at 'em, lazy ass." He put the plates on the table and went to the fridge to get some beer. "Well? You waitin' for an invitation? Siddown!" Clyde slowly sat down, looked at the food in front of him. "You okay? You seem weird." Clyde started picking at his food with his fingers and tearing the niblets off the corn and then squeezing the mashed potatoes through his fingers. He picked up the steak and sniffed at it. Mmmmm, medium rare bloody steak. Delicious. He leaned his head back and rung out the steak juice into his mouth, and when every last drop had dripped into his mouth he tore ravenously at the flesh of the cooked animal. "You need your medication or something?" Clyde would usually grin a big sloppy grin and shake his head up and down furiously when someone asked him this, saying, "Ya ya ya!"

It had darkened considerably. The sun had gone down and Jerome's apartment only had the kitchen light on for illumination. Jerome got up and got Clyde's medication from the cupboard. He handed the pill bottle to Clyde, looking at his sweaty, beady forehead. Clyde looked at the bottle for a moment. Jerome pulled away for a second to open the bottle for him. Clyde grabbed hold of his wrist. A lightning quick snatch that belied his slovenly demeanor and large frame. His grip was ice and steel. Jerome tried to shrug him off but couldn't. Clyde was on his feet now, and he stretched out Jerome's arm and pulled him off balance. He twisted Jerome's wrist like it was a rag and then bit into the stretched and vulnerable flesh. Jerome cursed in pain, and by this time had begun to strike at Clyde's head with his free hand. He was still a little off balance and couldn't get a serious blow in. Not that he wanted to; this was his friend after all.

Clyde had ripped a good chunk of flesh off of Jerome's arm with his first bite, and began warding off the blows with his other arm. They gripped at each other's arms and reached a stalemate of strength. But Clyde's build was bigger, he was taller than Jerome and he was slowly starting to overpower. That, combined with his fierce and ignorant determination, while Jerome also wrestled with his remorse at physically quarreling with one of his best friends.

Jerome was pushed back to the countertop and he was bent so that his back was arched at a sharp angle, the tension tearing the muscle and causing the vertebrae to grind against one another. Jerome's arms were pinned to the counter and he struggled against Clyde's hold. Clyde kept his arms as straight as steel bars and Jerome was forced to try and lift his arms under the weight of Clyde's entire body. He could barely bend his elbows, and his neck was whipping left and right trying to avoid the snapperhead bites of Clyde's now vicious jaws. Clyde's breath smelled of hot pepper and rotten eggs, something unnatural. Jerome was struggling to get his hands free, grappling all over the counter from some sort of weapon to help him. His feet were dangling off the floor now, and the blood flow was cut off from parts of his body-his hands were blue and tingling from numbness, and his back was creased into a fold just above his waist where he was being pressed into the counter-and Jerome wondered how long he could maintain consciousness if his blood couldn't get where it should be. Added to the fact that blood was coming out of his open wound and making the torn flesh look as though some tyrannical king had been soaking up the blood with bread. Jerome finally struggled his way to his right and got his hands on a serrated kitchen knife. He was so pushed up and his entire upper body was stretched out under Clyde's bulk but Jerome's legs still had some room to move and he began thrashing them to push Clyde off of him. He finally got his legs bent up towards his chest and with a great thrust he pushed at Clyde; though Clyde's grip was so tight that they both were flung across the kitchen and they fell, Jerome crashing into the fridge and Clyde crushing the table.

They both stood up, at odds against each other in the small room, Jerome squeezing his knife and trembling with utter confusion and trepidation. Clyde moved slowly towards Jerome-he was big and didn't have to move fast, and intimidated purely on his size and brutishness. His mouth looked dark and hot, his lips and gums reddened with blood, his tongue almost hanging out with every weighty pant of his foul breath. His hands shook and the edges of his features looked as though someone had painted him in death; his eyelids, fingertips, and earlobes tinted a pale and ill blue, his cheeks and eyeballs crimson and his nasal cavity a dry black as though it had seen fire for a thousand years. Jerome stopped for one moment as he caught a glimpse of something beneath the raw and unmitigated force of evil in Clyde's eyes-a yearning sadness, struggling, in the merest twinkle of the fluorescent light that flashed in Clyde's eyes, to come to the surface. Could he bring this monstrous, mindless beast to tears? Could he cut open his heart with pity rather than steel?

As Clyde moved towards Jerome, with Jerome shoving obstacles in his way-chairs, a side table, an expensive piece of artwork he'd bought in Québec City-the single-mindedness of the attack became apparent. Clyde moved forward in a sluggish manner, practically walking through the obstacles that were thrown in his path, only the barest effort necessary used to push the items out of his way. His glazed gaze was fixed on Jerome's bloody arm, and the sadness flickered away as the source of light moved behind Clyde's head, taking the twinkle away from his eye. Jerome kept backing away, into his living room, trying to position himself in such a way that Clyde would follow him to a point where he could trap him with the sofa against the wall. He'd maneuvered Clyde to where he wanted and (Clyde moving slow enough and seemingly with little consciousness other than his own small spark of self-centered will) tried to shove Clyde up against the wall and trap him there with the sofa. As soon as the bulk of the sofa hit the side of Clyde's leg he was thrown off-stride and, as though by some force rather than any self-control or strategic counter-maneuver, his arm extended stiff and straight, warding off the further thrusts of the sofa by Jerome.

Clyde had now rounded the sofa and both were in virtual darkness but for the light of the kitchen. Jerome, desperate for some other plan, clicked on his freestanding living room light, a bright spotlight type lamp that was designed to mimic a stage light. When the light was clicked on, the brightness of it blinded Clyde, moreso than just a momentary adjustment; he crossed his hands over his eyes and covered for a moment as though it were the light of heaven become visible to him and issuing a brutal judgment, casting him down to Hell while burning away his eternal soul.

This was Jerome's opportunity-he still held the knife, and he could choose to strike down at his friend while he was now in this vulnerable state. He moved the light closer to Clyde. His first mistake. After several moments Clyde stopped trembling under the God light and began to uncross his arms. His painted death face was revealed, beaded with sweat, and he was obviously in some primitive, unsophisticated form of agitation. His Oakbrook High School t-shirt was yellowed and wet with sweat, his eyes returning to the unmatchable, unstoppable forcefulness they once had. He realized the light couldn't hurt him, that, though it was sun bright, it wasn't the sun and he could resume his death march. Jerome was too slow in processing what was happening, and Clyde, his quickness surprising, had snapped his arm straight and grabbed hold of Jerome's neck, lifting him inches off the ground so that his feet dangled lifelessly beneath his body. Clyde's big, clumsy hands, sticky with chocolate and blood, began to squeeze and squeeze and SQUEEZE until Jerome's black face turned purple and his muscles deflated and his veins bulged as though they would burst from the pressure. Whatever was left in Jerome, whatever wasn't so focused on the fact that his neck was being compressed to nearly a third its size, manifested itself as a pointless thrashing of his limbs. His eyes were slammed shut from the pressure, his head pushed all the way back, and the horrible snapping of his bones grinding began to make him nauseous. He felt the lack of blood flow and his ears felt as though they were going to burst. The knife still in his hand, with one powerful, blind thrust forward, Jerome stabbed Clyde though the ribcage and they both fell to the ground.

It was as though Clyde fell in slow motion, and when he hit the ground it looked as though he bounced three or four times (because of his weight) before he came to a rest and lay prone on the ground, the knife sticking out of his chest, like a burial marker.

I slowly realized they were everywhere, their numbers growing slowly as the calendar kept circling. It awakened some long buried desire within me, to feel them swirling all around me, through me. But still it was dark and I couldn't really move, except to float around in the dreams of others. I had a taste of it but I needed more, just a little more. That one piece of majic, that spark. Then I sensed him, and for the first time in a thousand years I was awake...

Jerome sat at the edge of the hospital bed, hands hanging between his knees, and said, "I killed a man today, Graham." He took a deep breath. It was so hard to suppress the emotions of reality when you validated them with your own words, with the sound of your voice in a cold, blue room, even if you were talking to what was tantamount to a corpse. "And he was my friend. I haven't decided if that makes it that much worse." Jerome got up and looked out the window, put his hand to his forehead. "God, what do you know, you might as well be dead. It's raining out."

It was midday, and the hospital room was reasonably well lit, sad grey sunlight coming in through the window.

"It's ironic, you lyin' there dead and I'm at your bedside confessin' murder." Jerome looked over at his brother. "But some would say you're not really dead, huh?" He leapt over to the bed and grabbed Graham by the collar.

"Wake up!! God damn you wake up!!!" Shaking him and his head bouncing back and forth on the pillow. Dropped him and his arms fell across his chest, strength sapped from stealing life. He raised his head up a bit and saw that Graham had opened his eyes, two dark dots devoid of strength. Graham's eyes looked not at Jerome but across him. There was no hope in either of their eyes, and only thick gobs of tears in Jerome's as he saw Graham's head loll around another all too brief moment before resting awkwardly on the pillow. He whispered tearfully, "God damn you wake up..."

A nurse walked in, not especially quietly, but Jerome either didn't hear her or had blocked out her presence. Until she put her hand on his shoulder, said, "Is everything okay, *monsieur*?"

Jerome dried his eyes with the back of his hand and said, "*Oui, oui, madam.*" He pardoned himself and excused the nurse from the room.

"I'm so goddamned tired," he said. "I've been up all night. You're up all night aren't you, Graham? I must say it isn't as much fun when you aren't drunk. Perhaps the darkness affects us in ways we don't know. But after seeing ghosts I couldn't sleep after I just killed a man. Superstitious, maybe. But I'm so goddamned tired." He took Graham's hand in his.

"Needless to say it was a long night. I had nowhere to turn. God, that's an awful feeling. I think for a moment I realized how you must've felt. I couldn't go to Julia. And I have lots of friends, but I couldn't go to any of them, either. Lots of friends, but all I really do with them is party. Not that they wouldn't have helped me out. But there was no deepness there. Maybe I wanted to be saved from myself, I don't know.

"I even thought of going to Isabelle. But I have no idea what her sense of duty is like. So I came here, to see you. The only person in the world. And I'm talking to myself. And still I can't thing of anyone who can match it." He sat in a chair near the bed.

"Needless to say, it was a long night, maybe because I'm still living it over and over in my mind. But I went back to the apartment later. Must've been an hour or so. I wandered around the streets wondering what to do. Maybe hopin' that it would all have been a dream. It felt like one. Still does. I can't bring myself to believe I'm a murderer.

"It was a nightmare though. Right when I drove the knife into his chest, I think-" Jerome buried his face in his hands "-I think I wished the worst for him. Human nature. I was in fear of my life, y'know. Can you dig it? I creaked the door open and he was still there. Have you ever seen the insides of a man? The knife was still in him, but God..." Jerome laughed. "I do seem to be saying God a lot don't I? If I thought he looked painted up in the Devil's ink when he was coming at me before, well this...he was like..." Jerome stopped for a moment, his throat constricted with nausea. He had to take several deep breaths, and his head throbbed as he stepped on all the guilt and revulsion, pushing it away from his soul. "Fuck, his chest was splayed open, the flaps of skin like wings, and the knife was sticking right out of his heart...like someone sat there and created a sculpture of a dark angel from Hell, all painted up in bloody red and black membrane."

Jerome leaned back in the chair, and leaned his head so he was looking downwards.

"Someone down there knows he was an angel and is laughing at me," he whispered. The rain beat harder on the window, its harsh lullaby making Jerome feel tired until he fell asleep.

He woke suddenly, as though from a nightmare, or as if he'd missed an appointment. Night had fallen, slowly replacing each raindrop with darkness, leaving Montréal's streets wet and the air chilly. Jerome looked at his brother, lying there with his eyes half lidded. He got up and went out into the hall, got himself some water from the fountain. Gulping it down until the hunger died. He went back into the room, leaving the light of the hall (why didn't anyone bother to turn on the lights at night in this room? Whenever the door was open it seemed as though the light were a rude invasion into the gruesome, funereal darkness of Graham's room) and he saw the bed empty, the sheets pushed into a crumpled semi-circle. Graham was standing at the window ignorant of the light and his brother standing in the door.

"You're up," said Jerome. Graham stood looking out the window, holding his elbow. Jerome picked up a tray of barely warm food and brought it over to him. "You've been out for days. You'd better eat something." He handed the tray over to Graham. Graham thrust out his arm and the food flew in the air, some of it splashing on Jerome, the tray clattering on the floor ten feet away.

Jerome said, "Shit," and went to buzz the nurse, but the wire had been pulled. He went over to the door, but before he could go through it the table with the ECG, under its own power, slid across the floor and jammed itself up against the door, pinning it shut. Jerome tried to open the door but couldn't move the table out of the way. The room had suddenly become so cold. All Jerome could say was, "Mother*fucker*," as he wiped some of the food off his cheeks. Graham turned around slowly and moved towards him, lifted Jerome's arm that had the bite wound on it.

"A man of impeccable taste, I see. Your friend has opened his soul to you."

"Did you do that to the door, Graham?"

"He survives..he survives." Graham kept rolling his head slowly to his right, closing his eyes as though tired. "There are so many of them...legions...thousands...I had dreams for a thousand years..."

"Dreams of what?"

"Dreams of darkness...and clutching tightly to a blue rose made of blood."

"What does that mean?" asked Jerome.

"It means the world to me." Graham moved over to the window, wrapping his arms around him as though protecting himself from the cold, perhaps the chill of his soul rather than the cold of the air. "For a thousand years I clung tightly to dreams. Do you know what it's like to sleep and not dream? Thousands of them. All crying."

Jerome asked, "Is that what woke you up?"

"It's like looking through other eyes. He came along and that was finally it. After a thousand years I thought I could do it again, but I just couldn't lose him, so I bit. But they were all there and crying and it sounds so terrible so I do what I can but my head hurts sometimes. Sometimes I'm so weak..." Graham made tight fists of his hands, so tight his muscles corded and his veins became blue-grey and visible under his skin, and he looked down at his fists and shut his eyes as though his soul were pained. He pulled his left fist back to his waist, eyes still closed, and punched through the double-paned window, shattering the glass. Blood seeped out of the lacerations on his hand which criss-crossed his flesh like a child's freshly scrawled X's on scrap paper. He looked at them for a moment, then slowly pressed his already torn skin to the broken, jagged edge of the hole in the window, cutting into himself. Jerome ran over to stop him, to pull him away from the window, but Graham shrugged him off with his other arm with a strength that belied his ailing condition. Jerome got up off the floor and began banging on the door-still blocked-and yelling for the nurses to come, but it was as though no one heard him. As though the room did not exist within the hospital anymore.

Graham began suckling on his wounds, lapping up the blood from his arm.

"You could come through here!" giggled the little girl in the red dress. Jerome, startled, backed into the Electrocardiogram and fell away to the floor, saying, "Jesusm utherfuckin'Christ." The little girl in the red dress stood hand out, beckoning urgently, fingers of black smoke clinging to her. "Quickly, before he sees!" she exclaimed in a whisper. Behind her was a mass of black smoke, shadows that swirled together on the currents of the air. The little girl kept urging him on, but all Jerome could do, when he regained himself, was bang on the door with increased fervor. Graham, lost in the ecstasy of the bloody rips in his skin, began to turn, distracted from his distraction. The little girl became very agitated, her expression sad and urgent, and she kept glancing over to Graham to see if he'd noticed her. Frustrated, the little girl withdrew her summoning hand and, before Graham could turn around to notice her, she turned with a flourish of her blond hair and disappeared along with the shadows, into nothingness.

Graham grinned at Jerome who was still on the floor, a dripping red grin, his teeth outlined in blood. He lost his smile suddenly, looking nauseous, his throat choking as his mouth sputtered blood and it waterfalled down his chin, splashing on his white hospital gown.

"It disagrees sometimes. It's not perfect. Nothing is. But let me tell you the sheer ecstasy is worth every bit of pain that comes with it. You get to feel power. You see things other people will *never* get to see in their worthless lives. The majic is almost as intoxicating as love. The exception is that you get to keep more control of your senses. Love almost destroys you with its utter singularity of purpose. You forget yourself. I have all the bitterness of love scorned and I've coupled that with the grand scale of vision provided by my drunken power! Now the voices don't just talk to me-they worship me. I am truly eternal..."

He moved towards Jerome, his hands splayed out like claws and his teeth bared and hungry to bite. Jerome rolled out of the way, and Graham crashed into the ECG machine. Though his attacks looked fierce, Jerome felt there was something... lacking...about them. Like they were missing the same strength and speed which was used to fling him away from the window when Graham was cutting himself. Not that Graham didn't keep coming, like a raging rhinoceros. Jerome had to keep dodging his thrusts, as liquid frothed from Graham's mouth, trying to splash Jerome's face. He was trapped in the room like a fly in a jar, bolting from corner to corner, grabbing every object he could and throwing it at Graham to impede his advances.

It became apparent to Jerome, after several passes around the room, that his only hope may be in further breaking the glass and jumping out of the window. They were on the fifth floor, and survival would be a likely option to contemplate on the way down. Nothing, not madness nor majic, could bring him to kill his brother.

Jerome hopped the bed and leaned his back up against the window. He knew he only had seconds before his brother would be upon him again and he had to grab something-he eyed the chair-to widen the hole in the glass. He was about to bolt for the chair when cold hands gripped him about the neck, intimately, antagonistically, one hand covering his mouth so he could not speak.

"Quiet. Do not scream. I can help you, if you'll give yourself to me." The voice was deep and sinister in tone, though the intent behind it didn't sound evil. Jerome, at an absolute loss, utterly helpless, could not ignore this second offer of assistance, despite the fact all he knew of his savior were cold grey hands and arms clad in dark brown suede. "Do not scream," said the voice, as the hand uncovered his mouth. Jerome wasn't exactly sure what he saw, just that the stranger whispered some words in a strange language and extended his hand to the air, as though pulling threads of the air currents together with the circles he made with his fingers. Out of nothingness came the black smoke, the swirling shadows, and the stranger's fingers seemed to control the darkness as plumes of the smoke traveled towards Graham, filling his eyes, his nose, his mouth. The smoke covered Graham's face as though it were an octopus, and he fell-though, what with darkness invading darkness, Jerome couldn't really be positive of what he saw-to the ground, choking and sputtering and blind.

It broke his heart to have to leave his brother like that, as the stranger's arms wrapped around him once more. He felt himself being lifted off the ground, and suddenly he was outside, his eyes filled with tears and his heart remorse. He would have been overcome with emotion and insanity if not for the narcotic swoon and the rush of icy wind that blasted his face. He tried to gain some control of his senses, to the point that he could crane his neck upwards and catch a glimpse of the stranger's face. It was difficult, and the same bits of shadow whipped around and confused the picture he tried to take. Though, in his deepest instinct, he knew who it was. It was obvious who it was.

As a bright light blinded him, the last thing he felt before he lost consciousness were cold lips kissing his cheek, the tongue deceptively sneaking a taste of his flesh. He felt his thoughts melt and everything went black and he fell asleep, as though he were drunk and had no other choice.

It took a moment for Jerome to come to the realization that the phone was actually ringing, and he had to drag himself out of his sleep before he found the strength to pick up the phone.

"Jerome spanking, how may I service you?"

"Hey, it is Isabelle," she answered, effecting a Francophone accent.

"What's up?" asked Jerome, shaking off the grogginess.

"Just calling to see how everything is."

Jerome was quiet for a moment, that is to say, he was recalling the details of the previous few nights, his homicide, his demon savior, his brother's madness.

"Jerome?"

"Uh, yeah. Still here." Where was here? Oh fuck. His apartment. It *wasn't* all a dream. He imagined himself asleep all night and Clyde's rotting artistic corpse out in the living room, sleeping with him.

"You don't sound too good, Jerome."

"Hang on, I gotta beep." Jerome clicked over to the other line. Dr. Mendelbaum was calling to inform him of the state of his brother after the previous evening (as they couldn't get hold of Graham's wife.) He'd become violent, cracking a window and cutting himself to the point that he dangerously diminished his blood supply. There was some minor damage to some of the furniture and equipment around the room as well. There was certainly cause to leave him in restraints and Dubois was with him now, and a decision would be reached shortly as to his mental state of mind, and further where he should be treated. Jerome was to call later for an appointment once he got hold of Julia to go over the evaluation and discuss a decision.

"Hey, sorry. It was the hospital."

"How is he?"

"Don't know yet. I gotta go there later to talk to the doctor."

"And you?"

"Livin'," said Jerome. They made plans to meet for a coffee and bagels. As soon as Jerome tentatively opened the door to his bedroom and made sure no body had used his living room as a tomb.

Integrity and honesty were traits that both Graham and Jerome held in highest regard, so it was with a little feeling of guilt that Jerome left out the part of his story that involved the murder and subsequent disappearance of his best friend. But, unlike Graham, he told of the demon who'd saved him from his brother's psychotic outbursts.

"And you think this is the same demon that appeared to Graham years ago and caused him to close in on himself."

"That much is obvious to me," said Jerome. "But I looked up and caught a glimpse of his face."

Isabelle leaned back again, somewhat disturbed by the answer.

Jerome said, "What always bothered me about what happened to my brother...it was that, knowing him how I do, he really focused on specifics. Very obsessive kinda person. I mean if some monster rushed up to him in a blur and disappeared than he would've shrugged it off for a while, but this...he had a *soul* to focus on. A face with expressions, eyes with emotions."

Isabelle put her finger to her lips, contemplative.

"What is it?" asked Jerome.

"I never pictured Graham's demon as being so close to *human*."

"What did you expect?"

"A monster."

"And that would've scared you less?"

"Perhaps it is that something like a vampire, it carries with it an intelligence, it creates fear on a different level. There's a lot more intimacy in the kind of killing a vampire would do, as opposed to a murderous monster which would be tantamount to plunging a knife into a man's heart."

"I think I better go see Dr. Mendelbaum." Jerome got up and left some toonies on the table to cover the bill, nodded an *au revoir* as he turned to leave.

Isabelle thought she might have offended him and called out after him, "Jerome, do you think maybe Graham is just bored with life because he caught a glimpse of the end?" but Jerome had already disappeared into the crowd.

Part 3: Dream and Awakening

I imagined my own death a thousand times in dreams. I would be walking down a long, grey hall, and everyone I knew would be lined up along the corridor wall, most of them statues. Years ago, it would be my wife bent over in tears, but now it was mostly Korson, or Isabelle, people who were briefly important to me in my moments of longing and loneliness, until the glitter of initial attraction wore off. Lately it was just Jerome.

The hall looked as though it were made of stone, the ceiling rounded off, the surface roughened as though carved out slowly over the course of years by the tears of mourners. There was just darkness at the end of the hall as I walked slowly to my death. I could never figure out if it was metaphorical or literal, that I was always walking to my death. That maybe one day I would reach the end and that would mean I would never wake up.

I had dreams of the darkness at the end of the tunnel too. Imagining death, perhaps. I'd be sitting in a circle of grey light, outside of which I could see only endless black. Living black, for I noticed tiny tentacles of the darkness fingering my ring of light, only barely, but with purpose. I had dreams of the shadow. And Korson had already told me that it was a dangerous, volatile majic, trying to control the whirling, swirling darkness.

From moment to moment I would see people walking through the edge of the circle, briefly coming into the light, then disappearing once more. This scenario had been played out a thousand times in fiction and film, and was nothing new to me. To confront one's own fears. But the twist, of course, was that this was personalized. Plucked from my very own mind, tailor-made for me, something that, perhaps, you might find a little mundane, or may shrug off as insignificant, but for me...well, for me I spent a lifetime creating these things, even if they only were in my head.

Sometimes I believe that we are born knowing everything. And we forget things, which is why we make mistakes, continually, until we learn. Why we forget, though, I'm really not sure. Perhaps our minds can only take so much, so we don't really make use of it all. I try not to be guilty of that. I try to use my brain. But I really am, maybe more so than even a murderer like Korson, an animal.

So I sat in these dreams, my death, and watched for a while as people walked by the edges of the circle. I figured I should confront my fears, and waited for the next person to walk by. I heard faint steps behind me. I shot up and turned, and chased my fear as it walked calmly, as though nothing were happening, and disappeared. A couple times I just went back to where I was sitting. I chased my fears into the darkness twice; once, I got lost and it took me what seemed like hours to find my way back to my circle of grey light. The second time I was flung back into the circle. Actually, I must confess, I was flung back into the circle twice. Lesson learned, stupidity ceased. I couldn't start running around my own mind.

The worst of it was, in my brief moments of lucidity, or wakefulness, was that I felt the madness overcome me when I tried to push the limits of my dreams, tried to breach control. As though my body were reacting violently to the energies I was being exposed to. Once I even woke in time to find myself looking through my eyes as though they were windows, as though I had no control over myself, attacking my brother, and it took a supreme effort from yours truly to find enough feeling in my limbs to slow them so Jerome had a chance.

I took the lesson, and I sat there. I waited patiently for my fears to come to me, and I would deal with them if, and only if, they manifested themselves to me in a threatening manner. Oh, I was so tempted to get up and run when I saw the face of the murderer walk through the edge of the circle and turn her head briefly to smile at me. The bitch was in here with me. I sat there, I seethed. She knew I was getting close. Still far away, but dangerously closer than any mortal had ever dared. I knelt there, in the circle, and did my best not to boil over. Something told me that if I did I would end up reported dead with a hemorrhage or something. I calmed myself, relaxed everything about my mind. Define my anger, my emotions. In essence, explained it out to myself till I understood the source of my anger at her, that I hated her, hated the fact that she indiscriminately murdered innocent children, and that if I let my rage blind me, I wouldn't be able to function. That anger would only squeeze my fists into balls and keep all my energy within me, until it destroyed me. Rage is such an adult emotion. I don't think I can imagine a child truly angry. Perhaps I just don't have that great a scope of imagination, and I'm thankful for it.

I knelt in my circle and waited. I focused on myself, relaxed myself, just thinking, or if that got tiresome or redundant, meditating in the death of silence. Perhaps this was a lesson in itself, about my boredom with life. The fact that I was in awe of Korson and his gift of eternity. That's what it felt like, all the waiting, it felt as though my mind were showing me a piece of eternity, seeing if I could deal with it. Maybe my mind would grow? The circle would widen so I could cast a light on my fears? So much of ourselves we keep in darkness, and knowing what I know now, despite the shortness of my life, I found that such a pity.

From time to time, after a long stream of consciousness, or after a particularly relaxing session of meditation, I would let myself become distracted. I can't say for sure, but if felt as though some God would reset a clock. Like I was starting over again. I decided to resolve myself, not to boredom, but to eternity in my mind, my dream. When everything blurred, when the fears walking by could neither cause my ear to twitch nor my head to turn, when I felt as though I were part of the raging river time, someone stopped. A blond, at first I mistook for my wife, but she moved different. She stopped and looked at me as though she were searching her mind for recognition. Then turned and began to walk towards me. I waited, I would not seek confrontation. I wouldn't force anything to happen, I would let them happen as they may. I do confess I did feel a little cowardly, but I had chosen my position and would not stray from it. She got close to me and half sat and half reclined.

"Long time no see." It was Heather Langden, the girl I saw on the street, who brought Korson back to me. She was different. She was a vampire. Still fucking gorgeous, though. Had to say it, I am a man after all.

"Are you real?" I asked her. She looked at me a little curiously.

"Do you mean am I really here? Or am I, a vampire, really real?"

I couldn't find the words to rephrase the question. "Are *you* real?"

"I'm sorry, I don't understand the question. I think I exist. I have come across people who don't, but then I kill them, if that helps."

"God, you're beautiful."

"Your honesty is refreshing. There aren't enough people like you in the world. Don't you feel better being honest?" I thought she was trying to ask me something, and I think she realized that from the expression on my face. "You always denied your feelings for me, you never had any thoughts of my beauty in your dreams. Yeah, I watched from time to time. I was curious."

I slowly reached out my hand, getting close to her cheek. I wasn't sure if this was really Heather. She seemed real enough, except maybe for what she just said. Heather was beautiful, no doubt, but the last comment she made seemed too *sexual* for her.

"You can touch me, I don't bite…well, I do, but not you, anyway." She giggled. Innocently. That much, at least, was her. I didn't actually touch her though. Perhaps I didn't want to find out that it wasn't really her, that I was just dreaming this. Well, I <u>was</u> dreaming this, but I clung to the hope that Heather could come to my dream. Maybe I should, though. Maybe that would end all this.

"I don't know if I'm absolutely sure what is happening," I said. Heather threw back her head and laughed. Beautiful teeth, exquisite, musical laughter.

"It's Korson, isn't it? Him and his big fat pride. He came to you for help, but he isn't giving much away. Secretive bastard! I love 'im though. To death. He did the same to me. I had to leave him. God, that hurt, to leave him, but I had to. He loved me too, but he protected me too much. He's caught between love and some oath he sealed in blood. There's no one with a truer soul than Korson, no one more loyal. He's like a Klingon. That damn oath, but he takes his blood seriously." She looked at me and smiled. I looked back at her blankly.

"Well?" I said.

"Well what?"

"What's happening?"

"Oh…" she smiled at me again, slightly sheepish. "A war is coming."

"Over what?"

"Souls."

"Whose?"

"Everyone's."

We both turned and looked into the darkness, then looked at each other as if to say, *Did you hear that?*

"Is she here?" I asked.

"Talissa? Yeah, she's here," said Heather, looking sidelong into the darkness. "We better be careful, she'd freak if she found us here. Jealous type."

"Ah." I almost chuckled. "Are you actually telling me this or am I imaging you telling me this?" Heather rolled her eyes at me.

"Good grief, said Charlie Brown," she said. "The Place of the Dead is getting crowded. All the souls that are dying now have nowhere to go, and they're a great source of majical energy. *The* source, better than the shadow. I-" Another noise. "Shit. She's coming. I gotta go. Sorry, Graham, this isn't the place for me to fight her. Good luck." She kissed me on the cheek and walked (faded?) away as I called after her to stay. But just before she disappeared she looked over her shoulder and said, "Just remember, people tend to forget their dreams…except children…" The darkness began to hug her. She smiled at me and said, "Sowen, Graham."

Then she left me in darkness.

And Talissa jumped out.

Jerome left Mendelbaum's office a little put off. First of all, Julia hadn't shown for the appointment. So all that really happened was a semi-involved discussion about what happened to Graham. He was suicidal. He'd lost litres of blood, and his wrists were on the verge of being crisscrossed with scars from failed efforts at self-destruction.

"Because of his history," said Mendelbaum, "we're trying to give him every opportunity to reintegrate into society." A police officer with a once good standing on the force was not someone they wanted to throw into the nut house without an extremely sound and thorough diagnosis. But Dubois was pushing. And Mendelbaum, a genteel Jew, tried to phrase this to Jerome in that delicate and political way that doctors do. Jerome caught the implications, though, and realized that if there wasn't a serious regression to Graham's predicament, and soon, then there wouldn't be much stone to stand on against Dubois' recommendations.

Jerome had only met Dubois twice, and he thoroughly disliked him, much like Graham did. And much for the same reasons. He was a smarmy, greasy little bastard. He was an obvious homosexual. His red and white polka dot bow tie was so *gauche*. Furthermore, Jerome was not overly convinced that Dubois really wanted to help his brother. He was a psychiatrist, and Jerome thought he'd seen a wonderful opportunity to psychiatrate, or whatever it is that psychiatrists do. He seemed so eager to have Graham committed, with reevaluations for release every six months. Graham could be stuck there for *years*. Then, one day he would be deemed fit for society, cured of his mental plagues, through therapy and drugs and electroshock treatments, whatever Dubois could think of to try that couldn't be attempted on his more mundane patients, as Graham walked out of the sanitarium grinning that prozac grin. And Dubois could stand there proudly, holding his brightly polished dick in his hands, impudently reaping the rewards from his accomplishment.

So Jerome left Mendelbaum's office a little agitated and with a sense of urgency. He'd stopped to check in on his brother for a moment before he left to go home again and eat a much deserved meal. Graham's eyes were half open, all glassy as though he were trying to keep awake. (He was fighting a losing battle as Mendelbaum had ordered him all drugged up so wouldn't be a danger to himself nor anyone around him.)

He got to Graham's house and Julia wasn't home. He called Isabelle and explained Graham's situation.

"Sorry, Jerome, I don't think I can be of much help."

"Well, I can't seem to find my phone. I got here and called the number but I didn't hear any rings so I have no idea where he left it. But I can't figure what he would have done with it."

Tap, tap, tap, tap, tap, tap, tap.

"Isabelle? You still there?"

"Yeah. Just thinking." Another quiet moment. "The killer called us up once, um...well, we sifted through the crackpots, and we came up with one that we figured was quite likely to be the child killer. She called from a cell phone."

"Do you think-"

"I don't know. I can't make any promises. Give me your number and I'll run a check on all the calls made to it, say, in the last two weeks. Might be something to go on."

Jerome said, "Okay, one down."

"All I can tell you to do is rifle through some of his personal belongings while you're at his house. Maybe there's something there. As far as his official papers, I've seen them all and I can't think of anything as yet. But I'll keep in touch."

They hung up and agreed to call every few hours and keep each other updated. Jerome began to go through his brother's house, lingering briefly on all the objects he'd seen hundreds of times before. He knew, of course, that whatever he was looking for wouldn't be found sitting out in the open. Though he hid it well, Graham was obsessively neurotic, cagey and suspicious as a black cat, and would have meticulously hidden something he deemed important. Still, Jerome felt the need to linger nostalgically, something he didn't normally do. He was normally very focused on the here and now, no matter what the situation.

A good hour or so passed, and Jerome, feeling the futility at a random search, flopped on the couch. He hadn't stopped for a moment's rest since...

...just wasn't allowing himself time to think...

...keeping his body occupied kept his mind focused...

...placid in the face of madness, fearless when confronted with vampires and zombies, the swirling brilliance of the unknown splashing all around him. Jerome was functioning on autopilot, moving from task to task to event until his body forced him to go home and have an insignificant amount of food and a restless and uncomfortable sleep. He was a very smooth person, and his personality was very pliant, though by no means weak. Any sort of trauma or emotional distress he could easily absorb, but the recent events were not of the everyday sort, and Jerome was beginning to feel the pressure on his sanity. He was suppressing his resentment at himself, his undirected anger at having been forced into becoming a murderer. And that scared him a little. Perhaps, because, in the black of his mind he felt that maybe he shared something with a creature like Korson that no one should ever have to suffer and he began to cry a little. A few tears dripped down his cheeks to his lips and he tasted the salt water and hoped for relief from the release, that resisting things that went on around him was a futile effort. He hoped his tears were an acceptance of everything he'd suffered through in the last few days-the madness, the murder, and the scars on his soul.

He lifted the bandage and looked at the wound on his arm. It was as though life had given him a tattoo invented out of the abstract myriad of fate's cold, twisted mind, set apart from a common tattoo because this kind could be wholly unwanted, unwarranted and undeserved. But not without purpose. Tears and scars criss-cross the mind numerous times whether they are manifested physically or not, and Jerome had never wanted to be like everyone else-that is, someone who hid behind a false layer of toughness because sensitivity was viewed as weakness.

With the thought in mind that Graham would be incredibly suspicious of everyone, including Julia, Jerome got up and decided to look for the keys to Graham's car. He would be the only one to use it, and it would be a much better place to keep a secret than in accommodations shared with a spouse. He found the spare set no problem, and went out to the car to search through it.

He turned on the engine to warm it up, as it was cold October. Sat in the passenger's side and began feeling underneath the seats for anything he could find. He found the book Graham had kept to himself and read the title. Then the author. Andreas Lurik.

A ratty old printing looking as though it were a shameless horror novel. He was about to go back into the house and use the phone, then, as an afterthought, opened up the glovebox. He had already determined to shut it immediately but for the faint bluish glow that caught his eye. Jerome reached in and pulled out the object, a delicate blue rose that looked as though it were made of crystal. It didn't feel as fragile as it looked though, it felt a little pliant, somewhat like jelly. Jerome looked at the rose with a little awe for a moment and then slammed shut the glove box, the car door, then the front door of the house and called Isabelle.

"Still working on the phone," she said. "Found it?"

"Nah. Nothin'. But I did find a book Graham seemed to think was important. I was wondering if you could check out the author for me."

Isabelle said 'sure' and Jerome listed the details for her, the year of publication, etc. Seemed to be more of a privately published book, much like something distributed by a cult, or a Jehovah's Witness. Hopefully she would be able to answer him within a few hours.

Jerome than turned his attention back to the rose for a moment, and decided he needed to find something to wrap it in to take it home.

Julia St.Croix had never been fucked up the ass before. So with every tentative step she throbbed as she walked up to the door and put the key in the hole and entered her dark and lonely house. Her underwear felt a little wet with blood and she was going to change it as soon as possible. But she was a little bit scared coming home. What if Graham had made a miraculous recovery and was sitting smug with anger in the living room because he knew everything?

She had, of course, met a man, and it was some source of concern for her that she didn't feel guilty for the right reasons. Was she so starved for attention that she fell into the arms of the first person that would provide affection, no matter how shallow? He was a nice guy, really. His name was Howard. Nobody could hate a Howard. Perhaps that's why she picked him, because when Graham found out and got really jealous and they sent him to the nuthouse then he couldn't in good conscience sit there raving and screaming at sweet and docile Howard without even the most deeply mentally ill looking at him funny. But, like all men, no matter how good his intentions were initially, all he wanted to do was fuck her. And she was hungry and desperate and when he turned her over she gave him something she never offered to her husband. She felt guilty for doing that, rather than the cheating, and that in itself was wrong.

Steve Zinger

The house was quiet and empty, and it made her feel sad. This wasn't the life she envisioned for herself, the scars of deception staining what was a perfect union. She didn't understand human flaws and therefore compromised her vows that were at one time thought of as cement for an unbreakable love. It wasn't necessarily her husband's flaws that she misunderstood as perhaps it was her own. Why would she allow her body to be tortured in such a way if she wasn't torturing her own mind?

Ignoring the discomfort and the wetness, she walked slowly in the darkness. Wallowing in the guilt and self-pity and wishing things could be different. But never blaming herself, just wishing things could be different. It never occurred to her that she should want to die. It just wasn't in her nature to be violent, suicidal and manic, so some confusion arose as to these feelings she inspired in herself.

The music in her head quickly died as she walked into the living room and saw a form in the darkness, lying on the floor.

"Don't turn on the light," said the form. Julia stopped, unsure. It was her house, why couldn't she turn on the light if she wanted to? But there was something *powerful* about the girl on the floor as though she'd entered the house by majic. "Sometimes I just love the darkness, don't you?"

"What are you doing in my house?"

"That's quite rude of you. Don't you even offer your guests something to drink?" Julia's eyes became more accustomed to the lack of light and she realized that the girl on the floor was lying completely nude, her legs rubbing together slightly and arms caressing herself as though thoroughly enjoying her state. Despite having just been fucked up the ass, she was just a little shocked at what she was looking at. "Don't you even find me attractive?"

Julia shook her head no and told her to get out.

"Now that...that is something I can't do just yet." The girl got up off the floor, and pressed Julia up against the wall with surprising quickness. Her lips were intimately close to Julia's now. "Say my name. I'd love it if you said my name," she whispered.

"I don't even know your name."

"Yes you do. Think..."

Julia search for a moment, then said, "Talissa..."

"Oh yes, that's it," said Talissa and she pushed her lips up against Julia's. Julia tried to resist but she cold barely move. Talissa's strength belied her smooth and inviting curves. She took one of Julia's hands and forced it downwards, then pressed a finger up into her. "That's it."

"Talissa..." Julia found herself saying, "Talissa... Talissa... Talissa," between kisses. It was moments before she snapped out of it and began to struggle a bit, though her flesh did enjoy the sensations.

"Stop it...stop..why are you doing this to me?"

Talissa pulled Julia's fingers out of her, but still held her up against the wall.

"Oh, I know," she said. "It isn't as beautiful as it once was. It's very cold there now. It's just a cross I have to bear. But that doesn't make my longings for affection any less than they were. You of all people can relate to that." It was clear from the look on Julia's face that she didn't totally comprehend. Not that she was dumb, but she was just a little scared and fear is the mind killer. It can make mortals out of Gods and cowards out of men. "Oh. I see now. You just haven't figured it out." Talissa released her hold slowly and moved away. "Look at me for what I am." She lifted her hands upwards and made her fingers into claws, stretched her lips apart as she leaned her head back to reveal her teeth. Her teeth were a bit bloody, outlined in red, tiny bits of flesh her plaque. "Can you see it now?"

Julia felt her fear rise higher. Her mouth was a little bit wet, and she felt the cuts and tears along her lip and shook because she didn't notice that it had happened before.

"I know why you're afraid," said Talissa. "Graham was right. All these years he was right and those precious little seeds of doubt you had just burst and now you feel like complete shit."

"Why are you even here?" asked Julia.

"He has something of mine. I know it's here somewhere. I smelt it. But I watched you for a while, and I smelled your betrayal, too. If there's one thing I can't stand, it's a betrayal of love..."

She moved toward Julia with obvious intentions, everything about her sharp, her nails, her teeth, her vicious look. Julia noticed more blood on Talissa's hands and couldn't match them to her wounds, but she screamed and backed away out of the instinct and fright.

Talissa said, "Don't run away, Julia! It isn't even your blood!" She laughed, mostly because she knew Julia could never escape. She was on her in a flash to prove her own point to herself. "Don't ever think you can outmatch me. You're nothing. You're mortal. I've slept longer than you've ever dreamed of living. And if you thought your soul was tortured earlier this evening, I'll show you what true pain really is."

Talissa slit Julia's clothes off with a claw, and she shivered there naked, in fear, in the cold. She cried a waterfall down her cheeks and kept screaming out 'why' and 'no' and begging for explanations. Talissa ignored her and threw Julia face first flat on the floor and spread her legs apart. She took her clawed hand and-oh, great cruelties not in the swiftness of punishment but in the painstaking art of deliberate and gradual administration-began to fondle her throbbing flesh, pressing on the nerves as though she had expertise in medical torture. All Julia could do was bite down on Talissa's hand as her mouth was covered to stifle her screams, and when she became desensitized to the pain Talissa found a new piece of her flesh to play with. It seemed like hours and Julia vomited from the pain and the realization that Talissa had slowly and meticulously placed her hand in up past the wrist.

"Don't take this too personally, Julia. It's Graham who I will kill. But I have to get to you first. I think some part of him still loves you for some silly reason. Besides, I'm hungry. And there's someone else who I think really needs a taste of human flesh for him to fully serve my needs…"

It had just gotten dark as Jerome neared his home, and he felt a little lonely, despite the fact the streets weren't in the least bit empty. He carried the rose in a small, rectangular box under his arm, and had slight apprehension at the fact that someone would jump up and ask him what was in it and he'd be forced to find excuses. He knew he had something special in his hands, though he wasn't sure what it was.

He took a deep breath to relax. To relieve himself of the pressure he felt. Though he did find himself surprisingly calm. Others…would go mad at some of the things that had been happening. And others, like the people who walked the streets around him, would remain ignorant. Jerome never lived by schedules, and didn't fall into the happy rut that most did. He found happiness in spontaneity (…he was rethinking that a little now, though…)

By the time he reached the door to his townhouse and put the key in the lock, it was almost perfectly dark, only broken by the streetlights and stars. The release of each breath left him with a little bit of an eerie feeling. He felt like a criminal going into his own house.

He walked up the stairs (he was on the second floor) and put the box on the table, then got himself something to drink, was debating on if he should have a bite to eat. He was in the middle of making a sandwich when he thought he heard something. Not that he had any anticipation of anything happening, he was just trying to make lunch. It might have been a little stupid, but he put down the knife he was using to cut his sandwich with when he thought he heard a similar noise a second time.

There were two doors to Jerome's apartment, one at the ground level, and one at the top of the steps that actually led into the home. He was slowly reaching his hand to open the door, wondering if the noise was coming from something at the bottom door, or nearer to his door on the second level. Maybe some rat or cat scratching away trying to get in? He debated just grabbing the handle and swinging the door open, but-well, it wasn't something as trite as fear or his own good sense of drama that stopped as much as the fact that he had the shit startled out of him by the sudden loud rap on the door. Which somewhat relieved him anyway.

"Um, who is it?" he asked, not wanting to stupidly open the door without some sense of formality. His query was answered by a thump. And Jerome, suspecting who it was, opened the door slowly. Korson half fell into his home, before regaining himself and taking a proper step in while Jerome took an instinctive step backwards. Korson wore his long brown suede coat, and held his left hand underneath the right lapel as though gripping a weapon.

"Jerome St. Croix," he said with a touch of evil delight in his voice. "Please forgive my lackluster entrance…I'm not feeling quite myself this evening." He smiled a bit, not at all hiding the fact that he was a vampire. "I must say I have the deepest admiration for both you and your brother." Jerome gave him a questioning look. "Because you are both alive."

"I have to admit," said Jerome, biting off the end of a cigar, "that even for a dead guy, you don't look so hot." It was true, even though Jerome hadn't turned on much lighting in his apartment (he was afraid that illumination may shed light on things he didn't want to look at, like the stain on his carpet.) Korson looked at him and then broke out into laughter for a moment.

"That's another thing I love about you two! You make me laugh! Indeed a true talent to make the dead laugh. Whether in virtue or mischief the true talent is to bring laughter to one's soul." And his laughter had never trailed off, it just ceased.

Korson started sniffing the air a little.

"Problem?"

"No. I just thought I smelled something somewhat familiar."

"And your name would be?"

Again a smile, and he extended his hand. "The vampire Korson," he said, and they shook hands. Jerome noticed that he didn't have nearly his saviour's grip of the night before.

"You might want to sit down," he suggested. Korson sat on the couch, still clutching his chest. "I notice we have something slightly in common." Korson raised his eyebrow, and Jerome blew out a great plume of smelly smoke from his mouth. "We both have shrouds," he said, gesturing to the smoke. Korson eyed the air around him, and saw that bits of the black shadow had swirled around him. He inhaled greatly and it seemed as though the wisps turned to ghosts as they entered into him.

"Forgive me. Sometimes I seem to lose control of my power." He said it with a distant look in his eyes as though he was maintaining a burden or secret of some sort.

"So. What exactly is going on."

"You're much more accepting of your situation than your brother is."

"He likes to torment himself. A lot of people do, in fact."

"Very true," said Korson. "I remember, in my days as a mortal, the harshest winters would hit the plains in New York State and my people would wander through the storms. I felt like shit and I loved it. I thought triumph over suffering was the ultimate achievement."

Jerome sucked on his cigar and said, "It does have its merits."

"To a point. But one does have to have pleasures in life. And now I find myself on the opposite side, filled with bareness and causing the torment. It leaves me with complete intoxication and it sounds so wonderful but there is no fulfillment past that moment of pleasure. Everything is as empty as it was before and I think I may have been happier when I was in pain." He clutched at his chest as he cringed a little.

"You don't look it. What happened to you anyway?"

He didn't answer immediately, just laughed, giggled almost, a little bit like the Joker, then coughed. "You must excuse me, Mr. St. Croix. As your brother is already aware, I'm quite a mysterious and secretive person. And it has cost me dearly." He pulled is hand out from under his coat and it glistened in the moonlight, covered with blood. Jerome didn't register any shock on his face, just kept smoking. "You look at me and all you see is a pale, grey dead Indian. Well, now you see my war paint." He smeared the blood across his cheekbones in thick streaks, giving his face some colour.

"And what are you fighting over," stated Jerome.

"Lots of things. The power of these shadows, the privilege to indiscriminately kill, petty bitterness between clans. Your brother's soul. It seems one person always has the power to create or terminate a war." Korson stood up and profiled himself in the moonlit window. "And the spilling of one person's blood is, as per the case, the signal that it has begun."

Jerome had a question upon his face that Korson read and answered.

"Some of it is your brother's blood," he said, holding his hand up to look at. "But most of it is mine." His legs quivered a moment before he collapsed next to the stain left by Clyde's corpse. Jerome jammed his stogie in his mouth and rushed over to the vampire, leaned over him and pulled Korson's shirt open to see his wound. Korson was breathing a little bit raspy, his voice was sour like cranberries. "Three years it took me to close a bullet hole in this chest. And a century later she rips it open worse than before. She was trying to kill him. She drank his blood for weeks and I couldn't prevent it. All I did was haunt him. Make everything worse. I should have just told him, but my pride…I don't even know everything…I swear I tried to save him." He waved at the smoke in front of his face. "God, that cigar fucking stinks."

Jerome laughed a little, his yellowed teeth clenched around his tobacco. He looked at the glistening, blackened wound in the man's chest. "We'll get you fixed up, somehow. Keep talkin'. Tell me how my brother is."

"Fine. A little scratched up. I chased her off, but she'll be back. She'll kill him eventually. I think he's become symbolic of the struggle between us, as though whoever wins his life will win the power."

"All about power, huh?"

"I've always believed wars are fought over grand schemes for the pettiest of reasons. It's so dangerous to play with the shadow. I guess I deserved this. Perhaps I should lie here for another hundred years and see if maybe I'll die…"

"I hate to tell you this, Korson, but I already have one stain on my carpet and I don't want another," said Jerome, trying to piece together the puzzle of the flesh on Korson's chest. "You're an immortal, there must be a way to heal you."

Korson gripped his wrist, and Jerome stopped his makeshift medical work, thinking some ritualistic revelation was forthcoming. Korson pulled him a little closer so he could whisper in his ear:

"Why don't you fear me?"

Jerome gave a hearty laugh that billowed smelly cigar smoke. "I'm a great judge of character. I think you would find it dishonorable to kill me without a good reason. You seem very clear of purpose."

Korson smiled, just slightly, still maintaining an air of evil. "Not at the moment, perhaps..."

"Just how powerful was that shadow you mentioned before?" asked Jerome.

"Quite. Why."

Jerome lifted Korson's head up and pointed out the window. "Because it seems to be pouring out of the top of Mount Royal."

Korson stood, partly pulling himself up by the window sill, and said, "By the Gods..." He then pulled out a knife from his inside pocket and turned to Jerome. "Get me a cup. I will need your blood to heal the wound in my chest. Only with your permission," he said, dipping his head in a respectful bow. Jerome got up, took a silver cup from his dining room cabinet, and picked up the bottle of scotch that was next to it.

Isabelle had gathered up the information that Jerome had asked for and, not wanting to leave it at station twenty, decided it would be more appropriate to slip it into Graham's mailbox. She didn't know where Jerome lived, and couldn't reach him on his phone or at the hospital, so she hoped he would pick up the envelope at some point. Inside was most of Julia St. Croix's body, and she walked in the newly born night not knowing all that had begun.

Even if she had, she would have been a little nonchalant if perhaps not unconcerned at the bad tidings that were unfolding, for she thought of her former colleague and friend Graham. She'd just left what she knew to be the home of his shattered marriage, and she hated herself for loving him. But couldn't help it.

She wanted this mess to be over and for him to regain his confidence and dump his faithless wife so they could at least try to be together, but she wasn't much of a dreamer at heart. She knew she seemed cold to him, because she knew she was hiding her emotions and trying to live strictly within realities confines. He was married, disturbed, emotionally unstable, his life was falling apart and everyone would no doubt question her as to her choice of mate when there were so many other more feasible alternatives out there. But she was stubborn and willing to suffer silently, pining away for what she couldn't have.

And perhaps, though she wanted to believe in the unbelievable, the whole reason she was attracted to him in the first place, she had doubts as to the authenticity of her faith, thinking perhaps she was blinded by her feelings. What made it all the worse was that she could tell by the way he looked at her that, in another time, under better circumstances, he would have loved her too.

She took a deep breath as she walked towards downtown. It was cool October, and orange and black was starting to predominate the store windows. The streets were full enough as Montréal was known as a place to visit, a place for night life. It was great working at night, living through the nightlife.

When she became bored of her own thoughts and started to look around a bit, she noticed that there were a large number of derelicts shuffling around in ripped, garbage-green coats, hair all scraggly, some wearing dirty hats. She thought, like most, that this wonderful city was going to hell. Too much conflict between the Anglophones and Francophones, and the economy was being driven downwards. It would lose all charm if it became strictly a tourist town.

A group of them were ahead of her and she had to walk through them, as they shuffled lazily on the sidewalk. She dodged between them, but ran out of room and bumped into the last one of the group. The light caught his face and it was black with dirt and decay and age-old cuts. She held her hand to her mouth, nauseous partly from the smell and partly from what she saw. The dead man gave a half-smile of yellowed, rotted teeth and then grabbed her hand before she realized he was going to touch her. She had enough professional calm in her to remember her self-defense and pull her hand away from his slimy, tight grip. His interest in her body died almost immediately when she put a few feet of distance between them.

"The dead have come out to play tonight," she said to herself, looking back at the corpse that was walking away from her. She gave a shudder and turned back to her path and began to walk again. Took a deep breath and tried to relax. She looked around at the other people on the street, just to reassure herself. Most looked normal enough. She kept walking, her heels tack-tacking on the concrete. Perhaps that noise, combined with the relative silence of the night, made her become a little bit apprehensive. She kept looking over her shoulder.

What she did find curious though, was the fact that some children seemed to be out late, wandering the street like spirits. One, in fact, did go up to her, giggling away, and when Isabelle asked if she was lost or needed help, the girl just fled quickly. Isabelle followed but after rounding a corner into an alley the girl was gone, disappeared as though she were a ghost.

Isabelle sighed and thought to herself, "Now you're seeing ghosts, too. Been listening to Graham too much," and scolded herself for thinking that about her friend. At the end of the alley she noticed a figure standing there. Perhaps shuffling slowly toward her? Like the dead guy she saw before, and she wondered just how long he'd been there before she'd noticed him.

She'd realized she'd cut through the alley behind the old Forum, and this made her shiver for a moment, for the ghosts, the cold air, and the sense of innocence lost when the city had decided to board up the old place. It wasn't like it used to be, a place for the children, where majic filled the air. Now it was just ghosts, and a sense of something sooty and grey.

Knowing what she knew about girls on the street at night, she turned to go back the way she came and stopped suddenly. Another dead figure was blocking the path to the main road, shuffling slowly closer. The alley had enough girth to allow her to pass, but for some of the bags of litter that lined the brick wall. Isabelle moved out of the way of the zombie and tried to go around him, but, though he seemed unintelligent and slovenly he angled his path towards her. She tried to move to the other side of him and again he angled his path to block her, and she got a little frightened and slipped on her heal and nearly fell into a pile of garbage.

Though the zombie seemed a little slow, he had a single-mindedness that provided his purpose with energy and Isabelle's half-second slip gave him the advantage he needed. As she got up and turned to run, he grabbed her wrist and held it tight. His strength was too great for her to release his grip, and she began to kick and thrash at him, but he didn't feel any pain from her thrusts. Others began to join him from either end of the alley, and they essentially trapped her as they swarmed to her like flies to a carcass. The one who first grabbed her pulled her closer by the arm and then bit into her forearm with his browned teeth and Isabelle screamed louder than she ever imagined she could. The others began to pull at her limbs and bite away at her flesh and she screamed and screamed but nobody seemed to care, nobody came to help her. She wondered if she would still be conscious when she was a skeletal mass with torn flesh hanging from her body like rags off a derelict. Suddenly they were off her. As though their purpose had changed in an instant. She thought she heard a voice. Someone lifted her head.

"Isabelle..."

She found the power to open her eyes. Every fresh opening in her body spoke to her in volumes of pain. She looked at the person holding her up by the head, and choked on the blood that began to fill her throat.

"You know quite a bit more than you should, Isabelle," said Talissa. "I should let them kill you." Isabelle was in such pain that she couldn't speak, but if she could she would have begged for death. Her eyes begged for death.

"I won't though," said Talissa, breaking Isabelle's heart. "Because you love him. I'm going to allow you enough breath to live because I believe that love shouldn't die. It's such powerful majic." Talissa kissed Isabelle full on the mouth, allowing herself a drink of the blood that Isabelle would have sputtered out. When she released the embrace, she was a mess of bloodstains on her clothes, as though a child had put sloppy handprints in thick paint on her dress.

Isabelle lay there, near death and in shock, and wondered at this cruelty. She knew this was Graham's tormentor, that she wanted to kill him. She could *smell* him on her. It was no consolation that she would be permitted to live, in this state, with or without love, when she knew the one she loved was going to die a horrible death.

She couldn't turn her head much, and didn't notice the shadow creeping along the ground, until it began to consume her form. It entered her body through her mouth and nose and dozen open wounds. Normally, it would have choked her and killed her, but for the majic of one last breath Talissa had left her with. It filled her up and instead of killing her it allowed her, on some level she wasn't aware of, to understand...

Jerome woke up because of the dry taste in his mouth. His legs hung over the edge of the couch and he was not at all in a comfortable position. He turned and sat up, put his feet on the floor and into something wet.

"Shit," he said, picking up the bottle. Woke up from a bender. Most of the bottle gone and clear from the weight in his head that most of it had been spilled into him rather than on the floor. "Son of a bitch stole it anyway," he said, reminded of the events by the throb from his forearm. The cut had been made over the previous wound, scars upon scars. And Jerome scolded himself for thinking that Korson would stick around after his blood had been taken. Even with permission given, Korson was a vampire and had to take something with him. How could he be so naive? So trusting? So pliant? To think that a creature such as Korson would merely receive such an offering without bowing to his instincts of being a pure bloodsucker. In some way, in some form, he had to take the blood and return to the shadows, forever bound there by majic.

He got up, rubbed at his wound which had been bound in white gauze. Looked out the window. The smoke from Mount Royal had begun to blanket Montréal, covering most of the city. From what Jerome could tell, it was dawn but for the fact that the sun was being blocked out.

"So the dead can walk during the day," he murmured to himself. But if that was so, why did it seem as though Korson had fled? Jerome not only had the bitter taste of stale alcohol in his mouth, but also the bad taste of being deserted, left to his death. He could smell war, he'd seen the zombies walking the streets. The dead beginning to rise. His phone rang and he picked it up.

"'Lo."

"Hey, Jerome, man, we been tryin' to get hold of you for a while now. You okay?" It was Mario.

"Good as can be, I guess."

"Lotta shit's happenin', man."

"Hm. Like what." There was pause for a moment on the other end.

"Bloodsuckers. I know it sounds unbelievable, but I seen it with my own eyes. Dead guys walkin' the streets, eatin' people's skin. And in the shadow there're these creatures with sick yellow eyes and-"

"Where are you?" Again a pause. Mario said they were hiding out. So distrustful he wouldn't even say where, unless Jerome agreed to join him. Said he would pick him up. Jerome said, "Nah, I think, I'm gonna chill here."

"I fuckin' warn you, man. We don't stick together and we start disappearin'. Already lost some people cause they wouldn't stick with us."

"Thanks, I'm fine."

"You change your mind you call my cell."

He began to gather some supplies together-weapons, such as knives from the kitchen, some food, and the blue rose he'd found in Graham's car. Put them in a bag and then decided to sleep off some of the hangover. Set the alarm for six p.m. and drank a few glasses of water. He slept then woke before the alarm could wake him, and set out to his deli, where he would get some larger knives in order to take them along.

He got there at about sunset (what he thought was sunset, the sun having been blocked out. The air just got a shade darker) and packed up some more food and a few large serrated knives. He called Julia but no one answered and no one picked up the phone at the hospital where Graham was staying. He'd make his way over there to find his brother. He slung the loaded backpack over his shoulders and turned to go out the door.

Part 4: Love for All Time

The closest experience with which Heather could relate to what she was feeling now was her burial that was a prelude her life as one of the undead. The difference was that she couldn't feel the same sense of dread. She had no disgust at her predicament, but she had serious concerns. Everything seemed bright and red and warm. But she couldn't open her eyes. She wondered if Hell was painted in blood on a canvass of flesh. Magog must be the living embodiment of Hell, and she'd welcomed the Devil with open arms. She'd invited him into her mind. And everybody knows that you're not supposed to invite a demon across the threshold.

Heather found her encounter with Magog somewhat curious. She felt perhaps he wasn't what he epitomized himself to be. He called himself a demon-a shadow-demon, whatever that was-and he had the booming voice, the surreal form. But what he said to her, it didn't sound Sunday School, there was no vengeance, no anger. His personality was heavy, fierce and scary, but perhaps that was just him?

Heather thought, *Why should I be afraid of God? Shouldn't God be helping me?* But Magog wasn't much help. She was in his belly now.

For the first time in a year, Heather rose to the noon sun instead of the night sky. She avoided asking herself whether she was asleep, how she got here, and other such unanswerable questions. She'd been witness to obvious majic. It was in her blood. What was the use on putting limitations on the majic in the world? Her own limitations were not the equal of nature's.

The weather was beautifully mild, the sky clear as she'd ever seen it, as she'd ever remembered the noon sky to be. She was a bit heartsick when she looked at the puffy white cotton clouds that dotted the sky. They reminded her a bit of her kitty, and she missed his companionship, the furry little ball of personality. Though the beauty of the clouds eased the little twinge of anxiety she felt. Everything around her was just a little more perfect than she remembered it. The trees greener, the leaves bigger.

There were mountains in the distance, looming over what looked to be a town. Heather walked towards the town, quite enjoying the sunshine. She didn't realize that she did miss it. That darkness had a profound effect upon her soul. It was prejudice that made Heather equate darkness with evil.

Heather approached the town. It was a quaint, quiet place nestled into the land in the face of a great cliff. A great stone church made an intricate piece of art in front of the canvass of the cliff. The church looked a little too big for the village, perhaps too complex a representation of theology for such a sweet and simple town. Curiously she saw very little activity. The odd soul perhaps tending a garden, tilling the land, or moving goods in horse and wagon. For all intents and purposes, a dead town.

She looked towards the church and saw a few Roman guards posted at the entrance, standing very still, almost like statues. They aroused a concern in Heather: was this some surreal imagining of a shadow-demon? Was this perhaps the past? If it was, was it really happening or was it a re-creation of what did happen? She could only concern herself with the present reality, or exposing the reality. It would do no good to loose her head in the clouds of philosophy.

Of more concern to her now was the sky. She deduced by listening to thoughts that no one else took notice of this phenomenon. (Or perhaps there were no thoughts to even be heard, the town being dead?) If she really was living in the past, then Magog spread his malevolent form across the heavens. She hoped that Magog wasn't God. She hoped he wasn't heaven. For just one moment she envied humans that their ashes returned to ashes and that death was a panacea for their tortured soul. What was it to endure the pain of a lifetime when death would save you from the pain of an eternity? But then, who was she to know. She'd never died human and she knew that children could *see*. Perhaps innocence lost condemned humanity to death in dirt.

Heather made her way to the forest outlying the village. There she could perhaps find a place of solace, of rest. Someplace secret she could return to.

It was unusual walking in daylight. Heather was used to seeing forests blacker than night. It still felt eerie though. She figured things could only be creepy at night, but it was foreboding to stand in the deadly silence and see spots and bursts of sunlight breaking the canopy of the trees. The branches worshipped her whenever the wind whistled through them.

Heather looked up though a break in the trees and saw the thin mists. She wanted to see if she could find an end to them. Perhaps they sealed the village in like a dome? If she could find the edge of this world, then maybe she would be able to use it as a way of escaping if the situation called. The thought scared her, though. *The end of this world.* She implied to herself that there could be many realities. From what she'd seen herself, what she knew of the process of growth-the fact that she discarded certain occurrences and relied on the ones that she was comfortable with-there were exactly as many realities as there were minds. Though this was less lofty than it seemed at first. Some things were indisputable, and realities tended to overlap between minds. Sometimes clash even. She thought her reality may be clashing with another. Her eyes fixed on the shadow thinly surrounding her present reality.

It was, of course, entirely possible to control the shadow. To pull the smoke down from the sky in a roiling coil of greys. But would the bowels of Magog come splashing down as well? Would Heather be drenched in the shit of an ageless demon? Or would she rip a hole in time and see such fearsome images as her own birth? Best to leave such volatile designs for when they were truly necessary.

Heather noticed a clearing just ahead and walked towards it. Upon reaching the edge, she took a look behind her and could just make out the looming presence of the cross atop the church. Montréal had a cross overlooking the city as well and it did no good in ridding the decadence. People still indulged in intoxicating drinks.

Entering the clearing, Heather saw the remains of a human mess. There was food and utensils and other such items, the remnants of a fire. She picked up a large bone, perhaps that of a leg or an arm. The blood on it smelled mortal enough. She saw pieces of animal skin torn away from the whole. Possibly a crude seamstress at work? Heather sifted through the debris on the ground, the leaves and twigs and dirt. She found more bones but these were tiny, they looked like children's bones. She thought maybe they were splinters from the large bone she held in her hand. Heather turned over the bone to see if any fragments were missing. She glanced up for a moment, her surroundings still calling to be investigated. She saw a tree with the bark stripped off, a design etched in the wood.

Heather knew very little about pagans. The word would repeat itself in her head. Pagans, pagans, pagans. It made her shiver a bit. Maybe because she knew very little about them. But when she saw the symbol etched into the guts of the tree, another word associated itself in her head: Witchcraft. The symbol was a circle, and in the centre eight lines intersected. At each end of the line was a circle with a dot in the middle and crude icons of lines and dots. Hebrew script ringed the outer edge of the circle. Heather lightly touched the etching, afraid as if something were to happen if she made contact. Heather didn't know that the symbol was a protective pentagram, designed to keep away malaise and misfortune. She looked around to the other trees and saw four more pentagrams enclosing the clearing.

Crunching leaves alerted Heather to the footsteps of someone approaching. A witch was returning to the camp. As Heather was upwind she couldn't catch much of a scent.

*I am shad-*she began to say but stopped herself. She was uncertain as to Magog's volatility and would rely on herself to hide. She moved away quickly quiet, almost floating over the ground though she hadn't learned to fly yet. She moved back far enough to get some tree coverage but could still see the clearing. She wished she'd had time to search deeper for secrets.

A man and a woman entered the clearing. Heather crouched low and looked on. She'd picked up a discarded blanket and wrapped it around her head like a shawl, to help hide her face. They looked mortal enough. They looked around the clearing, picking things up and moving them. Heather hoped she hadn't broken a ritual arrangement. If she did, then they would know someone had been there. It appeared as though they were randomly moving items. They made no indication as to whether or not they thought someone had tried to sleep in their bed.

Heather thought about approaching them. She turned down the idea, partly because she had just pried into their personal belongings, and partly because she wanted to approach them singly rather than in a pair. She didn't want to have to spill any blood. She felt as if she could go an eternity without drinking, and it actually felt good. The man and the woman left the way they came and Heather was left looking at an empty clearing.

Heather relaxed up against the bark of a birch. She'd lowered her guard while thinking about what she should do next. A sudden change in the wind, and she noticed the man from the clearing, his brown robe wavering in the wind, standing in direct view of her, looking right at her. Heather didn't turn her head, she just looked with her eyes. She remained perfectly still, hoping the brown of her cloth shawl would blend with the bark behind her. She lost that hope when the man moved closer to her.

"Don'tkill'imdon'tkill'imdon'tkill'im," raced through her head as she felt her claws tighten and the urge for blood well up in her throat. The thirst was so sudden it nearly caught her off-guard. The man moved closer now. Heather remained perfectly still, as though she were a tree.

The man moved differently than he did moments before. His motions were unnatural, robotic, though not still. His face was hidden, surrounded by a brown hood he'd drawn around it. As he drew closer Heather began to discern some features. Whereas before he looked somewhat skinny he now looked bulkier, especially his face. A nose like a fat round apple, a little bit red. Sturdy jaw and cheekbones, with black scratches as though he'd fallen in pebbly dirt. He was walking on the path directly to where Heather sat. She arched her eyebrow upwards, her look no-nonsense and defensive. As the man approached her, he didn't tilt his head down to look at her; he didn't seem to take notice of her. He kept walking, slowly, methodically, fists clenched. He took the carefully planned step that brought him directly in front of Heather and stopped...turned his head, his face registering a subtly wicked grin.

He said, "Sowen," to Heather. His hand thrust out and grabbed her about the wrist, the speed surprising and unforeseen. It caught her completely off-guard, despite having been battle-ready. His voice was scratched and throaty, as though it hadn't been used for a long while. He seemed, for all intents and purposes, a corpse.

Heather drew her free hand high and brought it across the man's chest. He had a scream in his throat, which finally released itself as a hideous moan that died when Heather removed her hand from his chest. Her hand was drenched in his blood and she held a broken portion of his ribs. He stared at his own mortality and it was a piece of his ribs in the hands of another. Heather ran her tongue along the reddened bone to savour some of his sauce. True blood-drinking with more misanthropy than he ever saw. He had been quite sadistic in his lifetime though he never drank without ceremony. And always from a cup. This was sheer murder he witnessed. And it would be the last thing he saw.

Heather let the man fall and he sat at the base of the tree trunk, his hands palm up on the ground and his eyes skyward.

Good, she thought. *Magog will like his supplications.* She disfigured his face so no one would recognize who he was. Though in a village his absence would be noted. And her presence would be suspicious immediately. She dropped his ribs in his lap and walked further into the forest.

It was not long before she realized that rather than moving away from the village, she'd actually been encircling it. It was difficult, but Heather could just see through the trees to the cross atop the church. And the huge, rocky cliff face loomed up in the distance.

Heather changed direction and tried to move away from the village. Because there was nothing to gauge direction by, it was hard to tell which way she was going. The cliff face was too large. The trees were helter skelter. Heather looked at the cross and put her back to it. She walked away. Before she could see if she had her bearings, she heard someone calling her name.

"Magog," thought Heather. His hauntings were disturbing. A mere voice in her head, some uncertainties surrounding her reality. It's really one's self that is the cause of one's haunting. Like a snowball gaining girth as it is rolled, able only to melt under the heat of logic. We really are our own demons. What if Magog was just another creature on the earth, albeit on a different plain? Would the laws of nature also apply to him? Wouldn't the laws of nature be absolute? A haunting is as much in one's own mind, in one's own perception, as it has to do with supernatural visitations. Seeds planted and overtaking such unused vastness have a tendency to grow uncontrollably. Tangled, thorny weeds spreading, eventually able to consume the host.

Heather tuned a half-circle to begin walking towards the village. But the cross! It should have been directly in front of her, but it was on her right. Something was definitely unreal. Perhaps Magog didn't want her to leave the village? Had she trapped herself in the gut of this...demon?

She righted her direction (finally!) and moved towards the village. She broke the edge of the forest and saw the village blinking in front of her. Little candle lights had popped up everywhere. Heather sped over with superhuman speed and hid herself behind a stone building. She found a barrel of water and dipped in her dirty hand to wash it. She scraped the bits of flesh from her fingernails.

She looked into the sky past the veil of smoke and saw the sun setting on the horizon. She smiled and she wished she could run to it and catch the golden strands of light. But she saw the roil of mists rear up, and the fearsome eyes of the shadow-demon just peeked through the smoke. In her head she heard a laugh and she realized for certain that, whether she was in reality or the bowels of a monster, she was Magog's prisoner.

Peeking around the corner of the building, Heather felt a little tug from behind. There was a catch in her chest, one of surprise at being snuck up on. She turned to find the little girl in the red dress looking up at her with innocent doggy eyes. Heather picked her up and spun around with the girl in her arms and said, "I'm so glad to see you!" The girl looked to be a little overwhelmed, what with being swung playfully in the arms of a vampire. Heather put her back down and dropped to her level. "How come you're here?"

"My monster sometimes brings me here, to keep me safe."

"Do you mean Magog?"

"SSHHH!! Don't say his name!" exclaimed the girl in a whisper. She was so adamant that she clamped her hand over Heather's mouth and nearly knocked her over. She glanced skyward a few moments before easing up. "It's almost night now. For sure he's out at night."

"But if he's protecting you, why are you afraid of him?"

"He scares me. Sometimes things that keep you safe scare you." Heather rubbed the little girl's rosy cheek.

"Show me around the village, sweetie," said Heather.

"It isn't safe for me. They don't like children here. I'm only safe when I hide."

"How about if I wrap you up in my blanket, and I carry you under my coat. Would that be okay?" The girl thought for a minute. "Do you know what I am?" asked Heather.

"A vampire!"

"So you know I can keep you safe no matter what, right?"

"I might be a little big, but okay." Heather picked up the girl, legs dangling, and wrapped her up in the blanket. She then hugged her to her breast and did up her coat as much as possible. The girl locked her hands behind Heather's neck and underneath her hair. Heather worried a bit that her bright blond hair my attract attention now that it was uncovered.

"Don't worry about that," said the girl. "They probably won't even pay attention to you." She was right. The sun was dipping down and Heather felt a little more comfortable in the familiarity of night. The villagers began to come out of their homes, wandering the streets of this ancient town. They had the same deathly pallor as the man who'd attacked Heather in the forest. All walking like zombies just risen. "Just don't come too close to them or they might attack you."

"Do you know where we are?"

"We're in a very old place in Italy. Called Iner..Inter..Interamna!"

Heather looked up to the mists of Magog. They had thickened in the night. Of course, no one would notice them against blackness. But Magog didn't let the twinkling of the stars come through. Could this be the source of madness in Interamna? The utter blackness?

Someone's looking at me, thought Heather. To her right, nothing. Someone was peeking through the myriad of walking zombies. She lost the feeling for a moment. Then it returned. She was definitely being scrutinized. From where though, she couldn't discern.

Blast Magog and his infernal powers! Heather thought to herself. She laughed, this stuff was serious but she still made jokes in her head. She didn't feel as powerful under Magog's canopy, though maybe it was just her imagination.

A man exited the church. He carried a chalice in both hands, raising it over his head as he stood at the top of the stone steps. The cup over his head, he kneeled and poured the contents so they flowed down the steps, like a red waterfall. Then he kissed the chalice and returned behind the great doors. The guards were still there, statues.

Heather noticed a pair of eyes from the window near the top of the church. The eyes that were watching her. She looked straight into the pair of eyes that hid in the shadow of the window. They were dark pools and only her vampire sight could spot them. Barely.

I can see you, Heather said in her head, and the eyes pulled away from the window.

"What are they doing?" asked Heather.

"I don't know," said the little girl. "They just come out when it's dark. They walk and walk and they don't seem to know anything." Heather held the girl tight to her, and in turn the girl tightened her frightened little hands around Heather's neck. They walked, Heather careful not to come within range of any of the zombies. The little girl looked at the zombies, and Heather watched her eyes. There was a lucidity in them of quiet understanding at what she was seeing, and Heather wished that the girl in the red dress was of an age where her intelligence would allow her to express that lucidity of thought. Though the rise of intelligence would likely mean the death of that innocent clarity that allowed the sweet little blond haired girl to understand something as complex as a monster. The monster itself may be simple, and simple of purpose, but each and every monster one comes across, be it in real life or in dreams, this reality or that, is always a product of one's imagination. And that is never simplistic.

Heather walked casually, cradling the girl as if she were a part of her. The zombies walked around the streets, seemingly purposeless, and Heather watched the pattern of the paths. One caught her attention, particularly because it had bumped another while it's head was turned and that seemed so out of place. They seemed mindless, but they did have a sense of direction, enough so that they never crossed paths at the same time. This carelessness extracted a curious reaction. There was a common shift in direction, a conscious, unified decision, as though their minds were one. Their path became patterned, slow, and as Heather looked at all directions she saw that the decision had drawn every zombie towards a centre point. The centre point, quite predictably, was the careless zombie. These amazing creatures, tortoise-like, dull-minded and plodding, had effectively trapped the careless one as though she were a jarred fly. She had her hands up as though pushing the sides, she let out a few small cries. If she would jump to an outer ring, the pattern of the path would re-focus and shift on her, and the reinforcements arriving from all sides ensured her doom.

Heather, despite being a murderous vampire, was a morally strong individual, of great conviction. Her first instinct was to save the fly, but she merely assumed the pattern and watched, circling the victim. Out of some morbid curiosity she wanted to see what would happen. Not to create a false suspense, she wanted to see how they would kill her.

Heather said, "It's like Night of the freaking Living Dead." The woman was surrounded, the zombies with some small glimmer of purpose in their eyes. They bound her at the arms, legs, neck, their dead, pale green hands sliced with grave cuts unyielding in their grip. They splayed the woman out, stretching her almost beyond her limitations, and Heather could hear the cartilage in her joints tear like cloth. The little girl just shivered in her arms. The woman began to call for help, but she didn't scream. As if there was no help forthcoming anyway. The zombies began to put their jaws around her flesh, biting off skin deep enough to reveal the white of bone. Still the woman withheld her screams, save for when skin was torn from a painful location on her body-her inner thigh, precariously close to her vagina, the underside of her upper arms, where the flesh was a little loose and a flexed tricep and clenched teeth offered no hindrance to the agony of teeth tearing through nerves. It was only a matter of moments before the woman was nothing more than a skull, skin patchworked over splintered bone, the lower lip torn and hanging almost to the neck, showing the smiling jaw structure. Portions of the rest of her skeletal structure were discarded in the area of her corpse, most of the meat eaten off her bones. There was barely a pool of blood, as that too had been meticulously consumed. As soon as the corpse had been completely consumed, the purpose was lost and the living dead went back to their aimlessness, dispersing to the directions they came from.

Heather had both lost and gained from what she'd witnessed. She had gained an insight into these creatures, witnessing first-hand how they reacted to a foreign element. And, with Heather's insight into the majic of the mind, she was able to grasp that these things were doing this because the force of purpose came from another source, one outside of their ranks. Who was this source? What was the purpose behind the purpose? This was pure horror show, an obvious genocide to anything mortal, towards anything alive. But she'd lost a possible ally. What if valuable information had died with that woman? What if she had held all the answers? At least to what was going on here. It was very likely that if there was still one mortal among these then there were others. After all, if that was the last mortal, why didn't impending doom finally come crashing down on this microcosm of the past? Was it Heather's own prejudice that made her think that the end of mankind would spell the end of the world? Was it so disheartening that when the last of these apes who'd devastated the planet had died that everything continue? She was still here, after all. She was linear, not subject to petty resurrection, to hanging on to the suffering that accompanied the bitter resistance of the end. Man's fear of what was beyond the great door. Man's anger at losing control. Man's egotistical view that his death would have a significant impact on the whole.

Thankfully lacking the usual stupidity displayed by the central maiden of such films as a Friday the 13th, Heather looked at the church and consciously told herself that the source of the mental energy emanated from behind those walls. Heather *would* have gone right in there, too. She was about to ask the little girl in the red dress about the church...but-

"I have to go now," said the girl, starting to struggle out of the blanket and Heather's arms.

-the sun was coming soon, about to rise. "It's almost sun-up. My monster will be looking for me soon. I'd better go. I'll be back soon, I promise." She kissed Heather on the cheek. Such a darling little girl, haunted, running from monsters. Brave, as she could only play at night. She ran off behind a stone house and there was a flash of white light, an extremely pure and unsullied white. The white dimmed away as the familiar black smoke of Magog flickered out from around the corner. The edge of his cape of smoke flowing as though in wind. Heather ran to the corner and then around it, reckless to the fact that a demon was there. All she saw was a spot on the ground that looked as though it had been burnt, a black spot, like a star with innumerable points, and the thick eerie smoke rising from its centre. From the sky above, Magog let out a deep titter.

Heather looked to her left, she saw the vast forest. She wanted to find the edges of the great mists overhead. She had to know where Interamna stood. If it was in Magog or the past. As well she wanted to look for some shelter among the trees.

Heather walked towards the forest. She thought about how to maintain her direction so as not to get her course skewed. She decided it was best to move straight forward and not make any turns whatsoever. Hope the trees were kind and left a clear path to follow. And it was night, she was most powerful at night. But wasn't that also true of Magog, a shadow-demon? Or were the shadows more fearsome when they stole pieces of the light of day?

Heather broke the rim of the forest and it was like breaking into a new world of darkness. The dark was different, it was thicker, like smoke, or Magog. But Heather loved it, she could see with her vampire eyes. Even now, after experiencing daylight after death, she still loved the night more. Daylight was about inequalities. The nuances of the light lied to you. Its brightness could blind you; its dimness could fool you; it could cast a shadow and only show you half the truth. Darkness was equal because everything was in simple colours, black, blues, purples and greys. There was no distraction by the rainbow of tones of the rainbow of colours. Heather's talent was being able to see in the darkness, to obtain utter focus in the lucidity provided by the night draining the world of its varied colours for half the rotation.

Reality folded in the forest. There was only her direct route away from the village. Her journey throughout the black forest reminded her of her journey into Magog's intestines, though without the same extremity. It was as though the darkness became a tunnel because it couldn't lie to her.

And then she saw the wall. When she'd tried during the day to find this edge, the confusion of colours, amplified by her preternatural eyesight, had forced her into circles around the village. The wall was roiling smoke that crashed straight down into the ground. She could see the tear in the rock and grass. Heather felt as though she were moving but when she took notice of her surroundings she knew she stood still. And the way it looked to her, the smoke of shadow ripping into the ground, she felt as though Magog had picked up a piece of history in the cup of his hand. Heather could see him now, holding the ancient village of Interamna aloft in his hand, crumbs of dirt dropping from between his inhuman fingers, his cape alive and slithering around him in the vastness of nothing. His laughter echoing demonically across his blackened heavens.

Heather thought, *He must have ripped out a piece of time and put it in a loop.* Her mind was racing at possibilities. She didn't want to underestimate him, but neither did she want to overestimate him. It was unlikely that even one such as Magog, who exuded such power, who existed in incorporeal form, could dip his filthy, smoky hand into the stream of time and tinker with it without befuddling the flow. The perfection of nature was the delicate balance between the cycle of life and death, the linearity of time.

This answered nothing for her. What did she think she would see? The other side? A man and his animal pulling a wagon in the true reality of the past? Something sane? Like a shadow-demon would ever let her figure out the crux of a puzzle in three easy steps! The key to the netherwold was not something so easily gained. But this time, Heather was inside the netherworld. This time she'd found it. And to get out she had to make another journey. And the scariest thing was that everything was real. The zombies. Interamna. They could all be dead lost souls and they were real.

And no children were in the village. That had to be a lie, the children could see. They would be able to see the monsters no matter what face they wore! They would see what these zombies were! There must be children hiding somewhere in this chunk of history.

Heather picked up a stone and threw it into the roiling wall. Nothing happened. The stone could be half way around the world now. It could have shattered a window in the church in Montréal. All she saw was smoke.

The smoke coughed and the rock burst out and struck Heather above her eye. She cursed out loud to herself. The blood dripped off the stone but she didn't lick it up. She felt the wetness ooze and moisten her eyebrow. What bastard that stood on the other side would throw a rock at her head??

Heather turned her back on the wall. She saw only darkness ahead. Not the night that she could pierce but utter nothingness. Utter meaninglessness. The forest was gone. Interamna and the cross on the church were gone. Had the mists seeped around her? There was no point walking into the blackness. There was no point losing her direction. The only true unknown was the wall. And Heather flung herself into it like a stone.

She woke with an ache in her head and it felt as though someone had snapped her neck. Dirt clung to her and she realized that it was because she'd been flung into the ground. The chill of exposure gripped her shoulders, but her preternatural body had saved her from the elements. And she shivered as she saw the sun rise, she was sick of it after only a day. Heather put her head down for a moment and when she opened her eyes she realized that the light ebbed. The sun was setting, not rising. She'd slept the day away, as usual.

She tried to recall the events of the night;

Forest.

Blackness.

Wall of smoke.

The pieces of her journey reconstructed themselves. She remembered that she had entered the wall. The mists were alive and they closed in on her, making her think she would be crushed, or implode. They tried to enter her orifices, but she resisted them with her mind. She almost controlled the shadow. And it had flung her out. Back to Interamna. Weak little Heather. The shadow laughed because she wouldn't do battle with it.

The sun had still not completely set when Heather had returned to the town of Interamna. Some people were on streets, walking around. A little aimlessly. A little groggily. But with more lucidity than Heather had seen before. A small twinkle in the eye. Some intelligence. Some life. Real life, not just existence, as though they were cabbage. Heather cursed to herself that she'd slept through the day. Perhaps she cold have seen some difference in the people. As it was now, she was witnessing the end of a transition. The lessening of light brought about the zombification. Heather couldn't help what she was. Whether this was real or not her nature was to wake nightly. She was more aware of the changes that occurred with the transition from day to night.

Heather stepped over the mess of the previous nights kill she'd witnessed. The church, backed by the impressive cliff-face, looked at her as she walked. At the whole village in fact. It displayed the hierarchy of the town, the church God, and the stone houses the sheep. Nothing was above the church, save for the natural creation of the cliff.

It felt good, the sun receding to allow free reign of darkness, and Heather let her silk hair free to flow in the wind. The zombies had begun to roam the streets, ignorant of her. She didn't think of herself as a dream when people were looking at her. Perhaps she wasn't completely real. But a nightmare was more powerful than a dream and if people feared her when they looked at her, then she was more powerful. But a creature such as Heather could only exist as a dream. The zombies, therefore, had to be a dream too. Who, though, was dreaming this? Magog? Talissa? Even Korson or Cat? Had Heather died and become the product of a dream, of majic, of Talissa's, and she in turn a majical dream of her murderer and so on and so forth down the line? There had to be a beginning and an end. Such a human thought! So linear!

Heather looked at the Magog-sky. The Russian doll. Were they still inside the universe? Which led to thoughts of what that universe was inside. What was before it. What was after.

No! she thought. She wouldn't be distracted by daydreaming. Vampires were night creatures, they didn't dream, except for waking dreams. Which could be the death of them, oh so distracting. Once, Heather had spent a week daydreaming. She'd wake, take a feeble victim with a nonchalant and distracted air as her fangs pierced flesh. Then she would sit somewhere. In the *Vieux Port*. Walking through *Oratoire St. Joseph*. Sitting atop the Jacques Cartier bridge. Chased home only when the sun made it absolutely necessary to flee. From then on, with only slight difficulty, Heather made it a point not to dream. Rather, to live. The interpretations of petty philosophizing nearly made her sick, and she shunned her current predicament. She thought it best to not dwell on anything that couldn't be deduced empirically. That in itself was philosophical. Paradoxical as well. She had majic in her veins! She'd seen the shadow-demon Magog manifest itself in the very church of God! Would she not have to believe that there could be more?

The patternless wanderings of the zombies were a curious phenomenon. Were they sentinels guarding the village? If Heather approached the church, would they attack her to keep her from the source? Heather neared the church, looking up at its oppressive size. She noticed the illusion. That the church looked large due to the architectural design. That it was set upon a grade of increasing height. After some study it wasn't as big as it first seemed. The Roman looking guards at the front door were wax. Stiff, unnatural, unmoving, unbreathing. Most certainly real, the intestines having evacuated the debris at the heels of the soldiers. Perhaps, though, their lives had been frozen.

Heather listened to the walls of the church. Tried to hear what was going on inside. If there were children there.

"They get taken inside," said the little girl in the red dress. "Not me, though. They can never find me. But the others don't have much time. The others get pulled apart piece by piece."

"There are other children?" asked Heather.

"In the church. That's where you're going, isn't it?"

"Yes. What other children?" The little girl jerked her head up.

"The others like me. Why don't you know? Why don't you understand? If you don't understand Talissa's going to win."

"Do you know where Talissa is? Is she here?"

"It's so, so simple! Haven't you ever seen a horror movie?"

"If it's so simple, why can't I see it? Can you explain it?"

"...no..."

Ssssssssssssssssssss!

What fell with night was a great mist from above, shadow darkening the dark. This was the mist, living smoke, a gathering of all the sinister night. The shadow-demon: **Magog.**

"Magog, you're scaring her. Stop it." The great cape roiled and swirled, licks of smoke whipping out like lizard tongues. There were little shadow-pets, just smoke and teeth and legs to chase children with, the mites of Magog, giggling a high-pitched giggle: heeheeheeheeheeheehee! The form of Magog was crouched, as though wrapping his cape of smoke around him, and his eyes were a slight white glow, the light almost eaten up by his very substance.

Am I your supplicant? May I not scare who I wish?

"Not her, Magog. I won't let you. She's just a child."

She comes with me.

"No! You've done enough. She doesn't deserve to live in fear."

Why do you care for her vampiresss? You will be here long after she is dead. She is already dead. Why do you care?

It was an important question Heather never asked herself. Why would she care for the girl? Why did this girl keep running from reality to reality to help her. And just to be with her?

You are as afraid of me as she!

"Like hell! I'm not scared of you!"

Then why do you cling to her?

Heather didn't even realize she had clutched the girl so tightly that she'd broken the flesh on the girl's shoulders. The girl, in turn, had wrapped her arms around Heather's leg and squeezed her fingers into the back of Heather's thighs.

She's a tricky little sly one, she is, said Magog, with some unveiled contempt. Though he (it?) always spoke in those tones. Intuitive, Heather understood.

She knows majic! The girl was born with some innate skill, a talent of the mind for conjuration. More so than other children, who could merely interpret the majical manifestations of the world. Interpret and forget, as innocence lost blinded the ability see. The little girl had learned, out of necessity, how to fold the barriers, how to find Heather in this time and Heather's own. The little girl looked up with sweet innocence in her blue eyes and Heather saw that there was majic there. That the girl could hide it. The little girl, in all her sweet innocence, was unable to explain to Heather what Heather needed explaining simply because she didn't know! She had no idea she knew majic! No more than a dog knows that it can bark, it just does. And so did the little girl in the red dress. She just conjured. Without knowing it. Without knowing a name for it.

I must take her back.

"Absolutely not! I wont let you!"

The mites, small but fearsome nonetheless with their bright sharp teeth, advanced from some unheard command. Heather, with a wave of her hand, flung them back. They popped out of Magog's massive flowing cape, two, three, even ten at a time. If Magog did indeed have bowels, then this must be his shit. Holding on to the girl, Heather thrust the mites back, kicking them, exploding them with a thought. They continued forward, beginning to surround Heather as she retreated before the very numbers of them. To the only place she could possibly retreat to. The great doors of the church behind her. She flung them away and destroyed them by the dozens, but there were more and more every second. Heather tried to attack Magog himself but he had already put up his defenses. She couldn't even sense with her mind what she saw with her eyes.

Heather was flush with the Roman guards now. In a flash, Heather saw what the guards really were. An imitation of life. Art. Carved from stone in such intricate and stunning detail, the flesh painted in tones so perfect so as to accentuate all the nuances of flesh. Another lie, a lie within a lie. A misrepresentation, as perhaps the church itself was. The mites could only surround her on three sides now, the fourth owned by the doors of the church. Thinking her trapped, the mites heehee'd some more. Heather, with great strength in one arm, and force of will, swung open the door that would normally require three men to open it. Slammed it shut, once inside, and leaned up against it, chest heaving from breathlessness, though not fatigue. It was the little girl in the red dress, stuck to her breast, that caused her anxiety. She'd actually feared for her. It was like an arrow in her heel.

There was not a sound from outside, not of Magog nor mites trying to burst through the door. The little girl trembled slightly in Heather's arms, each breath short, accompanied by a wheeze, small, high-pitched, her shoulders jerking up in spasm. Heather had lived not two decades of life, shortened by undeath, and she cared for few. Her father, who'd wait in his den like a king for his little princess to visit him, to tell of her day, to leap on his lap no matter how old he was. Korson, who'd shown her much, yet apparently very little. She thought of him as the anti-Heather, so unlike her, and they rubbed against each other like sandpaper. But she loved him, like a brother. And she loved Catherine, her love, her mate, who knew her and how to look at her. The greatest affection for Cumulous, her little puff-ball, her spunky sidekick. But clinging to the little girl was like hugging a part of herself. Perhaps it was maternal instinct?

She'd gone into shock, and Heather, trapped in the church, knowing Magog and his legion of fiendish little shadow shits were waiting outside, carried the girl to a place where she could be hidden away. There were few sounds about the church, perhaps only a few people. Hopefully no zombies. Heather tucked the girl away behind a curtain, and found something soft to put her head on. She could still see the doors, large and quiet. Why didn't they attack? What was preventing Magog?

Heather drew the curtain. The little girl lay in shock, her twinkling blue eyes had darkened and she stared catatonically upwards. Majic in her eyes. The child, a little elf, who had achieved a level superior to those who'd grown up.

What is it that I lost? thought Heather. *Or that everyone loses?* And the question begged of itself, here in an old, old church, where it all began. Perhaps not <u>the</u> it, but <u>an</u> it. Who was really to say which force drove the universe? That it wasn't the lot of them? It wasn't philosophical. It was theological. Philosophy didn't serve any purpose but to ask questions. Any idiot could ask questions. Theology answered them, at least made the attempt. It tried to say where those precious little losses go. Through the diversity of the mind one can choose to follow a path. As Heather had chosen hers, had chosen one of majic. Of being preternatural. It doesn't exist. For those who don't want it, they won't have it and it doesn't exist. They will live and die within their own boundaries, and Heather had chosen no boundaries, to flirt with death forever. She felt her loss, had always felt it, the conflict, the confines of her mortality. She'd snatched this existence, and fought with it in a different way, to find what she felt was missing from her. Had someone stolen that? Where did the intangibles go to?

She had to be honest with herself. This world was so large, there was so much, and why would she find her answers in a church that may or may not be real? Heather walked along until she'd found an altar. It was different than what she was used to imagining about a church. Candles were lit for light. Everything was poor, there was no gold, nothing too ornate. It was a very bare place.

I could never be inspired here, thought Heather. It was very dreary, a place where no distractions could interfere with thought. Kneel before the alter and pray. The glitter that had attached itself to the church was meant to evangelize, to attract people with the misfortune of no education, who couldn't decide for themselves and couldn't distinguish the glitter from the truth. In all of his teachings Christ never adorned his body nor his words with gold.

In the door to Heather's left-unlit, therefore merely a black rectangle in the brown stone wall-a man had taken quiet steps forward, just enough to be caught by the light. He was quite emaciated, his ribs sticking over his stomach like an overhang jutting out from a cliff-face. His face had a reddish glow in the cheeks. He put his hands to the door frame, perhaps to balance himself. He wore nothing but a loincloth, white but for the stains, which also ran down his thighs. He had a small beard, quite out of order, and his hair was shoulder-length and brown. A wreath of thorns was on his head. He smiled at Heather, he had admired her as she stood at the altar. Heather enjoyed admiration but was quite used to it by now.

"Sowen," he said as he walked over the threshold. Heather took it to be a Latin greeting. He wore a pentacle necklace and he kissed it, then crossed himself. Heather thought he would fall over, his legs were so skinny, like stilts, and he swayed as though his inner ear was unstable. He caught Heather off-guard with his next words as they also sounded Latin. Heather had to decipher them from his thoughts.

"The Bishop of Interamna-St. Valentine," he said. As Heather had a small glimpse into his mind, she sensed a madness about him, one also obvious from his manner and eyes. The patron saint of love, an obscure figure in history. He carefully took Heather's hand to kiss it, a tear dripping from his eye. His grip tightened, he nearly dragged Heather to the ground with him as he fell, convulsed into a ball.

Shit, everyone's collapsing on me, thought Heather. The Bishop was putting his hands up to defend himself. As though he were looking at something completely different. He kept ducking behind his hands. Whimpering as though long tormented. Heather dragged him into the dark room. It was so dark, darker than the forest even. St. Valentine seemed to calm down a bit. Perhaps he felt safer here, in his room. Heather layed him out on the bed. She saw a candle on a dresser and lit it. And jumped, startled that she wasn't alone in the room. Lying in the opposite corner, curled up on some blankets, Talissa quietly slept.

Heather saw the familiar mass of chocolate hair. Was this a choice she was faced with? To kill Talissa before she ever had a chance to become a vampire?

Talissa had begun to stir. Heather raised a claw, out of instinct, out of self-defence. Then relaxed her hand and just put it behind her head casually. Nothing could be solved though anger and murder. (Or maybe she just didn't watch enough horror movies...)

This isn't the same Talissa, thought Heather. *This one isn't a vampire.* But why should that make any difference? Talissa, shocked, frightened at an intruder, had pressed up against the wall.

"It's okay...it's okay," Heather cooed. She extended a hand to Talissa, as one would to a squirrel. Could there be cruelty in Heather's kindness? She was at an extreme advantage over Talissa, mostly because she knew what was supposed to happen. Again the philosophical argument about Heather's choice. Heather had no regrets about actually becoming a vampire. It therefore followed she would eventually kiss Talissa's neck.

"He doesn't seem to be too well," said Heather, gesturing towards St. Valentine. It made Talissa forget her fear, she rose urgently to the bedside, pressing her hand to the Bishop's forehead. Her expression became more so agitated.

There was a shelf and table laid out with stone jars. Talissa gathered together some jars and a bowl and began transferring the ingredients from the jars into the bowl. Heather could smell the herbs whenever a jar was uncovered. Talissa crushed them together and carefully dripped some water into the bowl, as though measuring out the amount by eye. She crushed the dampened contents together with the pestle. Talissa swirled the concoction around, testing its consistency. It was a sandy paste, greenish in colour. Satisfied, she removed the lid from another jar and removed a yellow sprig that had an odour that was sharp and a little nauseating. In another ceramic bowl she placed the sprig, and this bowl was put over a flame. The herb, after mere moments over the heat, turned from yellow to a liquidy burgundy. She transferred the herb to the green paste and again crushed everything together with the pestle. The burgundy herb had bled into the green, almost overshadowing the original colour. Talissa reached for another bottle and poured its contents into the paste. It too was burgundy, a sweet, fruity wine. It made the paste smoother, drinkable.

Talissa took the bowl over to the Bishop, and before tilting his head up to drink it, she lit it on fire then blew the flame out after a moment. St. Valentine drank of the potion, the lump in his neck bobbing up and down with each gulp, a stream of burgundy running out the side of his mouth. When he finished his head dropped down, as if fatigued from the activity. He let out a few heavy breaths and seemed to fall into a slumber. Drugged he seemed, and Heather wondered what narcotic was contained in those leaves. Not wishing to disturb Talissa until she'd finished her cooking, Heather finally broke the silence and said, "Will he be okay?"

Talissa was patting the Bishop's forehead, her eyes sad, pleading silently. "I don't think he has much longer. I can't bear to lose him." Heather had to gleen the translation from Talissa's mind.

"What's wrong with him?"

"He sees...spirits." Heather gathered that by spirits Talissa meant demons. "I think he is trying to force his own natural death. He hardly eats. Hardly bathes. He just prays. And sometimes..." Talissa broke off, choked.

"Yes?" Heather probed.

"...Sometimes he sits in the corner, just talking to himself. Telling himself strange tales. I've heard him. But I usually can't listen to them." Talissa continued to pet the Bishop's forehead. Heather empathized and put her hand on Talissa's shoulder, pulled her away.

"Come. Over here. What's your name?"

"Talissa."

"That's a beautiful name. I'm Heather." Talissa smiled and took Heather's hand, kissing it gently.

"Are you from out there, Heather?" Meaning the village, Interamna.

"No, I've traveled from far away. What *is* going on out there?"

Talissa pulled a necklace, a pentacle, out from her top, kissed it. She crossed herself as well. She sounded a little different, perhaps naive, but not without intelligence. Heather realized that people here were not likely to be formally educated. Except a man of the cloth, like St. Valentine.

"Talissa...?" Again Talissa held her silence for a while. Then beckoned Heather back to the light, to the altar. Heather followed. When Talissa turned to face Heather, for the first time in adequate lighting, she let out a slight gasp.

"My...your eyes..." Talissa put out her fingers to Heather's face. "There are veins around your eyes." Heather jerked away a little. She was generally uncomfortable about being touched. She softened her aura, made Talissa less enamored with her. Her grey-white skin and saffron hair were very attractive to mortal eyes.

Upon the altar was a white cloth, tented, and Talissa gently pulled it away to reveal a chalice. It was carved smooth out of marble, polished, and etched around the mouth in black and white swirls were strange and crude little symbols. Talissa held the cup with both hands, reverently.

"It took me abut three weeks to create this. I carved it with the utmost care, knowing I would give it to the Bishop for the church. My heart skipped when he fell in love with it. He was so anxious to use it. But he saved it for Lupercalia. The festival of fertility. The congregation had their eyes fixed upon it during the whole ceremony. And finally he poured the wine into the cup to drink of it." Talissa's hand squeezed the chalice. "I had cast a spell over the cup to make all the wine within it the sweetest ever tasted.

"I should have noticed. I should have noticed..." Talissa put her face in her hands, angry at herself.

Heather, unwilling to empathize, didn't offer any words of sympathy. She just waited for Talissa to continue, and when she appeared unable to, Heather told her that she could only be of help if she knew the whole story.

"It was me on the altar!" cried Talissa. "I was the one who lay there! I loved him so much! So I lay there, bearing my womb for the Gods!" Heather had conjured the image of Talissa lying upon the altar, face up and arms out, white and naked. Eyes closed preparing to receive a God. "I still love him."

Heather said, "What exactly was supposed to happen, then?"

"It isn't what you're thinking. He was just going to anoint me with the wine. Then he would conclude the ceremony. I would try to have his child later that night." The words themselves sounded heretic to Heather. Who but heretics would mingle sex and religion? Who but heretics would lay a woman naked on an altar, only to be fucked later by a Bishop? The festival of Lupercalia was about fertility, and they were trying to mimic the art of creation, the ultimate art, perfected by God. Shouldn't zealots consider this the utmost form of love and devotion? Mimicry is truly incredible flattery. "He drew the cross upon me, from my neck to my womb. And a pentacle upon my very womb itself. I was so absorbed in the ceremony, with love, that I didn't bother to notice how the wine felt. So much that it became blood."

"There are certainly," said Heather, "things a lot worse than drinking blood."

"You don't understand? It was a ritual bound by blood. My blood!"

"Talissa, you can't know that."

"Really? The Bishop did." Talissa pulled back her sleeve to reveal a slice upon her wrist. "I woke to find him sucking on my wrist. I don't know how long he'd been there but I woke dizzy. I think I was lucky that I'd woken when I did."

Heather put her fingers to the scar, said, "What's this?"

Talissa pulled her arm away. "Nothing."

"When he drank it the first time, didn't he notice? Didn't he spit it out or something?"

"He nearly choked swallowing it. It dripped off his chin. The congregation was shocked, but he gestured as though he'd recovered. But I could tell from his eyes, from the way he returned the chalice to its place, that something was wrong. It was then I realized that the wine had indeed turned to blood.

"I waited in his chamber for hours. Then I found him out here, kneeling before the altar. Just staring at the chalice. I was afraid to interfere. He didn't seem right. Then he picked up the carafe and poured some wine into the chalice. He looked at it, sniffed it. Then he drank it."

"Even if there was blood in the chalice the first time, who was to say it was there when the Bishop drank the second time?" asked Heather.

"Because I tried it myself! He passed out and I dragged him to bed and I took a different carafe. I poured it out into the chalice. It looked and smelled like wine. Until I drank it. When I drank it, it was blood. My blood."

"Talissa, you don't know if it was your blood."

"I know my own blood! The Bishop knows my blood!"

"Fuck off. Blood is blood." Heather didn't mean to debase the importance of blood, only that blood didn't know the boundaries of flesh.

"This thing," said Talissa, holding the chalice up, "is cursed. It has cursed the village, this church, the Bishop. I created a cursed object. And cast a spell in blood!"

Talissa began to throw the chalice to the ground, but Heather, lightening quick, stayed Talissa's hand with abnormal strength.

"Don't! That won't solve anything." They stood eye to eye, the cup above their heads.

"I want to break the curse. I want everything to be back to normal."

"This cup isn't the problem. This is just something you made. It's beautiful. Why would you destroy it? Why did you put so much meaning behind an object?"

The chalice was more than a symbol of the destruction of Interamna. It was, in Heather's eyes, the beginning of vampirism. Essentially she came from that cup. The blood in that cup would eventually find its way into her veins. Heather put the chalice back on the altar, her fingers excited by the touch.

"You don't understand. You don't know the power of blood rituals," said Talissa. "This happened two years ago, and he's since polluted the entire village. One by one, on every holy day, on every sabbat, he would call the villagers in and they would drink of the cup. They would see the visions the Bishop saw, they laughed like Devils, they screamed. They went mad, tore their own skin. And when they reached a certain point, where they not only looked inhuman but there was no intelligence in their eyes, the Bishop would kill them. If they hadn't already done it themselves.

"That isn't even the worst of it. I watched as Interamna dwindled to nothing, as the roads became empty. I stupidly thought that that was horrific. That these innocent peasants were being slaughtered. And who were they to protest to the Bishop of Interamna? Who was, essentially, their God? Then, when the veil between the living and the dead was thinning, they began to rise. Maybe it was because it rained a lot, and the Bishop had them in shallow graves. The graves slowly rose. You could see the bumps of earth dotting the town. And one night, they began to climb out of their graves. Nobody knew what to do! What would you do? Some people ran, others fought-but most couldn't leave their possessions behind. They seemed harmless enough for a while, especially when the sun rose. When it was light out they all but stopped and fell down dead again. Then night would fall and they roamed. It was only a matter of time before they crossed paths with a villager. And when they did, they would tear them to pieces and drink up their blood and eat their flesh."

Heather raised an eyebrow at Talissa's explanation of the sickness of Interamna. "So they died insane, viciously, and with a taste for blood," said Heather.

Talissa nodded. "And then their dried and rotted corpses rose up because they'd consumed majical blood." Talissa breathed out a sigh filled with so much fatigue and frustration, expelling the burden of fouled majic. "I haven't left this church in two years! I've nearly starved at times! Oh God...!" She shook, holding herself, and Heather took her in her own arms and asked her to lead her to her chamber. Heather laid Talissa to bed, Talissa crying, finally feeling able to release herself, able to be weak, to break down, rather than being strong as though she held up the walls of the fortress of the church.

"It's okay, Talissa," said Heather, kissing her forehead. "Just sleep, you'll be okay. Everything will be okay. I promise."

"I didn't even ask how you got here. I don't care anymore. I've been alone for so long."

Heather used her power to make Talissa fall into a deep and dreamless sleep. She also cursed herself for being soft-hearted, for having sympathy for what she knew would become her demon. And it followed that she did haunt herself! She could easily have ended it here. Heather was determined to seek out truth-no, not truth, for truth is as beauty, bright only in the eyes of those who look upon it. Heather wanted to seek out her own understanding, to carve herself a history, an identity. Fierce independence, a unique identity, a nightmarish reality. Though she wasn't outwardly aggressive, she was as a tiger-sleek, quiet, fierce. It was, in fact, her birth sign. She had all the qualities of a leader, mixed awkwardly with her introvertedness. That made her all the more dangerous, for she was a quiet leader.

Heather, conniving as a tiger, was not without an ulterior motive, though. When Talissa had fallen deep into her sleep, unwakeable, Heather lifted Talissa's sleeve to take another look at the scar on her wrist. Instead of leaving the scar as a permanent mark, a permanent reminder, Talissa had used her remarkable artistic skills to beautify the mark. She'd pushed green and red ink under her skin, tattooed a thorny rose vine reaching from her wrist to her shoulder, little flowers at intervals on her arm, culminating in a large-petaled rose on her shoulder. The work looked as though it would have taken days, many tedious, painful days of one-handed needlework. And she wouldn't let Heather see it. It was so personal. Her art was so personal.

Heather tucked her in and examined the artifacts around the room. Talissa had spent her time carving and drawing upon the walls. The theme of nearly every picture had a cross or pentacle with it. Especially the simpler ones, the whimsical ones. One was of a child in a field of sunflowers, and the yellow-haired child was seen only because of cunning, thin black lines that accentuated her image among the yellow flowers. The sky was a plain, powdery blue and in it hung a bright yellow sun, subtly white in the middle. In the centre of the sun was the back 't' of a cross, in thick, angry lines. It didn't ruin the picture for Heather, but it made her wonder.

Perhaps it would be considered blasphemous if the cross were absent? she thought. Though Heather was assuming now.

The sun would be coming soon. Heather left Talissa and went back to find the little girl in the red dress. It came as no little surprise but with great agitation to Heather to find her missing. She hadn't sensed any movement, nor Magog's presence in the church. She had to hope that the girl was safe, she couldn't lose focus. She couldn't succumb to emotion. Now Heather had to concern herself with finding a place to lie. Likeliest the safest place, and the most gruesome, would be one of the upturned graves out in the village. But Heather wouldn't willingly put herself back into that position. She was much more intent on staying in the church, or if the need was great enough, going into the forest.

Heather walked through the corridors of the church, finding it quite devoid. Everything was very still, very quiet. Then Heather heard movement from the altar room. She spied in, seeing the Bishop of Interamna kneeling at the altar. The saint turned his head as Heather causally walked in, he smiled and quickly got up-actually, he was so anxious he shuffled on his knees to where Heather was. He took Heather's hand and she could see by his eyes that he was still drugged. He kissed her palm, his lips pressing hard on her hand. Then, quickly enough to astonish Heather, he pressed her palm to his cock.

Heather thrust him away and said, "You fucker!"

St. Valentine lay prone, bewildered. The Bishop began to twist his head from side-to-side. It rolled like a ball, Heather could hear the madness swishing inside his skull. "My suck love, the twisted thing go chomp lick! Ha!" He made a song of it: "The twisted thing go chomp lick! The twisted thing go chomp lick!" He rose from the floor, gangly, his limbs jittery. From behind a curtain at the altar, he pulled out a young girl with thick red hair and a dirty, tear-stained face. He grabbed the chalice off of the altar and gave it to the girl to drink. Then, after a few moments of expectant silence, the girl went over to Heather and gently put her teeth upon her wrist. She bit, though not nearly enough to break the skin. St. Valentine laughed hysterically, slapping his hands on his face and knees. He quickly sobered up and stood reverently at the altar, his hand crossed neatly in front of him.

He beckoned and the red head dutifully obeyed. As though programmed. He took the girl by the shoulders and turned her so they were facing the same direction, then refolded his hands in front of her. He pressed her close, her head up against his cock. The Bishop took the chalice in one hand and kept the child close with the other. He drank from the cup, swished the contents around and smelled as a connoisseur would sample the fragrance of wine.

Heather looked at the eyes of the child. Her eyes were a pool of deep brown, but empty of emotion. Dead to the innocence with brightness and vitality. The girl's light had been extinguished by the depraved mind of a mad Bishop. And with all the horrors that he must have reflected on her eyes, who was to say she was no longer innocent? Upon the altar were two who had consumed human blood.

The blood doesn't affect her! thought Heather. The girl had none of the vampiric madness that was evident in the eyes of the Bishop!

The Bishop pulled from behind the altar an athame, the witch's blade, and he stabbed it into the child's gut. Still the girl didn't scream. She fell to the floor and Heather, distraught, concerned, upset, rushed over to her. What harm could this child possibly pose to the Bishop? Why was her immunity to majic such a source of concern for him? Heather, empathic, felt her rage turn to tears. Why was all this happening?

Do I even have the right to be upset? she asked herself. *Yes. This is senseless. This is unnecessary.*

Movement at the door. Talissa had risen, groggy and swaying, her top hanging off her shoulder revealing the rose tattoo. She spied the chalice and went over and drank from it, reverently, like the Bishop did.

"Sometimes," she said, drunk, "it's so hard to resist." As the liquid filled her veins, so did the madness in her chocolate eyes.

Heather stroked the girl's hair, pushing it away from her face. She tried to pull the blade out but the girl convulsed in pain with every movement. Such a harmless child. It was unlikely Heather could do anything for her. But she had to try. She had to at least make the attempt and witness the failure.

The Bishop reached behind the curtain at the altar again, and brought out a child. And another. And a third. He followed by bringing out two more sets of three. In a circle around Talissa they stood, instinctively. They all drank of the chalice, and none, of course, were affected by the majic.

They joined hands, then paused, hesitant, all eyes focusing on one child. St. Valentine picked up a staff, and stuck one of the children in the back of the leg, below the knee. It was Talissa who spoke, as though they were unworthy to hear the voice of the Bishop of Interamna.

"Thomas. You have learned your lesson. Would you begin?"

Thomas got up, mustering the last ounce of his gumption, and cleared his throat. He was crushed, but trying to hold his head up. His soul on the brink of defeat, it was astounding that youth held such resiliency.

"Ring...around...the rosy," he sang, though barely any noise left his lips. Only raspy breaths that barely formed themselves into words. The words sounded dead and flat, like he'd just had his most precious toy stolen. "Pocket...full..." and he couldn't go on. Until prodded by a further threat from St. Valentine and one of his athames.

Talissa said, "Keep going, little Thomas. Come on, you all know what to do." The circle began to turn counter-clockwise. Talissa closed her eyes and began to turn against the circle, pointing to it. Thomas continued:

"Pocket...full...of...posy...ashes..."

St. Valentine had lit a fire in the small altar cauldron, sprinkling herbs over a bright orange flame. He uttered prayer silently.

"...ashes...we all-fall-down..."

All the children fell fatigued to the floor. Movement was too much for them. Talissa stopped turning and opened her eyes. Her finger pointed to Thomas and she smiled.

"It's ironic how the God's work. You've always been so much trouble Thomas."

For the first time Thomas spoke, hurling obscenities through tears at Talissa and the Bishop. Heather was about to go to him but for the dying girl clutching her arm. The Bishop surprised Heather though. He'd slit Thomas' throat without ceremony. He drained him of blood as though he were a swine, first filling the majic chalice to overflowing, then the altar cauldron. He pulled Thomas' head back by the hair, towards his spine, to keep the wound wide.

Heather had the dying girl in her arms, on her lap, and suddenly she giggled as though in a playground. Though to Heather even that sweetest of innocent noises was so disturbing here in sight of St. Valentine's rituals of blood. The most binding of all rituals. The titter was the last noise issued from the girl's lungs, and Heather hoped she would find solace in that sound, perhaps much, much later, perhaps in daydreams. Her head went limp in Heather's lap.

Rage filled Heather and with eyes a deep, boiling blue, her hair liquid gold, Heather lunged at St. Valentine. Caught him easily, a fly in her sticky, invisible web. She had exposed his neck by pulling his hair, his filthy hair, and nearly snapped him dead at that moment. Heather had her teeth ready to rip into the murderous beast, so devoutly religious with his athame and crosses and pentacles, but his reaction stopped her. Heather knew the human reaction so well, and even those who openly welcomed death resisted in some small way, a struggle, a cry of pain. The utterly broken resisted. The devotedly suicidal found fear. The afflicted and suffering renounced their cry for release. St. Valentine, his neck primed for breaking, had a crazed grin on his face, his heart raced in anticipation. He even let a small laugh escape.

"You want this..." said Heather. "You fucking bastard. This is what you want." Heather threw him, rag doll, to the floor away from her. They never questioned her presence because they knew what she was. Heather scolded herself for being so naive. People aren't that stupid! Everyone knows what a vampire is! She was kidding herself if she thought this life of hers, this vampirism, majic, the whole creatures of the night thing was really and truly a secret. No one on God's green earth ever kept a secret. The night just contained another small, quietly hidden reality that was ignored and dismissed by most, if not all, of those who were assigned to the day. Humans morbid need to be frightened! Just exercising unused knowledge of a reality. Denial due to agnosticism. How arrogant. "I'll never give it to you. Never." It stung all the more so that she said it without malice. Anger would have been a sign of emotion, and perhaps irrationality. Heather had made a cold, hard and final determination.

All the blood had been consumed. The chalice was empty, and the rest of Thomas' blood had been made part of the concoction the altar cauldron. The altar was a mess of blackened blood.

St. Valentine doubled over, letting out a grunt of pain. He looked as though he had a stone in his kidney. His legs buckled for a moment before he succumbed and dropped to his knees.

Talissa said, "Heather, help him! You have to help him!" It was as though she'd snapped, reverted to her sweet self that Heather was more familiar with. "There's no more blood left. He's been trying for so long...he's hardly eaten for two years." Heather looked at her, a little disgusted. Mortals shouldn't delve into blood majic. It was too powerful, too binding. The madness of St. Valentine was evidence of that. He was so emaciated from trying to subsist on blood alone, and blood that contained weak majic. If Heather didn't provide the majic, the oh so powerful majic that was hers, he would certainly crumble to ash.

Heather snatched up two of the impassive children and began to head out of the church. Better they take their chances with the zombies of Interamna. She could at least save some speeding in and out before Talissa and St. Valentine murdered them, if they still had the resolve. Heather didn't have to look back to see the image of the Bishop of Interamna struggling through the pain to regain his footing, and holding an athame to the neck of another helpless child. It wasn't Talissa's pleading that stopped her, though.

"Heather, please, don't run." Heather stopped dead in her tracks. She turned with the children under each arm, scanned the small altar room.

"Dad?" she said. The scene was as she'd seen it before, Talissa lamenting the mortality of her lover, St. Valentine, on his knees in pain and the children fallen dead in their circle.

Bits of smoky shadow began to swirl in mid-air above the altar. Above the chalice, the cauldron, the athame, all the majical objects present in three. The swirl quickly grew larger, almost a portal, a window. Though it wasn't a defined shape, it was just smoke, and it blurred the air, the reality of where it was. Majical smoke.

From it Heather's father stepped out, or through. He seemed to form out of the smoke, really. He looked much healthier than when he'd passed on, more robust. Heather put the children down.

"We need you, princess. It's really smoky here. I can see two ways to go, but I can't seem to walk to either of them. I don't really mind the smoke. After forty-five years of cigars, not much can bother you." Heather walked over to the apparition of her father. She touched his shoulder, more of a push, really.

She said, "Are you real?"

Albert Langden answered, "None of us blame you, princess. We all know how hard it is from your end of things. But some of the others, they're getting impatient, and well...you know how old people can be. Well, now just imagine people who are already dead!"

"Dad?"

"But you have to stand and fight. That's all we ask."

"How many fingers am I holding up?"

"I wish I could help you more, but if I were to tell you what I see from here, I-well I'm really not sure what would happen. Something bad. Don't ask me how I know. You just kinda know. Well, not *you*, you didn't really die."

"Nice try, Magog. I'm not going to fall for your tricks."

(Oh, Heeeaather!) The voice in her head.

"What is it?!" said Heather. "You're not supposed to be here."

(It's been a while, kid. I've missed you.)

"I don't want to talk to you."

(You don't have a choice. I'm right here with you. Right inside of your skull. Scary, huh? Can't keep running.)

"I'm busy. Go away." Heather was about to gather up the children again.

(Use your eyes Heather. I'm not in the room. You have another chance to talk to your father. Don't waste it!) The shadow swirled above the altar. Was that Magog? Did he take another form?

"This isn't real…" Heather clutched at the sides of her head. "None of this is real! Go away!" She was losing control. All her power was gathering, welling up, her fears shunting her self-confidence. She was trying to *think* her way through the majical realm, rather than letting her own natural instincts and power express themselves. She began to redirect the swirling of the shadow, her hand making clockwise circles in the air. The shadow slowly drifted to her finger, coming under her control. If Heather hadn't let herself become distressed, she would likely have easily banished the shadow. A distressed majician is prone to misdirecting the paths of spells.

St. Valentine had risen, brandishing an athame (he seemed to have stashed them all over the altar room!) He began to try and reverse Heather's conjuring. He was making circles, counter-clockwise, in the air.

Te deum laudums; te Dominum confitetur, he said. *Te aeternum Patrum omnis terra veneratur.* He was a sack of flesh hung on a skeleton, the only sign of humanity his patchwork beard and filthy hair. *Tibi omnes Angeli; tibi caeli et unversae Potestates. Tibi Cherubim et Seraphim incessabili voce proclamant;*

Sancuts! Sanctus! Sanctus! Dominus Deus Sabaoth!

Pleni sunt caeli et terra maiestatis gloriae tuae!

St. Valentine began to draw a circle in the stone floor. Though he hadn't stepped into the one the children had made. There was something solitary about his conjuring, and it was evident because Talissa stood isolated in the other circle, a tiny bit of incomprehension evident in her expression.

Te gloriosus Apostolorem chorus, te Prophetarum laudabilis numerous. Te Martyrum candidatus laudat exercitus. Te per orbem terrarum sancta confitetur Ecclesia, Patrem immensae maiestatus; He began to draw in the pentacle on the floor, in the circle. *Venrandum tuum verum et unicum Filium; Sanctum quoque Paraclitum Spiritum.*

Tu Rex gloriae, Christe. Tu Patris sempiternus es Filius. Tu ad liberandum suscepturus hominem, non horruisti Virginis uterum.

The shadow had reached a stasis, turning neither one way nor the other. She felt the pressure, the resistance and colliding of majic, and became aware that the Bishop of Interamna had been doing more than dabbling. He was going utterly mad, utterly drunk on power that was beyond him. But how did a mortal have access to it? Heather had met vampires who didn't even have an inkling of what Valentine was dipping his hands into.

St. Valentine had finished drawing out the circle and pentacle. It gave Heather hope that he'd reached the limit of his power, the edge, and now she waited for the crash, for she was far stronger. Though St. Valentine, his holiness, and who was to say it was out of utter madness or sheer intelligence or the stark collision of both that he could find Heather's heel? That he would swing the balance? He took the athame that had drawn the circle and sliced his skin open along his forearm, the satchel on his skeleton, and began to redraw the circle in his blood, tainted, vile, fire-engine red, so drowned in madness and majic. He concluded his prayer; his chant; his *spell*:

Tu devicto mortis aculeo, aperuisti credentibus regina caelorum. Tu ad dexterum Dei sedes, in gloria Patris. Index crederis esse venturus. Te ego quaesumus, tuis famulis subveni;

Quos pretioso sanguine redemisti!

Aeterna fac cum santis tuis in gloria numerari...

With his athame, he cut into his own chest the sign of the cross, and with the blood from his veins he drew out pentacles at all ends of it. Talissa had exited her circle of children and now held the chalice near St. Valentine's cock, catching the blood dripping from his wounds. (Mustn't spill a precious drop!)

The struggle that took place in the altar of the church of Interamna, in essence the First Church of the Sabaoth, the host, the army of madness and majic and corpses long dead, was not physical, not remotely. It was a struggle of majic, originating in the mind-and therefore the very soul-and it was from the depths of the mind that majic originated, from the subconscious. St. Valentine was not a shallow person. He was devoutly religious, a firm believer, zealous and aggressive in his thinking. It was this religious depth of soul that caused him to delve his hands into majic beyond that of anything that had been, was currently being, or would have been attempted by anyone Christian, Pagan, Vampire or otherwise. Though he was deep enough to find that hidden part within himself, he was drunk with the power, the ecstasy, the blood, literally blood, that bound him to his majic, that bound him to dark regions of the earth that were dark for a reason-not necessarily because darkness was equated with evil, but because the shadows had hidden things that mortals were not meant to study deeply during life. Parts of the universe that were there to be found once one *transcended* the mortal state. For, as evidenced by the Bishop himself, the tortures, the misinterpretations of the unknown, had emerged as physical manifestations-his thirst for blood, his madness, his self-inflicted wounds. Had he shed the physical self he could have avoided the tortures of the soul due to the fact that he would consist only of soul. The body tortured the soul because it was being tortured by the soul.

And Heather felt the torture of St. Valentine's soul. She'd experienced the challenge of physical battle, and it was nothing compared to the imagined onslaught thrown at her by St. Valentine. As the volleys of power slammed into her skull, she felt her knees buckle beneath her. She was being forced to the ground. More so, she felt her body beginning to contort-from the inside. She could feel down to the very cell the manipulations of excess energy filling her body.

She had to stare into the mind of a madman. How could she expect to defeat him? His thoughts were all randomness, while she tried to retaliate against his assaults with her own logic, her very sanity. Heather tried to throw him a loop by throwing back some of his own power rather than drawing on the weakness. He was dominating, full of guile in his mazed-up mind, leaping around the corners in quicksilver flashes and laughing like a clown holding a knife under the pale moon. He held an edge on Heather with every trick she tried, a long serrated edge.

The room had thickened with the smoke of shadow, but around Heather the air was clear. She was losing her access to the shadow, her one true source. Though she had the power of the vampire, her own witchery and her innate art, she was still young of mind as both mortal and vampire. And St. Valentine was very, very old, he who had extended himself almost two lifetimes on majic and child sacrifice. He knew his boundaries and extended them to breaking, he knew his depths and plumbed them. The effect could be seen upon his emaciated body, but in his eyes were only the power and madness. To look into his eyes was to see him great and powerful, as though he were a king, as though he ruled over life and death.

The children had died by choking on the shadow, and from their weakness. Talissa had sunk to the floor up against the wall of the altar room, delirious as she watched the purple electric volleys of majic fly between the two combatants.

Heather had sunk further to the ground. The Bishop of Interamna held his arms ahead of him as though physically pushing her. Evidence, unfortunately for Heather, that the battle had begun to spill from the majical plane into the real one-at the behest of St. Valentine. He could sense Heather's imminent defeat. He would bring the battle across the mingled realms, across the bridge of the surreal into the real. If the Bishop defeated her mind, her body would certainly and quickly follow.

Heather began to grasp at the shadow, drawing it into her as one does to water in a pool, slowly. It was St. Valentine's power that was overflowing her, spilling out of her and surrounding her in energy that was acid to her dark majic, her shadow. His energy, ironically, looked almost as light, quite white with a hue of purple. Her knees were almost touching the ground, and she resisted with every muscle in her legs and back not to touch the dirty stone floor.

"Oh shit, oh fuck, he's beating me!" thought Heather. "I'm gonna lose, I'll be dead before I was ever even born!" Heather felt the strain in her ligaments, her muscles tearing, the bones in her knees grinding together under the stress. Lost eternity flashed before her eyes. The moment before death, a moment she was familiar with in some intricate fashion, the moment when one's will succumbed to the inevitable cold skeletal grip, the shivering fear of the expected culmination of a lifetime of beliefs. Heather's heart almost beat for the first time in over a year, anticipatory (and, perhaps, as she felt her body draining of majic, becoming mortal again for one brief moment? Would that be her death, the loss of the majic that kept her alive?)

"Who will miss me?" she thought. "What will it matter if I'm gone?" She tried to look at her surroundings, at the room filled thick with shadow. She saw the town outside, filled with the walking, waking dead, utterly consuming everything alive that entered. Eating the flesh of humans. And when that was gone? Would they then die because they had broken the precious circle? Would there be nothing but trees and animals left? Was that the fate of her beloved Montréal? Of the world? "This is just some stupid dream of mine. This can't happen everywhere. I can just die and no one will ever know what I've done and everything will just go on like it did before." Heather was succumbing to her fears, Valentine made her feal weakness and she began to think only of weakness. He applied more pressure, he laughed, his madness reaching full tilt, his schemes coming to fruition in a way even his outlandish fantasies didn't dream of. Heather's left knee snapped, she felt the bone poking against the skin near the outer joint. She felt the muscles of her calf and hamstring rip painfully and her knee smashed onto the cold, hard floor of stone. Her eyes teared and she bravely tried to withhold a cry of pain, and she was successful in stifling all but the beginnings of it. Warranted or not, Heather felt defeated symbolically. "Oh, fuck, he's got me down! I'm gonna throw up, I'm gonna be sick from majic!" Her mind was on the verge of breaking and her body had begun to do so. St. Valentine hung his tongue out like a rabid dog, maniacally grinning, his eyes glazed as they filled with a supreme strength, a power of majic that was so strong Heather could see his flesh beginning to die as it hung from his skeleton.

Heather began to feel the majical acidity burn at her skin, her vision began to become clouded with white, and she struggled to see the purple hue, because it was colour, it was something to anchor herself to. Because it reminded her of Catherine. She pushed the thought out of her head. It would only make her sad. No one wanted their last moments of existence to be sad. Think of anything. The madness of St. Valentine filled her head. All his murders, all the blood he drank, twisted visions of...herself. He had seen her throughout the remnants. He had such power over her in his dreams, fucking her every which way, making her bleed and drinking her blood and fucking the hell out of her wounds.

"You perverted bastard!" She clutched the sides of her head. Whether it was warranted or not, she felt violated.

Think of Korson. He'd just stand here, he wouldn't even laugh, he'd just stand and live or die, just take it and nothing would bother him he's such a bastard he doesn't care about anyone least of all me he didn't tell me shit I can't believe this is happening ohfuckohfuckohfuck.

All white now, no purple, no nothing, this is it. Nothing to hang on to, no one to think of, no one to help, just all by yourself, like when you were born and when you die.

Holy shit, I'm on fire. It feels like my brain is already crumbling to ash.
(Heeeeeaaaatttheerr!)
Shit. Magog.
(That wasn't the usual sweet you.)
Could you fuck off please? I'm trying to die for real this time.
(You should have been my supplicant. It would have been much easier.)
I'm nobody's supplicant.
(Really, now? Oh, Catherine, it's all purple like you, my sweet Catherine! If only I could pretend I'm Korson! Then I could die like a man instead of like a little whimpering, pussy-hearted blond! HAHAHAHAHAHA!! What happened to your vaunted individuality? Where's your feisty spirit, the one that leaves you utterly alone and constantly fighting?)
Fuck you.
(I'd split your mind in two.)
I'm not listening to you anymore Magog. Leave.
(As you wish...supplicant...)
It's all in my head. There's no Magog, he's just some manifestation of my masculine side gone crazy. Yeah. Keep telling yourself that, Heather. Forget that you're shaking like jelly and about to not live forever like you wanted to.

She had to calm her nerves, her anger, her fear. Nothing good was ever accomplished in a fit of rage, though anger harnessed was deadly as ever. Direction of purpose and post-anger lucidity were what Heather needed.

It's like when Cumulous just walked up to me. He comes up to my ankle. If he has the balls to walk up to me, then I can beat Valentine. That reminds me. It's almost time to get him neutered. Poor lil' guy. Kay, no more Korson, no more Catherine, no more fucking Magog! It's just me! I have to think positive. No more of all this negative energy. I fell into his trap. Negative thoughts are draining my energy. I have to think positive and steal back the energy St. Valentine stole from me. No. He can have it. I am shadow, I am shadow, I am shadow. Come on! Consume all this light. I am shadow. Where are you? Oh shit. Purple. He's on to me. He's coming in here. No! Nothing negative. This is all a mind game. Reality, fantasy, whatever, it's all a mind game. I can't think myself into a loss. I can't think anything bad. You on to me, fucker? You in here? Come 'ere! You're less than me! You want to be me! I'll rip your throat out with my fangs!

Heather was further assaulted. She felt her mind being crushed under the power of his energy. It wasn't pain, it was the severing of the connections of her mind, like a computer breaking down. A vacuum ensued as her hearing was disconnected. Her heart, or whatever it was that kept her alive now, stopped pumping the majical blood through her veins. She felt herself begin to truly weaken, true death setting in. Blessing, to die in light.

He tapped into her spinal cord, the fingers of his mind reaching to the very limits of her body. He pulled at her nerve-endings like a man working the strings of a puppet. Each pull was the most complete torture, the nerves maxed out, receptors overloading. He pinched the backs of her arms, her inner thighs, her genitals, anywhere the skin was soft. Heather was forced to add to her own pain by biting on her own lip with her razors. St. Valentine administered a burst to her already tender and broken lower lip and Heather tore the flesh down to the cleft of her chin, the skin hanging loose, flip-flopping around like a fish thrown to dry land. Blood kept accumulating in a pool and spilling out, momentarily revealing her reddened, aching gums until another pool of blood accumulated, ready to spill. The nerves in her teeth and gums were being pressed upon as though she were chewing glass. In the real world, Heather was thrown against the stone wall of the altar room, lucky to have her spine remain intact. St. Valentine never touched the nerves in her eyes. Perhaps he just hadn't made his way there yet, savouring the anticipation of destroying the most delicate part of the body. More likely he was just being cruel by allowing Heather to retain her vision throughout the torture, not even allowing her lids to close.

Beaten, broken, lying on the ground, suffering in the white space allotted to her by St. Valentine, Heather did not once lose her faith, did not stray from her path.

I am shadow, darkness is the beginning...I am shadow, darkness is the beginning...I can feel pain. Fuck, can I ever! I exist. Pain is existence. The shadow is mine. It's in the room, right around me. Snatch it! Just a piece is all I need. To start. Nothing negative, just give me the darkness, hide me. For just a moment. Say the name? Will he come? Magog! Shout it for real:

"MAGOG!!"

Nothing.

Maybe he's really gone? Maybe he isn't just in my head? Gotta go, move somewhere, get away from this purple. No, wait. Don't give into fear. Fear is negativity. Confront it, make it positive. He hasn't killed me yet. If my mind stays positive, if I attract and focus the positive energy, he can't destroy my mind, and therefore he can't truly kill me. Great. I've got logic back. Fantastic. Now, if the energy is still flowing, where has the shadow gone? The energy is felt everywhere, it connects everything in nature. I can summon the shadow somehow. What is it that's blocking it?

The purple mishmash of majic from St. Valentine's mind was bleeding through the aura behind Heather, dividing the space between the two colours.

Oh fuck, this is it!

Though she still felt empowered majically, she needed the shadow, her element. This was Valentine's domain, he was in control. The shadow was Heather's domain, and she needed it to overpower the madman. She'd lashed out with a heavy brunt of energy she'd held in store as a last resort, to buy herself more time. Though, as she realized from the subtle recoil of energy, time had no real meaning in a reality where existence was sublime. A thousand times she had died and not known it. Her energies kept reforming, a drop of positive in an ocean held together by psychotic thought. Everything was infinite. The cloud of purple became reality, infinite. Heather turned towards it, and rushed head-on into the madness of the Bishop of Interamna.

"Darkness is the beginning! I am shadow! I am shadow!" Spoke the words instead of thinking them, as though volume would validate the spell.

Sssssssssssssssssssssssss!!

As though Magog had been summoned to arms. Though the malignant spirit was nowhere to be had.

Yes! I rule!

"Come on, Valentine! I've got you, you son of a bitch!" (Son of **a b**itch=Sab?)

Heather had astutely and correctly reasoned as to what it was that was blocking the shadow. Nothing in nature was complete, or perfect. There was always some flaw, or glitch, or exception, something that couldn't be reasoned out using established logic. St. Valentine's power here seemed absolute. It was, to Heather's own reasoning, a creation of the madness of St. Valentine's mind, woven from the majic and energy found in every cell. Therefore still connected to nature. To circles. And he was not absolute. She ignored the meandering of his mind. His reality was not hers, not the real reality, not even the one of his own making.

The more Heather ran, the more she feared, the further he defeated her, the further she *went into the light*. It was, obviously, a basic law of the behavior of light that was blocking the shadow. The shadow couldn't exist in the light. Just as Heather was weak during the day. It was a condition of her majic. As vampires were of the shadow, they couldn't be of the light. But it was light that cast the shadow, and with Heather's strong-willed determination to defeat the Saint by channeling the positive energy and disrupting his negative energy, he resumed his onslaught and gave her the very weapon with which she could summon her majic-a place to step out of the light.

Heather swam all over the purple mass, ignoring the incredible imbalance of equilibrium, maneuvering as though in a sea of plastic coloured balls that children played in. She was surrounded by shadow, thick, suffocating, utterly black, blacker than Valentine's purple, consuming it. She trailed it behind her, spreading it in thick, bold strokes to black out each one of the Bishop's warped fantasies. She would black out his mind, then escape into the corporeal again, her shadow in tow.

The glitch. Some of the Bishop's purple was pale like lilac, though most was dark violet. Heather thought she was consuming the madness of the realm. She was in fact mingling her majic with that of the madman's. Was she making him more powerful? Had he turned her advantage to his own favour through his diabolical manipulations?? Was he, as Heather had first thought, absolute in this actuality?

No! Hell no! I simply will not lose!

It was in simplicity that Heather found the proverbial plan B. Surrounding herself thickly in shadow, summoning all the positive energies her mind could control, she flew back towards the light. The acidity of it was felt immediately as her presence entered the realm. No matter how much shadow she cloaked herself with, it was slowly burning away in the light. Heather was split down the middle by the border of purple and light. One half burning her majic, the other mingling her with the evil she was battling. Her thoughts were racing through her head, trying to find some loophole in the circle of majic. As a vampire she'd stepped outside the circle of life, of living and dying, and each reality had its own circle to follow. Were the laws of nature absolute across realities, imagination, and perception? Could she rely on fact or did she have to make it all up every moment of her existence?

There has to be some clue. It's not like I don't have any knowledge. I must know something that can counteract this magic.

This had gone even beyond majic. They'd stepped into something altogether different than the known realm of blue-green earth. Heather had stepped into the mists of Magog and into the mind of a madman and could be absolutely unsure of where the hell she was if she was going to rely on certainties.

To my right is light. To my left is colour. I am shadow.

She was in a triumvirate, and it only took three to begin a circle. Which meant she was at least one-third of the power here.

To my left is one colour.

Simplicity.

To my right is all colours! Of course!

Though the white light made the shadow disappear, Heather had been focusing on positive energy as well. It was what had kept her alive. The shadow was more of a comfort zone gained through familiarity. She surrounded herself with shadow, but this time she made her aura the flow of positive energy. The connection was an astounding one. There was a small distinction between majic and energy, but the properties were based on different concepts. Majic was of the mind, of the individual, while energy was of everything. In everything. Everywhere at once, as though an atmosphere to be breathed in. With the shadow she was stuck in the realm St. Valentine had domain in, yet was unable to work any majic because she would be of him who she was engaged with. In the mirror realm she was unable to use the shadow because it could not be seen under light. The positive energy was what *was* the other realm, because energy and majic coincided, paralleled and complemented each other, like all things. Feeling the link with the absolute, the first time she'd felt it, Heather stepped completely into the white energy, confident. Yet she had only moments to protect her grip on the shadow.

Simplicity.

Now, how to split the light into colours? A giant prism. That would be nice right about now, if glass could even exist here. I wish majic was that convenient. Shit, how can I see colours?

She'd answered herself. This was all mind, all perception! Heather was looking at white light now. Heather was *looking at colours!* She closed her eyes and altered her way of thinking. Literally her way of looking at things. When she reopened her eyes again, it was as though a child had melted crayons all over everything. Abstract rainbows swirled and spun and popped everywhere. Heather saw every property of light that couldn't be viewed when the light energy was perceived as whole. For a split second she was mesmerized by the outstanding beauty of the scene. Nature at its basest form of existence and behavior. Completely chaotic. And it was the most beautiful thing anyone had ever seen. If Heather had realized that time had no meaning here, she would, without question, without hesitation, have stolen another eternity just to swim in the sea of what had to be the Mother herself before resuming her struggle. Alas, this would be a fleeting memory, and luckily so, for if it were more she may have spent the rest of her life trying to find this plane again and only to be whittling away forever at futility.

Now, he's purple for some god-forsaken reason. So no more darks. Purple is made of red and blue, so they're out of the question. Indigo and violet, obviously a no-no. Green is made from blue and yellow, so those are out too. And that leaves me with orange! Is that it?

Was that the band of energy that Heather had to tap into? What made it so special? Though Heather was trying to follow logic in her selection, she'd unknowingly selected the colour of the God. The colour of Samhain, of Halloween. Though Heather's logic was valid, it could be applied to all ends of the spectrum based on the intensity and resourcefulness of the majician. It wasn't the actual properties of the colour, but the <u>perceived</u> properties. It had the boldness of red, yet it overmatched it with a brightness taken from yellow. It could be bloody, sweet, offensive or delighted. It was very representative of the cheerfulness of youth, of birth, and Samhain was the birth of the God. Orange retained a dominance, a uniqueness and a fearsome quality. Summoning all the appropriate energy to her, Heather lashed out at the violent, violet madness of St. Valentine's mind. As though squeezing the energy of the sun, Heather struck over and over. She'd struggled to achieve the right state of mind, to summon the right energies for the right reasons. In her mind she'd erased the doubts, erased any possibility of defeat. Most people defeated themselves, and St. Valentine, though powerful, though mad, had achieved his status by feeding off the negativity of the weak, stealing from them, covering his own deficiencies with black majic. Heather, who had coloured herself orange, like a reborn God, thoroughly gouged the majic from every cell in the Bishop's body. The combatants both fell to the floor. If anyone in the room could recall the advancement of time, they would have seen a struggle that lasted no more than five seconds. Though the mind was limitless, it was also unimaginably quick. It was the body that delayed the mind.

Talissa immediately went to her fallen love. She lifted his head and saw that the only sign of life other than the one in his eyes was a slight twitch of his hand. A slight choke came from his mouth, but he could not speak or move otherwise.

"Help him!" cried Talissa. Heather could not provide any aid even if she desired to. She lay on the floor and couldn't feel anything but a mallet-like pounding on the sides of her head; then she lost consciousness.

Heather woke, surprisingly, to daylight once more. The sun was bright and high in the sky, noonish, and Heather decided to just appreciate it rather than debate as to its authenticity. She pushed herself up on her arms. Her lip throbbed with every twitch of muscle, as though she just had surgery and her brain hadn't figured out the limitations of the reattached skin. It was as though she'd woken from a dream. She'd never been a vampire, she never had to cope with a Host of evil zombies and demons didn't haunt the world; and night was for sleeping. It was that split second after waking where everything was okay, when the sun crashed its way into the room and then one realized what the world was again. Heather sighed when she saw her surroundings; a small barren room, with only the bed she lay on and a table of wood. Her clothes were in a pile in a corner, torn. For a moment the light of the sun had fooled her, but she now saw that everything was as it was when she had been knocked out: dirty.

She was stiff and began to get out of bed to stretch. She'd forgotten her knee had been smashed to bits and nearly fell over on her side and then said the word 'fuck.' Sitting on the bed, Heather lifted up the sack of a dress she'd been changed into.

"Well, I guess Talissa isn't too mad at me if she put me to bed," thought Heather. She began to examine her knee. It looked as a piece of metal did when it was severely dented. The skin over her kneecap was swollen and red and lacerated, and it looked as if lumps of bone had embedded themselves in all the wrong places. Painfully, it would bend a quarter of what it should.

"I may have to seduce a doctor into taking care of this when I get back. Maybe Korson knows someone *real* quiet." She touched her lip and cringed when she felt the huge gap. She didn't want to guess what that looked like.

There was no use delaying the inevitable, so Heather carefully rose to her feet. She kept most of her weight on her good (right) leg and took a few steps around the room. She bent to examine her clothes and saw that they weren't worth salvaging. She looked outside the window at the historical scenery. The veil of smoke that had surrounded the village was gone, a likely indication that Magog now allowed her to leave. But Heather wanted to see what kind of mess she'd made. Speaking of mess, looking out at the village, she saw the torn up ground and vandalized homes. As well as some people. They rummaged through the ruin of Interamna, a little dejectedly, but there was no air of fear, or defeat, rising from them.

Heather opened the door and limped out into the church. She was near the top, and she followed a winding stone stairwell down, step-by-step, favouring her knee. There was some movement from the altar room and Heather went there. Empty. As though nothing had happened. Very still, very quiet. Even the brown of the dirt looked lighter. There was a very small window at the head of the room and a sunbeam shone through, illuminating the floating dust motes.

The movement came from the room beyond, St. Valentine's quarters. A dark rectangle in the wall. Heather went to the room. It seemed sacrilegious to stand in the altar room, more so when one heard another's movement. Best leave it dead.

She entered the room and Talissa was working over the small altar cauldron, boiling up another concoction of herbs. The room was still dark, as though it were angled in such a way that light could never come into it no matter what the time of day. In the opposite corner lay St. Valentine, and Heather was a little startled when she noticed him, partly because the darkness hid him so well, partly because she did not expect him to be alive.

"Good afternoon," said Talissa. The dreaded confrontation, always awkward. Heather forced herself to experience it. It was existence, and she still existed.

"Hi." There, awkward moment over. "What's for dinner?"

Talissa didn't say anything. Just kept stirring and adding some leaves here and there. She didn't look angry. She just smiled as she looked down into the pot. She spooned some leaves here and there. She spooned out some of the broth, blew on it to cool it, then made sure it smelled okay before she tasted a sip of it. Then she put down the spoon and reached for a bowl, handed it to Heather.

"Pumpkin seeds? Thanks." Heather took a seat and munched on the slippery, gooed up seeds. It was the only food she could eat, and though it didn't satisfy the thirst, it made her feel full for a while. Ceremonial food, y'know.

Talissa said, "It wasn't a good harvest this year." Of course, since everyone was DEAD! "They'll have to ration out in the village."

"You look okay," said Heather, fingers sticky and orange from the pumpkin guts.

Talissa forced a quick nod. "I'm okay." She looked down into the pot mostly, forlorn. Stirring, needlessly, as though to keep busy.

"Watcha makin'?"

"A remedy. To heal the soul. If he has one left." Still she held a firm belief in majic. Heather looked over at his prone form on the bed, almost a crime to look. She'd put him there. Was he really evil? Or just sick? He didn't seem evil lying there, helpless and broken. It didn't even look like he was breathing.

"Everyone has a soul."

"I think his may be forfeit."

"Depends what you believe, I guess."

Talissa stirred a few minutes more, then Valentine stirred, a struggled moan. Talissa leapt to his side and lifted his head, her hand a pillow. She took some of the broth and tried to feed it to him. It seemed as though he swallowed it, but the liquid suddenly spurted out in a choke and soaked his chin and neck. It seemed too hot to drink, but the temperature didn't seem to be the reason the Bishop rejected it. Perhaps he willingly forfeited his soul? Talissa further tried to comfort him, whispering some ancient lullaby into his ear. A prayer, perhaps. A chant. She tried to feed him more of the broth but he wouldn't even swallow it, just let it dribble out the corners of his mouth. A long while later, he seemed to calm again, to become serene and placid. Talissa returned to the cauldron, began tidying up her herbs.

"He's dying," she flatly stated. Other than the lullaby, Heather had heard no emotion from her voice.

"Part of life, isn't it?"

"How can you be so cold?" said Talissa, lashing out. "He's going to be gone forever!"

Heather said, "You know what I am, don't you? Fuck, of course you don't, but you have a better idea than anyone else. You don't know where he's going. None of us do. Not even me. I was stopped at the gates, remember?"

"But, Heather, you could save him!" Pleading. "He doesn't have to die."

"Why would I save him? I don't care. Besides, he tried to kill me, remember? Let him die. The world's better off without him."

Talissa's eyes were wet, she shook with emotion.

"He wasn't always like this!" she cried. "This is all you saw of him! People can change. He can be what he was."

"So? What was he? How do I know what he used to be?"

Talissa said, "He used to bring happiness. Interamna was a faithless Hell, and he walked the Flaminian Way to bring joy to these peoples lives."

"Who ever said lack of faith had to be Hell? I have no beliefs. Every night I wake up, not believing in the majic in my veins until my lips drip red."

"You have to believe in something," said Talissa. "How can you float around in the world without anchoring yourself to something concrete? How often must you witness your own majic to believe in it? In all majic! There are some things you can't see, but they're there. And there are some people who can see those things. The Bishop was one of them."

"I can see as well," said Heather. "I know you can see things to some extent yourself. But there are some things mortals should not play with. If there is one thing I believe in, it is that the world itself is God, that Nature is the Goddess, and that it *should not be fucked with*. In one form or another, Nature will go on, but everything that lives is not eternal. Everything has its time. And the Bishop has had his time. He cheated, Talissa! He was supposed to be dead long ago. He cheated and it finally came back to him. That's why he's going to die in pain. To die a broken man. He brought it upon himself."

Talissa buried her head in her arm. She squeezed the Bishop's hand. He looked dead already, but for the extremely subtle rise and fall of his chest.

"Please, Heather! I don't have time to argue with you! He doesn't have time! From the bottom of my heart, you have to believe me when I say that a great man is dying. Please just trust me and save him!"

Heather stood up, slowly, and turned towards the door. She walked out, her left leg dragging a bit because of her shattered knee. She couldn't have rushed if she wanted to.

"Where are you going?" asked Talissa.

Heather stopped, said, "I'm going to find my way back home." And then continued to walk.

Talissa got up and caught up with Heather as she was at the door to the altar room. She put her hand on Heather's shoulder to stop her.

"Heather, please, just stay a while. You're not well. Please?"

Heather thought for a moment. She didn't want to stay. She wanted her home again. She wanted Montréal. She wanted reality.

Talissa said, "I have no one else. There is no one else here anymore. We've outlived them all. Just stay and keep me company for a little while? Watch St. Valentine die. Watch him be buried."

Heather, tersely, said, "Fine. I'll stay. But do not ask me to save him," then she continued her shuffle out of the room.

The staircase continued its winding path downwards. Perhaps the architect's instinctual sense of irony, of metaphor. Heather followed it downwards, into the darker, hidden reaches of the church. To see what an ancient church basement held.

The air was grey and dusty, and the floor was dirty. The stairs could be closed off by an iron gate. As Heather stepped off the final step, she felt a crunch beneath her foot. She picked up a shard of human bone. Half-sized skulls smiled from the corners, from niches in the wall, some even hung from the ceiling still dangling a spine. St. Valentine kept his dinner here. The last of the children had died in the altar room during the battle, as the Bishop had sapped their energy for his own purpose. The only evidence of their captivity were the skeletons of their peers lying about shattered and scattered in a dirty basement. Now they were memories. Now they were remnants.

It wasn't much of a room. Big, dark, with stone pillars here and there to hold up the church above. Iron chains hung from the walls, perhaps to confine the more rebellious captive. Or to see how long the hunger of children can resist.

Like the altar room above, it, too, was dead.

A dark red curtain hung against the wall near the middle of the room. Pulling it aside, Heather found a passageway leading sharply upwards, obviously a shortcut to the altar room. And another iron gate to seal off the passage.

Further along, the room arced around and Heather came upon a coffin. Dark oak and very ordinary. Just a box. Like the body, built to house a soul as it is ushered off to another place. The presentation was inconsequential.

Steps. Talissa. Everyone else had died.

"It's his coffin," she said. "It would take years sometimes for him to revive through majic, and he would spend most of the time dead in there." Conveniently among his victims. Their blood hopelessly keeping him alive. Such a futile attempt! Such vain grasping! Yet he did almost manage it. He did prolong his life. And he paid with a violent, lingering death. "When he finally dies, I will put him in there. Finally."

Heather looked at Talissa standing in this room of horrors, of tortures, standing there as though in the parlour, entertaining a guest. Like the room around her had no skulls on the floor, no coffin next to them. Desensitized to it all, to death, torture, pain. Numb to all but her own pain, the pain of losing her love, the grand Bishop, a madman who once was...who may have been...a great man.

"Come upstairs, please, Heather? He requested you."

They walked to the stairs and Heather had to climb the steps one at a time, very tedious.

"Here, let me help you," said Talissa, putting Heather's arm around her shoulders.

"No, it's okay, I can do it."

"Don't be stubborn." She helped her up the steps. They passed the great doors and Heather noticed one of them slightly opened, and torches lit in the village. As though in ceremony, though a quiet one. People seated around the warmth of the torches, the spectre of the church, drinking wine or beer and merely enjoying life, their own and of that around them. They reached the altar room and Talissa stood in the entrance way, motioning Heather to go on herself.

"What does he want?" Heather asked.

"He's in there," said Talissa. Heather crossed the room again, the absence of dread almost as eerie as if the dread were still there, and again entered the dark quarters of the Bishop.

Heather now stood at the threshold to the chambers of the Bishop of Interamna, his grace in twisted love, heated fervor and sickness of mind. Heather saw the bits of shadow that had crept into the room.

"He has a power over the shadow!" she thought. She saw the swirls entering throughout the Bishop's ears, his breaths becoming raspy. Heather listened to him and it became clear that he wasn't completely in control of his faculties; that is, he knew not what he did. It was possible that the shadow controlled him. If that was the case, then the simple explanation would be that Magog was the sickness of Interamna. But for life to be that simple! Heather laughed out loud. It was too easy to pawn off the world's troubles on a shadow-demon. Demons haunted people, not worlds!

Here was the man who preached to the village. In all his emaciated glory. His chest was a rack of ribs, the skin sucked tight to the bones. His stomach a rag of a sack that inflated and deflated prominently with each of his raspy breaths. His physical stature was a metaphor for his mental state; his mind as meatless as his ribs, and the airless nonsense expunged with his breath. Had he donned a red and white hat he may have resembled Saint Nick because of his beard. Though his beard was more of a dirty grey that could be found on a homeless man.

And soon as Heather made herself known-that is, moved into the room like an actress in a gruesome play-the Bishop sprang upright in his bed, psychotic eyes blazing red. He moved to a crouch, using the fingers of his left hand to help his balance, and with his free hand kissed the jewel that dangled from his neck. He seemed to have a strength in his body that belied his thin frame. Desire. It can push the weakest of creatures higher than heaven. The danger lay in the fact that, as mortals curse God, God may in turn look up and damn the skies above him.

"The Phoenix has fallen from the sky and will rise from us! Pray the Phoenix! Pray the Phoenix! Blood burns! Blood burns!" The Bishop took the jewel that dangled from his neck, he dug its pointed end into his body, marking it from thorax to pelvis. He dug another line from nipple to nipple, the blood dripping from his tattoo in great and small gobs, thick, and bold as cranberry sauce. He walked on his knees over to Heather, took her hand and licked the salt off the back of it. "To lick and love my flesh of passion fire. Lick my passion, love my fire."

Heather tried to pull her hand away, but the Bishop held on to it. He kept saying *love my fire* over and over again. Repetition is madness. Repetition is madness. He rubbed the heel of Heather's hand on his neck like he was bathing himself. Heather pushed him away by the shoulders. She wasn't sure what this madman was trying to tell her, his mind only showed splashes of colour, all shades of orange. Orange darkening almost to brown, almost to red, brightening almost to yellow, but always juicy orange.

"Has he regained his strength?" thought Heather. He was able to move, he practically hopped around, but still hadn't left the bed. "Maybe the moon is strong tonight."

As if in answer to her thoughts, the Bishop collapsed on the bed. Limp, powerless. Then looked up, and there was a glint of sanity in his eyes. Maybe a glint of what Talissa was trying to tell Heather he used to be.

"*Sanctus, Sanctus, Sanctus, Dominus Deus Sabaoth!*" he tittered and his face kept falling on the bed as he tried to hold it up. He lay there, mostly naked, wearing only a white loincloth, a diaper, really, as it had obviously been soiled recently.

"This guy is just fucked," Heather said to herself.

"Hi, Heather." St. Valentine. An as yet unseen moment of lucidity.

"Are you the one who has been talking to me?"

"No. I have seen you though. Looked through the...remnants, is it? I'm terrible with the terminology. It was the majic I was after. Now God has allowed me a few moments before I die."

"Which God?"

"I think I saw a goat."

"Which God?"

"I can't define God. All I know is it's in my head somewhere."

"Which God?"

"Don't do this to me, Heather!" he said, crouching and clutching the sides of his head. "You know I could snap at any moment!" Close, whispering. "I've fucked you every which way in my dreams...I'd like to rub my cock in that tear in your mouth."

"You're a sick bastard. I can't wait to see you die."

"Oh, shit! You're right! Look at me. Bleeding all over the bed!" He cupped his hands and ran the blood back up his body, trying to push it back into the wounds, trying to stop the wounds from bleeding. "I was wondering why I was feeling faint..." He fell backwards, looking weak again, his body shaking in tiny convulsions. "Can you see it? Can you see the moon?"

"Yes. It's mine. When it sets, you will die."

"Oh, you've cursed me!" A pause. "What are you doing? I can't feel it anymore!!!"

"I told you it's mine."

"Don't take all its light. That's cruel. I feel so tired now."

"Could use a drink, couldn't you, St. Valentine?" He'd retreated into the short, raspy breaths, shivering, his eyes losing their intelligence and staring blankly upwards. Heather watched him for a while longer, and he became much more still, like he'd looked before his attack of sanity. Heather turned and shuffled out of the room, hoping beyond hope that she really did curse him to his finality.

The real enticement was the little crack she'd seen in the door. There was life again in the village, and if Heather was to stay she figured she would see what had become of the town of walking dead. Her movements were slow because of her injuries, and as she poked her head out of the door Talissa rushed to her.

"You're not going are you? You said you would stay!"

"No," said Heather. "I was just going to see how things were out there."

Talissa looked at her a little tentatively. She stayed her with a finger and walked away, returning shortly. She handed Heather a cowl of dark brown material.

"I wish you wouldn't go. But put this on."

"Yes. I'm very scary looking right now."

"Come back soon, Heather."

Heather nodded and slipped out the crack in the door. She tried to hide her limp, but it was difficult. She couldn't get any movement out of her joints, and it felt like the knee had been fashioned from concrete. Slowly down the steps. Everything quiet. Towards the small fire lit in the square, sparsely circled with people. The survivors. So silent. Mourning, perhaps? They all wore hoods, somewhat like the one Heather wore. Protection from the cold night, and maybe they didn't want to be seen anyway.

"Looks like these people are into Druid shit, or something," thought Heather.

She reached the circle and there was no acknowledgment from any of the group. She sat on one of the logs, by herself, trying to be unobtrusive. Feeling a little self-conscious, she pulled the hood over her face a little further.

A pot hung over the flame, boiling some sort of drink. Heather smelled the aroma from the pot. Apples. Definitely apples. And some other fruit she wasn't too familiar with. Pomegranates? Most certainly there were apples and it made the night smell sweet. The cold air carried sweetness now.

"Tea. Or, um, cider," thought Heather. "Cider. They deserve some liquor after all that they've been through."

A man rose and stirred the pot with a wooden spoon. He poured some of the cider into a cup and it was passed around until it reached Heather, and the cup was handed to her with the gesture that it was for her. Heather, unsure if she was able to drink, politely put the cup to her lips and felt the scalding relief of the numbness of her wounds.

Everyone had their heads bent downwards and they seemed almost as though in prayer. Or thought. Everything was very still and serene, and the chaos that gripped the village was felt no longer. A sense of well being, of spiritual balance, was prevalent. It in fact emanated from the group itself, as though they had reigned in the tumbling energies after the dam broke and made the waters peaceful. Protected the calm lake, rather. Meditating in the energy.

A murmur of agreement issued from the group, and they all drank. Heather had caught no transmission of thoughts and therefore was forced to assume that they were all so incredibly in sync with each other in their meditations. How was it that a group of people cold achieve such a cohesive state? Was it their energy that connected them? Another murmur and again the drink. Heather was a little tentative and looked around. She noticed, across the fire and through the crackling flames that one of them was looking at her. A man, his hood a little father back so his features could be discerned; his head shaved bald and the lines of his skull very defined, and facial hair above his lip and on his chin. He looked at Heather and smiled a little, his stare still harsh. He raised his cup in acknowledgment and toast and drank with (to?) her. Heather put her cup to her lips and accidentally allowed some to be swallowed. Ignoring the choking enough to note the flavour, she could taste something extremely harsh, faint, but definitely a bitter aftertaste. Perhaps something more than the alcohol mixed into the drink. And the keeper of the pot crushed some dried leaves in his fingers and let them drop into the mixture.

Hours passed, melting away as though the sun's hot morning rays had mischievously found their way into the night before their time had come. It had been a long time since Heather had felt the pure relaxation that was brought on by the meditation of the survivors. Not that she'd never enjoyed herself (fuck yeah, it was such fun being a vampire!), but there was a great difference between personal enjoyment and spiritual relaxation. Not only did Heather's body feel the release of the chains of her wounds, of her cracked knee, but her mind was allowed to float, as though her head was filled with water. Did some of the cider she accidentally swallowed have an effect on her? Drinking, drinking, drinking, that's all it came down to...

"I can't think they're dead. I can't think they're defeated," thought Heather. And it didn't bother her. Of curse the Sab would be waiting for her when she returned. Right outside the church. It didn't bother her, though. It was a fight she was prepared to start. The seething mass of demons, waiting outside something deemed holy, sinisterly rubbing their hands together. The meditation gave her perspective. She was a warrior now. Much more than a killer. She had the knowledge, the awareness, that when her path twisted back home to her beloved Montréal it would be to a battle. Heather didn't trust what went on here. It would be too simple to think she'd simply defeated the Sab with the impending death of one man.

Sanctus, sanctus, sanctus, dominus deus Sabaoth!

The Sabaoth is the Host. The Army. If anything, what Heather had accomplished was to create a vacuum of leadership, she had disorganized the chaotic.

When it broke it was deeply felt by Heather. One of the meditators had risen and turned away from the fire, carrying the pot of cider. The rest followed slowly, one by one, walking in a line towards the forest. As though it were mad to remain in the village of Interamna to sleep. Like there were ghosts. Each took a piece of the fire with them, as though their presence held the energy to keep it lit. Heather sat alone on a log with dying embers.

Talissa was waiting when she slipped back through the crack for the great doors, leaving the dead village behind her.

"You should have slept," said Heather.

"I can't now. Not till it's over." Her voice flat and cold again, with death. "The villagers spoke with you?"

"No. They were...meditating."

"Of course." Talissa lowered her head, as though it was burdened, as though her essence had been trampled. "They have agreed to help with the burial."

Heather said, her voice betraying anger at the impropriety, "Why the hell would they? He all but destroyed their lives!"

Talissa, calmly, "They thought it best to honour the dead."

"Ghosts," thought Heather. "Their silent chants are a prelude to putting the ghosts to rest."

"Will you stay for the funeral?" asked Talissa.

"I have to go home," said Heather.

"Please?" pleaded Talissa. "It will be soon now. Only another day or two."

"Why do you want me to stay?" Heather was determined to see him die, to deny the gift of immortality that St. Valentine so openly tried to steal, descending him into madness.

"I just don't want to be alone at the end." Another plea. And who was Heather to turn down a direct request for friendship? She was, after all, very much a loner herself. There would be plenty of time for her to be alone. Why consciously isolate herself when it wasn't necessary? It was because of her pride that she wanted to spit at Talissa. The union between Talissa and the Bishop couldn't be denied and Heather still, quite literally, felt the wounds of the battle. With the Bishop lying sick in his quarters Heather found it difficult not to direct her anger at Talissa. The feral sadness in Talissa's wet eyes and the melodic, sincere request-*I just don't want to be alone at the end*-had softened Heather. It was also a much needed excuse to allow her wounds time to recover.

"Okay," said Heather. "I'll stay."

"Will you come to the funeral with me, too?"

"Why not? I could see them bury your fucking bastard lover and be done with the son of a bitch once and for all." (Heather didn't say this out loud.) "Yes, I'll come to the funeral."

"Thank you, Heather! Thank you so much! I really need a friend right now."

Talissa seemed to find a bond with her. No one said life was easy.

Heather again woke in the room shed occupied the previous day and was subject to a quick, dreadful flash of déja vu. It was only a moment before she realized that the sound of uncontrollable sobbing from beneath her was what had woken her. The sounds ebbed between wailing and curses of 'no!' and 'why?' and then degenerated back to a simplistic yet poignant gushing of tears that dripped out from between the fingers of the hands that the face had buried its misery in. She rose from the bed, donned the cowl, (she felt comfort in the anonymity it provided), and limped down the winding corridor of steps to see Talissa.

Talissa was in the Bishop's quarters, her face pressed to his lifeless chest. The blood of his wounds had coagulated into filthy dark red lumps that glistened under Talissa's rain of tears. He lay with his palms up, and Heather noticed he managed to carve pentacles into his palms before he died, and the wounds had made his fingers curl up in a twisted way. His eyes had rolled halfway up into his head.

Talissa looked up from her tearful mourning on the Bishop's corpse at Heather.

"You could have saved him!" she cried. She rose and rushed over to Heather and beat on her chest saying 'you could have saved him' over and over again. Heather didn't say anything, just held on to Talissa as she beat a tearful vengeance on Heather's chest before finally losing her strength and burying her face into the comfort Heather provided. Heather held her as tightly as her wounds would allow and Talissa just cried and cried until she choked. "It's finally over," she said. "Everything has to end, I suppose." She lifted her head off of Heather and looked at the skeleton body of St. Valentine. She wiped her eyes and breathed deeply and said, "I will bury him tomorrow," her words sounding automated.

"Have you made the arrangements yet?" asked Heather.

"Yes," said Talissa. "I've spoken with the remaining villagers. They will perform the ceremony out of respect to the dead. But it will have to be tomorrow. Before the sun sets. They won't bury him at night."

Heather nodded, agreeing with the decision. If his body still contained spirit, it would be strong at night. Burial beforehand would make it possible to seal his ghost.

"He will be buried in the graveyard behind the church?" asked Heather.

"No. We will walk the Flaminian Way and bury him on the treacherous path he traveled to come here."

"Mm. Poignant."

Talissa shot her a look of contempt. She was too sorrowful to be angry now. She didn't want to argue over the saint's dead body.

"You'd better get someone to take care of that body," said Heather.

"I must do it. I am the only one who can." And Talissa, in grief, became ignorant of Heather as she turned to her small altar cauldron and began concocting a potion for the preservation of the dead.

"It seems it always comes back to boredom," thought Heather as she leaned out the window of the great church. "If I ever start speaking to myself out loud, then I think I will definitely throw myself into the fire."

All that was left was to wait for the funeral. To finally bury that bastard St. Valentine. How could Talissa love him? Why was she so upset at the murder of this so-called saint? All Heather really cared about was the burial of his black majic. She'd never encountered someone so utterly, madly evil in her short life. It hit her pretty hard, the fact that she was so young, so far into the past. Enough trying to absorb the concept of everlasting future and she was flung so far back. And barely two decades of mortality to her merit to make her a part of the world. Maybe if this gift had come to after she'd *lived* a bit? So much was theoretical, she felt she had to make it up as she went along.

The stillness, the serenity, it was incredibly fascinating, intoxicating to look out and see nothing but endless green, and inhale clear air. Disheartening as hell, for the Interamna of the living dead had become dead Interamna. And everything that happened here would die too. With the burial of the Bishop. It was an endless circle, this living and dying. No one would be around to remember and it would happen again. It was all death Heather witnessed, she'd reached the village in time to see it dwindle to virtually nothing. What was left for anyone here? Who would stay? And her father. All she remembered of him was his drinking himself to death. And her mother killing him by dishonouring him while he was alive.

Heather reached down and massaged her knee, tried to move it. She had nearly half her range of motion back, but still very stiff, bone grinding bone. Healing, but not nearly enough. So many hardships, yet she never complained. She never thought of standing in the middle of Interamna and breaking the lucidity of the night with a scream. Or even atop Mount Royal, crying out, "Why me?! Someone explain this to me!"

"I love life," thought Heather, as she examined her wounds. "Or existence, rather, as I am supposed to be dead." As much pain as it was she went through, she never questioned it. Some would call her naive. And they would all be dead. Her survival was due to the fact that she allowed herself to experience. Despite her fears. Despite the pain. It was the prematurely dead that are naive, the ones that think they've figured it out. They die ignorant. Heather looked out the window again, and it wasn't so simple as being summed up in the perfect, ancient night. But it did provide a fulfilling satisfaction. To look out at nature and know that, despite the pestilence and war that flared from time to time, nature would always survive somehow. It would sleep and when everything had settled, out of the corner of one's eye one would detect-

Movement. Near the church steps. One of the villagers.

A wagon was stopped in front of the church, a hooded man standing to it. The one that had smiled at Heather in the circle the night before. Heather was thinking of going down to him, to ask him about the state of the villagers, of how it was possible for an entire population to descend into madness, the reign of one man's madness, but Talissa had rushed out and began gesturing frantically with him. Heather only caught parts of what they said.

...must be carried...

...too difficult, too far...

...mimic his suffering...

...disrespect for the dead...

The man pulled the wagon away, disgruntled. Talissa stood for a moment to watch him go, looked up at Heather in her window, then went inside. Heather hoped that the funeral wouldn't be delayed further, that the twisted priest St. Valentine would be buried as per the schedule. As though in answer to her thought, Talissa knocked on the door and gently pushed it open.

"Are you ready, Heather?" she asked.

Heather was a little taken by what she said.

"Now?"

"Yes. We're walking and if we don't get started soon we won't make it before sunset."

Heather nodded and took one more look out the window. At the foot of the steps lay the coffin of St. Valentine.

It was the general unspoken consensus that they were lucky when they left when they did. Six of the remaining villagers made two lines and carried the coffin of the dead (martyred?) saint. Valentine himself barely tipped the three-digit mark on the scaled, but the coffin itself was very heavy and imposed a terrible burden on the men. There were several tense instances where the coffin nearly came crashing to the ground. Talissa walked just in front of the coffin, and ahead of her was the leader of the village. There were a couple of villagers who brought up the rear and Heather was the last in the procession, dragging her leg because of her shattered knee. So there were many delays as they made their way to the Flaminian Way; the weight of the coffin causing the procession to stop for a moment, Heather's laggard walk slowing them down, even the choking sound Talissa would make, tears pouring out of her eyes and a moment needed for her to regain her composure.

All the villagers had their heads hooded and bowed in a respectful manner. Some had their backs bent due to the burden of the coffin.

"So this is death," thought Heather. How disorderly! The coffin of the saint might as well have been dragged along the rocks. Heather felt very out of place, and when she finally was able to maintain pace with the procession she found herself breaking from the line and wandering around it. It had slowed its pace considerably. The villagers who carried the coffin were becoming extremely tired. Talissa, but for tears, was silent the entire way. Heather found herself at the front of the procession, next to the leader.

"How much farther?" she asked. Her leg was beginning to hurt. He put his fingers to his hidden, hooded face and gestured for silence. Heather tried to look at his face and it was as though his hood had moved to cover it. Or perhaps he tilted his head away?

Her suspicions were cut short when she realized that they'd reached the Flaminian Way. It was a wide gorge, rock faces jutting up on either side of them. Essentially, as Heather felt, trapping them. And if she thought the journey up till now was treacherous, she was about to be taught a lesson. The ground was covered in rocks the size of basketballs, and the coffin of St. Valentine tilted this way and that under the gyroscope of the villagers. They'd already traveled nearly two hours, and it became worse. Talissa was determined to show the path that the saint had to take to get to the village.

Heather noticed that the village seemed to be in a pit. They'd traveled on an upward grade and it seemed as though the Flaminian Way was the only way out. Perhaps the village was doomed to die from its inception? None of the villagers would speak to Heather and, as her awe of the passageway subsided, her suspicions again rose. She felt it was not disrespectful to issue a whisper at a funeral. But perhaps these people had their own customs. Still, Heather felt uncomfortable about something. Maybe the spectre of death beneath a sun that may or may not be real? Perhaps she became wary of the daylight as mortals had of the night? And Talissa was too choked with emotion to lift her head.

They walked several more hours, the late afternoon sun becoming cold and casting great shadows because of the sinister rock faces that loomed over the Flaminian Way. Heather wondered, "Where does this place lead? Was it a direct path to a great place? Did it just fade out to nothing?" It seemed that this path was here to serve as a trial to anyone who would cross it. They'd traveled for hours and nothing was visible either behind or before them. Due to the depth of the path beneath the rock faces, the shadows were casting an early evening on the funeral procession. Even the greatest of men would not be shamed in turning back or dropping dead before completely crossing this unforgiving piece of terrain.

Talissa said, "Here," quite quietly, but everyone heard, as though awaiting her order and instinctively knew that this was to be the burial plot. Heather surveyed the ground and felt that it was about the worst place that Talissa could have picked. The ground looked to be mostly rock, and when the villagers had set the coffin down and began to dig (without even a break; how dedicated they were to their nemesis!), it was with great strain upon their weakened muscles that they carved out the rocky ground.

Talissa had sat upon a boulder about four feet high and Heather went over to her. She had to accept Talissa's extended hand to climb the boulder and perch herself next to the widowed lover. It got colder and a slight breeze picked up. Slowly but surely the hole grew in size as the villagers pulled away the gravelly ground. Talissa, grieving on the rock, put her head on Heather's shoulder. Though Heather offered no words. The silence had become a presence, looming much like the shadows of the rock cliffs that encased the Flaminian Way, and Heather didn't want to further break it. The mood had become thick and dreary and the darkness was etching its way over the horizon. They would be returning to Interamna in utter darkness.

The grave was complete and the coffin was opened to reveal the emaciated body of the saint. Each of the villagers took a moment to pay a final respect to St. Valentine. Bowing over the dead man's grave and making a small gesture near their chests. Their features and movements were completely hidden beneath their brown robes.

As the grave was slid into the hole in the ground, as the villagers began an eerie hum, as though praying in unison, the rise and fall of their voices synchronized perfectly, it seemed as though everything was timed perfectly with nature. The walk along the rocky path, the digging of the hole; the filling of the grave coinciding with the setting of the sun.

Heather was curious as to why Talissa didn't take one last look at the coffin. She just sat on the rock and became emotionless again. Had she been frozen by the spectre of the saint's death? Did his prolonged life give the false hope that he may actually fulfill his dream and live forever? She was clearly a slave to her numbed mind now, her eyes glassy with painful yet suppressed thoughts.

The only sign of life that caught Heather's attention, as the tired and mourning villagers began the long walk home, was the sight of two birds fluttering around on a rock near the grave, then taking flight down the path, back the way that St. Valentine had first come.

It was Heather and Talissa that walked home together. The other villagers had disappeared by the time the remaining two started out. They walked mostly in silence, only the dragging of Heather's leg the constant sound. The moon was high by the time they got back, and at the opposite end of the village a fire had been lit. They sat on the stone steps to the church.

"This is it," said Talissa. They both looked out upon the dead ruin of the village and thought the same thing. There was nothing left here in the pit, and it would remain forever dead. No one would walk the deadly path to get here. No one could, but for the one buried along its way. "We're trapped here, and soon we'll all die."

"I think you're being a bit melodramatic. You have food here, shelter. A second chance. From death there is always growth."

"We're doomed. The only one who could have saved us is dead."

Heather, annoyed, said, "I think I'll go inside." She was sick of hearing how great the dead madman was. As far as she was concerned he could burn in Hell and have his name stricken from memory. But the question begged in her mind: How could a man who'd brought about so much death be associated with love and fertility?

As far as she was concerned, it was time to go home. But what of the future? What of Talissa? They were surely trapped here, Talissa and the villagers. Heather decided to stay one more night. Her knee stung from the journey, she felt some inconclusiveness with regards to Talissa and she was just plain tired. She went up to her quarters and took one last look out at Talissa, sitting forlorn on the steps, before collapsing in her bed.

Heather rose the next evening, finally feeling some form of rejuvenation. She went down the steps and found Talissa in the dead saint's quarters, cooking a late meal of berries and meats.

"Smells delicious," said Heather. Talissa didn't answer in words, just gestured in agreement and then put a serving of the meat and berry stew onto a plate. Heather was neither offered nor desired any form of mortal sustenance. She'd abstained from drinking for more nights than she could count and the desire to withstand the urge for blood grew as though it were a snowball being rolled by a group of children-slowly but surely getting larger. Talissa ate ravenously, seemingly recovered from the emotional stress that subdued her during the funeral. "You seem a lot better," said Heather.

"I feel good. I really do. It's been so long since I've sat down and eaten a good meal."

"Things did get a little hectic around here."

"I've decided to rebuild the village. I feel its no use to let everything to waste. Things can move on here. Perhaps. Perhaps in his memory..."

"It seems so isolated here, though."

"People will come. There's lots of good land."

"The villagers will help?"

"Yes, absolutely," said Talissa.

"Are there are others, though? Those aren't the only villagers left, are they?"

"Of course there are others. Many others."

Heather got up and walked around, testing her leg. She looked out the small window, noticed very little light left in the remains of the day. Why didn't she feel powerful? What was it that made the coming night seem like just another passing phase? She felt as though she couldn't shed the weakness of the daylight hours, but she attributed it to her injuries, her fatigue, her tired mental state. There was something bothering her. Some feeling of *incompleteness*. It was mostly alleviated when she spoke the words, "I'm leaving now."

Talissa was cleaning off the table from her meal.

"Already?" she said.

"Yeah. It's time. I should've left long ago." How long had she been here? Weeks? Months? The clock ticked and Heather paid no attention to it. There was no more loss, no more urgency, no more passion. The linear existence of eternity meant constant and endless renewal. And Talissa was noticeably disappointed...

"I thought you might stay for a bit. Help out or something. Heal yourself. Watch the village grow again."

"I'm about as good as I'll get. I'm just too homesick anyway."

"Not even to keep me company?"

"It's a nice offer, but I really have to be getting back."

Talissa said, "It's your choice I guess."

Heather went back to her room and looked around at her belongings. Torn clothes was all, really. Nothing worth keeping, and her only keepsakes were the wounds on her flesh. She didn't need reminding of this place. So she left as she came, empty handed.

Talissa was downstairs. She'd changed into a silken dress, sleeveless, tinged with a pale blue. Her rose tattoo wrapped her arm tightly, the intricate beauty of each petal visible from a distance.

Heather said, "I'll see you around sometime."

"Promise?"

"Guaranteed." She went to the great doors of the church and pulled one open. She turned back and looked at Talissa, knowing that she would meet her again when she returned home. Not knowing if she was truly her nemesis or truly her friend, or what she would take with her. Or what the future would hold or if the Sab would be waiting when she rose from Magog's mists. There was no use being petty or bitter. Heather smiled at Talissa, leaving a bright image of herself as she left her alone. She turned and walked out the great doors.

On the stone steps of the church, one of the villagers was waiting, his face hidden by his hood, his hands crossed in front of him and hidden by his sleeves. The leader.

"Come to see me off?" said Heather. He didn't answer. He hadn't spoken a word since the terror of St. Valentine was crushed, since the survivors could show their faces in Interamna again. None of the villagers had. "Don't speak much do you?"

Heather saw several other robed villagers emerging from around corners, from behind trees, walking closer from a distance down the long main road that lead to Interamna's church. The man made some small gestures with his hands from under his robes. Friendly, soothing gestures. In moments, there were robed villagers lined in a 'V' formation behind the leader.

The man took slow steps towards Heather, his footwork hidden by his brown robes. He knelt at her feet. Took her hand and put it to his hooded forehead. Was this some form of worship? For freeing them from the evil clutches of the twisted St. Valentine? Heather felt honoured, a little embarrassed. Her hand hanging in his. After what felt like an eternity, she went to pull her hand away and finally leave them to their freedom. But, as though he instinctively knew, he tightened his grip on her hand and she couldn't pull free. How? A mortal?? Stronger than her??? Heather pulled and pulled and still couldn't free her hand. The other villagers began to pull their hoods away from their heads and they revealed their hideous, green, dead faces, scarred with earth from the grave. The survivors were the dead!

Heather pulled and couldn't break free. The leader rose to full fearsome height, towering over Heather (or was it just the fear of her mind making him seem larger than he was?), his free hand pulling his cowl away.

"Oh, God, no, please don't let it be him," thought Heather. They keep coming back, in horror, they do. He dragged her close to him, she nearly left her feet because of the force. He twisted her arm and she had to angle her back to keep her arm in one piece. She couldn't twist her head around to see his face. Was it him? Did he somehow prolong his life once again, cleverly eluding the grave with his evil majic? He bit down on her arm, tearing a piece of flesh out and chewing on it, each bite making a squishing, ripping noise. Heather pushed his face away. Wrinkled, gnarled and square, not thin like the saints.

"Not him," Heather prayed. "Not him." She could match his strength. She pushed him off. Looked at the large zombie in front of her. Big fucking Frankenstein. She could beat him. But the others swarmed around her and grabbed her, pulling her in opposite directions. Sinking their teeth into her flesh, ripping away large chunks of her dead vampire skin. They pushed her to the floor and their hideous, hungry mouths fell upon her like a pack of starving animals. It would only be moments before there was nothing left of her but pieces of bone...

It was with confusion that Heather looked at Talissa upon the floor of the altar room. She'd been kneeling and now her face and hands were pressed to the floor. The confusion was as to whether she was praying or crying. Talissa lifted her head and Heather decided it was both.

"What's wrong this time?" asked Heather, callously. After all, Talissa wasn't broken down in tears at the funeral. Was this some backlash of emotion? Had the death of her saintly lover finally set in?

Talissa tearfully related the emptiness of it all, blah, blah, blah, all that pathetic whiny shit, the heartfelt outpouring that is just so touching, the agony and angst, the burden of carrying all those painful memories, the gothic pathos of the innermost pain felt by all when a vampire enters the room and sucks the energy from those nearby. She cried and cried and Heather stood there, just watching, not saying anything, waiting for some form of rationality to set in.

Talissa calmed a bit and said that she was being left alone.

"What about the villagers? Rebuilding the village?"

Talissa said, "They've left. They left last night for Rome."

"You should have gone with them then. Instead of staying here by yourself."

"Don't you see? I can't go with them! I'll be killed! They'll blame me for this! As it is, there are probably soldiers on the way!"

Heather was exasperated with her by now.

"Give me one reason why I shouldn't kill myself!" said Talissa, brandishing a knife and pointing towards her chest. "See? You can't, can you?"

"Just think about it, okay? Stop for a minute and think? Why waste the rest of your life because of a few bad moments?" She'd taken hold of the knife and Talissa's hands shook in Heather's. If Talissa had a last surge of strength left to finish off her life, then Heather would've released her hand. She wouldn't make the choice for her. But Talissa couldn't find the desire necessary to call up that last bit of strength to fire the killing blow into herself. And as Heather released her hand, the tension in their arms eased and the knife clanged to the floor. Talissa followed it as her body sagged from fatigue.

Heather thought, "Oh hell. What's another few more nights?"

It was several nights later. In the preceding few nights, Talissa was mostly a shattered wreck, her body shaking involuntarily, her throat constricting and making her choke whenever she tried to speak. She mostly sat with her knees against her chest, holding onto herself as though it would keep her sanity from flying away.

Heather tried to be a comfort to her but she left her alone a lot, too. She sat atop the cliff above the church-it took her hours to climb to the top-and looked out upon the desolation of the village. It was a ghost town. Empty, broken down homes lined the quiet, dusty roads. Not even animals could be seen roaming around. If not for Talissa and Heather, life would have ceased to continue within the boundaries of Interamna. As it was, it seemed as though St. Valentine had taken the gift of life with him to his grave. Not a thing stirred in Interamna. The remaining villagers-by some miracle survivors of the ultimate evil that twisted the existence of the villagers into inhuman zombies-had left, seemingly almost instantaneously as the saint was officially dead and buried. And Talissa no longer had the will left to continue. Did St. Valentine hold these poor people so closely in his clutches that he not only controlled their deaths, but their lives as well? Did his power extend somehow beyond the grave, if that were at all possible?

Heather, in her wicked imaginations, sat atop the cliff many times and looked out upon the village, pretending she could just sit there for a century and stare at its nothingness. Just wait and wait for one single, solitary person to walk down the road and wonder if it was worth it to live here. To begin everything anew. But this was just Heather's imagination. It would never happen because the place was haunted. She could <u>feel</u> St. Valentine's ghost wandering here. She may have defeated him, but she didn't really win. She didn't completely crush his soul. Was that necessary, though? That was what she felt. The inconclusiveness to her victory wasn't just because of the wounds she'd sustained to her body. It was because of the strange presence she felt. Looming. He hadn't done anything-yet. Maybe he would just loom forever here, his evil spectre enough to destroy all hope, to deter anyone else from encroaching upon his domain. That was what was troubling Heather. All the wondering. The neurosis. She used the excuse of being worried for Talissa's sake-though she was, mind you-to remain here and keep a watchful eye upon the whispering mists of the saint. Why did Valentine continue to haunt this place, and her dreams? What really happened to him when he passed from mortality into majic? Was it his spectre that tormented Talissa? In some cleverly diabolical way, was the saint trying to keep Heather here, distracting her with his manipulations from the real war in Montréal?

She wondered about the way home, how she would get there, how she would find it. It would be silly for her to have to wait the centuries out until she returned to her proper time. But perhaps, just perhaps, that was what eternity had fated her.

The drop from the cliff was amazing. Heather never scaled it down, she always took the long way around, the way that brought her to the foot of the forest. Talissa would always watch her sitting upon the cliff from on the church windows, and when Heather would begin the long descent it was Talissa who would be waiting for her at the bottom.

"It must be beautiful up there," Talissa would say.

"Yeah, it's nice. Quiet." But Heather would never invite Talissa up there. Not only were they isolated, but Heather began to isolate herself, too. "You should consider going to Rome. Getting out of here. There's nothing left here. I can see that clearly from up there."

"No," said Talissa. "It isn't necessary. This is what was fated to me. This is how I will live." And Heather was stuck. Her heart was torn with sympathy for Talissa. So she remained many more weeks and watched from the cliff top as the ancient village of Interamna lay dead at her feet. And each and every night she had dreams, terrible dreams of trying to leave the village and St. Valentine coming back to life as a zombie, murdering her by eating the very flesh from her bones...

"You're keeping me from the forest," said Heather. She didn't plan to say it. The thought just spit out of her mouth before she knew it was coming. The hesitation of Talissa's answer only made Heather that much more suspicious of which she suddenly was wary of.

"I'm not keeping you from anything."

"Every time I come down from that cliff, you're there. You always take me straight to the church."

"You're being silly. You're just hungry."

"You know nothing of my hunger, Talissa."

"I know plenty. You visit me at night."

Heather looked at her and clenched her fist in anger.

"You're being neurotic," said Heather.

"No I am not. I have dreams. And when I wake up my neck hurts."

"I wouldn't bite your fat neck if you were the last person on earth."

Talissa grabbed a small cauldron and hurled it at Heather's head. Heather ducked easily and just looked at her with murderous blue eyes. Ready to kill her now. But that would leave her alone here. And Heather really wasn't sure how to get back home. After all, she had been unconscious as she fell out of the sky.

"I'll be back when I think you've found some rationality," said Heather. She walked out of the church, the echoing of her footsteps louder than she wished they'd be.

On the steps of the church, Heather looked out on the dead town of Interamna and wondered why the hell she bothered with it all. This wasn't really her, though, she was angry and still hurt and still wondering. She looked at the forest and decided-again, there was no logic or rationality to it-to walk towards it. Perhaps see what happened when she reached the spot where the wall of Magog's mists used to be.

Before she crossed the edge of trees and entered the blackened forest, she looked back at the church. Even with her great vision, she wasn't sure if it was Talissa watching her from the window or just her imagination. Heather didn't care, didn't give a shit right now. She just crossed into the forest.

It was all powdery, choking black with swoops of sinister, demonic greens painted around her. She walked for as long as she thought she had to to get to where the mists were. Then she walked even farther. There was no direction here. Nothing but black and green. At that, the green was barely visible, almost eaten by the black.

Heather stopped finally. Lost. She'd walked more than enough. And now, spinning around slowly on the spot, she had no sense of direction. She pointed herself towards Interamna-though, if anyone happened to be watching, they would be unconvinced as to Heather's certainty-and tried to go...home...where she was stuck. Was all this just Talissa's manipulations, trying to confound and confuse her? Did Talissa trick her into actually *going* into the forest just to scare her? Heather had convinced herself that, because Talissa *seemed* to be keeping her out of the forest, the way home was here. Now it seemed like she just fell for her tricks. Or was this the majic of the ghost of St. Valentine? Did he try to exact revenge from beyond the grave?

The faces of demons were subtly visible in the swishes of green that painted the black background. Did the dead saint mean to make her mad? Was his onslaught a gentle torture that would last the centuries?

"Just walk," thought Heather, trusting to her own instincts. "Ignore them." Them...Talissa? Valentine? The green demons swooshing in her face? What was all this? Where did the ground go? Were those the trees reaching in with their great arms?

"No. It's all black. Everything's blackened out." She couldn't see a thing. It required her focus. "Is it that my brain's coming unglued? Did I just imagine my victory over St. Valentine?" It felt as though the world would implode upon her.

Heather told herself to calm down. She didn't feel angry, but she could feel the anger still within her, like a hard pit inside of a peach. She didn't want to explode because of her own neurosis. So Heather walked and walked as though there were no demons swirling around her.

She found it more disturbing that the haunting was so subtle. That they just swirled and barely showed their faces. That she could see traces of their demonic presence but not *feel* it, as though they weren't part of the energies that made up everything. Dreams, perhaps? Her own? Or Talissa's? Did Talissa trick her into the forest so she could haunt Heather with her dreams? Was it the forest that held power?

"Maybe nature," thought Heather. Perhaps Interamna died because of a mortal's intervention with majic. St. Valentine must've upset some sort of natural balance. Heather didn't notice leaving the forest. The village (reality?) resolving itself.

She stood back in the square and looked at the great doors of the church. Then to the Flaminian Way. Where did it lead?

"Rome, as far as I can tell," Heather told herself. "What's there for me in Rome, though?" Not that there was anything left in the church, arguing with Talissa. So she set off on the Flaminian Way. Back the way the saint first came and on the very road he was buried. Visit his grave, maybe, Heather?

She reached the mouth of the Flaminian Way, its maw open and waiting for her to enter, its teeth rotten and rocky. It was less than impressive this time, though. She wasn't paying attention to it. She just walked in the gorged out path and forgot everything around her. The path itself, her vampirism, Talissa, the imagined presence of St. Valentine, her growing and increasingly feisty thirst for blood. Everything dimmed as though the spotlight were on her and no one was even looking at her.

When she passed the upturned grave of St. Valentine, the only remains some shards of bone, her feet kept moving, still a slight limp visible, and only barely out of the corner of her eye did she take notice of the desecration. Had the remaining villagers looted the grave when they went to Rome? It looked as though they stole the jewel that hung at the saint's neck, ready to ransom it as their prize for survival. But what of the body of the saint? Did they consume his flesh and bones for food?

Heather didn't really care anymore. She cared about finding the way home. This was the only way out of Ineramna. And it was in her very forgetting of herself, of her surroundings and her circumstances, that Heather Langden, the vampire, the witch, the majician, found herself back in the small altar room of the church of the dead town of Interamna, kneeling in front of the altar, the cauldron boiling away some herbs, and Talissa, on her knees and looking back at her, the glinting athame pointed at her own throat...Heather couldn't help but wonder if she'd forgotten or dreamed her way here...

"Are you awake, Heather?"

"Yes. I'm awake. Where's St. Valentine?"

"Did you think death would defeat his power?"

"He's gone. His body's gone. I don't feel him here. What are you doing with that knife?"

"It's an athame. A-tha-may, you say it. The witch's majical blade. I cut things with it. I'm going to cut myself with it."

"Really? Where?"

"First I thought I would just plunge it into my heart. But I wasn't sure if I could pierce my own ribcage. It's hard to kill yourself. The slightest hesitation in my arms, the slightest weakness in my wrist, and I wouldn't pierce my ribcage. So I figured on my neck. It's so soft. Easy to slice, like cutting through cheese. But that might be too quick. I though I might just torture myself, make myself bleed and wait for sweet death to cover my eyes. Would you like to do it, Heather?"

"No. I don't want to kill you."

"Such a soft-hearted vampire! You should be killing everything in sight!"

"Did you drug me? I didn't think I could consume anything but blood."

"My blood?"

"I don't want your blood, T'lissa. Why can't I move? Why are my limbs so numb?"

"I cut them off."

"No you didn't. I can see them."

"Can you feel them, Heather?"

"No. But I can see them. They're still there. What's that smell?"

Talissa laughed a nervous little titter.

"Stop laughing. What smells?"

"The first time I tried to do it, while you were daydreaming. I kind of had a little problem. I...I scared myself a little too much I guess." She lifted up her dress to show the bandaged up wound on her stomach. Her nakedness was distasteful. She was dirty and caked in her own filth. "I had a little accident, you could say. I had to bandage myself all up and start over again. Now I'm just trying to think of a better way."

Heather tried to shake the grogginess from her head. Was she drugged? Perhaps the scent of the boiling herbs from the cauldron. Maybe it was a potion that made her sleepy. The knife. It would kill her. Talissa would kill her.

"Gimme it," slurred Heather. "Knife."

"It's an athame. Much more than a knife. Do you know what happens when you commit suicide with one?"

Snap out of it, Heather! Heather said to herself. She could see the surface, just a peek of light from the murky depths. She cold almost touch it. Just touch it...all it took was a moment.

"D-don't," said Heather. She could almost think.

"What."

"Don't kill yourself."

Talissa said, "Tell me you love me."

"No. You just don't need to die. You can't do anything dead."

"You're dead, though, aren't you?"

"N-not the same..." Her head, heavy and pressured. Squeeze your eyes and shake. Make it go away.

Why can't I hear??? Why can't I see???

Talissa yelled, "Surprise!" Heather's eyes snapped open and her ears popped so she could hear again. Talissa lay before her, the knife again lodged in her belly, her body lying twisted on the floor, across the two steps raising the altar above the rest of the room. She didn't renounce her promise-her skirt was torn asunder, revealing the hundreds of little and large wounds made by her knife. The only part of her body left unscathed was her left arm, the one with the rose-vine tattoo encircling her forearm and bicep. It said something about her, that she would protect her art while at the same time creating a masterpiece of her body in death.

Through all the sinister and gruesome events, Heather had been the callous one. St. Valentine's dying? Fuck 'im! You're all alone in the village? Fuck you! You've lost all the love in your life? Fuck off! But it was Heather, the last soul left in Interamna, but for Talissa's barely lingering life-force, that showed emotion, that shed tears at Talissa's impending doom. This was her mother, after all, her friend, and it tore her heart to see her about to die on some rotten, dusty floor in an unknown and God-forsaken church. The only thing left beautiful about her form a rose inked into her arm.

Heather leaned close to Talissa's face, her own hot with tears while Talissa's was stoic and expressionless through the pain, the Reaper's cold and bony hand tugging faintly on her shoulder. Ironic, that it's the living who show sadness and shed tears while the dead go quietly and peacefully across the veil of shadow. Talissa's dark eyes looked obsidian, glazed over with a thin film of wetness. Heather shook Talissa's body, trying to get some reaction out of her. Trying to get her to stop abandoning her mortality until the time was right.

"Oh shit, oh fuck, Talissa, how could you actually do it, all over some power-drunk madman! Wake up! Please, please, don't die, don't end it, you don't know what there is on that side of it. None of us do, none of us know, just stay here for as long as you can." But it was too late. Talissa had already peeked through the veil. Most of her blood was dripping down the steps up to the altar like a small, indolent and sanguine waterfall. "Please wake up..."

Heather told herself it was pointless to shy from the truth. She wanted to save Talissa, but to do so would seal her fate. Why did she feel this way though? Wasn't the true evil defeated? St. Valentine dead and buried, his presence no longer sensed in the air?

She almost choked lapping up the blood off the steps, choked through her tears. She'd never made another vampire before. Never gave up a part of herself to create another. Now, she had no choice. It was so touching to see someone who held the power of life through death actually create an existence. Heather's heart actually beat. Talissa lay at her feet but her essence was now in Heather's hands. Heather felt that power with each lick of her tongue. She didn't even care that she tasted the dirt of the floor. It had been longer than she could remember since she last drank someone's blood. And she'd only tasted of Talissa's blood-albeit barely-once, years ago.

Heather had soaked up most of the blood off of the floor. Only the barest drops dripped from Talissa's wounds, and the blood had already begun to cake. But how to give it back? Talissa had absolutely no strength left. She was so devoid of liquid her lips had cracked from dryness.

Heather removed the athame carefully from Talissa's gutted belly. Her only hope was to slit her own wrist and let Talissa's blood drip back into her mouth. Hope she had enough strength to swallow. Heather made a cut in her wrist, the cold blade becoming hot as the skin was sliced open, the blood appearing as though by majic, gleaming against her chalky white skin. Heather lifted Talissa's head up, holding her gently by the cheek, and she put her lacerated wrist to Talissa's parched lips. Talissa's mouth filled with the blood until it overflowed and dripped out the side like vomit from a collapsed drunk. Heather leaned her head further back in hope that the blood would seep down into Talissa's body. She crossed her fingers and prayed she was in time to save her.

"Come on...come on..." she said. Mists of smoke clouded the church altar. The shadow was coming, and Heather wasn't sure if she was calling it or it came of its own accord. It made nasty streaks all over the room and then squeezed itself around Heather. The thickness of it nearly blocked everything out. She could only see the barest outline of the room, Talissa's near-dead form on the ground, and only the brightness of the blood shone through. The shadow enveloped her and it felt as though she were lifted up. Was this her failure? Did night come to claim her? Or was it Magog? As much as she tried to control the shadow she couldn't get a grip on it.

It choked off her senses, but Heather, in one last desperate attempt, caught a glimpse of Talissa, the barest traces of a smile playing upon her lips as life returned to her, just enough, though, to mock how soft of a heart the so-called killer Heather had...

Book 4:

Blood War, Blood Feast

Part 1: Night Stalker's

Heather Langden woke on the church floor, feeling a little bit nauseous. She'd remembered being consumed-or consuming-the shadow, and when she now rose it was as though the power was so great it made her stomach sick. She had to put her hand on a pew for support. But her mood brightened a bit after a moment-upon the realization that she was home, finally home. She thought it was mostly her will that had brought her back here. That, fact or fiction, she'd let the story be told to the point where Magog's hold on her soul was released. She took a deep breath, certain the air was real.

    The church was as she'd left it. That is to say, the candles were still lit, giving the room a dim golden-brown glow, the air smelling a sterile, lemony scent of cleanser, and the room empty. This wasn't the First Church of the Sab, turned demonic grey, the air filled with smoke and the weeping, praying bodies of the dead kneeling, hands on the floor, pleading in supplication to the chaotic powers of the evil vampire Talissa. The church was as she'd left it. And that comforted Heather. For a moment. Then she looked at the wooden double doors of the church, and wondered what lay beyond them. Magog and his mites? Unlikely. Magog was evil, sinister, mysterious and utterly malicious, but certainly not a coward. He wouldn't wait behind closed doors with a sneak attack, he would let his victim's fear reach a zenith and then appear in a **hissss** of shadow, bringing untold of pain and suffering beyond the fly's comprehension. Perhaps the evil zombies of Talissa's master plan? Were they waiting outside, ready to consume Heather, while Talissa laughed merrily like a jester, because Heather just had to search for why's and ease the torment of her soul while her nemesis was busy plotting and scheming?

    Heather thought of the little girl in the red dress. Had the demons devoured her? She pictured them, the horde of them, standing at the bottom of the steps to the church, a sea of dead flesh, fists clenched and the blood of the little girl dripping from their protruding fangs, bits of her flesh clinging to their chins. She shuddered.

She could stay in the church forever. Under the eyes of God. Just sit here and feed and hope the multicolored illumination of the stained glass windows was enough to keep out the sun during the day. Or just hide in the confessional and listen as the whispered secrets of mortal souls were disclosed to a sleeping Devil, the anguish filling her dreams and soothing her sun-baked sleep.

This was anticipation, giving way to unfounded, unfactual fears. Here, in the reality of realities, was only the ethereal silence of the church. Had the floors been desecrated by the sacrilege of supplicants of the evil Sabaoth praying inside these walls? No. The sacrosanct essence of the church was more in the mind than in the architecture, and what better place to expose the lies of Magog and Talissa and the entire dark side of majic than under the watchful eye of a deity? What better way to pay homage to a God? But there was no war in here, and Heather cold not cower in the church, nor behind the book that lay on the altar, could no longer use her fears as a shield, as an excuse to run. Horde of demons or no-and she had yet to prove this to herself-she had to leave and find Korson and Catherine and Cumulous so she could, at the very least, save them from the war. She took the image of the horde of demons to be metaphor; she was scared of leaving the building, of seeing what had happened to Montréal in her absence. She knew she'd taken too long in trying to find Talissa, and though she killed to survive, she was most certainly not a murderer-she had to know, before she killed Talissa, of the origins of her purpose. And if that delay meant it had cost her...well, if that meant the price was mankind, then so be it. She was not indiscriminate. She could not base her actions on the doings of others, make her plans around their schedules.

It had run it's course, though. She inhaled, shrugging off the nausea. It meant shadow, it meant power. Heather stood up and went to the door of the church and, glancing at the large cross on the altar for a moment, opened the door, slowly, listening to the creak and smelling the change in the air. She didn't look out immediately, her eyes fixed upon the ground for a moment. Then she looked out upon her beloved *rue Ste-Catherine*. Empty. Dead. No hordes, but horrifying enough. She didn't see dead people walking the streets, but it was much worse. Talissa actually *killed the city itself.* Heather walked out and let the wooden church door thud closed behind her. The hue was a little brown, pale, the air lifeless. The skies were filled with Magog's smoke, and nearing the horizon was a blood-red moon. Not actually a moon, but the sun, blotted out by the smoke of the shadow, as Heather would realize momentarily. Vampires could walk the earth by day without fear of the sun's lethal ultra-violet burning their volatile blood.

She walked the empty streets, looking at the utter desolation. It was, after all, daytime, and zombies, demons and vampires did sleep during the day. Mortals would likely be holed up in their homes in fear. If they knew what was going on. Talissa was likely infecting them all with the shadow, choking their minds until they died from fear of the visions provided by the majic of the shadow. Which meant that they were lying on their living room floors dead, waiting to be resurrected with the coming of night. Those strong enough to resist would become food for the immortal, walking dead, their blood wine and their flesh bread.

Mount Royal came into view, and Heather saw the smoke of Magog pouring out of it. He knew she was here, he tittered a little from his perch. (Heather thought: Perhaps it was merely Montréal shaking in slight mania at the madness of it's predicament.)

"Ah. That's what I did," she said aloud. Talk about sacrilege! She felt a shiver in her spine at the sound of her own voice, breaking the solemnity of the dead city. Such reverence given to those who had no existence to speak of! Such respect! She herself was dead, yet she inspired fear rather than respect, though some would argue that there is a fine line between the two, or no distinction at all. But to fear her? Sweet little Heather? Pretty, blond, angelic, merely beautiful and only doing what she was dictated by fate to survive the tide of time? It wasn't logical, but then again, neither was nature, and she'd seen enough chaos from St. Valentine's mind to know that the only predictable thing about the chaotic nature of nature is that things keep happening again and again and again.

She called out to Korson, another sacrilege. He might not even realize that it was day. He'd either be asleep, or weak and wondering why. And when night fell, the dead would begin to rise and the Sab would start to conquer the remainder of mankind.

Eyes were upon her. Yellow and evil, for some of the demons were cunning enough to brave the blackened day. Heather pretended not to notice. They were the knights of the Sab, but she wasn't concerned abut them. They would be for the likes of Korson and Catherine. She was concerned with finding her friends and then finding Talissa. As well, some mortals did wander the streets. Some conducted themselves according to their normal routines, as though nothing was wrong. The ignorant. The destitute still rested on cardboard beds, begging for golden dollar coins. Some listened intently to priests as prayers were handed out, street corner salvation. Most, though, cowered-or rather, hid, for they did more than just huddle in a darkened corner of a room-in their homes, only rushing out to the closest *depanneur* for some supplies when absolutely necessary. (Julia St. Croix, just before she was murdered, saw the smoke begin to pour out from the top of Mount Royal and blacken the day. She pulled back the curtain to the window of her living room and looked out at the scene in confusion and concern, for she was faced with the unexplainable. She searched for a plausible explanation-forest fire, car crash, plane crash-but caught only a glimpse of her husband's madness before whooshing the scene to the back of her mind with a swipe of the curtain.) And why shouldn't mankind be fearful of the events? The words of priests began to carry more weight than ever, rabbis stroked their long, grey beards triumphantly and the vampire Heather walked the streets in broad daylight and people could get a little glimpse of what she was even though she was trying her best to hide it.

"You's one a dem, ain'tcha?" This one had a bed of cardboard he sat upon, and a sign that said: "Your salvation lies in your generosity." The other side of the sign said: "I'd rather beg than steal," but that was scratched out for the more appropriate slogan. His teeth were a spectrum of filth, going from pus yellow to rotten flimsy brown and then burnt black stumps. His skin was dirty and his face unshaven and unkempt.

"Do you speak French?" asked Heather.

"Uh dun spik nun a dat frog shit," he said, and spit brown saliva on the sidewalk. Judging by the stains, he likely soiled close to his nest when no one was around to care. He patted the space on the cardboard next to him, and Heather sat.

"So why are you so happy?"

"Cus uh ain't th' munster anymer! Pipple yus ta wulk by here an throw pennies at muh head, an' spitun me. Bu' since thet smoke sterted cummin' dun ut th' mountin', they's dun care much boot me as mere'n a 'noyance.'"

Heather said, "You must be from Newfoundland. You miss it?"

"Wall muh hart!" said the bum, beaming his rotten smile. "Dey's uhnest folk dere, betcha dis nun apennin' down where's fokes uhnest and good t'nuver. Pipples here's brickin' wit nis an nuver evry two zecuns 'n God's witchin but nun cares, an nows tim t' pay d'piper! Bu' you's, you's one a dem, to, huh?"

"Depends on who you're talking about."

"Yeh, you is. See's bout th' time smuk sterted cummin' dun, pipples was gooin in thet metruh un nuhver c'min oot. So's uh witched 'n witted 'n den duh tall one kem in an' kem oot all bluddy. So's uh kin see's ut now-"

"What tall one?" interrupted Heather.

"Big, tall fuckin' injin guy wit a braid un is 'air. Din luk t'good shape nither, but wulked uff dem ways." He pointed. "Yikken iv sum uv muh blud if y'wunt," he said and held up his arm.

"Nah. God's watching."

"G'pint. But uh knows tuh pay muh dues, too. N'ah gut this lil feller here too." He pulled out a tiny, malnourished cat from under his coat. "His kin see, so's if'n uh's slippin', h'cud warn 'n pruteck meh."

Heather said, "Children can see, too, ya know."

"Yeh, but lass tim uh's hid a kid unner muh coat they's hulled muh in ta jail."

Heather laughed and got up, looking at the direction which Korson went.

"Word of advice. Hide. The Sab's coming." She dared utter such a sacred name to a mortal, but he was certainly not a threat to her, nor would she burn in hell for a heresy such as this. The veil had, after all, been pulled back and the creatures of the night walked the earth without the cover of shadow. Or rather, the shadow was a continuous entity now, spreading everywhere, therefore, paradoxically, hiding nothing.

Heather walked away, following in Korson's footsteps, catching faint traces of his scent, hoping there would be enough to lead her to him. She dropped to her knees and sniffed with her nose close to the sidewalk.

"Christ," she said. Intermingled with Korson's scent was that of the Taint.

"Christ will not help you child," said a shadow that loomed over her. "Not while youre down there, with your face in blood." It was the priest from the street corner, adorned in ceremonial white robe with golden trimmings. "Rise up," he commanded in soft tones. Heather had thoughts of just killing him, and hell, why not? She was a little hungry anyway, and figured he would be no fucking problem. But some of the sidewalk servants had gathered with him and Heather, not wanting to waste her time, looked up with an annoyed and dismayed look on her face. She *could* kill them all, and hell, why not? Bloodshed was fun and she was a vampire but certainly much more concerned about the Taint, the Sab and Korson rather than her belly. She stood up and before she could put him off as though he were a telemarketer there were some hushed whispers that she had the sickness about her. "You can still be saved," said the priest, and began to chant from his bible at her. Heather said she didn't need saving, but he continued over her voice. All eyes were on her and she knew she couldn't hide what she was, but neither did she wish to scare the living shit out of the parishioners. All she wanted to do was get away as quietly as possible. "Let Christ save you, child," said the priest, and splashed a vile of holy water across Heather's face. Heather recoiled and cursed at the priest, and a gasp of shock rippled through crowd

"See, my children? She is cursed! She feels pain from the blessed water!"

"No, you got me in my eye, you bastard!" yelled Heather. She said, "Asshole," and wiped her eye and cheek. "You think a book is gonna save you? Pieces of paper?" She grabbed the priest's bible and ripped it into two pieces. "Really, your faith is admirable. But it's blind. You don't know what you're following and you don't know what's coming. When it comes down to it, God or no God, a bible won't protect you from this!" She exposed her claws and then raked the priests chest like a teacher scraping chalk down a chalkboard to quiet children, and his robes shredded themselves into curly, bloody rags of material. Heather gave him a good shove and he thudded on the pavement, quivering towards death. She wondered if she was the only one who could see it, the bits of shadow creeping into him, and then looked at her bloody hands and knew that the murders she'd need to commit would lead mortals to become the zombies of the Sab. And she'd just added to their number. The rest of the supplicants began to back away, some looking with morbid curiosity at the priest, at Heather, and some just turning away and running, not looking back at all. Heather turned her back on them, arrogant and uncaring. She was no longer concerned about mortals, about each individual. She no longer cared much. She'd rather they lived and died by fate, though some guidance could possibly have saved their lives.

After continuing on, trying to determine the scent of the Taint, Korson's scent and trail, Heather came upon a dead body lying at the edge of an alley. A vampire kill, with Korson's scent on it. He'd gotten hungry. But this was sloppy, unlike him. Heather took a taste of some of the coagulated blood from a wound and shivered.

"Cold...bitter..." she thought to herself. "More than recently dead, just a little." The scent of the Taint was mingled here, too. Had Korson become one of them? Something must be wrong with him. Heather continued on, trying to find him. There were drips of blood leading away from the body, making the sidewalk look as though someone had carelessly dripped red paint as they walked. "Shit," she thought. "He's hurt. I should never have left. I should've stayed. Talissa's going to destroy everyone I care about."

As alone as Heather felt, walking across the battlefield that was once her beloved Montréal, following the blood drops, she thought of losing everything important to her-Korson, Catherine, even her kitten. Talissa would kill them all just to break Heather's will. Stubborn, though, and if Heather couldn't prevent it all from happening, then she would never let Talissa take her. Or take her happiness, even if it meant trudging through a war zone littered with zombies, vampires, and the bodies of dead mortals as Talissa sucked the blood from the very earth, because that's really what she wanted to do, take the biggest drink possible.

The blood drips diminished, but she still had the scent, and she walked into the doors of Montréal General, and, thankfully, the scent was clearer. He hadn't been taken over. Heather tried not to anticipate, because it led to hope, and hope to disappointment. She may seem bleak and emotionless, but she was, after all, dead, and throwing her hope to the wind, took a deep breath and called once more for Korson.

I woke up and I thought I was dead. I was still lying in the hospital, and I had machines hooked up to me. I tore them off, pulled out the intravenous. It was no way to live, on machines. Kept alive by something other than one's own will. I might as well have been kept alive by majic, become a vampire.

The first thing I did was look out the window and the streets were empty and the black smoke I'd first seen coming out of the murdered child was everywhere. Death had become the atmosphere. So naturally I thought I'd died. But I'd seen the face of the murderer, the woman who'd invaded my dreams. I'd defeated her, and if that meant my life than I could take solace in victory. In the fact that she no loner controlled me. It hurt that she was using my blood as her power, but she couldn't manage to steal my soul. And I saw her *face*. But what did I plan to do with that information? Come back as a ghost? I knew that ghosts couldn't speak.

I went to the bathroom and looked at myself in the mirror. Shit, I must've been dead. No one alive could look this *awful*. My skin was sickly, especially under the sterile fluorescent lighting, and it made me realize that I looked as weak as I felt. I felt bloodless, and I hardly had any energy to move. Even when I called up some desire as simple as walking across the room, it took a great effort on my part to do so. I touched my face. I looked at the scars on my wrist. Distant memories of someone else, they were. Someone trying to escape. I couldn't be dead, the dead didn't take their scars with them, did they?

One thing was clear: I needed food. I went out of the room, and it was further proof that I was living though I was walking among the dead, especially with the effect of the fluorescence. The staff was dead. Doctors were slumped over gurneys, nurses collapsed in chairs at the reception desk, and those who'd been standing had fallen face first on the desk itself. There were some people shuffling about, mostly old and infirm who looked to be on their last legs. I have to admit I was a little lucky. I would've gone right up to one of the living, but for the fact that I saw one hunched over the body of a pretty young nurse, taking healthy bites of the flesh on her arm as one would eat bread. It did look up at me for a moment, it's face monstrous, something that used to be human, but was no longer. It was more concerned with it's meal and took no interest in me. I checked some of the slumped and dead bodies. Some still looked human enough, but some had begun to deteriorate, turning grey-green and rotten as though they crawled out of a grave. It seems that people had dropped dead and begun to morph-or rather, rot-into zombies. One nurse, presumably because she'd caught a scent of my blood, had risen moments after I had dropped her head back onto the desk. She got up with a hungry look in her eyes and began to shuffle around as the dead did. So it wasn't necessarily the old and infirm who were walking around as much as it was the fact that people were turning into corpses.

I found some food and ate it, ignoring the fact that each swallow was filled with nausea. I knew I wouldn't throw up. It must've been weeks since I'd eaten solid food, and I was ravenous, so I ate my fill. I wouldn't let myself throw up, no matter how much I felt like I had to. I got up and felt woozy, took a deep breath, and began to walk. All I was really thinking about was getting showered and dressed. Not so much about the fact that I was walking among the dead. Afterwards, I would get the hell out of here and try to find a familiar face.

And that damned phone kept ringing. I'd forgotten that I still had Jerome's cell phone, and wondered if it was Talissa who was haunting the phone lines again. I didn't want to bother finding out so I kept hanging up without answering it, but the ringing wouldn't stop. Kept calling back. It was annoying. I finally answered it. It was Jerome.

"I met up with a friend of yours," he said. "You were pretty fucked up."
"I'm okay now. I think I finally got whatever it was out of my head."
"Sounds good brother man. Just watch yourself. Don't let it come back."

"Yeah," I said. "Madness has a way of creeping up on you, doesn't it?" From the shadows. "So where is Korson, anyway?"

"No idea, Graham cracker. He kinda took off on me. Then this cloud descended over the entire city. You know what it is?"

"Yeah. A war. The dead have nowhere to go."

Jerome said, "I think we should hook up."

"Jerome, I can't. I got some stuff to do."

"Graham, you idiot, let's just get out of here. Forget about vampires, forget about all this shit, let's just leave."

"I don't think I can, Jerome."

"Try. At least try. This isn't your war. We don't belong with Korson and those kinds of creatures. Frankly, I'm sick of seeing ghosts, myself."

"Even if I could leave, Jerome, I don't think I would ever be able to leave it all behind. I'm part of this now. I might as well play my part instead of fighting it." I could tell what Jerome felt by the fact that there was silence on the other end of the line. He wasn't one not to be talkative. "I am coming back," I said.

"You take care of yourself," he said after another moment's pause.

"I'm coming back."

"Take care," he said, and he told me to answer the damned phone when it rings. "Graham, I never told you this, but I always remembered how much it meant to me that you found me that day. Whenever I feel like shit I remember how fortunate I was to have been found by you. If not for that I'd be wandering the streets forever like some dead man," he said, and then he slowly hung up the phone.

If I thought I was dead when I woke up then I felt more so that way after the conversation I'd just had with Jerome. Perhaps he was right, though. I was chasing majic that was reserved for the likes of demons and dead men. Perhaps my only possible fate was death due just to the fact that I was throwing myself into that realm.

I had nothing but the clothes on my back and my dreams to guide me. Not even that stupid little majic book I'd gotten from the occult shop. I resolved to open myself up to the majic, to the impossible. Not that it was necessary, it seemed to be all around me now. Thick, sick shadow, blocking out the sun. Soon, very soon, vampires would be walking the streets whenever they wished once they'd seen what was going on and mustered enough courage to brave the daylight hours. As highly as I thought of Korson's character, I certainly didn't want to see that son of a bitch walk the streets whenever he wanted to. He didn't deserve it, not in the least. So, I stood at the window and watched-rather, *sensed* the sunset, as the shadow kept the skies dim-and let myself open up to the darkness that had been invading my nightmares for years now.

Funny. I didn't *feel* any different.

Except...except that there was a relief from the constant pressure that was put on my head. I'm not sure if it was the fact that I'd won the war inside my head with that monster Talissa, or the fact that all the majic seemed to have poured out of the mind's of majicians and into the streets. And that war inside my head was certainly real, not a dream, because Jerome had seen me last night and Korson had come to save him. Well, maybe I imagined something different in my head, but it did come out real. It *manifested* itself as a physical representation of my being. Instead of the pressure-the pressure that stopped me from functioning, from thinking, the pressure that made me see demons even when Korson or Talissa weren't visiting me-I felt a pull. Several, really. Tugs, and in different directions, and none were calling to me to come to them or anything like that, just my mind could sense these tugs. The sense got more acute as the little light left on earth dimmed, leaving the night of nights in its wake.

I tried to follow the tugs of energy, but it was like playing hot/cold with an obnoxious brat who would suddenly yell freezing just when you thought you were close to your goal. Every time I thought I was moving closer to a source of power, it would disappear only to be replaced by a tug in a further and opposite direction. The problem was that I was *thinking* too much. There was a difference in what I wanted to happen and what actually was happening in the world around me. I had to release my consciousness and submit to the whims of the ebbs and flows of the energies around me rather than rage against them. Not an easy thing do. Like letting yourself flow with the tide while risking the wrath of a nearby storm. But I tried to focus on the power and perhaps find something I knew, something familiar. Korson, even the girl Heather, if she still existed, or even the murderess vampire Talissa. Something to help weave my thread into the tale of the dawning war.

The air stank outside. It jolted me back to reality. I had to have some semblance of control over myself. I was no majician. I was no creator. I envied women at that moment. Absolutely envied them. Men were always warriors and leaders, but no matter how oppressed women were over time, the were and always would be goddesses. No wonder Korson felt such torment as a vampire. Being a majician was about controlling power, about being a creator. Perhaps women would make better vampires than me, sexuality merely being a means to an end. Death being an art form.

I-had-no-art.

It hurt to say that to myself. That I could not weave myself into this thing called war, and that the Sab was pulling me in as a pawn of some sort. I looked at the zombies wandering around the streets. In my despair I was ready to just give up. Forget all thought of majic. I would, of course, have to learn to live like one of them, because soon vampires would rule the world. I would feel like one of them, hiding for fear of my life, of the blood in my veins, stealing bits and pieces from the world just to exist. Maybe one day I'd slip up, a stupid little mistake as I wallowed in bitter depression and disgust at my own stink and filth and one of those brainless risen corpses would get it's hands on me and tear the flesh from my bones. And that would be the end of my story. Not that anyone in the world would remember me, or know about me or what I almost tried to do. They would just live and die in fear and confusion and ignorance and eventually rise up against their own kind. I felt so crushed by the multitude. So many people and these were the dead ones and there would only be a spark of mankind left. Perhaps they would breed us. They needed our blood.

Or did they?

The smoke pouring out of Mount Royal was definitely of great power, and perhaps this was just one sick creature's twisted plan to make herself a true goddess, <u>the</u> goddess and then write her own tale. Start it all from the beginning again. It all started from darkness and maybe this time she would leave it that way. And maybe my hell was that I would be the one lone voice of madness left in the new world, who knew of the old, and cursed with the one spark of mortality flickering to the point of death.

It pulled me. It pulled and I was so goddamned scared and I don't know why because it didn't feel at all sinister, perhaps just my preconceptions of majic from childhood fairytales and the fear of change and the unknown. I followed and ignored all my instincts to turn and just run and all those other little tugs from people who didn't even know they were using majic.

It took me to a place of majic, where ghosts had always roamed freely in Montréal. And, ironically, a place where childhood dreams came true...

It was through fate that events came together to create what was war to the eyes of the beings who roamed the streets of Montréal. It wasn't a typical war per se, but a struggle of power, and it manifested itself in the real world as a battle between the demons who controlled those powers. So it was that fate had a hand in bringing more of the weave together, in the fact that both Jerome and Catherine were looking for those beloved to them.

Catherine was standing at the foot of Mount Royal, a speck of pale purple skin under the big, billowing black clouds of Magog that poured out from the mountaintop. She wondered if Heather was atop the mountain, if she was in her death throes, in torment, and she listened for the screams of a vampire dying. Terrible screams she'd heard before, in the time of the Great Purge, when rampant slaughter decimated the rising number of young vampires making up the Sab.

But it was nothing like *this*. As terrible as the screams were, it was even more sinister to listen to the silence of the city, bound thickly by a cloud of evil smoke that came down from the heights of the mountain that overlooked everything. Just as every door in Montréal creaked, so now it was replaced by the occasional creaking of graves opening and pushing up from under six feet of earth.

She'd tried to keep Heather all to herself. She truly loved her, and hoped to protect her through love. But it only sheltered her, and one night Heather just walked out and never came back, when October had dropped, and the leaves turned rusty orange. Catherine had kept to herself and sat in self-pity and torment and wondered if Heather had just wisped away like a shadow in sunlight.

That's when Catherine cried her delicate amethyst tears, when she thought of that pitiful ending to her love's existence. And then the shadow poured out of Mount Royal, descending a darkness on Montréal. It brought Catherine out. Didn't give her hope, but brought her out, and her tears dried a little as she looked at the smoke-filled mountain top. All her logic told her it was the Sab that had done this, that brought this terrible darkness on. She scolded herself for feeling just a little bit mortal now. For feeling small beneath the grandeur of the majic before her for not seizing the opportunity of being able to roam free of the constraints of day.

She stood now at the *parc Jean-Mance*, the foot of the mountain, and the smoke didn't billow out of it in big puffs like it did at first. Now it seeped out, creeping along the streets as if to be sneaky after the first big blow. All her logic said that it was the Sab that did this, and she was right. She knew of Tailssa only from Korson, and possibly from glimpses of the vampire at Prince Arthur and *boul. St. Laurent*. Vampires could pick each other off in a crowd once the skill was acquired. She would see a white-skinned corpse glowing it's way among the mortals and she would say to herself, 'the vampire Talissa.' Though, of course, nothing was absolutely certain, not even the heat of the jealousy she felt in those glaring looks. Jealous, perhaps, that it was Korson who'd loved her and made her eternal.

"Heather," she whispered as she looked up at the shadow. It was her hope that this meant Heather was still here, though her logic defied that hope. She knew Heather had played dangerously with the shadow and that the Sab's wicked fingers were tantalizingly and longingly reaching for Heather's neck. She wondered if Heather was actually *up there*, but she dared not tread into the heart of the shadow. As a vampire she wasn't very powerful. She'd seen glimpses of Heather's power, *knew* that Heather had hid the true limitations of her power, and that inkling was enough to ward off any thoughts of jumping to the centre of the fray on her own. She looked up at the black smoke longingly, pining inside for her Heather.

Her worship was interrupted by the sound of someone approaching. She glanced off to her right, down *rue Parc*, and saw a mortal approaching. A live one. She causally walked up the few steps to the parkette, and sat on the ground, her back leaning up against the statue of the saint. She folded her arms across her knees and put her head down a little. Not that she feared mortals, not that she was running, she just didn't want to deal with it now. So she backed off to a shadow and hoped that he would pass.

The man stopped in front of the parkette, looking at the shadow of the Sab that came down from the mountain. Catherine glanced up a little and took a good look at him. A black man. He stood looking at Mount Royal, his hands in his pockets, a knapsack slung over his shoulder.

Jerome had come here because he was at a loss. He'd been left with a second scar on his arm from Korson stealing his blood then deserting him, and Graham off God knows where. He'd tried calling Julia but no one answered. Tried Isabelle but no answer. The friends he managed to get a hold of were gathering up in vigilante groups, hiding out in places like the underground mall, sometimes engaging in petty murders of the lifeless zombies that roamed the streets.

Sheep, he thought. Those zombies were just a distraction from the real cause and people were letting themselves become preoccupied with the pointless endeavor of slaughtering hundreds of them when thousands were rising from the graves every night. So, at a loss, he came here. To the source. Just to look, to give him something to do while he waited for...whatever...to happen.

He wondered at a few things as he stood there. One was what would happen once this was all over. If everyone would remember this at all. Or if they would each have their own version of the story. Like some saying a terrible fog had covered the city for weeks, and that people started going crazy.

And what was with the impotence of the government anyway?? The area around Mount Royal was devoid of any sort of organized civil defense. But, looking at the power arrayed before him, Jerome had to figure that whoever was behind this would have been smart enough to take care of that sort of thing before hand.

Then he saw the girl. He tried to look at her inconspicuously, and in a moment he saw her for what she was. A vampire, but not deathly white like Korson was, more of a purpley-white pallor to her. He looked up at the sky and saw the faint orange outline that was the blotted out sun. Still daytime, though it didn't feel like it. The girl had her head down and he moved towards her. He walked up the three steps and towards the statue, as if to get a closer look. Then changed his path and walked up to her quickly, thrust a cross in her face.

"Vampire," he said.

"That won't work," she said, and batted it out of his hand. "What are you trying to do, anyway?"

"I need a hostage. You're it," said Jerome, and he reached into his coat and pulled out a large knife he'd taken from his deli. "Come on, get up," he said, threateningly.

She got up and when she lifted her head he could tell that she'd been crying. But then she suddenly smiled and said, "Okay. I'll come with you, then, Jerome."

"How did she know my name?" he said to himself, dropping his guard a bit. She moved and he stiffened again.

"You can put that away," she said. "I told you I'd come along peacefully."

"If it's all the same, I'll keep it, thanks."

"Whatever you desire. Where are we going?"

The question perplexed Jerome. "Um...that way," he said, and gestured south. "Away from all this. The mountain."

She began to walk, and he came up behind her with his knife. The way he held it it was obvious he was an amateur.

Catherine said, "You do realize that if I wanted you dead I could kill you before you would realize it."

"Just walk," said Jerome, trying to be a hard-ass, but the tone in his voice said that he knew she was right. She looked back at him and smiled a warm, fanged smile.

"Why do you need a hostage anyway, Jerome?" asked Catherine. Jerome didn't answer her. After about twenty minutes of walking, when they were a solid distance away from the mountain, he began to look around and he stopped her. The road had hit a skewed intersection, all forks and turns, and he told her to cross the street. He'd seen a lighted patch and he told her to move towards it. Catherine, lax, perhaps because she'd let her guard down to daylight. And they were suddenly in the light, though faint, but Catherine let out a death scream and her skin smoked as her hands flew up in the air, fingers taut. Jerome grabbed hold of her, feeling the charring of her flesh beneath his fingers, and dragged her out of the patch of light, so hard he practically threw her and flew after her himself. They were both on the ground and then slumped up against the wall of a building, tired from the effort. Catherine's hands shook, and her skin looked burnt slightly. She took a moment to let her body relieve itself of the agony, her breath heavy and hot.

"I'm in your debt, Jerome," she said. Jerome picked up the knife and looked at it in his hand. Too soft-hearted to be an abductor. In his head he called himself a sucker for a pretty face. He looked at her and she looked dead, she looked burnt, she looked purple. And she was still beautiful. Her hair black and luxurious, her skin still with that olive oil sheen, though darker now.

"I'm sorry," he said, and threw the knife away. "That wasn't me."

"I know," she said. But he'd quieted down, and she was too tired and too much in pain to console him further. They sat there several moments in silence. Jerome just thinking, trying to build up his confidence, in himself, in the world. He reached into his pack and pulled out a cigar, bit the end off and lit it up.

"You know, Jerome," said Catherine, "if you really wanted to take me hostage you would have been better off blowing cigar smoke in my face than holding a knife to my back." And she waved away the smoke with a hand. Jerome looked at her blankly for a moment, then let out a big, bellowing, smoke-filled laugh.

"Ya know my name, so what's yours," he asked.

"Catherine," she said. "But you can call me Cat."

He smiled at her and said, "Cat. I like it, suits you."

"You know, you don't have yellow teeth. I always picture cigar smokers as having yellow teeth."

He smiled, trying not to show his teeth.

Catherine asked, "So why are you taking hostages anyway?"

"For about five years, my brother had been haunted by a vampire. I chose not to believe him, and now he seems to be walking into his own death."

"I've killed many mortals over my lifetime, and I can honestly say that nearly each one ends up running from death. Perhaps he's just distraught."

"Looking back on it," he said, then stopped. "Are you okay? I don't feel like staying here." Catherine nodded and they got up. She asked where they would go, and Jerome, after a moment's thought, decided to head over to Graham's place because it was close and his brother may eventually decide to go there. He told her of the years of his brother's self-induced isolation, his distrust of everyone around him, then the recurring of the hauntings. The suspicions he'd had of the psychiatrist Dubois.

"I just didn't trust the guy," he said. "Seemed like he just wanted to throw him in the nut-house. I mean, Graham seemed like a prize catch of a study, y'know?"

"People who are so consciously attuned to their dark side are intriguing. Perhaps there is a beauty in death, in the obscene."

"About things being hidden in shadow."

They arrived at Graham's house, and Jerome felt a little awkward as he slid the key in the lock to let a vampire in. He paused for a moment and took another look at Cat, then pushed the door open. No sooner had he taken one step inside then Catherine had put a hand on his shoulder and stopped him. The smell of death had wafted to her when the door was opened.

"What is it?" asked Jerome, but Catherine had moved past him like a gentle breeze and towards the smell. She gasped when she found the body of Julia St. Croix spilled over the living room walls and carpet.

"Jerome, don't," she pleaded, but it was too late. He'd already entered the room.

"Motherfuck-" he started, but then just clenched his fists and touched them to the wall as he bowed his head down to choke off the tears. Catherine put her hands on his shoulders but he didn't really feel them there. Just gritted his teeth in helplessness. "How..." he began.

"Say it," said Catherine.

"How could they have taken off her skin?" he said, as though God's head was turned as he pleaded skyward in vain. The only thing left recognizable about Julia St. Croix was a shock of blond hair stained mostly black with blood and a portion of her face around her left eye and cheek that still remained. Chunks were missing from her, her arms bitten through almost to the bone and her little bits of blood-soaked skin hanging off her body in other places like the sticky larvae of insects from a tree branch.

"Come on," said Catherine, and she pulled him away and into the kitchen. Sat him down and made him drink something. She told him she would get rid of the body, but she saw an image in his mind of the permanent stain that would remain on the carpet. She went over to the woman's body and, just before picking it up, took a little taste of the blood by dabbing her finger into it. Dead, dry and cold, and she shuddered in disgust at it. She picked it up and dragged it outside as quickly as she could, passing the doorway to the kitchen and trying not to notice that Jerome noticed. She ended up dumping the body at the side of the house, stuffing it up behind the air conditioning unit. Came back in and washed up quickly in the kitchen sink, scolding herself at the rudeness of her morbidity. Hadn't been around mortals in a while. Should've used the bathroom sink. She got herself some water and sat down across from Jerome and smiled at him; death didn't bother her.

"Sorry," she apologized. "Sometimes I forget what it's like to be a mortal."

"You still remember?"

"Yeah," said Catherine. "It's been about a hundred years. But some things never fade."

Jerome said, "So what do you suggest we do."

"I suggest you stay here. Out there you'd just get yourself killed."

"I have a feeling that that's inevitable."

"Perhaps," Catherine said, looking away and smiling. Jerome slung his knapsack onto a chair. "What do you have in there anyway?"

He thought for a moment then pulled out his cigar and said, "I have something to ask you about." He pulled out a small rectangular box. He put it on the table gently, and opened it, hoping the contents hadn't been broken. He cleared away the newspaper packing and tilted the box up for Cat to see. She picked it up gently and looked at it, the blue rose. "Do you know what it is?" asked Jerome.

Catherine lightly breathed on it and the colour reverberated between the original, startling blue to a rich purple and then a deep, thick red and back again. She manipulated the stem with her fingers, and Jerome made a gasp as though to stop her, as though she would shatter it, but it was somewhat pliant and didn't break. Even though it felt like crystal and ever so delicate. Then she sniffed it, her expression a little curious.

"What is it?" asked Jerome.

"Smells a little like...blood," she said. "Vampire blood looks a little bit blue sometimes." Then answered the question on Jerome's face. "Because our bodies are without breath it looks a little bit blue. When we feed it becomes red again." She rested her chin on her hand and looked at the rose.

Jerome said, "You're thinking something."

"Yeah," said Catherine. "This is Talissa's blood. The vampire up on the mountain. I was just wondering if when we drink and see the soul of the victim, it could work backwards. If she was connected to her blood. Where did you get this?"

"My brother had it. Are you saying that this was the connection, the reason he was haunted?"

"It's possible she was able to find him through the rose." And because Graham had stolen it from Heather, Talissa couldn't get her wicked fingers to stay around Heather's neck. Jerome asked her about Korson, and they realized the connection, that Graham was the mortal Korson had always referred to.

"He spoke highly of him. I don't think Korson would intentionally do anything to him." And Jerome silently agreed, because it was Korson who'd saved him.

"It's just something I can never hope to understand, being a vampire. Why my brother seems like a target."

Catherine said, "Sometimes our majic just haunts a mortal. Part of our nature. To hunt and haunt. This war brews out of love and jealousy. If Korson coveted your brother for whatever reason, Talissa would likely become jealous. She used to love him. I'm surprised she never came after me."

"So what should we do with the rose?"

"Destroy it. It's ironic, something so beautiful having to be destroyed. But we can't fall prey to our eyes deceptions. "She lifted the rose up and then smashed it on the floor, and when it broke it looked more like water splashing than crystal shattering. It made the most incredibly beautiful sound, like quartz shattering, but neither of them heard it over the scream that split the silence of Montréal.

Atwater and *rue Ste-Catherine*. The Old Forum. They'd closed it recently, and it was all boarded up and it felt as though it were dilapidated now. Even though it didn't look that way. My father took me here when I was a child, me and Jerome, and once we even saw the Rocket waving at the crowd. Even though he was smiling there was still a force that could be seen in his red eyes. It was said that ghosts and Gods lived among those walls. It was certainly a place of majic, and I think that Montréal lost something when they boarded up the doors. Lost something because it was one less place for the children to go.

I stood at the corner and looked up at the building, remembering. In all this filth and smoke that filled the air it was strange to just stand there and remember and try to feel the happiness I felt at those innocent moments of childhood with my brother and father. I felt something and perhaps it was a piece of majic because I looked to the left and right of me and the dead began to gather. Zombies walking towards me. Creepy, and I felt myself shiver at the sight of them. At least there was an eroticism to the death that vampires brought.

I tried the doors, but they were barred shut. Couldn't force them. I didn't want to break the glass, it would be sacrilege, so I went around the back way, slipping around the corner just barely out of the reach of the snatch of a zombie. I began trying the doors around the side and back, and the zombies were closing in. The slow, methodical death of mankind, one-by-one, blood for blood. I certainly didn't want to end up like that. I kept shaking and jarring the doors and finally, when I was about to give up hope and run for fear of the very flesh of my skin, I found one that opened. The lock had already been smashed. I closed it behind me and couldn't find anything to jam it shut with. I had to hope that they wouldn't get in, or I'd have effectively trapped myself.

It was here that ghosts could be seen clearly. I walked in some ways, trying to focus in the darkness. I lit a match when I thought I was far enough in that no one would catch the light. As far as I could make out, I was in a boiler room of some sorts. Except for the orange flame at my fingers, it was quite cold here still, and I don't know if that was because of the dead majic here. I tried to make my way around the place, trying to find perhaps the empty rink or maybe the famed dressing room. I had to relight a match every so often, and once I was so enthralled I let my fingers get burned.

Clang! it went and I jumped. Someone was here. That was a definite noise and not my imagination. I kept moving. The noise came again. I doused my match so as not to be seen, I felt a little woozy at trying to see through he darkness. I tried to follow the noise but it was elusive and when I thought I was going towards it I heard it behind me, then beside me, then all around me. Behind me again. I nearly froze. I felt my limbs stiffen, my back chill and straighten up, the darkness caving in upon me. Every nerve in my body began to crawl around as my flesh got colder and the noise began to sound ethereal. It felt as though something were pushing down upon my shoulders and I couldn't resist it. I tried to move, I think I actually did move but couldn't sense the fact, and each clang might as well have been a blow to my head.

Who put this blue glow here? That rose...the glow was like that blue rose I'd stolen from Heather Langden's room. Oh God, she was here with me, the murderess, the vampire Tailssa, she came to finally kill me and take my blood! After months of torture, though, she would never have broken me and she would finally leave me alone. Perhaps madness was better. It was so much easier to fight the things in your head, because you always knew where they were. I hate the real world, I fucking hate it because I have no control over it. I could've given in to madness and Dubois would have put me away and I would have lived off drugs and my imagination. So much prettier! The glow was brighter. Was I moving or was she? My blood, what was so important about it? Was it just a petty vendetta against a mortal? Against Korson?

Right on the back of my head, a *clang!* at the base of my skull, striking at the very Hell of my mind. Majic. I knew, I felt it now, I felt the power. Something in the mountain. I wasn't supposed to know...I wasn't supposed to know...

I felt surges and swelling all around me, from the top of Mount Royal to the shores of the island of Montréal. It took me a moment to realize that it only felt as if I were pushed to the ground, that I was still standing straight up. I held my breath and tried to clear my head of the various pressures, of all the pulling and pushing of majical energy upon me. Perhaps it was sunset, a time of change and power? I felt like I had a terrible headache. And that damned clanging, still going off around me from time to time, making every nerve in my body freeze up. The blue permeating the darkness, sickly cold blue.

And hands on my shoulders, gripping so tight I couldn't move and I knew, *I knew* I was dead and it was just a matter of time and I couldn't even turn around and I saw flashes of my own death before my eyes and-

"Sowen," said a voice in my ear. I *felt* it. Breath hot. And I fell to the floor, and when I looked up it was the ghost from the library, the nameless saint, and he could speak and be felt in this world and I hoped to whatever God there was in this world that it wasn't me who had called him up. He looked tired. Sick. As though whatever had brought him here had sucked up all his energy. I could sympathize. It was hard to exist without energy. And I think I knew why vampires lived off blood, because it contained the energy that kept us alive and they were forever thieves of that majic. "I...am not long for this world," he said.

I wanted to act shocked and gasp the words you can speak or something like that but it was war time and I had a sense of urgency about me. But I think he read the questions that were dancing in my eyes and he spoke before I could ask anything. Or maybe it was that he hadn't spoken in years and had much to say.

"It was a habit of mine that I kept lingering here beyond my time. Yet I remain a mortal. How dangerous to play with the shadow. Majic is quite volatile, as you have seen."

"Who are you?" I asked, almost frustrated at the query. He knelt before me in utter humility, his eyes cast downwards and his hands pressed flat together in front of his face, and he bowed his head to me.

"St. Valentine of Interamna, what you know as the city of Terni in Italy."

"I couldn't find any pictures of you in any books."

He laughed a little and said, "No. I foresaw the deceptions that the tale of history could tell, and I remained in the shadows of it. And I was also a recurring character in the scenes." He looked me up and down with a studious interest. "You were not subject to the same depths of madness as I for delving into the dark world of majic." He got up and looked away, as though looking outside. "I remember the last time darkness descended upon the world like this. I have lived many lifetimes. If you look into your history books you will see me appear two or three times. Such majic to keep me alive, and such noble intentions of using it. To spread the word of the gospel of love. God's word. But the majic is too much for mortals. That kind, anyway. The shadow. It all almost spilled out before. What you see happening now has been waiting one thousand years to happen. People would have *known*. Vampires, majic, the Place of the Dead, everything. Of course, that may have been disastrous. That kind of power being out in the world. But it was stopped, I gave my life away in battle for it, and a darkness descended upon the world, upon mankind. Knowledge became scarce as water in the desert. And people forgot and myths grew. I left my mark on the world with a myth.

"Did I tell you I wrote the bible? Many people had a hand in it, but like I said I foresaw many things and knew I wouldn't outlive this kind of majic, this power that was overtaking me. I couldn't stop either. I was being driven by some fervent force, some desire that made me continue to the bitter end. But the passage, and this would be known to some of those *vampires* and demons who now stalk after the majic of the shadow, it would be known to them as a myth that was handed down. And those who remembered it from the bible and have found it would laugh, perhaps because they sensed some of the deception." He lifted his hands and looked skyward.

"*And shall go out to deceive the nations which are in the four quarters of the earth, Gog and Magog, to gather them together to battle; the number of whom is as the sea.* Revelations, 20: 8." The earth rumbled a bit at his naming of the shadow-demon. "The earth has been deceived, my friend, and not only is the demon all powerful, his armies are legions and will overwhelm by sheer force. And finally the majic has exploded into the living world and I can come to you, the one who shares a soul for majic like mine, and ask you for release." He knelt at my feet and bowed his head, making the request in complete humility. What could I do? Deny a man who'd been in limbo for over one thousand years the release of his soul?

"I...don't know what to do," I said. I wasn't sure if I ever had the abstract creativity required to be a majician.

"My mind still lives. You must destroy it." If that meant going to Italy, he had to be shittin' me. But this was about majic, and not so literal. I raised my hands to his head, but he took my arms, stopped them and held them high, as though he felt such relief at touching human flesh. Perhaps he hadn't been able to touch human flesh in a thousand years, either.

He said to me, in a whisper, "I leave you with the final warning, in a word older than I: Sowen." He then released my hands, and I wanted to stop myself for another moment, to ask him what the word meant, but he had set the events back into motion-I think he'd used a remnant to stop the moment for his final words-and I couldn't stop it from happening. My hands gripped his head and there was a surge and exchange of power, then a final, furious squeeze and his head burst in what looked like an explosion of flesh and bone and brain, and his essence disappeared after the splashes of grey and red subsided into the shadows. My hands felt dirty and sticky, but I couldn't see anything there, and there was only a faint yellow stain on the ground, mucousy. Everything got quiet and dark again, and all I was left with was the occasional clanging on a pipe. I followed the sound and found Korson, lying in pain, holding a wound in his chest.

Catherine was certain she knew grief. Her beloved Heather had been gone nearly three weeks and her tears pained her as much as the vomit she endured every year of her undeath. She would pick up the grey little cat and sit by the window, petting his forehead and watching, hoping beyond hope, that Heather would come home. But she knew that she wouldn't. She knew that the moment Heather had called to her as she was leaving and closed the door behind her suddenly. Catherine had come down the stairs but Heather was gone, and she *knew*, but couldn't explain why she knew that Heather wouldn't come back that night.

Each night was agony and eternity, waiting and waiting for the blond sweetness of her love to come back. She felt the majic return to her soul with Heather around, and now that she was gone Catherine was left with more than loss. She was left with wanting. She would've been happy for the fact that she still had desire left, but it was an empty, heartbroken desire. Much like the nadir of love she felt when Korson had saved her from certain death at the fists of fate.

Ah, love. Where once it had made Catherine feel eternally wondrous and joyous, it now left her pining and tearful and bitter, sitting by the window clinging to a cat that was the only living possession that was a substitute for Heather. She wondered why Heather didn't care enough for her to just stay, to ignore the temptations of fate and Talissa and plumbing the depths of majic to find the soil where her blood first came from. Heather had been her majician.

She had phoned Korson, and in her anger she blamed him.

"She's gone. Been gone for weeks now." The tears had dried but the sadness never left her voice. Her face looked beautiful when she was sad, more so when her cheeks dripped with amethyst tears.

"I know. I felt it. I've been listening through the remnants for a while now."

"You bastard! You could've stopped her! You could've saved us all!" The line was silent for a moment, then she began hurling curses at him again. He kept quiet, accepting her arrows though they hurt, because he knew how deep they went.

"Catherine, you're angry. You know this isn't my fault, that Heather's gone."

"You think I don't hear things, too? I've heard the rumblings of war before, and I hear them again now. Different now, there's something so oppressive about them, not like the last time."

The last time. It had ended with Korson collapsing on Catherine's doorstep, the only thing that saved him from the coming sun the fact that he slid down the door with a sharp scraping of his claws. He'd endured the murder of hundreds of his own kind, and with it the wounds that came from demons resisting death with the fear-fueled innocence of a child, as well as the thousands of souls who'd been murdered to keep these beings alive. It had to be done, though, and if Korson thought he'd had any friends among the dead they'd been killed, most of them that very night, others within the next few nights, as recompense for the destruction of the schemes of the Sab.

Talissa had come to him, during a lull in the battle, his hands dripping with blood and the white flesh of vampires, her imminent defeat literally on his hands, and she mocked him.

"You're a fool, Korson. We could've had it all, the two of us. But you're just stubborn. Clinging to your mortality, to your *humanity*." She sneered, making the words derisive. "Why do you care if they live? Aren't you sick of hiding in shadow all the time?"

"This is so unlike you. It lacks all subtlety. Just makes work for me," he said, gesturing at the ground littered with the seared limbs of vampires.

"Perhaps I'm more subtle in love than in war," she said, smiling just a little bit arrogantly. Korson succumbed to emotion, feeling the power of his anger cut through his fatigue from his belly, and he picked up a decapitated head by the hair and hurled it at Talissa. It struck her on the side of her face as she turned to avoid it, left a bloody mess dripping down her cheeks worthy of an artist, or a doctor. Then he flew at her, but she was stronger than he. She'd been the one to give him the majic in his blood, and would hold that as her final advantage over him. She stepped aside and pushed him away, to the ground. He got up and wiped his bloody, broken nose, watched as she walked away.

"Kill them all, Korson," she said. "I could care less. But you know I'll be back. And you know my power grows each time." In a wisp of shadow she disappeared.

He hung over the bodies of his fallen, wondering if it would be grief that struck him down. She didn't care who fought alongside her, as long as they were ruthless and cunning and evil, willing to die so her soul could become powerful. He, though, was an honourable warrior, and would not offer up the bodies of his fellows before his own.

"You could've stopped it all, Korson."

"Catherine, if not Heather, than who? You know she has the soul for it."

"None of us have souls!" she cried. "God, why couldn't you just let me die?"

"Because I love you."

"Bullshit! You left me with nothing!"

Korson said, "I told you to stay away from Heather."

"You told me to watch her," said Catherine.

"I told you to make sure she was safe, not fall in love with her. You got too close, and now it's killing you."

"Korson, you son of a bitch. You let that girl die. You could have told her to leave."

"The less she knew the better. Running away wouldn't solve anything. Please, Catherine, we could argue in circles over this forever. What's done is done."

"You don't know what it's like to be so utterly alone," she said tearfully. But he did, for he knew what it was like to lose love and try to make majic again without failing from fear. He tried to make majic with Catharine but had only caused her to live on through emptiness and suffering. Then, through her tears, "By the shadow..."

"Catherine, what is it?" Catharine didn't respond for a moment, and Korson's worst fear flashed before his eyes, Talissa's claws striking down Catherine to complete thirty years of vengeance. He screamed her name into the phone. He was still capable of showing anger, reacting to his fear.

"It's all coming out of the mountain," she'd said. "So much smoke. It's like the myth. The legend of-"

"Don't," said Korson, so firmly it felt like he'd twisted her wrist. "Don't even say his name."

The line went quiet, then dead after a while. Korson, of course, left immediately, but Catherine was no longer home when he got there.

It was quite difficult to walk out from the guts of a demon and try to find a friend, especially when a thick and surreal fog had choked off the life from the air. It was as though Heather hadn't escaped Terni, though she knew she had. The easel had been prepared for the dark sketchings the demons would illustrate upon the cities, and the zombies, the recently dead who had risen because of the manipulations of the evil Talissa, had chased most of the mortals to their homes, where they remained. Those who dared go out, for food, for air, for defiance, were quite hard-pressed to return to their homes unscathed. The zombies had a bit of the dark magic in their veins, and therefore had a hunger for blood to feed that majic. They were the disposable warriors of the Sab, resurrected to pave the way for the malicious, the decadent, the eternal vampires who would eventually cover the earth and walk when they pleased. They would be Talissa's children, and those who opposed them would be crushed under foot and fang.

Though, as is expected, no triumph is ever complete, and there is always some spark of mankind left flickering. Some people did go on through the darkness, and still roamed the streets without being harmed. There were pockets of humanity that, albeit small, for one reason or another, were determined to go on. It was here that Heather went, to a pub just off *rue Ste-Catherine*. On those nights she grew bored of eternity, she would spy on the comings and goings of the famed and feared Night Stalker's biker gang, sharing the secrets of their trade. She'd even spoken to one or two, and, though their bombs went off during high points in the gang wars, found them to be a likable and entertaining bunch. But she'd never dared walk into their midst, for obvious reasons. She was a vampire, secretive and distrustful, and they were in danger of being raided and such by the M.U.C.P.S. It was enough for her to just watch some of the other creatures of the night. It was her t.v.

So it happened that Heather went to their hangout at the pub, and not that it wasn't easy to spot, the lights blinking around the window and the music blaring and what-not, it was just that there weren't too many around to spot it, and those who did didn't have much reason to care anymore. It wasn't like walking into any old bar, and not because of the darkness that descended upon Montréal. In the best of times there was a careful count and watchful eye upon who was coming through the front (and back) door. No sooner had the door slammed shut behind Heather than the music ceased and all eyes were trained upon her. She was a little more than uncomfortable at being in the spotlight among a large group of mortals, more so at these stone-faced, leather-clad biker types.

"Um..hi," smiled Heather, almost a question. She was glad for the fact that none of them had marked her for what she was.

"Bloodsucker!" shouted one, and Heather scolded herself for getting her hopes up that this would be easy. Chains, knives and guns made sounds like cutlery as they were drawn. A man from the shadows behind her slung a chain around her neck. But he was mortal, and therefore extremely slow in Heather's eyes, and despite his surprise attack she was able to get her hands beneath the chain before the grip became like that of a python. She cold have broken the chain or flung the man over her head and across the room, but she opted for acrobatics and majic. She swung forward and upwards, her toes stretching for the ceiling, as she hung onto the bar for leverage. Someone, perhaps quick enough to catch onto her movement and figure on her escape, fired a shot at her, but because she flew out of the way so fast it blasted a hole in the chest of the chain-wielder and he fell in all his grace to the floor with bloody streaks marking the way to the ground. More men came at her, knives making whipping sounds in the air as they swung and missed, Heather's acute vampiric senses easily allowing her to be two steps ahead of them. She flung them away into walls, tables, each other, and some couldn't be spared their lives because, after all, Heather was a murderer by blood. And she felt her face contorting into the demonic, her mouth becoming large with fangs and death reflected in her disconcertingly blue eyes; though it was not her intention to strike fear or claws into their hearts.

Heather moved to the middle, letting them circle her, and she never once struck the first blow; she was completely surrounded yet she waited for them to attack her. It was painfully obvious that knowledge of the disease of vampirism had begun to creep into mortal society, beginning from the depths and night stalkers and eventually moving its way up to the higher classes. And once the knights of the Sabaoth, those who would spread the word, or more accurately, the horror-blood dripping, fang ripping, flesh eating misery!-came out from hiding, out from the shadow, no one would be safe. Some, sensing the sheer futility of war as an endeavour, may even begin to bear their veins in homage to the Queen vampire Talissa, and she would make the beautiful her brethren.

She tried not to kill them. But sometimes she didn't know her own strength, and there was nothing much she could do about the guns. Heather would leap to the ceiling and cling there for a moment, then drop back down and lie flat to the floor, arms spread out, to avoid the bullets, and those who caught them were always Night Stalker's. Then a loud voice from the back called for a cease-fire and the barrage stopped.

The circle remained around Heather, but stood obediently still. A small opening formed and allowed two men to come through before closing again. It was sheer bravery, and everyone in the room, to a man, stood in awe of the gall that was displayed by their leader; though Heather, with her acute senses, knew that inside he was scared stiff. He was a big man, arms all tattooed with skulls and daggers, and he was also fat, but no one would dare stand up to him because of the sheer size and girth he carried. To a mortal he would be quite fearsome. But he also knew and bore witness to the fact that Heather could kill him in an instant.

He introduced himself as Hawke, then looked around and said, "Look what you've done to my beautiful bar. You've put holes all over the place." He picked up a piece of wood from a broken able and dropped it again after studying it in dismay a moment. Then the customary threat, "You make one move, and my men kill you, even if they have to take me with you." Then he waved everyone away and the circle broke off, people going back to their seats and pool tables and drinks. Eschewing formality he kicked away some debris and pulled up a chair and sat with it face backwards. Heather did the same, and the other man stood by Hawke.

"You'll have to excuse my men. You obviously know what's happening lately, and there have been rumors for nearly a year of a blond ghost who's been killing off some of our guys."

It didn't take much for Heather to put two and two together, to figure that Talissa had killed the few Night Stalker's that she'd spoken with, and let the blame fall towards Heather's fangs.

"That wasn't me," said Heather, but knew it was pointless to reassure him.

"I stopped the fight because I saw it was getting us nowhere. But, despite this night's sloppiness, be assured we have already killed some of your kind. So state your business."

Heather was leaning back in her chair and she had to look up to him. Despite the mismatch in size, the fact that Hawke was so overbearing physically, Heather was quite overwhelming because of her startling beauty and the hypnotic glow of her eyes. Though Hawke wouldn't let any weakness register on his face.

She said, "I have a proposition for you. The darkness that descended outside is a result of a war between…vampires. It really comes down to just a few of us, and some of the reasons behind it are petty, and jealous and all that. And there's much more behind it really, some cosmic shit, but that's besides the point. There are some of us who would stop what's happening. Friends of mine, but I don't have the time to look for them. What I want from you is for your men to get out there and kill each and every zombie that you can."

"And why should I," he interrupted. "I like things this way. We do what we want, and we don't worry about the cops. Why should we go back to the way things were."

"Because if things stay this way then it will become very bad for you. All that smoke out there is uncontrolled majic. Majic comes from the dead, and if it's in this world soon you'll be living in Hell."

He got up and said, "I have no reason to doubt anything you say. But you come in here, destroy my bar, kill half of my men-my *friends*-and expect help? You don't even have the respect to introduce yourself." And he turned around and stepped away. It was gang turf she'd entered, and she knew that there were so many strict lines of respect and vengeance and justice. But she could afford to seem weak and follow him to appease he anger.

"I'm Heather," she said, dashing in front of him so it looked as though she'd appeared there. She held out her hand and he took it, cringed at the feel of it.

"So why should I want things to change," he asked.

"Hawke, look around you. Look what I did in self-defense. Imagine what happens when the war gets going, when all those vampires come looking for you mortals. You don't stand a chance. What I propose is a truce between myself and your gang. All I ask is that, in the meantime, your men start killing off the zombies so no more people die. You guys have the means and bombs to do it. And any children you see are to be kept safe. Once everything goes back to normal, no vengeance will be exacted upon you from a vampire without them having to go through me first. And if you ever need me for something, so long as it doesn't involve killing an innocent person, I'll help you out too. Think of it Hawke. A vampire of your very own."

It would be the Night Stalker's that took the brunt of the blame for any damage upon the city. When the shadow was sucked back into the realm of the dead it would be a gang war that the rest of mortality remembered, and the forgetting would be woven by majic.

He rubbed his chin a bit, knew it would be silly to turn this down. So it was that the Night Stalker's went out into the shadow and began to hack and slash away at all the zombies with glee. And Heather went out into the shadow, towards the centre of Montréal, the centre of the circle of power, and to her final, bitter destiny with Talissa, the Queen of the Sab.

Standing nearly seven feet tall he still weighed much more than I would have guessed he would. We're talking about three-hundred fucking pounds of thick dead flesh here, and I gathered him up and dragged him through the streets. I was still feeling the sources of power pulling me, and the biggest one was coming from Mount Royal, where the explosion of smoke doused the entire island in darkness. The circle of power was open, the dead were rising, ghosts walked with the earthly feet, and I carried a wounded vampire in my arms as though a tiger would carry a cub in her teeth.

He grasped at his chest and said, "The sun. It's still daytime. If I ever thought I felt weak, then I've forgotten what it was to feel the sun." I stopped for a moment to allow both of us a rest. It had been hours since we'd heard a deafening scream rip the silence in two, and Korson knew it to be Talissa's voice, as though it were issuing a death scream. As though something had been torn from her very skin. My phone rang and I just prayed it wasn't her again. I just didn't want to deal with that kind of shit right now.

Jerome said, "Hey, man. What's up," and I could tell from his voice that he was, for one of the few times in his life, distressed and uncertain as to what to do. Usually he was full of energy, positive and upbeat. It hurt me so much to hear something like that in his voice. It was a part of myself that I hoped and prayed, as I lay in bed waiting for sleep to overcome me, would come out more often. "I'm all alone here, man." It killed me not to go to him. But I had to see this thing through to the end. I couldn't go on if I ran away from it all. It's something to run away from your fears, your demons. Especially when they've already been inside your head.

"I hope to God that you can forgive me, Jerome. But I have to finish this."

"It's all in your head!" he said, pleading with me. "Why can't you just let it go, leave it alone and save you own ass?"

"You've never been seduced by a vampire, Jerome. It's one thing to give your blood to them, but to have them stay there, to walk beside you and have a grip on your soul, that's different. I couldn't walk away from this if I wanted to. She has my blood and I couldn't run away from anything if I even wanted to. This is inside me already."

I knew how women felt, why they were so distrustful of men. To have someone inside of you, your body helpless in their arms while the look in their eyes tormented your mind. It was the same when a vampire clamped it's teeth around a victim's neck, the victim shuddering in utter agony, more so because of the bitter betrayal to the body rather than the pain; because of the brutal violation to the soul. No other theft was so dear to the heart as the theft of one's life, drop by bloody drop.

He told me of Catherine, that she'd been attacked and taken away by the Gargoyles of the Sab and that I should tell Korson because they were close. I told him I'd meet up with him later, probably my house or the deli or something. I also asked him if he'd ever heard the word Sowen, but he said he'd never heard of it. I told Korson of his friend, and it seemed to hurt him more than the wounds in his chest.

"It's because it's daylight, you know," he said, "that the wounds have opened up. If it was night they would have remained healed. But the shadow...it's against me now." He said it as though he'd lost love, that the shadow should be floating around the very air. So blatant! So sinister! It had not the subtle nuances of the majic that I'd first seen from the likes of the vampire Korson, from Heather's incredibly blue eyes as she was being changed into the kind of creature I came to know as a vampire. "Perhaps you should just leave me be," he said, sounding defeated.

"What? Leave you here to die? You would just give up? What happened to your honour? Great warrior of the plains, my ass."

He laughed at me, one of those pain-filled laughs that people force out when they're suffering too much to feel the joy of laughter.

"There would be no honour in that death. And I can't die. I'm eternal. I would just lie here forever, watching the silhouette of the sun behind the shadows. I would just lie here and starve and never die."

"There would be even less honour in that than dying. How could you live with yourself?"

Korson said, "You know not the torment that eternity causes. To know that vengeance can last more than a lifetime. Perhaps I can end it here now, by doing nothing."

"Korson, you can't let the obsessions of others drive you down. You can't let the fact that you've lost your majic destroy you. You have to react. If you do nothing you might as well be dead. You would be a coward, and worse off than dead. You'd have to live as a coward." And I could see the word stung him. I picked him up off the ground, so heavy yet I lifted him up anyway and held him up against the wall. "You are Blackfoot, proud, powerful and an honourable hunter. It's in your soul. Start acting like it." His head lolled around on his neck, as though he were groggy from drink. I still held him up by the shoulders and I had to look up at him though he was slumped a little. I was scared to Hell of him, his skin white and dead, and even though he was probably at his weakest, I saw death in his face and it was my own. He straightened his head a bit and looked at me from under half-lidded eyes and his mouth stretched into a smile, his fangs ivory white and teeth dark and bloody red. He began to stand up and the strength returned to his muscles. His hands moved slowly upwards along the sides of my body and took hold of my head and tilted it sideways to expose my neck.

"What are you laughing for," I asked, as he tittered away, his laughter the laughter of a madman. He didn't answer, just bent his head lower until I felt his cold, dead breath on my neck, and a quiet hiss like that of a snake issuing from the depths of his throat. At first I submitted to him, let my body go pliant in his grip, and all this despite the shudder down my spine that signaled to me that this was wrong, that I couldn't let myself become enraptured by him. That I couldn't just die in his arms as suicide. I pushed against him and tried to get out of him, but it was all in vain. I think I had my arms extended all the way, pushing with all the strength I could think of, but he was too strong for me, a mere mortal. If my life hadn't been in such danger at that point then I would have laughed in his face. No majic? He could still enrapture my mind! Make me fear the look in his red eyes! He was still skilled in the arts of the dark ways, and it was only in his forgetting that he found weakness. Though I hated to admit it, we had a trait in common; that of self-denial. Like the word of Christ told, it was the pious that found harmony in their souls and poverty was the way to the Gods. But what of the self-denial of rightful vengeance in the name of justice? Did the destruction of evil make the destroyer himself evil? Was not God a vengeful and angry being himself when he protected his children? I looked at the demon in front of me and saw the qualities of an angel. I hated him for a moment, for the first time in over a year. I truly hated him, but it was a bitter and petty hate because of the fear he'd put into me for my life. By the time it passed he'd begun to walk away, thrust me on the ground and I watched him go and knew instinctively that I couldn't follow him. He'd tried to cling to the last thread of the mortal world through me and all he'd caused was for me to be haunted. When he'd lost the shadow it was a painful reminder of how it felt to be mortal and helpless and now he'd left me for the darkness again, only this time it was all around us. I should have been angry that he rejected me so suddenly and like so. But I looked at him with only respect as he walked away. In his own eyes he'd dishonoured himself by not crushing the Sab over a century ago. Though I couldn't blame him for that. But now he went to fight a battle to regain his honour and his pride and it would be certain death against the legions of monsters that were coming out of their graves and out of the shadow.

    He left me there on the ground, with nothing and nowhere to go and every reason to be angry, but I almost shed a tear as he left. I knew I would never see him again.

    "Such tragedy..." Familiar words. Jerome was too laconic to answer and too forlorn to be startled. He'd gone to Graham's home to sit and wait. Gone back actually, as Catherine had forced him to flee when they'd heard Talissa's death scream squeal through the darkness. But hours later he'd returned to the scene and didn't much care anymore if he'd run into the arms of the enemy. Perhaps it would bring him to the arms of his brother again. It took him a moment to place the voice, and when he did he looked up. And wondered if he was seeing ghost again.

    "I felt his death," said the Majician, bowing his head in courtesy. "Your friend. Such a pure and innocent soul made to murder and forced to an early grave. Like killing a child. I don't know what saddens me more, his death or the stains of blood that have been forced onto your hands."

    "No more carnivals for me, sir," said Jerome.

    "Oh, please, don't say that. Don't ever let go of the child in you. It's the reason you're here now, while others are slowly choking on the majic in the air. The children can *see*. It's that precious innocence in mankind that will allow it to survive this war."

    "Survive? Why do I care if I survive? I'm left with nothing. I have no place in this world. Existence is meaningless to me."

    The Majician straightened himself up and pulled his black cape around closer.

    "Would you have the blood that is the root of this war?" he said. "It's a very different desire than you're used to. The quest for eternity. And it would never resolve what you're feeling now. The losses would keep compounding over the years."

    Jerome said, "Is that what it's all about? Suffering through loss? You'll have to excuse me. I'm really not all that used to this. I've never lost anyone I cared about before. And now everyone close to me is falling apart. Every*thing* close to me. My brother had a great marriage and it just disintegrated over the last couple of years, something I could never see happening in my worst nightmare. I just can't seem to remember who I am anymore."

"And would you let all that cost you your happiness? Your exuberance? You used to live life without a care for the why's. That's the most beautiful thing I could ever think of in all the world. With all the majic I've practiced in my long time on this earth, it has been something I could never find in any spell, the means to simply exist without torment because some God decided to give us an intellect with which to wonder with. To exist and look at things and just accept them if understanding is not possible. You had achieved this state and-"

"This is my brother I'm talking about!" interrupted Jerome. "It's not some bad mood, or phase, or anything like that. He's walking into a lair of vampires and never coming back."

"But would you let loss break and destroy you as well? You feel the pain strong as ever now, and it will never go away. But it will lessen, with time."

"Yeah. But it won't ever go away. Not even after I die. It's something that will always be with my soul."

The Majician lowered his head when he heard this. Not a bow, but from sadness. Out of respectful mourning and melancholy he lowered his head and looked to the ground. It seemed he weakened a moment too. Like his form flickered a bit, as though someone had passed a hand over the projector.

"If you only know how long I've lived. The loss I've felt in seeing the years melt away before my eyes. It certainly wasn't an eternity but it felt like one. I was an aspiring witch at the turn of the century. I dipped my hand into the shadow, into this dark thing called majic. So powerful. So dangerous. Such a druidic sickness to want to walk into the darkness and see what it holds." He squeezed his hands shut as though his palms were in pain. Jerome saw blood coming out of them, an orange-reddish blood, so thick and deep of colour. A subtle thing happened as he spoke; he slowly lowered to the ground in a crouch, so subtle that Jerome didn't catch the movement until the Majician was halfway to the ground. "I came because I am not long for this world anymore. I have extended my life beyond the years I should have passed on. I can feel death at my shoulder. But I felt the loss of your friend, and I came. And your brother..."

"What about him?" demanded Jerome.

"Long ago I studied the history of the patron saint of love, Valentine of Interamna. I tried to do what he did, to dip into the majic of the dead, the shadow, and extend my life, my vision of the world. And I succeeded...albeit only for a decade or so. I fear I strayed to dangerous territory, and now I will pay the price with my life. My soul, perhaps," he said, with a slight laugh, "forever barred from the place of the dead or any sort of heaven. If I'm lucky enough to be buried I will stare forever at dirt. All because I tried to chase after the ghost of some mad saint. I saw the ghost..."

"But my brother..." prodded Jerome.

"I sense his betrayal, too. I-" The Magician slumped with weakness. "I am the one, he read the words...Andreas Lurik. He tried to see that majic. All those years of research...I never did die, I *transcended* death."

They both were thrust to the ground as the air crackled, and a sick smell overtook them. The Magician, the one who was the witch and cult leader early in the century, was crouched right to the ground, wrapped in his cape, his head bowed so Jerome could see only the top of his black hat. He lifted his head slightly, and Jerome could see his skin wrinkling and aging and death slowly overtaking him. The light around them slowly dimmed as whatever little sunlight that got through was fading away...sunset.

The Majician held up his bloody fists to Jerome and opened them slowly to show him the wounds. When he spoke his voice sounded gargled and throaty and old.

"The druidic symbols, for tonight is the night of the dead, the time of All Souls, Hallowe'en. The dead shall rise freely and the children shall tremble in fear, warding off evil with their masks." His wounds bled in the shape of Jack O'Lanterns, scabs upon scabs that the blood poured out of. He'd lost the battle and the majic was being forced out of him, his body catching up with time and dying slowly. His insides were slowly catching fire with pain. Jerome went to him as he fell to the ground. A man he'd known for years as a source of thrill and joy and now it was just another loss. He didn't envy the vampires their eternity if it meant all this loss. "Promise me you won't go out tonight. The vampire, he will come to you. Don't seek petty revenge at the risk of your life. Let this night play itself out." Jerome heard the words and knew it to be a dying man's plea to him. He would honour them, though it hurt so much to know his brother would be betrayed. And he knew who, knew all along because it was his worst suspicions that he didn't want to believe.

It was bad enough with the bombs going off around them. Once in a while a tower of flame, black and orange, would shoot up as their ears popped with the sound of the explosions. It was bad enough and the sun hadn't even set yet.

"The fires," said the Majician, his voice fading and gurgling away. "It's happening...I fear I may die before the night arrives. My soul will never have anywhere to go." He took his bloody hands and put them to his face, smearing his goatee and mustache. "So many dead souls..." he said. "So many, and they have nowhere to go. And all their majic will be lost to the world."

Korson kept a house within the city of Montréal, and he went there now. He hadn't been there in thirty years or so, having abandoned it after he'd orchestrated the Great Purge. It was an usurping of power that had taken many long and painstaking strokes to strike down, to lash out at the rising forces of the Sab, but it had been nothing like this. The last time it had been all young vampires who were easily defeated, this time it was about sheer and cosmic power. Talissa had control of the shadow and Heather was gone and now he returned to the place where he'd last left when it was crushed before. He searched out his weapons, the one he thought he'd stored away for good. He used a scythe last time and caused no end of fear as he walked through the streets with it. But it didn't matter, because people would forget. He lifted it now and didn't much like the weight of it in his hands.

He brought some others, a carving knife, ceremonial, one his nah tova had given him. And his lacrosse stick, he brought it with him, for luck. So the Gods would be with him, if they'd ever abandoned him. But still it was an unenviable and reluctant task he now assumed, and he didn't like the taste it left in his mouth.

He left his house carrying the scythe, but it was the feel of the lacrosse stick against his hip that was more acute. He reached the main roads of Montréal and began to hack and slash his way through the zombies, not stopping to wonder at the futility of the task. He hacked away, among the bombs that were going off, and he gave not a care for the fires that could easily have destroyed him as well. He'd found purpose and was determined to see it through no matter how hopeless and daunting the task seemed.

He did come across the odd gargoyle or vampire of the Sabaoth, and he disposed of them swiftly, slicing right through their bodies like they were made of soft bread. He found a quiet sense of joy through the fact that he had given himself much work to do, more so than the last time he'd initiated a purge. And this time he was all alone in it. He found his strength growing and returning the closer to sundown that it got, but he ignored the small part of him that said something was not right.

Just focused on the pleasure/pain in his arms with each swing of the scythe, basking in the heat of the flames as well as the soothing cold of the dead blood he'd covered himself in. He'd run into some of the Night Stalker's, and once they'd seen that they shared the same purpose they left each other to the task. But still it was so overwhelming, the numbers of zombies that were growing, and the army hadn't even yet come down to battle.

Once Korson thought he was too tired to go on, but he scolded himself and in an instant he found renewed strength and began to hack away further, side-to-side with fury and overhand strikes that put holes in the pavement beneath the fallen of the legions. He fought through so much fatigue he felt almost drunk, as though he'd consumed the blood of three or four bodies that night.

Still something kept telling him there was something just not right, or *complete*, and still he ignored the feeling. He was not the majician he once was, did not feel the majic the way he did when he could control the shadow. And perhaps that was the source of his anger, that Talissa had stolen the shadow from *him*. That it was in the air around him and he couldn't grasp hold of it. All he could do was hack and slash away and hope there were no setbacks and fight away at the futility. Hope he wasn't overwhelmed. And finally he saw it.

Through the haze and the heat of the flames, he moved away from the legions of zombies, from the Night Stalker's and their fire-bombs. He'd caught a glimpse and it *moved* him, inside. Finally he felt something, and it was in his soul and he went out to it, hoping he didn't lose it. So fleeting. Like majic, and from the glimpse he caught he remembered just a little the pain of loss and deeply envied mortals the forgetting. It was the pain of remembering over the eternity's that was the most difficult.

It was all flame and blood and hacked up flesh and he rounded a tower of flame to get full view of the vision, of the true majic, a piece not of the shadow, but of the energies that bind us all. A piece of his past long dead and something he never dared himself to think of, otherwise his revenge on the Sab be all that much more brutal and sweet. He saw the Shaman, his spirit standing there, hands afire and his long feathered headdress glorious. He could see in the eyes of his master that he'd spent all these years trapped between here and the other world, his soul in limbo. But it wasn't just the Shaman that was there. It was his dog, Meetah, the wolf and spirit animal that was there too. And a different sadness in it's eyes. That of the sadness of a child being forgotten by it's father. Korson had begun to live by the shadow when he became a vampire, and ironically it was Meetah who'd given her life so he could be free. And he'd forgotten her majic and her spirit he so loved as a boy up to his last days walking the winter plains of New York State up to chilly Québec. He'd forgotten her and her kinship when he died, and dishonoured himself in doing so. He felt it more so now that he looked into her eyes, her grey-blue ghost eyes of the wolf, and he nearly cried when he opened himself up to what he saw. Friendship, endlessly loyal companion, who'd fought to the death for *him*. They both fought futile battles, but he lost sight of the nobility of his cause when he remembered that this was more for himself, for his own vengeance rather that something he would give his life for.

The Shaman's hands were still afire and he lifted them high in the air. He chanted but had no power of speech, no sound was heard from his lips, but Korson could guess at the century-long forgotten prayers. He stood holding his dripping scythe and watching the vision, for the first time wondering at reality, if this ghost was real. The Shaman's hands slowly came down and Korson gasped when he realized what he was going to do. Real or not he didn't like this dream anymore. He tried to move but was rooted to the ground, for the first time unable to do anything though he so desperately wanted to. The Shaman's hands moved to the head of Meetah, and he placed them flaming upon the wolf's head. The dog didn't seem to feel anything but the head burned, and Korson could only hope beyond all hope that it was because his spirit animal's soul was being released rather than condemned. He'd closed off his heart to friendship when his truest friend in the world had given her life to save him. He'd closed his heart to friendship and therefore to love as well. And it was just as painful as any betrayal he could think of because it lasted centuries, whereas betrayal really lasted only a moment. It was all left to memories and he didn't have even those.

He didn't even have the courtesy nor respect to keep the dream catcher his nah tova had give him, because he was afraid of dreams.

"Korson!"

He turned his head at the sound of the voice and he didn't know if it was the blood of the dead or tears that were down his cheeks right now. It was Graham St. Croix, walking towards him, face covered in soot. He turned back and saw the image fading away, but the last thing that happened was the Shaman crushing his spirit animal's charred head. Would the Shaman be so literal in trying to tell him something? Would the betrayal be so blatant? The wolf-dog, the symbol of his *best friend* and all the loyalty one could ever know. He looked back at Graham and heard his name being called again. Graham broke into a slight jog to come to him, his face a bit of a smile. It was obvious he had tried to follow Korson and now came to help him in the war against the Sab.

Then Korson's eyes widened in a moment of shock, the fading image of his spirit animal burned into his mind.

"No!" he yelled, but his voice was drowned out by the bombs going off all around him. He put his hand out as he yelled 'no!' again, but Graham couldn't hear him over the constant and rising noise, and he kept coming towards him, ducking the flames and braving the heat. All Korson could see, despite his preternatural vision, was one knife-wielding arm raised behind Graham, and he realized what was about to happen. The fires burning on Hallowe'en, the sun just setting, barely visible behind the shadow that covered Montréal, and the majic that Graham St. Croix had spent so much time looking for would be the final sacrifice to the spirit's to mark the beginning of the time when the dead would walk the earth forever.

He began to run, his warnings not heard, but after only several steps he was struck down. He looked up from the ground and saw the face of the vampire Paul standing over him, grinning like a madman. Forever faithful and blindly loyal. Korson was about to rise but he was bound at the arms by the other servants, Antoinette and Clarisse, and their combined strength was enough to hold him. They'd grown stronger in the many years since he'd last encountered them. The moment stretched into an eternity.

"The Sab will rise, Korson," said Paul in his adenoidal voice. "And you get the pleasure of watching your friend die...again."

Korson struggled and his mouth was gagged by the dead vampire's hands. Graham actually stopped for a moment when he saw the vampires bind Korson, and all it did was hasten the inevitable. A hand clamped itself around the face of the mortal Graham St. Croix, turning his head sideways and exposing his neck. Just to make him vulnerable. The other hand, the one wielding the knife, came over his shoulder and stabbed into his heart, and again so as to make Graham's blood splash out of the wound and into the air. It wasn't mortal blood that came out of his heart, it was filled with majic, and it splashed into the air as though gravity ceased to have a hold on the majic that had found its way into Graham's veins. It flowed into the air, a piece of his soul, and in one final explosion, one final clash between mortality and death and the shadow, each molecule of the air burst from the sheer darkness to a greyish-orange colour, and the smell of rotten eggs choked those who still needed breath to live. Graham St. Croix had been the final sacrifice on the eve of Hallowe'en. The sun now set, but the lingering of its orange light was left, mingling with the powdery grey of the shadow. And the form of Magog burst into being above Mount Royal, the shadow-demon laughing and laughing as the mites poured out of his cape and down into the streets of Montréal.

Paul, smug as he ever was as a young vampire, told Antoinette and Clarisse to release Korson. He knew Korson would be more worried about his friend than attacking them, and it mattered not if they were killed anyway. The Sab had arrived and was now beginning to see it's evil plan to fruition. It was Hallowe'en night and the time of the dead had arrived. They left him, and took the mortal with them, the *murderer*, and Korson of all people used this word with derision. They didn't go far though, and he could hear them begin to kill the remaining mortals with glee.

The Night Stalker's, upon the change in the tinge of the colour of the shadow, had retreated form the battle scene.

And Graham St. Croix, one of the few mortals to have ever seen a vampire and lived, now lay dying on the streets of Montréal. The last thing he saw before his killer had let him slump to the ground was the man's face, and he registered only mild shock because the piercings to his heart had left him numb and devoid of further emotion. The vampires Paul, Marie, Antoinette and Clarisse had taken the man with them, protecting him from recompense at the hands of a vengeful Blackfoot warrior.

Korson ran over to Graham and knelt next to the dying man, cradling his head in his hand and resting it in his knee. Graham shook and trembled with each ragged breath he expelled-they were laboured breaths and Korson secretly made a fist when he heard the last breaths of a dying man.

"I...remembered...the word," he said, struggling to speak, and Korson wouldn't deny him his last words. "We...say it Samhain, but it...was a druidic word...pronounced...Sa...wen..." He coughed between his words and his hand went to his heart, clenching it. "Doesn't... matter, though, because it was...only...warning...couldn't have prevented all this...if we tried..."

Korson took one of Graham's hands in his and clenched it as tight as he could. He seemed to keep losing his friends, and always just after he'd abandoned them because of his callousness, his lack of emotion. It was self-denial of joy, of feeling, and it ended up costing him more in the end rather than the risk of pain by opening up to another.

"It's yours," he said to Graham, "just ask for it." Graham understood what he meant and coughed and laughed as he looked away, at the orange and black shadow, at the fires going around them.

"I would make a terrible vampire!" he said. "No...I know...what she was doing...she opened a circle of power...the mountain in the middle...using the blood of children...and I was her final sacrifice..."

Korson said, "So let me save you, Graham!" He'd never called him Graham before and it felt funny to hear it. His claws squeezed a little blood from Graham's hand, and he bit down on his friend's hand in anger, but didn't pierce the skin, didn't taste of the blood because he had not been given permission. "Just take it for one night, then you can end it tomorrow, when it's all over. Let's win the war first." And Graham shook his head once more.

"Can't..." he said, "'cause this way I can just die. The other way I would just keep going...don't...*want*...that..."

"*Please*, Graham! Don't let her win! You can't die! You're my friend! Truly my friend!" Korson felt the tears streaming down his face, bloody and hot, tears he'd never shed for the Shaman, nor Meetah the faithful wolf-dog, and now he shed them for all three of his lost soul-mates. For the past hundred years of grief and release denied he shed them, but mostly for Graham, and he screamed. First in the face of the dying man, he screamed that he was so sorry that he'd ever played with majic and that he went to find him and dragged him into all this and then he screamed to the sky and the wolf asking for forgiveness. Asking the fates to stop and think for just one moment and stop this from happening. To save the one pure soul who absolutely didn't deserve to die, not with this torment. Then he just screamed, his war cry, so loud, louder than Talissa's scream. He only stopped when he was out of breath and his voice too hoarse to continue. He looked back down at Graham and could only whisper: "Please..."

But Graham was adamant. He didn't even deny the request this time, just said, "Not...dying for her...I'm like a tuning fork...*feel* the power...now...the power...isn't Talissa's...and...Heather is here..."

He was rapidly running out of breath, of life, and Korson was desperate to make a decision. He could force eternity on him. But as much as it hurt he couldn't do it. To deny the man his dying wish, even if it meant his soul would be forfeit, would mean he would be further condemned. His tears were homage enough, and the honour was so much more that it was the tears of not only a vampire, but of Korson, who hadn't laughed in joy nor cried in grief for over a century. Graham tried to speak further, but he couldn't manage it.

"You're truly a powerful spirit," said Korson, "and may your soul find peace wherever it goes." Then he bent lower, to Graham's ear, and whispered the only other gift he could think to bestow upon him. "Caquay ahpacee," he said. "That's my true name, my friend. I want you to be the only mortal on the earth to know it, if only in your last moment."

Graham's eyes glassed over, and one last rough breath spit out from his lungs. Korson bowed his head down and took the hand of his dead friend and touched it to his forehead. He hoped to the spirit of the wolf that the last little twitch of Graham's lips before he died was the beginning of a smile.

Part 2: Weavings

Heather had begun to make her way up Mount Royal, walking the steep, snaking road towards the graveyards. It was actually quite placid here, the eye of the storm, so to speak. There was still the shadow, it's mists lurking through the air in thick wads of darkness. She was about halfway up the mountain when she stopped, felt a disturbance. She sensed Korson, sensed a great loss, and then the smell of the Taint came strong upon the air. The Sab was here. She looked down the road to the bottom of the mountain at her beloved Montréal. With her preternatural vision she saw the hordes of zombies take to the streets and the fires of the Night Stalker's bombs going up in towers of orange flame. As well, the demons and gargoyles began coming out, as the true army against mankind took to the street to wreak havoc. She began to hurry.

The *cimetière Mont-Royal*, the one where she was buried, had half the graves upturned and corpses crawling out of them, animated by the shadow. Heather hadn't been back here since she'd risen from her grave, and, as she walked through the cemetery, she found her stone. Cringed a little when she read her name, and the inscription:

Beloved daughter of Albert and Susan

She sensed Talissa here, so close, felt the power that had been opened here. *Her* power. The grave brought back memories, of a time when she thought it was only about drinking blood all night and having fun. But she felt the loss that Korson just endured and now she had to go to him, once this was finished. Heather took another step closer to her grave. And the earth sunk beneath her feet, softening like butter on a hot plate, and she fell through the dirt that she'd risen from. After a moment she passed from the hands of the earth with a squish and fell into an open chamber, landing hard on her ass. This was Talissa's lair, where she'd been hiding the whole time. Quite an impressive feat of architecture, considering it was essentially an extremely large grave. Carvernous, rather. The shadow was quite thick here, and she stood up and passed through it, coming into a larger chamber. The throne room.

Talissa sat upon the throne, and at her side was her dog, John Hartley Watkins, still suffering on after all these years. Talissa patted him on his greasy hair and smiled. He sauntered off, as though in search of food.

Heather said, "It was you all along," and Talissa leaned her head back and gave a little laugh as though it all should have been obvious.

"All that's left is to call the shadow-demon Magog, and then the destruction of mankind will be complete. It's too late to stop me, Heather. There are others who want this as much as I. Kill me now and they will complete it. Fate's hand has it's fingers in too deep now to be defeated."

"I'm not here to stop you. I just want to know why." Talissa looked a little perplexed at the simplicity of the question. "This can't be just about power, Talissa. You've tapped that vein and you're going mad with it already. You don't *need* anymore power."

"It has already been prophesied in the Holy Bible of God that this will happen, that Magog will go out and deceive the nation in the four quarters of the earth and gather them to battle-"

"Don't give me that shit," said Heather. "I was in Valentine's mind. I know he wrote that. His lie didn't gain very much steam to only garner one passage in the bible."

Talissa gave Heather a sharp look, her brown eyes hot with rage, her mouth tight and angry.

"Have you ever felt loss, Heather? True loss? Endured it throughout the centuries. I endured loss for *one thousand years!* I was trapped in darkness, condemned to live forever and all I could dream about was that terrible grief. You condemned me to this eternal Hell, and you killed the man I loved with all my heart."

"I didn't condemn you, Talissa, you wanted this. It was the majic you were after. But you lied to get it and it ended up costing you someone dear to you. Don't put the blame on me, just because I couldn't see through your lies and because I wouldn't fall for them either. You're just pissed off because you couldn't make Korson love you, you couldn't make me love you, and now you're bitter and jealous. This is about love before power, but you just want to take it out on the world that you condemned *yourself* from."

Talissa shuddered and put her head in her hands.

"Heather, please, don't fight with me. I don't want to have to kill you. Please, just join me now and we can be together for all eternity."

"Would you kill me? You know you love me, but would you kill me out of anger because I rejected you? I was the one who was betrayed, Talissa. If you believe you were condemned than you have to remember who was lied to."

Talissa went down the three steps from the throne to floor level. With a wave of her hand the candles within the pumpkins next to the throne came to life. She neared Heather and pulled up her sleeve.

"You see this scar?" she said. "I spent nearly six months with a pin and ink pressing this rose into my skin, and when you gave me your so-called gift the majic rejected the herbs that the ink was made of. It bled out of my skin and it hurt like I've never felt anything hurt in my life. You should have heard me scream. All I was left with was this scar down my arm. *It never healed.* With all that vampire majic in me, wounds that would close up moments after I opened them, trying to kill myself, this one never healed no matter how much I tried. So I finally went to sleep for a millennium, until I felt that Place of the Dead getting clogged up with souls. I felt the power of these souls-"

"But you would have forgone all of it had Korson not rejected you, right? Don't try and justify it to me, Talissa, you're mad, drunk with power. Stop this right now. Look around you. You've *won*. You have more than enough. What are you going to do when you destroy all mankind? Where will you get your blood?"

Talissa's fingers played with bits of the shadow, and the smoke clung around her, caressed her cheeks and shoulders.

"Don't you see, Heather? The Place of the Dead is closed. There's no more room there. And with all this overflow of souls, there's so much energy floating around. An explosion of power. All the energy has to go somewhere, and I will have it. I will go beyond vampirism, beyond the need for blood. To finally get to the Place of the Dead. This existence is worse than Hell, Heather, it's limbo. I'm trapped, and I'm finally going to release the chains."

Heather said, "Talissa, we're forbidden from that place. What you seek is dangerous." Heather could foresee Talissa's plan. There was much power in the place of souls, and Talissa would have it as her own, but she would keep the dead mortals trapped here as she was, as zombies, only letting in a few souls at a time to maintain the swelled state of Tir Nan Og. The Place of the Dead would forever be sitting on a precipice, waiting to explode from over flowing. Majic so desired, so dangerous. The avarice of power. "We're not angels, Talissa. You're trying to get close to God, to come back into the light, but you know that isn't possible. There's a price for all this, and it means no God, and no love. Maybe that's what all this loss is trying to teach you."

"His ghost walks the earth. And he never comes to me. He never sees me! He goes to that mortal of Korson's! But whenever I get close to him he leaves! Maybe, just maybe, I can find him this way too. And be reunited with my true love."

"True love," said Heather. "You're a liar, Talissa. You have no majic in you. You could never love. All you can do is steal. You had love and you threw it away with your lies."

"I'll show you loss!" she said. "I'm so glad you're here, Heather. You can feel what I felt all those hundreds of years ago and then you can watch me become more than anything on this earth. I don't care if the cost is mankind. But first I'll show you loss..." she said, and she pulled down the black drape behind the throne. Hung by chains digging into her flesh and gagged at the mouth by the thick hand of the shadow, Catherine shook as she saw Heather standing face to face with Talissa. The chains began to rip her flesh apart from the rib cage, splaying her skin open so as to make it look as though she had wings. Her skeleton glistened with blood and a strange, white milky substance also seeped from her veins as well.

"NO!" cried Heather, and she began to dart towards her lover. The dead and dirty hands of John Hartley Watkins wrapped themselves around Heather's face and he stopped her thrust. Heather struggled and staggered around with the zombie on her back, but he had quite a tight grip and Heather was so distraught at the sight of Catherine bound on the chains that she couldn't find the strength to throw him off.

"GOOD boy, John!" exclaimed Talissa, like the parent of a child who'd just accomplished a good deed. Upon hearing Talissa's voice Heather grabbed the zombies head and thrust forward with all he strength, throwing him to the wall. But the head she hung on to, and the body twitched with final release as the bits of shadow flowed out from it. "My zombie..." said Talissa, dejected and sad. "You killed my zombie..." She looked up at Heather and scornfully said, "He was one hundred and twenty five years old!"

Heather tossed the head over to Talissa, a memento. Talissa looked at it mournfully, her mouth pouty. Her emotions were so enigmatic because of the corruption of power in her veins. But it wasn't enough to distract her from Heather and before Heather could even move towards Catherine again, her arms were bound by two female vampires who'd come out from the shadows, out from another chamber in this cavernous grave.

"You've met Antoinette and Clarisse, haven't you, Heather. I'm afraid poor Marie didn't make it though. You scarred her too greatly, and she just couldn't bear it. She left herself out in the sun just a few days ago..." Talissa went over to Heather and bent close to her ear, said in a whisper, "Frankly, I don't really care for either of them, but Paul is an ever faithful servant and he seems to find their companionship amusing." Not that it was much of a secret with the two girls standing close by. Talissa turned in a flourish and faced the bound Catherine again. "You said we weren't angels, Heather. I completely disagree. Look at your beloved Catherine hanging by those chains up there! Her skin is all pulled apart and spread out. Like wings! Glorious wings! All pink and white and dripping with her blood! Angel's wings are always dripping in blood. That's how I know I'm doing God's work, because of all this blood." Talissa bent her head down and lowered herself to the ground a bit, as though the years had made her tired, thinking of the years had caused her pain. "It isn't just you I was doing this for

Heather. It was Korson too. He deserved all this...he betrayed me too..." Her voice got quiet and the sadness began to bring her down. She put a hand to her head.

Heather could have easily broken the grip of the female vampires, but it was too late. Catherine was already beyond salvation. Heather saw in her eyes a duality: the agony of the torment of her second death, and the ecstasy of release from her hundred year old prison. She actually hadn't even reached the century mark yet, counting her mortal life. And it had been too much for her. And from the tensed expression on Heather's face, Talissa could tell she was pushing it, but she had not the scope of Heather's power, otherwise she'd have let her go out of respect.

But she had one final nail to hammer into the coffin. From behind the throne, wrapped up suffocatingly tight in a purple sack, Talissa pulled out Heather's little grey Cumulous. Despite the tears on Talissa's face, she wore a grin full of red-cheeked anger, her nose dripping wet as she caressed the soft-furred kitten. She could sense Heather's suppressed reaction, that Heather's eyes were ready to explode with blood and tears. Talissa petted the soft, soaked fur along the cat's back, then gently began to clutch his neck with her claws, and began to twist and twist and TWIST until his bones cracked and splintered, his neck looking like a fuzzy corkscrew, and his squeal was muffled by the pressure of Talissa's thumb upon his throat, by the death shuddering through his tiny body.

"Let her go," said Talissa. Hesitantly, Antoinette and Clarisse released their hold. "Go out and play. Go show mankind the meaning of the word Sabaoth." They complied, eager to kill with glee, and left the lair. "You know what tonight is, Heather? Hallowe'en. Samhain. The night when the souls of the dead are free to walk the earth and the veil between worlds is lowered. I spent years manipulating the shadow until I could gain control over it, and I certainly lowered the veil this year. I tore it down! Pass through the veil with me, Heather. Please, join me. Don't throw it all away over bitterness over Catherine. You should know by now that eternity means loss. Come see the other side with me and taste of the fruit that is forbidden to us. Taste of true power."

Heather clenched her fists and looked at Talissa with a harsh, hardened gaze from under her brow. Every ounce of her tormented heart wanted to lash out at Talissa, to show her what true power was, to tear her piece by piece with the shadow and leave her blasted, bloody soul in darkness forever. But she didn't want to succumb to emotion, no matter how raw it felt. No matter how much she knew how good it would feel to shred Talissa in her claws for what she did. But she wouldn't give in to the darkness in her soul. She told herself over and over that Catherine had found the release she wanted all along but was unwilling to take for herself. It didn't much make her feel better, didn't clear that sick feeling from her throat. But it gave Tailssa her answer.

"So you would choose love over it?" she said. "Dead love at that. What would you do now, Heather? Stop me? *Destroy* me? It would be quite a battle."

"Yeah it would," said Heather, trying not to choke. She turned toward the cavern from whence she came, and made to leave. Stopped, then turned back for a moment. "All that's left for you now is to call the demon. Maybe you should look around you and decide if you really need that power." She went back up through the grave, waiting until she was out of sight to use her preternatural speed to leave. She had so many emotions raging within her that she didn't realize the shadow was seeping out of her skin, and when she spit herself out of her grave, wisps of smoke followed her out. They clouded her vision for a moment and all she could see was the deathly, angelic image of her beloved Catherine, her skin being peeled off her body to form the red and white wings, repeating itself over and over. She called to Korson as she descended Mount Royal, her sight clouded over with emotion. He heard her call, and was there to meet her with his arms as she flew to the bottom. He carried her at preternatural speed, away from the onrushing avalanche of little Gogites that poured down the mountain, and only stopped when he'd reached Graham's house, where Jerome was. They could, all three of them, mourn together.

Talissa showed no little disappointment at having been left alone by Heather. She was a little stunned as well, by the fact that Heather made no show to stop her. Had she utterly defeated her spirit? It saddened her that the fiery blond showed no spark of emotion and vivacity that would have made for a beautiful battle. But nonetheless a victory was a victory and it was time to bring it to completion. She would have loved to have Heather with her through to the end, but there was something special about performing a majical ceremony alone. Something serene and obscene.

There were three steps that lead up to her throne, carved out of the dirt beneath the ground. At the top Talissa placed the chalice that she'd kept from her days as a virgin saint in Terni. And next to it her blade, with its jewel encrusted handle. Then she knelt at the bottom of the steps and looked at the items she'd placed there. Then bowed her head down, remembering. It was the remembering that hurt the most, of all the love, for Valentine, for Korson, for Heather. She'd caught glimpses of Valentine's ghost, only the barest of glimpses with gaps of decades between them. She'd sense the presence of his ghost and would always chase it down to no avail. She remembered fleeing the torment of memories and flying and crying across an ocean to put distance between herself and humanity. She began to hate the smell of blood and all the pleasures it brought, a lifetime of joy and heartache. There was hardly anyone around and she buried herself into the dirt anyway, so tired of it all, and spent many years alone with her dreams to keep her company.

But what Talissa remembered most of all now was the altar room back in Terni. She'd never gone back to that place, never had any longing in her heart to see the wonderful landscape, the rocky paths of that passionate and romantic land. She thought she woke to a new start but only realized that the ghost had stayed close enough for her to sense it, but just far enough so she could never catch it. It was her own personal Hell, and she'd made it for herself. Too good at falling in love perhaps, and she was the one who'd turned both Korson and Heather to the ways of the dark majic, and been spurned by both. Why did they reject her so? She only offered to give them anything they desired. Was that not true love? She would have screamed out her frustration had the wind not been so placid now. The only thing lurking about her were mists of black smoke from the shadow. And she knew the demon was here, all she had to do was summon him.

Talissa said the *Te Deum* in her head, over and over. She'd never forgotten the prayer, nor the prophecy that St. Valentine had written into the bible. After all her manipulations it had been him that had seen deep enough into the chasm of dark majic and seen the world of the shadow-demon. Had gotten a glimpse of a God and knowledge of what true power was. So vivid a picture of something so vast that he'd gone back and forth from the verge of being utterly mad. Something had gone so deep into his veins, such a dangerous piece of majic and it gave him a taste for blood before his body had been turned to the way of the vampire. She said the *Te Deum* over and over in her head and wondered if these prayers were really just spells and if she could ever get close enough to see <u>the</u> God. It had been so long and she felt the pain of being denied passage through the gates to the Place of the Dead. She didn't care what it was called, nor what was waiting when she got there. It could have been like a graveyard, with monuments to the dead and grey grass and a rusty wrought iron fence that creaked when the wind blew. All she wanted was to be at peace. To not have to listen to <u>his</u> name being mentioned every time someone fell under the swoon of another. She hated hearing them worship the man they knew nothing about.

"*O God, we praise thee, and acknowledge thee to be the Supreme Lord,*" she began, her voice echoing on the depths of the mountain, though she didn't raise it very loud. "*Everlasting Father, all the earth worships thee. All the angels, the heavens and all angelic powers.*

"*All the Cherubim and Seraphim, continuously cry to Thee: Holy, Holy, Holy Lord God of Hosts!*" She raised her voice up a bit as she made call to the Sabaoth, and she put the first cut across the inside of her forearm and watched the blood seep out for a moment, the hues glistening between deep red and a suffocated blue. She shuddered a bit, feeling a different kind of majic flowing through her, a much deeper, darker feeling from the shadow. She thought she saw the mists swirl a bit on their own and she continued the prayer.

Heaven and earth are full of the majesty of Thy glory.
The glorious choir of the Apostles,
The wonderful company of Prophets,
"*The white-robed army of Martyrs, praise Thee.*" She looked up at the hung vision of Catherine as she said this, a sickened, twisted metaphor for her prayer. Catherine's wings still dripped with blood and white mucous.

Holy church throughout the world acknowledges Thee;
The Father of infinite majesty;

The adorable, true and only son;
Also the Holy Spirit, the comforter.

"O Christ, thou art the King of Glory!" She let her voice get loud again and made a cut across her other forearm, mingled the two halves and allowed them to drip into the chalice before her.

Thou art the everlasting Son of the Father.
When thou tookest upon thyself to deliver man,
Thou didst not disdain the Virgin's womb.

"Having overcome the sting of death, thou opened the Kingdom of Heaven to all believers." She made another cut, this one down alongside the middle of her chest, over the spot where her dead heart lay. The marble chalice was almost full of blood.

Though sitest at the right hand of God in the glory of the Father.
We believe that thou whilst come to be our judge.
We, therefore, beg Thee to help Thy servants whom Thou last redeemed with Thy Precious blood.

"Let them be numbered with Thy Saints in everlasting glory." She finished the prayer and drank of her now sacred blood from the holy chalice. It had been carved in the name of God, as God carves each being in the name of art. And she lifted her head high and leaned backwards and let every last drop seep down her throat, save for the tiny amount that clung to the surface as film.

St. Valentine was a creative writer. She wondered if he actually saw the savior Christ or if he even existed; if it was not all metaphor and prose for the mortals to forever contemplate. She put the chalice back down. The prayer had been said, and the shadows truly came alive for her now. She felt the darkness of the shadow ready to rage, and all that was left was to call the demon by name. She lifted her arms up and blood dripped down them, and out of her chest as well, the blood her offering to the powers, be them God or Devil, in exchange for true majic. The offering taken within herself in hopes the majic would follow. So satanic and selfish of her! To take an offering unto herself!

She said aloud, "I call thee, by the shadow and the powers of darkness, by name: Lord Magog of the shadow-demons!"

She expected thunder and explosion of shadow like the ones she'd summoned herself to cover Montréal. But she foolishly had not counted on the subtlety or the guile that a God (or Devil) would show. She sat there many moments and nothing happened.

"Well," she said to herself. "Don't I feel like a fucking asshole."

Then she noticed the pair of white eyes in the cavern to her left. The eyes that came towards her now that she saw them and in the bare light of her grave she saw the smoke take somewhat of a shape of a large man, his mists making a cape as though of snake-like smoke around him. She shivered with anticipation to hear him speak.

"I can see the power in your eyes..." she said, having trouble raising her voice above a whisper. Magog's cape seethed despite the fact that there was no wind, and a faint, high-pitched giggle was heard in the distance of another world. His mites weren't far behind. He floated in front of her there, and it was becoming painfully obvious to her that the words she thought were forthcoming were being withheld. Would a God, so full of power, enter the world riding trite words as though he were a political leader? Would he not arrogantly boast his power through his mere stride?

"Lord Magog, King of the shadow-demons, I ask you to fulfill the prophecy and go forth with your legions and destroy mankind for his sins." Talissa felt her grip on the shadow as a much more tenuous thread than when she wove its intricate little wisps into patterns with her fingers. The shadow-demon Magog floated there for another moment, then his eyes increased their glow.

Am I your supplicant?

Talissa felt true fear for the first time in a thousand years upon hearing his voice. Such a simple query! Yet his tone so bold, and his voice boomed as though in her head. She felt her insides shaking. After all the torment and pain and anguish over the years, she'd never had any opportunity to feel fear nor humility. It froze her there for a moment, under the gaze of this God or Devil who would await her answer.

"Yes," she said, feeling meek, and that feeling being reflected in her voice. "I control the shadow and I command you to send the legions out to walk among man." If someone had asked her at that moment, she would honestly not have been able to proclaim that she herself was the one. Talissa stood before Magog and felt crushed by his presence.

And he smiled! If it was possible to see a mouth upon his black face than one would see a smile. His forms expanded as though he took breath, and the light in his eyes throbbed.

Then it is yours, my little vampire! The doors are now open to you, and you may pass through to the Place of the Dead as you please. Leave this vain and petty world of mortals behind! Join a new kind of existence! Transcend flesh! Despite your immortality you still have the limitations of flesh, and therefore do not have *true* immortality.

"Where is the Place of the Dead, Magog? How do I find it?" He spread his arms in answer. His cape took up the whole of the cavern, and Talissa took a few steps forward, accepting the invitation. The Place of the Dead was within him. Pity those poor mortals who didn't have the shadow! A small price to pay, the wait of a millennium and the anguish of lost love. Talissa moved forward, into the shadow, letting it overtake her. It took only moments for her to cross the veil...

Magog laughed and laughed and laughed.

"Shut the door, quick!" Heather pushed her way past the black man and if he hadn't known to spot her for a vampire he would have easily been offended by her impetuousness. Plus, she was with Korson. And he'd obviously been crying. If one had saw them then one would think Heather the emotional and expect the tears to be from her. Normally, they would be right. But things aren't so clear cut in the real world, nor so in the darkness of the night. The beautiful, youthful blond quickly removed herself from the presence of the two others, peeking out the front window from behind the curtain.

Jerome said, "You look like shit," and Korson nodded in agreement, wiping his tears away. It had bean so long and felt so good, the relief of the water dripping down his face. Ironically, he couldn't stop the tears, after so many years of stoicism. He enjoyed them now because he knew they would eventually dry up again.

"I come with regrets and my deepest apologies," he said, as he put his hands on Jerome's shoulders. And Jerome's eyes were wet too now.

"I know. It might sound funny, but I sensed it. When it happened. I think he called to me in his last moments, with all that majic he was getting into." Jerome looked away, as though he had more to say but wouldn't say it. As though he wanted to swear but didn't want to mingle Graham's memory with that of profanity.

"I am so sorry, Jerome. I feel as though I could have prevented it from happening. Maybe if I never went to him in the first place…"

"I know what you mean," said Jerome. "I feel like I could have stopped him, too. But maybe there's something to be said 'bout fate. I just hope he found what he was looking for on the other side."

Korson said nothing, just looked down to the ground from his lofty height. At the last few tear drops hitting the ground as his tap dripped out.

Jerome said, "Just tell me who," and Korson looked up with a question written on his face. "I told you I sensed it. My brother didn't die, he was murdered. With a knife. I want to know who." But Korson said nothing, and by the expression on Jerome's face as he looked back at the vampire it was clear that he didn't need the answer to validate his suspicions.

"Please," said Korson gesturing to the couch. His composure was returning. "No more bloodshed for now. It's too dangerous to go out now, with all that majic raging." But he knew he could only placate Jerome's vengeance for so long. Heather and Korson sat on the couch, all of them fatigued from the height of the war the last few days. Jerome took a look out the window before taking up on a recliner with the other two.

"What the hell are those things?" He had seen the mites of Magog, the Gogs of War, the little bits of shadow with teeth, tittering along the road looking for tainted majic to consume.

"They're from the shadow-demon Magog," said Heather. Korson shuddered at hearing the name of vampire legend aloud.

"Are you sure you should be telling him, Heather?"

"Yeah," she nodded. "It's very rare to find a person who has seen his form and lived. But Magog's mine, Korson. I dreamt him up as a child, when I began to find too much power in my dreams. His majic is mine. And Talissa had defeated us all. All she had to do was rule. But she got greedy. She had a glimpse of the power that drove St. Valentine mad, and his prophecies *were* lies...to her. She believed them and called the demon and ended up defeating herself. The mites are sent out to destroy all the tainted majic in the world, the vampires and zombies of the Sab. She had her army, and she destroyed it."

Korson said, "And what of us, are we safe?"

"Yeah. You remember the Taint? The mites can sniff it out better than us. They'll eat it all up then go back into the demon, to their world. It cost a lot of people a lot of souls, but now the dead can die happy again. The overflow of majic has been broken."

"You look like a fucking monster, Heather," said Korson. He referred to her scarred lip and crooked leg. He had her lean back and he used some of his blood and chanted quietly in Blackfoot as he applied the universal ointment to her wounds. He showed he knew of some majic himself, healing her within the space of an hour, so there were almost no signs of scars. She winced as he pushed the bones of her leg back into place. "The pain you must have endured walking on this thing," he said.

Jerome said, "There's such a fucking mess out there."

"No shit," said Heather. "I'll have to take care of that before sunup." Korson was finishing up his healing arts, and he looked over at Heather.

"Just what do you have planned to cover all that up?" he asked. Heather looked a little regretful for a moment, and she sighed deeply before she spoke.

"Something I think I may regret doing," she said. "I'm going to weave a forgetting. People won't remember these events as they really were. The story will get all jumbled up. And eventually it will fade. All those Night Stalker's bombs, the damage will be theirs. It's going to come down to a biker's war in the real world."

"Sanity from mundanity," said Jerome, but Korson was much more silent for a while.

"What about Jerome," he asked. "Will he forget too?" It didn't seem fair to him, that this man would lose so much for nothing and become dumb to it all.

"Maybe," said Heather. "But maybe he's seen too much already to forget." She got up, looking mostly healed now, and went to the window. "Looks a lot more safe out there. I've got a huge mess to clean up." She went to leave and the other two watched her go, but she stopped a moment as she stood in the doorway. "A couple hours before sundown, you two make sure to get inside, ok?" Then she left, the door thumping closed behind her.

It was with humblest apologies that Korson had left Jerome. He felt bad about leaving him alone, but he just wasn't comfortable being around mortals for too long. He said he would consider the standing offer to crash at Graham's place that night, if he needed a place to hide from the sun. But with the forgetting on its way, it wouldn't have been the best of ideas for them to be together.

Korson had left Jerome to retreat back into the shadow while it was still all around him. He didn't know whether he would have access to it after this night, nor if he would want access to it. So he left and went out just to lurk and creep, like vampires do.

But he didn't *actually* leave Jerome. He stayed close to him, hanging off his shoulder like a cobweb in a corner. He knew that Jerome had vengeance on his mind. And it scared him that it was a vengeance so placid and born of intelligence rather than emotion and anger. He watched Jerome go out of his brother's home, and, admittedly, was quite curious at the intricacies of man in the moments leading up to murder. He noticed Jerome's hand touching a spot on his jacket. A weapon, possibly a knife of some sort.

He stayed close to him, in the shadow, and felt a little guilty after a while. Guilty at his selfishness, at the fact that he, the voyeur, didn't feel alone, but Jerome had no inkling of his presence and the loneliness could be read on his face. It would be his second murder he was going to, but this one wasn't something he was forced into. This was his conscious choice.

Jerome hid as well, and watched and waited, until he saw the man who'd stabbed his brother walking up the sidewalk and go into the building. Korson saw his fist clench at the sight of him. A moment later he followed him in, but Korson didn't go after him, didn't prevent him. Something inside of him wanted to see if Jerome would go through with it. Korson stood below the window, and saw with his preternatural vision the murderer sitting smugly in his big chair, looking out the window. Even from that far away he could tell he already had some blood in him. Not enough to cause Jerome any trouble, but enough for another vampire to notice. And from there, Korson could tell he was nothing more than a pawn. Given a mere taste to entice, but not given the gift.

Then another figure appeared in the room, Jerome's figure. There were only a few words exchanged. The murderer showed off the beginnings of his fangs, and made a vain attempt at being a monster. Jerome moved over to him and stabbed him, his arms going up and down, up and down, several times in a vigorous motion before the room became still. Korson wondered, all too late, if he should have stopped him. If he should have a last moment savior, staying his hand. If it would've been all around better or even just the same if it was himself who'd exacted revenge. But it was moot, much too late to leave murder to the murderers. He watched the window a moment longer and realized Jerome wasn't coming down soon, he was fixated there. So he went up.

He opened the door and saw Jerome leaning over the very dead body of Simon Dubois. The knife was still sticking out of the man's heart and there was some blood on Jerome's hands that he absently wiped at, trying to get it off him. He looked over at Korson, one who'd seen much more murder than Jerome had in his life.

"Was it worth it?" asked Korson. "Did it make it better?"

"I don't know," said Jerome, and he huffed out a laugh. "It certainly didn't bring him back. But he didn't deserve to live. Not in a million years, he didn't deserve his life."

"You don't have to stay here you know," said Korson. "The moment's over."

"Maybe I just want to feel like I'll stay like this forever. I'll have the rest of my life to think about it, but I'll never feel this way again. I don't think a day will go by without me trying to remember what this feels like."

Korson moved over to Jerome and looked down at Dubois' body. He pulled the knife out of the man's chest. He might-just *might*-rise again.

"Get out of here, Jerome. Go home. Plan a big, beautiful funeral. And maybe pray that you're part of the forgetting. That you won't have to live with this, and you won't have to be a victim of the sickness of the majic in the air."

There was no hope in Jerome's eyes at those words. He knew torment wouldn't be dismissed so easily with a forgetting, and that there would always be pieces of this murder coming back to haunt his dreams, the same way that the memories of his brother would constantly flick back and forth across his mind. He took one last look at Dubois' body, then turned and left, the only sound heard that of limbs being ripped from the whole as Korson dismembered the betrayer-just as a precaution.

Having woven the forgetting, Heather took one last look at the darkness that covered Montréal. The thick smoke of Magog descended upon the city, further smothering the inhabitants with the choking smoke. In the right concentration, the shadow could be deadly to mortals. But this...this would just place an anesthetic fog over the people's minds. She felt it was necessary. She hoped she was entitled to make that decision. And maybe she was, simply because she had the humility to question herself on it.

It saddened Heather to do this, no matter how much she felt it was necessary to do so. She still brought the fog down, but to have to erase this type of experience could only mean that these events would be somehow repeated in the future. And she would with most certainty be around to see things come full circle again, whether it be ten years from now or if it took another thousand years for the cycle to renew itself. That was the danger with being of the shadow. The darkness. The secrecy, the seclusion, the suspicion of those around you. It was like her situation with Korson, how his distrust manifested itself, how he withheld his knowledge from her. That lack of enlightenment had caused the situation to be dragged out for decades longer that it should have been. Though he nobly suffered the symptom of the Sab alone, he could have possibly prevented the torment of the events. Then again, the hand of fate...Perhaps the unseen intelligence of majic, of the shadow, had merely been waiting for one like Heather to come along. Perhaps it was majic that was the ultimate form of existence and it was the ghosts of our fathers who were constantly testing the limits of our souls.

The worst of it was that this wasn't the first time this had happened to man. If man was to achieve anything, it would be through enlightenment and fellowship rather than conquering. The threads of that bond were much more pliant, but, if constantly woven together could prove much stronger in the long run. Heather felt the shadow flowing through her, the darkness making her mind black as she felt the power, and she slowly pushed it down upon man. The last time a fog like this descended upon mankind was the time after openness of the Roman Empire. It was when the word of Christ began to be spread across the globe, and also just after the time of St. Valentine and his prolonged lives. The time when majic started to sweep the earth, when man started looking to the stars. When Valentine had brought the shadow into this world-probably the first one ever to do so-his confrontation with Heather had brought a dark fog to the minds of men. Enlightenment stopped. Learning stopped. Secrets to the world became lost in the shadow, and the Ages of Darkness were born. So much was lost, never to be recovered, that terrible price of forgetting. One would never know if those things lost would ever be found again. It made men separate, this forgetting, by making them suspicious of each other. As well, man would weave little forgettings of his own: wars born of ignorance.

"No," she told herself. This certainly wasn't going to change anything. The cycle would continue. But as sure as she was that she may not be the one to make such a grand decision, she was just as sure that if the cycle was meant to be broken that it would have to be man himself who did it. Until then the vampires would lurk on the edge, in the shadows. Maybe they were more than man, but maybe it just seemed that way. Talissa wanted to get closer to God. She fancied herself a dark angel. Heather had no such ego, and neither did Korson. The bitter irony is that Talissa had God-like aspirations because she was drunk from the majic she saw and it ended up costing Heather and Korson people that they'd held dear. And Talissa just killed indiscriminately, and it was their morality that prevented them from taking the violent initiative against the hungry vampire Talissa.

She wanted to go to Korson, to tell him that she truly loved him and he should stay with her in Montréal instead of returning to the country. She so desperately wanted to, just to run into his arms, but she wouldn't, partly because of her pride. Because she felt the sheer power of the dead within her and knew that she was something just a little more than a vampire, just as she was something more than a mortal. And she knew he wouldn't come to her, but she hoped that maybe he would soften his heart and find her. Heather was certain they would meet someday, and maybe be together. But mostly she didn't want to go to him now because she had just lost Catherine. She felt vulnerable, as well as the fact that she didn't want to feel the guilt she would feel by using Korson as a replacement for Cat. She thought of all this as the veil of smoke descended upon Montréal. It wasn't as great a forgetting as the one during the Ages of Darkness, but it was enough. It would give her something to think about for quite some time over the next century, whether she had done right.

She'd gone to Hawke, the leader of the Night Stalker's, and told him to leave Montréal for the night. The next day he would show up and fulfill his part of the bargain. He would certainly be exempt from forgetting all this, but they had a tenuous trust between them, and he wouldn't betray her. He'd gained a sharp increase in notoriety for a minimal price.

Heather looked at Mount Royal in the distance, noticed that the smoke still seeped out of it, but in a different way. More like the last drops of water dripping out of a hose that had been shut down. The smoke settled out of the mountain and became part of the forgetting, and eventually would be returned to where the shadow belonged, across the other side of the veil, where only Heather would have access to the true depths of the power.

It was through the smoke that Heather looked for the veil, after walking for a while. Where did one go to search for a doorway so abstract? So surreal? Everywhere and nowhere, and Heather had seen the depths of the shadow, walked in it now, in the smoke, and could not fathom where Talissa might have gone. Back through to the past, like herself perhaps? To start this again? But no, those were Heather's dreams and fates and it was her majic now, that of the smoke of Lord Magog of the shadow-demons, and it would not be pliant to Talissa's will. Never was, in fact, beyond the petty little weavings of those leftover, forgotten bits.

Heather turned around in the shadow, lost in it, within herself. All round her was darkness and drifts of black and grey smoke. She didn't become agitated, nor was she suffocated by the utter darkness around her. She knew where she was, that she was still in Montréal, and could step back out into reality at any moment she so desired. But she didn't want to leave. It was like flowing through warm tropical waters, so easy to lose oneself and forget the surroundings. She kept walking through it. No doors, no lines, no distinction of anything but clouds and plumes of shades of darkness. Each step was as though she moved not an inch from her spot, yet she knew she had walked quite a distance. Into the thick of the shadow.

She pulled it through her. Not literally, not especially, but more with her mind made the wisps go hither and thither according to her whim. She manipulated the power, and not with chants or anything from theology or paganism to drive a mortals mind towards the right state. Heather was beyond that kind of poetry.

And she thought of the kills. Surprisingly enough, because it didn't feel as though the murder and the blood would feed the majic in her veins. But it was the torment of the shadow, the duality, the irony of it, that made the thirst come to her. Such rage to find serenity! Such blind, unmitigated passion of the heart to find lucidity of the mind! She felt she could stay here forever.

Like the song, just me and my shadow, thought Heather, but she knew it too good to be true, that one would wither and shrivel in this serenity as one would in the warm, blue tropical waters. The thirst would call to her and she would have to be a monster again, be a vampire. That was the deadly loop, to be forever drawn back to the earth, to never achieve that true angelic, God-like state that Talissa sought.

Maybe that was why she was wandering here now? It was the shadow that was her teacher, that manifested itself-from the depths of her own psyche-to push her in directions that perhaps her conscious self was afraid to step towards. Perhaps that was another loop, the lessons that kept repeating themself. Perhaps vampires still retained some mortality because they were also able to forget. It would be here to this nothingness that she could come to learn, to see things that could be seen where there was no light. It was another majic trick, to see through the darkness to the light; because where there was shadow there was always light.

It wasn't all Heather, though, that could control such majic. No one being could for it was also an entity on its own, an entity beyond that of Magog. She noticed the murmuring, hadn't realized she'd heard it until the buzz of the hum irritated her ears. It was the shadow that had subtly drawn her in as well, as a vampire draws a victim, with sweet caresses of the senses. The hum reminded her of the prayers of the dead she'd heard in the Church of the Sab, and a part of her feared to step on a fallen body of a supplicant. Though they should all be dead by now.

But it had been a while since Heather heard voices in her head, and in some twisted way she missed it. Missed the dark, disturbing companionship of those friends we mortals so take for granted. It was a little different this time, though. She couldn't make out the words, though the voice itself was more distinguishable as a singular entity. It screamed and writhed and Heather couldn't figure out if it was in her head or if it was coming from somewhere around her. There was something disquieting about the sound, luring yet causing a vibration not that unlike a spasm of fear in Heather's spine. It was a wailing that, for all the qualities of the sound, should have been deafeningly loud, yet was like an intimate whisper in Heather's ear. The tone and emotion of it fell and rose, going from the wailing to a weak choking, as though the pain that was being felt couldn't inject enough energy in the sadness...that the pain made everything tired.

Heather could never survive here. Not for too long, though she felt so drawn and linked to this place. She didn't really know why, she just knew she was not of their world as much as she was not of the mortal world. As the sun would burn her in the mortal realm, the utter coldness of this majic would cause her to whither like a flower that went unwatered. And she would become nothing, or the stuff of dreams, until she again found the strength to return for blood to warm her soul. She ran her hands through the shadow and it looked to be of her, and she felt it permeating her. It wasn't as though she made a simple request, nor any sort of calling. She just wove with her mind the shape from her dreams, and in swirls and funnels of smoke the elusive shadow-demon Magog appeared.

He was his usual arrogant, haughty self, merely hovering in front of Heather. It was true that he was of her, that the shadow was of her, but he'd become something more than that too. Something of his own, as though he were a representation of a secret. That's what separated him from Heather's dreams, more than the majic, the fact that he had become a part of the secret and its defender. Who, of all people mortal or vampire, could destroy the shadow? It could survive in anything and the light didn't burn it away, only hid it. The danger came when it was mixed with the flesh, when the majic had to struggle with mortality and the ills of life and the mind. And though Heather had control of the shadow, she had not a thing to do anymore with Magog, the demon that she'd dreamed as a child.

I can feel her inside me, he said. Stated it really, his voice still booming and having a ghostly, foreboding essence but not the sheer overpowering volume anymore. Heather studied the bulges of the surreal formlessness of Magog, and matched them up with the wailing she heard. Talissa was there, trying to push her way out.

"Why have you trapped her in there, Magog?" The shadow-demon issued a low, guttural snicker.

She has gone there herself! She is just thrashing for the way out…but perhaps I have trapped her as well, not knowing I have done so.

"Does it hurt you, with her in there?" asked Heather. Magog's white eyes looked away, turned slightly green. He seemed somewhat contemplative, as though debating the meaning of the word pain. Perhaps the demon had picked up some traits of Heather's in his creation.

Do you like pain? he asked.

"Is that a proposition?" asked Heather with a smile, hoping to draw Magog out. "I like to cause myself pain. I like my own torment. I bring things on myself, put myself in a hole just to see if I can dig myself out. But I don't care to watch Talissa hurting there. I know I probably deserve to enjoy it, but I just don't need to waste my time with her torment. It's not like she's a kill or anything. You might as well let her out."

Am I your supplicant then? Magog's deadly question. Heather didn't grab the bait though. Just tilted her head and shrugged her shoulders, gave a little wave of her hand. She didn't care either way what happened to Talissa. But she did have one regret. In the moment she turned here head, blinked her eyes, Magog had disappeared. She couldn't draw him up again either. But the wailing was still there, increased in fact. It was slowly getting louder. The forgetting had been woven, the shadow whipped around in torment. The swirls became a black funnel, and Heather felt she would very soon be sucked into the vortex. She tried to settle the storm down, but her efforts had little effect. The magic had to be returned to its own realm, now that the purpose was served.

At the bottom of the vortex a form appeared, at first difficult to distinguish because it too was black. Heather took a few steps towards the form, but it crawled towards her, too, away from the diminishing vortex. It was not nearly recognizable as Talissa, every inch of her charred black, and her head bald. The only thing that stood out were here eyes, still bright white with the soft brown irises. It seemed to be the only thing left unharmed upon her return from where she should not have dared to tread.

Heather stood over her, looking down at the burnt corpse. Still living, still eternal. Talissa raised a hand upwards in a plea for help. It was obvious every move was torment for her, and every move loosened a piece of charcoal from her body. Perhaps she would slowly disintegrate, until there was nothing left? Perhaps eternity was her doom, that she couldn't get to death, and couldn't cease to exist? She'd tried to find the place where the dead go, and it had known her and spit her back. Had marked her body with scars that would last forever. The wailing had stopped coming from her mouth, and her hand quivered as she held it up for Heather to take. She tried to speak some words, trite phrases perhaps, such as 'save me.' Heather just bent down to her and when she told her no, that she couldn't do it, the black, cracked smile that was appearing on Talissa's face ceased. She hadn't even had fangs with which to feed anymore.

"It's going to rain, Talissa. To wash all this away. And then the shadow will be gone. The sun will come out. I hope you have enough strength with which to flee from it. I don't care if you die, but I won't save you."

Heather brought the rains down, the sheer pantheism of nature. So much water that it nearly flooded the city. Her hair stuck to her neck and shoulders and she stood there a moment, letting the water flow over her. The shadow was being washed away slowly and for the first time in weeks Heather saw the rays of the sun making a thin, yellow-orange line around everything. The choking smoke of the shadow realm was gone, and Magog wouldn't come even though she beckoned him. The shadow was melting away and it was hard to tell if it was the rains or the coming sun that rid Montréal of a majic that didn't belong in this place. Heather walked away from Talissa's burnt corpse, feeling the rain but having trouble enjoying the cold splashes of the drops that pounded down upon her. She didn't look back at the corpse, but she could tell by the sounds what Talissa was doing. The thousand year old vampire couldn't find the strength to wail further and only isssued moans and grunts, barely audible. Followed Heather by crawling with shuffles and splashes in the rain. The last spark of the Sab still struggling for life. And perhaps, even if Heather had the will or nerve or vengefulness to turn around and rip Talissa limb from limb, there would always be something of the Sab left in this world, just as there was something of shadow where there was light. Maybe, when finally and fully dead, someone would pick up Talissa's essence or see her ghost and find in the look in her eyes the concept of evil she wanted to promote. It wasn't a bad thing. Not all a bad thing. For when the shadow descended upon Montréal there was a last spark of mankind left, enough for it to continue on after the most fateful of Hallowe'en nights. And neither was that a good thing, for there was a forgetting woven.

Heather had less than an hour to find a place to hide from the sun. She didn't rush. She walked away, knowing Talissa would follow her path until the rays of the sun came out to burn her to dust completely. Heather decided not to debate on whether Talissa would find release. She figured after a thousand years she would be beyond that, that maybe vampires had paid the price and were forever barred from release. Heather thought of murder, of the absolute agony each mortal felt upon receiving their death. Thought that maybe, for some, eternity was just that one moment of agony stretched out forever. Perhaps it was just the effort of existing. Heather knew how difficult that could be, how much pain one could feel when it was directly related to one's soul. The pain of loss, and she thought of her father and how no one would care but her, but to her it hurt so much because it was so personal. It was something she would have to endure forever, and for some they would see the end and begin to crack under the strain, but a small part of Heather would always rage against being broken by that. Against being broken by someone else's death because she didn't want to let anyone else but herself decide her fate.

The Sab was gone and the dawn was coming, but there was still an emptiness that Heather felt within herself. Tomorrow she would come back here to see what was left of Talissa's remains, and if there was anything it would only be a meaningless little coating of dust on the sidewalk. If anyone mortal did happen to see anything strange-perhaps the silhouette of a body just before the wind blew it away or the rains turned it to muck, or the stench of the Sab as some of the dust reached their nose- they wouldn't question it for more than a moment. But it wasn't Talissa's passing that caused Heather's stomach to feel hollow. It was the fact, that though she controlled the shadow, Magog was gone, and just as she thought she got closer to something she'd lost, it seemed more elusive than ever. She wanted Korson to be here for the last possible moments of Talissa's existence. She didn't want to feel so alone, here at the end of the night of orange and black. It wasn't so much desolation she felt as she reached her home, nor so much as loneliness or despair, but there was a sense of loss because she couldn't get close to Magog, or to the place of death, where things would be finally ended; and she just couldn't figure out why.

Book 5:

Epitaph

Part 1: The Veil

Standing atop the cross on Mount Royal, one could see everything. A cool breeze blew, and Heather hugged herself, but more for own comfort than because of the cold. She could feel winter coming on, and could hear the innumerable thoughts, alternately in French and English, about how the year was winding down, that things were coming to an end. She knew that people were blissfully ignorant of the war that had raged mere nights ago, how the city, and most of the world, was on the verge of destruction. How people were ignorant, through no real fault of their own, that the winter was not an ending, but a beginning, a renewal, a dawn. Indeed, her dawn, as the nights got brighter as summer neared. Heather looked out on the cityscape of her beautiful Montréal, and it had been more than restored-it had been renewed. The bridges, the *vieux port*, *boul. St. Laurent* and Prince Albert, all breathed life, and none more so than *rue Ste-Catherine*. If *Ste-Catherine* was strong, then so was Montréal.

She could see everything from here. As the forest dropped away along the mountain side, giving way to the parks, cemeteries and twisting, bumpy roads, to the flats and townhouses, winking their lights, showing life, Heather tried to imagine what would have happened if she had ran away. If she had lost. Don't ever, ever, ever give up on Montréal! The possibilities were moot. Only heartache resulted in giving up Montréal. Anyone who has ever left has always been heard to remark, 'Maybe I'll go back to Montréal?' and said it with a longing in their eyes. She could see everything from here. And it was hers. Whether anyone knew it or not.

The mists swallowed up the forest around her, creeping like snakes around the fat bellies of the trees. Heather hadn't called them, but now she began to beckon. Such a precious commodity as majic wasn't to be denied, wasn't to be thought of as an inconvenience. Heather had noticed the pattern of majic throughout the year, and would become more familiar with it in the coming eternity. There was an ebb and flow, all connected to the earth, and as the veil had just closed, she felt her majical energy at a low point. Not a weakness, a low point, a calm water.

Sssssssssssssssssss!

Rising, becoming (somewhat) substantial, from the mist, a soup of black and dark, bold grey, the caped form of Magog rose, riding the snakes of smoke, going through the trees as though they didn't exist to him. His presence loomed in front of Heather. She was almost intimate with him, he was so close. His eyes were a brilliant white light that was suppressed by his shadowy form. Heather tried to look into them, but his vaporous form sent licks of smoke lashing across his ocular cavities to distract anyone who might be lucky enough to get a glimpse of him and survive. By nature, Magog was imposing and aggressive, his voice deep as though it issued from the depths of a canyon, his form, if one could make out its limitations, equal to that of three or four well built men. Not that he couldn't spread himself any which way he wished.

Heather spoke first: "It's been a helluva year," she said. And she actually made Magog laugh! So deep and loud she wondered if anyone walking by the foot of the mountain could hear it. He always seemed so humourless, but for his own morbid sense of comedy. "I didn't think you'd still be around."

I am everywhere. Like God.

Magogianly cryptic. "You don't have anywhere to go?" For the first time, Heather thought she sensed feeling in him.

If I am everywhere, I have no need to go anywhere.

"True." Heather had finally relaxed in the presence of this imposing being. And it didn't bother her that he saw this growth in her character. Perhaps because there was no one else who'd seen her with Magog, who could judge her on what she was rather than that she'd become. That was important to her, she denied her past enough to almost be dangerous. Her encounter with St. Valentine and her own creation was lesson enough in that regard.

Heather continued to look out at Montréal, to savour the very existence of it. How many other vampires was she ignorant of? She directed no anger at those whom she knew, at this very moment, were celebrating the end of the War of Sabs. It was her battle and hers alone, and she was in fact grateful for that fact. Grateful that the few other vampires in Montréal had kept their counsel and let the fates run their course.

Magog continued to hover silently near Heather, looking at her as she looked at Montréal. She noticed a change in him. In his skin. He had a slightly greenish hue about him. And though she knew that everything was connected with the earth, it reinforced the fact that even Magog had been born of earth. Albeit of the intangible, invisible elements, the ones that can't necessarily be proven by science, or perhaps can't even be seen in shadows.

Am I your supplicant? Magog must have asked that question thousands of times, and nearly all who heard those words ceased to exist. It wasn't the question that hung in the air, it was Magog. He seemed, for the first time to Heather, to have no sense of purpose. Did he reach his death? His end? He was too quiet, and said, as if he'd read Heathers thoughts:

I am awaiting an answer.

Heather smiled. The cold and gruesome demeanor had returned. Some things never change, and no matter how disturbing that could be, it could also be a comfort. Magog seemed as though a dark knight at the foot of the throne of his queen, awaiting some form of direction.

"Are you my enemy Magog?"

No.

Despite the utterly evil veil that surrounded him, Heather had realized that Magog had done nothing but help her. Rather, push her in the proper direction and let her find her path. It took death to allow Heather to truly define herself. In all its glory, she was still unknown to the world. Her accomplishments were global, perhaps even universal. So what if she didn't receive her true recognition? Who the hell needed it? It was far more important that Korson knew, that Catherine died knowing. That was all the more evident when Korson was with her. It was the loneliness that diminished her strength, and to survive she to overcome that. She had to find her anchor.

"Stand next to me, Magog." Magog's form floated over to Heather and reversed itself to come abreast of her. Amazingly he complied without his usual arrogance. They hugged. That is Heather stood close enough to be virtually surrounded by the ever-swirling mists of Magog. She felt the shadow creep through every space in her body, wrapping it's limbs around her arms, her neck, even her fingers like rings, as though binding her. It surprised her that it actually felt completely natural to be touched by Magog. Nothing unholy. Nothing obscene. From neither her mortal perspective nor her vampire one. She knew the shadow, controlled it. She knew when others controlled it. Heather even sensed when Magog himself was mustering power.

She smiled and thought to herself, "Wow! My own shadow demon!" She thought that because Magog had done what she'd told him, because he seemed...affectionate. Coldly, slightly, but no one expected even as much from him.

"I was never inside of you in Interamana, was I?"

Perhaps not.

"Not much of a conversationalist either, you bastard."

Silence.

It was worth saving.

Was this emotion from Magog? Did the Montréal cityscape, viewed from Mount Royal, tug at his proverbial heartstrings? Perhaps a more open-ended question?

"What is inside you?" Magog didn't answer. Maybe he couldn't. Perhaps he was a well, one that Heather had to draw upon by pulling the rope herself? Though he did tease a bit, his eyes glowing a little brighter, overpowering the shadowy ocular cavities. "Don't move, Magog. Okay?"

Again silence. Heather scrunched up her shoulders, said, "I am awaiting an answer."

Yes.

Heather began to step into Magog, into the very demon himself. He seemed to increase his size, in order to accommodate Heather's form. The smoke thickened quickly-the edge of his form more clearly defined when one walked through it rather than trying to discern it visually. Heather found herself in the inky blackness, almost lost, for it was a directionless medium-no ups, no downs, just tones of gray and splats of black. Heather kept her nerve, kept walking where she thought was straight. The smoke brightened, and quickly she was in a medium exactly the opposite of the one she had just left. It was bright, the light mostly white, but with a hue of oily yellow. Again all Heather could do was keep walking straight, this time blinded by brightness rather than the absence of vision the darkness provided.

Would she be disappointed? Would Magog merely be light surrounded by shadow, a being of pure majic? Hell, most people wouldn't be disappointed by half that.

Heather's eye focused, and she realized she'd come out of the light. That she was in some sort of field. Her eyes were hurting, more so than she'd gathered before the light dimmed to something bearable. It took her a moment to adjust. The first thing she did notice, that she actually had no choice of noticing first, was that the light was very much the light she remembered as the sun. Though much, much purer, more vibrant, as though it had enough intelligence to be accommodating to the desires of whomever it bathed. She regained her focus and looked around her. She was in a sunny field, virtually endless, but for a faint vapor on the horizon. She could not discern any other limits, and it was as though Magog were limitless on the inside. The field was covered in saffron reeds that swayed in the breeze, the sky a clear, crystalline blue.

"Ow!" Heather was struck on the side of her head by an orange ball. She followed the bounce and saw that it came to a stop back in the hands of its owner, the little girl in the red dress. The little girl sat on a grey rock, and it looked a bit out of place among the brightness of the field. Heather smiled eagerly, walked over to where she sat.

Before Heather could say 'hi,' the girl said, "You're not supposed to be here." She said it with all the innocence of a child, in no way derisively or maliciously. She bounced her ball between her feet.

"Should I go?" asked Heather.

"Mmmmmm," teased the girl. "No, you can stay for a bit. It'll be alright out here, I guess."

"What's this place called, anyway?"

"It's Tir Nan Og-the Place of the Dead. But some people who come here have other names for it. Doesn't matter though. It's all the same place." She stopped bouncing her ball. "This is just the entrance. The rest of it is over there. It's so beautiful, I wish I could show it to you." The girl's voice saddened a bit. Heather picked her up and swung her around in her arms.

"Hey! None of that! We hardly see each other, I don't want you unhappy. Especially in a place as beautiful as this!" The girl giggled, for once a truly happy giggle, one without fear of being snatched from place to place by Magog. "So you're dead, then?"

"Well, kinda. I can't really explain it." As the conversation took a more intelligent turn, so the little girl seemed to get older, on the cusp of puberty, closer to womanhood. Never too close, though, always a child.

"I find that a little confusing," said Heather. The little girl in the red dress asked her why and Heather answered, "Because I thought that if you were dead, I would be too."

"You are dead silly!" giggled the girl. "Some majic can be dangerous. There was so much of it, and sometimes it can be too much." The images flashed strobe-like in Heather's mind, bits and pieces returning. She'd dreamed all of them. She saw a thick stream of smoke swirling out of the night sky, funneling into her bedroom window, and little threads wove in and out of smoke, twinkling like pixie dust. It was too much for any mortal, much less a child, and it had overwhelmed her. With her mind on the brink of explosion, out of the shadow emerged Magog. He then latched onto the child Heather.

"Come on!" yelled Heather and she grabbed her ball and ran off. They traipsed through the field of saffron reeds, tossing the ball between each other, laughing, enjoying the intense purity of beauty that endured in this endless majical place.

"How high can you throw this ball?" challenged Heather.

"Pretty damn high."

"Let's see!"

Heather took the little orange ball and reared back, launched it nearly straight up in the air. It rose until it was a mere dot, barely visible in the vivid light, and it took a moment for either of them to realize it was actually coming right at them. They jumped out the way, Heather shielding the child, and watched the ball dent the earth mere metres from where they stood.

"Wow! Didn't even break!" said Heather. Then, "I wish I could do that."

"You'll be able to one day."

Heather became saddened and subdued. She hung her head, looked down at her favourite orange ball. They both felt the same pain.

"What is it?"

"I can't ever grow up." She said it as if it was a bad thing. Most of the time she was a happy, contented and well-adjusted young girl, but was afflicted with strong pangs of childhood depression. She could never consolidate her experiences, interpret her feelings in any complex way, understand or vindicate the suffering she saw when she returned to reality. She said it best herself: she could never grow up. Her development was stuck.

Heather realized that she'd subconsciously made a decision to protect a very precious part of herself. That, under the strain of powerful and forbidden majic, with the weight of it upon her and about to make her burst, she'd thrust one part of herself forward, and the other into this realm. She picked up her little self and squeezed her as tightly as possible, rocking her body side to side.

"I think you're incredibly lucky," said Heather.

"Don't you see?" she cried. "I know everything you do! But I can't experience it. Sometimes I barely understand it!" Heather had, inadvertently, become two, each part an opposite. One forever a child, the other a survivor of the trials of growth that allowed her a deathly eternity. Though each were whole in their own way, the split carried a price, that of true, eternal happiness. Heather could only recall bits and pieces of her childhood. Her childhood, in moments of boredom between the hours of endless play, would long for that which she would never attain. "That's why I come here. To be with the dead. To be happy."

"That doesn't sound like too happy a thought," said Heather.

"Silly! Everyone's happy in Tir Nan Og!" she said, her mood brightening immediately. "The dead come here to be happy."

Heather faced the minute mirror of herself. She had broken the cycle, and now stood in pieces. Should she not be grateful? To have this part of her live on, the part of everyone that experiences that first little death? If her childhood could live, then she could never-ever-die. She never had died. Though she drank blood to live forever, death was a metaphor. She put her little self down and the severing of contact she felt-actually, <u>they</u> felt-was as though tearing open a wound.

Little Heather picked up the orange ball again and began to run, tossing it up in the air. Heather followed her, navigating through the saffron reeds, the ones that matched her hair, matched every sway in the ever-present kissing breeze. She thought about how it sounded-endless childhood. Sounded so perfect. Nothing is perfect. As happy as her little self always seemed, there was a sharp twinge of sadness that accompanied her phenomenal gift. The spiriting away by Magog for her own protection. Living among the ghosts, among the loneliness, among all the fears that every child brings to bed with them. Among the ghosts who never spoke.

"C'mon!" yelled the smaller Heather. She took Heather's hand and led her in a run over a small rise in the field.

Hell, despite the imperfections, people would kill to be a child forever. It was the rock of the cycle, the foundation everything was built upon. There was a careless excitement in having everything to look forward to. Waking early on Saturday morning for cartoons. Imagining what you're going to be when you grow up, then changing your mind the very next day. Stealing the raw cookie dough when your mom pretends she isn't looking, thinking yourself so clever. Toys!

Toys! And more toys! Each one a thrill as big as the previous.

"C'mon!" urged the little Heather. "It's just over here!"

Heather said, "Slow down, Heather!" Her spine tingled just a bit at addressing herself by name for the first time. She'd avoided it. It may have been a little silly, a bit petty, but it was a line that had been drawn. By crossing it, she'd validated the situation, and everything became suddenly clear and real, like the light that bathed them. With one last tug from her doppleganger, Heather broke through the saffron reeds.

"This is my absolute favorite place," exclaimed little Heather. "The punkin patch!" There were fat orange pumpkins resting all over the brown earth. The green stalks looked sinister growing out of the crown. Some of the pumpkins were so large, they came up to Heather's waist. Some had already been carved as Jack O'lanterns, each face evil and scary in its own way. Heather picked one up, very unique. It's shape more square than circular, the skin surface very uneven, it looked though it had been fashioned out of fire. The face, with it's sharp eyes pointing upwards, it's nose a slit, enhanced the image even more.

"I'll show you my favorite," said little Heather. It took several minutes of searching, of losing themselves in the orange and brown and green punkin field, but the little Heather finally snatched one of the fat orange fruits off the ground. "This one rocks!" It had evil eyes, the brow furrowed in hellish anger. Scrunched in the middle of the face was a tiny shapeless nose, full of contempt, deformed from the imperfections of the orange skin. At first glance the mouth looked like it had been carved to show numerous jagged teeth bared in malicious grin. In actuality, Heather saw that it was a bat, leathery wings spread wide in the smile, a creature found flapping about in the cobwebbed castles of imagination.

It began to get dark, and they were both tired from hours of playing. They sat down on a pumpkin, Heather in Heather's lap, and the Jack O'lanterns began to glow as though each housed a candle.

Heather saw a plume of smoke in the distance and got up, said, "Who's that?"

"Don't go there," said little Heather. Then exclaimed in a whisper, "Injuns!"

The wind became a little violent, and the light dimmed further. Even here the cycle had to be obeyed to some degree, the energies had to run their course, and a wintry night would fall for a few hours, the wind becoming icy.

The two Heather's found themselves near a veil of greenish mist, evidence that Magog existed here.

"Tir Nan Og," said the little one. They had reached the gate to the place of the dead. There was a whitish glow beneath (within?) the green-hued smoke, the formless doorway a misplaced plume materializing out of nothing. The ground encircling the door showed no growth, no life of any kind. "I have to go now." It was so sudden. So final. The pumpkin patch, the field, the sky, seemed a little angry.

"I'm going to miss you, Heather." She picked her little self up and they hugged tighter than ever before. "Am I ever going to see you again?"

The little Heather's bright eyes teared. "Maybe. Maybe on Hallowe'en. I'm not sure. I'm sorry." Heather wiped the tears out of the little one's eyes. She felt the emotions within herself, but did not cry. It wasn't out of any cold, callous suppression of emotion, nor because she was a powerful dead witch. It was because of understanding. The longer they remained together, the stronger the bond between them would grow. Who was to say what would happen to them if they fused together? Childhood would die. And vampirism? Would that be allowed to continue? Would the price be the gift of eternity?

The wind blew a strong puff, some dirt and leaves raining on the pair. They could purchase no more time. For the last time, they would feel this tearing separation. For the last time they would lay eyes upon this half of their self. It was freedom, bitter freedom, that they each felt, that would allow each of them to grow in their own way. Continue, rather, in their own way; each existed as a continuance, linear, not bound by literal growth which invariably included death.

"Take care of yourself, kid. You never know what kind of monsters you might run into running around in the shadows."

The little Heather smiled. "Yeah, but not all of them are mean." She waved, returning to her carefree demeanor, and glanced over her shoulder. "If you ever do find this place again, stay away from it. It isn't meant for you." Quickly she stepped into the greenish smoke, her blond hair, scraggly, bouncing up and down on her shoulders with every eager step. A moment's entanglement in the mist, then she disappeared.

Heather stood at the gate to Tir Nan Og, forbidden, alone. The wind, along with the door of smoke, calmed. Heather turned to look behind her. Even in the dark, she could see the field of saffron reeds beyond the pumpkin patch. Though she could cover that distance in less than an hour with her preternatural speed, she saw a long journey ahead of her.

I'm going home to nothing, she thought to herself. She still felt some of the pain of losing what had gone through the door, more so because she still stood at the very place. A thousand years later, she would still daydream of this moment as if it just happened. Time meant nothing to her, and could not deaden whatever wounds she'd acquired. Her love, Catherine, was gone forever. The one she thought she'd share eternity with. Talissa, mad with her lust for power, crazy with thoughts of absolute love and romanticism (such unreasonable things!), was finally dust. It hurt because it was Heather's first real link to the world; she was essentially Talissa's daughter. And she hated her. Still she missed her, what could have been there, what was supposed to be there. Who knows if she would have gone mad herself had she not found Catherine to fill the void of her needs?

Poor Cat, she thought. *Are you in there behind me? Are you now allowed to be happy?*

Heather dismissed the idea, though it disheartened her to do so. Catherine had been a vampire for nearly a century; she'd broken the circle of life, the great cycle, and had likely lost her soul in doing so. Heather could only find solace in the fact that Catherine, kept alive by blood majic, had returned to the infinitely connected energy of the universe. That she now existed as majic, and perhaps that was a purity that was greater than being forever happy in Tir Nan Og. But it still left her alone.

No! thought Heather. *I'm not going to do this to myself. I'm not going to focus on the negative. I don't deserve this. I'm not alone in the world. I have Korson.* For if the dead could be forever happy, why couldn't she? At least she could try, make the attempt. She didn't wish for endless happiness. That would be unreasonable. Even drugs couldn't provide endless happiness. She would end this self-deprecating loathing. There was a difference of loneliness and being alone. Heather was perfectly content being alone, in fact she thrived on it. If she did get lonely-and understandably so-there was always Korson. Her sibling, her knight. She wouldn't be petty, she wouldn't feel as though she had to swallow her pride to go to him. It didn't make one weak to reach for a rock when they happened to be floating aimlessly. It was difficult to admit weakness, and therefore it was strength to do so.

She decided she would walk the journey home as though she was mortal, slowly, taking each precious step carefully. Alone, but not lonely, she began her journey back to reality.

"Heather!" The little one was emerging, shrugging off the entanglements of the smoke. "Silly me! I almost forgot. I just thought you shouldn't go back with nothing. You don't deserve to lose everything." The little Heather was carrying a bundle, and from it emerged the bewildered fuzzy head of a grey and white kitty.

"Cumulous!" said Heather. "My precious little boy!" She snatched up her kitten and squeezed him till he squeaked. She kissed him all over his face, but he ignored her, putting a paw on her shoulder and propping himself up, looking at his surroundings, shrugging off his bewilderment in favor of curiosity.

"Sssh!" said the little Heather. "Don't tell anyone! It's a secret!"

"You little thief! Go back to where you belong!" The little girl giggled, putting her hand over her mouth. Heather heard her name being called several times, and looked towards the doorway. There her father stood, looking young, fit and healthy as he did before the years of booze withered him and did him in. The little girl went over to him and he put his hand on her back to gently guide her back through the door.

Heather walked through the pumpkin patch and shortly reached the saffron field. The weather was cold, yet calm, and she hugged Cumulous to keep him warm. The reeds afforded adequate protection. She walked and walked, and she knew she'd been walking quite a while when her muscles stiffened and her legs felt weak. As well, the pure white light began to flood the sky. It came from everywhere, spread randomly like melting butter. Heather began to watch her feet as she walked and then began to think that the light came up from the very earth itself. She saw translucent waves shimmering upward from the earth and as she followed them they looked as though they dispersed into little radiant explosions. It was quite a fantastic phenomenon, although an unnoticeable one at that.

It became quite apparent that Cumulous, back from the dead, had rediscovered his appetite. Heather, devilishly clever, discovered she could nourish him with drops of her own blood. He would steady her finger with his paw and lap up the seeping blood, which would sate him for nearly an hour. She had no idea how long he was without nourishment, nor how much longer till she found her way back to her reality, and (unfortunately!), had no other choice but to feed her starving kitty. If that meant he would share her curse with her...well, Heather pretended it was out of sheer necessity, at least that was her excuse. She was more than pleased at suffering the possible consequences.

If, by some chance, no doorway back to mainstream reality appeared, she would try to use her majic to return home.

She passed the time playing with Cumulous in her cradled arms, tickling his belly (which he hated.) He hissed, growled and bared his claws, but Heather could see him smile, vicious and malicious, petting his head to soothe him, telling of her adventures in the shadows up until he'd been returned to her. She noticed some scratches on his forehead, and she playfully scolded him.

"You naughty boy! Have you been starting trouble in Tir Nan Og?" He yawned and licked his nose in answer; his gaping maw revealing the cutest little fearsome teeth that were reddened by blood that clung to his gumline. He became restless and tried to climb out of the blanket clawing his way up her shoulder. She struggled to keep control of him, soothing him with her thoughts. Her concentration had been diverted from her journey for a while now, and she focused on calming down Cumulous. That accomplished, she noticed the cause of his excitement. The surroundings, the field that led to Tir Nan Og, had lost its substance, the colours becoming a blending of pastels. Before she could wonder at what happened to the ground, she felt herself floating, more directionless than when she'd entered his realm.

Rather than give in to the obvious fears, she opened herself to the energies of this place. Just a little. She was dropping, slowly, the realm turning from a faded banana cream yellow into black crayon. She felt the energies shift-there was no break in the connection-as the energy changed from one form to another. She felt the absolute, pure, virgin energy of Tir Nan Og (was this the source of all energy? Did the dead come here to shed their majic, to release it so their souls could truly become one with the earth?) become the familiar raw power of the shadow. There was something perhaps...uncontrollable in the place she just left.

That must be why I'm not truly dead, thought Heather. *There is something beyond the shadows. Something that wasn't meant for anyone who has a corporeal form. Pure, utter majic, pure energy. Existence as thought.* It was the most comforting view of death Heather could possibly imagine as she drifted slowly down, back into the familiarity and comfort of her shadows. It was something she'd never dreamed possible, to be able to tap into the energy that held together the very soul. By nature, an energy that could not be accessed before the very destruction of the body. It was that connection, the physicality of her existence, that kept her from being truly immortal, for nature stated that energy could neither be created nor destroyed.

A bright spot resolved itself among the mists, retreating from close to Heather's face. It was, in fact, all of reality resolving itself, and if it seemed as though Heather were cradled in the arms of the shadow-demon Magog, then that fact was invalidated by the more immediate fact that her descent took on a greater speed than was evident in the tranquil realm of the dead. The result was, unfortunately for Heather's ass, hitting the thankfully soft ground, leaving a six inch deep niche, and more unfortunately for her breasts was the painful evidence of Cumulous' claw marks as he clung for dear life. Magog still hovered just above the cross (presumably her intended target; nobody said nature was perfect.)

Heather said, "Shit," real loud and checked to make sure her kitty was okay. She looked up at Magog, hovering purposeless.

"You gonna stay up there all night?" Obediently(!), he drifted down, all smoke and shadow. He looked almost formless when he moved from place to place, and to mortals would likely look more so for he never let them see his eyes. Heather looked at the glowing white of his eyes. (He even averted his eyes when among vampires, offering only a tantalizingly swift glimpse of them. Unless he wanted to kill someone, it was likely that Magog would have his back turned on whoever he was with.)

Heather descended Mount Royal, walked along *chemin Remembrance* and passed the *Cimetière de Notre Dame de Neiges*, looked at the piles of earth and upturned graves where many of the members of the evil Sab has risen. Rows upon rows of graves, a sea of graves.

"The world's gonna have a hell of a time figuring that one, eh, Magog?" Magog remained silent, following Heather, making her look as though she trailed wisps of dense smoke. In fact, she felt him very close to her, his shapeless form brushing her ankles and shoulders as she walked. "Hmm. Just me an my shadow."

The lights of Montréal twinkled then disappeared, as the altitude of the road decreased. Heather walked briskly, eyes front, not taking in anything around her. It was quite late, and as it was most people were loathe to leave their homes, what with the remains of a supernatural war littering the streets of Montréal. It was a city that had endured much turmoil over it's history, as well as it's present. Heavy rains flooded an underpass on the Decarie, killing several people in their cars; storms knocked half of the population out of their homes; the FLQ kidnapped and murdered politicians over language. Despite the chaos Montréal remained a city fierce with pride. It wasn't a violent city, but rather violently proud. When Maurice the Rocket Richard was unjustly suspended from N.H.L. competition angry Montrealers took up flaming sticks and rioted across *rue Ste-Catherine*. It was out of pride. This was the power that emanated from the streets. To instill it's own citizens thus and be able to survive it's self-inflicted onslaught.

    Heather neared St-Catherine Street, and could feel its presence before she realized she was near it. For years people were saying how it was dead. Now, that could be said literally. She'd traveled that street frequently, out of boredom, out of purpose, for whatever reason. It was always *Ste-Catherine*. Start from there and then work your way out. There was an air of resiliency. And finally, almost appropriately, perhaps even ironically, she stood at the corner of Atwater and *Ste-Catherine*, in front of the now defunct, boarded up old Forum. Where the ghosts were. If *Ste-Catherine* was the artery, the old Forum was the heart. Such majic, earthly majic, emanated from here, even though it was now dormant. It was the center of daily discussion, of pride, of power, of dynasties, of gods. A place where children went, a place that never left them. Even dead, there was a resiliency. When an old man would remember the Forum, he would remember what it was like to be a child. Childhood memories always gave mortals a piece of majic to hold, for just one fleeting moment-and perhaps that would be enough.

    Neither did she bother to hide herself the way she used to. What was the use? It was late, there was hardly anyone about, and if someone did see her-well, who would believe? They would forget. For Heather, it was a logical explanation for the existence of ranting, zealous homeless wanderers who unfortunately turned up in just about every horror story.

    Perhaps it was the familiar scent of home, as Heather neared wealthy Westmount, which caused Cumulous to prop himself up on her shoulders with his front paws, and hang his tongue out like a dog, a crazed look in his eyes.

    The flashing lights of *Ste-Catherine* receded, and the energy along with it. Even when there were no people there the residual energy could be felt. Pride? Majic? People just being alive? Heather smiled to herself.

    Isn't that what it's all about? Just being alive? Existing? Was that why she felt so comfortable roaming the night up and down *rue Ste-Catherine?* If it had been in her nature she would have shouted. Instead she just skipped a step in her walk and clenched her fist as she said, "Yeah!" Because she existed. Even after going to death and back, she could still see the pointlessness of it all. She bore no disappointment at losing the chance for eternal happiness. She was in fact luckier in her own eyes anyway, hell, the only ones that mattered to her, luckier because she had eternity and happiness was hers to find for herself. On her own. Tir Nan Og was for ghosts who were too drugged up on majic to realize that there was anything else. If they were lucky enough, they could shift into energy and become part of the cosmos. But would they lose their identity, their intellect? These were most important to Heather. She wanted to leave some sort of legacy to the world, and it turned out to be herself. From a path she'd chosen. She had the foresight to look late into her life. She remembered thinking how fast the years went by, and in her mind she accelerated herself to old age constantly. Almost two decades as a mortal, and wow!, two more and she'd be almost forty and that was half a life and certainly no fun if her own parents were any indication and it nearly made her crazy until she reviewed the concept of time.

Sometimes we shock ourselves with what we are by discovering it. Heather was a true born witch, someone with an innate talent for harnessing the majic all around. Who else could survive the shredding of one's childhood from the soul? Who else would seek out vampirism among the energy and the chaos of Montréal? By no means had Heather found everything that there was to be found, but she'd shattered many of the misconceptions she'd been brought up with. Black, shadow, night, magic, witches, vampire, death, hell, all were words that had negative connotations associated with them. Perhaps that was merely the misinterpretation of the concept that the words were meant to convey? Perhaps the cancer of Christianity, while suitable for many, was not suitable for those who were not content with the Sunday school teachings, of a Satan with horns and pitchfork, of a God who was vengeful when angry yet loving only when one followed his word. The very state Heather was in could very well be deemed the Hell everyone was talking about-but-she was usually quite content with the path she'd chosen. It was all her own choice. No one forced her. As well, did the people she killed not go to be happy forever? As well, despite the fact that she murdered to live, she was actually doing a service to her victim. Heather would pick her victim with more care than ever now. As Korson did. Though he did so for different reasons. It didn't matter. (Did that mean all paths led to the same...?)

She rang the bell to her house. It was nearly four a.m. This would have to be quick. Some things would have to remain dead for awhile before they were resuscitated. It took several rings before someone answered. A man, in his bedclothes, unshaven and groggy eyed.

"Hey! D'ja miss me?" Heather kissed him on the cheek-MWAH!-and walked passed the bewildered man into the house. "*Love* what you've done to the place. Could use a vampire's touch though."

"Listen, I think you better go." His wife came down the stairs, followed by two children. In the living room stood Heather, holding her grey kitty, standing among the fearsome unnatural mists that wafted around her.

The man said, "I don't know who the fuck you think you are, but get the hell out of my house!"

"Um, no. My house. I was the previous tenant."

"Great! I'm happy for you! And the key word is previous! Now get the fuck outta here before I call the cops!"

A thick-fingered lick of shadow reached out and slammed the door shut. The quartet jumped, startled into shock by the cinematographical phenomenon. Mortals were so easy to scare!

Ssssssssssssssssss!

Heather filled the room with the shadow. She wouldn't drink from these four. She'd send them to the ecstasy of Tir Nan Og.

"This isn't anything personal, please understand. It's just this house has to have a myth about it. I know, I know, police will investigate, but they will never turn up anything concrete. And-" Heather lowered her voice and put her hand to the corner of her mouth as though protecting her words from an eavesdropper, "-just between you and me, the only cop who would've believed is no longer on the force!"

The shadow grew large, making a knee high pool in the room. The mortals couldn't navigate through the smoke; it weakened their legs and essentially forced them into remaining frozen.

"It's ghosts I'm worried about. No one's going to live here for a very long time. I just can't have that. I have a secret to protect. More so now than ever before."

The man said, "Look, just take whatever you want! We can be out of here tomorrow. I'll give whatever I can!"

"Money, money, money! This has nothing to do with that! I need your lives! You can't leave with the knowledge." Heather went over to one of the children, who stood, belly out, in his nightclothes. "You know what I am don't you?"

The boy nodded, said, "A vampire."

"So you know why you have to die, right?"

The boy nodded again, clung to his stuffed animal.

"I'd like to tell you that I'm sorry, that your lives mean something. But I'm not much of a liar right now. I can tell you that you will find solace in death."

The man told his family to run and stood valiantly between them and Heather. Of course, they could barely move in the smoke. One of the children was sucked beneath the surface of the smoke. The mother screamed and lunged to grab her other child, but snatched only air as he too was sucked away to his death. She tried to run, and even managed a step but was lifted up into the air and thrown against the wall, her spine and skull cracking as she hit. There was still life in her eyes as she fell face first into smoke and was consumed by the darkness.

The man had much more spirit in him. He lunged and managed to move close enough to the stairwell to grab the railing. There was hope in his eyes as he felt himself pulling out of the cake-like mass of smoke. Suddenly, he stopped. He could move no further, the grip of the smoke had tightened. He readied himself, and with a large, quick thrust of his arms he pulled. He hung from the railing, feeling freedom from the nonsense that covered the floor of the house where Heather Langden had been born and died. The man looked down and realized what it had been that he'd felt as he lunged free. The cold tightening that had grabbed his legs. He looked down and saw skin hanging loose as the stumps of his legs thrashed wildly, dripping blood and ligaments. He screamed and hung to the railing for dear life. He felt like a war veteran who was trapped in a nightmare.

Licks of shadow rose like snakes and entered his body through his mouth, his nose, and his ass. The snakes even squeezed their way through his eyes until they were useless. His scream was stifled and if he had any thoughts of voiding himself due to fear, that option was also unavailable. He was filled with the shadow, majic too powerful, too volatile for mortals, especially one unprepared. The indescribable taste, incredibly disgusting, almost as distasteful as strawberry Quik, made him vomit, and as he was choked by the shadow, the flow of bile stifled in his throat, further choking him, making his throat bulge, looking like a snake who'd just consumed a rat. In death his muscles constricted and his grip on the railing froze. The railing tore away as the man was sucked beneath the shadow. To be preserved until morning.

The limbs of all the victims were severed partly to fuel the fear of the myth of the Langden house and partly to prevent the corpses from rising again. Heather had learned one could never be too careful with majic...

Over the next several nights, Heather rose to find Magog's presence fading away, and she went to bed with his image resolving itself as she closed her eyes. How was it that he existed during the day? Was he not a demon of the night? The shadow-demon seemingly utterly evil, spent the days guarding Heather. From St. Valentine, from Talissa, who knew? Perhaps from herself. Though he would not appear at night anymore.

There were, of course, shadows during the day, for it was the light that cast them. Night was merely a giant shadow cast by the day from the other hemisphere of the globe. Nothing in nature was separate, or singular, or not susceptible to the chaotic disciplines set out by the Mother. The rules were so complicated that no one could figure them out. Not even Heather, with all her powers, one step outside the circle. The complexities transcended her mind. In simplicity, her fangs dripping blood, there was more enlightenment, more insight. And yet, and yet...it would die with the victim.

Rue Crescent. Trendy clubs clumped together, and everyone went there, and then to Burger King at the corner of *rue Crescent* and *rue Ste-Catherine*. Heather had not walked this street since she was a mortal girl. And she and Patrick had gone into Thursdays for a few drinks. Too crowded. Too many people. It was ego that kept her away. She lied to herself saying it was because it was too dangerous for her to be around so many mortals when her hunger could well up at any time. Ego that made her think everyone would turn and notice her. Who would notice her? A short blond girl dressed rather plainly with pale veined skin. Her hair bright. But no one would notice! Heather had the power to make people see something she was not, to confound them. She walked; hands in her pockets, and it was impossible not to brush shoulders with the crowd, so thick on the sidewalk. And no one noticed her! The odd glance and all it took was a flick of her hair to distract her face and the look would be gone. Some called her a goddess and no one noticed. After a war, no less. Secular society had indeed paid a price. It wasn't a lack of religion. It was a lack of faith. Of belief.

It was so easy. A small bump and pretend to fall, and of course unable to get up without any assistance.

"I'm sorry, I didn't even notice you!" And he helped her up.

"Oh, that's okay!" Bat an eyelash, feign bewilderment, and let the fingers touch the base of the neck in a delicate way. "I think I'm alright." Turn your ass towards him as you brush it off. And the two friends already gone as they sized up the developments, gesturing up the road.

"Let me buy you a drink. Please. Least I could do."

"Oh, um well..." Playing those female games. "Okay. Let me make sure I didn't lose anything."

Pull him to the side and slip into the little alcove.

"I didn't think you had anything with you. Did you drop a purse?"

"Yes, that's it."

So close to the sidewalk, people could certainly see. Um, hmm let's see. Shadow? Good choice.

"Magog."

"Pardon?"

"You heard me. I said Magog."

Sssssssssssssssssssssss!

That ole black magic, you got me under your spell!

"How 'bout that drink now, hmm?" File the nails against each other. Quick and easy, this one. Snick, snick! A slash across the neck, another for good measure. Pull the head back by the hair and slurpslurpslurpslurpslurp!! Drop him on the ground and he slumps against the wall with a look of horror on his face. They all do that. In every movie. This is reality and this one just looked dead.

"Put a smile on his face, Magog." The demon moved forward on the air and covered the body. Nothing to it really. The flesh breaks down so easily. Months of work for nature taken care of in moments by majic. The demon became formless, just a mass of smoke, and then dispersed, leaving only an empty alcove. He hadn't spoken since the day after the war ended.

Back home to Catherine's, another empty place but for a sweet little cat. Flop down on the pillows and watch a movie. The shadows were near to her, but it was Magog, the living embodiment, that was elusive lately. Just faded in at dusk and dawn and whenever there was a kill. Claimed the body. Perhaps it was uncouth of one such as Heather to leave a mess.

"I miss you, Magog. You always made things interesting." She would never see him again. This she knew, and therefore spoke the words of parting while it was still possible for him to hear.

"I wonder where he went."

Everything was so peaceful. The remnants of war littered the city and people looked at wrecked and crumbling buildings and scratched their heads and kept walking. There was bewilderment to be sure. The city was noticeably damaged. People could not be ignorant of that. There was physical evidence that *something* had occurred. But rather than get bogged down in explanations and hypothesizing over the cause, people moved on. Some helped rebuild. Most had to move on. Life moved on. It never stopped.

"He was always there in my head. It was him. I'm sure of it."

Heather and Korson sat in a cafe at *St. Laurent* and Prince Arthur. Mercifully one of the few places that was left untouched by the war. The place where the vampires went at night. Some made themselves known to Heather. More accurately, Heather had made herself known and she knew who was there. They couldn't hide from her anymore. More so, they weren't being hidden.

"I'm sure he's still around somewhere," said Korson. Heather laughed. She didn't really care who noticed her and some people did look and she laughed.

"Everything's connected somehow, right? But he's dead. I'm sure of that."

"I can't say I'm sorry to hear that. Magog was...the ultimate bastard." He lowered his voice as though the shadow-demon might hear him and rise from the dead. One of the few who made Korson tentative.

"He would never had hurt you."

"How do you know that?"

"Because I would never hurt you."

"You don't know his way."

Heather leaned her head back and looked up at the sky and over everything and out over the square. There were some vampires wandering around, mixing with the mortals, and it seemed like a lot. Only a handful really. When you looked at the population of the world, only a meaningless handful. No. Not meaningless. Everything was necessary to create the puzzle that was the earth, nature and life. Every saint and every rapist and even the infirm. Everything was balanced on a polarity and the delicacy was too intricate even for vampiric minds to fathom.

"Do you see it Korson?" Heather held up her arm to him and he nodded. "Sometimes it just flows off me. There's so much of it. Do you know what it is?"

"The shadow. It's a well-worn rumour among others that you have control of it."

"It's Magog. It's his body. He epitomized the shadow. But you know what it really was? He was a piece of me. My soul was fragmented. And he was a manifestation of my fears become real. Mostly he was power though. There was too much power flowing in me and it shattered my soul and the strongest piece became sentient and resolved itself as Magog. When he died I got his body. Somehow, though, he developed a soul. And I wonder where that went."

A vampire slowed in front of where they were sitting, keeping respectful distance. If Heather was not already known then she could be recognized for who she was. And Korson was legend among the undead. Not that Heather couldn't aptly defend herself, but Korson was deterrent enough to maintain one's distance. He looked at Heather and bowed his head and kissed his index and middle finger to his lips. Made some sort of gesture almost-but not quite-like that of the cross on his chest. Who knew how many denominations of the religion of vampirism there were? He shut his eyes a moment in reverence and then stepped back a step and walked away.

"It's great to have you here, Kor." He smiled. Actually smiled! A rarity in Korson, though he was by no means emotionless. That much was obvious. He just didn't convey his inner thoughts and feelings.

"So your subconscious mind was strong enough to realize there was a power too great in you and it created a shadow-demon."

"I said it's great to have you here."

"I had some business to attend."

"Okay. Don't admit you came to see me. I don't care."

"Among other things...I came to see you."

"Wow, you almost conceded the point. Good boy. How's your arm?" Korson lifted his sleeve a bit.

"It healed pretty quick. I don't think it suits me though."

"I think it looks great on you."

"Why the hell did you make me get this anyway?"

"Kind of my religious irony about it all. The mark of the beast and such."

Korson said, "What kind of idiot gets a pumpkin tattooed on their arm?"

"It isn't a pumpkin, it's a jack-o-lantern, silly! It marks you as one of mine. That mark has to be earned. That's in case there's ever another war. I will know which Sab is which."

"It's all about Sabs isn't it?"

"Not even close! A sabaoth is just an army. It has two meanings really. The Host and the Army. Talissa's was the Host, mine's the Army. I figure everything will be quiet for awhile. But someone's bound to rise up and start some shit. Way of the world, you know."

"I have very clear definitions of the way of the world."

"Korson, you wouldn't believe what I've seen. I went to the gates man!"

"The gates?"

"Heaven. They call it Tir Nan Og."

"I've heard the stories. An old witchcraft legend. The place where all the dead go to be happy."

"I don't think all the dead go. It is selective about who comes in. We'll never get there. Even if we die now we'll never get there. It's only for those in the circle. But man, if I didn't feel the energy there! It was definitely crowded."

"I felt something too. The remnants. I tried to see the events but couldn't catch more than a glimpse. Ironically, I think it was my glimpse that helped start these events..."

"Sorry, I forgot. We have the same blood."

"Did you feel Graham in there?"

"Korson..."

"No, I want to know that he received justice in death. He earned the right to eternal happiness. I want to know that he's there."

"I have no way of knowing the Korson."

"Heather, you have the power. You could look for me."

"It's forbidden, Korson. We're banned from that place forever. You just have to have faith. Please. Have faith. He could walk there if it was what his ghost wanted to do."

Korson sat in silence, angry and forlorn. The injustice of the world on his face. If he ever ceased to exist, he wouldn't be able to walk among the ghosts, among his few dead friends. Perhaps he would share hell in limbo with Catherine? So many uncertainties of death, so many fears. The ultimate and forbidden knowledge acquired only if one were to sever their ties to the real world. And if you were disappointed? No going back.

Heather said, "You're thinking."

"Nothing wrong with that. Thinking is good."

"But I'm here now. You should be talking."

"Did you ever wonder that maybe the dead started to rise because they had nowhere else to go?"

"Can't say I have," said Heather. "I figured it was Talissa and her twisted desires."

"There are two things in this world that man can't figure out. Religion and nature. What about the pieces of the puzzle that we do know? Who's to say that religion isn't just fiction that tries to explain the reality of nature?"

"So who's the writer, Korson?"

"Us."

"Us, vampires, or us, mortals?"

Korson thought for a moment, said, "I haven't figured that one out yet."

"What are you telling me about all that happened? That we're merely playing out parts on a stage?"

"All this would have happened anyway. It's possibly happening elsewhere to other people."

Heather said, "And it's happening because nature is making it happen and we're just here to be pushed along the path."

"I can't think of a more piognant way to epitomize the mad ramblings of all the fools who scribbled sanctified words and were shunned by the masses. Maybe some mortals saw a piece of the shadow?"

Heather interrupted, "I can't believe what you're saying. What about our free will?"

"That was the big mistake; our emotions. We look at this with our bleeding hearts and make metaphors and stories for that which pulls at our heartstrings, but really we're all just parts of the machine. Haven't you done anything you didn't want to, then wondered why you did it?"

"And you're saying that heaven was overflowing, and someone had to empty it."

"Yes."

"Why, thank you, Korson. That would make me heaven's toilet."

Heather swallowed audibly thinking of the entire grand scheme and the great cycle and how the world motored on despite the machinations of man. How, despite the innumerable losses of life, everything kept moving forward through time, constantly renewed.

"I didn't do anything, Korson!" Heather said, pleadingly, almost pleading not to be a heroine.

"Did you ever wonder where you got that extra energy to decide the fate of the war? Not to dishonour your power-you control the shadow completely and have incredible power-but you fought for that control and you had an extra resource that you called upon when you needed it. And Tir Nan Og was filled with souls just waiting to become energy."

"That's impossible, Korson, I can't get into Tir Nan Og. Heaven is denied to the undead. I didn't do anything."

"Talissa sensed the vast energy of the place of lost souls, and as the population grew exponentially, that energy grew with it. She tried to tap into it and the more powerful it became the madder she became. Perhaps there was a part of you that was pure and innocent and was able to harness that power and accomplish something good with it. Nobility comes in the strangest little packages..."

Korson got up and kissed Heather on the forehead.

"Korson? Could you do me a favor?"

"I would be honored to."

"Come back to the city. Come back to Montréal."

He thought for a moment. Just looked at her. Which wasn't difficult. She was very pretty, even more so in death. But ultimately he said no. He told her no and she just looked at him with sad eyes, helpless and almost pleading and questioning why he wouldn't want to be with her. That's what she was asking, for him to be with her. As isolated as she felt, she felt more so than ever now because of the one who willingly isolated himself. He did nothing to alleviate her, no soothing words from his mouth. Heather waited for those words and they didn't come, not even a smile, nor another kiss. Maybe he was mourning. Maybe that was why he was always on his own? He was forever mourning. Perhaps he would spend the rest of his life in mourning, loathing the chaotic world and subsisting on the barest amount of blood.

He was a warrior, though, her knight. They shared the same blood. And soon, when it felt right, Heather would go back to him and bring him here, if only for a while. He stopped and pulled his hair out of the ponytail, and it flowed as the wind picked up around him. Heather had visions of a blood-soaked field, and nights under a starry sky. Then he walked away. They would always be bound by blood, but right now it felt like she would never see him again...

Part 2: A Note From the Dead

It was a terrible thing I did as a child. Though it gained me so much, it also cost me more than most would be willing to give. I was tormented by dreams of monsters and demons and ghosts and vampires. Like every child was, but these dreams, I knew, were much more to me. See, I was born a witch. It had nothing to do with pointy black hats and warts and eye of newt and oil of frog's legs. Though I must admit I do have a great love for cats, those thoroughly evil and fanged creatures who always plot the takeover of the world during their many naps. These monsters were in my dreams and I knew I was seeing something, and the older I got, the more I saw. There was something theological creeping into it, before I even knew what theological meant. I began to see things from the past and had a glimpse of something that might happen.

  I knew I had some sort of power inside me, and it only came out in my dreams. It didn't haunt my days and I sat in a classroom with many other children, leading a quite normal childhood. Birthdays with cake and candles, Easter with painted eggs and lots of chocolate and cold Christmases blanketed with snow on the streets while I was safe inside in front of the fire with my mom and dad. But it was Hallowe'en that I absolutely loved! I always dressed up and ran from door to door trick-or-treating for candy while my dad huffed and puffed along the sidewalk trying to keep up with me. It was the one time of year that I was an absolute brat, rather than my normal sweet little self. But it didn't matter. After all, who couldn't love a pretty little girl in a red dress?

  I always wondered why we had to dress up on Hallowe'en, and my dad would always tell me:

  "To ward off the monsters and evil spirits, princess."

  I never told him that I saw those all the time anyway. At least I don't think I did. And if I ever did I'm sure he would have shrugged it off like most adults would. That stuff was for horror movies and the rambuctious imagination of idle children. But there was something in me, in my dreams, that was talking to me. Some sort of power.

  I was born a witch, and it was not out of any logical or meaningful choice. It was just fate's cunning little hand piecing things together. Who knows why? My parents didn't have anything that set them apart from other people, but I guess the combination was all that was asked for. Sometimes

Steve Zinger

fate is funny, and just makes things happen and those of us with a consciousness will always sit and wonder why.

I've always thought we were actors with a designated part to play, and that whether or not we knew what that part was, we would play it out. We really didn't have much of a choice as to the direction of the role or much opportunity to ad lib and make a great change. Perhaps I'm being a bit fatalistic. But I do think certain things have to happen for the world to keep turning, and though it may seem a surprise to us, it really isn't anything new and it keeps happening over and over again because the world is a cycle.

Sorry, I was talking about Hallowe'en. You will have to forgive me as I will always have a bit of childhood in me. You know kids!

So it was Hallowe'en, and I think I was eight years old, and as usual I dressed up. As a clown I think. Nothing is so reminiscent of childhood as a clown, nor can anything be so scary at the same time. The most sinister evil is always the most brightly coloured. I dressed up, I trick-or-treated with my dad, and saw some of the other kids. Then I got an idea. It was dark anyway, and I would have to go home soon. But I faked sick and went home early.

I sat up in my bed, using a little flashlight to see by. My dad let me take some of my candies to my room. And I sat up and waited for them to go to sleep. When their light clicked off I knew they were asleep.

I had taken a small, sharp knife from the kitchen and hidden it in my room earlier that day. Under my pillow. It was still there. I didn't dare sleep that night. It was the night when ghosts and ghouls roamed more freely than others. The night when majic was at it's strongest. Come to think of it, I usually tried to stay up on Hallowe'en. I think I would doze off at dawn, as the sun rose and washed all the majic away, wiped out all the bad stuff. If Hallowe'en was the day of the demons, then I'd have to guess that the day after must be the day of the angels.

I really can't explain why I did what I did, and I think that that's what majic is really all about: trying to achieve something without really knowing the intricacies of how it was done. That's what separates it from science. I would hope that you would be somewhat impressed with that thinking. I think you would be, if you could see my little eight year old body.

Hm. Maybe I did fall asleep. Or at least a part of me did. I felt the majic rising up and I knew in my heart that to all majic was from the soul, and therefore could be bound with blood. So I cut into myself. I had never even dreamed of suicide but I just wasn't ready for what I did. Just the copper scent of my blood in the air brought forth the majic that had haunted me in my dreams. I think I began to draw symbols with the seeping blood on my flesh, but I'd become woozy and wasn't sure if I was asleep, or dying. If my father had burst into the room at that moment than he would have screamed to some God because all he would have seen was his pretty little daughter lying on the floor bleeding, a knife dropped a few inches from her hand. And from her mouth the murmurs of a prayer in age old Latin that know one would ever have thought she would understand.

But I resisted sleep, and as I mumbled the prayer against my will the thick smoke filled the room. Rather, the shadows merely came to life and became more than darkness; they became the very depths of every nightmare I ever had. Like thick, puffy clouds on a sunny day, though these epitomized black instead of brightness.

Needless to say, if I had fallen asleep, I'd woken myself quickly and gotten to my feet. I was so scared at first that I didn't run. I hopped into my bed and went under the covers clutching Bear, my stuffed animal, unconcerned about the little drips of red blood I left on my sheets. I was scared, but these weren't the monsters. I lay there frozen, wondering if they would come. Wondering if I had made my nightmares come true. I peeked my head out from under the covers.

"Oh, no! Oh, nonononononono," I cried, not caring if anyone had heard me. In fact, I wanted my parents to burst in now and wake me from this nightmare, for my mother to run in all worried and cradle me in her arms. A pair of white eyes began to form from the shadows, small slits like snake's eyes, and they began to move forward towards me. I kept shaking my head and crying and it wasn't until more of a shape began to form that I got scared enough into action, that I burst out from under the covers and ran towards the door of my room. I put my hand on the knob and took a look over my shoulder, trying to see through the tears in my eyes. The shape in the shadows was huge, as though it was somehow bigger than my room while still being in it, and it wasn't so much an actual body as a large cape of billowing smoke and many tentacles and snakes and souls making up a whole of some sort. I opened the door as fast as I could and fell out into the hall in a burst of smoke.

I must have inhaled more of the stuff than I thought, as I coughed it out of my lungs as I lay on the ground on all fours. Remember I was-am-a child and this was a lot harder on me than it would be to someone fully grown. I relied on others quite a bit more to help me through life. But I got up quickly, fear being the motivator, and I noticed that the hallway in the upstairs was coated in a film of blackness, as though the smoke had been absorbed into the very walls out here. If I'd had a moment to stop and look I might have had thoughts that this wasn't even my house anymore. But I was more worried about this monster that was chasing me. Sorry, I mean demon, he doesn't like being called a monster.

He came out of the plumes that flowed out of my room and I had only taken a few steps, and now I just followed my instincts and ran right for my parent's room. I swung open the door and was ready to burst in and jump into their safe and waiting arms. But all that lay there as I reared up in utter shock and tears and fear were their dead and rotten corpses smiling at me. The demon came into the room after me. I had trapped myself.

I turned around and began to back towards the wall as he floated toward me and I kept glancing over at my parents half expecting them to rise up and come after me as well. But they didn't. They just lay there dead. He came towards me and he trailed so much smoke that I couldn't see what was behind him.

My child... *he said to me.*

"Leave me alone!" *I screamed at him.*

You called to me, *he said.* **You called and I have come for you.**

"I don't wanna go!" *I was still breathing heavily and my face was all wet.* "I want to go back."

Impossible! *he bellowed. For a moment it looked as though he pointed a finger at me and I thought flames would come out of it and burn me to Hell.* **To return with knowledge of such power would mean you would burn in the sun. Playing with majic has it's price, child. You must remain...**

I had calmed a bit and wiped my face of the wetness. My cheeks were hot and I began to ignore the heaving in my chest. "Where are we?" I asked, my curiosity getting the better of me... again.

Tir Nan Og, *he said, ominously.* **The Place of the Dead.** *He spit the last word at me with his forked and smoky tongue.*

"I don't want to stay here," I said, determined and resolved.

The Well of Souls awaits you, and you will be happy there, *he said, and moved towards me to take me.*

"No! I called you and you're mine," I yelled at him, and from my still bleeding wound threw my blood at his foul white eyes. He stopped. Perhaps that bound him to me, my blood...I looked down at my arm and finally realized that I was still bleeding. "I'm bleeding to death," I whispered, and for the first time in my entire short life I think I didn't sound much like a child when I said that. His eyes glanced over his shoulder of smoke as though he'd heard something.

Someone is coming. We must leave now. *And he moved towards me again.*

"I demand you send me back!" I screamed. I was practically asking to be sent to my room.

She will seek you out for your power. She already roams dangerously near the Place of the Dead.

"I don't care, I demand you take me back where I belong!" I thought he would take me to Tir Nan Og anyway, but he stopped. Perhaps my innocent child's eyes could pull at the heartstrings of even a demon. Perhaps a child's majic is strongest. I looked down at the bleeding cut and squeezed my arm to stop the pain.

My child, *he said, and he actually sounded a little bit sad, rather than ominous and gruesome.* **You have called such power and do not know that you are already dead. That you belong forever in the Place of the Dead, Tir Nan Og. She now seeks you.**

"I demand!" I screamed again, and I think that I might have actually caused some fear in a demon with the unfettered and fearful determination in my childlike voice.

So young, *he said,* **you know not what price you ask to pay.** *It was as though he were remembering. And he granted me my wish.* **I will return you to the world of the living, but this part of you that sits before me now must remain in the Place of the Dead, and the part of you that returns must return to the world ignorant of the power it has. It must return to the world and die and live off blood to exist, to keep it's majic alive.**

I was still a little scared and he told me that I would be forever happy, for the dead go to Tir Nan Og to be happy. It sounded fair enough to me at the time. But I was too young to realize what he really meant. That I would lose my childhood and the few moments I had to myself between that and adulthood would be spent haunted by Talissa as she sped me to my death. That my real self would forever be barred from the Place of the Dead because vampires had no souls that could go there to be happy forever. And my soul would be forever chased from that place by the monsters who could get their fingers to reach out to the power of the shadow. The cut on my arm turned a sickly olive colour. And, as though extending his arms, billows of smoke puffed out to me and became tentacles that teased inches away from my face.

Rise, he said, and somehow I had enough majic within me to know what to do. I got up, out of myself, and went along the shadow to the bosom of Magog. **To name me is to call me,** he said, **Magog, the shadow-demon, concubine to the Lord of Hosts.** Then took the most precious part of me forever to Tir Nan Og, yet doomed to run from hungry monsters like Talissa. Even that part of me, the part I had to give up to remain in the world, had paid the price of not being able to enjoy the eternal happiness of the Well of Souls.

It isn't often that I get these moments of lucidity, that my mind can reflect upon the years as an adult would. I make the most of them. They aren't so bad really, but I can't say I hate being a child forever. It's usually fun to live out the fairy tales of demons, even if it is my soul that is always the price. Sometimes such majic is chains and I have to regret not just dying like everyone else. But I know Magog will forever protect me though, and he's pure shadow and nothing corporeal can defeat him. So I take every advantage to write down my thoughts, because I know that soon I'll forget them and just be a kid again, and that does hurt a part of me, that I can't ever become more than I am. No matter how much fun it can be.

I sit here and write in this secret little place I carved out for myself in the Well of Souls, at the centre of Tir Nan Og, on parchment of flesh and ink of blood, and here the souls of the dead live in blissful happiness. Maybe one day I'll find a way to send these little scraps out to the real world. Maybe one day someone will read and understand my story. And then I remember the part of me that's trapped there forever, the vampire Heather, and that she is eternally writing for me.

And it was St. Valentine, devilishly clever as only a priest could be, who hid the name of Magog and the prayer that could call him, in the Holy Bible.

-Heather Langden, Age 8

Part 3: French Onion Soup

The door slammed shut and it was pretty dark in the place but neither of them cared. One could see clearly in the dark and the other one, he felt comfortable in the dark. Secretive, alone, private, and all one could see if one looked closely was an ebony sheen on his cheeks from the buzzing street light outside. Otherwise he was hidden in the shadow and that's the way he wanted it for now. He didn't even look up when the door slammed open and shut.

"We're closed," he said, his voice not too loud but echoing in the emptiness.

Korson walked slowly to the counter and sat down on a stool and steepled his hands, elbows on the countertop.

He said, "Thought I had a few more minutes. Figured I could pop in for a drink."

"We don't cater to your kind in here."

"S'okay. I brought my own."

"How you doin', Korson?"

"I'm good. No real bumps or bruises worthy of a warrior, to tell the truth. You?"

"Livin'. That's good I guess. It will get easier. Just keep movin' forward in life and leave my mark and all that. Run a good deli."

"No shame in that."

"Seems a little mundane after the recent events."

Korson said, "This is life. This isn't the movies. Sometimes you have to sit on a toilet and just shit. As boring and disgusting as that seems. It's all made up anyway. I think you live well for yourself. You're good to people."

"I try. I guess that's the least I can do." Jerome lit up a fat cigar and poured some bourbon from the bottle under the counter. The door wasn't locked but it was late and it was unlikely anyone would come in.

Korson said, "I'm sorry about your brother." It seemed so out of context. An apology for the death of Graham St. Croix.

"Wasn't your fault, man." Jerome tried to seem casual and it was apparent that there was emotion choked in his throat. He burned it clear with a shot of bourbon and a pull on the cigar.

"He died a warrior's death, proud and valiant. In battle. You should be proud of the life he lead."

"I miss him like hell," said Jerome, holding back tears. "It kills me that I didn't believe him at first. Maybe he would still be alive if I did." Korson reached under his trench coat and pulled something out, held it up in front of his chest to show Jerome.

"This is my lacrosse stick. I fought many battles as a child with it. And I fought my final battle as a mortal with it. That's why it's in two pieces. I lost it when I died my human death. First it found the Shaman. Then he gave it to me. And when this war of the Sabaoth began I was going to give it to Graham St. Croix to aid him in his battle. To provide him with the bravery to die the most honorable death imaginable. But as it turns out he didn't need it. And now I'm giving it to you, Jerome St. Croix. I was going to bury it with your brother, but I thought it should remain in the world of the living. With you. As a reminder."

Korson presented the pieces to Jerome and he carefully took them. He felt the power of his brother's soul when he held the pieces of the broken battle stick. Or rather, the power his brother felt. There was so much power in ideas. Korson bowed his head in reverence to the dead. He put his hands on the table and pushed himself up, readying himself to leave, not waiting for Jerome's thanks, and not needing it.

He stopped, turned back, said: "A vampire walked into a restaurant, much like this one. Sits down at a table. He waited a moment for the waiter to come over to take his order. A sturdy-jawed kinda guy, much like you. So the waiter asks him what he wants to order, thinking the answer obvious.

"The vampire says, 'Waiter, bring me a cup of boiling hot water.'

"The waiter says, 'Water? I though vampires only drank blood...'

"The vampire smiles at him, pulls out a tampon and says, 'Yes, but I'm having tea.'"

Jerome just stared at him for a brief moment, then burst out into laughter.

"Sonofabitch! Get the fuck out of here!"

Korson, half turned to walk out, pointed towards Jerome, said, "You're right. I'll work on it."

Then left.

Heather returned home, to Catherine's house. She stopped in next door to the old lady, Mrs. Dumont, who was taking care of Cumulous in the real world.

It was painful to tell Mrs. Dumont that Catherine had befallen a great tragedy and met with her death.

"Oh that's such a shame," said the old lady as she put on her glasses, adjusted her robe. "She was such a wonderful lady, what with her being a social worker. I think she stayed late every night, I hardly ever saw her before dinner time."

Heather smiled. Catherine seemed to touch every life she came near.

Mrs. Dumont continued: "She would sometimes bake me a banana bread, wouldn't even take a piece for herself, no matter how much I offered. The world is less of a place for losing her."

They talked a little more, Heather saying that she would continue living next door, that she would most certainly stop in and would learn how to play rummy so they could pass the time the way she used to with Catherine.

"She really was terrific, she seemed very humble and devoted like the woman in the story," said Mrs. Dumont.

Heather asked, "What story is that?"

"Oh, the story of her namesake, St. Catherine. She would just blush and brush it off when I told her, but I think she actually liked the story.

"There was St. Catherine of Alexandria, and she escaped death through a miracle. The Roman Emperor beheaded her instead, and it was said her veins produced milk, not blood. Our Catherine seemed like someone who would risk her life for others, to give her life purpose.

"I think they even have a statue of her at the *Parc Jean-Mance* at the foot of Mount-Royal."

Heather felt a tear run down her cheek and she wiped it away, picked up Cumulous and thanked Mrs. Dumont, promising to stop in very soon.

She took Cumulous next door, noticing he was already looking fat because he was overfed.

"Diet time for you, kiddo," Heather said, and he looked at her with a sidelong glance of contempt. She called Korson but he still wasn't home.

"He must've gone over to Jerome's right away," she thought. She'd try later, or maybe stop in at the deli.

She left the kitchen, where the phone was, and walked towards the living room. Cumulous sprang out from under a chair in the dining room, standing on his hind legs looking like a Frankestein monster, and he wrapped his paws around Heather's knee, playfully biting at her skin. She picked him up and laughed because he left his mouth open and his tongue hanging out like he was a crazed freak, hell-bent on destruction despite the fact that Heather cradled him like a baby.

"I missed you too, kiddo," she said, and kissed him on his ink black nose.

She looked out the window, at the beautiful November night, put on a light coat for the chill and went outside.

Time for one of my famous walks, she thought.

She went to the *Vieux Port*, with its cobblestone roads and Victorian architecture. People cluttered the sidewalks, the cafés, even the streets so that cars couldn't get through. She stopped where the street artists were, looking at all the caricaturists, and she went up to one who drew real pictures, not cartoons, handed him a crisp, red fifty and said, "Immortalize me."

He worked for forty-five minutes or so, his pastels making broad, waxy strokes on the paper. The crowd ebbed around her, young men enthralled with the angelic beauty who sat there displayed for all. Even middle-aged women would turn to their husbands and say, "My, she's gorgeous." The husbands would say something like, 'Mmmmm,' or, 'I didn't notice,' and smile when their wives weren't looking.

While she was sitting there, Heather noticed the little girl who she watched TV in the shadows with. The girl looked at her with familiar eyes, and Heather smiled a malevolent little smile, boldly bared her fangs for the girl, and the girl alone, to see.

The little girl clung to her mother's thigh, pulled her parents away from the painter's easel so she could make them buy her an ice-cream or a toy.

When the picture was finished, Heather was amazed at the way the man had captured her, the shine of her hair, the fullness of her cheeks. The playfully devilish smile that she thought only the girl could see.

She'd already overpaid the man, but she gave him another ten bucks anyway, and he rolled up the picture and tied it with a blue ribbon.

Heather felt that art was important, and hoped that the picture would last as long as she did, longer if necessary.

She walked a few blocks towards the *Vieux Port*, and walked down a short but steeply sloping sidewalk. Nestled into the ground, half-buried because of the hill, was a restaurant that looked out at the hansom cabs, at the water, at the *Jacques Cartier* bridge.

She sat down at the table, ordered a glass of water and a bowl of French Onion soup. When it came, she sat and felt the warmth of the bowl through her hands, smelled the smooth, tangy broth and the hot, bubbling cheese. She wondered if the waitress would think her crazy for ordering food and not eating it.

A young man came in, ordered an ice-cream from the parlour that was at the front of the restaurant, very close to where Heather sat. He looked strong and healthy, he was unattached and free to do with his life as he pleased. He noticed Heather looking at him, smiled back at her. She glanced at him, then at the empty chair in front of her, then back at him, and he took it as an invitation to sit, which he did. He would make a fine feast this evening.

Indeed, thought Heather as she fumbled the little jewel in her pocket. *A feast fit for a Queen.*

About The Author

Steve Zinger was born in Montreal in 1974. He is the author of Ray McMickle, the Kentucky Vampire Clan and The Sab, both published by 1st books. He is currently working on his next novel, entitled Man of Ash.

Visit his website at www.stevezinger.com to find out more!

Printed in the United States
19799LVS00003B/31-168